The Prophecy

When the Marked is found amongst the Maples,
And the armies of the east shall walk again,
With the Enderdetag alignment in the heavens,
Then shall be the end of good men.

When the Oracles crypt shall be opened,
And the choices we make must thrive,
The powers of evil shall be woken,
And no one alive shall survive.

From the innocent the savoir shall waken,
To the Bards he shall appear,
To reunite the Gems of Thamous,
And destroy the Lord of Fear.

1.

The bean cane man, dressed in the most oppressive of blackened robes, slammed his fist down upon the gnarled oak table amid the confines of the musty bughut into which he had the misfortune to have been summoned. He had travelled far along an arduous old road with two others from the Citadel of Parandor. Now he was both tired and irritated.

"It's just a cart of bear's bollocks!" he exclaimed, his eyes fired with anger and confusion.

The man looked across the table at the three others who sat opposite him and then over towards the one woman who stood in the small space that passed as the kitchen at the far end of the rustic farmhouse. There she busied her dirt encrusted hands in the menial work that was her life.

"I don't know how she does it!" replied a rotund man whose ginger hair crept down the sides of his face and threatened to join together under his chin. "Thinata has developed a strange ability to infiltrate people's dreams and for no obvious reason that I or others can think of."

"And does she know what she is doing?" asked the dark haired man who sat to the right of ginger whiskers.

"What do you mean Rukave?" asked the round man before sipping from his tankard of ale.

"I'm sorry Enguerrand, let me be clear," he replied. "Your dear wife, the most honourable Lady Fullbane; is she aware that she can act in such a way? Does she even know when she is doing it? I mean, is it a conscious decision to infiltrate the nocturnal meanderings of people's thoughts?"

"No, my dear Lady does not," sighed Lord Enguerrand Fullbane. "I thank the gods each day that she has no awareness of her abilities. It would give her dangerous ideas and fuel her decadence should she ever become mindful of her unique skill. I would fear for all the young boys across the Realm if she discovered that she could infiltrate their thoughts. I tell you this, one of these days, even though I love her with all my essence, I fear that my dear monstrous mathulath will be the very death of me."

The other three responded with embarrassed laughter as Enguerrand Fullbane took another swig of ale from his tankard. It was then that the fourth man present at the table spoke and caused the laughter to stop. He was of similar age to the man in the black robes although nowhere near as thin. His face was more wizen and full of the sort of lines that reflected a lifetime of worry. Each wrinkle had been forged over years of study, argument, and the longing for a lineage with which to carry on his name.

"So what does this all mean?" he asked in his usual curt manner. "Will this witch-skill pose a threat to our conspiracy?"

"Shush!" hushed the woman from the depths of the kitchen in which she toiled, the noise somehow finding its way around the finger that she held to her lips.

"I'm sorry, I have always had tendency to speak louder than needed," continued the wizen man. "It seems to me that the Lady's practice must have some deeper intent. I find it hard to believe it is just coincidence that your wife is reaching out to Lyrusa through her dreams Fullbane. You know our beliefs. You know what they say about coincidence."

"Oh come on Mathias," sneered the black robed man. "You cannot in all honesty believe that Enguerrand's globular glutton…"

"Show a little more respect for my good wife if you don't mind."

Enguerrand Fullbane was clearly irritated by the insult, despite the fact it was one of his own well used terms of endearment for the woman he had married.

"I'm sorry to have offended you and of course I should not be so disrespectful to the delightful Lady Fullbane, that vision of perfect form that I must endure so often," continued the thin man. "As I was about to say, you cannot believe that she has any influence over the unfolding of the Prophecy."

"You forget she is the current guardian of one of the keys to the Underworld," said Mathias Amberstone. "She holds one of the five Gems of Thamous that underpin the Prophecy."

The man in the black robes did not speak yet his jaw dropped a little as he sought to understand how he could continue to contribute to the conversation without a stream of expletives leaving his venomous mouth. He stared with less than benign intent at Rukave Emgar as Lord Amberstone continued the conversation.

"You're the Historian, Rukave. You dragged us all into this this conspiracy. What does this dream interference mean to you?"

"At this moment I find it difficult to give a clear answer. I hesitate to suggest what's going on for fear of saying something stupid."

"Most times that doesn't stop you," sneered the man in black.

"Okay, if you want my opinion, it would seem that someone or something is trying to connect with us and is using my wife as their preferred means of communication," added Fullbane while ignoring the insult. "If the Moirai are trying to reach out to us…"

"For fucks sake!" snapped back Blackfayer as his face flushed. "Don't tell me that that we've been dragged all the way out to this shithole called Maplehill to listen to more religious drivel. If I had wanted a debate on theology then I would have stayed in the Capital and listened to holy-fucking Heward."

"And yet Xix, like us, you are Cuvar," added Mathias Amberstone. "You follow the teachings of Anyle Belanore just as we do and…"

"All this dream shite is nonsense, it's all bear's bollocks," hissed Xix Blackfayer but Fullbane was ready for him.

"Remember where you are," he replied. "Remember who Rukave is and what he has done."

"You cannot go back on your oath, the pact that you made in our presence," added Amberstone. "It's you're your duty to continue to support our goal."

"I know it's my fucking duty and I don't need a book minder to remind me," growled Blackfayer. "Just because I swore allegiance to your cause and spent time learning the teachings of Belanore doesn't help me get my head around why Rukave has summoned us all to meet in the dung heap of the Realm. I am still waiting for an answer. There are many in the Capital who will miss us and all this fucking secrecy is messing with my head. Rukave, you told us that you fled Parandor because of your fear that a traitor was at work amongst us, someone that threatens the existence of our conspiracy and watches us night and day. Is this why you have brought us all this way out here? I cannot believe it to be about three old crones or the nocturnal fancies of Fullbane's wife. To begin to suggest that the fabled three are speaking through your lardy Lady and effecting others dreams is more than I am prepared to tolerate. Enguerrand, you need to stop talking such drivel."

An uneasy silence fell across the room until broken by the sounds of Lyrusa working in the kitchen. The four men continued to stare at each other and the tension rose. Finally Fullbane could endure it no longer.

"I hope you have finished spewing out your bile?" said the ball of a man.

Blackfayer did not speak but instead took a drink from his tankard.

"I'm sure Rukave had a very good reason for summoning us all here at such short notice. We all know what he protects and what his sworn duty is. The Marked of..."

"Hush, Mathias please," exclaimed Lyrusa as once again she held her finger to her lips. "He's asleep in the next room. We must not wake him."

The eyes of the four men followed the movement of Lyrusa Emgar as she crept to the closed door on the other side of the room and put her ear to the wood. The sounds of snoring from within confirmed that Amberstone's volume of voice had not disturbed the occupant of the bed chamber. More ale was drunk and the four resumed their conversation.

"Rukave, we three have answered your summons as agreed, but we need to understand right now why we are here before Xix succumbs to apoplexy," began Fullbane. "What is so important that you had to drag us to your place of refuge?"

All eyes fell upon the muscular man who rose from his seat and started to pace the cramped room while lost in his thoughts. Rukave then turned and spoke at his fellow conspirators.

"I received a bird several days before I summoned you all here. It came without warning in the midst of a gale that blew in from the west. It was from another of our order."

"Oh really! I didn't know there was one of us out there," said Blackfayer. "Who sent the bird? Did they have the decency to put their mark upon the message?"

"It was from one of the appointed Guild Musicians," continued Rukave Emgar, returning to his seat. "For some reason that I am yet to understand he decided to make contact with me."

"A name Rukave," demanded Fullbane. "How may we assist you if you keep details from us my friend? How did he sign his message to you?"

"His name is Ulthirn, or that at least was the name he gave me when he passed through Maplehill some two months past. I had met this bard by the fireside of the Red Mare after he had triggered a conversation on the subject of coincidence. It was at once obvious that he was Cuvar and that he searched for the boy, one he said the Fates would present before the Bards of Valameer. "

"To the Bards he will appear," added Amberstone in a whisper.

"That infernal prophecy still haunts me," replied Rukave as he sighed. "There is not a day that passes when it is away from my thoughts."

"Quit stalling Emgar," demanded Fullbane. "What did this message from Ulthirn say?"

"That the time of Enderdetag is fast approaching. It is almost upon us."

"Bullshit!" exclaimed Blackfayer.

"You servant of Kha," spat out Amberstone. "If you haven't got anything constructive to say then keep your festering orifice shut. I am most grateful that you procured this place in which Rukave has hid for the past five years, ever since that awful business with Tullage; and I am sure that our Historian also appreciates all that you've done for him, but for once just shut up and listen to what others have to say."

"Well said Mathias," added Fullbane as Blackfayer fell silent, sulking into the folds of his robes.

"Let us get back to your story Rukave?" continued Amberstone. "How can this Ulthirn fellow be sure that the time of the Prophecy approaches? What was it that convinced you he was Cuvar and not someone who would seek to bring about the End of Days?"

Rukave Emgar reached into his pocket and pulled out a small device. It was made from the ivory of the long nose beasts that roam wild in the Dragonas. The object had been fashioned into two flat discs, one a little larger than the other, and both joined together at their centre by a metal pin. The other three looked with deep interest when Rukave placed it down on the table. Lyrusa joined them for she too wanted to hear what the others thought of it.

"His credentials were good enough for me. This object convinced me that the bard, this Ulthirn, is one of us," said Rukave while the others had examined the ivory object.

"Is it what I think it is?" asked Amberstone with childlike excitement.

"Yes Mathias," replied Rukave. "It is indeed?"

"What the fuck is it?" demanded Xix.

"It's a legendary Cuvar code wheel," continued Amberstone. "A device to help keep secrets in times of peril. I've always wanted to see and hold one of these."

"And now you have; it's yours if you want it," answered Rukave but his mood darkened when Blackfayer then spoke.

"How do you know this Ulthirn character didn't kill a Cuvar and steel it from the corpse?"

"There you go again Xix," sighed Amberstone. "How many times do we have to tell you...?"

"Lord Blackfayer makes a good point," added Enguerrand Fullbane while picking up the device to study its detail. "May we be sure that this Ulthirn fellow is who he says he is? Possession of a device proves nothing in my mind."

Rukave Emgar sighed and then responded.

"The Ulthirn I met here in Maplehill was a beanpole of a wimp with about as much meat on his limbs as found on a gnat's thigh. It is impossible to imagine him hurting anyone. He made a more appealing woman than Lyrusa and that's not too hard to do."

"Piss off Rukave," barked his wife from the corner of the kitchen.

"I'm sorry my pet, you know I never wanted any other but you," he laughed back.

"If you were not such a moron yourself I would take offence, but seeing as... " she began.

"Rukave, Lyrusa, please," interrupted Fullbane. "What made you so certain he was Cuvar?"

Once again Rukave Emgar sighed, closed his eyes, and continued.

"He knew the words of the Prophecy and knew too much about what was at stake. There was also something else. He swore he would never ignore a coincidence. As far as I was concerned he knew the true purpose of the Cuvar, to find the Marked, to protect him, and to ensure that he reaches the Oracle described in the Prophecy with the Gems of Thamous in his hands."

The room fell silent until Fullbane passed the code wheel back to Amberstone

"I won't say that I'm convinced but I am willing to accept your assessment of this bard for now," said the librarian. "What more did this Ulthirn have to say?"

Rukave looked across the table towards his three companions. He checked that the door to the room where his son lay asleep remained closed.

"Have you heard what is special about the highest tower of the Bards Guild?"

"You mean the Orrery of Anyle Belanore," replied Fullbane, somewhat puzzled.

"Correct," continued Rukave. "The coincidental fact that Ulthirn was tutored in the stars and the orbs of the gods was not one that I could ignore When we met here he confirmed his specialist knowledge of the working of the Orrery. He had long studied the movements of the heavens and the teachings of Belanore. No one in the Realm knows more than he on this subject, or so he implied. He was convinced the Marked would soon show up in Valameer as foretold."

"He'll only end up there if you take him," added Amberstone, tapping the edge of the code wheel on the table in rhythm with the words that left his mouth. "From what I have heard your lad carriers too much self-doubt to ever set out on a quest by himself. Now, if he was to spend some time with my daughter Tonousa then perhaps she could make something of him, toughen him up a little. Maybe then he would have some chance of fulfilling his destiny. I am sad to say this Rukave but you have not invested enough of your time in ensuring that Llyat can hold his own in a fight."

"And that's because I choose to keep him that way," replied Rukave. "I know the importance of his bloodline and what those cunts in Calistorn and Avolire would do if they ever got their hands on him again. I have kept him away from swords and anything to do with magic and quests. I did it for his own good and have sought to keep him well hidden. My way was to avoid any attention being drawn to him for although we maybe in a shithole far from the Capital, those who seek to resurrect Urthanock will have eyes and ears everywhere. The Knights of Avolire continue their search..."

"And they'll keep searching," interjected Fullbane. "However, with Sanura Silverwynn, or whatever she is calling herself these days leading them, their focus of attention will be elsewhere."

"Why so?" exclaimed Rukave. "What is keeping them occupied?"

"Some of their number have been causing havoc in the north beyond the Grey Mountains," continued Fullbane. "Court Judge Emeny received word that Griginor was in trouble and Sir Byddin, the new Head of the Royal Guard, dispatched Britta Rainmark with a significant force to put down the insurrection."

"That is at least some good news," mumbled Rukave as he pondered the information.

"Yes, indeed," added Fullbane, "but you still haven't answered the question. What did this so called Ulthirn of the Bards Guild have to say that is so important to our cause?"

"A month past he had been watching the movements of the stars across the heavens and noted something very significant," answered Rukave in haste. "That was two weeks before I received his message and it led me to summon you all here. Just as I said earlier, he saw that the alignment of the orbs as predicted by the Prophecy was just five years away from its enactment. We therefore do not have long before the stars are aligned and that which we fear most will be upon us."

"Bullshit!" spat out Xix. "Urthanock is long dead and nothing can bring the foul lord back.

"And you call yourself Cuvar?" replied Amberstone before any of the others could respond.

"Sometimes I wish that I had never allowed myself to become involved."

"Well Xix, no one is keeping you here," snarled Amberstone as his patience crumbled. "Fuck off back to Parandor if that's how you feel."

"Gentlemen, order, please," said Fullbane. "This isn't taking us anywhere useful. The success of our mission to protect Emgar's lad depends on us being able to trust each other and respect our collective decisions. You are involved Xix whether you like it or not. There is no way we can let you back out now. Let your venomous tongue rest in its foul pit and allow Rukave to finish what he has to say. We need to understand why he has brought us all the way to Maplehill?"

"So be it, have Rukave tell all," snarled the Sovereign Advisor.

"At long last and by the benevolence of the gods we have got there," exclaimed Rukave, pushing back into his creaking chair. "That is what I have been trying to do these many minutes past and you would have known all by now if you had listened with ears not mouths. Ulthirn of the Bards Guild confirmed that the time of the Enderdetag is almost upon us and that we need to put our plan into action. We have protected the boy for too long and must now prepare him to fulfil his destiny. Somehow we have to help him locate the rest of the Gems of Thamous and deliver them to the Oracle. Only then will they reveal the location of the door to the Underworld and how to use the power of the jewels to seal the cracks between the realities. Already those from the Eastern Marsh are tapping the energy of the Rift. I fear what will happen should the Knights of Avolire harness its true potential. Sanura Silverwynn will stop at nothing to retake that which she feels belongs to her by right."

"I cannot believe that evil bitch could ever control the power of the Underworld. The very mention of her name revolts me," said growled Fullbane as his demeanour darkened.

"That may or may not be so Enguerrand but perhaps you now understand why I fled Avolire with the Marked," sighed Rukave. "If the Silverwynn ever manages to collect all five then without hesitation she would seek to force the Marked to open the portal to the Underworld. Who can guess what terrors we would then face? When I first read the words of the Prophecy in the Dirmark I was persuaded to take up the cause of the Cuvar and I am still fully committed to that end. We cannot permit a return to the days of fear when Urthanock held sway over this Realm."

"That embodiment of evil was defeated once and can be again if need be," said Amberstone. "There are those that will stand firm against him should his reign of terror return."

"Well I wouldn't wager on Byddin and the Royal Guard," sneered Blackfayer.

"I have to agree with you," continued Amberstone. "However there are many in the City Watch that would fight to the death to defeat such a threat."

"Like your bitch I suppose," added Blackfayer.

"Yes I do mean my daughter. I am aware that you and my child have equal scorn for each other. You need to realise, like most others do already, that women can do more than cook and raise children. I declare to you now if front of all present that Tonousa is one of the most loyal and honourable individuals that walk the streets of Parandor. She would only have to raise her helm and shout out to have others to rally to her side."

"Gentlemen please, we are losing focus again," said Fullbane, "If the time of Enderdetag is imminent then we need to act soon. We have to locate the Gems before our enemy finds them."

"And where do you suppose we even start looking?" asked Blackfayer. "Apart from the one that sits around your wife's neck we have no idea where the others could be."

"That is not entirely true Xix. You have forgotten that one is reputed to be buried in the mines below Avolire," added Rukave.

"Yes, well, apart from that one," answered Blackfayer.

"The Emerald said to be within the hands of the last remnants of Death Tubaria," said Amberstone.

"Yes, yes, okay, that one too! Yet the precise location of the others is unclear to us and all could take an age to find," continued Blackfayer. "The mines of Avolire are vast and even if we found one there, it still leaves three hidden from view. That is unless there are clues buried deep within the tomes and scrolls that you guard in your library."

Once again silence descended on the small dwelling built amid the smell of pigs and maples. Lyrusa who had listened to the conversation of the aging conspirators felt the need to speak out.

"What about Thamous?" she asked. "Couldn't we seek him out and ask him? That idea came to me in a dream, in words spoken by your wife Enguerrand."

"That is a possibility Lyrusa and perhaps we should have thought of doing that some years ago," replied Rukave as he turned his head towards the woman he had once found attractive. "To do that now would require us to undertake a long and treacherous trek. Given the state of unrest in the north of the Realm, a journey to the Dragonas is not possible. The eyes of Avolire would soon detect our presence."

"Then what about that book?" asked Lyrusa.

"What book," exclaimed Blackfayer as he refocused his attention?

"You know the one I mean, that one full of shit... oh why can't I remember its name. Enguerrand, you must know the one to which I refer, the one that Tullage found in the Harico Hills. It's the tome with which he tried to resurrect his wife after he had killed her. Rukave, you must also remember its name, the one that started all that Death Tubaria nonsense. For some reason, and I know not why, the location of the Gems should be mentioned within its pages."

"Of course I know the one that you speak of Lyrusa," replied Fullbane. "It is called the Lore of the Dead but I do not agree with you that Death Tubaria was nonsense. In fact I would say that it was one of the darkest evils of all time. It almost brought us all down."

"Tullage was a most malign influence and so typical of his profession," added Amberstone as he took a great gulp of ale. "They are either motivated by a desire for money, or else a quest for control. That evil swine was the lowest of them all and will suffer for his sins for eternity. It was a coward's caper that the gods will never forgive him for. His deluded followers were so gullible in their belief that he could resurrect the dead using the spirit of Kha. Death Tubaria, the child's bane as they called it..."

"Say that again Mathias?" interrupted Fullbane. "The child's what?"

"Death Tubaria, the child's bane?" repeated Lord Amberstone. "It was so called because the majority of the victims that fell foul to Tullage's fiendish rituals were young children. Many were poisoned by mushrooms. However, he is no longer of concern to us for he now rots in the Grey Keep under the very watchful eye of our Sovereign's brother."

"Gentlemen, once again, please let us bring some order to our conversation," said Rukave having lost patience with rambling discourse. "We must return to the reason why I asked you all here. Let us refocus on the task that we face, to guide the last descendent of Sir Raulyn to Harico and somehow help him present Thamous's baubles to the Oracle."

"It seems to me that the Lore of the Dead is the one practical option left to us," said Fullbane.

"That's if we can trust what is written on its foul pages," replied Blackfayer.

The Sovereign Advisor cast a knowing glance at Amberstone who, having acknowledged it, continued to play with the code wheel. It was as if some deep secret had passed between them.

"What other option do we have Xix?" snapped back Fullbane.

"I mean..." added Xix while hesitating. "What I want to say is..."

"Oh just spit it out man and be useful for once."

"We had some of the pages burned," said Xix. "Amberstone and I...'

"It was your idea," barked out Amberstone and as Lyrusa glared and once again held a finger to her lips. "I'm sorry Blackfayer, but I'm not taking the blame for it. You said it had to be done. "

"Are you two admitting that you burned some of the pages of the Lore of the Dead?" gasped Fullbane as he held his head in his hands. "Why would you do such a thing? By the balls of Belanore, what possessed you act in such a way?"

"Certain individuals had been sniffing round the book ever since it came into our possession," growled Blackfayer. "Sir Byddin, Lady Emeny, and even the new Archmage of the Wizards Guild, now what's his name... Iqotrix. You know the one I mean, stick-tall, spiky red hair, and one who doesn't look old enough to act as my arse wipe. I decided it was a necessary act, for as Gylewu's Sovereign Advisor I needed to ensure that Death Tubaria would never again surface amongst us. Mathias agreed with me at the time, no matter what he may say now, and together we burned the pages that contained the key incantations."

"So not all the pages were destroyed then?" uttered Enguerrand.

Blackfayer and Amberstone failed to respond.

"Well man!" shouted Fullbane. "Were all the pages destroyed or did some survive?"

The two looked to each other as if deciding whether to reveal all.

"We did not burn everything," said Blackfayer at last. "There were other pages that we left in place. Spells, maps, histories and other incantations which could well indicate the likely locations of the Gems. The remainder of the tome is safe within the walls of the Citadel and away from the prying eyes of those who would seek its knowledge."

Amberstone turned a ghastly shade of grey and his hands trembled.

"Well that is at least some good news," said Rukave.

"There's the answer for you Emgar. Come back to the Citadel with us and interrogate the book in your own time," said Blackfayer. "You are after all a Historian and if anyone can make sense of the shite it is you."

"That is never going to happen and you know it," replied Rukave.

The former Historian slammed his tankard upon the table causing its contents to cascade out.

"I meant no offence," said Blackfayer as he raised his hands in a submissive posture.

"Then none is taken," answered Rukave, "You know why I can never return to Parandor. Remember what I saw in the hall at the feet of Phauless. I remain convinced that I saw evidence of a changeling. The Court has been infiltrated and I can never risk going back and being recognised. Llyat must never visit Parandor or cross paths with those that slither in from the swamps. The prophecy is quite clear; the Armies of the East will rise again."

Blackfayer shrugged his shoulders while his face failed to hide his disbelief. His head began to nod from side to side as he mumbled 'bollocks' several times.

"You have never explained what you saw that day Rukave," began Fullbane. "We value your great knowledge of the Prophecy, having been tutored in the lore of the Realm and as a Cuvar; however, it is difficult to expect us to follow your guidance if we remain unaware of certain key facts. For the sake of our cause if nothing else please tell us what happened that day at Court, just before you fled for your life."

"The Great Hall of the Citadel was crowded that day. The Council had just confirmed the priest Teulu as a new member and Gylewu threw a feast in honour of the occasion. You know how our Sovereign needs little excuse to partake of the best of food and wine. I attended as your guest Enguerrand you may recall I spent much of the time out of the way in a quiet corner."

"Yes, I think that I can confirm that," said Fullbane as he leaned back into his chair.

"Do you also then remember that incident of madness that involved the Fool and how he managed to embarrass several members of the Council?"

"Yes of course I do. Nobody present that day will ever forget how Lolly contrived to make such an arse of himself," replied Fullbane.

"The moronic idiot had been in the midst of one of his useless tricks, the precise one eludes me just now, when madness seemed to spread across the floor. Several members of the Council then fell down, all on top of one another in a heap of tangled limbs. Although I cannot be certain there were at least four others in that pile in addition to the Fool."

"And who were they?" asked Fullbane.

"I am sure the four were Sir Byddin, Lady Emeny, Sir Richemanus of the Nightfall, and the guest of honour, Heward Teulu."

"So fucking what!" snarled Blackfayer.

"Give me chance Xix. I'll get there if you cease interrupting. When they were lying intertwined I swear by all of the gods that I saw an inhuman limb amongst those that floundered. It was reptilian in form and it disappeared almost at once. At first I thought my eyes had deceived me but then it flashed before me a second time. I had heard of something similar happening long ago in the time of Sir Raulyn; having read of it in a dusty tome somewhere. There was no doubt in my mind, one of the magic users of the Marsh was amongst us. Whichever one it was must have realised its mistake for the scale covered limb never appeared again. I knew it had to be one of the Council and afterwards I felt their eyes never left me. I have to tell you know, I feared for my life and I ... "

"You suspect just those four from the Council," interrupted Xix. "Why not Lolly? On what grounds have you excluded him. He must also have been a possible suspect."

"To be honest, it was information that Enguerrand's wife once told me," said Rukave. "I recalled that Thinata had said that there had always been a Lolly from the same family in the Citadel as far back as anyone could remember. Each new generation replacing his own father as the years rolled on. The tomfoolery, jokes and annoyances never changed and were passed on like the idiot's clothes and mannerisms. It is inconceivable that such a tit is anything but genuine. No shapeshifter could be so ridiculous. No, it has to be one of the four I have mentioned. Their positions would give great insight and knowledge to such a spy."

"Bear's bollocks! That's the biggest load of tripe I have heard this year," snorted Blackfayer.

In a hiatus of quiet each of the conspirators sought to evaluate the implications of Rukave's revelation. Then the silence snapped.

"Now do you see Xix," said Rukave. "You must understand the reason why I can never return Parandor. I escaped the armies of Avolire in order protect Llyat and I will not allow the repulsive reptiles to take him."

"I have to say Rukave, from what I have seen and been told, you and my dear sister have done an excellent job in shielding the lad from the evil that stalks him. As the last surviving member of Sir Raulyn's bloodline we should all be forever in your debt. You have disguised him well albeit at the expense of his emotional development."

"I hope that is not irreversible," said Fullbane.

The rotund Lord then smiled to Lyrusa who still listened from the back of the room.

A creak from the shadows in the opposite corner caused the four men to hush. They scanned the gloom yet saw nothing amiss. Paranoia, it seemed, was beginning to get the better of the conspirators.

"Should those from the Eastern Marsh or the Knights of Avolire come looking I am ready for them," added Rukave. "Some time ago I dug out a deep space beneath this building, in secret, at night, and its presence remains hidden from the inhabitants of this sad village. At the first signs of trouble we can at least hide. They will not find us down there."

"Good. Let us hope your efforts of concealment will be as robust as they need to be," added Amberstone while fingering the code wheel. "You have indeed done well to protect Llyat but he remains unskilled in the use of weapons which may yet still be required to save his life. I hope you know what you have done. He will hear of the Knights of Avolire one day and you will have to explain why they may come looking for him. How have you managed to keep their name away from him all these years?"

Rukave looked to his wife and smiled. Then he began to laugh.

"Is something funny? Are we missing something? " asked Amberstone.

"Not at all,"

"Then spit it out man," snapped back the librarian amid his frustration. "You talk in more riddles than fork tongued Xix."

"I'm sorry if I offended you Lord Amberstone," continued Rukave. "The truth is..."

"Is what?" snarled Xix.

"If the Sovereign Advisor will let me finish. Once we fled Avolire I protected the lad with a simple memory charm. The Kundalish Aura that flows through him enhances the spell and blocks all memory from the past, although it will always leave him with an interest in stories of old. He is already fixated with tales of dragons and fabled knights but any inherited knowledge relating to Avolire, the fall of Calistorn, and the Enderdetag Prophecy has been supressed. Furthermore, I intend to keep it that way."

"Well that will be difficult given the presence of that garrulous cretin at the other end of the village," said Lyrusa moving towards the table.

"To whom do you refer sister?" asked Fullbane.

"An impoverished drifter came to this village some time ago," replied Lyrusa. "Some say he came from the Capital but no one knows the truth. I think he is just full of bullshit but he loves to tell stories of the old days and of his travels across the Realm."

"And does he have a title, this tramper," asked Blackfayer?

"He goes by the name of Denius Castor," added Rukave. "I'm sure the simpleton's motives are innocent but I do fear his continued storytelling, more so when the idiot has filled his belly with the Blessed Beast."

"Then you will have to keep a close eye on this Castor," replied Fullbane. "At least until you are sure of his intentions."

"Yes of course, I do understand that. I will do my best and continue to serve and protect"

Another subtle creak seeped out from the darkest recess at the back of the rustic building. It floated across the air and seeped into the ears of the four men and the woman. All turned and looked to the direction of its origin yet saw nothing.

"I sounds like you have rats Rukave," said Fullbane grinning.

"No doubt another of the joys of rural life," sneered Blackfayer.

The others laughed for none could ever imagine Xix living such a rustic existence.

Further movement in the dark went unnoticed. Three ethereal figures looked on with great interest as the conversation came to a close. Their presence remained hidden from those who talked, just as the three had intended.

"This is the history I told you of sisters," began the first of the crones.

"So these are today's Cuvar?" said the second. "Not quite the heroic figures I expected."

"Yes dearest sisters," continued the first. "Behold the protectors of the Marked."

"Do you think it is these men who have been threatening our game?" asked the second as she watched Mathias Amberstone place the ivory code wheel into his pocket.

"I don't think so. Then was then, and now is now!" replied the first. "The Cuvar have always been part of our game throughout all its iterations. No, there is something more powerful at work and it impedes our intentions. This game is different to any we have ever played before. Whatever or whoever is behind this interference has a power equal to our own.

"Do you think it time for the boy to see all?" added the second, glancing to the mute third.

"No," said the first, dropping the hood of her cloak over her face. "It's time for him to wake."

2

Llyat's eye lids flickered as they sought to recover from their long enforced sleep. They opened, not knowing if they should, and as a film of sticky mucous was swept off the surface of each globe the youth stared up at the night sky. The sudden realisation that he was alive caused Llyat to gasp for air. He sat up while panic took control of his senses. His breathing became rapid and shallow while he attempted to fill his lungs with the cold air that enveloped his body. He had no idea where he was, how he had got there, or how he could still be alive. For some reason his memory seemed difficult to access as if lost in the swirling mists of the marsh lands. After some time in this state of suspended confusion he began to recall his escape from the tunnels that spread like giant wormholes from under the Eastern Marsh. A flash back vision popped out of his mental fog as he remembered running into the dark night amid the lands of swamp and reeds. His leg twitched as the memory of being gripped by a slime covered tentacle returned to challenge his sanity. Shaking his head in an attempt to clear away his confusion Llyat then remembered hitting his head on a rock. At last it all came back to him, including the last thing he saw before he had fallen unconscious; the great shadow had covered the heavens and blocked all light from Mona's face. Llyat knew that he should be dead and yet somehow he was alive and in one piece. Struggling to work out where he was he started to shiver. The body tremors were part caused by his fear but mainly from the cold and the damp of the air that filled his waking. Scanning his immediate location he noted the cause of his discomfort. Snow was all around him, not deep, but it covered the rocky ground upon which he had lain until his awakening. The clothes he wore were however free of damp and did not have the lingering stench of marsh water and mud. Being both clean and fresh, Llyat concluded that some other must have been caring for him as he slept.

The youth from Maplehill jumped to his feet in order to seek any sign of his saviour. That was when he became aware of a warmth that emanated from an amber glow that sneaked into the edge of his vision. Turning his head to the left he was gladdened by the sensation of heat that broke through the frost filled air and caressed the tender skin of his youthful cheeks. A small campfire burned and as it did so it crackled and sent smoke and impish sparks into the darkness of the sky. The weak flames cast a small amount of light which fought to illuminate the ground upon which Llyat now stood. There was no sign of any other present but the nature of the fire's construction confirmed that it had been made by human hands. Llyat moved closer to examine it and there found several utensils of the type a man would use. They were too small and delicate to belong to either ogres or Lizardmen and too big to be of use to a dwarf.

"What is this place?" Llyat exclaimed as he continued his search.

He scanned the sky and land but saw no distinctive landmarks that could offer any clue as to his current location. From out of the swirling mist his eyes fixed upon yet another surprising vision. A once great watchtower emerged from out of the gloom. It was an ancient construction and had not well endured the passage of time. Then it dawned on him where he was for the stars seemed to be much closer than he had ever seen them before. Llyat was somewhere high upon a mountain top.

"Where am I?" he shouted out into darkness.

Confusion flooded his brain as he once again tried to piece together his flight from the Eastern Marsh. A blackness descended into his thoughts and filtered away all the positivity that he felt at finding himself still alive. An intense state of sadness came out of nowhere, washed over him, and filled his soul with grief. He recalled images of his friend, Einar the Berserker from Falahorn, being dragged beneath the surface of the reptiles' arena by their pet kulkulkath. Such was the depth of sadness that crushed him that he spontaneously began to sob. Tears flowed and they froze upon the icy surface of his cheeks. He feared they would stay there forever and so wiped them away with his sleeve. In the midst of his grief another train of thought broke through. He had travelled to the Eastern Marsh to search for one of the Gems of Thamous, the amethyst that was hidden deep within the reptile's temple. It was only reason he would have ever contemplated visiting that loathsome foul-smelling place. At the moment that he had been dragged to certain death he had held the jewel in his hand. He remembered his fingers coiling around it as the tentacle of the wisp did the same to his leg. Llyat knew in that moment that he would never be able to find that same remote corner of the fetid swamp where he assumed it must have fallen into the brackish water. With his heart sunk to ocean depths he realised he had failed. The jewel stone had been lost for all time. His quest, his journey, Einar's death, had all been for naught. As if on cue, Llyat sensed the cramp that burned in his right hand. As he looked to his coiled fingers he could not believe what he held in his hand. In complete confusion he unfurled his grubby digits.

"No fucking way!" he exclaimed aloud as he looked at the purple rock which had brought him so much danger. "This can't be possible."

The amethyst was there in his hand and Llyat was stunned by its presence. Against all odds he had not let go of the stone when he had hit his head and drifted into unconsciousness. Somehow it was still in his possession, far away from the malevolent hands of the Knights of Avolire and the slimy swamp swine of the Marsh. Yet he struggled to see a way forward and still had no idea of where he was or what he would do next.

A spicy aroma crept into Llyat's nostrils and drew his attention to a simmering concoction inside a pan that had been placed above the small fire. Whatever the food was it smelt divine and was far better than the bland meat served up by the Lizardmen and on which he and Einar had been forced live off. Without hesitation Llyat walked towards the fire. His feet crunched as they passed over the snow that had turned to ice on the high peak of this unknown region of the Realm. On nearing the flames Llyat saw that the heat from the burning wood had melted the ice in a circle and revealed a hint of vegetation beneath the otherwise white veil that covered the mountain. He pulled his right sleeve down over his hand and with the protection that the fabric offered, lifted the lid off the pan. The full force of the fresh and succulent scents infiltrated his nostrils and clung to his nasal hairs with no intention of leaving. The smell was one that he recognised although he had never sniffed goat stew that was as good as this.

Without hesitation he placed the amethyst deep within a pocket of his trousers and looked to the pewter bowl that lay on the ground beside the fire. He picked it up, looked around to ensure he was not being watched, dipped the bowl into the pan, and scooped up some of the stew. The buds on his tongue savoured the various tastes that hit them as his first mouthful was taken in haste Llyat detected the presence of numerous spices and herbs that had been used to mask the strength of aging goat. There was a hint of wild garlic, mint, and thyme, along with several root vegetables, strong onions, and pine nuts. He took a second mouthful and sat down beside the fire to warm himself from the outside while the stew worked its magic on his innards. Several minutes later he felt much more comfortable, more so than he had in days. He had not felt this well since before the unnatural cold weather had drifted down from the Dirmark on route to the town of Fallguard. Llyat then recalled the last time he had felt the warmth of fire, within the cage in the ogres' encampment; the night that he and Einar had escaped into the ruins of Calistorn. It was the last time he had seen his two great friends. The bard Thias Calavan had been like a brother to him and the young warrior Irabo Basequin a source of steady reason.

Llyat sighed as the memory of his friends threatened to destroy his appetite despite the quality of the food. He began to contemplate a multitude of hideous tortures inflicted by Brosizrug and the Knights of Avolire on his two comrades. Soon his eyes closed as they attempted to hold back the tears that formed in response to the loss of his friends. Llyat was not a true believer in the ways of the gods but in his desperation he prayed that one could still be awake and able in some way to watch out for his companions. Whatever torments they faced, he prayed their suffering would be short-lived. His three valiant friends had sworn to protect him to the end but one was now dead and the other two lost to the enemy. Despite his anguish Llyat hung on to the one fact that mattered above all others. He was at least free. This is all that Thias, Irabo, and Einar would have wished. The survival of the Marked mattered above all else.

The dark mood lifted as Llyat took another mouthful of the goat stew from his bowl. At the instant that the nourishing bolus slipped down his gullet he began to ponder over all that had transpired since that fateful night in Maplehill when his family and all who he had grown up with had been slaughtered. He contemplated different outcomes had he been taken alive by the Knights of Avolire and then delivered to the Lady of the Silverwynn. The fates of his comrades may well have been more benevolent and his thoughts began to explore what alternative paths their lives could have then taken. Perhaps if his father had given him up or he himself yielded to the Commander with the skull helmet then things could have been so much better for all. Soon he realised the futility of his thinking. All such ideas were but nonsense and ghost plagues from the past. He could not change anything for such power was beyond anyone who ever walked the Realm. All he could do now, in memory and gratitude to his friends, was to ensure that they had not died in vain. He had to push on and finish what he had started, for the sake of the Prophecy and all who believed in it.

Amid his next mouthful Llyat became aware that something was moving towards him in the dark. His pulse quickened, his sphincters tightened, and the hairs on his neck stood on end. He sensed a large man approaching from the way in which a heavy footfall crunched across the icy ground. Llyat jumped to his feet and looked to the direction from where the sound emanated. From out of the dark shadows cast by the ancient watchtower a giant man strode into view. This visitor was dressed in a manner that Llyat recognised. From his head cascaded the typical nighthowler pelt favoured by the Berserkers of Falahorn. The giant man was bare chested and he carried a spear in his right hand. Llyat blinked several times for he could not believe what his eyes told him. There was no way it could be his friend for he had seen him die.

"Einar!" shouted Llyat as the rugged giant stepped ever closer.

"Do I look like fucking Einar?" snarled the Berserker in an ice cold manner that competed with the snow for effect.

Llyat looked closer. He soon accepted that this giant had different facial features.

"I'm so sorry," added Llyat as he dropped his head. "I thought you were someone else."

"Mistakes happen to those who have not yet learned to use their eyes as Fatumai intended."

The Berserker moved to the fire where he began to examine the cooking pot. "I see you found our supper."

Llyat's face flushed and he held his bowl high in confirmation that he had already started.

"If you would allow me one question, who are you?" asked Llyat.

"Just a friend; someone willing to aid you on your quest," replied the emotionless Berserker "Before you thank me, it was another who brought you to the summit of this mountain called Feorhraed and to the base of its great watchtower. It is that other who has had me care for you these past two days."

"Who are you taking about? Who brought me here? Tell me who saved me from the terrors of the Marsh?"

Llyat waited for an answer as the Berserker poured stew into a second bowl that had lain on the floor besides the fire. No answer left the giant's lips as he sat and began to consume his supper with great relish. As the minutes passed in silence Llyat became ever more frustrated and yet he knew the ways of the Berserkers from the time that he had spent with Einar. As much as it irked him he realised that if his new minder was not prepared to divulge the name of his savour then he had no other option than to wait for the return of this other. Llyat looked through the flickering flames of the campfire and as the minutes passed he became consumed by trying to work out who had saved him. He considered the possibility of it being the ancient half man, Cvyler Olin, or perhaps even Eerickk Jarl or his beautiful daughter Arnkatla. Many other possibilities scuttled though his consciousness and it took Llyat several minutes before the most important clue to surface. Whoever had rescued him had known of his exact location within the endless Eastern Marsh. This new insight perplexed him while he studied the giant's appearance in more detail. Llyat then spotted a small white oval stone set within a framework of crafted metal and attached to a chain around the Berserker's neck. It was identical to the one he had given to Thias.

"Is that a Dragon Whisper?" asked Llyat as he pointed to the pendent.

The giant did not answer and instead took another mouthful of stew. He chewed it for some time before allowing it to slide down into his stomach. He then belched and wiped his sleeve across his mouth.

"You're not much of a talker are you, even for a Berserker," said Llyat.

"I've not got much to talk about."

"Well you could start by telling me your name. I mean, it would be nice if I could thank the person who made this wonderful stew and who has looked after me these past few days. I am most grateful for all that you have done for me."

Yet again an awkward silence passed between the pair as they sat in isolation upon the desolate mountain peak. Llyat was about to abandon all hope of meaningful conversation when the Berserker decided to speak.

"Halor," he mumbled before filling his dish from the pan. "My name is Halor."

"Well I thank you Halor the Berserker," replied Llyat. "I will forever be indebted to you for caring for me and I must tell you something else; you make the best goat stew that I have ever tasted."

The Berserker did not answer and the sound of the wind over the mountain peak filled the void that followed. Llyat decided to try a different tack in an attempt to engage with the man of very few words.

"You said that we were at the summit of Feorhraed," he began. "I have never heard of such a place. Can you remind me on which mountain range it lies?"

"We are in the Grey Mountains," replied the Berserker. "At the foot of this mountain is the town of Griginor and the start of the canyon that was once the point of the mighty river called the Wistulla. We are also close to the source of the Awyth. These two rivers, now one, feed the waters of the Eastern Marsh. This watch tower once guarded the entrance to the old pass through the mountains."

"Why have you brought me here?" asked Llyat as he sensed he was at last getting somewhere.

The giant continued to eat his supper. This pissed Llyat off for he had never encountered such rudeness before. Many minutes passed until Llyat could contain himself no longer.

"Your friend, where has he gone? What is he doing? When will he return?"

The Berserker lowered his bowl and raised an eyebrow.

"You have a lot of questions for one so young. He said you would have many when you woke and he was not wrong."

"I am getting really fed up now! Who is this sodding friend of yours who saved my life? I demand to know his name!" shouted Llyat as he jumped to his feet and reached for the sword that should have hung from his side.

"This is how he said you would behave," laughed Halor. "He said that I could pass on a message to you. My friend will answer all of your questions once you are awake and when he returns."

"For fucks sake quit stalling. Just tell me who he is!" exploded Llyat.

The frustration at the lack of a response to his questions fuelled an anger that was different to anything Llyat had felt before; save for the time he had pummelled Rhaizen's face to a pulp. He no longer felt comfortable waiting at the will of others. He need to take control and part of him urged an assault upon the Berserker. With some difficulty he allowed the feeling to pass for he doubted it would help him make progress. Although the youth now felt more in control than ever before he knew it would be foolish to act on impulse; he had to think each situation through, evaluate the consequences of his actions and make the right choices. Llyat jumped as a deafening screech fractured the air around him. It was followed by the sensation of something circling overhead in the dark night sky. Whatever it was, it cut through the air with ease and was far larger than any of the skyfawn that Llyat had ever encountered.

"Shit! What was that?" he called out while his eyes sought the origin of the sound.

"My friend returns," said the Berserker without lifting his gaze from the fire.

Mona's light was extinguished as a dark shape passed in front of the goddess's face. It reminded Llyat of the dark cloud he had witnessed back in the Eastern Marsh before he had lost consciousness. Training his eyes to the sky he watched as the shadow circled around the mountain peak. From its front end it emitted a bolus of fire that formed an arch of illumination around its body as it flew past. Llyat then recognised the distinctive form of the beast. He marvelled at its brown scales, leathery wings, talon tipped legs, and serpentine neck and tail. As it swooped back and forth Llyat realised what had saved him from a premature end beneath the foul waters of the Marsh.

The wyvern circled once last time before gliding to the ground. Llyat looked up in awe at the magnificent beast as it completed its descent. The creature placed both feet upon the ruins of the old watchtower and then retracted its wings into the sides of its great body. Dropping its head it pushed towards the youth and smiled.

"Thamous," exclaimed Llyat. "So it was it you who plucked me from the Marsh?"

The head of the Wyvern snaked forward and the great creature stared out through emerald green lidless eyes. Thamous spoke but his mouth did not move and the distinctive voice of the beast passed with ease into Llyat's mind.

"Who or what else did you think could have saved you? The snout of a greynose perhaps?"

"But how did you know I was there?" shouted Llyat, forgetting in his excitement that he did not have to speak. "How did you know that I was in the Eastern Marsh?"

The voice laughed and the tone of its voice changed."

"I have been observing your quest ever since you and the bard left the Gathering," began Thamous. "I suspect you recognised some of my watchers during your travels. The geckos are my eyes and ears across the land. Yet for the majority of the time you were oblivious to their presence as they monitored your every move."

"So you were with me the whole time," added Llyat, still speaking his thoughts.

"Yes I was; throughout your journey to Fallguard, your passage through Thengar Forest, and then on into the Eastern Marsh. All your footsteps fell under the scrutiny of my watchful army of eyes. I've have monitored your progress with great interest as you evolved from the runt that first walked into my cavern into the young confident man that I now see before me."

"But if you had been watching the whole time, then you could have prevented what happened with the ogres and the splitting of our group!"

Llyat began to feel angry again. He was not sure why but he was certain it had something to do with the ogres. If only he and his companions had not been taken captive by the monstrous thick skulls then they would all still be together.

"You could have saved them," bemoaned Llyat as he raised his voice "Thias, Einar, and Irabo would all still be alive if you had come to our aid earlier."

"No Llyat that was not possible," hissed the wyvern. "I could not intervene."

"Bullshit!" screamed Llyat.

"For certain I could not lad."

"Go on then!" exclaimed Llyat. "Why couldn't you have saved us all?"

"I will explain some other time; we have work..."

"Tell me!" screamed Llyat. "Tell me the fucking truth. I deserve an answer."

In the next instant the Wyverns expression changed from its benign calmness to that of a fearsome predator ready to destroy its prey. Thamous rose to full height and expanded its leathery wings. All the while it remained on its perch, its talons gripped onto the ruined crenulations of the ancient watchtower. Then it emitted a belch of fire from its snake like mouth which Llyat was thankful had not been directed at him. The beast's head snaked back down only to stop inches from Llyat's face. Llyat jumped back in shock and fell to his arse. The beast snarled and its lidless eyes threatened to pierce Llyat's soul. He heard the creature's voice again, this time more powerful as it sought to express its anger.

"Do not take me for a cold hearted beast. I have lived a thousand generations and have dealt with more issues than your simple mind could ever come to terms with. I've seen stars fall and stars born. I've seen gods replace gods. I was there when Urthanock rose and I was there when he fell. So don't fuck with me lad!"

Llyat felt a warmth in his trousers. He did not know what to do or how to react. He just wanted to run and get as far away as possible. Then he had a great insight; that had been his old self. Now he had a new presence and he wanted to know what it would have him do. Refusing to flee, he stood fast and allowed the Fates to dictate what happened next. He was after all the Marked....

"I hear you. If you were the Marked then of course I would never kill you?" said the Wyvern. "Would I have left you to die in the festering swamps had you not been the One?"

The jaws of Wyvern snapped forward and forced Llyat to scuttle backwards across the icy ground.

"N... n... no." he stuttered. "I don't believe you would."

"Then get your carcass off the ground and let me gaze upon the hero you have become."

Thamous's neck retracted out from Llyat's personal space and allowed the youth to move. The youth did not hesitate and jumped to his feet. As he rose to full height he glanced over to where Halor still sat in silence, tending to the fire. Then he looked in to the emerald eyes and Thamous stared back.

"You called me a hero," said Llyat. "Why was that?"

"Because that is what you are," said the voice as it penetrated his mind.

"How can I be considered a hero? I've done nothing."

"But that is not true," said Thamous. "You have accomplished much over these last few weeks and have exceeded my expectations, even though I always knew you were the Marked. I still however detect too much self-doubt and a gamut of destructive traits. You must drop these thoughts for you are no longer a simple farm boy. Get over your issues and move on lad."

"I know now that I am the Marked," answered Llyat. "But I didn't choose to be and it is not of my doing. It is daunting to think of having to seal the door to the Underworld and stop Urthanock from entering the Realm."

"Tough! I know," said the voice, "but that is the fate of the Marked."

"I just wish that it wasn't me. Why couldn't it be some other simple clodhopper? Why can't things go back to being how they were? Life was so much simpler then."

"The past is over and done with," continued Thamous. "The future remains but a mystery. We can only focus on the moment at hand and you have a destiny to fulfil. Right now we need to think how you are going to destroy the evil that is preparing to decimate the Realm."

"Do you refer to those from the Eastern Marsh or the Knights of Avolire?"

"I'm sorry to say, it's the reptiles," replied the wyvern and Llyat sensed the sadness in the creature's response.

"What do you mean? What else do you know?" he asked.

"The Realm has been deceived and it has made a great mistake. The Eastern Marsh has grown stronger than Parandor could have believed possible. You have seen evidence of this yourself."

"Yes I have," replied Llyat as he thought back to his time with Ssobekk. "I have seen their army and the one legged beast that leads it."

"Then you know first-hand what marches against Parandor?"

Llyat recalled images of the armoured reptiles and the weapons that they carried. It was a formidable force and a match for any army of men. If as Ssobekk had told him, they were intent on attacking both Avolire and Parandor, then their numbers must be even greater than he had witnessed. There had to be many more of the vile creatures hidden in different locations, some no doubt under the marsh land, and others hidden elsewhere. This realisation caused Llyat's stomach to churn. He looked towards the wyvern and as he stared into the beast's eyes he became convinced that there was something else that the wyvern was reluctant to disclose.

"What is it you're not telling me?" asked Llyat using his mind and not his voice.

"In your travels throughout the northern lands did you ever hear mention of the 'Vessel'?"

Llyat recognised the phrase for it was one that Ssobekk had used before he had pushed Einar into the kulkulkath's pit.

"Yes, I believe I have. I have heard the word spoken with similar importance placed upon it."

"Who was it who uttered this word?" asked Thamous.

"It was during my time beneath the Marsh. Their general, a foul creature called Ssobekk, spoke it. He was the bastard who took Einar's life."

"And what did he say exactly?"

"Something to do with the Lady of the Silverwynn who he said now lay dying," added Llyat as he struggled to recollect crocodile beast's exact words.

It took some seconds for his memory to return but soon he was in a position to answer the question with authority.

"The Lady of the Silverwynn was being used by the Lizardmen to harness the powers of the Underworld, the very same powers that the God Kha bestowed upon Urthanock. They had found a way to channel it as it leaches out through a crack in the Rift. It was said that it had rejuvenated the old hag and allowed her to return to the strength of her youth."

Llyat hesitated as he tried to recall any further relevant information.

"Say more," said the wyvern.

"Just give me a second to get my head around this shit," snapped back Llyat. "Now... yes...the Knights of Avolire say they have found another who can serve their needs. It seems the Rift has taken a liking to this person who was discovered deep within the mines of Avolire. He is also marked in some way and is now the preferred agent of those who hail from the Marsh. The Lady of the Silverwynn and her Black Knights are being sacrificed like counters in a more complex game. Their new 'Marked' has become the focus of their plans for they believe he can absorb all the energy of the Rift and still survive. So you see..."

Llyat hesitated and looked again to Thamous whose snake like neck swayed from side to side.

"You already knew this didn't you?" said Llyat.

"Yes, I did," replied the beast. "The man the reptiles wish to use as a vessel to contain the powers of Kha came to me just after your visit to the Gathering. He is different from any other mortal and has a great magic of his own, the curse of immortality. He has been tapping the power that now leeches out of the Rift and is growing stronger by the day. I thought I had killed him but was soon proved wrong. Something most evil has awoken inside him. At first I believed that those from the Marsh wished to use him to open the door to the Underworld and therefore release the Urthanock, the Lord of Fear. I was however very much mistaken?"

"What do you mean?" asked Llyat as his thoughts turned to the horsemen he had seen during his flight from the three peaked mountain.

"The powers of the Gathering kept the young man's magic in check, or so I thought. As with you I saw inside his head but he had the unique ability to also examine mine in detail. We stole each other's thoughts and I saw the power that gestated in his being. I saw the enormity of what he had sucked out of the Rift. It was a great power and it had a name."

"A name?" questioned Llyat although he had already guessed what it was.

"Yes Llyat, that is right; I saw Urthanock. The evil one has escaped the confines of the Underworld through the cracks of the Rift and had chosen this other as its Vessel. I have been blind for too long. I had assumed that the Lady of the Silverwynn was the one we should all worry about. She was a difficult enough to manage but is nothing in comparison to Urthanock who walks amongst us once again; only this time in human form."

Llyat closed his eyes as the Wyvern spoke. His role in the Prophecy was becoming ever clearer. According to its words and the inscriptions on the side of Sir Raulyn's tomb, it was he who would have to stand up to the one who had been taken over by the Lord of Fear. He, Llyat Emgar, had been revealed to Bards during his visit to Valameer and his mission was clear; to destroy Urthanock for all time.

Then without further warning the wyvern opened its wings, rose from its perch on the watchtower, and soared into the air. It circled the mountain summit several times while the eyes of Llyat and Halor followed its movement through the night sky. At last it came back to land amid the icy scattering of snow and dropped its spine low before Llyat. The youth spotted a leather saddle fixed upon the back of the great creature and then realised how Halor and Thamous had carried him to the summit of Feorhraed. Llyat moved over to where Thamous lay and as he did so he heard the voice speak again.

"You are troubled and I am too tired to see all," began the wyvern. "What bothers you?"

"It's just that..." began Llyat, but in truth he did not know what to say.

"Then let me answer the question you have yet to ask. You are struggling to understand how you can accomplish all that is expected of you. Is that not the case?"

Once again Llyat hesitated for he still felt lost and bewildered.

"You're right, but..."

"But what?"

"Is it really possible?" asked Llyat. "I mean, all that I have to do. I get that I am the Marked and that I must unite the five jewels. I also know I have to kill the man who carries the essence of the Lord of Fear but it all seems so overwhelming. Are you sure that I can do it?"

"Of course you can," answered the wyvern with a granite sternness that demanded obedience. "As I have stated already, you have accomplished much in such a short period of time but I cannot keep interfering in your fated path. That is why I only intervened to ensure your survival."

"What do you mean?"

"The journey of the Marked was set out by the ancients, the heroes of a long past age. Your strength as the true saviour must come from the gathering of experience and by making the right choices. That is why I named my three peaked home the 'Gathering.' If you make a wrong choice, learn from the mistake and move on. Just never repeat it. With each chapter of life that passes you will grow stronger.

Others my help you get there lad but in the end you will have to face the Lord of Fear alone."

"So who is this man?" asked Llyat. "What did you learn about this other who has become a vessel to carry Urthanock's essence? When you looked into each other's minds beneath the Gathering you must have seen his true identity."

"My young friend, in truth I do not know the answer," replied Thamous.

Llyat glared at the Wyvern. He was not sure if the beast was being honest.

"Thamous, are you lying to me?" he said but the wyvern did not answer.

Llyat sighed and his mind went blank

"So what do I do next?" he asked. "I have no idea where the Gems of Thamous are. This is the extent of my knowledge. The Lady of the Silverwynn will by now have taken possession of the sapphire we found in Barad Elestor. Apparently she already had another two, the emerald and the diamond. The ruby is in Parandor somewhere and I have ownership of the amethyst which lies here in my pocket."

Llyat's hand touched the stone through the course fabric of his pants while the memory of Heliana holding the ruby came back to trouble him.

"I see that you have answered your own question," said the voice.

"So it would seem," replied Llyat as he feared for the woman he craved. "Heliana has the ruby, the last of the five, so that puts her in great peril. As long as she stays in the Capital there are some who will do all they can to protect her. As for the three jewels that have fallen into the clutches of the Silverwynn, well they are another matter altogether. Even if I could unite all five, how would I ever find the coor to the Underworld? What bait would I use to trap the Lord of Fear inside?"

"One step at a time. I have seen an opportunity that could benefit our cause..."

"Now you're just talking in riddles," said Llyat using his voice, forgetting for an instant that Thamous could hear his thoughts.

"That is my role in this quest," said the creature. "Do you remember my parting words when we first met; the first riddle that I left you with?"

Standing within the glow cast by the fire at the summit of the remote mountain Llyat began to reflect on his time at the Gathering. His gaze switched from the ruins of the watchtower to the snow and then to the rocks. For some reason his mind would not recall Thamous's parting words that day. Perhaps it was the numerous bumps to his head over the course of his journey that accounted for his poor recollection for it was not often that he came over so dull of mind. Llyat's gaze turned to Halor who still sat by the fire, still consuming the goat stew that he had cooked with such care. He began to think on who this Berserker was and why Thamous had brought him to the top of the mountain. The insight came in an instant. A wyvern could not care for an unconscious boy.

"Your thoughts are correct," said Thamous. "He was the first of the Berserkers to heed my call for help once the geckos had revealed the seriousness of your predicament in the Marsh."

"For which I am most grateful," said Llyat.

"Your appreciation is most welcome and does not go unnoticed," uttered a second voice.

The addition of another voice in his head startled Llyat such that he slipped on the icy ground and only just managed to keep himself upright. .

"Who is that?" thought Llyat after which he turned to Halor "Have you been listening to our mind talk all this time?"

"Of course he has," answered Thamous while his snake like head swooped in between Llyat and the campfire. "He wears the answer to my first riddle. Look around his neck."

Llyat's eyes homed in on the small white oval stone around the Berserker's neck. In that moment the words that Thamous had spoken at the Gathering forced their way into his memory.

"You told me to give Einar's Dragon Whisper to Thias the Bard," said Llyat. "I'm right, aren't I? That's what you told me to do. Why was it so important to pass on the stone?"

"Your head was not the only one that I searched when you and your friends traversed the Dragonas. Ever since you arrived in Falahorn to your time at the Gathering, I monitored the young bard's thoughts to be sure of his intentions. I have examined his life through all its ups and downs, its twists and turns, and the depths of his darkest hours. I know of the pain that he carries in his heart. I sense the loss of all that meant so much to him."

"So why give him the stone, or do I have to work out for myself?"

"I saw a glimmer of hope in a fleeting moment," continued Thamous. "In one brief part of my examination I understood the impulsiveness of the bard's character, his tendency to act without thinking through the consequences of his actions. I saw the possibility that he could place the success of your quest in jeopardy. In that moment of insight I sensed that his behaviour could lead to many problems and that the bard could be our undoing. He may yet allow the Fates to add further mischief to their game; one which is still far from over."

"What is it that are you trying to tell me?" asked Llyat somewhat confused.

"Have patience my young friend for I will explain all. The Dragon Whisper which you gave to Thias after he had used his bronze pendant to purchase provisions in Fallguard holds many secrets of its own. As well as allowing direct communication, it allows me to track and focus in on the wearer's presence; to know the exact location where the one who carries it is at any point in time; to see and listen into all that goes on around it. Since you fell afoul of those monstrous ogres in Barad Elestor I have kept a close eye on your friends just as my gecko spawn have watched over you."

Llyat could not hold his excitement and words burst from his mouth.

"Do you mean to tell me that you know where my friends are? Can you see if Thias and Irabo are still alive?"

"Of their fate I cannot be certain," continued Thamous, "They have been separated from the Dragon Whisper. I do know however where that stone lies. At present it rests in the ruined city of Avolire."

"In the hands of the evil Lady?"

"So it would appear."

Llyat stood in the freezing snow and tried to work out what this meant for his future. The wyvern coiled itself around its body as if crushing some memory of significance. A sudden thought popped into Llyat's head and he then knew what he needed to do next. Without pause for reflection he mind whispered to the slumbering beast.

"I have just worked it out."

"And what is the answer you have come to?" teased Thamous for the creature had already seen the thought.

"I have to go to Avolire and snatch the jewels away from the Lady."

"Good, very good. You are so much more a man than before. But you will not go alone."

Thamous looked towards the Berserker who still sat by the fire.

"Is he coming with me?" demanded Llyat.

"No he isn't but I thank him for looking after you."

"It was an honour," whispered the Berserker's voice.

"I have one more task for you Halor," added Thamous. "You must return to Falahorn and talk with Cvyler Olin. Tell him that I have gone with the Marked to free Avolire from the control of the Lady of the Silverwynn and her followers."

"Of course, if that is your wish," replied Halor. "I'll just finish up here and be on my way."

"Also, ensure Olin sends a host of Berserkers to Parandor. They will be needed in the great battle that is to come."

"For sure," mindspoke the Berserker.

While Llyat listened he realised that Thamous intended to accompany him to Avolire.

"I take it you have decided to help me further. I thought you said that I had to complete this onerous task alone. Why have you decided to come to my aid?"

"Because I choose to play against the game," replied Thamous. "You are the Marked and you will have to face the Vessel alone. But you will never penetrate the defences of Avolire without my help. It is vital that you reclaim my Gems and make your escape from that evil place. I have decided to aid you in this next step despite what the ancients and the Fates may have dictated. I expect to pay a heavy price for breaking their rules but that is a risk that I am prepared to take."

Llyat sighed and felt overwhelmed. He began to think about his three friends Thias, Irabo, and Einar. The latter was already with the gods but it was possible the other two were still alive. Then as he looked into the eyes of the wyvern he remembered the dream that had passed through his subconscious just before he had woken on the summit of the mountain.

"I saw my father and his fellow conspirators," said Llyat. "They were in deep discussion over the Prophecy and how they intended to help me. They seemed to think the key to the defeat of the Lord of Fear would be found within the pages of the Lore of the Dead."

"Hmm..." pondered Thamous. "The dreams of men are mysterious things at the best of times and you cannot place great trust in what they reveal."

"But this one was different," continued Llyat. "Those that were present and my mother also appeared to be members of some cult that was formed to protect me. They call themselves the Cuvar. The people in the dream had journeyed from the Court of Parandor and I am sure that I had seen two of them in its library. The dream was sent to me by the same three crones who have been guiding me on my travels. I suspect they intended to tell me something important."

"What three do you talk of?" hissed the Wyvern.

"The same crones that guided me from Calistorn to the Eastern Marsh. I swear they have been following me for I even saw them in the tavern we stayed at in Fallguard."

"Do you know who they are?" asked Thamous.

"Einar gave them a name. It was the same one I have heard in my dreams. They are called the Moirai. Irabo told me that they are the daughters of some goddess called Fatumai."

"That proves beyond all doubt that you are the Marked of the Prophecy. They would not otherwise visit you and display their magic in such a way."

"I'm not sure that I understand you," replied Llyat.

"Dreams are just the way man's primitive brains cope with subconscious thoughts. They try to give them meaning and purpose. But to enter someone's dreams and manipulate them requires a power of magic equal to my own. Are you yet aware of what the Gems of Thamous can do?"

"Yes, I think so," said Llyat with confidence. "They can open and then seal the doors to the Underworld."

"Correct, but there is more to them than that. I protected the jewels with the magic of dragon fire in order to dampen down their individual powers. They each can do far more than you as yet realise but we can talk of that later for now we must move on. We have wasted far too much time on this mountain and Avolire beckons. I will explain more on the way."

The Wyvern uncurled upon the icy mountain while for a second time Llyat focused on the leather saddle upon the beasts back. He was instructed to climb upon it and he did not argue. Things were now starting to make sense, his dreams, the information passed from the three crones, and the realisation that a greater magic was at play. It was imperative that he recovered the jewels and if he could locate and save Thias and Irabo then all the better. He knew what he had to do and yet he still had no idea how to begin. Snapping his eyes closed he prayed that the Moirai would once again come to his aid.

3

The jeering crowd cursed with intense enthusiasm as the body twitched and then jigged on the end of the thick rope wrapped around its neck. The man dangled from a set of scaffolding that had been constructed in a space between several buildings in the southern quarter of the city. Some minutes earlier, the dishevelled long haired wretch who had been beaten beyond recognition had been dragged to meet his end in this most unholy of places. He had then been forced to stand in his tattered rags upon a milking stool and await his own execution. An officer from the City Watch had kicked the stool away without warning and two nearby eyes wept. A weak voice mumbled a makeshift prayer to any god that may have still been sober. The body jigged for what seemed an age before one climatic convulsion signalled the end of the dance. The skin of the man's bloated face became mottled purple while two lips turned blue. From the depths of their cumulative depravity the expectant crowd roared as death arrived to claim its latest victim. It had been a highlight event for the low life of this quarter of the city, for such sport was usually reserved for the Richemanus Folly that stood on Stukeley Knoll. Their roars drowned out the distress of the small child who stood at the front of the crowd and watched his father's last seconds of life evaporate into the stench of the city. Tears of loss left his eyes in endless torrents. The child clenched his fists and dug his dirt stained fingernails deep into his palms with sufficient force as to draw blood. The tears of sadness then gave way to those of anger and then to hate. It was a most powerful hatred and it was directed towards the man who had kicked the stool from under his father's feet, a ginger haired youth who went by the name of Danisun Dain.

"Thias!" cried the voice of a woman from somewhere within the crowd.

The sound caused the young boy to turn and scan the faces of the charlatans, beggars, whores, and shits of every other conceivable kind. These were the kind of scum that always turned out to witness the impromptu executions conducted by the City Watch of Parandor. The highborn reserved their attendance for performances at the Folly.

"Thias!" cried the girl once again.

The child continued to look around, trying to see who was calling his name. He thought perhaps it was a member of the Thieves Guild that his father worked for and that maybe she was about to offer care and relief from his misery. Then he imagined she was one of his father's paramours or even his mother who had long since abandoned him out of a lack of love. The child was uncertain of the nature of the voice, one which projected both confidence and vitality.

"Thias," said the woman again, her voice rising above the din of the crowd. "Thias Calavan, Bard of the Guild, listen to me now."

The child did not recognise some of these words but he did know his own name. The woman who was calling him knew who he was but his focus refused to be drawn away from the lifeless corpse that hung from the end of the rope. It dangled like the meat in the abattoir on Shaylotte Street.

Thias watched as another from the Watch, one who went by the name of Townsforth, drew his sword and moved towards the corpse. In a single movement he cut the rope and caused Thias's father to drop down onto the cobbled ground. As the body hit the hard surface yet another cheer rose from the crowd.

"Let it be known that all members of the Thieves Guild will end their lives this way," shouted the man called Townsforth, his sword held high in the air. "No one is above the law, no matter what their status. Remember that when I visit you in your nightmares!"

"Thias," shouted the woman.

"What do you want," cried the child.

"Thias," continued the woman. "Wake up."

"Who are you?" cried the child.

"Thias," repeated the woman with an even greater urgency to her voice. "You need to wake up right now."

A stinging pain erupted on his face as if someone had slapped him. A second spasm followed, then another, and another. The young boy begged for his nightmare to end but it did not go away.

"Thias," screamed the woman. "Wake up this instant."

The bard's sleepy eyes opened and he sought to take in his surroundings. He stared at the vision before him, a young woman in a dirty blue dress and a white servant's apron. Her golden hair cascaded over her shoulders as she stared down into his eyes.

"Thias, for fucks sake wake up," screamed the girl as she raised her hand to strike again but paused once his eyes moved. "It's getting much worse out there. The battle is getting close."

The confused bard looked through the gloom of the prison cell while his tired and crusted eyes sought to make sense of his predicament. The only light came from a hole in the ceiling that opened onto one of the streets of Avolire. A silver beam of Mona's light poked through this oculus and illuminated a section of stone wall. It created a sharp contrast to the remainder of his cell which hid in the shadows. Minutes passed and Thias began to make out the detail of those who shared his place of incarceration. The feisty young girl stood over him and continued to attempt to bring him back to full consciousness. By the wall and lit by Mona's beam his gaze focused on the pitiful sight of his friend Irabo Basequin. Just like Thias, the young warrior had been stripped naked and was shackled to the wall by an ankle.

It had been three days since the master of the dungeons had removed Irabo's wrist manacles. This life saving act had been carried out after Thias had used his hypnotic voice to coerce the gaoler into carrying out the task. Such was the strange magic hidden in a bard's voice, although Thias had never used it other than when singing. Irabo sat back against the wall for he too was now awake. When Heliana had asked Thias why he hadn't ordered the gaoler to release them all, Thias's response had been *'that is not how the magic works.'* He had gone on to explain that the voice spell can only work by enhancing a desire that recipient already holds. He had sensed that the gaoler felt some pity for Irabo and deep in his soul, wanted to let him down from the wall. The warrior of the Watch was however in a most sorry state. He had suffered much torture at the hands of Ventes, the mercenary who had crossed their paths back in Fallguard. He was also weakened from starvation and from the filth and squalor that his naked body had endured. Yet still he refused to surrender into death nor give up hope despite being delirious for most of the time.

Thias then began to focus on the cries of battle that poured in from the street above. The sounds of metal upon metal, the screams of the dying, and the battle cries of the combatants left a distinct impact on the bard's eardrums. From within the prison's interior the three fearful cellmates listened as the battle unfolded. It became even more apparent that the Knights of Avolire and the Lizardmen of the Eastern Marsh were engaged in a fight to the death and that this was no simple skirmish. The war had been raging for three days and nights and had started soon after Heliana had been thrown into the cell by a hideous creature. No man nor beast had visited them since save to leave bread and water.

"What is it? What have you heard?" moaned Thias as spittle drooled down from his mouth and into the matted tangle of his dirt encrusted beard.

"Something bad is happening up there," said Heliana. "The sounds of war are more intense now. They pound away inside my head. They are coming ever closer and there is some other great evil out there."

"What do you mean? How can you be so sure?" asked Thias as he sought to try and make sense of her words.

Thias and Irabo had at been stunned when Heliana had been thrown into their cell. Both had recognised her at once as the young woman who had accompanied Llyat Emgar and the Grand Physician on their journey to the Bards Guild. They had not forgotten how much the youth that they were sworn to protect had been attracted to this maiden. On first seeing her face Thias had thought that he had died and that Heliana was a messenger from the gods, sent to collect him and guide him into his afterlife. He had imagined it was what his father would have experienced at the end of the rope.

Heliana's first instinct had been one of great sadness on seeing the shocking nakedness of the two wretched men. She had to fight the will of her eyes, drawn as they were to the prisoner's privates, and exposed to the harshness of their cell. She had prayed aloud that Llyat had not been subjected to a similar degradation and had been shocked to discover Thias and Irabo's identity for they were not now so recognisable and their stench prevented clear thinking. In fact it took all of Heliana's self-control to stop herself from throwing up. The morning pukes that accompanied her condition had not yet left her. The first few hours of her incarceration had been wasted by repeated banging on the cell door. It took much coaching from Thias before she at last relented and was willing to exchange stories. Histories were then swapped as each gave an account of their separate journeys after the destruction of the Bards Guild.

Thias had done most of the talking for Irabo was not up to the task. He told Heliana of their travels through the Ivory Pass and how Llyat had become sick. After that he told of the journey to meet with Thamous. Heliana had laughed for she found idea of conversing with a Wyvern to be beyond belief. Thias had then taken the opportunity to remind her of all the strange things that she had experienced at the Bards Guild. He then told of the journey to Barad Elestor, the finding of the

Sapphire, and Llyat's subsequent flight to the Eastern Marsh in search of the Amethyst in the company of a Berserker. Throughout the telling of his story Heliana appeared to marvel at how brave Llyat had become and on more than one occasion said her love for him was stronger now that he was less of a runt.

After Thias had finished, Heliana related all that had happened in Parandor once she had returned from the Bards Guild. Despite some misty memories she explained events as best she could. She told of how Tonousa's team had managed to work out that one of the Sovereign Council was the infiltrator from the Eastern Marsh. There then followed a description of how over the days that followed, Tonousa had interviewed each of four key suspects with help from her select band of trusted investigators. Thias listened intently when Heliana talked of how she had found the Ruby, the last of Gem of Thamous that had lain within the rolls of Thinata Fullbane's body. The vision of its discovery turned the bard's bowels and he would have puked were it not for the fact his stomach was empty. Heliana had then gone on to describe the events in the pantry and how Tonousa had found a hidden room. All thereafter was a blank and she assumed she must have been hit on the head.

Shocked that she no longer had the Ruby in her possession, she could only guess that her attacker must have taken it. Irabo later asked what had become of Tonousa but the serving girl did not know. The knowledge that the ruby was now in the possession of the Lady of the Silverwynn crushed the bard's hopes although he tried his best not to show it. Thias knew he could not permit the others to give up on their quest despite their difficult situation. He wept for he had failed and left the Marked out in the wilderness with only Einar for protection. The Berserker did bring a brief glimmer of hope for there were few who could challenge such a giant and live. He felt sure Einar would stick to his task and protect Llyat at all costs. Heliana had then dropped the most painful of words into the conversation. Phauless Gylewu had been murdered and the bard then realised the full extent of his failure.

Thias refocused on his present predicament and looked deep into Heliana's eyes.

"How can you be so sure about the battle?" he said.

"Can't you hear it, that other evil sound?" said Heliana, trembling.

"What is it like?" replied Thias, looking up to the roof hole. "What else am I listening for?"

A moment later a deafening roar was followed by the sounds of people screaming. Thias sat upright and sought to tune in to the new sound. Yet another roar followed, then another. Whatever thundered above was both large and fierce.

"What the fuck is that?" exclaimed Thias.

"I don't know but it scares me. Just listen to the people screaming," said Heliana.

"I've never heard such a sound before," added Thias. "We came across nothing like that on our travels through the Dragonas, but if I was to hazard a guess then I would say it was..."

"What?"

"I think it's the bestial bellowing of a dragon, and a big one at that."

"What the fucks a dragon doing here in Avolire?" she exclaimed. "Why has it ventured out from the Dragonas and come this far to the east?"

"I don't know," added Thias as he shook his head. "But a dragon is…"

"Wyvern," whimpered Irabo.

The warrior of the Watch drifted in and out of reality. A lack of sustenance had taken its toll on the young man. Thias realised that if help did not come soon then Irabo would surely die. Once the wyvern word had left his lips Heliana moved over to where Irabo lay. She sat beside the once proud warrior and despite the filth on the floor, lifted his head and rested it on her lap. She began to stroke his matted hair and her fingers moved through the grime and the lice that had chosen to make their home there. She began to soothe the young man and to percolate compassion. Thias watched on with a growing respect for the girl who gave freely from her heart.

"Welcome back; you've not missed much," said the bard.

"If I had, then I'm sure you would have written a fucking song about it," moaned Irabo.

Thias was not fooled by the extent of his friend's bravado. He sensed the young man's pain.

"You know me too well but what makes you say wyvern?"

Once again a deafening roar reverberated through the room and caused all three to look again to the hole. Then as the noise subsided Irabo moved his head over Heliana's thigh and looked to Thias.

"It is not the voice of a dragon," he said, wincing from the pain. "That is the call of a wyvern."

Irabo then began to cough and the effort sent agonising spasms through his body. He felt the need to cry out but he was made of sterner stuff. The warrior knew that death was imminent but he would not let his flame blow out on the first breeze.

"When the Moirai come, I am ready," he said softly. "I've made my peace."

"Enough of that sort of talk," snapped back Thias.

"Be quiet and keep still Irabo," whispered Heliana as she continued to stroke his head.

"I'm going to get you out of here," continued Thias. "You will get through this."

"Stop talking shite," snapped Heliana. "We're stuck in here until we die and you know that bard. It is cruel to give him false hope. Let the poor sod die in peace."

"I'm not giving him false…" began Thias.

"Yes you are." she growled. "You are so caught up in your own self-importance to see it? If we stay one more day in this rat hole then Irabo will certainly die and I intend to comfort him through his final hours. I don't give a toss what you think Thias, I know what has to be done"

Thias's thoughts drifted away but he knew that Heliana was right. Giving Irabo false hope would not help and his head dropped with shame.

"I'm sorry Heliana," he said, "I'm just trying to keep strong and…"

"And another thing," she snapped back. "Why didn't you use magic to get us out of here?"

"I know but a few limited spells. As I said before, the technique I used on the gaoler to drop Irabo to the ground worked because he himself wanted to do it. The magic can only work on those who deep down know what ought to be done. I'm certain our keeper doesn't harbour thoughts of setting us free given what the Lady of the Silverwynn would do to him should he even think of it.."

"You know what," she screamed back, "I've had enough of this."

Heliana lowered Irabo's head back down to the floor, jumped to her feet, and strode over to the metal door that kept them from the world outside. She began to hammer with both of her fists and vented her frustrations in the same manner she had displayed when first being thrown into the cell.

"Let me out of here!" she screamed each time her fist struck the door. "I demand to speak to bitch in charge. My friend is dying and he needs to see a healer. Open this fucking door."

"Heliana please stop," moaned Irabo.

"Heliana, we've been through this several times already..." began Thias.

"Then fucking do something instead of sitting there like a stinking turd ..."

Heliana did not finish her rant for another great roar echoed down from the street above. It was very close, if not directly above, and was followed by more terrified cries. Without warning an armoured reptie fell with a thump through the oculus. The creatures hand released the blade it had carried and it lay motionless amid the three prisoners. The sounds of the fighting grew even louder and were accompanied by a loud gush as the air above was disturbed by the flapping of mighty wings. Glowing streaks of fire shot across the small section of sky that was visible from within the confines of the cell. Thias had no doubt that there was a great beast on the rampage.

"What's going on up there?" exclaimed Heliana.

"I dread to think," replied Thias, his eyes fixed on the hole.

The bard struggled to make sense of all that was going on and two specific thoughts began to trouble him. He could not understand why the Lady of the Silverwynn was keeping him alive when she had four the Gems of Thamous and he had nothing further to offer her. The second was the fate of Llyat Emgar and what the Lady may have done since he had broken down and told her of the youth's intentions. He had given away the location of the amethyst and that Llyat had gone to claim it. The shame filled bard had only talked to save Irabo's life and he now realised how futile and stupid that action had been. The body of the Lizardman soon gripped Thias's attention. As he focused on the creature's blade it trigged an ideas as to a way to end his dilemma. A surge of energy pulsed through his body as he realised the Fates had sent a gift, an opportunity to make his escape. Years ago when his father was still alive, the Thieves Guild had taught him how to pick the locks of doors and restraints using the tip of a dagger. Now he saw his chance to use a skill that he had tried so long to forget.

"Heliana," he shouted. "Fetch me the creature's blade."

Heliana did not answer but retrieved the dagger at once and passed it over to the bard. Thias took hold of its hilt, thought for a few seconds, and then inserted its point into the lock of the shackle upon his leg. He manipulated, twisted, and poked with the tip. Then a sound from the metal door broke his concentration. The portal was thrust inwards and two figures stepped into the cell. The largest of the pair then closed the door while the smaller of the two made his way to the fallen Lizardman and kicked it to ensure that it was dead. Thias watched as the two figures, dressed in the distinctive black body armour of the Knights of Avolire, took stock of the sight that greeted their eyes. Thias recognised the taller of the two for he was the same knight that had accompanied Rhaizen to the ogre's encampment near Calistorn. There was also no mistaking the bearded dwarf and even though he had never met the Despoiler, Thias knew it had to be him.

"Grovrouk I presume?" he said.

"Tell them that we are here to help them get them out Oedd," began the dwarf in the language of the Dirmark.

"Don't worry. I understand what you are saying," said Thias in broken dwarf tongue.

"You speak the language of my people; I am most surprised," said the dwarf.

"I learned a little some years back but it's not the easiest to get your mouth around."

"Will someone please explain what's going on?" exclaimed Heliana, "and tell me in manspeak for all this spitting and hocking is making me feel sick."

Thias looked towards the bewildered girl.

"Heliana, please," he begged, "I can speak this language, so I'll figure out what he wants. Please have some patience."

Heliana sneered and returned to attend to Irabo.

"So we get to meet at last. My long search has finally ended," said Thias.

"I didn't realise you were looking for me?" replied Grovrouk.

"Phauless Gylewu sent me to the Grey Keep to seek you out, in part because I knew something of your language," continued Thias as he sensed the dwarf's growing disquiet "To be precise, I was to interrogate you regarding your knowledge of the Lore of the Dead, to discover what exactly Jonas Tullage had passed on to you before you murdered him."

"Do we have to do this now?" exclaimed the frustrated dwarf.

"I guess now is as good a time as any given that the Lady of the Silverwynn has..."

"She is dead," shot back Grovrouk.

The words shook Thias for he had not expected her to die so soon. His mind raced and he thought it may be something to do with the battle outside. Perhaps the dragon had killed her or maybe he had mistranslated the spittle words.

"Did you say that the Silverwynn is dead?"

"Thais!" added Heliana as she recognised the change in his demeanour. "What's going on? What is the short one talking about?"

"I'm working on it Heliana."

"Listen well bard," began Grovrouk. "We don't have much time and looking at your friend, he hasn't long for this world. There is a chance to get you out and we need your help. In return you will get the freedom you so desire.

"You would let me go, just like that?"

"We've been deceived," continued Grovrouk. "The Eastern Marsh rises and Avolire falls. The Lady of the Silverwynn has been killed by her pet."

"Her pet?" questioned Thias.

"There is no time to explain. We must leave now," ordered the agitated dwarf. "There is a remote possibility of escape but we must act at once. It seems you are the only one who can put a stop to this madness. We cannot allow the repulsive reptiles to take over."

"Thais?" exclaimed Heliana. "What are they saying?"

"They're here to help us. They're going to get us out of here."

"We have to go now!" insisted the dwarf while signalling to the knight. "Release the chains."

Oedd, who had stood in silence since his arrival, dropped the bundle of clothes that he had carried onto the floor. Thias watched as the knight approached, bent down, and then unlocked the restraint that was fixed to his ankle. It left a ring of excoriated flesh around his naked leg. The release of the pressure brought great relief but Thias did not have time to savour the moment.

"Thank you Grovrouk," said Thias as he regained his feet and somehow managed to support his own weight.

"You're welcome," replied the dwarf as he pointed to the clothes on the floor. "Now put some of those on."

Thias examined the pieces of cloth which were little more than rags. They were however better than nothing. As he began to choose his attire he noted that Oedd had not unlocked the manacle from around Irabo's ankle.

"What about my friend, he is very weak?" said Thias.

"Your friend is as good as dead," replied Grovrouk.

"What is he saying?" asked Heliana.

"I won't leave him here," asserted Thias.

"He won't make it," replied Grovrouk. "There is nothing we can do."

"Then you must leave us all in here," ordered Thias. "It's all or none."

"Would you give up your life and that of the girl for a dead man?"

"Yes, and I will," said Thias with a force that convinced the dwarf of his sincerity. "I would die for him and him for me. That is the strength of the bond between us. You said you needed my help, our help. We come as three or not at all."

As Grovrouk pondered on the consequences of the ultimatum Thias focused on the dwarf's eyes and waited for a decision. Then the dwarf nodded to Oedd and the Harbinger unlocked the manacle from around Irabo's leg. All the while Heliana looked on with great suspicion.

"Thank you sir," muttered the warrior after which he groaned the call of the dying.

"Heliana, help me dress Irabo for we are about to leave this shit hole," ordered Thias.

The girl did not wait to be told a second time and at once began to dress the distressed young man. Irabo's cries only added to Grovrouk's fears. The dwarf realised that Thias was barely capable of supporting himself let alone his dying friend.

"Oedd help that man to move. He's your responsibility now."

Once Irabo had been dressed, Oedd picked the warrior up and slung him over his shoulder as if carrying the side of pig. Irabo screamed in torrents which competed with the cries from the battle that still raged above. Thias sensed that the war was reaching its climax. He watched Grovrouk look to Oedd, his eyes glazed and filled with anxiety.

"We must leave now," exclaimed the dwarf.

"We will need weapons," said Thias.

"Yes, but first things first," continued Grovrouk, peering past the now open door into the tunnel beyond. "I'm sure there is an herb store somewhere down here that has potions and such that may be of help to your friend."

"I hope you are right," replied Thias. "We are in your hands now."

Grovrouk strode out from out of the cell. Oedd followed with Irabo suspended from his shoulder. Thias then turned to Heliana and smiled.

"You see, I told you I would get us out of here," he said.

"Oh just shut up and move your fancy arse," she snapped back before pushing past the bard and entering the dark beyond the door.

The tunnel was cold and dank, lit by a single brazier fixed to one wall in the distance. The bricks of the passageway were crumbling and covered in a mould like substance that collected water from the breath of those and frequented the subterranean maze of tunnels. The strange vegetation emitted a stagnant damp that permeated the stale air and smelled of wet river moss. The floor was of simple earth, uneven and rutted in parts. The sounds of the battle were at least muffled by the walls of the dungeons but an occasional high pitched scream somehow made its way into the narrow conduit. The dwarf led the way while Thias brought up the rear, a position that somehow seemed appropriate given his ignorance of the prison's layout.

Each passageway they entered looked the same and the eerie atmosphere continued to feed Thias's growing apprehension. Despite Grovrouk having released him from his cell, Thias prayed that he was not leading him into a trap and while he trudged on trembling legs he was troubled by many thoughts. Wondering if the beast above was indeed a wyvern as Irabo had suggested, it could only mean that Thamous had decided to join the battle. Why the beast would do that seemed an impossible conundrum to answer. The Lady of the Silverwynn had been killed and Grovrouk had said that he needed Thias's help. Wondering what the Despoiler required of him, he decided that it had to have something to do with the Enderdetag Prophecy and the Gems of Thamous. Methladon Heyn still lived and according to the dwarf had killed the Lady. A veil of confusion descended.

As the group moved forward through the tunnels Thias's trust in the dwarf's motives evaporated. In a state of heightened vigilance he was determined not to be led like a blind man in fog. Heliana in contrast obeyed all orders without question and her unquestioning obedience added to the bard's concern for her safety. When Thias turned next turned to his right he collided with Heliana's back for she and the others had all stopped walking. At first he could not see what they were looking at and so he pushed himself past the young woman.

"What is it? What's going on...Oh fuck," he gasped.

Before them lay a heap of dead amid the narrowest part of the passageway. The pile of comprised the remains of both Lizardman and knights, some limbless and still bleeding from their stumps. Others had been decapitated and some pierced through the chest. Yet more had been eviscerated and it was they who stank worst of all. Thias scanned beyond the slaughter and was relieved to see no further danger ahead.

"Are you going to tell me what's going on?" he whispered.

Grovrouk did not answer but instead stood in silence as he surveyed the carnage.

"We are not going to get far if we don't know what we are dealing with," grumbled Thias.

Still the dwarf remained silent and Thias saw the fear etched upon his hairy face.

"The Rift took control of the boy," mumbled Grovrouk. "The power that fed the Lady switched its allegiance and latched on to him. Then something else came through, something evil and long thought dead."

"Now you are talking in riddles," said Thias. "Explain what you mean. Why are they fighting each other and why has the beast got involved? What is that you want of me and...? "

Thias cut short his words for he spotted movement ahead in the darkness. Soon he made out two figures, both dressed in dark cloaks and each with a sword drawn.

"What we have here L'Fare; it seems the cunts are trying to escape!" said the tallest.

In that moment Thias knew who approached and fear welled in his heart. Grovrouk shouted out in the unique language of the Dirmark. Ventes sniggered and spat back copious amounts of saliva in mockery of the way the dwarf spoke.

"At last Grovrouk, we have found you," called out Ventes.

"Out of the way," ordered the dwarf. "I have no quarrel with you."

"Can anybody translate the shite that comes out of that creature's foul mouth," replied Ventes as he and L'Fare continued their march forward. "Someone put us out of our misery and explain what his throaty farting means."

"He said get out of the fucking way," snapped back Oedd, who still carrying his load, stepped forward in front of the dwarf.

Ventes and L'Fare stood still beside another burning brazier.

"Where the fuck are you going with my prisoners?" snarled Ventes.

Grovrouk made as if to speak but Thias placed his hand over the dwarf's mouth.

"Let me handle this."

"The prisoners at least are smart," said Ventes. "What do you say L'Fare?"

"Yeah," grunted the second mercenary as he readied his blade.

"We are indeed smart and what is more, we are no threat to you. My friend needs urgent attention from a healer," said Thias in the hope that he could detect some compassion.

"Just hand over the dwarf and the rest of you will be free to leave," ordered Ventes.

Thias looked into Grovrouk's eyes and knew he could not give the little man up.

"Not for all the gems in in the Realm," he replied.

"Then I will have no choice but to gut you," snarled Ventes. "Isn't that right L'Fare?"

The second mercenary kept silent.

"I said, isn't that right L'Fare?" bellowed Ventes.

"Yeah!" came a hesitant reply. "That's about it."

"Listen bard, I will say this just the once," continued Ventes. "I'm going to take the dwarf with me. If you want to fight over him then so be it. Just recognise that given your weakened state our conflict will not last long. Are you sure you are ready to die?"

Thias knew that without energy he would soon be cut down and he had little idea as to the skills of the dwarf and the knight. Just because they wore the black orichalcum did not mean they were both proficient warriors. Yet Thias knew it was now or never. He had detected a weakness in L'Fare's voice and noted his hesitation. As only trained bards can do, Thias sighed, closed his eyes, and focused his thoughts. He stepped forward until the tip of Ventes's blade connected with the grime coated flesh that covered his windpipe. Having felt the point push against his skin he spoke in a strange ethereal voice.

"You don't want to do this," he ordered as the blade dug further in.

"Then hand over the dwarf," replied Ventes. "The reptiles are offering good money to see his head on a spike."

"You don't want to do this," repeated Thias, emphasising each word with great clarity.

"Let me repeat my offer. Once I have the dwarf, you and your friends will be free to go where you please," said Ventes.

"But he is one of us," said Thias as the point of the blade drew blood.

"I don't give a shit," replied Ventes who then took a step back.

"There is no other way," said Thias. "Do it now or let us go."

"Thias!" exclaimed Heliana. "What shit are you playing at?"

"Either do it now or turn around and let us go," repeated Thias with a quiet authority that demanded compliance.

"You have not listened to my words…"replied Ventes as his voice began to waver.

"And you must understand the message," ordered Thias, staring into Ventes's soul "Either do it now, or turn around and let us go."

The mercenary laughed weakly and then continued. "You have fucking balls. I'll give you that bard. I saw that when we met back in Fallguard but you forget that I am now the one dictating terms. You weren't strong enough to protect your friend and I found much pleasure inflicting pain on him. You are nought but a string plucker and we broke your will. How pathetic you were to reveal the intentions of your friend. The Lady..."

"The Lady is dead," shouted Oedd. "The Eastern Marsh will turn on you just as it did her."

Thias knew that Ventes had understood Oedd's message. There was nothing to stop the Lizardmen killing the two mercenaries once they had possession of the dwarf.

"The knight makes an important point," added Thias as Ventes began to lower his blade.

"It is true, the Knights of Avolire have been destroyed," continued the mercenary. "Their reign over this city is over and the reptiles now hold power."

"Then I repeat for the advantage of us all. Either do it now, or turn around and let us go."

"No matter how many times you spew out the same words in that dumb voice of yours it will make no difference. I am not leaving without the head of the dwarf."

"And I'm telling you one final time!" shouted Thias while his eyes began to flicker in their sockets. "Turn around and go away."

"Fuck this, I've had enough shit for one day," exclaimed Ventes.

The mercenary raised his blade and prepared to strike at Thias's neck. The blow stopped mid thrust and Ventes's eyes opened wide in disbelief. A violent cough expelled a bolus of blood from deep within his chest cavity. Thias saw the shock expressed in the mercenary's eyes as his blade crashed to the ground. The bard then spoke the last words that Ventes would ever hear.

"That was for my friends," he snarled before softening his voice to address L'Fare. "You can stop now."

The sound that the blade made as it was pulled from the chest was almost inaudible, so quiet in fact that it seemed Heliana did not hear it at all. The mercenary dropped to the ground and lay still. Thias's voice control trick had worked and he had even surprised himself by its success.

"I killed him," moaned L'Fare who then dropped to his knees. "I had no choice. I had to do it. I just had to fucking do it."

Thias turned to the others who stood in awe of what they had just witnessed. All shared a collective expression of disbelief as they tried to work out how the bard had managed to make the dull one kill his friend. However, before any of them could question Thias further, the sound of a man's footfall caused them to look ahead into the distant gloom of the tunnel. This time a single man approached and a smile of recognition spread across Thias's face

"I'm so pleased to see you again bard," echoed words from off the walls.

4.

Cold blasts of air shot across Llyat's cheeks as he hung on for his life. His tight young hands gripped the reigns while his thighs ached from squeezing hard against the leather saddle. He had ridden horses on old Chirth Hadra's farm and Cleath Mark had taught him well, but horses are horses and not flying reptiles. Llyat had never once believed he would sit astride a Wyvern, bursting through the late afternoon clouds with Solaris setting in west. At this moment he felt infinite. He could accomplish anything.

The flight on the back of Thamous from the peak of Feorhraed had taken most of the day. Llyat had marvelled at the magnificent vistas that rolled out before his eyes. To the south he saw the Grey Mountains with their snow covered peaks and beyond them, glinting silver in the light amongst the verdant grasslands, the Tiaryer and Valmuhsh. To the North he saw the distant ruins of Avolire and beyond that city the even greater mountains of the Dirmark. To the east he made out Thengar Forest, the strange lands around ruined Calistorn, and of course the Eastern Marsh. To the west across the vast plains of the Dragonas, he spotted the three peaked Gathering. It helped him realise the extent of his travels and reflect on all his suffering.

The ice crystals grew on the surface of his cheeks. Blasts of cold air bit into his face as the wyvern swooped from side to side, rode updrafts, and then dived again. During the most violent changes in altitude Llyat closed his eyes and gripped even tighter. Yet for most of the time he enjoyed the ride. What stories he would have to tell his friends and for a moment he wished that Methladon Heyn was still alive. The blacksmith's son would have been so envious of Llyat's flight into the heavens. His expanded thinking then focused on his friends, Thias and Irabo. Thamous believed they were still alive although the creature was unable to locate them with any accuracy. His task now was to find them in Avolire, take back the Gems of Thamous and somehow make his escape. Daunting as it was and with no real certainty of what he would do next, Llyat sought to strengthen his resolve. He would not allow the Lady of the Silverwynn block his path to destiny A sudden turbulence jolted Llyat from his thoughts while sickness welled in his stomach.

"I thought I told you not to do that!" mindspoke Llyat.

"I'm sorry," replied the amused Wyvern.

"No you're not, you enjoyed that."

"Yes I did lad. I was just trying to keep you alert..."

"Well don't," snapped back Llyat as his face turned leaf green.

"You shouldn't have had that last ladle of goat stew."

Llyat tried not to respond but the wyvern heard his thoughts. It was true that he was a glutton and he should not have emptied the pot. If the wyvern continued with its aerial acrobatics then he knew that he would have to vomit. He would aim for the back of the creatures head for that would teach the ancient beast a lesson. He then began to try and alter his thoughts, focusing on the difficult tasks ahead while the wyvern continued to laugh. He concentrated on the Gems and recalled that Thamous had earlier said that each possessed a unique property. He felt for the amethyst in the pocket of his leather trousers and wondered what magic that particular stone contained.

"An interesting question," projected Thamous.

"What is?" answered Llyat, wondering if the wyvern had heard all his thoughts.

"What properties do each of the gems possess?" teased the wyvern.

"It might help me if you told me more about them," replied Llyat. "How do they work? What unique magic does each possess?"

"At first the five stones were but ordinary jewels, dug from the earth in different regions of the Realm. Sir Raulyn presented them to me long ago when Urthanock first rose and cast its scale edged shadow across the Realm. The Oracle of Frasteria had told Raulyn of the secret of dragon fire; that it contains inherent magic in addition to its destructive capability. That knowledge was exchanged for the gift of a child but I sense you know this already having seen the marks on Raulyn's tomb."

"Yeah, I saw those markings. Thias said it was the language of the ancients."

"And the bard was correct. Sir Raulyn gave the Moirai a child and in return they taught him an incantation. He brought it to me as instructed in order to meld the gems into one, the ultimate key to seal the great portal that guards the entrance to Kha's dimension. Together we created it."

"I guess I knew that too!" thought Llyat.

"After casting down Urthanock with Fortune's Edge and sealing the swine in the Underworld, Raulyn then decided to separate the key and hide the five components should anyone be foolish enough to seek to use their power. He visited me a second time and with my breath the Gems were then separated. The bonds between the components were strong and the task drained most of my energy and magic. I have not been the same since. Once split, Raulyn and I examined the five and found they had retained much of the magic required to cause their separation."

"So what powers did they retain?" asked Llyat.

"The ruby gives the wearer the ability to infiltrate the dreams of others. The Emerald's magic is the most evil for its brand foretells death and is the necromancer's stone. It became a weapon used by those who sought to resurrect Kha."

"You mean Death Tubaria?"

"That is correct," continued Thamous. "The diamond was stolen by the followers of Urthanock and it gives those who dare look into its centre potential visions of their future. But it is a power of false prophecy. The sapphire, Sir Raulyn took for himself and he fixed it into the blade of Fortunes Edge. The gem has the ability to hide its owner from the prying eyes of others. That's why he wanted it; he did not want to be found."

"But that's not it all," added Llyat. "I touched it? I saw things. I saw where to go next."

"Yes," added Thamous, "it is a power they all share. They give the Marked the ability to see where the other Gems lay hidden."

Llyat thought for a moment. He recalled touching the Sapphire and then what happened; it had shown the way to the amethyst. The same thing had happened when he touched the amethyst for he had then seen the ruby in Heliana's hands but he could not understand why the red stone would be in her possession and that troubled him. Perhaps it came to her by chance and he strove to remember if he had ever seen it during his time in Parandor. He hoped she hadn't stolen it from old Marus's belongings and his heart sank at the thought that the girl that he loved could now be a thief. Then another thought popped into his head and he sensed that Thamous had heard it.

"What about the amethyst? What power does that hold?"

"Another dark one," replied Thamous. "The stone in your pocket has the ability to manipulate the dead. It can raise them from the ground and contro them until such time it sends them back below the soil."

Llyat was stunned and was sure he must have misheard the wyvern's thoughts.

"Do you mean that with this jewel I can bring people back to life? Would it work on my parents and friends? "

"No one can resurrect people as we once knew them," laughed Thamous. "Not even the greatest of wizards and necromancers can restore life back to the dead. Once the strings of life are cut they remain severed from the consciousness of the heavens. There is no coming back from the darkness and the reanimated ones are devoid of thought."

"So what does the gem do?"

"It lets you become a puppeteer," said Thamous. "The holder can manipulate the corpses of the dead as if they were alive. They are the undead and they bow to their master's command. They move or remain motionless depending on the will of the one who controls them. They are but shells."

Llyat's hopes had been crushed for his greatest desire was to resurrect his loved ones.

"I need to tell you something else," interrupted Thamous. "It concerns the Vessel, the one who houses the spirit of Urthanock and who is being helped by those from the Eastern Marsh."

"What about him?"

"The man is immortal and cannot die in this dimension," continued Thamous. "Despite being cursed by the emerald he survived, the only one ever to do so. His essence has been compromised and it is leaving him. Kha and Urthanock have replaced all the goodness in his soul. Having become the Vessel he had to be filled and those from the Eastern Marsh recognised his potential..."

"Yes, yes," groaned Llyat. "You've already said as much but you still haven't told me who the Vessel is or what he plans to do."

"Those questions must wait for now."

"Why?" Llyat demanded as the ice air stung his face.

"Because Avolire approaches."

Without further warning the wyvern dived to locate another upwind. Llyat once again hung on for his life as Thamous plunged and soared. Then as the creature levelled out into a long smooth glide Llyat found that he could think once again. He realised that Thamous had refused to name the Vessel on at least two occasions. Could it be that the wyvern didn't krow who it was or perhaps it was someone Llyat knew from his past? There had to be some connection with his father's betrayal of the Lady of the Silverwynn. The uncertainty threatened to overwhelm him and he knew that the wyvern was following his every thought. Then there was Sir Raulyn and his own connection tc that warrior. Perhaps the Vessel could also be a descendent of that long ago conflict, one from the evil side and determined to hunt Llyat down and end the fulfilment of the Prophecy. Yes, that had to be it. Llyat was sure that had to be the secret behind Thamous's cryptic messages. History was repeating itself and he, Llyat Emgar, had been chosen to lead the side of the good. The bad was out to destroy him.

"Fuck it all, I want to go home," he screamed into the wind.

Llyat then thought about the Moirai who had visited his dreams and wondered what their motive was in interfering in his life's stream. They had not yet declared if they were friend or foe, if they were out to protect him, or lead him into further dangers. In his last dream they had revealed the extent of his father's conspiracy but it may have been just fiction as most dreams are. Specific words from the Enderdetag Prophecy then returned to trouble him.

When the Oracles Crypt shall be opened.

He remembered that both Thias and Irabo had said that the Oracle, the Fates, the Daughters of Fatumai, and the Moirai, were all one and the same. If the Prophecy was to be taken as intended then he, like Sir Raulyn before him, would need to face the Oracle and ask for their help. However, unlike that ancient knight he swore he would never sacrifice a child in the fulfilment of his quest.

The banks of cloud that had hidden the ground at last cleared. Looking at the snow covered earth and the ruins of a once great city, Llyat knew that it had to be Avolire.

"There's something wrong," mindspoke the Wyvern. "All is not right."

Llyat focused on the ruins below and tried to make sense of a strange black mist that rose up from its crumbling structures.

"What is it?"

"Avolire burns," replied Thamous.

As they flew closer Llyat began to make out the amber glow of fire as it leapt from building to building, part hidden by the expanding and extensive dense smoke.

"What could have caused it?" asked Llyat. "Did you send a dragon ahead of us?"

"No. That fire is not the result of dragon breath. The pattern is not right and this is something much different. Ready yourself Llyat, your day is about to get even more interesting."

Thamous swooped down while uttering a deafening roar. Llyat hung on as best he could, trembling in fear as the wyvern flew ever faster. He may have been singled out as the Marked but that would not save him from the consequences of a fall at such speed. An image of his entrails splattered across the snowy ground appeared inside his head. Thamous saw it and laughed.

The Wyvern flapped its leathery wings and then glided on towards Avolire. Llyat hoped that Thamous had a plan for he did not. He knew what was expected of him but he still had no concept of how he could begin his search for the Gems. The city was huge and it was on fire. It would be like looking for a groat in a granary. Yet even with all that was stacking up against him, Llyat knew that he somehow had to succeed.

"What do your eyes see Thamous?" asked Llyat "What is the cause of the fire?"

"A battle rages down there," replied the beast. "Man against reptiles; most unexpected."

"But I thought they were on the same side."

"The Knights of Avolire are at war with the spawn of the Eastern Marsh," continued Thamous. "All who the Silverwynn gathered to her cause, now fight with her to the death. The Lizardmen betrayal has been swift in coming."

Llyat squinted at the ruined city ahead. It was still too far away for him to distinguish individual fighters amongst the ongoing battle.

"I sense you struggle to understand why the Lizardmen would turn against the Lady," said Thamous. "I assume that once the new Vessel was chosen the Silverwynn and her followers were of no further value."

"Well... I think I follow you..." began Llyat.

"The reptile army must now be at full strength. They no longer require the support of Avolire."

"Ssobekk told me that Avolire would fall. I see now understand he meant," said Llyat.

"Hmmm, I think you are right. This battle has been underway for several days. Getting you inside the city will be easier than I expected."

Llyat swallowed hard for it was the last place he wanted to go.

"And how will I get in without being seen?" he asked.

"There is an ancient sewer that spews out under the hill on which the city is built. That will be your starting point."

"Where? I cannot see it," mumbled Llyat while scanning the ground. "My eyes are..."

"Don't bother with your eyes. Trust in my greater knowledge. The sewers will take you to where you need to go but once inside the city you will be on your own. Gird up your courage and prepare for a bumpy landing, I'm going in fast."

Retracting its wings and dipping its head the wyvern dived to the ground. The thrill of the ride was exhilarating even though Llyat kept his eyes glued shut. The youth never saw the entrance to the sewer appear in the distance, nor did he see it become a gaping chasm as Thamous closed in on it. The journey down was bumpy and it took all Llyat's strength to remain in the saddle, one which had been built to accommodate the more ample size of the Berserkers of Falahorn. At the height of a man above the ground the wyvern spread its wings, tilted them back to break against the wind, and thrust is clawed legs forward towards the dirt. That was when Llyat opened his eyes and a second later closed them again as the ground rushed to meet both man and beast. When Thamous's feet h t the stony ground in front of the sewer's entrance Llyat's momentum carried him forward like a shot from a pult. Somehow, despite his eyes still being closed, he managed to grip hold of the wyvern's neck as he flew out of the saddle. Thamous came to a halt and snorted through its great nostrils while Llyat hung in the air, relieved to have not soiled himself.

"You can get down now lad," ordered Thamous.

Llyat opened his eyes slowly, the right one first and the left followed soon after. He could not believe he was still alive and vowed never to ride a beast again. The experience was not how he had imagined it in his fantasies when smashing evil foes from the past.

"I said you can get down now Llyat," repeated Thamous.

"Right!" the youth answered, not knowing what else to say.

Llyat relaxed his grip on the wyvern's neck and dropped the short distance to the ground.

"We are here and behind you will see the entrance to Avolire's sewers," added Thamous.

Turning around Llyat stared towards the dark tunnel entrance a short distance ahead. From out of its mouth trickled a stream of foul smelling fluid with the consistency of treacle. Its odour carried a strong stench of shit but also of something else. It was reddened and lumpy for the sewers now ran with blood.

"I cannot stay here with you; I must leave now," mindspoke Thamous. "From here you are on your own and I pray the Moirai are with you today. You will need both their favour and much luck if you are to complete what has to be done."

"Oh Fuck!" exclaimed Llyat, his thoughts racing. "Get me out of here!"

"No Llyat. Your destiny awaits. You must enter the dark before you will find the light. "I cannot stay for I am too vulnerable down here below the city walls. I will however do all I can to distract those above from your presence. My fire begs for release and I have unfinished business with the Vessel and the armies of the Marsh."

Llyat turned as a noise from within the sewer entrance broke through his thoughts. Screeching sounds, mixed with the splashing of mire in the bottom of the ancient drain, grew in intensity as an armoured Lizardman staggered out into the open. It was in severe distress with two arrows embedded in its breastplate and a third that penetrated its left eye socket. Still armed and despite its injuries the creature approached at speed. Preparing to run away Llyat looked to left then right, seeking the path of best retreat. Thamous opened his nostrils but dared not exhale lest he fried his friend. Then Llyat froze but the Lizardman never reached him. It fell forward, dropped, and did not move again. Walking forward with care Llyat reached the scale covered corpse and kicked its head with his foot. Then, given that he was sure the creature was dead, he reached down and picked up the blade that had fallen from the reptile's hand.

"Move aside lad," mindspoke Thamous. "I will clear the way for you."

Llyat stepped several paces to his right. The wyvern stretched its serpentine neck forward until its jaws faced the entrance to the sewer. Without further warning it took a deep breath and then exhaled. Vast amounts of dragon fire belched forward into the tunnel entrance. The fiery ball shot through the tunnel for a significant distance, burned its walls, and boiled the effluent on its floor. Steam roared out of the stone work while Llyat fell to his stomach to avoid being cooked.

"That should help you. The tunnel is now clear," added Thamous.

"Then I best get moving," replied Llyat

"I wish you good fortune. We will not meet again lad and you must remain strong to the end."

"What do mean, why will I not see you again?"

"I have interfered in their game. They will not forgive me and their punishment will be both swift and severe. But until such time as they come for me I intend to rain fire down on those that continue to wage war in the city."

Llyat's eyes moistened but he said no more. His throat choked and his mind turned blank. There were no words that could describe his impending loss. Thamous did not need to hear words for he felt the emotion ripple through the youth.

The great and ancient beast retracted its neck away from the sewer's entrance and then took two giant steps backwards. It turned sideways to the hill and stretched out its mighty wings. Lifting its head high it flapped with great force and somehow raised its mountainous bulk from off the ground. Within less than a minute it was circling near to the few clouds that now gathered overhead. Llyat stood in awe while Thamous swooped and then rose again as if in salute. He sensed the creature speak one last time.

"Do not let me down Emgar, the Marked of Maplehill, and descendant of the Ancients."

For several minutes Llyat stood in silence and listened to the cries of battle and the intermittent screeching of an incensed wyvern. It was time for him to move into the sewer. There was nothing else he could do.

Squeezing the hilt of the Lizardman's blade in his left hand, Llyat walked forward into the opening of the ancient drain. The heat from the wyvern's breath had left the floor dry and for that the youth was most grateful. As the light of the day faded behind him he thrust his right hand forward and called up the flames.

"Promethelumous" he shouted as his energy illuminated the passage.

Feeling the strength of his isolation, Llyat strode up the drain as it inclined towards the subterranean levels of the once mighty city of Avolire. At first the tunnel was straight but after several hundred paces it began to twist and turn. Side tunnels joined it and from that point the ground became increasing wet, sticky, and foul smelling. Blood dripped down from vertical openings in the roof that connected with dark spaces above. Had they not been so narrow and noxious then Llyat could have climbed through one of them and into an ancient street, bathhouse, or latrine. Through these channels the sounds of battle fell alongside the crimson clumped fluid of those being slaughtered above. A fear began to fester and the more he thought on it the greater it became. There was no obvious way of getting to the surface, let alone finding his friends or the Gems he had come to reclaim. He contemplated turning back but the thought of Irabo and Thias needing his help caused him to press on. If as he feared, they were alive and being tortured, then he owed it to them to do his best enact a rescue. He sensed he could succeed; he just had to.

Llyat then began to think about Heliana. He focused on the memory of her beauty for it fed his courage and kept him moving forward. Hoping she had escaped Valameer he then remembered looking into the amethyst. He had seen a vision of her with the ruby and although he could not explain her whereabouts he at least knew that she was still alive. His hand dropped to his trouser pocket for he had not checked on the amethyst for some time. Much to his relief it was still there. To keep his heart from despair he began to focus his memory of Heliana's body. The visions would not help solve his current predicament but they would at least take his mind away from danger. He recalled the times they had been naked together, the softness of her skin, taste of her lips, and the smell of her hair when washed. His cock began to stiffen despite his fetid surroundings and as Llyat was just about to savour more intimate thoughts his dreams where chased away by a hint of a breeze against his face.

Hope surfaced in his heart for if the Fates were with him it seemed he would soon find his way to the surface. The force of the wind on his cheeks came and went but soon he was convinced that the air was getting sweeter. He hoped that somewhere along the way there would be a hole large enough to permit his passage. If he had to retrace his steps it would take him forever and he was not even sure that was possible. Surely the Moirai would not desert him when he most needed them. A moment later he felt the energy in his magic centres hit empty. The light from his fist flickered twice and then disappeared.

"Fuck!" he shouted into the black.

With no other option possible, Llyat placed both hands upon the slimy walls and began to edge his way forward. It was all he could do for he could not turn back. Nor could he believe how dumb he had been to depend on the light from his hand. Along the wall he edged until in the distance his eyes focused on the hint of a glow. The chance of escape spurred him forward and soon he became convinced there was an opening in the wall ahead. Then he tripped. His foot had caught the corpse of yet another Lizardman and while falling he lost hold of the blade he had been carrying. Dropping to his knees he pushed forwards with his hands and just before they hit the ground Llyat felt his fingers pass through the sticky effluent that covered the base of the sewer. It took him longer than it should to get back on his feet for every time he pushed with his hands he slipped forward again. In the end he turned, sat back against the tunnel wall, and inched his way up with his thighs. Once erect his hands searched amongst the stinking sludge until he found the reptilian blade.

And so he recommenced his slow progress towards the distant hole in the wall. Sometime later he came to a collapsed section of tunnel that linked in to a different set of underground passageways. Although also dark they were at least lit by intermittent braziers fixed half way up one wall at regular intervals. Given the number of doors with bared grills opening into the long passageway Llyat realised that he had entered a subterranean place of confinement. Unless he was mistaken it was Avolire's notorious prison which even he had heard of in stories told in the Red Mare. His heart began to pump with anticipation for if Thias and Irabo were being held prisoner then this had to be the place of their confinement. It seemed the Moirai had not deserted him after all.

For another half an hour Llyat continued his long slog through the maze of passageways that made up the prison. All the cells had been emptied and he could only wonder for what purpose. He assumed that anyone once held there must have been freed to serve in the armies of Avolire or else in the search for the Sear's stone in the mines below the city. He passed one particular brazier which was almost detached from the wall, its fixing bolts having been corroded over time. Llyat paused and studied it while trying to work out if there was any pattern to the crisscrossing of the tunnels. He was disappointed when fifteen minutes later he found himself before the same brazier. Realising he was lost and walking in circles he sought to work out a more logical method of finding a way through the maze. His aimless changing of direction had so far failed to bring results and in the end he settled on an idea that seemed to make some sense. He would go forward and at each junction alternate between turning to left and then right. Sometime later while approaching one of the many change points he saw a shadow cross the tunnel ahead of him. It passed in an instant and he failed to make out any of its details. He assumed it to be another Lizardman or perhaps a warrior from the army of Avolire. Neither prospect filled him with cheer but if he chased the shadow perhaps it would lead him to the surface.

Picking up his pace he strode forward to the junction in the hope of tracking the shadow figure. On turning the corner he managed just two paces before bumping into the back of a Lizardman that had stopped to extract a crossbow bolt from its right arm. Both were startled and each jumped from the shock of the impact. What happened next passed in halftime for Llyat's thoughts raced. His eyes stared forward as if watching a farce in which he was part of an attentive audience.

The reptile turned and with its good limb gripped Llyat by the throat. Its slitty eyes projected hate and its lips curled to revel the foul interior of its venomous mouth. A split black tongue licked at the air. Llyat stared back as the creature's grip tightened and stifled his attempts to breath. The Lizardman however had failed to notice the blade that Llyat carried and which he had slipped behind his back at the onset of the confrontation. Around came Llyat's arm and it thrust upwards with all the strength the youth could muster. The blade's point entered the Lizardman's throat below its jaw and then surged on before exiting through the top of its skull. The creature's eyes crossed as the blade passed behind them and the last thing they likely saw were the stone walls to either side of the passage. The reptile then went limp and its unsupported weight dropped it to the ground taking Llyat's blade with it. Several seconds later and having composed himself, Llyat pulled the sword from the creatures severed skull and prepared to move away.

On he trudged without aim or sense of direction, all the while distracted by the consequences of his confrontation. Blood continued to drip through the shitholes and drains in the ceiling and the floor became as tacky as the pigsties back in Maplehill. Through the orifices seeped the sounds of war where men screamed and Lizardmen screeched. Every few minutes the wyvern's roar bounced off Llyat's ear drums. Heat from the fires that raged above and blasts of dragon breath created upwinds that moved the air within the passage ways of the ancient prison. Amid a hiatus in the clamour another voice drifted down the passageway. A short distance ahead the tunnel again split. Llyat cupped his left ear in his hand, turned it in the direction of the noise, and began to make out the words that made their way into his head.

"I killed him," moaned a voice that Llyat knew he had heard before. "I had no choice. I had to do it. I just had to do it."

It took a few seconds for him to recall where he had heard that voice, back in the Three Sisters of Fallguard. It belonged to the quieter of the two mercenaries who had confronted Thias and forced him to sing. At least it wasn't a Lizardman and if the mercenaries were there then so perhaps might Thias and Irabo. Despite his fears of what lay ahead Llyat moved on towards the sound.

Turning the corner he saw a group of misfits gathered in the midst of the passage. They surrounded a cloaked body on the ground and another dressed in the same manner that knelt beside it. Llyat smiled for he recognised the one nearest to him despite the long growth of hair that sprouted from his face. Striding forward he shouted out as the others turned to see who approached. His words echoed a greeting off the decaying walls.

"By the will of the gods, I'm so pleased to see you again Thias."

Heliana and Llyat spotted each other at the same instant as the young woman stepped out of the shadows at the sound of her lover's approach.

"Llyat is that you?" she squealed. "I must be dreaming. Solaris strike me down rather than deceive me!"

"What! I cannot believe it!" answered Llyat while the greatest smile he had cast in weeks fixed itself upon his face. "What are you doing here? How did you get to this place from Valameer? You're not supposed to be here but back in Parandor. Oh fuck what am I saying? I am so pleased to see you again. You have no idea of all that I have been through. I have suffered so much in my travels."

"If you think you've had tough times then just wait until you've heard my story Emgar," snapped back Heliana while reminding Llyat of her fiery temper. "We can argue which of us has had the worst of it later. You left me in Valameer and I could have died for all you cared. You are a prick Llyat. All you wanted to do was to piss of north of the Grey Mountains in search of your fortune while I was left alone to face the evil that stalked Parandor."

Llyat moved forward and stepped over the body without further acknowledgement, so preoccupied was he in seeking to embrace Heliana. He took no notice of Thias nor of the armoured knight that stood beside him. He cast a cursory glance to the dwarf but moved on without making comment. He never even noticed how sick Irabo was or enquired as to why he was being carried by the knight. All he wanted was to connect with the woman he loved for a passion had resurfaced in his soul and it fired bolts of desire from his heart. Without warning Heliana thrust herself forward and began to hammer her fists against Llyat's chest. Her anger flowed in waves while Llyat sought to ride them as best he could. Her insults hammered into his ears but he ignored them as he gripped his love with his arms. Heliana struggled at first but then her fury began to abate. Within seconds they held each other in a tight embrace of love.

"Right now I just want your arms around me for ever," relented Heliana as her eyes filled with tears of joy. "I prayed every day that the Fates would not take you. Come, let me gaze into your eyes for I have missed them so much,"

Oblivious to all around them, the couple stared at each other, locked lips, and lingered so long that soon they gasped for air. Then their lips locked for a second time and Heliana licked and sucked on the tip his tongue. Out of the edges of his vision Llyat sensed Thias, the knight, and the dwarf looking on, embarrassed but unwilling to intervene. Then at last Heliana broke from her embrace, pushed her head back a few inches, and rolled her tongue around her mouth. She savoured the taste she had detected for she had not eaten for days.

"Goat stew. What I would give for a bowl of that. Have you brought with you?"

"No, but I would have done had I know you were here," replied Llyat.

There was something about Heliana's appearance that did not seem right and Llyat was sure that her face had grown fatter during their enforced separation. His gaze then fell upon her breasts and he reckoned they were a handful bigger. Then he looked down upon her swollen belly.

"I see you have not skimped on the pastry since we last met," he said grinning.

Heliana threw a punch and it landed with force on the right side of Llyat's jaw. The blow knocked him backwards and he staggered while trying to clear his head.

"What the fuck was that for?" he moaned. "I meant no disrespect Heliana. I like plump women. There is more to hold on to."

Heliana kicked forward with her right foot and connected with Llyat's groin. The youth sank to the floor while the girl turned her back, buried her head in her hands, and then began to wail. Llyat looked up to Thias but the bard just shook his head with scorn

"What was all that about?" Llyat demanded of his friend. "It wasn't that bad an insult. I can do much better than that!"

"You are a thick turd Llyat," replied the bard.

"Who is this this tosser?" asked the dwarf. "What do you know of him?"

"He's just a young lad I once met while travelling the Realm," replied Thias as he sought to dismiss the question.

"My name is Llyat Emgar and I come from Maplehill. Are you the one they call the Despoiler? If so I have heard about you from my friend Thias. I always thought you had a great name and I wish that I had one as interesting."

"Like Loose Lipped Llyat perhaps," answered Thias before the dwarf could respond. "Can you understand the little man's language?"

Llyat detected the surprise in Thais's voice. "Yes I can but don't ask me how. Anyway, what kind of crap is that you just spewed out? What's going on with you lot? Have you all been at the mead?"

"So this is the Marked!" said Grovrouk. "It is imperative that we know how you got here lad and what your intentions are."

Llyat then realised that he had been too free with his information and it dawned on him that the dwarf may not be as benign as his demeanour had first indicated. He looked from Thias and then to Grovrouk who had raised his eyebrows in anticipation of a response. Thias did not speak and Llyat eyes flicked to the knight and his load. The shock of seeing Irabo's near death appearance caused his knees to tremble and a great concern robbed him of his senses.

"What happened to Irabo?" asked Llyat. "Is he badly hurt? He looks like shite."

"He will die by the end of the night if we do not find something to begin the healing process," said Thias. "He is weakened through torture and lack of nourishment. Parts of him are festering and that may be the beginning of his end. Grovrouk says he knows of a store, a place where healing herbs and potions are kept. We need to find it soon or it will be too late to even try and salvage his brave soul."

"The let's get going then," said Llyat with concern for the man who had pulled him from the Tiaryer.

"First tell us why you are here," ordered the knight. "Did you come to rescue your friends? If so, how did you know where they would be found? Do you possess magic vision lad? And if it wasn't to perform a rescue then why else you are here?"

"It's a long story sir, but in essence I have come for the Gems of Thamous. I was told that the Lady of the Silverwynn has three of them, the emerald, the diamond, and the sapphire. I don't know where she is other than the fact she is in Avolire somewhere. I hope you can all help me in this quest,"

"She now has four; she also has the ruby!" wailed Heliana.

"But in my visions you had it," said Llyat.

"I did but some fucker took it from me and brought me to this shithole,"

"Who," demanded Llyat? "Who brought you here from Parandor?"

"I've no idea and if I did I would have told you already."

"We haven't got time for this," mumbled the knight.

Llyat looked to the floor as he considered the implication of the ruby's presence. He then noticed the two others present, one very dead, the other on his knees and rambling.

"What happened between you lot?" he asked.

"We have much to discuss but we do not have time to exchange stories," replied Thias.

"But before we move away from here, tell us what you know of the location of the fifth, the amethyst which they say you tried to take from the city of the Lizardmen," demanded Grovrouk.

"It's in my pocket," replied Llyat.

"Show me," ordered Thias.

Llyat took the stone from his trousers and held it aloft for all to see.

"Okay. Now put it away and don't get it out again," ordered the bard.

"Then let's stop wasting time; let's get the others," said Llyat replaced the Gem in his pocket.

"Wait! Let me think..." began Thias but the dwarf interrupted.

"We don't have time for that either."

Llyat watched as Thias paced in circles, trying to decide on what to do next. When the bard stopped Llyat prayed he had thought up a good plan.

"We cannot allow the Marked or the amethyst to be taken from us and Irabo is in a desperate state. We have no alternative but to split our resources some of us will seek the Gems and the others will take Irabo to the place of herbs and potions.

"I'm with the jewel hunt; I have risked all to come here," said Llyat.

"I cannot allow that," replied Thais as he raised his hand. "Grovrouk and I will search out the Gems of Thamous for he says he knows where they are. If we fail at least the Vessel will only still have four. You will go with the knight Oedd and Heliana and seek to do all you can to help Irabo. Heliana has knowledge of herbs and Oedd is of the ancient order of Avolire who have the ability to perform some limited magic."

Llyat looked to the knight and Thias continued.

"The three of you have to come up with something to arrest death's progress until such time as we can get Irabo to a true healer."

Llyat pondered the bard's words. Given Thias's own state of health he was not sure the plan was a sound one.

"I will go along with your plan for now. But if you do not return soon I will set off and find them myself."

"I see you are a decision maker," sneered Oedd.

"Yes indeed," replied the dwarf.

Llyat glared and the little man looked away. A moment of awkward silence cut through the tunnel before Grovrouk explained in detail how to locate the herb store. Once his instructions were understood the dwarf tugged on Thias's sleeve and the two set off into the darkness in search of their prize. As they moved away Llyat tuned in to their whispered words.

"I have an idea how I can get you all out of Avolire."

"Tell me then," replied Thias.

"Once we have possession of the Gems I propose…"

The bard and the dwarf, turned into yet another passage and their words were lost behind dark walls. Llyat meanwhile took Heliana by the hand and the pair began to follow Oedd down a passage in the opposite direction to that taken by Thias and Grovrouk. Irabo, amid his delirium, looked down at his own hands as they dangled below his head. He moaned with such softness that Llyat found it hard to follow his words.

"There are strings of light coming from the ends of my fingers."

"What did he say?" asked Llyat.

"I'm fucked if I know!" replied Heliana. "Something about strings,"

"Yes, that's what I heard."

The passageway emptied save for Ventes's corpse and the still sobbing L'Fare whose mind had given up on the world. Llyat squeezed Heliana's hand and sensed there was something important that Thias had kept from him. He wished he knew what it was.

5

Evil pervaded the small room that sat atop the highest vantage point of the once multi-tiered city of Avolire. It was a malignant demonic evil and had it smelled, then it would have reeked the stench of a thousand decaying corpses. Within the room's crumbling walls, empty windows faced in all directions, and yet the space was devoid of furnishings. From the centre of its base, a circular stone stairwell broke through the surface. It was surrounded for most of its circumference by a small balustrade. Although now unstable the once formidable watchtower, the pinnacle of once mighty Avolire, allowed the dark all-seeing eyes to assess the progress of the battle playing out in the ruins below. Globes that were devoid of all humanity refused to glint in the glow of the fires of war. They were eyes without soul and were intent on overseeing the destruction of man. Such foul eyes had not looked upon the world for over a thousand years and their presence was disturbing the balance of realities. They fed from the energy of the Rift and they liked what they saw.

Stood before the three arched south facing window the Vessel's demonic pupils moved like fireflies within in their sockets and relished the demise of Avolire's army and inhabitants. It was not yet a rout but the Lizardmen continued to press forward and their victory was assured. A great darkness pervaded the thoughts in the young man's head. There was no residual evidence of the spirit that had occupied the boy on its journey from birthing bed to adulthood. It had been replaced by something much more powerful. The Vessel was now full and its destiny usurped. Through the cracks between the dimensions the collective perversions of the Underworld sought to see the images that the Vessel's eye's beheld. Even Kha himself took interest as his disciple, the spirit of Urthanock, sought to adapt to the ways that men's minds worked.

The body that held that essence had climbed the ancient tower dressed in the typical ramshackle armour of the forces of the Marsh. That was how he had dressed in times long past and that was how he would do so in the future. From the hip, held in a scabbard of no significance, hung the sword that had been brought with the sapphire from the base of the temple in Barad Elestor. It was the blade taken by the ogres and presented to the Lady of the Silverwynn along with the Gem of Thamous. He had claimed it for his own for there was something about its metal that pleased him; something that made his fingers fizz and call out 'destiny'.

The Lord over Fear, the one devoid of dread who demanded to be followed, watched with immense pleasure the death and destruction he had initiated. It mattered not how many of his kin fell as long as more men than lizards died and the battle was won. He was immortal and would replenish any of the reptile losses over time, no matter how long that took. Man however would not be so fortunate. One by one he would exterminate them all. That is what the Underworld demanded of him. The more souls he took, the stronger he would become. He would deliver what the Eastern Marsh expected for there were past defeats to avenge and the Vessel had many memories.

"What do you plan next Urthanock, once Avolire has fallen?" whispered words inside the Vessel's head.

"What do you want? Identify yourself."

"It matters not. Do you intend to soon march on Parandor?" asked the voice.

"I think not," thought Urthanock. "First we must win this day. The Armies of the Marsh fight well but the Knights of Avolire will eventually succumb to the death I have unleashed upon them. There are still pockets of resistance that the reptiles must subdue. My brothers from the swamp are not the force they were when I first took on the Ancients. Once this battle is over I will need to mould them to my will, reskill them in art of war, and stoke the fire in their gizzards."

"But what of the force that masses in the east? Is it not ready to attack? Its numbers are said to be great and were it here now this battle would have long been over," said the voice.

"I am not yet sure of its capabilities and await reports from those who know the truth. If the news is as good as I expect then it will not be long before those in Parandor feel the full force of my fury. They say the Marked was taken captive in the Marsh and that is good. Once he has been brought before me, made to beg for his life and told me everything I need to know, I will drive his spirit out from this existence and the next."

"And Ssobekk has the amethyst they say. When and how do you intend to unite the five? Then what will you do?" enquired the voice.

"When all are in my possession I will seek to re-forge the gems as was done of old, although as yet I do not know how. Once the forces of the Marsh are fit and ready I will unleash them on Parandor while I seek out the Oracle to confirm the exact location of the portal to the Underworld. Those interfering cunts, the pox ridden daughters of Fatumai, have hidden the memory of its location well and there is something else that disturbs me."

"What is it that troubles you so?" asked the voice.

"I'm not sure. Something seeks to interfere."

"Do you think it is the Marked? Is he capable of such meddling?"

"No, not yet, however there is also something else, something with equal power to my own," replied Urthanock, closing his eyes and focusing on that thought. "Something seeks to disrupt the game."

"Too long in the Underworld has addled your thinking. You are all powerful and nothing can stop you. You are the Lord over Fear," said the voice.

"I do not fear it!" bellowed Urthanock, his eyes snapping open. "Once I understand it I will destroy it."

The possessed body of the youth looked down to check on the progress of the battle. Many fires raged and dense smoke rose to fill the sky, blackening it as if it were night. The screams of the warriors, the dying, the mutilated, and the terrified, rose to a deafening crescendo. The streets of the ancient city ran with blood, forming rivulets of coagulating treacle that coursed their way into drains that had not been blocked by the passage of time. The smell given off by the red flow, mixed with the shit of the disembowelled, seeped into the Vessel's nostrils and Urthanock savoured its scent. All was going well.

"He did well in killing the Silverwynn bitch," said the voice.

"Yes he did. I felt it wasn't easy for him, at least until the last minute when I gained control of his feeble mind. He served his purpose and this body will prove far more useful to me that that of the ancient whore. Although I did learn much about the way that women think from taking her essence. Tell me, does Methladon Heyn's spirit torture itself, now that it has been condemned to drift through the Rift for eternity?"

"As you so desired, its pain is immense," replied the voice "We have buried it deep."

"Now that I have control of his body I am omnipotent. The boy's sword skills are now mine as are his unfulfilled needs. However, I have two strange desires that grow within. I seem to need beer and to fuck a woman. These primitive drives distract me and I need get them out of my head. Most of all I desire to kill something. All the time in the Underworld I dreamt of a vessel such as Methladon Heyn with which to enact my return. Each and every day through all those long years I willed what I now possess. At last I can enact my revenge."

The eyes of the Vessel stared once again at the battle below but no longer noticed its ebb and flow. The evil that filled the youth had begun to recall the detail its long war with the Ancients. It remembered its first incarnation when at the head of the forces of the Marsh it had fought many battles. It recalled every limb it had severed, every skull it had smashed, and every belly it had opened. It savoured the joy of the slaughter in the days when it was worshipped as a god. It remembered the scent of the terrified woman it had destroyed and the innocents it had ripped from those whose bellies were full.

Through eyes that did not see the present it looked back to the fierce fights with the champion of the enemy, the mightiest of their knights, Sir Raulyn. For so long they had been each other's equal until the day the knight turned up to fight with an axe said to have been fashioned by a greater magic than Urthanock's own. Despatched to the Underworld, its spirit had plotted an early return but had been thwarted when the five gems were combined to seal the portal. It vowed that long day to avenge itself on all of Raulyn's descendants, even if it took until the end of the world. Urthanock's essence had waited aeons for cracks to appear between realities and for the Lizardmen to learn how to manipulate the Rift. The choice of the Lady of the Silverwynn as the first Vessel was one of expedience. She was alive, if not old, and she had an army to supplement that of the Eastern Marsh. Back then the reptile force was small in number, lacked equipment, and its warriors untrained. Now she was dead but she had served her purpose. The Rift had rejuvenated her long enough to locate the Sear's Stone deep in the mines of Avolire.

The spirit of Urthanock then thought back to the time that it had first become aware of Methladon Heyn, the day that the youth had travelled the Rift, confined in a cage with Grovrouk the Despoiler. That was when the hidden power of the youth, marked by the brand of Kha, had made its presence known. The energy generated by the interaction of the mark with the Rift set in motion the chain of consequences that created the ultimate Vessel for Urthanock to take as its own.

"Someone approaches," whispered the voice.

"Friend or Foe? Do you know which?" asked the Dark Lord.

"Not yet but they are almost here."

The Vessel's ears heard the heavy footfall ascending the spiral stone steps that led to the summit of the crumbling watchtower. The sound grew ever louder as large feet slapped against the cold stone. So precarious was the ancient structure that Urthanock feared the weight of the one who approached would cause it to collapse and yet it did not. The tower swayed a little but it did not fall. Before Urthanock could think of taking evasive action, the monstrous frog-like Ssonsh appeared at the top of the steps where it paused and gasped for breath following its long ascent.

"Oh it's just you," the Vessel sneered. "What do you want?"

It took a while for the priest to be able to answer as he looked into the eyes of the youth, one whose face was part covered by a unique half helm and which exposed his damaged flesh.

"Methladon, I have come to report on the progress of your order to kill the men of Avolire," croaked Ssonsh.

"Never call me that name again should you wish keep your webbed feet walking upon the dirt of these lands. I am Urthanock, Lord over Fear," barked the Vessel's vocal cords so loud that they threatened to disrupt the foundations on which the tower stood.

Ssonsh stepped forward and made to join the youth by the window. The room tilted and swayed and Urthanock screeched.

"Don't move another step. Your obscene bulk threatens to destroy us; retreat to the steps."

Ssonsh took two paces back realising the gravity of the situation. The tower stopped swaying and the priest spoke again.

"As you will have witnessed from your vantage point, I set in motion the battle that continues as we speak. The fight progresses well on our side. We have sustained many casualties but they have many more. The Knights of Avolire fight for their very survival but their hours are numbered and what is left of their city is burning."

"You tell me naught that I haven't already observed. If you have nothing else to say then leave. Your presence continues to put us both at risk."

"As you wish Methladon. I will return when..."

Ssonsh's words ceased as the Vessel's arm pointed forward. A surge of power snapped from its fingertips. The frog priest rose, its limbs stretched apart in the shape of a cross as it hung in the air. Excruciating spasms passed through every piece of the priest's flesh. Ssonsh screamed.

"Call me that name ever again it will be the last word your foul mouth ever utters. I am Urthanock, Lord over Fear. That is who I am; that is who you reptiles now obey. You see before you 'The one devoid of dread'; 'The one who must be followed'. Drop to your knees and address me with respect. I am the Lord Urthanock and you will call me such or by the ancient power of Kha I will destroy you where you stand."

Urthanock released his grip and Ssnosh fell to the floor. One leg slipped backwards under the belly of the priest and the creature cried out again as pain shot through its twisted knee.

"Kneel or die!" barked Urthanock with glowing eyes that pierced.

With great difficulty and much distress the frog priest forced itself onto bended knees. Then without instruction it prostrated itself before the evil that commanded the room.

"My Lord Urthanock, I am yours to compel," it croaked. "My followers await your commands. We will enact them all without question."

"And so you shall, but recognise they are not your followers any more, they are mine. The sooner you understand that, then the less pain you will suffer. Is that clear for I cannot speak in plainer words?"

"Yes Lord Urthanock, I do understand," whimpered the trembling Ssonsh. "My Lord, I give my whole self up to you but at the risk of incurring more of your wrath I beg that you allow me a couple of questions for the answers will make the news of your second coming easier for your followers to believe."

"The threat of death is all they need. That will make them trust in my words."

"Yes My Lord, but the answers will make compliance easier and with less pain and suffering of those who born out of our eggs," groaned Ssonsh as he knelt upon one knee with his eyes focused on the ground. "I beg you to consider my request."

"I will indulge you this once Toad for you do not yet comprehend the true nature of the force that stands before you. Stand and spit out your questions before I change my mind."

The frog priest manoeuvred its large bulk and with difficulty rose once again to face its master. "My Lord, is there any of Methladon Heyn still left inside the shell that you have occupied?"

"You test my patience and I say this one last time. Should you or any other Lizardman mention that boy's name again in my presence it will result in instant death, an act which I shall carry out myself. Just so you can pass it on to those who may dare question my power, there is but one spirit in this Vessel, the other I have dispatched to the Rift where its pain will be eternal."

"Thank you for confirming that My Lord," quaked Ssonsh. "My second question is this; you refer to yourself as the Lord OVER fear and yet the great Prophecy of Enderdetag refers to Urthanock as the Lord OF Fear. Questions will be asked as to why the discrepancy and I would like to be able to answer with authority when asked by your followers."

"The answer is simple; the ancients who first wrote down the Prophecy mistranslated the message from the stars."

"Yet my Lord the words have been checked and held to be true by many scholars over the years that have passed since it was first chiselled into the stone of memory."

Another surge of pain rippled through the priest's body as Urthanock's anger shot from his hands. Ssonsh fell to the floor a second time. Once the screaming stopped Urthanock smirked and without a hint of concern, continued his explanation.

"Your dare to question my words!" he yelled, causing the stones to shake. "Never do so again. Stop displeasing me, there will be no more questions. You have been loyal so far and for that reason alone I will explain the significance of the word change. The prophecy points to one who leads by fear and as you have just witnessed I am more than capable to doing that, if fact demanding respect through the infliction of pain will be the key to my control over this reality. Yet I am more than that. I am the Lord OVER fear for I have conquered that emotion. There is nothing that I will ever fear, either in this dimension nor the Underworld itself. It is that mastery that makes me unique and indestructible. In addition, I now inhabit a body cursed by the mark of Kha. My spirit is immortal, my body is immortal, and there are no limits to my power. That is what it means to be free from fear."

Ssonsh remained prostrated on the floor. He breathed hard and yet despite being terrified of Urthanock's power he dared to croak again.

"My Lord, there are some who would dare to say that being without fear may lead a person to make the wrong choices. This could..." continued Ssonsh

"Are you such a one who would dare to say that to me?"

"No Lord Urthanock, I was just..."

"Stop your fucking croaking. Get to your feet and stand still."

With considerable difficulty Ssonsh rose from the ground. Once erect he lifted his head and with fearful humility uttered his submission to the will of Urthanock.

"We, the Lizardmen of the Eastern Marsh, have waited for generations in the expectation that one day you would walk amongst us again; to lead our army to victory against the men that have so long ruled these lands. Forgive me for testing you with questions Lord Urthanock, I had to be sure it was you. Now that I am convinced of your second coming my cold heart is warmed and I rejoice in the glowing future that you will bestow upon our race. I swear to you now that I will serve you until the end of my allotted lifetime. I am yours to command and will do your bidding, whatever that may be."

"Then no more nonsense. I will hold you to that vow so break it at your peril. Is there any else you have to say? If not, you can fuck off and let me get back to watching the battle. It's a long time since I had such entertainment."

"Lord there are a couple of things I would seek to bring to your attention," croaked the trembling priest.

"Well?" demanded Urthanock, drumming his fingers.

"First my Lord, I am able to report on the readiness of Ssobekk's Army of the Marsh. We received a message through the Rift a short time ago. Despite the fighting in the streets and buildings, the herald still manged to materialise into a secure and safe place. You should know that we have taken control of key strategic areas including the regeneration chamber that we built for the Silverwynn."

At the mention of her name the Lord over Fear turned and displayed his wrath.

"She is dead. I destroyed her lest you forget. Do not talk of her again. Now cease your evasion and get to the gist of your message Toad."

"Of course Lord," continued Ssonsh

The frog priest bowed low despite the hindrance of its belly, its tight loin cloth that disappeared into its arse, and the continuing throb of its swollen knee.

"The messenger carried a note with the seal still intact. It was one which Ssobekk had written himself. It was address to me for he does not yet know of your rebirth."

"Show it to me then for I am sick of listening to your voice," snarled Urthanock, thrusting a hand forward in expectation.

"I did not bring it with me Lord for I feared amongst the chaos it could have fallen into the enemy's hands. That would have been a most unfortunate development. The last thing I wanted was to undermine your plans before I even knew what they were."

Urthanock's anger flared and the mark on the Vessel's neck burned.

"Then go and get it you feckless turd." snapped Urthanock while the tower rocked. "When you have it come back at once with an armed escort if need be."

"That I cannot do Lord for once I read the message I destroyed it. Again I did not want the enemy to gain any advantage. I can however remember what was written for my memory is acute and well respected."

The Vessel's hand rose but Ssonsh was spared more pain.

"I am getting weary of threatening you," hissed the Lord over Fear while turning his back on the priest. "It seems you are the most devious of the lizard spawn. Tell me what was in the Gator Lord's message but in future any such document must come before my eyes. Do you understand?"

"Yes Lord," croaked Ssonsh, his voice trembling. "Ssobekk confirms a number of important facts. His army has swollen to a number close on ten thousand. The breeding programme the Lady initiated has been most successful and the juveniles are now of an age they can be sent into battle..."

"I told you not to mention her again," snarled Urthanock as he turned to induce further pain.

"Forgive me Lord. I am trying to follow your wishes," croaked Ssonsh "Ssobekk has had them all fitted with traditional armour, which I am so pleased to see you deem appropriate to wear yourself, and of course the weaponry that our race has always gone to war with. The Gator Lord stated that with his one good leg he is ready to march at the head of his army and requested instruction as to where and when he should strike."

Ssonsh paused and Urthanock stared in silence.

"What message should I send back Lord?"

Urthanock turned away and looked again to the battle below. In that moment he contemplated the next phase of his strategy. He did not need the eyes of the Vessel to gaze into the Seer's Stone and decide what to do next. The visions were false and being all powerful he, not Fate, would dictate the details of his own future. After several minutes he turned back to face the priest.

"Send a message back to this Ssobekk and confirm my regeneration. Also write that I am still working on my battle plans. I am thinking that the best option could be for the General to move out of the swamps and mass at the Keep in the Grey Mountains. How many lizard spawn can pass through the Rift at any one time?"

"Dozens but not ten thousand," replied Ssonsh without pausing. "Let's say fifty. That was the number we managed to push through to the Bards Guild which then fell with ease. We do not have enough bracelets as yet. I myself can take about fifty through with me so that would make a hundred but there are not many with my skill at manipulating the Rift."

"I thought perhaps it was so. Have him report back with his view on moving to the Grey Keep. I will lead what remains of our forces after the destruction of Avolire. I will take them through the old pass south of Griginor and from there descend to the wildlands and join with Ssobekk by the banks of the Tiaryer. Have your smiths set to work and create me a thousand more bracelets."

"You remember the lay of the Realm well my lord," said Ssonsh. "I will pass those orders on as soon as possible. But first I have some difficult news to relate."

"And what is that?"

"Lord, I am just the messenger and I fear you will inflict further pain on me. Please try to hold your temper," mumbled the fearful priest.

"What is it Toad?"

"Ssobekk has allowed the Marked to escape into the Marsh and the youth somehow took the amethyst with him. The lad has been missing for several days. Ssobekk swears it was not his fault and claims that it was due to unplanned consequences of sport with his pet kulkulkath. I would have thought the Gator Lord would have learned his lesson when the creature took his leg. He was lucky that day..."

Urthanock erupted into another rage. As the red fog flushed his thoughts, an aura of intense energy exploded in all directions. Waves of magic rolled out and they felled the priest and rattled the ancient stone work. For a brief moment the tower almost toppled as the blocks that formed its walls moved against each other and ground the mortar between them into dust. The edifice swayed and groaned and yet somehow it still did not drop. Once the aura dissipated a deep sense of darkness penetrated the room.

"You imbeciles!" roared Urthanock, giving no care to the failing structure. "I need that jewel for my own ends. The Prophecy threatens me."

"I'm sorry my Lord? The boy can do little with only one of the Gems. I am sure Ssobekk will track him down. No one knows the marsh better than he does. I would wager that..."

"Shut up you fucking idiot and let me think," spat back Urthanock as he looked out to the burning city. "The boy is the last descendant of the Ancients and he must be stopped. He is the only one with power sufficient to interfere with the destiny I am creating for myself. Find and eliminate him. Send a message to Ssobekk as soon as you are able for he must locate and kill this Marked. That is his priority and once done he can he proceed to the Grey Keep."

"Lord I will do your bidding without question but what is it about the Marked that worries you so much?" asked Ssonsh while regaining his feet.

"I feel something important," pondered Urthanock. "It has passed down through the blood line of Sir Raulyn and has strong magic of its own. I sense its presence, and yet I cannot grasp what it is. Something is being hidden from me; someone is interfering."

"Do you think it possible that the Marked could unite the Gems and seal the portal to the Underworld?"

"That was what was written but I will not allow it come to pass," boomed Urthanock as once again his voice caused the room to shake. "The bastard may have powers that I am not yet aware of. Perhaps he is planning to get to the Oracle before me in which case I must enact my plans with a greater urgency. Something has been passed down to this boy through the seed of Sir Raulyn's balls and the fruitful fucks of his descendants throughout the many years that passed while I was forced to watch from the Underworld. I need to find a way to discover this secret of the Marked. Whatever his power, it must be stopped. The line of Raulyn must be terminated."

"I am not sure I have much knowledge that can add insight to your dilemma Lord," replied Ssonsh. "However, I was once told a legend. It spoke of something interesting written on the side of Sir Raulyn's tomb. Perhaps the messages contained there could enlighten you."

"Do you remember what you were told for I cannot afford the time to search Barad Elestor?"

"As I recall, it predicted the return of the Marked but also that Raulyn gave a child to the Moirai in payment for knowledge on how to create the key jewel. The so called good Knight seems to have been willing to make a sacrifice. It was a bit of a surprise to us all," replied the hesitant frog-priest.

"Raulyn, sacrifice an innocent! I find that hard to believe."

"And yet that is what was written Lord," affirmed Ssnosh while looking to numerous deep cracks that had appeared in the walls of the old watchtower.

"I have not wasted centuries to be thwarted by some snot of a lad. Long ago my armies of Lizardmen were put to the sword and defeated by the Ancients. I saw too many of them slaughtered to be able to forget what happed and I will never forgive their attempt to wipe us from this Realm. I will have my revenge of that you can be assured. Look at me; I have returned for one purpose only, to destroy the descendants of the Ancients,"

The Lord of Fear paused as a gust of wind threatened to shake the integrity of the tower.

"Did you ever hear of the battles and the losses that befell our spawn? I guess they were never written down but I have not forgotten a single life that was extinguished. I led our brave warriors through five major battles and lost upwards of five thousand of our kin in the first three without gaining any decisive advantage. In the fourth I lost ten thousand, and most of my senior generals, creatures long descended from the highest of Lizardman families. Always that damned cunt Raulyn planned and dictated his forces and fought me hand to hand. I vowed after that last war in which neither side won the day that I would not return without sufficient numbers to ensure victory. It took years but then our armies clashed one last time on the killing ground between Thengar Forest and where the ruins of Calistorn now stand. I brought with me one hundred thousand and until the end the outcome hung in the balance. The battle had raged for seven days until the point when I fought my way through the ranks to Raulyn. That high and mighty bastard caught me with his axe on my helm. Its magic enhanced the blow and dropped me to my knees. Further strikes then rained down and I still feel the pain from the wounds they inflicted. My neck was severed, my chest cleaved open. My entails were then displayed for all to see and trample into the ground. Once I had fallen my lizard spawn lost courage and they were slaughtered to a one. Their bodies sank beneath the soil and so many died there that the rocks began to boil. It is said in the Underworld that just below the surface of that field of death the ground still burns."

"I have heard that myself," said Ssonsh.

"Now I am back. With the aid of this Vessel I will spill so much man blood that their grasslands and forests will turn red," ranted Urthanock.

"We will be there with you Lord," affirmed Ssonsh.

"Tell me priest, is this history news to you?" he muttered turning to look through the window.

"My Lord, much of what you said, although never written down, was passed on by word of split tongue through the generations although I must confess that our stories cover a great deal more detail of your prowess and victories. Your memory became a cult and long have we worshiped your memory,"

"Then tell me the version of today. What detail..."

The heavy footfall of another ascending the stone steps cut off Urthanock's words and both Vessel and priest turned to face the stairwell. A minute later a second Lizardman, one dressed in battle armour and splattered with crimson, rose through the hole in the floor and began to speak in haste.

"Oh Mighty Ssonsh I bring word of the battle and other news. May I speak with an open tongue before this man?"

Those last few words did not travel well through Urthanock's thoughts. An unseen bolus of light left the Vessel's hand and gripped the Lizardman's throat. It tightened by the second as the creature's eyes bulged and its head turned blue.

"Please Lord, release him for what he has to say could be of great importance," pleaded Ssonsh while seeking to save the messenger's life.

"So be it but if he demeans me again it will be the last thing he ever does," snarled Urthanock.

The Lord of evil released his control of the reptile's neck and as the seconds passed it began to recover. Its legs had weakened but somehow it found the strength to keep standing.

"This is Lord Urthanock," shouted Ssonsh to the new arrival while displaying what little authority he had left. "You will humble yourself before him and address him as Lord should you wish to live. Urthanock now leads us and we are all his servants. Tell him your news and then fuck off back into the hole you just crawled out of."

The Lizardman bowed low and spoke with a fearful hiss while its body trembled with fear.

"My Lord Urthanock, Mighty Ssonsh, first news of the battle. Our army has the upper hand and the Knights of Avolire are falling back. Their numbers and capabilities have been much degraded and although final victory is not yet ours its inevitability is beyond doubt. I predict you can declare your triumph by the end of the day."

"You should have saved yourself the climb for I have seen the evidence from this window," snarled Urthanock. "I hope the rest of your news is of more value for if not you will regret the day you were hatched."

"Oh Mighty Ssonsh..."began the trembling herald.

"Don't ever call him mighty again. I am the one with power now," growled Urthanock.

"Oh... Ssonsh, you ordered us to locate the dwarf Grovrouk. We have searched the battlefield and the burning ruins at great danger to ourselves. The little man is nowhere to be found. We checked the prison and it appears that those captured by the ogres have escaped. We must assume that they have all fled the city and ..."

These were the last words the Lizardman ever spoke.

Ssonsh looked towards the frightful Lord that seemed to grow ever larger before his eyes. The Vessel stretched tall and thrust out its right hand. From the essence of Urthanock and amid an explosion of anger, a blot of intense blue light shot across the confined space of the square stone room. It picked up the Lizardman and flung him with great force against the northern three arched window. The stone work shattered with the impact as did the back of the reptiles head and spine. As it hit like a projectile from the greatest of pults, the north wall of the watch room exploded outwards and showered missiles of rock onto the warriors who fought below. The whole tower shook and Ssonsh gripped the balustrade around the stairwell lest he should fall down into the darkness.

"I am sure we will find Grovrouk Lord," said the trembling priest. "We just need more time to conduct a thorough search. If we do locate him, is your wish that we take him alive? It may be easier to kill him."

"Bring the squatwaddler to me skewered, head at one end, cock at the other," screamed back Urthanock with eyes afire. "I don't give a fuck if he is alive or dead when you chop him and stick the spit rod through. I just need to recognise his face and piss on it before I roast his flesh and feed it to the mathulath. Do you have anything more to tell me for I have grown weary of your presence?"

"No Lord Urthanock, but I remain a little confused. What is the message that I should send to Ssobekk. What are your orders? Should he search for the Marked and the amethyst? Should he stay where he is or depart for the Grey keep? I could order him to set off for Avolire if that pleases you."

"It would please me to see the dwarf dead, like all men of the Realm. Don't bother Ssobekk just now for your role is to seek and destroy all who are not of the lizard kind. Men, women, their children; all must be put to the sword or the torch. Do you understand me priest?"

A large black shadow passed over the watchtower and darkened the room.

"I sense another danger," said Urthanock as he turned to look out through the gaping north window.

"This tower will fall soon. It is becoming more unstable by the second. Take your bloated body down to the ground. If you idle you will not make it. Now fuck off and find the dwarf."

"But what of your safety Lord, should you not go first?"

"I have other plans. Now go before I send you through the wall like that last fool."

Ssonsh did not hesitate and moved as fast as his injured leg would permit. To the stairwell and down the steps he raced. The walls creaked and swayed and despite the unlit darkness the priest knew the structure was about to fall. An intense and bestial screech shook the stone and caused Ssonsh to trip. Down the spiral steps he tumbled but at least he was moving fast. From his precarious high vantage point Urthanock watched the wyvern dive and breathe fire on the Lizardman warriors below. Realising that the course of the battle was about to change unless he somehow intervened, he thrust his head through the middle arch of the south facing window. The watchtower tilted forward with his weight but he had a plan and was confident that what he was about to do would suffice. As the wyvern swooped and rose, Urthanock fired bolts of dark energy from his fingertips towards the tail of the soaring beast; one connected. The wyvern's tail flicked in discomfort and its head turned to seek the origin of the insult. Urthanock's voice boomed out above the raging battle as it sought to gain the wyvern's attention.

"I am waiting for you. It is I, Urthanock. Come and get me dragon fucker."

Thamous turned in a circle and the creatures eyes honed in on the tower.

"I said I am here, you bag of shit. I am reborn and have come to avenge my years of incarceration. Your precious fucking Gems cannot help you now!"

Thamous continued to circle the tower while two minds connected. The wyvern screeched as Urthanock penetrated its thoughts and spewed out further insults.

"You have grown fat and lazy while I have been away. What have you been doing all these years; playing with yourself inside some dark mountain. Yes, I sense that is the answer. Well I am back and soon you will join that cunt Raulyn in the Underworld."

Thamous swooped at speed towards the window as it sensed the presence of its nemesis. As it passed at speed Urthanock knew that that the creature had recognised the body of the Vessel and made the connection with the voice projected inside its skull. The beast pulled up at the last moment, overflew the watchtower and then dived over its opposite side. Then circling again it made ready to bring fire and destruction down upon one that hung from the window. It dived a second time, its mouth spewing forth fire as it closed in on the watchtower and its evil occupant. In a flash Urthanock moved away from the orifice and hid behind the adjacent stone work. A second later the air filled with intense heat and flame. Up Thamous soared over the room and then began a descent over the opposite side. Having anticipated this move, the Vessel's body sprinted across the room and leaped through the gap created by the absent north wall. The timing was perfect and he jumped just seconds before the wyverns claws kicked against the roof of the tower and caused it to fall. Landing on the neck of the dragon Urthanock held on with all the strength that the Vessels arms and legs could muster.

The wyvern then proceeded to do all it could to dislodge its assailant. It swooped, banked, looped, and stalled. It dived, shuddered, shook, screeched and screamed. It whipped its neck from side to side, flicked its tail over its body and flew as close as it dared to the flames and fighting that still continued at a pace on the ground below. Everything the creature tried was to no avail for Urthanock refused to let go. Thamous screeched and roared again and again as the ride to tame the beast continued for minute after long minute. As the ancient lizard began to tire its movements became slower and less fanatic. It descended towards the ground and just for a brief second settled into a glide.

"You're going to die worm, you're going to fucking die. Prepare yourself for an eternity of nothingness," mindscreamed Urthanock.

In that transient moment of calm flight Urthanock removed the sword from his side and held it aloft. The evening sky suddenly crackled with bright blue lightening which drew in and engulfed the sword with its awesome power. The blade crackled with the essence of the gods while Urthanock thrust it deep into the hole on the right side of Thamous's neck, an arm's length behind its eye. The pain induced was intense and caused Thamous to swoop even lower. The beast hit the ground at speed and slid forward for some distance on its scale covered belly until finally coming to a halt amid a fountain of crimson spray. The blade had destroyed the wyvern's ear and destroyed the beast's ability to fight on. The damage from the blade had set up an intense dizziness within the creatures head which Urthanock could sense through their connection. Though stationary on the ground, Thamous's world span around in circles.

The wyvern thrashed for several more minutes before the intense distress began to take its toll. At last it stilled and that was the point that Urthanock chose to strike. Extracting the blade from the hole that was the wyvern's ear, Urthanock channelled all his strength into the metal of the weapon. It began to glow with a fierce white light and the air around it began to fizz and crackle. With a demonic grin etched upon the Vessel's face, Urthanock drove the blade deep into the mighty wyvern's spine. Thamous's neck, limbs, and tail fell limp and its head crashed to the ground. Urthanock leapt from the falling neck, rolled in the dirt and then immediately regained control. The Lord over Fear moved to the side of the creature's head and stared into the still open right eye. The wyvern was dying but it not yet gone. It tried one last expulsion of flame which shot forward causing no harm save for the destruction of several inquisitive warriors who had come to gaze upon the fallen beast.

"You tried to kill the Vessel with your fiery breath yet even then you failed," mindspoke Urthanock. "I believe you are the last of your kind. Let it be known for eternity that it was I, The Lord over Fear, who ended the last of your race. You sealed me in the underworld with your magic but you will not go there yourself. You will be no more. Your powers are mine to take and without them you will never reap an afterlife."

Thamous's eyes flickered and began to fade. It had lost and the end had come. As the beast breathed its last gasp of air, an aura flowed from its right eye, formed into a beam, split into two, and then forced it way through the vessels eyes. There amongst the spirit of the Urthanock two sources of great magic mixed and the power of the product was something never before felt in the history of the Realm. It was a power great enough to contemplate taking on the gods themselves. A great tremor radiated away from the feet of Urthanock and buildings began to fall as the ground quaked.

The Vessel's right arm reached out and took back the blade that had killed the wyvern. The sword cleaned itself and the Vessel replaced it n the scabbard of no significance that still hung at its side. Urthanock climbed onto the wyverns back and atop of its great hump began contemplating events of the past. Thoughts of a cavern deep below a mountain and the pain of burning flesh lingered long and confused him for it was not his pain but the Vessel's. There Urthanock pondered his destiny and watched on as Lizardmen and the Knights of Avolire continued to end each other lives. From out of the nearby rubble of the fallen tower he saw the unmistakable frame of Ssonsh limping away amid a great cloud of dust and ash. Urthanock laughed at the sight of the lame frog-like creature. Beneath him Thamous's eyes, though still open, had clouded. There was nothing left inside its scale covered skull.

The Dark Lord saw the battle move away as the forces of Avolire retreated in to small pockets of resistance in the south of the city. Intense magic swirled inside his vessel and he savoured the new sensations. Seeking to try and distinguish what was new, he sought to work out how the ancient power of the wyvern could be harnessed to his own ends.

Amid the ongoing battle he sensed something different. Somehow he could feel the presence of one of the prisoners; the bard called Thias Calavan that he had heard so much about. There was also something else, a memory neither of his own doing nor that of the wyvern. It was an image of that same bard singing in a tavern far away in a village surround by maple trees. Without doubt or question, he knew where to find this other. He could sense him and he could see his face. If he so wanted he could infiltrate the minstrel's thoughts but that would just give away his advantage of surprise. Jumping down from the back of the dead beast, Urthanock set off the find the bard. The dwarf would be with him and he knew the exactly where to find them.

6

"Keep to the shadows and try to avoid the glare from the braziers," whispered Grovrouk the Despoiler as he led Thias Calavan on through the dark foreboding passages of Avolire's prison.

"Yes, but that's not so easy for me with my long legs," whispered the bard. "Even more so as we approach each of the fires. The smoke they make is beginning to irritate my eyes and it seems they are getting more numerous the further we walk."

"That's because we are approaching the centre of this hateful place where men, dwarves, and beasts have suffered for a thousand generations."

"Hush, do you hear that!" said Thias as a thunderous crash above his head caused dust to sprinkle down like pepper-fine snow. "The noise of battle is growing ever louder and the fighting seems of a greater intensity."

"Again, that is because we are nearing the centre of the city. The stench of the dead that seeps down is confirmation of a great slaughter," replied the concerned dwarf.

Amid the deep gloom and fetid air, the cries of the dying echoed down the ventilation shafts in the tunnel's roof. The sounds were dulled by the copious clumps of coagulated crimson that fell with the noise. The crash of metal hitting metal created a distinctive clamour that masked the bloodcurdling sounds of the dying and battle cries of those who fought to survive. The cacophony continued to swell as the pair of strange companions trod with stealth amid the darkened passageways.

"How did a dwarf from the Dirmark come to be linked to the likes of Avolire and the Eastern Marsh?" quizzed Thias as they stopped at yet another junction in the tunnels.

"Does it matter?" replied Grovrouk, "I am here and you should be grateful for my assistance."

"And indeed I am and yet it would help me to trust you if I were to know how your involvement with Avolire began. The last thing I want is to be walking into a trap set by a stump."

"It is of no relevance to our current situation so stop bleating bard," interrupted the dwarf. "I am just trying to ensure the downfall of the one who is determined to destroy both the Realm and this world. We must keep moving and take possession of the Gems. Above everything else, we have to put an end to the plans of the Dark Lord who seeks the power of the gods themselves."

"I am not inclined to travel further unless you explain your involvement Grovrouk."

The bard's stubborn streak surfaced again. Despite being released from his cell by the little man, there was little else that Thias could call on to trust in Grovrouk's intentions.

"Not inclined to travel further!" exclaimed the dwarf with disdain. "What kind of nonsense talk is that? Do you think you are on some ale house wander? Right now we are in great danger and if we don't succeed this world that we have come to love will be forever destroyed! Now move your feet before I piss on them."

Thias moved on into the passage way to his right.

"Not that way string plucker!" exclaimed the dwarf.

Thias turned at once and followed his diminutive colleague into the opposite tunnel.

"I'll tell you this much," moaned Grovrouk. "I only ever wanted to see Parandor fall. I was disowned by my own people. Although they too are not adverse to plunder and rape, the extent of my lust to despoil was too great for even them to tolerate, so once I turned the impulse to thieve on my own race. I was exiled from the Dirmark with instructions to live out my life of crime on the sworn enemy of my people, the long legged shits like you who rule the Realm from Parandor. For too long your kind have plundered the wealth of the Dirmark and it became my mission to take what I could for myself."

"But Avolire, why link in with them?" asked Thias.

Another torrent of screams from above was followed by an eerie silence.

"Let's just say I fell into their control for we had similar aims. At first I did not understand what they were up to, nor what Sanura Silverwynn wanted. I worked it out in time but by then it was too late. In the end I understood the importance of the Lizardmen to her scheme and grew ever more concerned."

"But what was your specific role in the Lady's plans?" asked Thias as his interest grew.

"To gain the information that would lead to the discovery of the Gems."

"The interrogation of Tullage at the Grey Keep?" pushed Thias.

"Correct!" replied Grovrouk. "That was my prime task."

"Yet I am still not sure why you would risk so much to help me."

Both man and dwarf then stopped and looked up to an air hole as an earthquake like tremor shook the roof and walls of the passageway. It was followed by a prolonged screech, so deafening as to cause both to hold their hands over their ears. Then, just as quick as it had started the noise disappeared and an eerie silence fell. For several seconds even the sounds of battle ceased.

"I don't like that one bit!" said Thias with nerve ends tingling.

"Me neither so let's keep moving. Whatever it was it was not good."

"Why do you risk so much to help me?" asked Thias.

"Because that shit from Maplehill turned up and everything changed. Quick, back against the wall! There are several lizard men ahead."

Thias dropped to his knees whist pushing the small of his back against the stone wall of the tunnel. There ahead, illuminated by a brazier, walked three Lizardmen in full armour. They were too busy in their own conversation to notice those who followed.

"They are heading for the old guard room where the Knights of Avolire store their black powder," whispered Grovrouk. "I hope they have moved it for if that stuff goes off the noise you just heard will sound like a sleeping mouse in comparison. We need to wait a few minutes and see if they intend to stay there or move on."

"Ok, I understand, but while we continue to hide in the shadows I would like to hear more," whispered Thias. "You were talking about the one from

Maplehill. What do you know of this person who gives you so much concern? What did he do to cause you to switch your allegiance?"

Thias looked to the little man and stared into his eyes. Deep in his own soul he knew the other that Grovrouk spoke of was the child of the blacksmith Heyn. His heart began to pound while beads of perspiration formed on his upper lip.

"He must have a name; what is it?"

"He went by the birth name of Methladon Heyn," replied Grovrouk. "I first met him after the reptiles raided the Grey Keep, slaughtered all except me and set off towards Avolire. I shared a cell with the boy on my journey to this city and then my audience with the Lady of the Silverwynn. She soon realised the significance of the three circled curse mark that the lad carries on his neck. The bitch forced him to look into the Seer's stone and that corrupted him to the point of wanting all her power for himself."

"I knew this lad of old and he was the furthest thing from evil you could ever imagine," replied Thias. "Something else must have happened to twist him away from the path the good folk tread. His mind has been warped by something most evil."

"There is no time for me to tell you all but he cannot be killed; the bastard is immortal," growled Grovrouk.

"He was not a bastard. I knew both his mother and his father."

"If anyone is a bastard it is him," snapped back the little man with such speed that Thias struggled to understand the meaning of his words. "He survived the Lions of Avolire and a blast from Thamous's fiery breath. He even looks like a reptile now. Yet, what changed him was the long periods of time he spent confined inside Sanura Silverwynn's room, that which feeds off the power of the Rift and was gifted to her by the Lords of the Marshes. During those long hours the greatest of evils made contact with the lad and took control of his thoughts. As his friend I tried to turn him away from the dark but it was no use; his future path had already been lain. The person you once knew is no more and pure evil courses through his body."

"But he's still just a boy. Why do you fear him so?"

"As I said, he is immortal," continued Grovrouk. "He killed the Silverwynn and destroyed her spirit. He leads the Lizardmen now and ordered them to turn on Avolire. The slaughter above is of his doing alone and I sense there are just pockets of resistance left to combat his growing power. He has to be stopped before he destroys everything."

Thias spent the next minute in deep reflection. He could not come to terms with all that had been said about the boy he had known and called his brother. A sudden chill coursed down his back and in that second Thias feared for the farm boy, the Marked of Maplehill, who would have little chance against such a powerful enemy.

"The one you just met, the boy called Llyat, he must never know of Methladon Heyn's survival," ordered Thias. "From what I know and understand they were once friends but Llyat is weak in courage and lacking in common sense. He believes that Methladon fell in battle and that is how it should be left. I have sworn to protect the Marked, pledged myself to his survival in the manner demanded by the Cuvar, just as they have conspired over the years. I must keep the truth from him at all costs. Promise me you will not speak the name 'Methladon Heyn' again to anyone."

"I promise," replied the dwarf without any real conviction as he readied himself to move off into the dark. "Enough of this wasted talk. The reptiles have not left the powder store and we must move past it to take possession the Gems. I hope you have been making a note of the way we have travelled for if we become separated you will need to find your own way back to your precious farm boy?"

"I have made mental images and could easily find the point where we all split our two groups."

"Good! The store with the herbs is but a short distance from where you left the lad."

"But where are you taking me? Where are the Gems?" asked Thias.

"They are in the Lady's room that sits upon the crack in the Rift. The Gems will be feeding off the room's power, just as the evil one does. Once beyond the powder store there are steps that lead to the surface. Then I will take you to the place where terror seeps into our world."

"I have seen black powder used with great effect by the Lizardmen in their sacking of the Bards Guild," whispered Thias "I know what it can do."

"No more talking bard until we have passed," ordered Grovrouk while lifting his hand high and placing it over Thias's mouth.

Thias moved his teeth together but held his bottom lip between them lest he should be tempted to utter further words. The dwarf then removed his hand and led the way forward as their four feet trod lightly across the dirt impacted floor made slippery from the by-products of death. It took a minute to get level with the part open door and Grovrouk did not stop. Thias watched the little man pass the portal and stooped as he too moved to pass. A quick glace to the light surrounding the door edge was all the recognition that Grovrouk gave to whatever was behind the wood. The bard however could not stop himself from pausing. As the dwarf continued on alone Thias stood up straight, moved to the edge of the door, and peered behind it. The noise of Lizardmen talking and the occasional tap of pots touching each other intrigued him and he felt a strong need to investigate further. Given that he was in the dark and the room was well lit, Thias calculated it would be almost impossible for the Lizardmen to spot him as long as he did not reveal too much of his face.

On peering behind the wooden barrier he saw a group of five reptiles busy filling small pots with black powder that they took from a lone barrel. If as the dwarf had told him, this was the main store for the Knights of Avolire's explosives, then most had already been consumed in the battle above or elsewhere. The reptiles it seemed were using the last to make hand thrown missiles. The floor about the reptiles was covered with a sprinkling of spilt powder and this observation gave Thias an idea. He would give the creatures something to think about and exact some degree of revenge for the destruction of his spiritual home and his brother musicians of the Guild. Thias pulled away from the door and whispered a word of the ancients.

"Promethelumous," he chanted several times and his right hand erupted into flame.

Thias then looked to Grovrouk who had stopped and turned at the sudden appearance of a new source of light. The dwarf's look of horror made Thias question whether to continue but as Grovrouk opened his mouth to shout, Thias threw a ball of flame into the room. Wasting no time he then threw himself to the ground and as far away from the door as possible. At the same time that he hit the dirt a blinding yellow flash shot around the door, the wood of which then exploded outwards in a myriad of splinters. An instant in time later, Thias felt the shock wave push him several feet along the ground. His ears began to throb with the force of the air and a dense cloud of acrid smoke burst out from the store and rolled through the passageway. Thias's head span, his ears rang, and all went black as he slipped into unconsciousness.

The length of time that the bard lay oblivious to the world was in the order of a minute, but when he at last opened his eyes he had no idea how long he had been out. After another minute drifted away with the settling smoke Thias manged to sit up. He felt a small hand grip him by the throat.

"Do anything like that again without my agreement and I swear by Fatumai that I will kill you," screamed Grovrouk. "I've done well to keep us hidden so far and all you can do is try to fuck things up."

The words were too muffled to hear but Thias understood the message.

"I wasn't expecting such power. Do not worry, I won't do it again."

"Move your arse, we have to go," ordered Grovrouk.

The hand left Thias's throat and the dwarf waddled on towards the stairs.

Thias stood up and looked around as the smoke cleared around his head. Where the door once stood a pile of splintered wood rose from the floor-fog like the peaks of the Grey Mountains pushing through clouds. Upon that pile and spattered against the opposite wall dripped raw Lizardman flesh and unrecognisable scale covered parts. At his feet lay half a reptile's head, its forked tongue hanging out as if in some final desperate cry for the mother who had laid it in the nest. Thias turned and as the smoke cleared further he noticed the walls to his left and right were fissured. They did not look like they could remain standing much longer. As his confusion lifted he raced after the dwarf and caught him up at the base of steep an ancient set of steps down which the noise of conflict flowed.

"We must be careful once we gain the surface," ordered Grovrouk. "The reptiles have been ordered to take me dead if need be. My height means it is impossible to create a disguise and so my presence will give us away. You look neither Lizardman nor part of the forces of Avolire and so too stand out. The shits will be swarming in packs up there and we are going to be hard pressed to get to our goal unseen. But I tell you this bard, I will not be taken alive."

"And yet we must try to complete our task," replied Thias as both began their climb up the mountain of steps. "Tell me before we go any further, why are you risking your life to help me; you could just try to escape and save yourself? Have you been completely honest with me?"

At the midpoint of the climb Grovrouk paused for thought and tried to catch breath. Then at last he turned and answered the question.

"I understand the words of the Enderdetag Prophecy. It may surprise you to learn they have been talked of in certain parts of the Dirmark for many generations. It is even said by the sages of my race that the words were etched in stone by the Ancients. Some even claim to have seen such writings although I am myself sceptical. The Silverwynn claims the Enderdetag is upon us and the 'End of Days' approaches fast. The Gems are congregating and a great evil has returned to these lands. The prophecy is playing out line by line and I have come to realise that no one but your friend Llyat Emgar can destroy the Lord of Fear. But he cannot do so alone for it is clear he has neither the mental strength nor the physical prowess to defeat his onetime friend.

"Be careful, you promised never to mention his name," interrupted Thias.

"Yes I did and I will help you protect the Marked. You have the skills to take on the evil and you must help Llyat to fulfil the Prophecy. I need tell you my most precious secret for you have spoken of the need for truth."

"Then share it," said Thias, taken aback by the little man's comment.

"Many years ago, at the time of my expulsion from the Dirmark, I swore a sacred oath to a dwarf sage who helped turn my hatred onto those who dwell in Parandor."

"And what oath was that?"

"That of the Cuvar!"

Thias's jaw dropped in disbelief. He questioned his hearing, perhaps the explosion had caused him to hear untruths.

"But come now," continued Grovrouk. "We talk too much and your constant prattle is putting our mission at risk."

The dwarf continued the second half of the climb. Thias followed, his head still spinning from the explosion and from the revelations of his co-conspirator. By the time Thias reached the surface his hunger for air forced him to tap on the dwarf's shoulder and call out for respite. Grovrouk did not argue. The stone steps had alighted into a ruined building, its roof having long ago caved in. Its four stone walls were just half the height of a man and yet in the direction that Thias faced a single arch had somehow remained intact. He assumed it to be the once feared entrance to the prison of Avolire. Its door was long gone, no doubt used to fuel the cooking pots of those that walked the wastelands. Yet the low crumbling walls provided a degree of cover and from behind the stonework two sets of eyes observed the battle that surrounded them.

Bodies of men and reptilian spawn lay scattered in all directions and created a gut wrenching stench that was almost intolerable. Thias retched numerous times yet still managed not to vomit as his eyes scanned the field of evisceration. Significant quantities of drool dripped onto the thick beard that now grew from his chin. He looked to the dwarf who appeared to show no such discomfort and wondered what great slaughters the little man had encountered in his past. Peering for a moment over the stone wall that formed their hide, Thias watched the war move away as the Lizardmen forced the army of Avolire from this central point of the city. Groups of armoured reptiles moved across the ruins to either reinforce their battle formations or to drop back for a moment's respite. Despite the distancing of the fight the intensity of noise created caused Thias to shout in order to be heard.

"Where are we heading for?"

"Do you see that old ruined church on the opposite side of the square?"

"Yes I do, is that where the special room is?"

"We need to enter through the main body of that building. At the rear behind it's alter there are passageways, one of which leads to the fractured Rift and the room that sits above it. There are far too many of the scale skinned bastards between here and our goal."

"I've had another idea Grovrouk," said Thias as his gaze fell on a nearby fallen Lizardman. "I think I know how to increase our chance of crossing the open ground."

"It had better not be like your last one or I swear I will kill you right here."

"Please hear me out," demanded Thias. "There are dead everywhere and just outside the archway there are two reptiles of my height and build, both felled by crossbow bolts to the throat."

"So..."

"Please let me finish," snapped back Thias. "If I were to put on Lizardman armour and one of their helms I could march you forward with a sword to your back; then just perhaps we could convince any we pass that I have captured you and have been ordered to take you to the special room... to receive punishment... or something similar."

Grovrouk paused while Thias waited for an answer.

"I think your plan may actually work," replied the dwarf as he grinned. "It's worth a try and I cannot conceive of a better one."

Thias moved along the wall to the opening of the arch. There he scanned to left and right before jumping forward and dragging the first of the corpses back within their place of hiding. With help and instruction from Grovrouk, Thias dressed himself in the unique mix of leather and scrap metal that was the standard battle dress of those from the Eastern Marsh. The garb fitted well and Thias was pleased that his estimate of their size had been so accurate. Then, as he ripped the helm from the creatures head, Thias noticed a glint of gold under the blood and mud that part covered the creature's right arm.

"Grovrouk, when we first left my companions with your friend the Harbinger, you spoke of how perhaps we could use Rift bracelets to escape, once we had secured the jewels," said Thias in a heightened state of excitement.

"So?" replied the dwarf.

"Well this buggers got one."

"Check if the other one also has one," replied Grovrouk. "Two would be enough to get us all access to the Rift."

Thias moved out through the archway and examined the second body. It too had a golden bracelet and he took it without hesitation. Having secured it within a recess in his armour he picked up the Lizardman's jagged blade and returned to his diminutive companion. Grovrouk smiled for he had removed the first that Thias had spotted and he pushed it into the bard's hand.

"Keep them together for we need both. One alone will not suffice."

"Then you must tell me how they work," insisted Thias.

"It's simple in a way, but then it's not so easy," began Grovrouk. "First you place it around your wrist. If you are transporting more than one then the harder it becomes. The bodies of all must remain connected at all times during the process. The bracelet is then rotated one full circle forwards and then two back while the traveller or travellers focus on an image of where they intend to go. If that image is broken several unfortunate outcomes then become possible."

"Such as what?"

"If more than one are travelling together and their physical link is broken, or they are not under the guidance of a travel master like one of their bloated priests, then there is a risk that both may drift through the Rift for eternity," continued Grovrouk, his voice dropping to a whisper as a group of Lizardmen raced passed the arch. "If their focus of attention, the image of the intended destination, is lost then the traveller can end up somewhere different or indeed worse."

"What is 'worse'?" asked Thias.

"I have heard it said that various parts of the same Lizardmen have arrived in different places and that of course means instant death. I have also been told that lack of focus alone can result in the endless drift between the dimensions."

"I'm not so sure it's a good idea to use the bracelets," replied Thias, troubled by the consequences of such an event. "Have you ever travelled the Rift alone? How long does it take to train someone in their use?"

"No, I have not. I have only travelled the Rift once and that was under the guidance of Ssonsh, he who controls the Eastern Marsh. I have been told that it may take months to teach the reptiles how to use the bracelets and that some can never master the technique. The Lizardmen are however small of brain and much inferior to we that do not spawn."

"And you expect me to take the Marked through the Rift without training or knowing what we are doing!" exclaimed Thias.

"It is an option; that is all I am saying. Keep the bracelets with you and use them only if there is no alternative. I am just trying to help but if we don't move from here soon we may never secure possession of the Gems. Silence your mouth and we will go with your plan."

With nothing further said Thias stood up from behind the wall and placed the Lizardman helm over his head so as to complete his disguise. He pushed the dwarf ahead with the tip of his new blade and marched out under the old archway. Prodding the dwarf's back with force he sought to make the deception look as real as possible to any eyes watching their procession towards the old ruined church. They progressed at a pace that Thias deemed appropriate for one forcing his prisoner on to punishment. Several groups of Lizardmen rushed to and fro amid the chaos of the battle and some even crossed their path. So preoccupied were they in obtaining victory for Urthanock that none took more than a cursory glance towards Thias and his captive. The plan was working better than the bard could have hoped but as they approached the steps of the church the leader of the last group they encountered shouted towards them. Thias did not understand the tongue of the Eastern Marsh and once they had moved away he spoke.

"What did they call to us? You winced at their words so I know you can understand them. "

"They said that the wyvern has been killed...killed by the Vessel whose name you do not want me to speak of," replied Grovrouk.

"But how could a mere blacksmith's son destroy a wyvern? That seems impossible."

"I told you the boy could not be killed," replied Grovrouk as the two began to ascend the stairs of the old church.

"Did they say the name of the wyvern?"

"There was only one still alive, the great and mighty Thamous. If that beast is dead there are no more in this world," answered Grovrouk with much sadness. "To defeat the demon, you must become a demon."

"What," said Thias as he gripped the dwarfs arm?

"Only by channelling the evil of Kha could a man defeat Thamous."

"But why would Thamous intervene in the battle between men and reptiles," asked Thias? "As far as I understand from the lore he has never done so in the past, not since he helped Sir Raulyn banish Urthanock's ashes to the Underworld."

"You do not understand the importance of Thamous to the conspiracy that you have sworn to uphold."

"Then tell me now," ordered Thias, "or I will go no further with you."

"You are so naive bard; you must start to trust me. Thamous was the first of the Cuvar. He and Raulyn are the ones we have all followed, even though some are ignorant of that fact. If he has intervened in the battle, it is something the Moirai would never forgive. I assume the beast's sole purpose was to aide you in your quest. But come, we cannot delay longer."

"You also know of the Moirai!" exclaimed Thias.

Trudging on behind the dwarf the bard's mind filled with questions, some were answered, but more came.

"For the last time, be quiet," ordered Grovrouk. "Speak no more. Just follow me to the crack between the realities and focus on the fulfilment of your destiny."

"You must answer one more question. This vessel my foster brother has become, what is its purpose?"

The dwarf stopped, anger forged upon its face as its lips began to move.

"Methladon's essence has been replaced by that of Urthanock with the help of Kha. That is who the Lizardman said killed the wyvern, Urthanock, the Lord of Fear. Your brother has abandoned his old name and all reptiles now call him by that most ancient of titles. They recognise the second coming of the beast that they now accept as their master and they will follow his orders without question."

"You swore never to mention his real name again," snarled Thias as the pair approached the raised platform of the church.

"And I told you to shut your fucking mouth," replied Grovrouk. "Look over there. Do you see the entrance to the passageways? Now, say no more and let us finish what we came here to do."

Grovrouk moved at pace and led Thias through the dim light of the passageways and on towards the doors that guarded the entrance to the room where the Gems of Thamous were said to lay. Thias did not speak further for he had much to think on and did not want to give warning of his approach. He had had enough of dark tunnels and longed for the time he could once again roam across the green and verdant lands of the south, feel the heat of Solaris on his back, and sing out ballads while resting feet in pools of cool water. He trembled as he sensed those days were gone forever. There would no doubt be many more dark places to negotiate before his quest would end.

Thias snapped out of his day dream as Grovrouk turned into the short passage that led up to imposing arched doors over which a dragon had be carved into the stone.

"We are here at last and the room is unguarded," whispered the dwarf as he pointed at the entrance. "We are fortunate indeed for all have joined the battle. Follow me in as I know this room well and stay alert for we may not have much time."

Thias nodded his understanding and the two would-be thieves moved forward towards the twin doors. Footsteps caused them to duck into an adjacent niche in the wall that was hidden from light. In an instant a group of lizard men stood before the doors and began conversing. Thias did not understand their words but recognised their lack of agitation. Soon they began to drift away.

"Grovrouk, before we go inside, tell me why the Rift chose my foster brother over the Lady of the Silverwynn?"

"Do you never give up bard?" sneered the dwarf. "It recognised the curse brand of immortality and discovered a much better vessel for Urthanock's essence.

A sudden realisation struck home. In the seconds that followed the bard's thoughts scattered, his heart raced, and his leg began to shake. Some unseen force caused him to reflect back to his visit to the Grey Keep and how he had been deceived by a Lizardman disguised as a knight. The words that the changeling had spoken hammered away inside his head. *'The House of Gylewu will fall from within and our armies will sweep across the Realm. The race of man shall be extinguished and only those loyal to our cause will be deemed worthy enough to survive.'* It then all seemed to make sense. It was all about the Eastern Marsh. Everything else was a distraction.

"So this is really about the downfall of Parandor, the desire of the Eastern Marsh to destroy the house of Gylewu," Thias whispered as he unveiled his new insight. "I once thought it was about the resurrection of the cult of Death Tubaria and the infiltration of the Court of Parandor by a changeling spy. Then it was a quest for the Gems and the resurgence of Avolire. But now I see the truth."

"You had no real idea bard," said Grovrouk. "Your mind has been walking through the mists of ignorance. You still have no fucking clue! You..."

"At long last I get what all this is about," interrupted Thias before Grovrouk could insult him further. "It's the final war between the realities, good versus evil. I understand how the Prophecy fits in. The knowledge of this battle has long been predicted by the Ancients, by Thamous and Raulyn, right from the beginning. It's a war between those who were once friends, one now evil and one carrying the torch of the righteous. It's between Llyat and Methladon, or Urthanock as he now calls himself. The farm boy from Maplehill is expected to defeat the Lord of Evil as dictated by the words of the Prophecy. We two are but bit players in this game of the Fates and yet I fear Llyat is not up to the task."

"Then we must find another way or somehow put steel in his marrow," replied Grovrouk. "There have been many other 'small bit players' as you put it over the many generations since the Cuvar were founded. All have done their bit and so must we. There was a man that your brother befriended before being turned to evil. This man and another fellow prisoner we lost to the Lions of Avolire but the deed was kept secret from your brother. They like me were Cuvar and through their own foolishness and ineptitude they failed to live long enough to play their part in our conspiracy. I will not let that happen to me. Come, there is nothing more you need to know."

Grovrouk moved towards the twin doors and Thias followed without hesitation. He became aware of a strange sense of power that seeped through the cracks in the wood and felt both fearful and intimidated. As the little man pushed the portal open and stepped into the chamber the room lit with a magic of its own. As if from nowhere numerous candles flickered into life and remained burning once Thias had closed the doors. His body tingled as it sensed a connection with something evil beneath the room. Knowing he was in the presence of the crack between the realities he felt more afraid than at any other time in his life.

"I will find the gems," said Grovrouk with confidence. "You have a quick look and see if there is anything else that could be of value. Then let's get out of here."

Thias walked over to the bed that occupied the far wall of the mysterious chamber. He sat on its edge, removed his helm, and placed it down upon the blanket that covered its surface. Then he watched as Grovrouk approached what appeared to be a small dresser and from off its surface began to collect objects. Thias felt most strange and forgot the dwarf's instruction to search the room but soon Grovrouk joined him by the bed. An old leather bag with a strap was thrown to his side having been taken from beside the dresser. Thias's eyes lit up as one by one, a sceptre, a dagger, a necklace, and a large sapphire were placed inside the bag.

"Put this bag over your shoulder, the Gems are now your responsibility bard," said Grovrouk. "Guard them well. Now get of your bony arse off the bed and help me look for anything else of value. You take this end of the room and I will look by the doors. Come on."

Thias had moved only a couple of steps before Grovrouk spoke again.

"Oh! One last thing, by chance do you know what this is?"

The dwarf held up a white stone attached to a chain and as Thias stared, the object glowed.

"I have seen it before," he replied.

"When and where, tell me now!" demanded Grovrouk.

"Llyat gave it to me. It is the means to communicate with dragons and wyverns. It was passed to him by a Berserker in order to speak with Thamous. Somehow he didn't need it. I'm not at all sure how it works and the last time I saw it was in an ogre's tent outside of Calistorn. It glowed then and spoke my name."

"Fuck!" exclaimed Grovrouk as he snatched the stone away and raced back to the dresser.

Thias watched bemused as the dwarf searched the surface of the furniture until he located a small metal box into which he then thrust the stone. Having secured its clasp he returned to Thias.

"What are you doing, what does all this mean?" asked the bard, his concern mounting as the heavy presence of the room bore down upon his shoulders.

"Listen with care bard. We have little time. I can but say this once and you must understand and act with all haste and with no more questions. I have heard Ssonsh talking about this stone that some call a Dragon Whisper. He said it was powerful but also dangerous. Not only does it communicate with dragons and wyverns but it acts as a kind of locator, a type of beacon. If Thamous spoke your name then he knew of your existence. He had been monitoring your progress."

"Why are you so scared of it?" asked Thias.

"Thamous is dead and yet it still glowed when I held it before your eyes. It is possible that Urthanock has that power now and that he is watching you. He could know where you are."

Thias exhaled and looked to the double doors, expecting them to open at any moment.

"I may be just overreacting but I fear the Lord of Fear will come here soon," continued Grovrouk. "He may well know of your plans if he now has Thamous's insight. This small casket was created by the creatures of the Eastern Marsh. It is made of a metal called lead and I have heard that it blocks the power of the stone to see and communicate. Now place it in your bag with the jewels and never open it through curiosity. It may be of value to you one day if you use it with care and much prior thought."

Thias complied with the instruction and placed the casket inside the bag with the Gems.

"Now we have no time for stealing," ordered Grovrouk. "I once overheard the Silverwynn talking with Commander Rhaizen about a hidden exit from this room, one that the Lady could use should she need to escape or leave undetected. I don't know if it is true but we must find it for it will be too dangerous to leave by the way we came. I will search the end by the doors and you take the area around the bed."

Thias did not question the dwarf's order. As Grovrouk headed towards the doors the bard jumped off the bed, adjusted the bag that hung from his shoulder, took hold of the Lizardman's blade, and then looked beneath the bed. Finding nothing but a broken looking glass he then stood and began to examine the walls to either side of the great bed. As he approached the tapestry that covered the wall behind the bedhead a hint of air moving across his face caused him to stop and contemplate its origin. He soon noticed that the bed was not positioned right up to the surface of the wall hanging and that with a squeeze, if he moved the decorative material forward, he could just about manage to slip behind it given his slight of stature. Pulling the tapestry forward he poked his head behind it and there saw the black circular opening of a tunnel. With great luck he had found the exit Grovrouk had heard speak of and in his excitement Thias turned around and took several paces towards his companion. The double doors burst open and an intimidating figure swept into the room and strode amongst the shadows cast by the candles. Beyond this figure Thias caught a brief glimpse of the dwarf as he slipped behind the door to hide. Thias's legs began to tremble and he dropped the lizard man's blade that he had held in his hand. In the next instant he lost control of his fingers and then of his limbs as he rose into the air, suspended by some unseen force. His vision was drawn to the reptilian eyes that stared at him.

"Who are you?" screamed the bard through the intense pain that spread through his body.

Thias stared at the one before him, dressed in reptilian armour and with a unique half helm that revealed part of a scarred face which resembled the skin of Lizardmen. Then he noticed the sword at the creature's side, the very same one that Llyat had used to kill the ogre in Barad Elestor. The coin fell and as his fear erupted as he realised who he was talking to.

"Do you not recognise me bard," snarled Urthanock with great viciousness. "Perhaps you do not since I have grown out of the body of the youth you last met in Maplehill.

"Methladon, I know it's you," screamed back Thias through the few muscles he still had control of. "Brother, it is me Thias Calavan. We shared part of our lives together. Your father took me in as his own."

"Do not mention that name again or I will terminate your life sooner than a whore can piss," snarled Urthanock with great venom. "The brother you knew of old is just a memory. I captured most of that as I banished him from this Vessel."

The Lord over Fear sneered with contempt and he took several paces forward in order to examine Thias in more in more detail. The bard hung in the air, suspended as if by invisible strings which could be cut at any moment.

I know who you are," laughed the creature. "I know who you seek to protect and I know what you are up to. You have failed bard, for you will never leave this room with what is in that bag. You should never have tried to interfere in a game as powerful as this one."

Thias tried to fight the pain that now consumed him, vowing that whatever happened next he would not divulge the whereabouts of the Marked.

"Where is the boy!" demanded Urthanock as he reached out and gripped Thias by the cheeks."

"That I will never tell you," spat back Thias as the intensity of pain in his face matched that of the rest of his body.

"Oh yes you will, but before I have my sport with you and extract all I need from your pathetic mind, my memories remind me of unfinished business."

"And what would that be?" snarled Thias as the creature released its grip on his face.

"The last time you met this body you refused it something most important, well important at least to my Vessel. He asked you to sing a certain song and you declined. You will sing it now, one last time. It will be the last you ever utter so you had best sing it well."

"I have no fucking idea of what you're talking about," screamed Thias.

"My Vessel asked you to perform the 'Sparrow and the Lark' and I would like to hear it. I want to understand why the boy liked it so much."

"Fuck off!" screeched Thias.

"You misunderstand me bard. This is not a request. You will sing it in the end. All I need to do is increase the level of your discomfort."

Intense spasms of pain shot through Thias's body. They were unbearable and broke his will.

"Stop, please stop" he screamed. Then as the pain abated the bard began his rendition of the Sparrow and the Lark. It was not his strongest voice as it trembled in terror, but Thias was buying time.

> *A long time past in the fledging city,*
> *When men lusted for quim and firm titty.*
> *Two men vied, for the women they spied,*
> *Whether ugly, pockmarked, or pretty.*

Thias paused after the first verse and as perspiration fell from his face he shouted; "Do you see why I refused to perform it in the Red Mare? It is cheap and vulgar and has no musical merit."

"I did not say you could stop; finish it!" bellowed Urthanock and so Thias continued.

> *The first, known to all as The Sparrow,*
> *Was a short arse, the shape of a marrow.*

In that instant Grovrouk jumped from the shadows and smashed a heavy iron candlestand upon the back of Urthanock's half helm. The beast fell to the floor and Thias followed him down, released from the power of the dark magic. The fall from his suspension was a heavy one but apart from winding Thias it did no significant damage. He was back on his feet in seconds and he reached down for the Lizardman blade that he had been forced to drop moments earlier. Then without thinking, he secured the bag of Gems upon his shoulder. Looking quickly to Grovrouk he saw the little man was shaking, part in fear, and part from the effect of striking one so powerful.

"Is he dead?" shouted Thias as he began to hear the sound of many feet.

"He cannot be killed, run for your life. I will stay behind and delay the bastards as best I can. Do not argue for there is not time. Go now. I am but another bit player in this ancient quest but you are the Guardian of the Marked. Protect the boy at all costs. You are Cuvar!"

Thias opened his mouth to speak but no words came. As the sound of the footfall grew ever louder and the creature upon the floor began to moan, he raced past the bed, snatched up the discarded lizard helm and slipped behind the tapestry at the end of the bed. Something then made him stop, a simple curiosity and a desire to witness events. He pulled the fabric back an inch and peeped back into the room. There he saw a group of some ten Lizardmen race through the double doors. Grovrouk lifted the iron candlestand and made to swing again at the head of Urthanock as the creature rose to its hands and knees. At the same time several of the Lizardmen moved to restrain the dwarf's arms. Urthanock's right hand stretched out and gripped one of Grovrouk's ankles. Then to Thias's shock and amazement a bolt of intense red fire left the Lord of Fear's arm and Grovrouk the Despoiler exploded. Bits of the dwarf were scattered throughout the room and a drop of something even hit Thias on the forehead just above his right eye. The few Lizardmen who had restrained the dwarf dropped also and never moved again. Urthanock rose to his feet and Thias fled.

"Fuck!" he exclaimed under his breath.

Thias moved into the foreboding entrance of the tunnel and all the while he heard Urthanock's anger roar. Amid the dark his thoughts turned black and he muttered: "I hate these fucking tunnels."

Urthanock's voice thundered and forced its way into Thias's ears.

"Find and kill the bastard for he must have escaped before you cunts arrived."

"We didn't pass him on the way here," hissed a quieter voice.

"Like all bards he is a cunning shit and hides in the shadows," continued Urthanock. "Look to the prison for that is where he would likely have come from. Do not dare comeback without his head."

"Yes my Lord," hissed another.

Thias had continued to make slow progress within the dark space. When he deemed he had travelled far enough he thrust out his left hand and muttered "Promethelumous".

The light that arose from his limb illuminated the way and the bard then moved as fast as he could through the old passage. Forcing his way through a forest of spider's webs he disturbed more geckos than he would have ever believed existed in the Realm. After some minutes the tunnel opened up to the surface a short distance from the ruined archway he had left a short time earlier. There he extinguished his flaming hand and looked in all directions. There were several Lizardmen still crossing the killing ground but none took notice of what appeared to be just another of their kind. Thias stepped over the corpses of the fallen and soon reached the top of the steps. Down he went. Once he had reached the bottom he paused to rest for his thighs pained with the effort of the descent and his lungs burned with exhaustion. He turned and looked to the surface where to his horror he saw numerous Lizardmen at the entrance. One screeched on seeing Thias's shadow far below and soon the rest joined in. The chase was on and Thias ran as fast as his feet could move. He had to escape, he had to keep going despite his weakened state.

The bard had no initial difficulty in retracing his journey through the subterranean prison for his mind map of the place was still vivid in his memory. He slowed when he approached the black powder store and with great care negotiated the pile of splinters and still slippery remnants of the Lizardmen he had earlier destroyed. Once past the place of carnage he raced on again and a few minutes later heard the distressed shouts of the chasing pack as they approached the scene of death and the crumbling stonework. Thias stopped and turned. The walls then collapsed without warning and showered the tunnel with debris and smoke. He prayed that all his pursuers had been eliminated but several appeared out of the dust cloud and the chase continued.

Approaching exhaustion point Thias passed the spot where he and Grovrouk had parted from the others. Two mercenaries lay dead upon the ground, L'Fare having joined Ventes in the after world by taking his own life. Thias then turned to where he understood the herb store to be located. In the distance he continued to hear the sound of those that hunted him. He passed numerous openings and peered inside each of them. Realising that his disguise would alarm his companions should he ever manage find them, he stopped, threw down his helm, and stripped himself of the Lizardman armour. In the process he took the two gold bracelets from the recesses of the armour and placed them inside his shoulder bag. Taking hold of the sword and the bag of Gems he returned to his search of the rooms. Some minutes later, looking into a door to his right, he was wrenched backwards by an arm that grasped his shoulder. Thias turned, ready to thrust his blade forward only to have it knocked from his hand by the large muscular knight whom Grovrouk had referred to as Oedd.

"Get into the room opposite bard, we have been worried for you," ordered the Knight. "Your friend Irabo is dying but we found some stuff to keep him going a little longer. The girl with child knows her herbs."

A noise from behind gripped their attention.

"You have allowed many to follow you here; what number do you think they are?" asked Oedd as he looked over Thias's shoulder.

"No more than a handful and more cannot follow for the passageway has collapsed near to the old black powder store."

"Give me that blade and I will see to them," ordered Oedd. "It is the least I can do for you. Get in the room and bolt the door. I hope you have a good idea as to how to get out of this mess."

Thias did as instructed. Once inside he closed the door and slipped the bolt. Then he turned to greet his companions but was struck by the sight of Irabo slumped against the shelves on the far wall. The warrior's pallor indicated death was imminent.

"Do not worry Thias," called out Llyat moving out of the shadows. "He is fucked but not yet dead. Where is Oedd? Where is the dwarf?"

Oedd's sudden cry indicated the attack by the Lizardmen. There was no need to answer Llyat's first question.

"Grovrouk is dead," said Thias with some sadness. "The beast that leads the Lizardmen slew him with explosive magic. There is nothing left of him."

"You are wounded Thias," said Heliana, moving closer. "There on your face. Does it hurt?"

"No, I'm not injured," replied Thias.

The young woman reached forward and wiped a large globule of red tissue from Thias's forehead and then stood bemused when there was no wound beneath it.

"I don't understand," she said as she held the blood and tissue before Thias's eyes.

"It must be a bit of Grovrouk! His bits were scattered far and wide."

Heliana rushed her right hand to cover her mouth, turned to her left, and then emptied the few contents of her stomach onto the floor. The sound of fierce hand to hand combat travelled through the door and it was obvious that the knight was outnumbered. Thias turned to Llyat and Heliana and in his severest voice he began to enact their escape. Pulling two gold bracelets from his bag he explained that their only means of escape was to pass through the Rift. Heliana was in support of the idea for she had travelled it as a prisoner of the Lizardmen, even though she didn't remember the journey. Llyat quaked when Thias began to explain what needed to be done. Slipping one bracelet on his right wrist he passed the other to Llyat and encouraged him to do the same.

The intensity of Oedd's screams added urgency to their preparations.

"I'm done! For Avolire!" the knight bellowed, "Death to the Eastern…"

Oedd fell against the door after which crimson fluid oozed in between it and the floor. Following the sounds of a body being dragged away, Lizardmen began their pummelling of the door.

"We do not have much time," ordered Thias. "Hold on to Heliana and travel with her, I will take Irabo on my shoulder, so come and help me lift him."

Once Irabo was upright and linked to Thias's side the bard continued his final instructions.

"We must do this together when I say 'Go'. Listen well, I will repeat the instructions once again. There will be no time to question your understanding. The bracelet is rotated one full circle forwards and then two back while we all focus on the image of where we are going, The Murdered Wolf in Parandor. It's the safest place I can think of and it is where Heliana told me the City Watch conduct their investigations."

"Okay," replied Llyat, concerned at what was about to happen.

"You must not break your concentration," ordered Thias as he closed his eyes. "Ready?"

Count us in then," shouted Llyat as he gripped Heliana's hand.

"One…Two…Three…Go!"

7

Isambard Hotch rolled his lardy frame around the interior of his tavern. Sweat dripped from his forehead, tricked in small rivulets over his cheeks, and then streamed on into the thick bushy beard he had been cultivating over recent weeks. The thin shirt that tried to contain his flesh had not been changed for some considerable time and the stains under his armpits had expanded outwards such that they reached down almost to his elbows and waist. Similar dark and offensive patches of stale sweat covered most of his back and the area under each of his sagging breasts, the size of which were envied by the few malnourished woman that dared drag themselves around the slums of Parandor.

Hotch's trousers were also stained around the crotch and arse but being of a darker material the discoloration was not as impactful to the eye. It was perhaps just as well that his customers could not see the build-up of congealed sweat that hung like bunches of grapes from the thick tangled hair of his armpits. Had anyone dared to stop and asked the barkeep why he had worn the same attire for so long without washing the answer would have been straight forward. They would have heard that it was due to how busy The Murdered Wolf had been of recent weeks, ever since the threat from Avolire had reached the ears of its patrons. It had created a sense of 'let's get pissed now, it could be our last chance' within the collective mind-set of the low life and it was a pattern of behaviour that was replicated across the vast extent of the Capital. So much drink had been consumed that Hotch and the other tavern keepers estimated that they would run dry within days should urgent supplies of the basic materials for brewing and distilling not arrive soon from the surrounding farms. It was said that some establishments were already collecting buckets of the heaviest drinker's piss and distilling it to capture residual traces of alcohol. The Murdered Wolf however was not yet one of them.

It was not Hotch's appearance that gave most offence for that alone would have been tolerable to the desperate inebriates that frequented his tavern. What made him the monster of revulsion that he had become was the smell that accompanied his passing. Even noses hardened by a life time in the fish markets, the pig farms, or the covering of death pits, recoiled as Hotch passed them on his way to serve both food and drink.

"Fucking hell, Isambard, you stink a lump," shouted Ligart Highroar as the barkeep rolled past his table. "Which pigsty did you wake up in today?"

"Go suck your own dick if you can reach it!" snorted the sweaty man as he continued on with his labour.

"Perhaps we should find another place to drink," suggested Highroar's dark skinned companion after Hotch had disappeared amongst the throng still prepared to tolerate his stench.

"I wouldn't give that vile cunt the satisfaction of knowing that we are that bothered," sneered Highroar once sure that the barkeep was out of earshot.

The Captain and First Mate of the Banshees Wail had entered the tavern some thirty minutes earlier and were already on their third mug of Blessed Beast for they too had heard rumours that the beer may soon run out. The poor wine and the little mead for those with more coins had long since been consumed and the meagre food on offer would turn even the stomachs of the starving. Highroar had suggested a visit to The Murdered Wolf for it sold one unique drink worthy of mention. Isambard's homemade spirit which he passed off as firewater. It was called 'Hotch's Nectar' and it was distilled in one batch, once a week if demand was high, and so popular was it that enough was made to fill a single enormous barrel the height of the tallest of men. That barrel sat upon a flat topped boulder behind the serving counter at the furthest point from the door. Yet even that special spirit was no longer available due to the upturn in customer demand; much to Highroar's disappointment. Hotch used his fingers to percuss the level of its contents each and every hour. Earlier that morning had declared it empty but no one knew if this was true or whether Hotch was saving the dregs for himself.

"Make the most of this day Theo," said Highroar, his nose still stinging from Isambard's assault. "Our last voyage was profitable but we must make ready to leave at the slightest hint of war."

"But I have unfinished business in this city," replied the First Mate. "I still have things to sort out with Tonousa Amberstone and I need to understand how her investigations have progressed."

"There was a whisper in the docks this morning, from the shadows by the dead collector's door," mumbled Highroar such that just Theoplous could hear. "Some say she is dead, murdered a few days ago within the Citadel. Another Death Tubaria... "

"You know that's horse pizzle."

"Take it as you will, friend," replied Highroar

"It cannot be true. I will not believe it. If that were the case it would be the talk of this tavern. Hotch would have said something as those two never saw eye to eye. Given that her investigations were ran from one of Hotch's back rooms he would have come and gloated over her death as soon as we had entered."

"Perhaps he doesn't know; perhaps it isn't true," continued Highroar, "But let's see if we can pull him to one side and ask him."

"You're not bringing that stink over here," said Theoplous while holding his nose. "No, with your leave I will go later and seek out the Commander of the City Watch. He will know the truth; that is of course unless I bump into Tonousa first!"

"Do I have a choice?" replied the Captain as he began to laugh.

The two sailors lifted their earthenware mugs, laughed some more, and then returned to their drinking.

"Fancy a game of dice," asked Theoplous. "I feel the need to lighten your purse."

"Perhaps a quick one, but I really need a fuck; if Hotch has any whores left who are sober."

"When has that ever stopped you before?"

"Never lad," laughed Highroar. "Never in a thousand lifetimes."

A sudden and strange noise, followed by a blinding flash of blue light, distracted both the sailors and the rest of those that filled the tavern. All stopped and stared at the great barrel of hooch which now glowed in a most peculiar manner. Then the giant keg shook as if moved by an earth tremor and it was followed by a crack so loud that it ignited terror amongst the gawping onlookers.

"Fuck, the barrel's about to explode!" shouted one fearful customer.

"No it's a manifestation of evil from the Underworld," screamed another.

"That shit Hotch has replaced his spirit with a tub of black powder and the bugger's about to blow," screamed the customer nearest to the phenomenon.

"Run for your lives if you value your scrawny arses," bellowed the oudest of the calls.

All further warnings were drowned by the cacophony of panic that then filled the room.

The next minute passed in complete pandemonium. In the mad rush to exit the tavern a stampede of terrified souls flattened Isambard Hotch and trampled over his lardy body. Several kicked him in the head as they passed but soon all had departed except the barkeep and the two sailors from the Banshees Wail.

Theoplous had been swift to evaluate the situation and once the barrel had begun to glow he had dragged Highroar from their table and pulled him against the wall opposite to the serving counter, his blade drawn and ready for whatever would happen next.

"Captain, it seems the war has begun!"

"What do you mean?" stuttered Highroar, trembling and confused.

"I have seen this before at the Bards Guild of Valameer. Ready yourself sir for we have visitors. This is how the Eastern Marsh breached the Guild and it appears their attack has started."

"Let's run like the others," shouted back Highroar into the empty tavern.

"No Ligart, it is time to earn our share of the glory. We must do what we can to aid Parandor and repel the reptiles; but why they should target a barrel in this particular shithole none but Fatumai could know. If we can destroy their portal then perhaps you will be rewarded beyond your dreams. Just think on that Captain, a ship loaded with treasure."

Theoplous watched Highroar's expression change as he mulled over the possibility of great wealth. In that moment that the Captain was with Theo to the end. Then amongst the sudden quiet of the emptied room, where the only sound came from Isambard's moans, the two sailors crept with stealth towards the still glowing barrel.

Llyat, Thias, and Heliana had focused upon a collective image of The Murdered Wolf as the two bracelets had been rotated. All had followed Thias's instructions but it was Llyat who had found the task harder than the others. In the seconds that followed the turning of the gold he had struggled to control his desire for a stiff drink with which to bolster his courage. Moments later he felt the shock from a sudden blinding flash that surrounded him and which sent a surge of uncontrollable pain throughout his body. He felt as if his guts were being spun on a spindle into a fine thread before being reconstituted within the dark confines of a malodorous tight space where the air stung both his eyes and nostrils. He lost consciousness and drifted into nothingness. All of a sudden amid the darkness he was shook by a rough hand that had gripped his shoulder and despite the dizzy waves that rolled through his head Llyat manged to pick out words from a voice that he recognised.

"Llyat wake up," shouted Thias over and over again from within a polluted space. "We haven't got much time if we are to get out of this place alive. For some reason we seem to be in a large barrel of spirit as best as I can tell and will soon be as pissed as tavern rats. Now move yourself."

"What? What are you saying?" mumblec Llyat.

"We are going to die unless you help me you thick skulled dimwit," bellowed the bard. "I cannot let Irabo drop for there is fluid at the bottom of this vat and something else under my feet that doesn't feel good."

"Where's Heliana?" demanded Llyat, his thoughts racing.

"I feel sick," moaned the young woman while retching. "I heard the voice of a friend amid the darkness of the Rift and she said 'look to the ruby to reveal all'... Oh fuck, I feel ill."

"What do you want me to do Thias?" asked Llyat as his head cleared a little.

"Feel in front of you until you locate my bag," replied Thias. "Then reach inside and locate the Dagger of Kha. Pull it out for it may be the one chance we have to get some better air. Once you have it, bend down into the liquid and locate the bungtap. It must be there somewhere and you must push it out to allow the residues of spirit to drain away. Poke around until you find it and then use the dagger to push it out. Come one lad, do it now, my senses are beginning to addle.

Llyat did not argue and reached forward until his hand located the bag as Thias had ordered. Without further hesitation he slipped his hand inside it. The shock of warm vomit hitting his arm caused him to pause but then he continued. Several seconds later his hand gripped the hilt of the infamous weapon and he pulled it clear of the bag. Then, as if enchanted, one of the emeralds in the daggers hilt began to radiate a green light. It lit up the confines of the space and confirmed Thias's assessment of where they had arrived.

"Firewater!" exclaimed Thias as he looked down towards his feet.

The four travellers had materialised inside an enormous wooden barrel and were knee deep in strong liquor. Llyat looked to his companions and saw concern etched on Thias's face. Irabo looked like a cream corpse whereas but Heliana was rosy cheeked and had begun to giggle from the effects of the enriched atmosphere.

"*There was a young man from Longbarrow,*" she sang. "*With a cock just as big as a marrow!*"

Staring down into the hooch below, Llyat gasped at the sight of a pickled head by his feet. Wasting no further time he began a desperate search for the bungtap as ordered. The glow from the emerald soon helped him locate it below the level of the spirit and he repeatedly pushed the dagger at it. Heliana vomited once again and then set about singing another bawdy song whose words were so slurred that Llyat could not understand them. Thias began to hiccough and Irabo began to stir, woken by the reviving effects of the firewater that seeped up his nose.

"Strings," muttered the young warrior. "I see strings."

With an air clap and a whoosh the bungtap popped out. Liquid then flowed out of the barrel. Once the level fell below that of the bung a draft of fresh air crept in but the atmosphere still remained poisonous and Llyat's eyes began to roll in their sockets.

"Help! Please Help!" Llyat heard Thias cry. "If anyone is out there please help us now."

The amplified sound of Thias's voice battered against Llyat's eardrums to the point where he felt they would burst. Then as the echo died Llyat heard another voice, one much quieter as it seeped through the small hole he had created in the side of the barrel. It was a voice Llyat had never expected to hear again.

"Is that you bard?" asked this other. "Are you the one called Thias Calavan?"

"Yes is me, please help us. I have Llyat, Heliana, and Irabo with me. We are all in a bad way and unless you soon release us from this barrel it will be too late."

"I understand what you say," replied the voice. "Hang on, I am going to tip the barrel over in an attempt to break it open. Come on Ligart, give me a hand for it will take all our strength to move it."

A few seconds later Llyat felt the great barrel rock and edge forward inch by inch. He heard much grunting from the efforts of those who attempted their rescue. The barrel toppled and then fell. Llyat bounced off his companions and Heliana vomited again but at least the fall had stopped her caterwauling. After the barrel had rolled several times it came to a stop. Its wood had cracked in several places but its basic structure remained intact.

"Use this," said a voice that Llyat did not recognise.

The booming sounds of an axe striking the base of barrel caused all to cover their ears.

Theoplous swung the axe with all the energy he could muster. It was a substantial two handed weapon that Isambard Hotch kept behind the serving counter of his establishment should he ever have the need to subdue difficult customers. Once the monstrous barkeep had recovered from his trampling he had moved at once to where his prized spirit barrel had begun to speak. At first he thought it was dark magic but then realised there was someone in trouble within its confines. He had wasted no time in thrusting the axe into Theoplous's hands. Several blows later the base of the barrel split into two and it caved inwards. The First Mate thrust his hand inside the barrel as the residual spirit gushed out and then he removed the two halves of the wooden base. A pickled head was the first thing to slide out and it came to rest by his feet.

"Fuck me!" exclaimed Theoplous. "By the balls of Belanore, what is that doing in there?

"Fuck indeed!" uttered Highroar.

The Captain looked down to the pickled globe while Theoplous grabbed it by the hair and began to raise it for a closer inspection.

"Shit," exclaimed Isambard. "I forgot about that and I should have warned you."

"I know this bugger," shouted Theoplous having studied the face of the one that he held. It's the bastard Nedes Karoly."

"Who," shouted Llyat?

"Just someone I knew who is now of no importance," replied Theoplous.

"It was in here when we arrived," shouted Thias from inside the barrel.

"Isambard, what have you to say about this? Can you explain?" demanded Highroar.

"It is what I use to add the distinctive flavour to my hooch," replied the barkeep as his face turned the hue of a ripened plum. "A fresh skull gives the Wolf's grog its unusual musty flavour that is so beloved by those who frequent my place of business. You could say it gives it a good head"

"That's not at all funny you murdering bastard," shouted back Theoplous as he took hold of Irabo's feet and sought to pull the young warrior from out of the wooden container. "How many have you killed over the years?"

"None, and why should I?" answered Isambard. "No one knows of this secret save for Cassius Underscroft, the dead collector. It is he who provides a head once a week from the back of his cart, or less often if business is slack. I only ever use those already dead and if you must know, the tastiest are those unfortunates who died from starvation for they seem not to sour the flavour as much. It is a well-practiced and honed recipe but you must promise to keep it a secret. If others in Parandor…"

"You sick fuck," screamed Theoplous was he managed to extricate Thias from the barrel. "Dispose of it before any of your customers return. Should any see it and realise what you do they will lynch you and drop you from the Folly without so much as stopping for a piss. Throw it on the fire."

"Is it worthy of a snog?" slurred the inebriated girl and the question echoed around the barrel as if trying to find ears willing to acknowledge its dreadful implication.

The question remained forever unanswered as the lardy barkeep picked up the slippery object, licked a pool of residual firewater from out of a sunken eye socket and then moved to the dying fire in the tavern's hearth. Once the pickled head hit the embers the flames roared into life and the spirit soaked ball was sent on its final stage of destruction. By the time that Isambard had returned to the barrel its blue glow had ceased, so also had the green light that had become obvious once Theoplous had broken into the great tub.

"I always enjoyed Hotch's Nectar," said Highroar in complete disbelief. "I guess I'll still buy it!"

"You are one sick fuck!" snarled Theoplous with disgust.

"How is Irabo?" shouted Llyat as he swayed back onto his feet. "Is he still with us?"

"Just about," replied Thias, kneeling to examine the young warrior. "We need to get him to the healers in the Temple of Fatumai as soon as possible otherwise he will be lost to us for ever. The firewater has at least made his pulse bound which must be a good thing.

"All praise the spirit of the Wolf," slurred Heliana before once again breaking into song, this time a wench ditty about how a girl can best use her quim.

"Ligart, lift Irabo onto the counter and raise his head a little to help him breath," ordered Theoplous as he grabbed hold of Heliana's feet and began to pull.

"Once we have got the other out, you and I will take this man to the priests of Fatumai. There's not much time left if we are to save him."

"It's a fortunate coincidence we were here to rescue you land buggers," said Highroar. "

"Never ignore coincidence Captain, how many times have I told you that?" replied Thias.

"Far too many," came the muffled response.

Ligart Highroar knelt down in order to lift Irabo. Just at that same moment Theoplous pulled Heliana out. Her dress rose to her waist in the process and Llyat noticed Highroar staring at the girl's most prized possession. The old sot whistled before pausing in his task of lifting Irabo.

"Why don't you look to the man while I care for the girl?" drooled the lecherous old sea dog.

"I swear I will poke your eyes from their sockets should you not step up to the mark," snarled Theoplous as he threw his Captain a look that left no doubt as to his anger.

"And I will cut your fucking cock off if you ever so much as look at her again," slurred Llyat as he steadied himself against the counter top.

Llyat had followed everything that had occurred from within his place of entrapment, even though most of it had been hidden from his gaze. The effects of the spirit clouded the reality of what was happening but once out and into the room his head had begun to clear a little. A kick in the small of his back from Thias's foot caused him to move forward and then cradle Heliana in his arms. She too seemed a little less muddled in thought and had at least stopped singing. Another bonus was that she had not vomited for some minutes. Somehow the four companions had made it through the Rift and Llyat sensed a feeling of great achievement even though the outcome had almost been a disaster. Soon the three stood together, gathered in a group with their rescuers and their dying companion.

"What is that stink?" asked Llyat as a new insult hit his nose.

"Hotch," replied Theoplous.

"Blood and guts, that's an awful reek," added Thias as he retrieved the Dagger of Kha from Llyat's hand replaced it inside his bag. "I'm most happy to see you again Theo my friend and I am mighty pleased you made it out of the Guild."

"Just look at the amount of hair that you and Llyat have grown," replied Theoplous. "I wouldn't have recognised you had you not spoken. It looks like you have been through much shit."

"We have," answered Llyat, "but we haven't time to speak of it now.

"We must try to save Irabo's life," interjected Heliana.

"And we have to warn the Court of the dangers we have uncovered," added Thias.

A cough from behind caused all to turn.

"I heard this morning from Sir Richemanus of the Nightfall that there is to be a meeting today of all the highborn, somewhere inside the Citadel," began Isambard Hotch. "Out executioner said it was something to do with developments in those Death Tubaria murders. I'm not sure what but the whispers hint at further deaths and the identification of the true poison used in some of the crimes. He said it wasn't Nightshade after all."

"Did your informer say who had died?" asked Theoplous.

"No he didn't," replied the barkeep, "but the meeting is due to start within the hour."

"We need to be there," said Thias. "Theoplous, please can we entrust Irabo's life to you and the Captain?"

"Of course and we will leave at once. Come on Highroar, grab his feet."

Within seconds the two sailors had picked up Irabo's limp body and raced through the tavern's entrance. Following their departure customers began to return, most inquisitive to see what had transpired since the barrel had begun to glow. Others came in and continued with their drinking. As the number of inebriates and fornicators began to swell, Llyat sought to clear his head by helping Heliana towards the door. He watched as Thias threw a last glance to the fire but no trace of the head remained.

"What about Hotch," growled Llyat as he too looked towards the hearth?

"Right now we have more important matters to deal with. We must go to the Citadel before any others dare to enter via the Rift. It won't be long before Urthanock sends his reptiles after us."

"Llyat my head is still spinning. May we rest awhile?" pleaded Heliana.

"I wish that we could my love but we are still in the greatest of danger."

The three companions raced through the southern quarter of Parandor. It would be more accurate perhaps to describe their progress as a stagger in haste and yet as the minutes passed, heighten by anxiety and fear of what was to come, their minds began to shake off the effects of the firewater. Llyat was pleased that the many citizens they pushed past were not armed nor intent to do them harm. Many sneered at the smell of the drink that pervaded the threesome's tattered clothes and several even called out in disgust at what they thought were drunks running from the Watch.

The journey continued on without significant incident and no one bothered to speak. There was no need to do so for all three knew where they were going and the news they had to impart. Llyat's thoughts returned to Irabo and whether there was any possibility he would ever see the young warrior again. He was sure that he had done all within his power to aid the young warrior but he then thought how angry Tonousa would be if she were to hear of her colleague's demise. Llyat was determined that should the worst outcome prevail then he would not be the one to inform the fearsome woman of the Watch. He prayed that the two sailors were true to their word and would deliver his sick friend into the hands of the priests who were said to be able to perform great miracles of healing. If there was anyone who deserved to be kept alive then it was Irabo Basequin for Llyat had never met a more honourable and honest person.

After some twenty minutes Llyat, Thias, and Heliana arrived at the Barbican and the first of the manned gates that led into the Citadel. The imposing portal was however closed and the armour clad knight that stood before it was well armed and not in a mind to permit the passage of three dishevelled tramps into the space reserved for the Highborn of the Royal Court.

"Let me do the talking," said Thias as the three approached the knight and caused him to unsheathe his sword.

"Of course," said Llyat smirking. " You are known in the Capital, even if you look and smell so bad that you never would have been be made welcome in Maplehill."

"You don't smell so good yourself Llyat," moaned Heliana, proud to make comment without slurring her words, the rapid walk having sobered her thoughts sufficiently to give her back control of her lips.

"Excuse me good sir knight," began Thias as he stepped forward and offered a hand of friendship. "We have urgent business with the Sovereign Court. I understand that they are about to meet to discuss matters of most importance for the security of the Realm. We three have vital information that they need to hear. We have travelled from the great battle of Avolire and at great haste in order to relay messages of great value. Please let us pass and allow us immediate access to the Citadel."

"Fuck off before I stick you with my sword," bellowed the knight who tightened his hand on his blade.

"Please sir, you must listen to me," continued Thias, taking a couple of steps back just in case the guard decided to carry out his threat. "I am Thias Calavan, personal bard to Phauless Gylewu. He sent me away on a secret mission and I now return with the information he ordered me to discover."

"And I am Ruler of this gate, so fuck off before I get angry," roared the knight who then waved his unsheathed sword before the bard.

At the sight of the blade Thias retreated to discuss the predicament with his companions and as he did so Llyat struggled to think what they could do to win over the trust of the gatekeeper. Then out of the corner of his eye he spotted someone approaching from the Barbican. As this other got closer Llyat called out to him.

"Commander Townsforth, it's me, Llyat Emgar, the youth that Irabo Basequin pulled from the Tiaryer and sent to old Abrahamus Marus as a servant; the boy you sent to Valameer."

"Fuck off, I don't give money to beggars," snarled the Commander as he marched forward. "Move away while I enter the Citadel or by the fists of the gods I will rip that tongue from out of you stinking throat."

Thias turned at the sound of the Commander's name and as soon as Townsforth's words had finished the bard drove the conversation forward.

"Brynn, although you may find it difficult to believe, it is me, your old friend."

The Lord Commander looked at Thias and despite recognising the voice he failed to make the link with the wretch that stood before him.

"It is I, Thias Calavan, bard and confidant to the Ruler. Please help us gain access to the Sovereign Council. We have much to tell and explain if Parandor is not to fall."

Llyat watched in silence as the Lord Commander of the City Watch paused for a moment and pondered on Thias's request. After what seemed an age the Commander spoke.

"What was the name of the strumpet procured for me on the eve of my sixtieth name day?"

"Saddle-lipped Sonya," replied Thias without hesitation. "Brynn, it is me and this is Llyat Emgar. The girl beside me used to be a servant of the Grand Physician and she has played a key role in gaining the information we need to place before the Sovereign Council.

The Commander looked at the three friends with great curiosity and then his stern face broke.

"Well, bugger me, I do believe it is you Thias and I have indeed seen the wench around Court. I even met the young lad you speak of once before, when the old Physician set off for Valameer. He doesn't look much like him though for like you he was clean shaven and shorter of hair."

"Brynn, I swear it is the same youth," snapped back Thias with great urgency. "Please help us. Tonousa Amberstone will vouch for us."

"Erm..., Yes... You could have at least washed and shaved before coming here," continued Townsforth while ignoring the mention of Tonousa's name. "That could have been more to your vantage than going to some tavern and getting pissed. By the bowels of the gods you all reek. How much spirit have you consumed? It is pouring from your pours and assaulting my nose."

"We have not been drinking Commander," chipped in Llyat. "We fell by accident into a barrel of firewater."

"That's the honest truth sir," added Heliana after which she began to hiccough.

Brynn Townsforth stood and contemplated what he should do next. Seconds later he turned to address the guard and gestured to him to open the gate.

"I know these two of old," he began. "In particular this filthy bard. I will vouch for the three of them and take them with me. The Sovereign Council must hear their news."

The knight did not reply yet replaced his sword into its scabbard. He then moved to open the gate with a shrug of his shoulders.

Minutes later the four burst into the marble throne room where a significant crowd of highborn had gathered to hear important news. Llyat was the third of the four to enter into the regal space and was once again struck by the opulence of the majestic room. His eyes, now cleared of the effects of the spirit, scanned the multitude of faces before him and noted that the meeting was just about to begin. An odd rotund man with enormous side whiskers stood beside the throne and made ready to open his mouth. Yet his words refused to flow as his gaze fell upon the four who had just entered. Llyat then watched with trepidation as two knights in armour approached.

"What is the meaning of this Townsforth?" demanded the first. "How dare you bring these vagrants inside the Citadel? My god they stink. Are they pissed?"

Both knights gripped on the hilts of their swords and Llyat knew that the slightest provocation would lead to an immediate slaughter. He looked into both warrior's eyes and sensed they were unwilling to listen to reason. Commander Townsforth then held forward his right hand and shouted as loud as his voice would carry. His words were directed to the whiskered man who was preparing to make a speech.

"My Lord Ystafell, forgive me if I am a little late," began the battle-hardened Commander. "All is not as it seems. These three who look like the detritus of the Realm are important messengers and I know them of old. You also know two of them, one very well indeed. They have endured much hardship to bring us important messages that impact upon the continued safety of the Realm. I beg your permission to hear them out. That is of course when you have finished your business."

"Commander, if you deem it to be of such importance I will grant your request," replied Ystafell. "However keep them to the back of the room for their stink has reached my nostrils. Is that the girl Heliana? The wench that works for Fullbane?"

Llyat then spotted a whale sized Lady, kept upright by six strong muscular men, suddenly turn amongst the crowd and begin to eyeball Heliana. He guessed her to be the infamous Lady Fullbane.

"Yes Gilebin, it is and the others are..." began the Commander before being cut off.

"Sir Lightmain and Sir Cragtalon, guard those three foul stinkers and keep them against the back wall for I do not want any mischief carried out this day," ordered Ystafell, his lisp struggling to keep up as his voice bellowed out into the room. "Brynn you come closer for I also do not wish to continue shouting. First I will deliver my decree and only then entertain the words of your guests."

The three dishevelled companions were pushed back to the far corner of the room by the sword points of those ordered to stand guard over their presence. Llyat then watched as Townsforth strode forward and took his pace amongst the highborn. Thias then turned to Llyat and whispered such that none but he could hear.

"All who are important have gathered here," he began. "All that is except Phauless who is I am sad to say is dead."

"What!" exclaimed Llyat as the words hit him hard? "When? How?"

"Heliana told me while we were confined in Avolire. It's a secret being kept from the Court"

"Fuck me, what else have you kept secret? Who else is here that you say matters?"

"There is nothing more being kept from you," replied Thias as he began to point out some of those present to his friend. "Over there is Sir Byddin and next to him Lady Emeny. The tall evil looking swine over there is Sir Richemanus of the Nightfall and the priest stands to his right. You must have heard of him, Heward Teulu, he who leads the followers of Fatumai and to who's care we have dispatched Irabo. The tit balancing on one leg over there in the multi-coloured doublet is the arsehole known as Lolly."

"Yes, I know him; we met once," whispered Llyat. "I have seen the others before, when I served in the feasting hall."

Llyat then noticed an absurd young man with bizarre clothes who was staring at him.

What about that that one with the spikey hair?" he whispered while pointing to the stranger.

"That Llyat is Iqotrix, Archmage of the Wizards Guild..."

"My Lords and Ladies and other esteemed friends..." bellowed Ystafell.

The intervention caused Llyat and Thias to cut short their conversation and the wizard to break the focus of his stare.

"... I will keep this short for I know you have many important tasks and pleasures which you will no doubt be in a hurry to get back to complete.

"Dogs bollocks Gilebin, get on with it!" shouted Sir Byddin. "What's going on man?"

Ystafell coughed while revealing his nervousness to his audience.

"I have two significant pieces of information to pass to you today. One has been a well-guarded secret and the other is my decree.

"Why are you issuing decrees, why not Phauless himself or at least Emeny as his Sovereign adviser?" asked the enormous woman that Llyat assumed was Heliana's new mistress.

"The health of Lord Phauless is the first point of my message," continued Ystafell, his lisp enhanced and his fingers twiddling against his palms. "Although a select few witnessed the event the majority of you have been kept in the dark for some days."

"Spit it out man, what are you trying to tell us?" roared Lady Fullbane.

"Phauless died a number of days ago," stuttered Ystafell, his nerves suppressing his ability to talk coherently. "We believe he was poisoned. Lady Emeny along with a small number of others remain key suspects."

Gasps filled the room and evolved into a tumult sufficient to sting Llyat's ears. Some Ladies of the Court fainted while many of the older Lords rested against the walls to steady their legs. Llyat assumed that the fat lady would drop but she did not; which was good for no one would have been able to pick her up again. At last the noise dropped to a level whereby Ystafell could be heard once again.

"He was marked with the three circle brand of Death Tubaria. The murders continue."

"If Emeny is one suspect, who are the others?" shouted a voice from the Court.

"Byddin, Richemanus, and Teulu," replied Ystafell while inducing another shock wave.

"Then why are they here and not dangling from the Folly?" demanded one voice.

"Where is Tonousa Amberstone" shouted another Lady who Llyat did not recognise. "Let her answer here for her failings. She was supposed to put an end to these despicable crimes. Phauless appointed her himself so why isn't she here?"

"I'm afraid she too has been murdered and once again we suspect the hand of Death Tubaria," bellowed Gilebin.

"What! No way, I will not believe it," exclaimed Llyat in disbelief as the air resounded to the wailing of women and angry cries of men.

Llyat looked to his friends. Thias, having been struck dumb, leaned back against the adjacent wall. Heliana dissolved into a deluge of tears.

"Was she also poisoned?" demanded another from the crowd.

"No she was not," continued Ystafell while trying to gain control. "She was stabbed and bled to death down in the pantry of the Underkeep. The 'Warrior' card from a pack of Fortunes Fate had been left in her mouth and we struggled at first to understand what that could mean. However, Commander Townsforth has given us an insight into Tonousa Amberstone's investigations and we are now a little wiser as to its implications."

"Shit, it must have happened after I was knocked senseless and just before being taken to Avolire," sobbed Heliana as she laid her head on Llyat's shoulder and her right hand over her belly. "The murderous fucker must have been there with us all the time."

"It seems the Amberstone bitch liked to play cards with an uncouth crowd of late night eaters," giggled Lolly as he pulled a pack of playing cards from a pocket in his doublet and with a high jump threw them into the air.

As they dropped to the ground the Fool continued with his bizarre intervention. "All fall down! Who can pick them up again? She should have asked me to show her a trick or two."

"Open your fucking mouth again Fool and I will slit you from scrote to throat," snarled Byddin.

The knight gripped Lolly by the scruff of his doublet and threw him down to the floor such that he landed with a thump.

"Ooo, you are so forceful," sniggered the Fool.

"Llyat," whispered Heliana. "Lolly was in the pantry when I was attacked."

"Silence, I demand silence" ordered Ystafell and a deep hush fell upon the room. "For the past few days the wizards, under the guidance of our great friend the Archmage Iqotrix who is here amongst us today, have sought to identify the precise poison used by the murdering bastard that still moves amongst us. He or she is present in this room right now but let me tell you this, whoever you are; we are closing in on you and will reveal your identity one day soon. You will slip up sooner or later and by all the gods that I can name, you will be cursed forever."

Llyat watched as Ystafell's gaze drifted to the strange wizard.

"Iqotrix, step up here for a moment and tell us of your findings," he lisped.

Silence fell and Llyat watched as the wizard rose to stand beside the Lord Chamberlain.

"Lords and Ladies of the Court and all others deemed worthy of hearing my words," he began "My first task was to look at the evidence surrounding the first poisonings associated with the resurgence of Death Tubaria, those who had also been branded with the three circle mark of Kha. You may have been told that their deaths had been the result of ingestion of the plant called the Nightshade. However, the descriptions of the deceased when found indicated to us that it was in fact the administration of a rare mushroom poison that finished them off. Then we examined the body of Lord Phauless, may the gods look over his soul. His body resides in the temple of Fatumai and on close inspection we are certain that a different poison was used."

"Which one man," shouted Lady Fullbane?

"Lillywort," replied the wizard, triggering more gasps and the feigned fainting of Ladies. "We have therefore come to the conclusion that our murderer is skilled in the use of a least two natural poisons and this has led me to offer some advice to Lord Ystafell. It forms the basis of his decree. We still do not know how Phauless ingested the Lillywort for Lolly had been designated taster and sampled all that the Sovereign later consumed. As you will see, the idiot is still with us."

"Dickdangle!" shouted Lolly.

"I've warned you once already, speak again and you are dead," growled Byddin.

At that the wizard stepped down from the raised platform and returned to his place in the crowd. As he did so Llyat heard Thias whisper to himself. "I'm sure that Ulthirn once told me Lizardmen are immune to the effects of the Lillywort."

Llyat felt Heliana straighten as if transfixed with some deep thought and he wondered if she had also heard Thias's comments.

"What's wrong?" he asked.

"Shush and let me think. This is important."

"By the powers laid before me in the absence of suitable others," bellowed Ystafell. "I do hereby decree that from this day hence mushrooms of any kind and the products of the Lillywort are banned from this city. Anyone found with them in their possession after Solaris rises on the morrow will be consider a traitor and will end their life without trial on the executioners block. I hope that is understood by all and there will be no further debate on this matter."

Muffled mumbling spread through the room as everyone, including the guards present, swore under their breaths. The widespread impact of Ystafell's decree did not go unnoticed by Llyat, nor indeed the few others who were not already misusing the substance. Llyat was sure that Lady Emeny was about to faint but somehow she held herself upright. Then Llyat noticed the Lord Chamberlin beckon the Commander of the Watch forward.

"Now Townsforth bring your stinking friends forward and ensure they introduce themselves before they speak," ordered Ystafell. "Make it succinct and be quick for we will not be able to tolerate their stench for long."

The Commander waved the three forward and the crowd parted as the three moved as one, followed by the sword points of Sir Lightmain and Sir Cragtalon. Lolly danced a jig in front of Ystafell and as Llyat approach the whiskered man the Fool bent double, kissed the first two fingers of his right hand and with great drama touched his arse. A kick from Townsend's boot pushed Lolly back to the ground where he then sat in silence and stared ahead. Llyat found this all very amusing and winked at the fool who had once befriended him. Lolly smiled back.

"Okay Thias," ordered the Commander. "This had better be good."

Thias cleared his throat and stepped forward. As he did so Llyat caught Heliana's gaze. She was staring at Lolly.

"Gilebin, although you may find it difficult to believe as you gaze upon me here and now, it is Phauless's agent that stands before you," he began. "For all others present who cannot see me close up, I am Thias Calavan, Royal Barc, and I left here many weeks ago on a secret mission at the behest of our Great Sovereign, may the gods protect his essence."

"I do at least recognise your voice Thias, if not your stench." replied Ystafell. "What important news do you three have for us? What do you know?"

"Being aware that the spy we know is still at work in the Citadel and the fact he is no doubt here in this room, I will not tell all that I know, just enough to ensure you take me at my word and agree to meet later in perhaps reduced and more trusted company," answered Thias.

A murmur of discontent reverberated against Llyat's ears. Byddin snarled, Emeny hissed under her breath, Richemanus spat on the floor in front of his boots, but Heward Teulu shouted;

"Here we go a-fucking-gain."

Llyat watched as Lolly stared at Thias but then fixed his gaze on Heliana.

"Let me summarise the key point that you need to grasp," continued Thias. "The Death Tubaria murders are part of a much more sinister plot. It is all to do with the Prophecy of Enderdetag."

"Yes we have heard of it and have already realised there is some link to it," interrupted Iqotrix in a manner that displayed his arrogance.

"Good," replied Thias. "That helps a lot. Urthanock has returned and will soon lead the Lizardmen into war with the intent of destroying all that the Realm stands for.

Once again shouts and audible gasps filled the room.

"Dogs bollocks," shouted Byddin.

"You smell and look just like I always imagined Urthanock would do whenever the ballads were sung," shouted Lolly who did not once move his penetrating eyes away from Heliana.

"My Lords and Ladies, order... please!" shouted the Lord Chamberlin as he at last he gained some semblance of control. "Please Thias, do continue. Make some sense out of all of this for us."

"My friends and I bring before you the key objects that give us hope of defeating the evil one."

Llyat watched as Thias reached down into the bag that still hung from his shoulder and began to pull out items from inside is dark recesses.

"We three have done the impossible," began Thias. "We have travelled to the furthest reaches of the Realm and have returned with the five legendary Gems of Thamous, those referred to in the Prophecy and long hidden from the eyes of humble souls. This first is the Dagger of Kha which you have all no doubt heard of and feared in your dreams."

A collective gasp shot through the room as Thias held aloft the emerald encrusted dagger. He then passed it on to Heliana to hold.

"This second is the fabled Sceptre of Urthanock with the Seer's Stone at its head. Llyat hold this for me but wrap your hand around the diamond lest anyone should be tempted to look inside."

Thias passed over the sceptre and Llyat acted as instructed.

"This ruby on a golden chain is yet another, and believe me when I say that many of you have seen it before. Heliana, the girl beside me works for Lady Fullbane is the one to be commended for…"

"That's mine, you thieving swine," bellowed the large Lady but Heliana wasn't listening.

As Lady Fullbane's voice silenced, Llyat once again looked to Heliana and then to Lolly. Both stared into each other's eyes in a way that Llyat could not understand. Then the Fool's lips moved and Llyat read the silent message that he mouthed; 'The ruby as well, you are a clever girl.'

"This is the sapphire that we took from Sir Raulyn's axe in Barad Elestor and…"

Llyat's thoughts strayed and he again found himself looking down at Lolly. He began to wonder what the Fool would make of the Gems. He then saw Lolly's gaze switch from Heliana and fall upon the dazzling sapphire. The Fool's eyes widened and were followed by a smile. Heliana's hand flashed forward, still gripped around the hilt of the Dagger of Kha. In total disbelief Llyat looked on as his lover thrust the dagger through Lolly's left eye socket and on into his head. The Fool fell backwards and writhed on the floor below Ystafell's feet. There Lolly twitched in the most violent of seizures with the dagger embedded in his skull. The convulsions lasted no more than a few seconds after which Lolly lay still and a great hush fell upon those present.

"What did fuck you do that for?" screeched Llyat and as Sir Lightmain gripped hold of Heliana.

Cragtalon's blade danced between the backs of Llyat and Thias as if not knowing which to strike first should either move. Llyat's sudden gasp of horror was mirrored by most others present for the assault had been so unexpected. Ystafell retreated a few paces and almost fell backwards over the rear of the raised platform. There he tottered like an inebriate before finally regaining his composure.

"He's the fucking bastard you've been looking for," screamed Heliana with a shriek so high in pitch that it threatened to shatter the windows.

As Sir Lightmain attempted to drag the furious woman from the room, Heliana screamed at Lolly's corpse. "Die, you shit faced loon."

"What in all that is holy has happened to the girl?" exclaimed Teulu.

"Heliana" exclaimed Llyat. "What are you…?"

Before Llyat could finish his sentence, or indeed others could act or speak, the metamorphosis began. Within a minute the body and clothes of the once comical Fool had reformed into that of a gross and monstrous Lizardman. Then as Llyat stared with incredulity at the sight before his eyes, Thias swept his right hand down and wrenched the Dagger of Kha from out of the reptile's skull. Withdrawing his hand in a swift arc he then proceeded to wipe the residues of reptilian brain from off the dagger with his left sleeve before replacing the weapon with the ruby and sapphire back into the deep interior of his shoulder bag.

Llyat stood dumbfounded as Thias then snatched the sceptre of Urthanock from his hands and thrust it into the bag.

"Shit," exclaimed the Lord Chamberlin. "I wasn't expecting that!"

Llyat noted that Lady Emeny had fainted at the sight of the changeling and that Sir Byddin was vomiting which seemed out of character for one so battle hardened. Then Heward Teulu stepped forward. Llyat assumed the priest wanted a closer look but on staring down at the scale covered corpse Teulu also began to act in a most unexpected manner. The man of the cloth kicked at the dead creatures head, over and over again.

"You fucking cunt-swine of the swamp," he began as his anger spewed out in a torrent of blasphemy. "What the fuck have we been doing all these fucking years, letting this dog's dick of a mother fucker share the fucking ground that we honest folk walk?"

"Heward, control yourself," began Ystafell, amazed by the priest's sudden outburst. "You are reverting to your village roots and it does not become you!"

"Stick your roots up your fat arse Gilebin. We have all been made great fools by that fucking king of idiots. I say we dangle the dickdangle by his dick from the highest tower of Parandor. Let all see what the gods have spewed into our lap."

"It seems the girl has delivered the spy we have sought for so long, "shouted Townsforth amid the pandemonium. He then turned to Lightmain who still held Heliana his vice-like fist. "You can let go of the girl now."

In an instant the knight released his grip and Heliana threw herself into Llyat's arms. The youth held his lover in a tight embrace as further confused cries filled the hall

"Be quiet everyone, shut your mouths and listen with your ears," bellowed the Lord Chamberlain.

Llyat felt the presence of the Commander move up close.

"What made you so certain it was Lolly, Heliana?" asked Townsforth.

"I was in the pantry with Tonousa as she tried to spring her trap to capture the murderer. Lolly, I mean that fucking thing, was with us when I was hit on the head. It could only have been him."

"But what was it that gave him a way and convinced you of his guilt?" asked Ystafell who had moved to her side.

"The ruby, he mentioned the ruby that I had around my neck at the time," continued Heliana as she began a pitiful sobbing brought on by the shock her first kill. "It is a long and complicated story and I do not have the strength to speak of it now."

The body of the Lizardman twitched. Once again the gathered crowd began to panic. Ystafell cried out for order.

"Listen everyone. Given how shocking this revelation has been, we do need time to gather our thoughts. This is what we will do. Thias, take your friends and go and clean yourselves up. Put those jewels that you carry in the safest and most secret place that you know of. We will hold a Council tomorrow in the war room at the time of the first cock crow. You will attend the meeting Thias and tell us the detail of all that you know."

Llyat's head began to clear from the ensuing madness and he focused on the conversations.

"What about my friends Llyat and Heliana," asked Thias?

"Leave the servants to rest," replied Ystafell. "But ensure they too are kept in a secure and secret location. Byddin, Emeny, Teulu; given what we have just witnessed you are no longer under the same degree of suspicion and I expect your presence to make itself known at tomorrow's meeting. Do not on any account fail me."

Llyat watched the three nod in acknowledgement of the order and felt great relief at not having to attend the meeting himself. If only he knew what to do next. His party had possession of the Gems but they still didn't know how to find the door to the Underworld or how to defeat Urthanock. So many thoughts rushed through his head that he did not notice Richemanus push up alongside the Lord Chamberlin.

"Would you like me to attend the meeting?" asked the Royal Executioner. "Given that I was a suspect and all that?"

"No, I fucking would not," bellowed by Ystafell without the hint of a stammer or lisp. "This meeting is closed. Now all of you, go and do whatever you would otherwise have done this day. Commander Townsforth, arrange for the removal of that creature."

Some hours later as night took its firm grip upon the Realm, Llyat stepped out of the hot steaming tub in which he had lain in for the past half hour. He and Heliana had been taken and locked for their own safety within the chambers of old Abrahamus Marus, for a replacement for the Grand Physician of Parandor had yet to be found. After all Llyat's travels through the far reaches of the Realm it felt good to be able to once again remove the accumulated grime from his body. Heliana had cut his hair while he lay in the soothing waters and had then proceed to shave the long and patchy hairs that had grown on his adolescent face. With a towel around his waist he began to walk the chambers of his old master and as he did so he reflected on all that had passed since he had last visited the room. He moved over to a small mirror that was fixed upon one wall and he stared at his smoky image in the ageing glass. He was at least now recognisable as his old self although he seemed thinner and more wrinkled around the eyes.

Llyat then turned and saw Heliana proceed to empty the tub down into the adjacent hole which led via a lead pipe into the water conduits beneath the Citadel. He smiled as he watched her and realised how relaxed he felt in her company. It seemed easy to recall the time he had spent with her as their love had blossomed on the floor of the old man's chambers and his cock soon twitched beneath his towel. Then without reason his thoughts jumped to an image of the old sword that Heliana had first shown him as she had packed for the journey to Valameer. He had not seen Destiny's Song since Barad Elestor and he wondered where it could be, or indeed if he would ever see it again?

After some minutes Llyat wandered over to the bed and began to dress in a set of old servant's clothes that Heliana had lain out for him besides a clean frock that she intended to wear later. The young woman proceeded to refill the bath with steaming jugs of hot water which she had been boiling over the fire in his old master's study. Llyat closed his eyes, took in the peace of the moment, and realised how lucky he was to still be alive. The events of his quest flashed before his eyes and he relived their graphic details. He focused on the Gems of Thamous and began to wonder what secret place Thias would choose to keep them. The bard had eft as soon as he had ensured the lovers were secure and then rushed on to the temple of Fatumai in order to check on Irabo's progress. He had told Llyat that he would only disturb him during the night if the news was bad and the fact he had not so far returned lightened Llyat's heart.

The noise of Heliana's clothes falling to the floor caused Llyat to look once again towards the bath where he caught a glimpse of the naked girl as she stepped into the hot water. He looked with searching eyes and noted once again that her figure had changed. As was so often the way in his youth, his mouth spoke before his brain had considered the implications of what he had seen.

"I know your thinner in the face but your belly and tits are much bigger than they used to be," he blabbered. "I don't know what you've been eating that could have done that but perhaps you need to think about what you put on your plate for a while."

"I'm pregnant you dumb shit," replied Heliana. "You must be the only bugger in the Realm so blind as to not have noticed."

"What!" Llyat exclaimed as the new information shook him to the core.

"I am with child Llyat and before you embarrass yourself further, yes it is yours."

"What!"

"You are going to be a father, so you had better start thinking about names for your child."

"What! Fuck!" exclaimed Llyat as the truth sank in.

"Those are not the names I would choose," Heliana replied who then giggled.

Late into the night the couple lay in each other's arms. Once Llyat had recovered from the shock of his impending parenthood the couple had begun long and wishful conversations about their child, where they would live, and what sort of life they would create for their family. For most of the time they were able to think with much positivity despite the reality of the dangers they both now faced. Heliana had become the Vessel that carried the seed of the Marked and that heavy duty did not go unfelt by the pair as they hugged each other and shared the taste of each other's lips. Before he readied himself for sleep Llyat realised he had an even greater meaning to his life. He reaffirmed his vows to fulfil the Prophecy for the future of his unborn child depended on the success of his quest. Finally he felt like a man.

8

A clean and fresh shaven Thias Calavan raced from the Temple of Fatumai through the deserted streets of Parandor and on towards the Citadel. The first cock had yet to crow and he knew he could not be late for the War Council that he had been ordered to attend. His first task of the morning had been to check upon Irabo's progress at the hands of the healing priests. The young warrior who had just a few hours before been fighting for his life was much improved. The holy men had not only arrested his demise but turned its course such that Irabo showed signs of stirring. The two in charge of his care, Fathers Atropos and Lachesis, had told the bard that Irabo would be sat up and conscious by the end of the day although still far from being restored to full health. Their expressed view was that the warrior had been delivered to them just in time and had it not been for the stimulating effects of the firewater into which he had materialised then he would have died before the priests could have begun their magic.

When Thias had asked how they had arrested Irabo's life-threatening illness the priests were more than a little secretive and refused to divulge the mysterious processes that they had guarded for many long years. Thias appreciated their response and he did not press the matter for he knew the bards and the wizards did much the same whenever asked about their own rituals and potions. All that the priests did let slip was that their most effective remedy contained an extract of the Lillywort which surprised Thias for he had always consider the plant to be a poison. However, it had been explained that small traces of the marsh flower, when mixed with other extracts of herbs and exotic animal parts, worked miracles in the restoration of the almost dead.

Running on towards the Barbican Thias began to reflect once again on the surprise news he had heard at Court the previous evening. He had not known Tonousa Amberstone long, just a matter of hours during the revelations and destruction of the Bards Guild of Valameer. Yet those few hours with her had convinced him of her valour and he mourned her passing, no doubt murdered by the changeling that Heliana had despatched before the highborn. He knew Tonousa's father of old and wondered how the old man was taking the awful news. His eyes had failed to spot the Royal Librarian at the meeting and soon a sense of foreboding rattled his mind. Perhaps something terrible had also befallen him. He didn't know why, but he sensed that Mathius Amberstone was also dead and he made a mental note to check with Commander Townsforth whenever a suitable moment arose.

Some minutes later he stopped running and took several deep breaths in order to regain his composure. While so doing he began to think back to all the others who had already sacrificed their lives as the events of the year had unfolded. Far too many had died and he felt sure there would be many more who would perish before his quest was over. At the current rate of attrition there would be few left to hear his songs should he somehow manage to survive the impending battle with Urthanock.

Darkness remained and the clouds were thick and heavy when Thias at last reached the Barbican. He had to hammer with his fist upon the door of the guardhouse for the solitary knight that manned the main gate was deep asleep inside its stone walls. After much persistence, a rustling sound from within indicated the guard had stirred was moving to open the door. A minute later the wood was pushed open and the same bleary-eyed knight from the previous day stuck h s head outside.

"What the fuck do you want at this hour?" moaned the knight. "What business do you have?"

"I have been summoned to attend the War Council in the Citadel before the first of the cocks' crow," replied Thias with great urgency. "Please check your admission list for the day."

"I will, don't you fucking worry," replied the knight as he scuttled back inside his dingy hole and shouted; "Just don't go anywhere!"

"Do not fear good knight, I am going nowhere!"

"Now what did you say your name was," said the knight as he reappeared at the door.

"I didn't give you one."

"Don't try and be fucking smart with me lad," growled the knight. "Piss me about and I will come out there and stick you with my sword."

"I meant no offence sir but I am in rather a hurry for I sense the poultry will let loose their throats before you let me pass. My name is Thias Calavan, Royal Bard to the House of Gylewu."

"I met that bugger yesterday," said the knight as he checked his list, inhaled, snorted, and then swallowed a glob of mucous from the back of h s nose. "The one I remember did not look much like you. He had long hair, a beard, and stunk like a skyfawn's arse. How do I know it's the same person who passed here yesterday under the protection of Lord Townsforth?"

"Look, I'll sing for you to prove that I am a bard," said Thias and just as he had threatened he burst into song.

When all were touched by the fall of Aquaris,
And my thoughts were....

"No more I beg you. Just shut that shite up," groaned the knight as he moved to signal the doors of the Barbican to be opened. "I believe you! A bard you may be but you're songs are dreadful."

It took several more minutes to rouse the second knight on duty. This other was positioned high above in the room that housed the mechanisms that worked the doors and the several portcullises that would need to be opened. When yet another sleepy head appeared though the high window, the knight besides Thias shouted out.

"Open a way for this sullen faced crooner. He needs to get to the Citadel and is on the list!"

Some five minutes later Thias pushed open the doors to the War Room. He was the last to arrive and no sooner had he closed the doors than the sounds of a crowing cockerel drifted in through the one window that had been left open to keep the air fresh. Many eyes looked to the young bard and a few eyebrows rose at the timing of his entry. The Council had gathered and all were already sat around the large wooden table that almost filled the thick stone-walled room. Thias's eyes flicked from one member to another as he checked out all those present. He listed them in his mind to ensure there was no one that he had forgotten. At the head of the long table sat Gilebin Ystafell, still holding sway over the rest of those gathered to decide how best to ensure the continued survival of the Realm. Adjacent to the head of the table and to Gilebin's left sat, Lady Emeny, Sir Byddin and the priest Heward Teulu. The three once under a cloud of suspicion had been rehabilitated into their roles, given the belief that the spy amongst them had been silenced. To the right of Gilebin sat Archmage Iqotrix and Brynn Townsforth. An empty chair had been left next to the old warrior and the Commander beckoned Thias over in order to take his place.

Walking towards the empty chair, Thias looked to the others present, ones who sat on chairs at the end of the table furthest away from the Lord Chamberlin. Clustered together were the most senior ranked knights in Parandor. Thias knew them all of old and nodded his acknowledgement to each in turn as he passed. These others, entrusted with supporting the defences of the capital, comprised Digory Bethellemy, Toby Cragtalon, Watcyn Dustfury, Wesmin Lightmain, Horace Mandelwoth, and Jasper Redglade.

As soon as Thias touched the seat of his chair Ystafell declared the meeting open.

"The Council is in session; Llys you take notes for the record. Welcome back Thias, I am so glad you made it for I was beginning to think you had stood us up. I must say you did cut it fine and only beat the cock by seconds."

"I do apologise Gilebin for I first went to visit young Irabo Basequin," answered Thias. "He is the member of the City Watch who came back from Avolire with me. He had been tortured and his life still hangs by the thinnest of strings. But Heward's priests are doing all they can for him and believe that he will survive."

"He will," snorted Teulu in response.

"I would like this Council to recognise the assistance given to me in this life saving act by another person," continued Thias, ignoring the rudeness of the priest.

"Who would that be then?" asked Sir Byddin as he stared out from his one eye.

"He is the First Mate of the Banshees Wail and he goes by the name of Theoplous Danmar."

"How do you spell Danmar?" asked Emeny, her quill moving across the parchment. "Just for the record."

"Dogs bollocks Llys, just make it up," sneered Byddin while puffing out his cheeks. "It doesn't matter how his name is spelt. And further more young Thias, we never recognise the actions of the low life in our Council records."

"Be more specific, who is he and how does he fit into what we are due to discuss today?" demanded Ystafell.

"He is a dark skinned traveller, an ingrant from the Lotus Isles," replied Thias but before he could say more Sir Byddin raised himself to full height and slammed his fist down upon the table.

"It will be a first if we ever recognise one of those black islanders in this Court...."

"Be quiet Byddin, you racist prick!" bellowed Ystafell, also jumping to his feet and seeking to contain the knight's outburst.

Then as the two retook their seats the Lord Chamberlin spoke again.

"Thias, please tell us about this sailor; this Theoplous and how he relates to our endeavours. Please take no notice of Byddin's poor remarks for they do not reflect the views of most of us here."

"Dogs bollocks" mumbled the Head of the Royal Guard, words which were met by an icy stare.

For the next five minutes Thias explained how Theoplous, with the help of Captain Highroar of the Banshees Wail, had set him and his companions free from the barrel of hooch in which they found themselves paddling having travelled from Avolire. Thias then managed to deflect questions about the Rift and its use until later while he went on to describe Theoplous's involvement during the sacking of the Bards Guild. To his surprise Commander Townsforth had then told of how this same seaman had been part of the team that Tonousa Amberstone had put together in her attempt to solve the murders attributed to Death Tubaria. All this while Thias and his friends were 'trotting round the north of the Realm.'

"And what of her father?" said Thias. "I have had a premonition that the librarian is dead. Say it isn't so."

"I am sad to say it is correct," replied Townsforth in a hushed whisper. "I will explain what happened another day for we haven't time to speak of it now."

Thias understood it was not the time to pursue the matter and his thoughts returned to Theoplous.

"I believe he is Cuvar," said Thias with.

"He is and told me as much himself," confirmed Townsforth.

"What the fuck's a Cuvar?" snorted Sir Byddin to the amusement of the other knights.

"I will explain if you will allow me the opportunity to speak Gilebin," began the Archmage.

Following a nod of approval from Ystafell and another snort of disbelief from Sir Byddin, Iqotrix rose from his seat and began a lengthy explanation of the known history of the Cuvar and all that they believed. Townsend followed this up by explaining the purpose of the Cuvar wheel that Tonousa had used to aid her investigations. That point did not go unnoticed by Lady Emeny, Sir Byddin, and Teulu the Royal Priest, those accused of treason on the basis of a note that the wheel had translated. Several minutes later Iqotrix had run out of things to say on all matters Cuvar. Thias finished off by revealing facts which no one else in the room knew, including the wise wizard. Sir Raulyn and the wyvern Thamous were the first of the Cuvar conspirators. The bard also spoke of Grovrouk the Despoiler being one of their followers and an ally after all. Then when all had paused for reflection, Thias admitted that he too, along with Irabo Basequin, had sworn allegiance to the Cuvar cause. They had joined the great conspiracy that had been maintained for so many generations that they were impossible to count.

"This is all nonsense and children's' fantasies," moaned Sir Byddin. "I believe none of it. It's a load of fucking pig..."

"I think for all our sake Thias you need to tell us the full story," interrupted Lady Emeny before Sir Byddin could launch into another tirade of abuse. "I want to know every detail of your journey beginning when Phauless sent you out on your mission to the Grey Keep."

"I support Llys in that request," added Sir Byddin, quietening in response to the Sovereign Advisor's authority. "I haven't got my head around what's going on yet."

"Then so be it," began the bard who then began to describe the details of his journey.

It took the best part of two hours for Thias to tell his tale. It could have perhaps have taken less time had there not been so many interruptions. Sir Byddin was the worst of the offenders and had paused proceedings with exclamations of disbelief at many parts of the story, in particular the ease by which the Lizardmen had destroyed the Bards Guild, the contact with dragons, that ogres still lived and walked the Realm, and that there was a hidden city in the centre of the Eastern Marsh. The Archmage had always questioned further when the Prophecy had been mentioned, and whenever Llyat had played some significant part in the story. He was most interested when Thias had described the finding of Sir Raulyn's tomb and the runes that covered its sides. Lady Emeny took copious notes with her quill and on numerous occasions interrupted to check or spellings and dates. This had irritated both Ystafell Gilebin and Sir Byddin to the point where they grumbled at each of her subsequent interventions. Lord Commander Townsforth had made positive interjections whenever points in the story confirmed all that Tonousa had earlier told him. Teulu for the most part remained silent but did raise questions whenever Thias talked of the debates he and Irabo had held regarding fate and destiny. The knights at the low end of the table were most interested in the descriptions and details of the battles, both at the Bards Guild and that which still raged in Avolire. They revelled in the gory bits and the vivid descriptions of slaughter.

After much speculation Thias got to the end of his saga and the meeting adjourned for breakfast and a piss break. Several servants entered with platters of bread, hog roast, and numerous flagons of sweet red wine. Soon the Council rose as one from their table and began to stretch and move.

"Tell us more of what you make of this 'Vessel' that you referred to," began Ystafell once the Council had resumed its business. "This boy who calls himself Urthanock?"

"What sort of things do want me to say?"

"I would like your views as to whether this is a village lad gone mad or something worse," said Ystafell as he tried to add clarity to his jumbled thoughts.

"Like what for instance," asked lady Emeny?

"Well, is he just a simple village dolt, a power crazy arsehole, or perhaps just insane," continued the Lord Chamberlain. "What I am trying to determine is whether the boy has been consumed by the essence of Urthanock or just thinks he has. I think this is fundamental to our understanding and how we should plan to counter his threat. It is hard for me to believe that the spirit of the Lord of Fear has somehow remained intact over the vast number of years since Raulyn smote him down."

"I concur," sneered Sir Byddin from across the table. "I would put my life savings on the lad being mad. I have heard of many and indeed met a few nutters in my time, some of who were so deluded and full of shit that they even believed in the existence of the gods."

"Fuck off!" snorted the priest, gesticulating that Byddin was fond of tugging his cock.

"Charming!" giggled Llys Emeny and as her cheeks blushed. "Remember where you are priest. You are not at one of our private parties now, nor indeed back in that pitiful village that you once squirmed out from."

"Order...Please," yelled Ystafell. "Thias, please answer my question."

"I would answer in truth if I knew what has happened to my poor brother."

Gasps of stunned disbelief left the mouths of all present.

"Brother?" questioned Commander Townsforth after which Thias spent some minutes relating his past childhood and how he had come to spend time with Vostag Heyn's family. Then he continued with his assessment.

"I would like to believe that Methladon has gone insane," continued Thias. "If it is pure madness then perhaps he could be healed by the likes of Heward's priests, or even one of your wizards Iqotrix. However, as I have already told you, I have met him and looked deep into his eyes. It is my belief that Urthanock has returned and we should not underestimate the power that he could bring to the war that's coming to our gates. The essence of the Foul Lord would have the ability to manipulate this world and all that resides within it. Only by the use of the Gems of Thamous, to seal the swine back inside the Underworld, may we have any hope of salvation.

"Dogs bollocks!" bellowed Sir Byddin as the war room quietened.

After numerous minutes of silence, punctuated only by continued grunts from the Head of the Royal Guard, Thias decided to change the focus of the Council's attention as an idea tormented his mind.

"I did not know Tonousa Amberstone very well nor indeed for very long but I am saddened by her death. Of course I am also distraught at the passing of our Sovereign Ruler and the Royal Librarian, but I would like to understand the circumstances of the young lady's death. It may have bearing on planning the defence of both the Capital and the Citadel."

"She was no lady," spluttered Byddin.

"Sir Byddin," hollered Lady Emeny. "Do not speak so ill of the dead or lower yourself to Blackfayer's level."

"Hypocrite," snorted Heward Teulu as he coughed into his hand.

"What did you say?" spat back Lady Emeny while turning on the priest.

"Council please!" shouted Ystafell.

"Allow me to fill in the details Thias," added the Lord Commander.

Townsforth then explained in detail the investigation that Tonousa had led, including the trap she had set with the assistance of one called Nedes Karoly, a horse rustler and scumbag with links to the Thieves Guild. He told of how Tonousa had been found dead in the pantry, taken by surprise no doubt, given she was well able to defend herself. The Commander then went on to describe the 'Warrior' card found in her mouth, one from Fortunes Fate, the game that Tonousa had linked to the Death Tubaria murders. He spoke of how Llys Emeny and Sir Richemanus had both seen Tonousa near the pantry but neither of them had seen Lolly there. The Sovereign Adviser acknowledged these facts with a nod of her head.

"Did you search the area afterwards?" asked Thias.

"What are you getting at?" asked Ystafell, his eyes squinting with suspicion.

"Call it intuition if you like," replied Thias. "I have grown a great dislike of recent for dark underground tunnels but we need to search the whole of the Underkeep starting with the pantry. We have to ensure there are no other ways for reptile scum to enter the Citadel while we sleep."

"That's a good point bard," said Townsforth as he at last understood the implications of Thias's words. "Tonousa believed there was a tunnel from the Temple of Fatumai that led to somewhere beneath the Underkeep so I agree with your assessment. If one changeling used it then its existence will be known to others."

"I showed Tonousa the only tunnel ever known to exist and it is blocked by a roof fall," added Teulu. "That passageway has been impassable since before you were born."

"That's not a good enough answer," said Byddin as he stared at the self-made holy man.

"Go fuck yourself Byddin," grizzled Teulu.

"We know what you speak of bard," said Sir Digory Bethellemy from his low position at the table. "While our esteemed leader was confined to his quarters, we of the Royal Guard met to plan our own actions and we came to similar conclusions. We have searched the Underkeep for hidden passages. Like you suggested, we started with the pantry and behind a set of shelves we found a secret tunnel that led to our infiltrator's lair. We did not know it was Lolly's until the changeling had been revealed. Then all became obvious. Beyond that secret room there was another tunnel that did indeed lead towards the Temple of Fatumai and as the priest just indicated it was blocked by fallen stone and earth."

"That's quite interesting," said Ystafell as Byddin scowled at his ignorance of the facts.

"But if the Fool used it so perhaps could others," added Lady Emeny.

"They cannot now," replied in Sir Cragtalon. "We have caused the whole tunnel to collapse using fire, brimstone, and much water."

"Good man," added Thias, heartened by Sir Cragtalon's actions.

"Did you find any other passageways?" asked the Archmage.

"Not we did not," answered Cragtalon. "We searched every inch of the Underkeep and found nothing other than the incarcerated and the tortured."

"I think we need another break to collect our thoughts," ordered Ystafell.

To Thias the discussion that had followed the description of Tonousa's death had at least focused the minds of the Council onto the dangers that they all now faced. Parandor was clearly at risk of attack from within. Much more work was needed to secure the Capital and he needed to convince the council of that fact.

"You mentioned the name Nedes Karoly," said Thias before the others could stand.

"Later, bard," snapped back Ystafell. "I need to squat and then consume more wine."

Some fifteen minutes later, following the delivery of pastries and spiced mulled wine, the Council reconvened.

"Now young Thias," began Ystafell. "What were you saying about Nedes Karoly?"

"During the break from our meeting I remembered where I had heard the name before," began the bard. "When I arrived with my friends inside the barrel of firewater that sat behind the counter of The Murdered Wolf, there was a head already inside it, pickled by the power of the potent spirit. The sailor, Theoplous, the one I have already spoken of being Cuvar, recognised its face. He told me that without doubt the features were that of a person called Karoly. He said he was someone of no importance."

"Well that is not quite true," replied Townsforth while he rubbed his chin to aid his thinking. "He was, as I too have already said, a key go-between in the sting that Tonousa tried to enact in order to trap our spy. She had promised Karoly an amnesty for his crimes and a new identity once he had revealed the place that Tonousa could meet with the bastard. After that he disappeared as expected."

"And a very good identity you gave him," sneered Lady Emeny.

"It wasn't the Watch..." began Commander Townsforth.

"Dogs Bollocks!" interrupted Byddin but Townsforth carried on regardless.

"I can only presume that his death and the subsequent treatment of his head was a punishment for the betrayal of the Thieves Guild."

"Say more Townsforth," ordered Ystafell.

"We have known for a long time that Karoly was involved in their work," continued the Commander. "We also knew he was behind the horse rustling and some other foul deeds. There is an unwritten law that is spoken within the slums. Anyone betraying the Guild will forfeit their life without trial. The creature must have convinced the thieves that he was the Fool for I'm sure even they would not deal with lizard spawn. Somehow they must have discovered Karoly's involvement in Tonousa's plot and that sealed his fate. I guess we may never have known of his demise had you not stepped on his head Thias."

"Why would the Thieves Guild side with the Eastern Marsh?" said Lady Emeny. "Their activities worry me greatly."

"Me too," added the angered Archmage. "Karoly had threatened us wizards and I suspect that the thieves were backing him."

"That's just another distraction. The greatest threat to us comes from a probable two pronged attack by the Lizardman and the evil Lord that now leads them," said Ystafell as he stood from his chair and began to pace the room behind the head of the table. "Townsforth, do you have the resource to secure the inside of the city and in addition root out these thieves once and for all?"

"No I do not Gilebin. My advice would be to try and seek a dialogue with the Thieves Guild and have the buggers come to realise that the reptiles will destroy everything that they too need for their continued existence. Better they are on our side than against us."

"I agree," growled Sir Byddin. "For once the Watch talks sense."

"How secure are we Brynn should the Lizardmen use the Rift and breach our walls?" asked Lady Emeny, her hands trembling as she spoke

"Not very, I'm afraid to say," he replied. "The Watch can only muster some two hundred. Many of those have been rushed through their training and have inadequate levels of physical and mental resolve. Even if I cover each gate with two or three, and then stretch those who man the battlements as thin as I dare, it still means there will be inadequate numbers to defend the Citadel and cover all the most important buildings in the city. That analysis includes leaving a handful of the Royal Guard inside the Citadel while the rest help confront the army of the Eastern Marsh. I believe we should arm the citizens, including the women and any child over six summers."

"Steady on man, I'm not so sure that's such a good idea," said Teulu as Ystafell took his seat at the table. "Once we give the lowlife the right to carry arms we may never be able to reverse the decision. Even if we defeat the reptiles we may have created another enemy within"

"Yes, I agree with you Heward," said Ystafell as he stared at the table. "What do you think Thias?"

"When the swamp swine arrive they will take no prisoners," replied the bard as memories of the attack on the Bards Guild flooded back. "By the will of the gods, I hope they have no more black powder for they are skilled at its deployment and Parandor will soon fall should they gain access to the underground sewers and cellars of this ancient city. There are no doubt many tunnels in existence that we have no knowledge of, even if as Sir Lightmain has indicated they do not access the Citadel."

"The old sewers do though!" added Ystafell. "I dumped into one myself just minutes ago."

"I have grown a great dislike for such places," continued Thias, ignoring the slurred words of the Lord Chamberlin. "Whatever we decide here today, please do not put me in charge of securing the underground spaces."

"No, we will expect Townsforth and the Watch to do that," sneered Sir Byddin.

"Let us hold off on such a decision for now," ordered Ystafell. "I think we can start to define our defence strategy once we have had your report Sir Byddin on the readiness of the army to repel an attack on the city. What do say, are you ready to give an update given your restricted movements these past few days or should I ask one of the others present to do so on your behalf."

"That may be a better idea seeing that you chose to deny me access to the ongoing planning," grumbled Sir Byddin as his one eye glared at the Lord Chamberlain. "Lightmain, you're best placed to update the Council. Go on, get on with it for you've always set your hopes on my position. Just remember however, I will reverse any decisions should I feel them inappropriate."

"Please Byddin, calm yourself and let's move on," said Ystafell as Lightmain rose to speak. "There is no need to stand in our presence sir. Just give your report and keep it succinct."

Thias had been fully engaged by the proceedings of the war council thus far. Although not filled with any real confidence over the decision making capabilities of those present, he felt at least as informed as the rest of them. He decided to watch and listen and at the end of the day assess whether he would follow the advice of the Council. After all, he was now Cuvar and the Guardian of the Marked.

Wesmin Lightmain was one of those people who could not cut his words to meet the impatient ears of an audience. Once he set off on any story he was unable to resist two ingrained traits that he had carried with him from childhood. The first was that he found it impossible to progress from one point to another without including every detail, no matter how minute or insignificant. The second was an uncontrollable tendency to divert the focus of his message by drifting down various rabbit holes and side conversations. This day was no different and Lightmain laboured on as the army's preparations were revealed in their most infinite complexities. Thias marvelled at the knight's ability to retain facts but he, like the rest whose ear drums were being tortured, began to lose concentration after the first half an hour. He even sniggered once when Teulu nodded off and woke with a snoring jolt.

Lady Emeny struggled to keep up with her note taking and in the end abandoned it save for recording just the most significant points. There were however several times when some of Lightmain's comments stimulated further debate. They included an update on the Narrow Gate's remedial work and the defensive palisade that had now been completed half a league from the city walls and behind which the army encircled the Citadel. That was of course, save for the south wall that was guarded by the natural course of the Tiaryer. The main point of concern for the knights and Commander Townsforth was the Narrow Gate. Despite extensive work on the mechanism that allowed the rise and fall its portcullis, the iron barrier would not remain in place once opened. It would often drop without warning and two stone masons had been crushed during one such incident. Thias thought this a great shame and perhaps a portent of similar problems to come. His concerns had been noted by Llys Emeny and supported by the others.

Townsforth and Sir Lightmain had continued to reassure the Council that everything possible was being done to fix the issue, including the forging of two new metal wheels that were considered to be the cause of the problem. After each debate the meeting had moved on at the now predictable pace of a snail. Two hours after he had started Lightmain concluded his report. With the need to stretch his legs and fill his belly, the Lord Chamberlain then called for the doors to be opened. Servants filled the tables with a light lunch consisting of jellied eels, mustard beef pasties, a mountain of figs, and a barrel of Blessed Beast. Thias's stomach had not seen as much food for so long that he refused anything other than a tankard of the Beast. He would not even have had that had Lightmain not bored him to the point of cutting his own wrists. So a rejuvenating lunch was taken and when the meeting resumed it was Emeny who took the lead while Ystafell busied himself draining the barrel down his funnelled gullet.

"I want to understand more about the boy Llyat," Lady Emeny began.

"As do I," added the Archmage.

"His full name is Llyat Emgar," said the Sovereign Adviser as she looked back through her copious notes and sought to find the specific reference she had made earlier. "Is that correct Thias?"

"Yes it is."

The bard shuffled with discomfort on his chair and felt pushed into to a corner. He knew that he had to be honest with the Council but he was still fearful of walls with ears and was reluctant to tell all that he knew. Even though he had mentioned Llyat many times during the recounting of his adventures in the north of Realm he had avoided adding detail that would allow others to understand the full complexity of the youth that he now guarded.

"Then he must be the boy adopted by my childhood friend Lyrusa and that man she disappeared with all those years ago," Emeny declared. "His name was also Emgar."

Thias paused before answering, still uncertain of all that he had deduced throughout his long observations of Llyat.

"Yes he is, what do know of the family,"

"I used to play with Lyrusa when we were children," began Emeny. "She, I, and Thinata Fullbane were the closest of friends until the large one got too big. I remember her husband introducing Rukave to Lyrusa and I watched their love grow. The child that Rukave brought with him was always shrouded in mystery and most of us were never permitted anywhere near him. I seem to recall that the only ones ever to get close to the infant, besides Rukave and Lyrusa, were Enguerrand Fullbane, Mathias Amberstone, and Xix Blackfayer. That was something that puzzled most of the rest of us and we even talked of their being some kind of conspiracy afoot between the five of them. Then in a flash the child was gone. The family just vanished one day any no one ever found out what happened to them. That is until you now turn up Thias and tell us the child was brought up in Maplehill of all places. That is what you are saying isn't it?"

"So it would seem," said Thias without hesitation. "What sort of a conspiracy did people talk of? Was the Prophecy of Enderdetag ever mentioned?"

"No, it was not," Lady Emeny replied.

"I am bored and Ystafell's pissed," snorted Sir Byddin. "I think all this talk of the peasant lad is an utter waste of our time."

"I'm not pished." slurred Ystafell. "I'm ss...sober cold ss...stone."

"It could be important to find out more about his childhood and education," added Teulu as he dismissed Byddin's words from the table.

"Tonousa told me that the youth she first met in Parandor had indeed been raised in Maplehill," said Commander Townsforth. "Furthermore, she spoke of a link to the Prophecy and that the bards themselves were convinced the lad was the one referred to in its text."

"I can confirm that is the case," added Thias.

In the hiatus that followed Thias took the opportunity to observe the others. The knights at the low end all looked bored, as did in fact Sir Byddin. Ystafell sat in a cocoon of quiet and tried to stifle hiccoughs. Only the Archmage, Teulu, Townsforth, and Emeny looked as if they wanted to keep the meeting going.

"Anyone else got questions regarding Llyat Emgar before we move on?" demanded the Lady.

"I have something to ask," said the Iqotrix. "Thias, can you go over again in some detail what you found written on the side of Raulyn's tomb."

"I mentioned that in the telling of my travels this morning," replied Thias as he sought to avoid disclosing more than necessary."

"Stop being so fucking evasive!" snapped Sir Byddin. "You bards are unbelievable, just like the fucking wizards."

The tension in the room ratcheted up another level. Even the Archmage looked unnerved as he twitched in his seat. Once again Byddin's obnoxious tones commanded the room.

"Well, go on then bard. Enlighten us with your tale."

"As you wish," replied Thias. "The first thing we noticed was an unusual pictogram. It seemed to show a figure and five stones surrounded by a glow like the Kundalish Aura. The colour of those stones had faded over the years but the figure did resemble Llyat Emgar."

"The coloured stones, do you believe they were supposed to be the Gems of Thamous?" asked the Archmage, his furrowed brow replaced by an excited smile.

"That is what we presumed. I then began to examine the runes and the glyphs on the stone. From what I could make out they spoke of Raulyn's personal history and in particular the slaying of Urthanock. The legend told of a series of battles over nine hundred years ago, a time when these lands were in a state of anarchy. It was an everlasting war between the armies of the Ancients and those that dwelt within the Eastern Marsh. To my surprise I discovered that the leader of the Lizardmen was in fact Urthanock. He was reptilian and not a man as described in our songs, sagas, and paintings."

"Dogs Bollocks," snorted Byddin

"Be quiet tosspot," screeched the Archmage. "Let the bard finish what he has to say."

"I then found something else, something most disturbing that I did not disclose to my companions at the time. The runes went on to describe how Urthanock had promised to deliver fresh innocent children as sacrificial offerings to Kha. With each life he took, Urthanock grew ever more powerful and after fifty years of such sacrifices he had grown invincible."

"Make-believe, that's all!" said Byddin to the further annoyance of the wizard.

"It would fit the story of Death Tubaria for those who worshiped Kha like Jonas Tullage were referred to as the 'Child's Bane'," added Sir Cragtalon only to be ignored as Thias continued.

"The story went on to confirm that Raulyn was one of the Ancients, sworn to vanquish Urthanock once and for all. The runes became a little vague after that but it seems a deal was struck with the Oracle of Frasteria in order to tip the balance of the battle. Somehow the Moirai were involved. From other information I gathered on my travels, it appears those three Fates are one and the same as the Oracle of Frasteria."

"Mumbo fucking jumbo," grunted Bydcin.

"Fascinating," squealed the Archmage as he ran his hand through his spikey red hair. "This all fits in with the Enderdetag Prophecy."

"Did it confirm the location of the Oracle?" asked Lady Emeny as she readied her quill.

"No it did not," replied Thias. "Certain texts held in the Bards Guild of Valameer seemed to indicate the Oracle is located somewhere in and around the Barrow at Harico."

"You are hiding something bard, what is it?" said Teulu. "What else did the inscription say? What is it that you are so reluctant to divulge?"

Thias took a deep breath.

"Sir Raulyn sacrificed a child to the Moirai," he exclaimed. "That was my interpretation. The true translation of the runes was that Raulyn 'gave the Moirai a child' but given what Urthanock was up to it is also probable it had also been a sacrificial offering."

"By the favours of Fatumai, they were all evil fuckers back then," swore the priest. "Praise the gods for the benign practices of Fatumai. How do you respond to that bard?"

Thias clammed up for he believed he had already given away too much information.

"Given these insights regarding Llyat Emgar, I ask for permission to speak to the boy. With the presence of his image on the side of the tomb, plus the involvement of the Moirai and the resurgence of Thamous, I suspect there are far greater forces at work here than any of us could ever have imagined. If the boy is the key to our survival we need to think what to do with him."

"Think about that while we have another piss break and order the cheese and port to be delivered," interrupted Ystafell whose slurred words reminded the others of his presence.

"Haven't you had enough to drink?" sneered Emeny.

"Not yet," slurred Ystafell. "We will reconvene in about ten minutes. Cragtalon, go to the door and have the food and drink brought in; you may yet be of use to our meeting."

The meeting broke up once again and Thias sank into his thoughts as he tried to assemble them into a plan of action. He did not know where to begin and yet realised that as each minute passed Llyat's presence in the city was a danger both to himself and everyone else.

The Council session resumed before a platter of malodorous cheese, goblets, and the large flagon of port had been placed before Ystafell. The Lord Chamberlain was at first disappointed when no one else agreed to partake in the mid afternoon snack for the cheese was the best pungent kind from the Badlands. The wine was even better, a great vintage from Phauless's cellars and created from the grapes of Griginor. Ystafell's surprise at his colleague's refusal to eat and drink did not stop his own whiskered jaws from chomping and slurping with gusto.

"Right, carry on, I'm all ears," he ordered as he resumed control of the meeting.

"Where do you want me to continue from?" asked Thias, snapping out of a daydream.

"The wizard was about to tell us what we should do with the lad called Llyat," lisped the rotund gourmand as his speech impediment worsened.

Thias took his seat and waited to hear what the Archmage suggested.

"It is my strong recommendation that the boy be delivered to the Wizards Guild for mind experiments," began the odd looking man. "We need to understand what insights he has, whether his mind is pure or corrupted, and to free up any important memories and knowledge that he may have suppressed. Only then may we decide what to do with him. Have any of you considered that he may be more of a threat than an asset?"

"I agree," said Emeny with force of voice.

"Well I don't." shouted Thias, reluctant to let go of the boy he had risked so much to save and despite the conflicts that raged inside his head.

"Look bard," continued the Archmage. "As far as I can deduct from all we have heard here today, there are two interlinked threats to our survival that we must address together. The first is the defence of this city but of greater importance is the fulfilment of the Enderdetag Prophecy. This boy Llyat Emgar is key to both. I suspect from what you have told us that Llyat is descended from the Ancients and as such may have hidden knowledge that he is as yet unaware of. I would seek to test that theory and discover if there is anything locked inside his skull that could help us. If there is then I may have methods to extract it. We will need the knowledge of the Ancients if we are to succeed against such a foe as Urthanock."

"I'm still not sure," replied Thias as he scratched his chin while pondering if the Archmage could be trusted?

"Ooo! What devious perversions do you have in mind for the boy?" slurred Ystafell raising his head up from the table where it had rested for several minutes.

"Be quiet and finish your cheese!" ordered Lady Emeny with nostrils flaring.

"I wish to inform you dear Lady..." replied the Chamberlain as he poured himself another drink. "I am delighted for once in my life to give in to your demands... What are you doing later tonight?"

Thias stared with disdain at the drunken oaf who had been chosen to lead Parandor through its darkest hour. All ignored Ystafell's comment including Lady Emeny whose face flushed with both anger and embarrassment. Sir Byddin,

Heward Teulu, and the Archmage grunted but did not seek to inhibit the progress of the meeting any further. The knights at the low end gawped in disbelief.

Thias took the opportunity to reflect on the future of the Marked. He knew he had to get Llyat out of the city as soon as possible. Urthanock's clear priority would be to find Llyat. Where the Marked went, so would the Lord of Fear. Llyat had to be secreted out of Parandor and taken by stealth to the Oracle and yet the Archmage's idea had great merit. If Llyat carried unlocked secrets it would be better to reveal them now before it was too late. In a flash a plan formed and a few seconds later he was ready to make an offer to the wizard.

"This is what I will agree to regarding young Llyat," he began." I will deliver him to your Guild once he has dressed and broken fast tomorrow morning. I will wait there while you conduct your analysis of his mind and memory. I too am interested to see if you can unearth anything that will help him in his quest to seal the door to the Underworld. You may have him until Solaris sets over the Great Ocean in the west. Please recognise that the lad needs to be out of Parandor before the war comes and we all must facilitate his escape. Indeed, I have formulated a plan which for at least today must remain a secret. The next stage of his journey has to be kept from the ears of drunks or those with loose tongues. He must leave Parandor at the earliest opportunity and take the Gems with him."

"I agree," replied the Archmage without hesitation. "I look forward to receiving him tomorrow and my fellow wizards and I will complete our preparations overnight."

"Are you having a party Iqotrix?" slurred Ystafell. "Will there be quim; I could go on all night?"

"Will he travel alone or with protection?" asked Townsforth. "Having gone through all you have to gather the jewels you cannot afford to lose them again."

"Have no fear Commander, I have factored that into my plan which I promise to reveal when Llyat is away and safe," replied Thias with an outward confidence that betrayed his racing heart.

"Who will accompany him? I guess you will be one but who else will travel with you," asked Sir Byddin. "At least you could answer that question."

"I will not go with him for my plan requires my presence in the Capital," answered Thias. "I will speak no more of it now, no matter how much you press me. I will deliver Llyat to the Archmage as promised tomorrow and we can talk more when we next meet."

"Then we should agree to reconvene again the day after next," suggested Lady Emeny, grateful that at least some decisions were being made, even if it had took all day. "Don't worry I will remind Ystafell tomorrow when his temples are throbbing from the effects of the wine. What a pig you are Lord Chamberlain..."

"I'm a fucking pig with a fucking pig like gob; I eat and I sup a lot, for that's part of my job..." sang the drunken lord as he emptied the last drops from the flagon of port into his goblet.

Thias winced in disgust and turned his head to Lady Emeny.

"Before I close the meeting there is one further update we need to hear," she said as she made a note in the meeting records of Gilebin Ystafell's behaviour.

"Commander, please could you report back on our requests for aid from the far reaches of the Realm. Who, if anyone has pledged to come to our assistance?"

"There is just the news from Falahorn that..."

Townsforth was immediately interrupted by the sot at the head of the table.

"Hurrah! The fucking Berserkers are coming to save us," slurred Ystafell, unable to control his mouth.

"It is true," added Townsforth before the Lord Chamberlain could say more. "We received a bird a couple of days ago. The message confirmed that Cvyler Olin has sent a force of wild men south and by now they will have passed through the Ivory Pass. Olin himself is too old to make the journey and has entrusted their leadership to one of the up-dwellers called Jarl."

"I met him once and he is a good man," added Thias. "If like me you had seen Berserkers fight you will realise that even a few will do a lot of damage to our enemy, if of course they arrive on time."

"Quite so," mumbled Sir Byddin. "But what of the two you sent to Valameer Commander? Have you heard anything back from them?"

"No, not a whisper and that troubles me," answered Townsforth with concern. "We should have done so by now and I worry that something unforeseen has happened, an ambush perhaps! Danisun Dain is a..."

"Are you sure you can trust this Danisun Dain?" said Thias. "I know him of old, back when I was a child. My assessment is that he would do anything to further his own ends. I myself wouldn't trust the man."

"I don't know where you're coming from bard," replied the Commander, marshalling his anger. "He is one of the finest and I will not sit here and listen to him being badmouthed by the likes of you despite your rank as a member of the Court of the late Phauless Gylewu. I would trust him with my own life and indeed any of yours present in this room today. The man is beyond loyal and you have picked the wrong one to accuse."

"So be it, I was just expressing an opinion," snapped back Thias.

"What about the other one, Darchus Arillius, how much do we trust him?" asked the priest having listened with great interest.

"He is a most honourable man and a model of goodness for others to follow," replied Townsforth. "I've got to know him well of recent. What makes you think he could be a threat to our cause?"

"Just something I picked up in Valameer," responded Teulu.

"And what exactly would that be?" asked Lady Emeny.

"The scarlet cockpox!" hiccupped Ystafell before reverting to his stupor.

"Ignore the bilious buffoon Heward," continued Lady Emeny. "What have you heard?"

"While in Valameer and helping those who managed to escape the Bards Guild, there were rumours, whispers in dark circles that speak of the Lady Flurdiana's quim being still active," answered Teulu as a wry smile formed on his lips. "It is said that she needs a regular servicing to remain balanced in her head. Furthermore they say she has a secret lover, someone else apart from our dear deceased Ruler's brother, one who manipulates her actions. Perhaps it is this Darchus Arillius who has advises the woman against coming to our aid."

"Bullshit." exclaimed Townsforth but Sir Byddin was quick to jump in and stir the mire.

"Whist having your ear to the trough did you pick up any rumours as to the identity of this mysterious shagger of the highborn?" he asked with a mischievous grin etched on his face.

"Some mentioned a sea captain, some an artist, while others said it was one of her Trident Guard. However one source did say a cordwainer! Is that not the profession of the one called Darchus before he joined the Watch? That's what my priests have told me. Perhaps the shoe fits, if you follow my drift."

"I won't believe it," snarled Townsforth. "You are just seeking to make mischief where there is none. Sir, you are as helpful to our cause as that drunken idiot over there."

"Cobblers," giggled Ystafell.

"So be it but don't say you were not warned," snarled the priest.

"Please, enough; stop acting like children," ordered Lady Emeny. "Observe the Lord Chamberlin, gentlemen. The dolt has passed out and so I take it upon myself to close this meeting. We will reconvene here the day after tomorrow."

No more was said and war room emptied. As Thias made his way through the corridors of the Citadel he became consumed by the plan he was hatching. It was obvious to him that the future of the Marked now rested in the hands of the Cuvar for the Court of Parandor were beyond redemption. He walked out of the main door and on towards the Barbican. Beyond that great gatehouse he raced to find the First Mate of the Banshees Wail.

9

The Lizardmen that he had been sent to kill the bard and recover the Gems of Thamous had not returned. The first place the Lord over Fear had searched had been the darkest hole in Avolire. Having descended the old stone stairs to the subterranean prison he had found the tunnel collapsed and assumed all were trapped below ground. It was then that he returned to the surface in order to search the city for the body of the bard, just in case Thias Calavan had not pursued that route of escape. Urthanock could not risk the Gems lying in the open for some other to find. If they too were buried below ground he knew that a way was needed to destroy them forever once he had gained access to the Underworld. However, he could not linger, not while the bard still evaded him. No longer was he able to sense the string plucker's presence as earlier when his farsight had located the bard within the room that sat over the crack between the realities.

Urthanock stepped over the dead and the dying as he surveyed the slaughter from the battle. It had been a long and eventful night and the Lord over Fear sought to assimilate the two streams of thought that interfered with the clarity of his thinking. Never before through the long years of his confinement in the Underworld had his mind been so bombarded with such strange thoughts. Despite being all powerful, the one thing he had no control over was the flooding of his mind with the history of the Realm and its accumulated wisdom as seen through the eyes of the wyvern. Then in addition there were the residual memories of the blacksmith's son who he had banished in order to house his second coming. The power from the Mark of Kha and the magic taken from the Child of Chalis fed his desire to conquer all; yet somehow he knew that unless he was able to rid himse f of the nagging chatter from the remnant essences he would struggle to remain sane. Then he laughed, for a monster such as he could never be considered stable. Determined that nothing would get in his way, he vowed to unify the Middle Realm of the Living with that of the Underworld. Reborn as Kha's gatekeeper he would open the portal between the two dimensions for all time. Evil would prevail and it was fast approaching. The end of all good men was nigh; the End of Days was coming.

Soft gentle rays from Solaris broke through the light cloud cover over the city as another morning broke. The redness of the dawn flooded the ruins and enhanced the crimson of the slaughter that fell before his eyes whichever way they turned. The dead lay everywhere, black armour clad knights and Lizardmen alike, intermingled as if in some final union of souls. Limbs were hacked and severed. Throats were cut, heads cleaved, and innards strewn far and wide. It was a massacre on a scale that even surprised Urthanock for he had not thought that those from Avolire would have put up such strong resistance. He cursed the dwarf for he knew that the little man had been responsible for much of that will to resist. It did not take long to calculate that the Lizardmen must have lost at least half their force but he rejoiced in the knowledge that of the army of men had been completely destroyed. The stench of the Lady of the Silverwynn and her followers lingered heavy in the air.

From out of the stillness and quiet he heard soft whimpering sounds that came from an area before the doors of the old armoury where once Grovrouk the Despoiler had taken his Vessel meet the Harbingers. Climbing with care over and through the dead he came across a group of three knights and a Lizardman, all injured but not yet dead. To his great surprise, Methladon's voice started hammering inside his head; "Revenge... Revenge.. Revenge..."

Not being able to rid himself of the word it drove him on with a lust to kill. At last he had stumbled on some who would bear the brunt of his anger. He stood before the first of the injured knights, one whose legs had been removed at the knees, no doubt from a blow from the Lizardman's halberd that lay a short distance away. Eyes reddened with hatred as he stared down at the unfortunate man.

"Do you know who I am?" he demanded.

"No sir I do not, but please end my misery with a quick slit of my throat or the point of your sword through my heart."

"Let me give you something to ponder on as you die," replied Urthanock. "Did you ever know Vostag and Ruta Heyn? No...I guessed as much... and if you want my help, then call me Lord."

"Please Lord, have pity. I do not know of who you speak."

"No, you would not!" snarled Urthanock. "Yet you fight for some who did. They are dead and you are not. Therefore you will suffer in their stead."

"Please Lord..."

In an instant and before the knight could move his arms, Urthanock stamped on both of the wounded man's wrists in quick succession and snapped them with a sickening crunch. As the unfortunate knight screamed out in pain, the Lord over Fear drew his sword from his belt and ripped open the crotch of the man's leather trousers. The blade slashed through the groin and then Urthanock reached down and held aloft the knight's severed genitals. The man screamed again but not for long. What was once his most prized possessions were thrust into his mouth and then down the back of his throat. Urthanock rammed the bleeding genital tangle as deep as he could into the knight's gullet with his gauntlet covered hand. Obstructing the windpipe he allowed a sly smile to form behind the half helm that covered the unburned side of his face. The vessel then stood back to watch the outcome of his work. The man choked slowly and died. Urthanock laughed and sneered.

"That was for Vostag and Ruta," he said before moving on the next unfortunate who had witnessed his comrade's demise.

"Please Lord, spare me torture. Kill me if you must but do it quick," he moaned.

The Lord over Fear stared down at his next intended victim. The wretch lay amongst the red mire with an axe embedded in his right shoulder. The arm was almost severed and perhaps the knight could have found the strength to run away were it not for the fact that his legs were pinned to the ground by the bodies of three dead Lizardmen, the result of his last encounter. Urthanock hoped the knight would linger long in agony and then his head noise started again.

"Revenge... Revenge... Revenge..."

"Did you ever meet Fiat and Grophaldo?" he growled while pointing his new sword forward, the one with which he had slain Thamous.

"I have no fucking idea who you are talking about; who are you anyway?" groaned the terrified knight. "Pull these buggers off me and let me be on my way!"

The blade flashed in the light of Solaris as Urthanock thrust it forward into the Knights right eye and twisted the globe inside the socket. Screams filled the square before the armoury.

"This one's for Fiat!" sneered Urthanock, "and this one's for Grophaldo."

The blade flicked forward a second time and continued in its task to destroy the knight's eyesight. The man screamed again while Urthanock struggled to understand why the desire to avenge the Vessel's family controlled his actions. He realised that a strange competition had begun as three distinct personalities fought for supremacy inside his head. Yet he knew which one would triumph for he was the Lord over Fear.

The third wounded knight saw him approach and in total panic he tried to wiggle away. This was not an easy task considering he had lost both arms but his fear of the mad creature was overwhelming. Urthanock stamped in the middle of the knights back and then rolled him over. Without bothering to acknowledge the screams of his victim he stripped the armour from the front of his body and then opened up his abdomen with the point of his sword. The guts spilled out and the knight screamed. The beast of three minds then scooped up the entrails and lay them across the knight's face and although not yet dead the unfortunate soul did at least slip into unconsciousness.

"That is for the Castors, the Darchas and my friend Cleath Mark," bellowed Urthanock as he spat at the dying man's intestines. "Fuck you and fuck all the knights of Avolire. Fuck all the men that roam this Realm and fuck those who believe in a pathetic prophecy. I am Urthanock!"

"Lord, I am lizard kind and am in need of your assistance," shouted a nearby wounded reptile who had watched the events unfold.

Urthanock looked to his right and his gaze fell upon an unfortunate Lizardman, tapped under a collapsed battering ram that his group had been using to gain access to the armoury.

"Please Lord, lift the wood," groaned the creature. "I know you have the strength and magic to do so for Ssonsh has spread word of your power."

"Revenge... Revenge... Revenge... Revenge... Revenge..."

The words pounded away inside his Vessel's head as Urthanock fought to remain in control. For an instant he clasped at his temples, tormented by the pain. Seconds later he stood to full height, dismissed his agony, and without warning thrust his blade into the lizard's heart. The creature died in an instant.

"That's for Catriana and Maria and all the times you bastards whipped me," he snarled with great contempt. Pulling the sword from the creature's guts he wiped the blade upon his tunic. A sudden wind howled through the ruins of Avolire and never before had he felt so alive.

For the next hour Urthanock wandered the ruins of Avolire and ended the lives of any injured knight or Lizardman kind that he came across. By the end of his task the voice that had demanded revenge had dissipated to an almost inaudible whisper and soon he began to feel like his old self. The revenge lust of the blacksmith's son had been satisfied and there was now only the background chatter from the wyvern's thoughts as they tried to rebuke him for his actions. The game of death had helped him come to terms with the union of the three minds. His weapon dripped with the blood of those it had been destined to destroy.

Sometime later the Lord over Fear came across a patrol of Lizardmen returning from their own extermination expedition. Urthanock raised his hand aloft and the warriors stopped at his command.

"Do you all know who I am?" he asked while looking at each in turn.

"Yes," hissed the leader of the group. "You are the Lord we now serve, Urthanock reborn, the one we have been ordered by Ssonsh to follow. What would you bid us do?"

"Go now and find the rest of your kind," began Urthanock. "Have them meet me by the fallen wyvern within the hour. It is time for me to address you all."

"Is there a message regarding the reason for this summons?" asked the head of the platoon.

"Tell them that we prepare to march on Parandor."

An hour later Urthanock climbed upon to the back of Thamous's carcass. The morning heat from Solaris had begun to dry out the wyvern's scales such that they had lost their natural smoothness and allowed the Lord over Fear's feet to grip with ease. On reaching the high point of the creature's bulk he looked down to the growing number of Lizardmen he had summoned in order to hear his orders. The lizard spawn stood in lines just beyond the point where the wyvern's left wing lay across the dirt.

"Ssonsh, step forward onto the foot of the beast so that all may see you as I speak and give praise," began Urthanock, his voice booming through the ruined streets. "My most loyal of subjects come forth and bestow your presence upon me."

The frog-like priest did as ordered and after appearing out of his kin, mounted the giant claw that had been Thamous's foot. It took some considerable effort to clamber up for his bulk did not aid his progress.

"My Lord over Fear, I serve your will as do we all," croaked the priest while catching breath.

"Enough of that, I shall do the talking this morning and all shall listen and obey. "Ssonsh, you led this force of reptiles in this battle, just as I had ordered and for that I am pleased. I am not happy that we lost so many of our kind while destroying the scum of Avolire. How many of our kin do we have left with which to march on Parandor?"

"Am I allowed to speak Lord?" hesitated the trembling Ssonsh.

"For fuck's sake yes, get on with it."

"About a thousand, that is all," replied the priest.

"What of Ssobekk's army? How may does he command in the east?"

"At least ten times that number Lord."

"I am pleased with your contribution so far toad but I expect more from you in the future."

A throbbing pain surfaced behind the Vessel's eyes and the three circles on the neck burned with an increased intensity. He had assumed he would not suffer the effects of the mark now that he was Urthanock, but he was wrong.

"Soon we will join up with the Ssobekk's army," continued Urthanock. "The Gator Lord will then take control of our combined forces, once the limper has located the Marked. It is he who will marshal our troops and lead us on to victory when we then strike at the gates of Parandor."

Great hisses of affirmation rose from the gathered Lizardmen as to a one they revelled in the prospect of taking the war to the Capital.

"He lives... he lives... he lives..."

A sound hummed behind Urthanock's eyes and caused him to rub his forehead; an action that did not go unnoticed by Ssonsh.

"Until such time as we meet with Ssobekk you will remain the head of this scale force," continued Urthanock as yet another great hiss of affirmation rose from the crowd. "After that I have another role for you. Given your mastery of travelling through the Rift and your success in the sacking of the Bards Guild, you will be the one to lead a force of a thousand reptiles into the heart of Parandor. That strike will commence once the Gator Lord begins our assault on the Capital's outer defences. We will slaughter them from within as well as without and to that end you are promoted this day to the position of Hochnar, warrior priest of the Rift."

An even louder hiss rose from the crowd.

"Thank you my lord, I am honoured," replied Ssonsh.

The frog priest tried to kneel but got stuck in the process as its belly obstructed movement.

"You are dismissed and can now set about your work," continued Urthanock. "Select your best captains and begin your plans. Then meet me one hour's brisk march to the south of Avolire. Be there by the time Solaris passes on his watch to Mona."

The promoted frog priest descended from the wyvern's claw and drifted back into the crowd.

"Now listen well, my bog-born brethren," began Urthanock. "Here are my orders that must be carried out by the fall of Solaris. You will follow them to the letter and Ssonsh, Hochnar of the Rift, will supervise how the work is done. Any who dare question my commands will be punished. Make no mistake, it will be the last thing you ever challenge."

While he bellowed, a voice thumped within the Vessel's skull.

"He has left the marsh... He has left the marsh... He has left the marsh..."

Urthanock shook his head in order to dislodge the torment. He then looked to his troops before his voice once again boomed out between the stone buildings.

"You have all fought well for me amongst the ruins of this ancient shit hole. The weapons that those under the Silverbitch have been collecting will be of great importance as we take our fight to the gates of Parandor. You will gather them together for use in the battle to come. As for the beasts of war, I value their strengths. Collect them together and we will use them to our advantage."

Urthanock glanced down to where Ssnosh stood awaiting his Lord's command.

"Hochnar, warrior priest of the Rift, take your most competent captains and herd the beasts together. I have seen numerous kulkulkath and skyfawn amongst a number of others. Bring only those you believe will either help in the battle or that we can eat on the way to Parandor."

Urthanock paused. The inside of his head throbbed as the voice returned with a vengeance.

"He has the stone... He has the stone... He has the stone..."

Shaking his head, Urthanock screamed out more orders.

"Find and strip all the knights of Avolire of their accursed armour and collect all their weapons. As we make camp on our journey to Parandor we will fashion the orichalcum into the style that we of the Marsh like best. The weapons we will use unaltered for they have proved most effective against us. You will collect all that you find, including any portable furnaces, and you all will meet with me one hour south of the city as Mona begins her ascent. Those that collect the beasts will do the same."

Urthanock paused for breath, pleased that his audience remained attentive. He adjusted his half helm which had slipped and thereafter continued to throw out instructions to the crowd.

"Gather together all dead knights and foot soldiers of Avolire and throw them down the mineshaft; every last one of their hideous race. Then collapse the shaft and the workings of the mine. That hole will be their tomb for eternity. There, buried with their Lions, they will be lost to history."

Urthanock hesitated as he sensed the memory of his Vessel remind him of all that had happened inside the Lion pit. For some reason he focused on the possible fate of the man called Nictis.

"Enough!" he screamed.

The Lord over Fear looked to his gathered crowd. Not one of them acknowledged his outburst while they waited for his next command.

"Send others to sweep across this city and scoop up all Lizardmen, both those that are dead but also those no longer capable of joining our march to Parandor. We have not time to care for the wounded so you must end their suffering. All must be placed inside the great ruined church from where the Silverbitch gave her audiences. You will have more than enough flesh to fill its vast space and those you cannot fit inside you must pile against its walls. Then burn the lot. We will have a fire of dark souls that will warm the very heart of Kha. The God of the Underworld will then favour our cause even more than he does now. We will have a cremation the likes of which the Realm has never seen. Hochnar, feel free to say some words at the burning, should you think it appropriate."

"Urthanock... Urthanock... Urthanock..." began the chant from the crowd and it did not cease until the Lord over Fear raised his right hand and ordered silence.

"The Marked has the Gems. He will put an end to your reign," laughed the voice inside the beast's head.

Urthanock contained the pain for he was Lord over Fear. Yet the voice was relentless. Then without warning Urthanock raised both hands to the heavens and shouted to the sky.

"Fuck you Thamous, you will torment me no longer."

The intensity of the noise that left Urthanock's mouth caused all who heard it to cover their ears with their hands. Several of the more unstable buildings shook to their foundations. Towers crumbled and walls were split. Most of the Lizardmen trembled with fear, certain that a final punishment was coming to all. The clouds darkened and lightning bolts shot through the cold night air while thunder roared overhead. Then all was stilled as Urthanock stood upright, took a breath and continued to utter his decree.

"Before you all depart on these tasks I have one last demand. Hochnar of the Rift, I need you to send the one called Ssnakash on the most important and dangerous of missions. He will take ten of the mine masters that helped discover the sceptre that bears my name. Together they must hack the body of Thamous into manageable pieces and transport them to the room that fed power to both myself and the Silverbitch. Any residual magic, either from the wyvern or the room must be destroyed."

"But my Lord," croaked Ssonsh. "The Wyvern is dead and we..."

"Such power cannot be allowed to fall into the hands of others once we have left this place. Keep the head, boil it, and strip it of all flesh for it will be the new banner that will lead us into battle. Behold, I am not just the Lord over Fear. I now bestow on myself a new name which you may call me as you please. I am the 'Dragon's Bane'."

"Dragons bane... Dragons Bane..." cheered the Lizardman horde.

"Ssnakash's group must also scour the city and collect all unused black powder. This will also be placed inside the room and the team will fire the powder the moment Solaris slips beneath the horizon. For the successful completion of this task you will be rewarded in this life and the next. Now all may leave, and other than those that light the powder's fuse, meet me at the agreed time to the south of the city where we will watch the effect of Ssnakash's labours. Avolire will fall and we will revel in its final destruction."

Urthanock stood atop of the wyvern and watched as all went about their allotted tasks. The hammering inside his head had ceased. He knew that it was Thamous trying to control his thoughts and that it would stop once the wyvern's carcass had been destroyed

As the last minutes of Solaris's watch covered the plain of Avolire, Urthanock sat astride a black mare upon the edge of the plateau that sloped up towards the snow-peppered Grey Mountains. Besides him on mounts they had salvaged from battle, sat the warrior priest Ssonsh and the three other promoted Generals who had gathered with their troops and beasts as instructed earlier in the day. Around them massed the remnants of the Army of the Marsh that had triumphed in the battle of Avolire. Behind, the chained beasts of war screeched, wailed, and roared at the impending darkness to come. Here in this place, one hours march south of the city, all eyes focused on the remains of a great fire that had consumed the old church in the centre of Avolire and which had been burning since mid-afternoon. Plumes of grey smoke and ash had risen high and drifted north on the strong breeze that swept on and over the srowy plains towards the mountains of the Dirmark. All waited in anticipation for the final act in the destruction of Avolire and the wyvern born from the tears of Chalis.

"Forgive me Great Lord, Bane of Dragons, but may I be permitted to ask of your future tactics," croaked Ssonsh. "Have you decided on the next stage of our conquest? Do we march on Parandor this day?"

"Yes, oh warrior of the Rift," replied Urthanock without moving his eyes from the distant city. "But first tell me what you think of that persistent green glow that seems centred close the smouldering church. Does it emanate from the room over the crack in the Rift?"

"I believe it does Lord. It may inhibit Ssnakash from completing his task."

"He will not live to see another day if he fails me," replied Urthanock without moving his head. "We will need a contingency plan should the coward not deliver on my order. Pray that he does toad, for you will lead the next group in if he falters."

"Lord, have you given any thought as to whether we will still be able to traverse the Rift if the fracture has been sealed?"

"No... have you?" replied Urthanock.

Ssonsh and the three Generals stared back with surprise.

"I cannot be expected to think of everything you bloated ball of mucus. It had better still be fucking possible to use it or I will blame you for our failure; and you don't want that do you Hochnar?"

"As it pleases you Lord," grovelled Ssonsh. "Assuming Ssnakash completes his mission, then what next?"

"When I am certain the power of Kha is out of the reach of all men who may come this way, we will make camp here for the night," continued Urthanock. "We will set off at daybreak and head straight for Griginor. We could reach it by the end of tomorrow if your aging carcass does not slow us down."

"Lord, remember that General Brosizrug and his ogres had been dispatched to clear the old route through the mountains," croaked Ssonsh. "The Lady Silverbitch gave them orders to ensure our safe passage. It is most probable that they have already passed through Griginor."

"As will we, if they have left anything standing," replied Urthanock.

"The people of the city would have fled at the first whiff of ogre stench," said one of the generals from behind. "They have always been runaways."

"Then let's hope they can run fast," laughed Urthanock. "Do not forget Sslondash that I look to you to disposal of such scum. Ssonsh, I expect you to exterminate any who would dare approach us on our way to and through the mountains. I suspect the Marked has escaped so there is no need for Ssobekk to waste time searching the swamps. Send word to him at once and tell him of my decision."

"What should I tell him Lord?" asked Ssonsh.

"He is to gather his full force together and leave the city of the marsh. Tell him to then destroy all traces of its existence, along with all the villages of the marsh lands. The old, the females, and the younglings of your kind will march with him for there must be no prospect of ever turning back. There must be nothing left to go back for. If the weak cannot keep up, bury them by the roadside. Only then will our army move as one rolling wave of destruction."

"But that is our home." said Ssonsh with great passion as he tried to come to terms with the order. "Must we destroy all that we have built over the centuries, the temple and your idol that we worship?"

"Are you questioning my orders Hochnar?"

"I'm sorry my Lord..."

"Just do it you bloater bugger or I will demote you to the lowest of the low. Tell Ssobekk to head at great speed along the road that skirts the Eastern Marsh. Order him to divert to the Grey Keep which he will turn to rubble as he passes. Then instruct him to descend into the southern plains between the Grey Mountains and the Tiaryer. We will meet with him at the base of the old pass as it enters the grasslands. Furthermore, have him realise that should he get to the meeting place before me then I will reward him with the City of Parandor in which to rule his kin. Now is all that clear?"

"Yes my Lord," replied Ssonsh without further question. "That would be an opportunity to test the Rift once the room above the fracture is blown. If I am not mistaken that time fast approaches. Darkness is almost upon us and by now the fuse must be lit."

Those besides Urthanock looked to the city in expectation of something wild and unknown. Night had indeed fallen and Solaris slipped away while they had talked. The temperature dropped over the snow covered landscape but this did not affect the Lord over Fear. His human body was strong and more robust than any of the lizard spawn that shivered close by.

A distant rumble shook the earth and Urthanock sensed an upsurge in the energy between the dimensions. He held onto the reigns of his mount and then spoke from the side of his mouth;

"So be it Ssonsh, test the Rift as soon as..."

The Dark Lord's words stuck in his mouth as a flash of light and the shockwave of an explosion shot across the land. A column of silver then exploded out from the centre of the ruined city. It was like a bolt of lightning and yet it was not. Perfect in vertical form and smoothness, it showed no signs of dissipating. A thousand pairs of eyes stared in reptilian amazement as the column rose to the height of the tallest of mountains. A second later an enormous ethereal globe formed and hovered at the summit of the column. Soon a multitude of dancing strings composed of red, blue, and green fire shot from the globe and connected with the ground below. They covered most of the centre of the ruined city and showed no signs of disappearing as they shimmered and maintained the connection.

"Fuck," croaked Ssonsh in disbelief.

"Fascinating," answered Urthanock.

The blue globe exploded and the column of silver was sucked back down into the earth. The strings of coloured light dropped to the floor as if to ignite a thousand barrels of black powder. The ground at the centre of the city rose in a single second to the height of the tallest mountain. Then before Urthanock's shocked gaze a wave of earth of equal height rolled out faster than a horse could gallop in all directions. It was followed by another and then another and then another. The Lord smiled at the show and thought how similar the earth waves were to those that travel in water after being disturbed by great boulders.

As the waves travelled from the centre of the city they began to shrink a little in height but the power they carried with them levelled the ruins as they passed through them. Nothing was left save for a flat shallow crater that continued to expand ever outwards. The army of Lizard men and their promoted Generals turned as one and fled in panic as the wave bore down upon them. Only Urthanock refused to flee. He jumped from his horse, sent it on its way, and then turned to face the fast approaching wall of death.

"By the powers of Kha, I command you to turn back!" he screamed into the night air while thrusting both hands forward. "Stop now before the presence of your Lord and Master."

The wave crashed at the foot of the tableland were Urthanock stood, just as its watery twin had done for eternity against the rocks around the Bards Guild. Vast clouds of dust enveloped Urthanock while all other reptiles continued to flee. It took a long time for that dust to settle and the beast then saw that nothing could have survived in the city. The fractured room that fed off the Rift had gone and so was all trace of Avolire.

Urthanock turned and emerged from the mist of dirt as his army began a slow and careful return to the place from which they had fled. Then as they recognised his emerging presence the chanting began, growing ever louder through the magnified hiss of the reptilian swarm.

"Urthanock... Urthanock... Urthanock..."

Some minutes later he stood once again before Ssonsh and his Generals and spat the dust from his mouth. With a grizzled look on his face he turned on the cowards that had fled.

"You pathetic mortals. Shame on you all. Learn from this for we have great challenges ahead. Ssonsh, go test the Rift and see if you can visit Ssobekk in person. Then pass on my orders."

"It may be safer to send a subordinate," replied the shocked frog-priest. "The Rift may not be in full order."

"You are the Rift expert and Hochnar. You will deliver my message." snarled back Urthanock, as his scarred lip curled. "But if you are not back within the hour I will assume the Rift is broken and that your corpse is with Kha. Then I will need to think of an alternative means of communicating with Ssobekk. Be on your way and say no more."

Ssonsh turned the gold bracelet on his wrist forwards and then backward but nothing happened. Then he tried once again and still nothing happened. Urthanock glared at the priest until on the third attempt a weak blue portal of energy crackled around the frog and his horse. Then with a pop they were gone.

"Lord, do you think he will ever return," asked the largest of the Generals.

"I've no fucking idea!" snapped back Urthanock, his attention taken by a noise from behind.

"And what's wrong with those buggers?" he barked out.

A group of four reptile warriors had detached from the edge of the crowd and had started to run towards the east.

"Fucking deserters!" yelled the large General.

"Quick, let's take them before the contagion spreads," exclaimed a second.

"Fucking bastards!" screamed the first again as he turned his horse and rode off in pursuit.

The other two Generals then followed this lead. Urthanock felt a great darkness surge within his core. No one could be allowed to question his orders, not even his own adopted kin. He would make an example of these deserters.

Fifteen minutes later Urthanock stood upon a supply cart such that all of the Lizardman of the battle group could see him and hear his words. They had been ordered to stand to attention while their Lord addressed them. Captains of the army stood around the perimeter of the gathering lest any more should seek to desert. Those who had ran earlier, captured by the Generals that had chased them down on horseback, stood in chains beside the Lord over Fear. Bodies trembled with sufficient force as to cause the chains which bound their wrist and ankles to rattle. Urthanock raised his right hand and called for silence. A deep quiet fell across the land and even the beasts stilled. The only noise came from the chains of the captives as the Bane of Dragons began to speak. The words cut through the wind that rolled down from the Grey Mountains

"Now is our hour. I am pleased with your endeavours during the days of battle against the scum of Avolire. Your triumph will be sung about for as long as Lizardmen rule these lands and that my brethren will be for an eternity. Furthermore, I am much pleased by the work you have carried out this day. The focus that you all gave to your tasks was admirable given the fatigue that I know you all share. We are brothers together in arms and though our number may not be the greatest that Lizardmen have ever put upon the field of battle, we will be triumphant. That is my promise to you all. Tonight we rest but tomorrow we march south to conquer the Realm."

The Dark Lord raised both hands and the chanting began.

"Urthanock... Urthanock... Urthanock..."

Then as he lowered his limbs, silence fell and a darkness descended across his presence. The clouds shut out the last of the light as evil manifested itself on the surface of the plateau.

"But these four are not my friends," Urthanock continued as he pointed to the manacled captives who shook in terror bedside him. "They are too fearful to add any value to my cause; mindless snakes. What are they?"

"Mindless snakes!" cried the army in unison.

"Now witness how I will now judge and punish any who decide to oppose my will. No matter how scared you may be, nothing will ever compete with the pain will inflict upon any who fail to carry out my orders or dare to desert my cause. Watch and learn from this demonstration and behold Urthanock's Knot!"

The army looked on transfixed, wondering what the Lord of Fear could mean. Before their disbelieving eyes the four chained captives rose into the air, level with the cart on which Urthanock stood. The metal restraints that had bound them clunked to the ground while the reptiles were forced to float in the shape of a perfect circle, the hands of each touching the feet and tail of the next. All were under their Lord's complete control.

"Remember forever how I tie the knot," bellowed Urthanock.

In an instant, the bodies of the captives moved closer together. Their limbs and tails were then dislocated and stretched to the point of rupture. All the while the Vessel's memory whispered:

"Remember the child and the horses..."

The captives screamed out in pain with an intensity no one had ever before witnessed through the long history of the Realm. So loud were their cries that the beasts of war joined in and howled in terror for they could not make sense of what was happening. Urthanock was not yet finished for his dark magic then drew the four even tighter and knotted their limp and malleable appendages until one great reptilian ball had been created. It was then held suspended in the air for all to see and marvel at its form. Screams of terror rolled out in shockwaves from the tight knot that bobbled before the army's attentive eyes. Not one of the troops dared to show fear lest they would be next.

"Now what would you have me do with this ball?" demanded Urthanock.

The chanting began again. It started from the centre of the army and then grew to include every last one of those gathered before him. All the while Urthanock stood with both arms raised in salute.

"Throw it... Throw it... Throw it..."

When Urthanock dropped his arms the chanting ceased. The ball of reptiles continued to scream even as it was shot from the tableland towards the shallow crater that was once the ancient city of Avolire. To those that watched it was as if some mighty and invisible pult had fired the ball with the power of the gods themselves. A good minute later the ball hit the ground. Such was its force and speed that the impact left nothing that resembled its origins.

"Now let us rebuild our courage," Urthanock continued as he turned back to face his horde. "You saw how I embraced the ground wave. I was untouched although dirtied. I did not let it harm a single one of you; such is my mastery of this world. My omnipotence and magic will act as your shield as we go forth to slaughter our foes. You have waited a thousand years for my return and I have not let you down. See, look at me, I am here amongst you once again and I will finish the job that I stated so long ago. You are my kin, my brothers in arms. We will gather our strength overnight and replenish our spirits. Tomorrow at the rise of Solaris we will head south towards Griginor."

The Lord over Fear raised both arms and once again the chanting started.

"Urthanock... Urthanock... Urthanock..."

This time it's volume had an even greater power, one so strong that the ground trembled and the gecko's that had watched from afar scuttled away in to holes so as not to be deafened by its noise.

By mid-morning of the next day Urthanock's reptilian army stretched out in a column many leagues long as it snaked across the tableland. The unstoppable swarm made its relentless way south towards warmer lands and the town of Griginor that nestled within the protective feet of the Grey Mountains. At its head rode Urthanock alongside Ssonsh. The warrior priest had returned within the allotted hour given to test the functioning of the Rift. Urthanock noted that Ssonsh looked much older and indeed thinner when it had declared the Rift to be functioning and the Hochnar had not yet recovered from its traumatic jolt. The message the frog brought pleased Urthanock for it was the first event of the day that had helped calm his temper. Behind these two rode Sslondash, the creature responsible for the cremation of the Lizardmen and he too sat high upon one of the few horses that survived the battle. This creature led the warriors on foot which comprised the main bulk of the moving battle caravan. These troops tramped forward, hour upon hour, never daring to contemplate dissention in the presence of their fearsome Lord. Most had throbbing head pains from the beer that had been downed on that first night of victory.

Following the reptile foot troops rode Sslondart, also fortunate to possess a strong and capable horse. He was followed by seven captains and a dozen warriors allocated to him in his new role as General of Armaments. Together they drove ten cart loads of orichalcum armour and weapons. A small number of battering beams, artillery pults, and two siege towers that had been built by the Knights of Avolire made up the rear of the army of destruction. These war engines were pulled at walking pace by teams of giant auroxorns, beasts which roamed free in several secret isolated regions of the Dragonas and which had never before been tamed by the likes of man nor reptile.

The rear section of the formation was led by the Beast General, the warrior called Sslashnash, and who rode a juvenile kulkulkath, tamed and equipped with a saddle which sat atop its hairy carcass. Its stinger had been removed lest it caused injury to its rider although its two gigantic pincers remained unbound. With the assistance of his seven captains and fifty allocated warriors Sslashnash controlled the menagerie of beasts that would support Urthanock's battle group in the coming war. Without exception, all the creatures were restrained by chains linking one to another as they plodded on in single file. Urthanock had inspected them all as they had departed from the edge of the tableland and had welcomed their diversity. He had smiled at the pack of skyfawn, the juvenile kulkulkath, a dozen or so mathulath, and several longnose that the Lady of the Silverwynn had accumulated. Sslashnash's allocated foot warriors marched beside the beasts, weapons drawn, and ready to strike should any become disruptive. They in turn were followed by some twenty or so carts loaded with whatever food had been rescued and scavenged from Avolire. These were also pulled by teams of auroxorns which would serve as additional meat once the siege of Parandor had begun.

It did not go unnoticed by those who marched at the rear of this war caravan that a league behind there followed an ever growing hype of geckos. Their number had swollen to around a thousand and more joined by the minute as they advanced like a dark cloud drifting over the plateau. As they passed they stripped the land bare of any creature small enough to fit between their jaws. The presence of these lizard like vermin had been reported up the line to Urthanock but the Lord dismissed their presence for he did not know what to make of the strange phenomenon.

"My Lord and Bane of Dragons, there is something I need to discuss with you," said Ssonsh as he rode closer to his master. "Do I have permission to speak?"

"I am in a benevolent mood this morning Toad; so what is it that you have to say?"

"It concerns Ssleptaz, the changeling we embedded in Parandor," croaked the Rift Master. "He has failed to check in today as instructed. It is most unlike Ssleptaz and I feel his identity must have been discovered. If he has been caught or eliminated it would put us at a significant disadvantage when we send our forces through the Rift into Parandor."

"The Fool served his purpose and it was only a matter of time before that arsehole gave himself away."

"I beg to differ, my Lord," replied Ssonsh as he trembled. "He has been in place for years and only once did he ever get anywhere near exposing himself."

"Why the fuck should I care about one shapeshifter?"

"Because he was to have coordinated the entry point for our troops as they materialised inside the Capital's walls," croaked Ssonsh. "Now it will be like firing a pult while wearing a hood."

"Will you still be able to get a strike force inside the city?" asked Urthanock.

"Yes Lord but they will arrive in places by chance and not as we had planned. We had hoped to target a single location in order to trigger maximum destruction as we did at the Bards Guild."

"Trouble me not with such trifles," sneered Urthanock. "You are the Rift Master. You figure it out. Bring me the answer when we next talk on this matter for I do not like problems. Stick another spy in amongst them if you must. Find a solution or we'll see what kind of knot a fat ball sack like you will make."

"I will think on the matter as you suggest my Lord," quaked Ssonsh.

"Good, I have more important things that concern me other than the future of a few reptiles."

The arduous journey south continued on until nightfall when the fires from the burning city of Griginor lit up the night sky. All afternoon a voice had nagged behind Urthanock's eyes.

"...to reunite the Gems of Thamous, and destroy the Lord of Fear."

10.

The morning's first rays fell upon Llyat and caressed him with their tender warmth. It was as if they had sought him out for their particular attention. The beams of yellow reflected off his light-coloured hair and transformed it into a golden crown. Tiny beads of perspiration formed on his brow and also on his clean-shaven upper lip. A small rivulet trickled from his hair line and down the back of his neck. The climb up the hill had not been too arduous for Llyat was both young and fit. The fact that he was still only half way to the summit surprised him for he had been climbing for at least an hour. When he had set off he had reckoned it would have taken him some thirty minutes or so to reach the top but he had miscalculated both the time and effort required.

The voices that had first sang out to him as the first of the cocks crowed still beckoned and despite his climb seemed no louder nor nearer. There on the hillside he decided to stop and take stock of their origin, to try and gauge whether or not he had heard the voices before and if he could recognise them. His ears tuned into their specific tones and he tried to decide whether they were men, women, or indeed a mixture of the two. Llyat could not make his mind up and in the end came to the conclusion they had to be female. No man could sing for so long a time without being bored or needing a drink. It was difficult for his ears to work out what language the voices sung in, and whether the sounds were happy or woeful. Once again, he failed to make any sense of what he could hear, other than the occasional repetition of certain words such as 'come child', 'we await', and 'sacrifice'.

The ascent had a been made easier by the fact that steps had been cut into the turf of the hill and they exposed the underlying chalk-like stone over which the thick grass grew elsewhere. Despite significant time driven erosion the steps provided a firm and secure foothold with which to climb with confidence. Llyat had begun counting the steps as he set off but had given up once he passed three hundred, in part because he was bored, but in truth because he then lost count and decided he would assess their number on the way down. Looking back to his point of departure, away in the valley below, his gaze focused on the roof tops of the ancient houses that made up the quaint and rambling town that he had admired so much when he first walked through its streets under Mona's silvery glow. Now that they too caught the light of Solaris their thatched tops glistened and sparkled and gave the hamlet the appearance of having been forged from gold. He watched for some considerable time as those who inhabited the ancient mystical place moved like dots amid their dwellings and the farms that surrounded the centre of the idyllic community. To the east of the village, no more than half a league away, lay a cluster of stone ruins which to Llyat resembled the buildings he had seen while walking near the Great Pyramid of Barad Elestor. He could also just make out the small river that ran through the centre of the town and the small stone bridge over which he had tramped but an hour earlier. The view was as perfect as a vision could be. It was as different from Maplehill as he could imagine.

After an age of self-indulgence and as he gazed upon the one place in the Realm he felt sure would be a perfect location to settle with his family, Llyat decided he needed at least to try and make it to the summit of his climb. Voices still called and beckoned him on. Minute after long minute as he continued to climb he began to repeat the words that he understood; come child, we await, and sacrifice. An hour later, just as he mounted a small overhang below the rock-strewn summit, he saw the crest of the hill and the structure that sat upon its peak. There rested a sausage like construction, old beyond time, and built of rocks and mighty boulders; no doubt dragged by some incomprehensible means from the valley and left there by a long-forgotten people. Above its rocky walls turf had grown over the millennia and created an emerald carpet upon the roof. At one end of the sausage, several even larger boulders created a portal into its interior. At that moment Llyat realised it had to be hollow. The entrance was as black as pitch and yet once Llyat stood before its opening he was enveloped by a dazzling white light.

The youth woke with a start, half blinded as Solaris moved across the open window in the bed chamber of the deceased Physician of Parandor. Llyat realised that he had been dreaming and sought to look away from the painful light. Rolling to his right he came up against the enlarged belly of the woman he loved.

"Be careful Llyat," moaned Heliana amid the confusion of being woken too soon.

"I'm so sorry, my little bog booby! I've not hurt you or the baby have I?" he mumbled.

"I wish you wouldn't call me that name Llyat" she answered as she rubbed her bleary eyes. "Can you not think of something more endearing, I mean, you make me sound like some creature that has waddled out of the Eastern Marsh."

"What about, dumpling chest?" he sniggered as he squeezed her nearest tit. "Your paps are growing by the day. I could play with them for ever."

"You are such an arsehole, has anyone ever told you that."

"Sure, often!"

A cock crowed outside the window and forced Heliana from her bed.

"I need to piss," she exclaimed as her naked form swayed across the room.

Not wishing to hear the sounds of Heliana's toilet drift in through the open door, Llyat covered his head with his blanket and thought back to the strange dream that had just visited him. He began to think that perhaps the ancient town he had seen could be Harico, nestled deep within the Howling Hills. He remembered so much wanting to look into the blackest of black openings before the blinding white light had woken him. Solaris had woken him many times but this light was far more intense and he sensed that the two could not be the same. The more he thought about it the more convinced he was that this new illumination meant something else. Not being able to decipher the message he took it as a portent of evil.

Thirty minutes later the young couple sat eating breakfast together at the old Physicians table. They had stayed naked for they now felt at ease in each other's presence. Heliana had scrambled some duck eggs and mixed them with the cream off the top of the milk brought by a servant, still warm and straight from the udder. She had cooked the mixture in lard and added parsley leaves to enhance the flavours. Fresh bread from the Citadel's bakery completed the meal and the young couple emptied their plates quicker than the slash of a skyfawn's claw. After they had eaten they drank a mint infusion and talked. Heliana had already filled Llyat in with all that had happened in Parandor when he was away tramping the Dragonas when they were locked in the herb store beneath Avolire. Llyat took this opportunity of calm to ask Heliana to repeat her story and the young woman duly obliged. Once she had finished Llyat gave a potted history of all that had happened to him in the Dragonas for he had not had the time nor desire to do so earlier. Heliana took in every word and even asked for repeats when she liked a particular part of the tale. However, her mood darken when he began to express his concerns regarding the resurgence of Urthanock. Both remembered the time on the Citadel's steps when they had stared at the stained-glass window depicting Sir Raulyn's defeat of Urthanock, now revealed as a reptile and not one made in the form of man. Their two hands met over the table where they squeezed together in the fear of what may come to pass. Soon they began to explore what all this would mean for their unborn baby, an innocent singled out for an uncertain fate. Both were in no doubt that Urthanock would kill the child should he ever become aware of its existence. The seed of the Marked could not be ignored.

After they had exhausted their fears Heliana left the room under the pretext of making more mint tea although the truth was she needed to weep alone. Llyat's thoughts drifted to the Gems of Thamous and the task he needed to complete. The responsibility he carried for his unborn was so intense that he felt it would crush him. One thing he was certain of; he needed to take possession of the Gems and set off to find the Oracle at the earliest opportunity. The Moirai had spoken to him again while he slept and directed him to a hill adjacent to the ancient town of Harico. He would do whatever was required to have them help him re-forge the Gems and create the single key. No matter what they asked of him, he would comply with their demands.

A sudden knock caused Heliana to cry out.

"Llyat get the door, there's a lovely. I'm still naked.

"Yeah ok, my little marsh mallard... Oh, sorry," giggled Llyat inanely.

"Piss off cockface and get the fucking door," she shouted back as further raps hit the wood.

Llyat jumped from behind the table and snatched his britches from the floor. He dragged them up his legs, over his bits, and then looked to tie the string at the front of his waist. It was then that he realised he had put them on back to front but he did not stop to remedy the mistake. He ran to the door as the knocking got ever louder and finally slipped its two heavy bolts. At last the wood swung open.

"Who is it? Is it Thias?" shouted Heliana.

"Yes it is. Come on in Thias. Sorry I was so long, she wouldn't let you in."

"You lazy wazzock," screeched Heliana from the back room.

Llyat ushered Thias over to the breakfast table and there the two sat and waited for Heliana to join them. Once the young woman had slipped on her dress and rushed a comb through her tangled locks she served up the tea to the men who had agreed not to discuss matters of importance in her absence. As soon as the infusion was poured Llyat began to question Thias.

"Have you seen Irabo this morning? How is he?"

"I have indeed. You will not believe his wondrous transformation at the hands of those two priests. They have attended to him without break or rest. This morning Irabo is propped up in bed, albeit with the support of many pillows. He was even able to recognise me and utter a greeting from his lips. The priests say he even managed a few steps in order to get to the privy and although still weak and tired he is taking food and water without assistance. I would not have believed the speed of his recovery had I not witnessed it for myself. By the gods we were lucky to have delivered him to the holy men's care when we did. Father Lachesis says he will have Irabo walking by this evening."

"That would be fantastic, I am so pleased," said Heliana as she clutched her hands to her heart.

Llyat was ecstatic but he lacked the ability, like most awkward youths of his age, to express the warmth of his feelings. Instead his thoughts jumped to Irabo's wounded hands and face.

"Will they be able to regrow the finger tips that that bastard Ventes hacked off?"

"No Llyat, they will not," answered Thias. "He will journey through life without them and also several of his teeth. The priests have already straightened his nose so at least he will not be as ugly as our pox-faced friend Theoplous of whom I also have news. But before I speak of him I need to fill you both in on discussions that took place at the War Council yesterday. There was a significant decision made that affects you this morning Llyat."

"Then you had better tell us all of it," answered the young man as his left hand reached out to take and hold Heliana's right.

Thias related the farcical events that had played out before the Council. Being a bard he was able to embellish and summarise the proceeding in the most comical and almost musical manner, including the Lord Chamberlain's descent in to stupor. But the mood plummeted once Thias revealed that he had agreed for Llyat's head to be examined by the wizards and that he had come to escort him to their Guild.

Llyat was furious. He could not believe that Thias had agreed to this without asking him first. He cursed and looked to Heliana to defend him and at first she did. However, Llyat had not realised how persuasive his friend Thias could be until Heliana pointed out that the bard was skilled in the handling of the highborn of Parandor. Slow minutes passed and Thias's reasoning worked its magic until in the end Llyat was willing to contemplate a visit to the wizards. What turned it around was the concept that parts of him could be hidden and that if released could help him fulfil his true potential. Llyat knew he needed all possible help if he was to defeat Urthanock and protect his loved ones.

"I will only go before the warlocks once you tell me where the Gems of Thamous have been hidden," said Llyat. "This is not up for negotiation. Tell me now or you can stuff the wizards and the poxy War Council up where the shit forms. I have had another message from the Moirai while I slept and I must leave for Harico as soon as possible."

"I too have been working on a plan overnight and believe it vital to get you out of this city and away to Harico," affirmed Thias. "Given what's coming to the gates of Parandor we have to get you far away from here."

"And I'm going with him," added Heliana. "He will not go without me. He has sworn never to leave me again, isn't that right Llyat?"

"It's true," confirmed Llyat with confidence. "No Heliana, no visit to the wizards. No Gems, then no fucking magic men."

Thias contemplated what to do but finally relented.

"I will factor Heliana into my plans as to how and when we sneak you out of Parandor."

"And the Gems? Where have you hidden them?" demanded Llyat.

"Theoplous has them locked away inside his chest on the Bar shees Wail," replied Thias, knowing the wizards would be waiting. "We will collect them later, once you have been examined. Then we will get both of you and the jewels to the Oracle as soon as possible."

"Will the wizards hurt him?" asked Heliana as she continued to squeeze Llyat's hand.

Thias did not reply for he did not know the answer.

Much later than Thias had intended, the two friends tramped their way from the Citadel towards the Wizards Guild. Neither took any notice of the people or the buildings that they moved amongst except for when Thias passed the Barbican's gatehouse and the Royal Guard that stood on duty. Llyat had no idea that this was the same gatekeeper that had permitted the bard access the previous morning. Nor was he aware of the tension between the two. The only words exchanged where 'nice day' uttered by Thias and something more foul mumbled by the gatekeeper.

As soon as they had passed the shadows of the Barbican and entered into the narrow streets of the Capital, Llyat began to talk.

"I have some most wonderful news to tell you Thias," he began. "Heliana is with child and I am going to be a father; I mean, how great is that?"

"No way, I am shocked to soles of my boots," replied the bard before bursting into laughter. "By the Bells of Belanore, I'm so pleased you have at last woken up to that fact."

"Are you saying you knew already?"

"Yes, Llyat; me and everyone else in the Citadel."

"Really, is it that obvious?"

"It is strange how those who fuck and leave their seed are so often the last to realise what stares them in the face as the belly grows."

"Bugger me!" exclaimed Llyat.

"No that's not how it's done Llyat, but I guess you already know that."

The friends walked on in silence until the bard felt compelled to speak.

"We need to talk about the blood line of Sir Raulyn."

"What about it," answered Llyat as he manoeuvred around a stink pile?

"Do you remember in Barad Elestor, when I told you what was written on Raulyn's tomb?"

"Of course I do Thias, the Rift has not destroyed my memory."

"The Archmage and I are convinced that you must be descended from the seed of Sir Raulyn," began the bard. "There can be no doubt about it in our minds and you must understand the implications of what this means. You are the last living descendant of the Royal Blood Line of Elestor. Your child, be it a boy or girl, will carry that line on and must be protected at all costs. Do you understand now how important it is to protect Heliana and her unborn? You cannot put her in danger and that must be key to any decisions you make in the future."

"I understand what you are saying Thias but I would rather we all die together than ever be separated again."

"I follow that way of thinking but I am now sworn to uphold the way of the Cuvar," continued the bard. "You must not make my task any more difficult than it is for I now have three of you to protect.

"I thank you for all you have done and continue to do in aide of my quest, but it is my quest. I now realise that I alone must decide what needs to be done and I intend to take Heliana with me to confront the Oracle. She will give me strength as I seek the way to re-forge the Gems."

"Llyat I sense that the closure of the portal to the Underworld, as critical as it may be, is secondary to the key task that the ancients carved out for you so many years ago. Your destiny has always been to confront the beast Urthanock. This is what it is all about, the ultimate battle between good and evil. You are the champion of all that is good in this world of ours."

"You think too fucking much Thias," laughed Llyat as he stopped and stared at the great edifice before him.

"You don't understand what you are up against. I stared into his eyes."

Llyat looked to his friend and noticed his hands were shaking.

"You have no idea of ...." continued Thias before hesitating. "Urthanock's power. He could crush you as I could a snail under my boot."

Llyat held his finger to his lips and requested quiet while his thoughts raced. His eyes scanned the walls and the great door of the building they stood before but the detail did not sink in. There was something about the way Thias always hesitated when speaking of Urthanock that he had at last recognised. It worried him and he suspected there was a truth that the bard withheld.

"You know something about Urthanock that you don't want to tell me?" he said.

"No I don't, what makes you think that?" replied Thias.

"I'm not sure I believe you but we will leave it at that for now," answered Llyat. "If you won't be honest on that score, then tell me of your thoughts regarding my journey to Harico. There are many questions to answer, such as where is it? Who do think should come with us, or is it just you me and Heliana?"

"Llyat, I have still to work out the details and that I intend to do while the wizards seek to interrogate your mind today. By the time we leave their Guild this evening I will be in a position to confirm my thoughts and share my intentions. There is one certain fact that I can divulge. I will not be going with you for my plan requires my presence elsewhere. Do not press me on that matter just now but I promise I will tell you by the end of the day. Walls have ears, windows have eyes and I will not speak again of it until we are somewhere more secure. You will just have to trust me. Tomorrow I have to report back to the Council and give some detail of your departure from the city but I will not tell them all of it. Did you ever hear that old saying; 'when the chatter is slack, you'll find a knife in your back'... well there are far too many slack tongues in this city. Tonight we will call on Theoplous and retake possession of the Gems after which I will tell all. But right now, let us seek to enter the Guild."

The walls of the wizards' home were as high as those of the Citadel. The building stood a fifteen minute walk to the east of the Barbican and about half way from it to the eastern wall of Parandor. Had it not been for the timber framed buildings that hid the inner wall that surrounded the Citadel, it would have been easy for Llyat to compare structures. The walls of the Citadel were constructed of smooth faced and undecorated stone but those of the Wizards Guild were carved from the ground stones to those that formed the crenulations of the mighty edifice. Llyat was fascinated by the strange markings and soon recognised them as being of a similar design to those on the ancient buildings he had passed in Barad Elestor. He noted figures in strange clothes with odd headdresses, and weird plants that he had never seen before. His eyes drifted upwards and as they did so he became convinced that the walls told an important story. Llyat thought of mentioning this to Thias but the bard was far too preoccupied with trying to gain entry through the magnificent wooden door that bared their way.

"Just knock Thias. That often works," suggested Llyat.

"There's no need to get smart lad," replied the bard as he searched for a knocker.

The wooden portal was just as ornate as the carved stone walls. Despite their age and the effects of erosion they reminded Llyat of his late master's study. The wood had been shaped to show plants, animal parts, bubbling cauldrons, strange squares that wizards stared at, and intriguing symbols the likes of which he had not seen before.

"There is no knocker anywhere to be found but there is a button hidden here in the middle of this great carved eye," exclaimed Thias after some minutes had passed.

"Push it then. We cannot just stand here like wazzocks."

"I hope that is not the level of your contributions once we gain entry Llyat," groaned Thias,

Thias shook his head, pushed his right index finger forward, and depressed the wooden bud. The great lump of oak then swung open. From out of the buildings dark interior a woman stepped forward. She was dressed in a coal-black habit with a silver cowl that covered most of her head. The hood however could not conceal the mass of iridescent purple dreadlocks that cascaded from her head, surrounded her neck, and cascaded over the front of her ample chest. Both Llyat and Thias were taken aback and before either could speak the woman's mouth moved.

"Welcome to you both," she began. "I am a nameless servant of the Archmage. You are late and that is something that he does not favour. You must both follow me at once for we still have a way to go before we will reach his study. If

I were you, and believe me I am glad that I am not, then I would begin thinking of a good excuse for your poor timekeeping."

At that the strange woman turned and beckoned the two friends to follow.

"Have you ever had a name?" Llyat shouted as the entrance to the Guild closed behind him.

"Once, hundreds of years ago in the great dell of time, but I have long forgotten what it was. Names have no relevance to us wizards."

"Then how come Iqotrix has one," demanded Llyat as he sought to catch up to the woman who looked to him in her thirtieth year.

"It is a name he invented to appease you dimwits. He too is nameless but once outside these walls he has to play by your rules."

"You said hundreds of years but yet you look so young," replied Llyat as he sought to reconcile what his eyes saw with what his ears had heard.

"I am older than you think but be quiet now. We wizards keep silent and our house must be mute. That is how we like it so follow without speaking."

Thias leaned forward and whispered into Llyat's ear, "It seems they are slow to age!"

Llyat could never have imagined the strange nature of the wizards abode. All the rooms he passed through were similar and equally bizarre. Their square walls seemed to be constructed from wooden frames between which thick paper or hide had been stretched. They gave a hint of transparency and yet they were opaque. The floors were of polished wood, again all the same and without a speck of dirt upon them save for what fell from Llyat's and Thias's boots. Some of the rooms contained small tables and what appeared to be foot stools. On those tables rested small earthenware jugs and cups. What fascinated Llyat more than anything was the fact that the rooms had no doors, windows or points of illumination and yet all were somehow lit without the hint of shadows. Llyat looked to his feet and then to Thias's and wondered if their shadows had been stolen by magic. The weirdest thing of all was how the walls slid open whenever the nameless purple one approached and slid back once the three had passed through the openings so created. It was as if the walls themselves were alive and sensed the presence of the three figures that moved amongst them.

The path through the Guild did not take a straight line. A different turn was taken in each room and on rare occasions they went back out through the way they came, just to find themselves in rooms they had never passed through before; not that it was easy for Llyat to be sure as they all looked so much alike. The youth felt a growing sense of unease. To find his way out of the bizarre maze would be impossible, even if the walls would have opened for him as they did for 'purple head' as he now referred to her. In about one in ten of the rooms there were other wizards present. Some were in pairs, but most were alone. There was an equal number of both sexes. Most held square shaped slates upon which their eyes focused. All wore the same black habit and silver cowl as 'purple head' and all looked the same sort of age. There was no one younger and no one older and this surprised Llyat for when Denius Castor had described them in his stories in the Red Mare, wizards were always old men with long lank hair and even longer wispy beads. Not one carried a staff or wand as he had expected but they all had one unique feature that distinguished each from another, their hair. Every wizard sported a head covering of different colour and style. Some Llyat thought too bizarre to be nice but there were others, in particular the bright coloured ones, that he was determined to try himself one day. Most he knew he would never dare copy for Heliana would just laugh.

Some considerable time later the journey through the moving rooms came to an end as 'purple hair' ushered Llyat and Thias into one final chamber. It was larger than all the rest, about twice the size and yet of identical design. Once inside the strange guide spoke again.

"Wait here and do not move. The Archmage will be with you soon."

At that the woman left and Llyat turned to Thias and whispered; "I'm not so sure I like this!"

"Me neither," replied Thias as like Llyat his eyes scanned the white cube.

Llyat then noted there was something else present. Ahead, on its own and camouflaged by being the same colour as the walls, was what looked like a large egg. The oval shape was joined to the floor by a thin white pole. Beyond that, in the far right corner, stood an empty chair of polished red wood.

"I think we are up some weird chicken arse!" said Thias in a whisper so as not to disturb the paper thin walls.

"It's too fucking big for a chicken, I reckon it's a dragon's pouch," Llyat answered.

"Not quite," uttered a third voice as the egg swivelled on its pole and revealed itself to be the strangest of chairs. Sat in the midst of object was the Archmage and he wore a smile so large it could have been seen in Maplehill.

"Welcome to my laboratory although I am disappointed you are so late," he began. "Were you anyone else I would reprimand you for your tardiness but we have no time to waste and must get on with the task that has brought us together. Come here lad and change places with me. Sit on this chair and I will begin my experiments a once. Thias set your arse down on that chair in the corner. Once on it you can observe everything but the chair will not release you until I have finished and given it permission. Do you understand?"

"Interesting!" answered Thias as he made his way over to the corner.

"Come Llyat, do not be afraid," said the Archmage.

"Will this hurt?"

"Not a bit lad."

Llyat walked over to the egg shaped chair where he hesitated before sitting down. The Archmage then swivelled the chair such that Llyat faced Thias who now sat on the red one in obvious anticipation of watching the experiments unfold. Llyat giggled as Thias tried to lift up from the seat only to find it impossible to move.

"Is your arse really stuck to the wood Thias?" shouted Llyat.

"Yes it is! This is both scary and strange, but you have my trust Archmage."

"Worry not bard," laughed the Archmage. "If I had wanted to do you any harm I would have stuck something else down. The spell is a weak but an effective one and you will experience nothing at all if you sit there and behave."

"Will I stick to this egg seat?" asked Llyat "What will the mind experiments will be like? What will I feel? Will you be able to see all things I do in private...?"

Iqotrix walked to a side wall and picked up a square slate coloured object and a stone stylus.

"It would be possible to see your personal practices but I won't be using that particular spell," replied the Archmage. "I am going to use two specific ones to look inside your head, if of course all goes according to plan. First I will..."

"What will I feel?" interrupted Llyat.

"Let me reassure you lad, there will be no physical pain," Iqotrix continued. "Many memories will be stirred and indeed released if you are who we suspect. We have no real understanding of what may be locked inside your head. It may be that we can release some or all of your hidden memories, if your subconscious mind will agree to let it go. First however we need to do a simple experiment to ensure you are not a changeling for it would be dangerous to release great evil inside this building. That first task will also reveal if there is indeed anything hidden that I can unlock."

"You talk of 'we'. Is it possible I will also see what is revealed?" asked Thias while trying to contain his excitement.

"If my method works you will. Just be patient, all will become obvious."

"And will I also see what's in my head?" asked Llyat

"You will see, hear, smell, feel, and experience all that you mind sees, if indeed there is anything in there and that remains a significant possibility.

"How will I see from over here?" asked Thias.

"The walls will reveal all," replied Iqotrix while he scribbled away on his square pallet with his stylus. "Now Llyat, close your eyes."

The Archmage placed the objects he held down onto the floor and stepped forward until he stood in front of Llyat. The youth from Maplehill sensed his presence and even the flow of the wizard's breath upon his face. Hands touched his head and sent a ripple of warmth across his mind. He relaxed at once, despite his concerns of what was about to take place.

"Budditon imon kambo kanxsma. Kom-ber-o brigos et gwhor marcosior," whispered Iqotrix.

Llyat felt the words bounce inside his skull and although he didn't recognise them he felt compelled to cry out.

"No there fucking isn't one in here!"

Llyat watched as the wizard rushed to his tablet, picked it up and began to read its message.

"Ok, that's good and also bad," mumbled Iqotrix, loud enough for both Llyat and Thias to hear.

"What's the problem?" asked Llyat, keen to know what was going on.

"The good news is that you are not a changeling," said the wizard.

"So what's the bad news?" shouted out Thias from the corner.

"According to the message that has formed on my slate, the Historian that was called Rukave protected Llyat's memory with a forgetting spell. It is wrapped tight and protected by a password phrase. Unless we can deduce that passcode we will not be able to unlock Llyat's memories. My spell has scanned the lad's thoughts for any evidence of the code but it is too well hidden to reveal anything. This may be the end of it I fear."

"We cannot give up just like that," said Thias in his frustration. "Llyat, don't just sit there like you've just seen your first pair of tits. Think lad! Try and work out what that phrase could be."

Llyat thought long and hard and threw out many suggestions none of which seemed to please the wizard. Then he remembered the strange dream he had experienced on the mountain top after Thamous had rescued him from the Eastern Marsh. Had the Moirai showed him the answer? The pieces were falling into place.

"I think I know the words that will unravel my mindlock," said Llyat with a glint in his eye. "I suggest you scribble them down on your square thingamafuck and see if I am right. They may not be in the right order and there are five of them."

"Ok Llyat, we will test your insight," replied Iqotrix. "What are the five? Say them as slow as you can and I will write them down."

"Rukave, Lyrusa, Enguerrand, Mathias and Xix."

The Archmage scribbled away with his stylus and then raised his eyebrows in surprise. Looking down at his square he saw it perform its magic.

"The 'eye of the fruit of knowledge' as I call this tool, suggests a different order. It seems to like a particular combination and it is possible we are getting somewhere," said Iqotrix after a brief moment of contemplation. "It believes the right sequence of the five to be; Rukave, Xix, Enguerrand, Mathias, and last but not least, Lyrusa."

"Try it without delay," shouted Thias from his chair of confinement.

The Archmage placed his hands upon Llyat's head. The youth closed his eyes and another ripple of warmth then rolled through his mind. In the distance Llyat heard the wizard say the words.

"Rukave, Xix, Enguerrand, Mathias, Lyrusa."

An intense explosion of white light then burst inside Llyat's head. It filled his skull and even though he then tried to open his eyes it did not go away. So intense was the white that he was sure it would leave him blind. Ears picked up the voices of Thias and Iqotrix as they shouted to see if he was still sane. Then the voices faded and there was just the white. Llyat thought for a moment that this could be his 'End of Days' and that he was journeying into the afterlife; but then he realised that he felt too calm for such a dreadful outcome. A small image appeared in the light and it grew larger by the second. Within perhaps a minute it seemed to fill his head like one enormous square. It was the image of a dusky knight in ancient armour whose face seemed noble and true. A moment later the image began to move and Llyat's limbs twitched. The wizard's words, about others being able to see his thoughts sprung back into his mind. He shouted in the hope that the bard was still listening.

"I hope you can see all this Thias. It is fucking awesome."

The mind lock had been released.

For the next four hours moving images flashed through Llyat's head at rapid pace. They were accompanied by the sounds of their time as the history of the

Realm was revealed in its entirety. It started with the childhood of the Knight who had first appeared in the square image and who had introduced himself as Sir Raulyn, greatest of the Ancients whose ancestors had travelled to these lands almost before time began. Llyat remained conscious throughout and was awed by the presence of his hero, in particular when the great man confirmed that Llyat was descended from his seed. Raulyn revealed in detail the blood line of his family all the way down to the present. One of the mighty warrior's first messages was to make Llyat aware that others would wish access the knowledge that was about to be imparted and that for added protection the story's unfolding would be delayed in time to any eyes and ears that somehow had managed to tune in to his thoughts. Llyat, the knight confirmed, would have the ability to block important messages and facts, clues as to the way to defeat Urthanock, for this was the purpose of the embedded memory and knowledge that was for him alone. The youth's mind questioned how to do that for he knew that Thias and the Archmage were listening in and watching his channelled thoughts. Raulyn's voice told him how to activate a time filter and Llyat tested it with success as soon as he could. Yet he reckoned that most of the new insights that swept into his mind would help Thias understand what had to be done and so the majority of what he saw went unblocked. Some messages however were so critical to the success of his quest that he kept them to himself.

When all had at last been revealed, the square of images faded and shrank back into the white. Several seconds later the white turned black, his eyes flicked opened, and he stared once again upon the face of the Archmage of Parandor. Llyat had returned and his mind was full of new insights.

"Welcome back lad," said the wizard with a beaming smile. "That was interesting!"

"Could you see all that I could?" asked Llyat, praying he wouldn't have to relate the hours of messages he had received.

"Yes we could," shouted Thias from the corner. "It was amazing, we saw and heard almost everything. Your mind was projected onto the walls of this room and it all played out on four enormous canvasses. I have never seen the like before and would not have believed it had I not witnessed it with my own eyes. If only the bards were still alive to see this place."

"Such is the power of the Ovumchair which can interrogate minds and share what it sees," added Iqotrix. "Now perhaps you will understand why all the walls in this Guild are constructed the way they are. The Ovumchair projects onto them all and every wizard here today has shared in your most interesting revelations."

"You said that you saw almost everything?" said Llyat, alarmed that so many could have witnessed his most intimate history. "What did you mean by that?"

"We understood from what were heard Sir Raulyn say at the beginning that there was a time delay in what we saw and that you had the ability to filter out anything you didn't want us to see or hear," answered Thias. "There were numerous gaps and interruptions in the flow of the story and it was soon became apparent that there were certain things you were holding back."

"Good," said Llyat. "Archmage, you had no right to share this information with others without my prior agreement. You are however correct Thias. I suspected you both would be listening and I did indeed block significant facts and messages that I will keep to myself, at least for now. You see, it's all about trust. It took a long time for you to build my trust wizard and yet it was so easy for you to lose it. I will be very careful what I tell you going forward."

"I understand lad, but please accept that I come from a place filled with good intent," replied Iqotrix. "We wizards are not all that we appear. We are many yet one and you will never see more than one together outside the walls of this Guild. You have the right to hold your own secrets as do I, but for the sake of all our safety and the success of your quest, then we do need to discuss, just the three of us, some of the implications of what we just witnessed. I will release you from the Ovumchair."

The Archmage then scribbled with his stylus onto his palate and Llyat was ejected from the chair. The four walls that had shown Llyat's face since he had returned from his spell all turned white again. Thias stood from his chair, free at last. After all three had stretched their legs the Archmage began to question Llyat.

For the next two hours, the three who sought to ensure the survival of the Realm reviewed what that they had seen and sought to make sense of it all. Llyat did most of the talking for it was his knowledge and he wanted to make sure he put his own mark upon all that was considered. When asked by the Archmage how he had deduced the five words that had released the mindlock, Llyat described his mountaintop dream in as much detail as he could recall. Both Thias and Iqotrix had then been keen to understand if Llyat had experienced any other similar and prophetic nocturnal experiences. So it was that Llyat recounted his dream of earlier in the day when he had experienced the dazzling white at the black entrance to an old barrow. Leaving out no detail he explained the image of walking up the hill that stood behind an ancient village. How he had found the barrow with the black portal and how he was convinced the place was at Harico. The wizard agreed for he said he had been there years some years before. Llyat's description matched what he remembered of the place.

"Did you see anything else when you looked into the black and before you were enveloped by the white?" asked the wizard.

"No," replied Llyat, feeling that he should have done. "Wait a minute, there are more images being fed into my thoughts... I see what's there... The Moirai sit within its structure and there is fissure beneath their feet that leads down into a maze of caverns and room hacked from out of the rock. Oh fuck, there is something else down there."

"What is it?" asked Thias with concern.

"The dead walk amongst the chambers and the Moirai shout to them by name,"

"And what name do the Three call out?" asked the wizard.

"The Children of Gebez!" replied Llyat.

"Son of a whore." exclaimed the wizard. "I was not expecting them to show up."

"What do you know of these children?" demanded Thias as his fear for Llyat grew ever greater.

"They're the real deal," answered the stressed Archmage. "But I know they are not children. They are dark beings, or so the legends say. Gebez is the god that is never mentioned. His minions are condemned to wander and lay in wait between the realities. They are the revenant dead not considered worthy to pass into the Underworld or to join the gods that inhab t the Heavens. The foul creatures wander without sense and destroy all at their will. Their pale flesh is said to be covered by dark sackcloth, their hands clawed, and their screeching most terrible.

"They don't sound good to meet in the dark," said Llyat.

"It is said they have a thirst for human blood and that they are grim eyed with the sharpest of teeth," continued Iqotrix.

"This quest is getting more fucking ridiculous by the day," muttered Thias. "How many more trials can be sent to test us?"

"Do you fear them?" asked Iqotrix as he witnessed a degree of calm in Llyat that he never thought him capable of demonstrating.

"No, I do not," replied Llyat as ripples of courage flooded out from his unlocked memory. "They and the Moirai may set traps and test all who enter their domain, but I am no longer the person that you knew before we entered this building. My childhood anxieties have left me. They were placed there by Rukave Emgar when he sought to protect me with his mindlock. Now I am whole again and my true potential has been awakened. For the first time since I began this journey I believe that I can succeed. The real I, the true Llyat Emgar, the one whose panoply of talents has been hidden for so long from this Realm, now stands before you."

"And so the prophecy comes into being!" exclaimed the Archmage.

"What are you getting at?" asked Thias.

"From the innocent the saviour shall waken."

"Llyat, what did you learn about the ways of defeating Urthanock that we may have missed," said Thias after the implications of the wizard's words had sunk in. "We saw much about how Sir Raulyn defeated Urthanock the first time but we gleaned no new insights that could aid us in the defence of this city. Did you hold anything back that could be of use? If you did you should tell us now for war is not long in coming. What do you know of his strengths and weaknesses?"

"I did hold back one piece of information that may be of value because I did not know what it meant," replied Llyat as he began to pace about the white room.

"You must tell us what it was Llyat. We may be able to help you make sense of it," said Thias.

"At first I thought it was nonsense; that I was expected to learn how to sing."

"What kind of tripe is that?" replied the confused bard.

"Let him tell us and we can evaluate whether or not it is helpful," added Iqotrix.

"Sir Raulyn told me that the way to kill the essence of Urthanock during this reincarnation is by the means of 'The Ballad of Predestination'."

"Codswallop," muttered Thias. "I have heard every ballad ever written and never come across one of that name. Are you sure you heard him right?"

"I'm certain, there is no doubt. That was what he said, word for word."

"Then we need to do research for the ballad must have been written down somewhere," squealed the excited Archmage. "Given that the library of the bards has been destroyed then let us hope someone kept a copy amongst the tomes of Parandor. Wait, let me check my slate... No, it too has no knowledge of such a song."

"Did you learn anything else that could help us defend Parandor?" asked Thias as his frustrations grew.

"No I did not."

"Archmage it is time for Llyat and me to leave for we have other business this day."

"Yes of course," replied the wizard. "But first tell me what do you intend to do next?"

While Llyat ruminated on the possible meaning behind mention of the ballad he noted that Thias had led the wizard into a corner and had begun to share his plans for Llyat's journey to Harico. Iqotrix nodded in affirmation and then the pair approached Llyat to seek his agreement.

"Listen with care," began Thias. "I have just bounced my ideas off the Archmage and he believes we have the basis of a good way forward. In truth the final decision will be yours but I have been thinking about this for a long time. So please let me finish before making your mind up."

"I am happy to hear your thoughts and then I alone will decide if I want to go with them."

"While visiting Irabo I have been talking with the two priests who are doing such a remarkable job in nursing our young warrior back to health," began the bard. "In case you have forgotten, their names are Atropos and Lachesis. I asked Lachesis if he had any ideas as how to secrete you out of Parandor, past the preying eyes of our guards, and deliver you to Harico undetected. He offered a way forward which is better than any that I could have come up with but for it to succeed no one else must know of it; that includes the idiots that sit around the Council's table. We will dress you and the girl, plus two others that I will send to guard you, as priests of the Temple of Fatumai. The two real priests will also accompany you to add credence to your tale should you be stopped and questioned. The cover story for your journey will be that you are in search of the herbs, spices, and resins that only grow south of the Tiaryer and which are vital to the practice of the religion of Fatumai. The hood and habits of the order will offer ample disguise."

"Who are the others you feel should accompany me?" asked Llyat with suspicion.

"Two men true of heart and who you will trust," replied Thias, confident that the names would sit well. "Irabo will soon be fit to travel and the priests will continue his care as you all traverse the lands south of the river. Theoplous is the other and as you now know, both are Cuvar and will continue to watch over you, your girl, and your unborn child. The priests have a boat ready in the docks and will row you across the estuary tomorrow tonight. A half a day's walk from Parandor, in a most remote and secluded copse known only to the two priests, lives an old hermit called Clotho, one who knows of a secret trail to Harico. Clotho, Atropos and Lachesis will take you via this path to within sight of that town but will then leave you. They agree to get you there undetected but will go no further. What happens after that will be down to you, Heliana, Theo, and Irabo. Does that sound like a plan that will work for you?"

"I will go with it unless I can think of another and better alternative," replied Llyat, "However, no one other than the three of us, the two priests, and the two Cuvar must know of these details. Do you both agree?"

"We do," answered the others.

"You have however omitted something Thias," said Llyat. "What if the Moirai ask for a child?"

"That was the reason I didn't want Heliana to accompany you," relied the bard as the colour drained from his cheeks.

"Don't worry yourself over that decision Thias, It is mine alone. I understand what my obligations are and what is expected of me."

Llyat thought back through his implanted memory and in particular to those parts he had kept from the bard and the wizard. He now had a much greater insight into the significance of the giving of a child to the Oracle, just as Sir Raulyn had done centuries before. Although he still did not understand its full implications he somehow felt sure that it would not be his child that they demanded and if they did he would not surrender it to them.

"If there is no other way you will have to give up the child. It is your fate, it is the fate of your unborn," said Iqotrix as he placed his hand on Llyat's shoulder as if to inject strength and resolve.

"No Llyat, you cannot contemplate such an act," said Thias as his tears welled.

"That's never going to happen and there is always another way," replied Llyat as he raised his right hand and signalled that he didn't want to talk further on the matter. "Come on Thias, we need to leave and seek out Theoplous. Time is getting on and we must make ready to leave."

"Yes you are right," began the bard. "Archmage, please escort us from the building for we will never find our way out alone. I will join you at the Council tomorrow where we can give an update of what we have seen and discussed here today. We will not however give details of how Llyat will travel to Harico, not even to Teulu whose priests will show us the secret way. Even they advised me against doing that!"

"So be it," replied Iqotrix as he ran the fingers of his right hand through his spikey red hair. "Stand by the wall over there and my colleague will come and escort you to the main door. I have much to think on and we need to begin the search for the mysterious ballad that may help us defeat Urthanock."

Llyat and Thias moved as instructed to the wall. They looked back one last time at the Archmage who climbed into the Ovumchair and then swivelled it around such that he could no longer be seen. In the next instant the wall besides Llyat slid back and revealed the purple haired witch.

"Follow me," she ordered.

As the three progressed through the succession of sliding doors and endless rooms, they passed through one that contained a small table on which a pack of cards lay in a stack. Llyat had by this time dropped several paces behind the bard and 'purple head' and he stopped and picked up the cards out of curiosity. 'Purple head' turned in an instant and shouted: "No!"

The cards fell from Llyat's hands for the shock of her sudden utterance had cause his fingers to lose their grip on the silky squares of parchment. All hit the ground but just three then lay face up to reveal their nature. In an instant Llyat reached down and scooped them into his hands. He reinserted the three and shuffled the deck such that the others would not see what had been disclosed.

"You shouldn't have done that lad," said 'purple head' with concern. "Do you feel okay?"

"What were the three? I couldn't see their detail from here," asked Thias.

"I didn't take any notice," lied Llyat as he moved to join the others.

The Marked followed on in silence as he was escorted out of the building. While he walked he reflected on what had appeared before his eyes; Truth, the Cutter, and the Lover.

11

Thias and Llyat made their way to the Banshees Wail, mesmerised by the day's weird experiences within the strange interior of the Wizards Guild of Parandor. As they crossed the southern quarter of the city they talked in length about all that they had both learned. Thias quizzed Llyat on both the reality of his new-found wholeness and of the inherited memories that his father had locked away with a mind incantation. Llyat was now different. He spoke with clarity, great authority, and impressed Thias no end. The bard marvelled at Llyat's the true nature, one that had been hidden from the world for seventeen long years. Moving with ease through the abutting buildings of the lower town, Thias reiterated the plan he had been formulating over recent days. The bard had first revealed it inside the Wizards Guild and the youth listened with care to ensure he understood all of its details and ramifications.

The short walk passed without incident and soon within the tight constraints of a small cabin on the Banshees Wail, three conspirators sought to plan the next phase of their quest to save the Realm from destruction. Theo's allocated space was cramped beyond belief. A dwarf could not swing a vole by its tail without hitting all four walls. A wooden chest, crafted in the ornate tribal style of the Lotus Isles and lying under a single hammock were the sailor's only possessions. This lockaway was secured with an iron padlock. The walls, floor, and ceiling, were formed from the solid oak planks that were part of internal structure of the seafaring caravel. With three adults confined in such a tight space there wasn't room for anything else.

Heat from the bodies raised the temperature to a level that both stifled the breath and caused rivulets of sweat to form on Thias's brow. He knew this would have to be a short meeting but he need not have feared for he noted that Llyat was in no mood to spend any more time than necessary inside the cramped cabin. The air quality was not helped by Theoplous's pungent body odour nor the dimness of the light given out from a single lantern, fixed to the roof behind the small door. But it could have been worse; they could have been trapped with Isambard Hotch and then they would have known true torture. The bard reckoned that the sailor had no change of clothes, nor did he often wash. Due to his fatigue from hours trapped on his arse in the house of the wizards, Thias was content to allow Llyat to lead the discourse.

"I understand from Thias that you are Cuvar; is that correct?" asked the youth, his face just inches away from that of the First Mate.

"Yes, I am and as such I have spent many years in preparation for what is to come. I swore my unswerving loyalty to you and your cause long before I knew who you were and even before you were born. I have studied the teachings of the Great Belanore and I place my life at your disposal. Say what you wish of me and I will do as you request."

"I glad to have you with us and most pleased you were in The Murdered Wolf when we dropped into that barrel," continued Llyat in a manner that amused Thias for it was so untypical of the youth. "However, we do not have time to waste on small talk. I have come for the Gem's and the lead box that Thias asked you to keep safe. The bard will soon explain his plan for he intends that you to play a significant role in it. I have heard it twice now and I like it the better the more I think on it. Thias, waste no more time, explain the next stage of our journey and how Theo fits into your plan. But first give me the Gems."

With considerable difficulty Theoplous somehow managed to bend to the floor, release the padlock with a key taken from his trouser pocket, and retrieve Thias's shoulder bag. The sailor passed it over and Llyat checked to ensure that nothing was missing.

"Excellent! Thank you for looking after them for me."

"My pleasure," replied the sailor, "but I desire to know what more you would have me do."

"Tell him the plan Thias. Do it now before we all pass out," ordered Llyat.

"Well, it goes like this..."

Thias related his thoughts for getting Llyat to the mysterious town of Harico where legend indicated the Oracle of Fasteria could be found. In order to get Llyat there undetected, a small team would travel disguised as priests of the Order of Fatumai. Two real priests from Parandor would accompany Llyat and Heliana along with two others in order to add credibility to the ruse should the group be stopped and questioned. Theo interrupted and asked who the other two unnamed members of the party were.

"We ask you to be one and the other our young warrior Irabo, if the gods are willing and he continues his speedy recovery," answered Thias. "I will visit him again this evening to check on his progress."

"Why the girl?" queried Theoplous. "She is pregnant and journey may hold many dangers."

"Because her presence is necessary to ensure the success of my mission," snapped Llyat.

"The priests have a boat with oars down in the docks and will row you all across the estuary," continued Thias. "They will then take you to an old hermit called Clotho who knows of an ancient secret trail to Harico. They will leave the four of you there for they are sworn not to enter the domain of their deity's daughters. From there on you will be on your own."

"I'm still not happy with Heliana coming with us," said Theoplous, his brow furrows highlighted by the lantern's flicker. "She has a child to protect and I have heard stories of sacrifices."

"She is coming and it is not up for negotiation," said Llyat.

"Are you not making the journey too Thias?" asked the sailor.

"The war is coming sooner than I would have liked," replied the bard. "I need to create a diversion and buy you time once the battle starts. Urthanock must be distracted but I first have to clear my plan with the Council. If all goes well with the war then I will seek to catch you up but the method of my distraction must remain secret, at least for now. You'd best warn Highroar to move his ship across the estuary and out of range of the enemy's pults. You should tell any other captains to do the same."

"No further talk then, let's just do it," ordered Llyat.

"As you wish lad and as I have already said, I will do all I can to protect you," replied Theoplous. "However, I do have one more question of you Thias."

"Then ask away."

"I assume Llyat will take the Gems with him on this journey, but what of that strange box?"

"That little trinket will gain us time to weld the Gems into the one key, should the Moirai prove helpful and when and if you ever get to meet them," replied Thias. "Only Llyat can know the plan for the box and what to do with it. No other can have that awareness for it would be a disaster should Urthanock understand my intentions. The foul Lord must not be allowed to track Llyat from afar."

"Do not fear such a possibility Thias," added Llyat. "I know things about the Gems that only Thamous and Raulyn knew. The wyvern explained it all to me on our way to Avolire."

Thias's eyebrows rose and Theo's jaw dropped.

"The Sapphire will hide us from Urthanock's gaze," Llyat continued with great authority. "The gem has the ability to hide itself and certain chosen ones. That is why the Lady Silverwynn and the Knights of Avolire could not locate it in Barad Elestor, even though it was in open sight. Once we have spoken to the Moirai, I will use the dragon whisper as per your plan and set a trap to lure the swine. Let us see what the three crones make of the beast of the swamp. They have been guiding me each day and cannot favour both sides in their game. Besides, I will not open the box until I have talked with the 'Three'. If I sense they have been playing me along then I will not act as you have suggested Thias. Your plan is a good one and we should act without delay. The time for talking is over."

"I'm with you Llyat," replied Thias, stunned by the youth's growing confidence.

"As am I," added Theoplous.

"Then Theo, be ready to leave Parandor once Solaris ends his trek tomorrow," said Llyat. "I will come and collect you with the others."

Thias escorted Llyat and the bag of jewels back to the Citadel and into the chambers of the deceased Physician. Once he was content that the Marked and Heliana were secured behind locked doors he set off back to navigate the narrow stinking streets of Parandor. His legs ached from the demands of his day. Once he had entered through the main doors of the Temple of Fatumai, he crossed the vast space towards the inner sanctum and then veered off to the right into a small room set back into the thick walls of the circular edifice. In that sparse stone space, he saw Irabo sitting upright on the single bed that almost filled the room. The warrior of the City Watch greeted Thias with a warm smile and a wave of his right hand.

"As you can see friend, my recovery continues at great pace."

"It's pretty amazing Irabo and I wouldn't have believed it had I not witnessed it for myself."

"Not only do I feel stronger," continued Irabo as he jumped off the bed, "but as you can see I have regained my legs. I have been moving around the temple this afternoon and I'm told that by the end of tomorrow I'll be considered fit to leave. The two priests for whose care I am under have hinted that I haven't seen the last of them, but as far as their healing is considered, well it is all over and done with."

"That's perfect," replied Thias as he stood by the edge of the bed and smiled. "I have come to tell you of the next stage of our mission and I am pleased that your recovery will allow you to play a full part in my plan. I hope you recall your allegiance to the Cuvar for now is the time we must both step up for the Marked."

Questions then sprayed from Irabo's mouth.

"How is Llyat; do we know if he is safe and well? Have you any idea where he is? What about the Gems of Thamous, are they still in Avolire? How the fuck did we manage to leave the Silverbitch's cell and end up in Parandor? How..."

"What have the priests told you," asked Thias.

"Nothing at all for they say it is not their place to tell of things that belong to others."

"At least I don't have to correct any misinformation," replied the bard.

Thias then sat with his friend and contemplated where to start. It was obvious that during his near death illness Irabo had failed to appreciate most of what had transpired. He took hold of Irabo's hands and began from the point of their recapture, back in the ogres' encampment on the outskirts of Calistorn. Irabo showed great surprise at several points in the story, including how Grovrouk the Despoiler had sprung Thias, Irabo, and Heliana from their cell and how Llyat had appeared as if from nowhere amid the prison tunnels. Thias took the opportunity to embellish his part in the recovery the four Gems, snatched from the Silverwynn's control.

"She only had three," Irabo interrupted.

The young warrior had no recollection of Heliana's appearance in the cell below Avolire, or that she had brought the ruby with her. He was also stunned that Llyat had turned up with the fifth that he had found in the Marsh. Irabo wept when informed that both Thamous and Einar were dead and his limbs shook with trepidation when told that Urthanock once again walked the ground of the Middle Realm. Thias failed to disclose the identity of the Vessel that carried Urthanock's essence; that he deemed he would keep secret lest Irabo let it slip. The young warrior laughed on hearing how he had been brought to Parandor and only saved by a barrel of firewater inside The Murdered Wolf. However, when Thias broke the news of Phauless's death and the revelation that Lolly, being the shapeshifter, had murdered him using poison, Irabo began to shake and his lips trembled as he whispered.

"So, that's why has Tonousa not been to see me? She is too ashamed at her failure."

"No Irabo, she is dead!" sighed Thias. "That bastard Lolly killed her."

Thias held on to his friend who wept in pails. Once Irabo's emotions began to subside Thias filled in the details regarding Tonousa's most dreadful demise. It took the bard what seemed a lifetime to console his friend and drag him out of a deep pit of despair.

"How are your fingertips?" he asked as he tried to switch the conversation away from images of the knife as it entered Tonousa's side. "Your nose looks almost straight and not shifted so much to the right as it did when the sailors brought you here."

"My nose is fine Thias and I appreciate your concern," replied Irabo as he thrust his hand forwards such that Thias could examine his digits.

"Your fingers have healed well but your skill with the lute will never be the same."

"Fuck the lute! All that matters is that I can still wield my blade. I will have my revenge on those bastards that crawled out from the swamps, and for your information bard, I never did learn the workings of that instrument."

"I know that Irabo and you'll never make a singer either," chortled Thias. "Do you think you can still grip your blade for it may be necessary as you journey on?"

"You bet I can!"

"Now I need to tell you my plan," began Thias. "But first I must let you know what Llyat and I have been up to today. This morning we went to visit the Wizards Guild. By the Orbs of Belanore that is some weird place. We were met…"

Thias recounted in great detail all that had occurred within the confines of the strange building. Irabo looked back with a deep suspicion when mention was made of the white walls that slid and the tablets of slate on which writing appeared by magic. He snorted with laughter at the description of Iqotrix's laboratory, the ovum chair, and the other to which Thias's arse had been stuck.

"He's not the person you once knew, Irabo," continued Thias. "Llyat's personality is almost exactly the opposite of the wimp we both once knew and steered through the Dragonas."

"Get to the point Thias," interrupted Irabo. "What is it you ask of me?"

"You will be travelling with him and he will lead and give you clear orders. Do not mess with him Irabo, he has the strength of Raulyn's memories and they fuel his thoughts and courage."

"Where is the lad now and what of the Gems of Thamous?"

Thias then told of how he and Llyat had just been to visit Theoplous aboard the Banshees Wail. There they had repossessed the five jewels that the First Mate had been keeping safe since their arrival in Parandor. He told how clear thinking and forceful Llyat had been and how he had agreed to travel to Harico and lure Urthanock into a confrontation with the Moirai, to pit one power against another. Explaining that the Gems were now secure inside the Citadel, Thias vowed to return to collect Irabo and pick up Theoplous as they left Parandor.

"I think you had better tell me the full extent of your plan," said Irabo, trying to take all in.

"Yes, it is time that I did just that," replied the bard. "This is what will happen…"

Thias explained his plan in detail. Irabo wanted to know why Thias was not going to Harico with Llyat. Thias explained the outline of his intended deception, how he would try and dupe Urthanock into thinking that the Marked remained in Parandor until Llyat triggered his presence in Harico. Having then heard that Heliana was pregnant Irabo questioned the sense in allowing her to travel with Llyat, despite her having been the one to unmask the changeling. When Thias explained that the two priests who had save his life would be there with him, Irabo smiled and whispered:

"That Lachesis is a sly bugger. So that's what he meant when he said that I hadn't seen the last of them."

"Be ready when Llyat calls for your tomorrow. I am very tired and must be up long before the first cock crows. Our paths will be full of terrors and should either of us fall, I must tell you now that I have been proud to call you friend."

The two sworn Cuvar stood from the bed and embraced in a hug of mutual recognition. A tear welled in the bard's eye.

Thias was not the last to arrive at the War Council of Parandor. He made his entrance some five minutes before the first cock had crowed and took the same place at the table as he had on his previous attendance. Busying himself in general greeting and chat talk, he waited for the last to arrive. Gilebin Ystafell had yet to show and Thias began to wonder if the acting Regent was still drunk or too ashamed to show his face. Thias turned to Commander Townsforth.

"Have you seen anything of our illustrious leader since he fell asleep yesterday?"

"No I haven't," smiled the Commander. "I bet he has one mighty head thump this morning. To think these are the depths to which we have fallen in our hour of greatest need makes my bile boil. I never thought I would ever say this but I wish Blackfayer was still alive. Despite being such a shit he at least knew how to lead. Old round whiskers isn't fit for purpose. He should stick to cleaning the bed chambers of the highborn that he so likes to fawn over."

The first cock crowed at the same time as Ystafell strode though the door, scuttled over to his chair at the head of the table, and there grunted a greeting to those gathered without so much as casting a glance in their direction.

"The meeting is in session, welcome one again," the oaf lisped. "Lady Emeny please be so good as to take notes as usual."

"You cut that entrance a bit fine, Gilebin," sneered the Sovereign Adviser. "Some of us didn't think you were going to make it!"

"Let's get on with it and let me stay this; I apologise for the excesses of our last meeting," squirmed Ystafell. "There will be no beer or wine served here today for we must all keep a clear head as we finalise our preparations for the war that is about to strike against our walls. I have drafted a simple agenda which I have on this parchment and we will stick to it. I will seek to finish our business before the end of this afternoon."

With that Ystafell thrust a scroll that he had been carrying down upon the table.

"Now first up to report will be …"he began, but Lady Emeny interrupted.

"Before we agree to any agenda, you need to understand that some here present feel you are not up for the task that has been thrust upon you. I volunteer to take the lead should you agree to step down and relinquish control to hands that are much more capable and competent."

The room fell silent as all eyes turned to the Lord Chamberlin.

"How dare you woman," snarled Ystafell. "I admit the wine got the better of me last time but it was a great vintage and if you buggers had shared it, and the cheese, then perhaps we would not be having this conversation now. Go swallow some Lillywort or just fucking shut up."

All stared at the red faced buffoon.

"Is there anyone else here bold enough to join Emeny in her treasonous assertions?"

Silence fell. Thias was contemplating supporting Lady Emeny's attempted coup but as no one else spoke up, he held his tongue.

"Good, that's settled then," continued Ystafell. "Stick to taking notes woman and leave the running of this Realm to us men, just as it has always been. Now, as I was saying before old Lady Law interrupted me; Sir Byddin, you are first up. Please report on your preparations to defend this fine city of ours."

Sir Byddin rose to his feet, pulled out some scribbled notes from a secret recess in his armour and began to address the Council. Just before he began he looked to Lady Emeny and smirked. She reddened in anger but said nothing more.

"Here is my report," he began, "and I would like to thank my fellow knights at the end of the table for all their assistance, both in preparing this report and for the work they have supervised in order to aid our long term survival."

"Get on with it man," heckled Heward Teulu.

"I have much positive news to pass on today and I will start with the most import..."

Thias leaned back in his chair and yawned in anticipation of yet another long and laborious speech. However, that was not how it turned out for Sir Byddin seemed set on being concise.

"First off, the preparations for the defence of the walls and gates of Parandor..."

The old knight continued as if on a horse charging into battle. He covered the key points that needed the attention of the Council and started with the outer defences.

"As you will all be aware we have constructed an outer palisade of oak staves that now surround the city on all sides up to the Tiaryer. Before it, some ten paces forward we have dug a deep ditch which we have filled with bush wood and tar. This we will fire once the enemy seeks to cross it in numbers. On the ground behind the palisade and in front the city walls our armies will make their first stand. We have been manufacturing arrows by the barrel full for weeks and by the gods' spleens we will rain them down on all who approach the ditch. The pults are tested and ready and will unleash boulders big enough to smash even the mystical armour that our spies say the shits now wear. The City Guard and the armies of the Fifteen Keeps are as ready as they will ever be. Should our outer defences be breached then we will retreat behind the city walls and continue the defence from on top of the battlements. We have sacks of rocks and cauldrons of boiling tar ready to drop on any that then make it to the stone ramparts that have kept us safe for centuries."

"All that is all excellent news," began Commander Townsforth. "Now could you give us an update on the Narrow Gate, the functioning of which has being causing us such concern?"

Sir Byddin sighed and Thias sensed that the great knight had hoped to avoid this particular issue. Byddin then puffed out his chest and answered with such authority that Thias was convinced he was telling the truth.

"The portcullis is fixed at last. The parts we had re-forged have been fitted and the mechanism tested several times. It now works fine so you can all rest safe in your beds."

"Forgive my interjection," said Townsforth "A couple of my warriors from the Watch who witnessed your trial gave me a less convincing account."

"What did they say Commander?" asked the Archmage, taking an interest in proceedings. "Does it work or does it not?"

"Of course it fucking works!" bellowed Sir Byddin.

"Come now, we must have the truth!" lisped Ystafell.

"Dogs bollocks. Dogs bleeding bollocks, you are such a bunch of brainless turds," snapped by Byddin. "For fucks sake Townsforth tell them what you heard."

The Commander of the Watch, raised an eyebrow and replied.

"I heard tell that it stuck mid descent on the first two times you tried it out."

"And did your gutter rats tell you it worked well thereafter?" grumbled Byddin.

"No they did not," admitted Townsforth as he dropped his head a fraction.

"Then I will say no more," replied the knight. "All of the gates are now functional. The plans for the external defence of Parandor are complete.

"In that case I suggest we take a pause to break our night fast," said Ystafell with relish.

"There it is my friends, laid out for us all to admire," sneered Lady Emeny. "Parandor's survival is dependent upon Gilebin's gluttonous gut. May the gods preserve us and pray we do not fall victim to a protracted siege. Then I fear our dear Lord Chamberlain would eat us all once supplies run out."

"And you'd be the first I'd eat, not for your meat because that's long past its best, but just to cease the prattle from your garrulous gob."

The two combatants glared at each other while all others smiled, part in disdain, and part from the ridiculousness of the conversation. A bell rang and a platter of bacon, fried eggs, and bread entered the room in the arms of several servants. The fast was broken and Thias noted Ystafell's mood lighten as the food hit his stomach.

Fifteen minutes later Gilebin Ystafell called the meeting back to order. As he lisped, drools of butter and bacon fat seeped out over his lower lip. His great whiskered sideburns were already awash with fat, for what the others hadn't eaten Ystafell had consumed with relish. Thias watched with disgust as the Lord Chamberlain's jaws chomped away on his last mouthful at the same time as trying to speak.

"Right then, now we are all back seated, it falls to you Townsforth to give us an update on your progress to secure Parandor against a sneak attack like the one the slit eyed buggers pulled off at the Bards Guild. Can you reassure us that nothing like that will ever happen to us?"

"No I cannot, and you must see that," began the Commander of the Watch. "If as we are told, the Lizardmen are capable of utilising the powers of the Underworld to move unseen from one place to another, then without knowing how to stop that act we are at a significant disadvantage. We have to focus our efforts on detecting such an assault and then trying to negate it, just as you do Gilebin whenever there is food on the table that threatens the rest of our stomachs."

"These no need for such sarcasm, Brynn, even though I agree with your words," interrupted Lady Emeny. "My mother always said a resort to such humour showed a man for what he is and she didn't think well of the privy perves."

"Point taken," replied Townsforth before coughing and moving on. "Following up on what Sir Byddin has already reported, I can confirm that all the gates into the city are ready, the battlements prepared and the Watch reservists mobilised. They are as ready as such a bunch of fill-ins could ever be. I will not resurrect issues regarding the Narrow Gate as we have already covered it during our earlier discussions. All portals are being manned in shifts and two warriors are posted to watch every building of significance throughout the city. They have been instructed to report any unnatural or unusual noises coming from underground cellars or the like. This is how we understand the reptiles managed to sack the Bards Guild, is that not right Calavan?"

"That is correct Commander," replied Thias as he listened with care. "They came from below, used black powder, and took us all by surprise."

"Well we will be ready for the buggers this time," snarled Townsforth.

The Commander of the Watch spent the next hour detailing the buildings where he felt the threat would come from should the Lizardmen dare to launch an underground attack. The Citadel was the most obvious place for them to strike and perhaps because of that fact alone it was Townsforth's opinion that they would choose somewhere else. He listed the buildings in his order of the most vulnerable.

"First up, if I were they, I would strike below the Barbican, destroy it in one great bang and thereby deliver a lethal blow to our defences. After that the Temple of Fatumai would be my second choice given the maze of tunnels under its foundations. I have not ruled out that my own barracks could be a target. Also, I would go for the cellars under the North Gate for f that were to go it would open the way for a full-frontal assault."

And on he continued until all other major buildings had been covered. The Commander then went on to describe how his men had been training the highborn on how to defend themselves. After that he proceeded to discuss the secret knock that all would from now on use before any door could be expected to be opened. The last message he gave concerned the previous evening when he had received a carrier bird confirming that a contingent of Berserkers would arrive in the Capital by lunch this day. The force was over a hundred strong and was led by one called Eerickk Jarl. Once he had finished his account, Townsforth sat down and drank from the cup that rested on the table before him.

"Thank you commander," lisped Ystafell. "Iqotrix you're next up. Be brief for I need a piss?"

"It may be long," replied the wizard.

"Then we will reconvene in five minutes," ordered Ystafell as he rose from the table and ran towards the privy.

It took Iqotrix a full two hours to report back to the Council on his interrogation of Llyat Emgar's mind. However, it did not seem so long to those who sat and listened to the wizard's story unfold. The strange man with spikey red head turned out to be a most excellent orator and teller of tales. His audience was captivated and that included Thias who knew the facts already. No details were left out as both the method and output of the interrogation was told in all its glory. Thias wondered what Llyat would have said if he had known so many had heard the account of his private thoughts.

At various points in the recounting of his saga Iqotrix had looked to Thias to confirm facts and observances, in particular when others present questioned the credibility of what they had heard. Thias always nodded back in agreement or added details from his own observations for he found no inaccuracies in the wizard's words that he could dispute. All were fascinated at the point when the Archmage described the mindlock and how Llyat himself had offered up the verbal solution to enable it to be opened. Heward Teulu caused a major distraction when he insisted on hearing details of how such a lock worked, not that the Wizard could answer many of the questions put to him for he declared the complex skills of the Ancients were beyond even his comprehension.

Iqotrix then went on to describe the outpouring of information that had been locked within the youth's subconscious mind, all of which had been projected onto the white walls of the wizard's laboratory. He then talked of the radical change in Llyat's personality such that the youth was unrecognisable from his former self. Thias was asked to confirm once again that all that the wizard had spoken was true, which he did for he also marvelled in the youth that had transformed before his eyes.

"The boy was an innocent dolt, when he came before me," said the wizard, pausing his long account. "But he is not one now. Remember the Prophecy!"

From the innocent the savoir shall waken

"Well he has woken my friends and no longer is he innocent."

"Dogs bollocks!" sneered Sir Byddin while the knights at the end of the table tittered. "And I suppose you played the key role in this fucking saviour claptrap."

"Put like that Sir, I suppose I did," replied the wizard.

"Dogs bollocks, that's all I say."

"Please Byddin, don't strain your extensive vocabulary," sneered Lady Emeny

"Fuck you!" snorted the knight; "Fuck you all."

Thias watched as most others burst into spontaneous laughter. The Archmage ignored the outburst and asked Thias to talk of what the 'Marked' intended to do next. Thias obliged and spoke of how Llyat was determined to visit the Oracle at Harico for advice, even though unsure of the route and despite the fact that war was coming. He was not deterred even if the lands to the south of the Tiaryer had already been taken by the enemy. The one issue that Thias omitted to speak of was the potential need for a child sacrifice in exchange for the wisdom of the Moirai. He thought the Archmage would have raised it but the wizard did not and that worried him. He began to think that Iqotrix was playing his own game but then Ystafell called a halt to the proceedings.

"Thias, I would like to hear your detailed plans for young Llyat but that will have to wait," began the Lord Chamberlain. "It's time we took a break for lunch which will be served in a few minutes from now. We all need to stretch our legs following the Archmage's most exceptional report. I think I must pay a visit to your Guild once all this trouble is over and done with Iqotrix. I would be most interested to see your methods and ways of working."

"You will be made most welcome," replied the Archmage as all rose.

Several minutes later lunch was brought to the room and laid upon the table by the servants of the Court. Composed in the main of pies of various sorts it was not long before sets of teeth sank into the pastries. Ystafell began his explanation of the basic offering.

"Given that war is coming we need to be a little more careful with how we utilise the food we have at our disposal. I think we are a way off imposing rationing but I wanted to set the tone and avoid waste. Therefore the pastry cooks have been up all night reclaiming what was left over from last night's communal feast. So, the pies on this first platter are a mixture of fish, fowl and red meats. You should find pike and ale, swan in port, and hot radish and hog. The middle platter pies are the vegetable offerings for those of you with more delicate digestions. I believe them to be carrot and parsnip, sprout and onion, and red cabbage with beetroot. The third plate is the fruit. These pies are all the same, apple and pear. This will be the final food offered to you today so make the most of it and ensure there is nothing left over for that would send the wrong message to the servants. I am told there are people starving in this Realm, so all plates must be left clean in recognition of their suffering. Oh yes, and something else. There will be no cheese served for I cannot abide it without the company of fine wine. Enjoy!"

"I wish to make a proposal Lord Chamberlain," said Thais as soon as Ystafell had finished. "Given that we are all busy and pressed for time may I tell you of my plans while you all continue to eat? That would be a more efficient use of our time and will allow me to leave earlier and get on with all that I need to. That will become more apparent once you understand my proposals."

"I have no objection young bard," replied Ystafell. "Does anyone one else disagree?"

No protests surfaced as the collective of jaws sank their teeth in deep. So Thias stood and spoke.

"But first I must tell you something of great importance that the Archmage did not cover in his most thorough discourse on Llyat Emgar's mind investigations. We discovered something that could be critical to our success. The way to destroy Urthanock is by the use of a ballad."

"Dogs bollocks!" roared Sir Byddin.

"No, the bard is correct and I am at a loss to know why I didn't mention it myself," added the Archmage.

"Please explain more Thias," ordered Lady Emeny with her quill poised to note the answer.

"Sir Raulyn's memory informed Llyat that the only way to kill Urthanock during this second reincarnation is by the means of 'the Ballad of Predestination'. I thought this rubbish at first but it would be foolish to dismiss the message out of hand,"

Thias paused and took a bite form his pike and ale pie. "One of the reasons I cannot leave Parandor with Llyat just now is because I have to find a copy of this ballad somewhere in the tomes that fill the Great Library of Parandor. I for one have never heard of it, have any of you?"

Following some grunts and murmurings silence fell across the room.

"I thought not," continued Thias. "So there you have part of what I must stay behind to achieve. The Marked will leave for Harico this night, in secret, and under the cover of darkness. I will stay here for now but seek to join him later once the battle is over and if by the will of the Fates I somehow manage to survive."

"Here we go again, more claptrap," sneered Sir Byddin.

"Be quite dolt!" shouted Heward Teulu as he pushed his empty plate away.

"Will the lad travel to Harico alone?" asked Ystafell with suspicion etched on his brow. "Who will you send to escort the youth to that long forgotten town of no importance?"

"It is the Barrow at Harico that is important, not the town," responded Thias as he sensed Sir Byddin poised for yet another outburst. "Llyat has agreed to the following. The servant girl Heliana who carries his child will travel by his side. Before any of you say anything against this, Llyat will not be persuaded otherwise. I have tried as best I can to do that but he now carries Raulyn's strength of will and like a mule refuses to listen to any advice on that matter."

"I know what he's up to," snapped back Heward Teulu. "He needs her for the sacrifice. The Moirai will not give up their secrets without the blood of a child. I remember what you said at our last meeting bard, that Sir Raulyn sacrificed a child to the Moirai. They will expect the same from Emgar. The sly bugger is going to give up his own unborn infant to ensure the prophecy is fulfilled."

"The clever bugger!" cursed Lady Emeny. "Had you already worked that out yourself Thias?"

"Yes, indeed I had, but there is no other option as far as I can tell,"

"Is the girl aware of what lies ahead of her" asked Teulu, wincing at the thought of the deed.

"No, she isn't," said Thias with great calm and amid an awkward silence.

"Who else will accompany them?" asked Sir Cragtalon breaking the quiet and pushing his plate away as his appetite deserted him.

"Two men who have sworn themselves to the great conspiracy of the Cuvar. One is the sailor Theoplous from the Banshees Wail of whom I spoke at our last meeting. The other is the warrior of the Watch who helped me protect the Marked when we travelled north of the Grey Mountains."

"Do you mean Irabo Basequin? I thought he was dying," said Townsforth somewhat confused.

"Yes I do. Two of the priests from the Temple of Fatumai have proved to be great healers and have resurrected Irabo from before the door to the afterlife. I thank you Teulu for allowing them to use their skills on one so valuable to our cause."

"Did you think I would do otherwise?" asked the priest.

"I would like those two, Father Atropos and Father Lachesis to travel and watch over both Llyat and Irabo. My intention is they all go dressed as members of your order to deflect attention and suspicion away from the truth of their quest. The six will tell anyone who asks them they are out collecting herbs to treat the sick and wounded once war comes to our gates. Will both of you agree to allow me use your people in this way?"

"If Irabo is fit to travel then I have no objection," replied Townsforth.

"I am not so sure I can release my most competent priests," said Teulu as he scratched his head. "They are rather busy just now, what with the battle due to start any day. They are booked solid with appointments, conducting Fortunes Fate readings for the highborn of the Citadel. It seems all are keen to know what the future has in store for them."

"Bollocks Heward, even I can see there are more important things at stake just now than the pampered paps of Parandor playing poker in your pompous palace of piety," roared Sir Byddin.

"Yes, you are of course right," responded the Royal Priest. "Please feel free to use them as you feel appropriate bard but they will not enter the sanctum of the Moirai. That would be against all our teachings."

"They will accompany Llyat to the edge of Harcio, that is all," replied Thias. "Then they will return here as soon as possible for I am sure their skills will be needed once the fighting begins. There is however one other significant part of my plan that you need to be aware of and for which I need your approval and help in bringing into being."

"We are all ears and I hope that includes you buggers at the end of the table who haven't uttered a word all day," said Ystafell as he reached over to sample a fruit pie.

The embarrassed knights at the low end shuffled their torsos and made faces that indicated a readiness to listen.

"I need to create a significant diversion, slip a hood over Urthanock's eyes so to speak, and buy Llyat a little time..." he began

"Then tell us at once Thias, what do you need our help with," lisped Ystafell. "Please make it short and be precise for my guts are beginning to churn. I fear that the pies are off!"

"Yes I agree, the pike was not at its best and I feel the rumbles too," moaned Lady Emeny.

Thias detailed the extent of his plan to dupe Urthanock. He would have everyone send messages across the whole of the city that he, Thias, was Llyat Emgar, the youth that the army of the Lizardmen had come to destroy. Everyone was to be told of the Prophecy and a copy pinned to the door of all taverns and public buildings across the Capital. Furthermore, the proclamation was to say that the 'Marked' would never leave the protection of the walls of Parandor. This message would also sent by a volunteer courier outside of the city walls. This herald had to believe that Thias was the Marked. Thias would need to meet with this messenger and pass over false information. The unfortunate volunteer would be sent towards Valameer believing he was carrying an important message to the Lady Flurdiana along with a further request for military assistance. The timing of the ceparture was to be such that the herald would be certain to be captured by the enemy. Given that he believed in the truth of his message he would repeat it when tortured; which no doubt would happen. Urthanock would then be convinced that Llyat remained inside Parandor until such point as Llyat left a signal that he had left the Moirai at Harico.

"I can see the merit in your plan Thias but how will Llyat convince Urthanock that he is not in the city and away in the hills of the southern lands?" asked Sir Byddin.

"He was given a special stone by the Berserkers of Falahorn," replied Thias. "It is like a beacon that Urthanock can read and see what is going on around it. Llyat has it concealed in a lead box that blocks that ability. He will open it once he has completed his business with the Moirai. Then he will race to wherever the Oracle directs him and we will force Urthanock into a confrontation with the crones."

"And what if the three sisters refuse to help Llyat," asked Teulu. "They are fickle by all accounts and may on a whim decide not to do so."

"In that case Llyat will not reveal his location and we will be stuck with Urthanock outside of our walls. Then we will need the help of all the gods," replied the bard.

"Who do you intend to use as the decoy to convince the beast that you are Llyat," asked Commander Townsforth as he too held a hand to his griping guts.

"I was thinking that you could offer up one of lower ranking warriors of the Watch. It has to be someone credible, someone who has never met me, nor indeed Llyat."

"Again I see the merit in your words bard," replied Commander Townsforth. "As much as it grieves me to lose one of my best, I do know someone who would volunteer for the honour of this mission even if he was to be given the truth of the matter. His name is Lolye Throissler and I suggest you seek him out when you are ready to spin him your yarn."

"Thank you Commander, I will do just that," replied Thias, grateful that his plan had been accepted without significant challenge.

The collective bellies of the council began to ripple and rumble. Ystafell rose to call the meeting to a close before an unprecedented disaster exploded within the confines of the enclosed room. A loud knock on the door was followed by a shout.

"Commander, Members of the Council, the Berserkers have arrived and Erik Jarl requests an immediate audience."

"Oh no!" grumbled Sir Byddin as he clutched his bubbling belly.

12.

Llyat and Heliana spent the day preparing for their flight from Parandor. They packed two back sacks of the type used by priests with a spare set of clothes and a selection of foods that would not spoil over the coming days. In the top of his sack Llyat placed the shoulder bag that contained the five Gems of Thamous and the lead box that concealed the Dragon Whisper. He had not once thought of opening that container for he understood only too well the consequences of allowing Urthanock knowledge of his whereabouts. Heliana packed as may herbs and potions as she could, left overs she had found in jars on the shelves of the Grand Physician's chambers. When Llyat asked her why, she told him that she wanted the means to cure simple ailments, for the two priests from the Temple of Fatumai would only be available to help them for the first phase of their journey. Both then checked the soles of their shoes to ensure they were fit for a long trek. To pass the time away until Solaris dipped from the heavens, Llyat sat with Heliana on the edge of their temporary bed and began to tease his lover over the name he would like for his unborn child.

"I have been pondering on some good ones for the next in line of Emgars," he said, as he smiled and wrapped his arm around her shoulders.

"Oh yes, and what wondrous insights have you had today my love," replied Heliana as her right hand stroked the lump under her light green dress.

"Well if it's a boy they are a few names I could call him,"

"Tell me just your favourites for I have also thought of some myself," replied Heliana as she rested her head into Llyat's chest.

"What about Brutus if he is born with strong limbs and big muscles, or Belinus if he is lanky and thin. If he is born with red hair he could be Redon, but perhaps if sick and poxy then we could call him Lludd."

"Are you being serious, you dimwit?"

"No, just passing the time!" replied Llyat as he stood from the bed, moved across the room and looked out of the window to the courtyard of the Citadel.

"I thought you were being sensible for a minute. Please be serious just for once. What if the baby is a girl, what name would you want to give her?

"I would call her Mead."

"What! Why of all the beautiful names to choose from would your pick that one."

"It's my favourite drink!"

"Pillock!" snapped back Heliana.

"There's always Lyrussa," added Llyat, "or if it is a boy, Rukave."

Before Heliana could respond Llyat spotted movement in the courtyard and turned at once to his lover.

"Thias is on his way. Come, let's get ready to leave."

Some twenty minutes later Llyat, Heliana, and Thias the bard walked up the steps and entered through the main doors of the Temple of Fatumai. They were all in good spirits now that the next chapter of their short lives had begun. Thias entered first and then Heliana. Llyat stopped for a second to fasten a lace of his boot and in that briefest of moments another young woman exited the building and almost fell over him as he bent double on the steps.

"I'm so sorry sir," exclaimed the surprised woman. "I did not see you there."

Llyat stood upright and stared at the girl before him. In a spontaneous expression of delight he gave voice to his pleasure.

"Arnkatla! Is that you? In the name of all that's sweet, what are you doing here?"

"Hi Llyat, I am pleased to see you looking so well," replied the girl from Falahorn. "I have followed my father and one hundred Berserkers who have answered Parandor's request for help in the war against the Eastern Marsh. We arrived in the city yesterday afternoon. I am here to help nurse and comfort the injured who will fall in battle and to pledge my assistance to the priests of this order."

"I so pleased to see you again Arnkatla. I can never thank you enough for a l your personal care and attention when I had the sweating sickness," continued Llyat as his face slid into an embarrassed grin. "Despite how much I want to stay and talk with you, I do have an urgent appointment inside this temple. Perhaps we will get chance to talk when the battle is over. Once again, thank you for your intimate attention."

"It was an honour and a great pleasure Llyat. Yes, I too hope we will meet again and can spend some time together. I long to hear of your adventures. However, you must excuse me for I must away to my father. I am late for a meeting,"

"Then do not let me detain longer sweet Arnkatla."

The young woman's face flushed and that did not go unnoticed by two eyes that looked out from the shadows of the open temple door. Arnkatla disappeared into the murky gloom of the refugee camp that spread out across the square before the temple steps. Llyat turned and made his way through the holy coor where he found Heliana waiting beyond its entrance.

"And what form did that 'intimate care' take, may I ask," she said with great suspicion. "I think you have some explaining to do young Emgar. Who the fuck was she."

"There is no need to be jealous my love. She is just the nurse who helped me get over my illness in the Dragonas. Can you not remember me telling you how much she helped me?"

"Ah, so that was the Arnkatla you mentioned in passing?"

"Yes, my love."

"The one you said had a face like a plank and the arse of a mathulath!"

"Did I really say that about her?" said Llyat as his face betrayed more than a passing liking.

"Yes, you fucking did. You are a brainless turd. Just remember that I am the one carrying your child," grumbled Heliana as she pointed to her bump.

"I'm sorry to break up your little spat," shouted Thias from across the floor of the temple. "Irabo is ready and waiting for you. He is well healed and prepared to accompany you on your travels. Come and reunite with the one who once dragged you out of the Tiaryer."

Llyat may have inherited Sir Raulyn's memories and strength of character but many of his basic behaviours were still those of an immature farm boy. He recognised that fact himself and vowed to act with greater honour towards the woman who carried his child. Seconds later he rushed to embrace the young warrior.

"Irabo my friend, I am pleased to find you so well."

After their brief embrace Llyat questioned the warrior on all that he could remember from the time they were separated at the ogres' encampment outside of Calistorn. Once Llyat had confirmed that Irabo was fit to travel, Thias called over the two priests who had been waiting in the shadows and introduced them to Llyat and Heliana. Father Lachesis and Father Atropos gave out priestly habits which Llyat, Heliana, and Irabo donned without question. With cowls pulled over their heads the five figures looked identical. Covered in rat-brown attire all would pass as devotees of Fatumai. Llyat realised how clever Thias had been to devise this means of leaving Parandor undetected. The youth then sought to engage with the two priests but only Lachesis answered.

"Brother Atropos has taken a vow of silence as dictated by his wishes and those of our Order. Please do not try and communicate with him other than by using your face and hands. He can of course respond to any messages you may decide to write down but it would be better to direct any discourse through myself."

Llyat nodded his understanding as he noticed Atropos's lip curl. Thias soon also donned the priest garb for despite not travelling on to Harico he needed the disguise to pass through the Southern Gate and then back again.

The narrow streets of Parandor were death quiet and devoid of light save for when an open window cast a candle glow out into the night air. By contrast however, when Llyat and his companions passed the door of The Murdered Wolf, light spilled out and lit up the surrounding ground. The shouts, curses, squeals, and screams that flew from its open door left the youth in no doubt that it was business as usual in Parandor's most infamous tavern. Llyat's hand moved and he patted Heliana on her arse. It was an involuntary action caused by his recollection of how the pair had almost succumbed to the fumes of Hotch's Nectar during his only previous visit to that den of debauchery. A drunk, whose legs had failed him, sat back against the tavern wall and looked on as Llyat's hand squeezed Heliana's cheek. The inebriate felt the need to comment as the holy group moved on.

"You dirty buggers. Man on man should be a fucking hanging offence, more so when such foul buggery is perpetrated by priests."

Heliana giggled and Llyat smiled but the rest just ignored the ramblings of the dishevelled sot.

As they approached the Southern Gate that would give them access to the waterfront, Llyat whispered forward to Thias in order to confirm the next phase of the plan.

"Are you doing the talking, or am I?" he asked.

"Leave this one to me Llyat for I have to come back and I want to make sure the guards understand that before I pass through the walls."

The group waited by the imposing portal while Thias moved forward to engage in dialogue with its keeper. Llyat watched, never once dropping his concentration while the bard negotiated the opening or the mighty wooden door. It seemed to take longer than he had anticipated but then Thias returned and the guard made preparations of open the gate wide enough to allow the group to pass.

"Was there a problem?" asked Llyat. "You seemed to take an age,"

"Not getting out," replied Thias. "It was getting back in that was an issue. The guards are twitchy and do not like admitting anyone in the hours of darkness. They have given me just thirty minutes to return before they lock the gate for the night. So, we had all best get moving or I will have to rest my head in the slums tonight, or worse still, share a bunk with a sailor."

"You never know, you might enjoy it," giggled Heliana

Thias did not rise to the bait. Minutes later the lechery of priests huddled at the bottom of the Banshees Wail gangplank while Thias raced up onto the deck of the vessel. Soon he scuttled back again with Theoplous Danmar close behind. As the sailor reached the dockside he was immediately surrounded by those he had come to join. Llyat squeezed Heliana's hand as Father Lachesis thrust a folded habit into Theoplous's arms. Thias ordered the sailor to put it on over his clothes and when the group pulled back the sailor had disappeared and been replaced by yet another priest.

"Never did I imagine I would wear such a garment," said the sailor as he laughed.

"Where is you rowing boat Lachesis?" asked Llyat as the group began to draw the attention of several slum dwellers who lurked with prying eyes. "I think we need to move for our presence here is being monitored."

"I agree," said Thias.

"Thieves and scum," whispered Theoplous. "Some of Underscroft's boys I guess."

"Father, where to next?" asked Thias.

"Follow me, it's down at the end of the Jetty, beyond the Masters Catch," answered the priest.

"That's the very same spot where I pulled you from the river," whispered Irabo as they moved forward. "Who would have thought back then what lay before us? I just wish that Tonousa was here with us now. She should have been with us to the end. If I ever get to meet with the Moirai then I will ask them why she had to die. She may have not believed in the Fates, but still..."

"I am sure her essence is with us and that she is looking out for us," interrupted Llyat. "Even in death, she remains in our hearts."

"Perhaps so," said Irabo and Llyat noted the tears that welled in the warrior's eyes.

"Come let us leave this place. We have much work to do," he ordered as he led Irabo by the arm down to the end of the jetty.

In stealth and at speed the secretive party at last reached their destination. The group had gathered by the rope ladder that dropped down into an old boat besides one of the pier supports.

"Master Irabo, you sit in the prow," said Father Lachesis. "Young woman, you go in next and sit on the plank behind Irabo."

"My names is Heliana," she tutted.

"I know that already young lady," the priest added. "You must forgive the formality for old customs die long. I have had few dealings with women given the vows of celibacy I swore during my formative years. Now, if you would be so kind, take your seat for we must depart before the tide turns."

Heliana winked and Llyat smiled back as his soul mate began her descent into the vessel.

"Sailor, if you could go in next with Father Atropos and sit beside the oars with him," ordered Lachesis. "I hope you do not object to sharing the rowing. Being a sailor I assume you will be the most proficient of us. Atropos has done it a few times but is still somewhat of a novice."

The mute priest looked at his companion and tapped his chest with his hand. Lachesis responded to the gesture.

"The mute wishes to demonstrate that he is worthy of joining your quest."

"Sure, no problem," replied Theoplous. "'I'll be delighted to assist and I will teach your brother the best technique; it is after all what I do for a living."

Llyat noted the scowl that formed on Father Atropos's face and decided that once alone with Lachesis he would get to the bottom of why the two constantly sniped at each other. The last thing he needed was two feuding friars given the enormity of the task ahead.

"When you have said your farewells to the bard," said Lachesis as he stepped onto the ladder, "come sit beside me at the rear of the boat while I steer for there are things we should discuss. You may also have many questions to ask of me."

Lachesis then disappeared from view without waiting for an answer. Danger stalked Llyat's thoughts as he focused on how he would protect Heliana and her baby. Whatever the Fates threw his way, he would be ready of it. When all were aboard save for Llyat, the youth turned to the bard and the pair embraced one final time on the dockside. Then as they pulled away Llyat spoke:

"I wish you could come with us Thias but I understand your reasons. Any time you can buy me away from prying eyes of the Lord of Fear will be much appreciated. I wish you good fortune in the battle to come. Wars are dangerous and brutal affairs; that much I know from the memories Sir Raulyn has passed down to me. My path ahead is also full of dangers and I don't know if I will ever see you again. I must thank you for all you have done for me."

"My plan is too good not to succeed Llyat," answered Thias. "Do not grow restless through anxiety caused by my predicament. I have chosen my course and I look forward to thwarting Urthanock's attempts to take this city. Who knows, I may yet meet the Lord of Fear himself. Now, you must speed on to the Oracle and demand that they speak the truth."

The bard paused and his voice became serious.

"I know what you intend to do with Heliana and her unborn but we must not stand here and argue even though I disagree with that part of your plan If you find some way to avoid that unspeakable deed then please seize the opportunity."

"What the fuck are you talking about Thias?" demanded Llyat.

"You know what I mean lad, I will not speak of it here lest my words travel on the breeze to her ears. The whole Realm looks to you to deliver the outcome of the Prophecy. Do not let us down. Now get into the boat and leave before it is too late."

Llyat wanted to stay and discuss the bards concerns but he knew it would serve little purpose and so into the vessel he dropped. It immediately pushed off from the pier and began its short voyage to the opposite shore of the Estuary of New Beginnings. While the wooden hull slipped with grace through the water Llyat heard Thias's last words float over the brine and slip into his ears.

"Once the battle is over and should I survive it, then I will follow and find you."

The priest's boat made soft ripples in the water as a light mist began to form in the estuary. The travellers passed in silence save for the whispered conversation that passed between Llyat and Lachesis. Irabo and Heliana stared out across the vast extent of water and as the tide began to turn they focused their attention on the wooded shoreline of the distant bank. Theoplous and Atropos feathered their oars over the water with the silence of a ghost ship. The First Mate was the most proficient but the priest soon improved as he mirrored the actions of his companion.

"I have never heard the names Lachesis and Atropos before," began Llyat as he turned to the old man beside him. "Did you make them up? Are they your real names?"

"They are titles we chose for ourselves. They fit better with the faith that we follow."

"What were your real names?" asked Llyat. "What were those you were born with?"

"We do not speak of them to anyone for they are no longer of relevance. Yours too is an interesting name Llyat. I sense it is an old one, passed down from the time of the Ancients. My studies tell me that its root is from the old word Edling which means 'noble child'. This is what happens as time drifts ever on like this river; names get distorted."

"That's very interesting but I guess I will never know if that is true," replied Llyat. "Had you been studying my origins before you met me?"

"Of course, ever since we became aware of your presence."

"And when was that?"

"A long time ago lad," answered the priest. "From the day, young Irabo pulled you from the Tiaryer and dragged you into the city, Atropos and I have also been monitoring the Cuvar and their conspiracy. When necessary we pointed them in the right direction with a small clue here and a coincidence there. Xix Blackfayer had..."

"I would like to understand more of what you hint at," interrupted Llyat. "You dangle half-truths and yet I sense you are reluctant to tell all. What else is there I should know?"

"Not now, maybe once your quest is over."

Llyat made as if to speak, but the priest raised his hand and Llyat relented.

"Let us change the subject of our discussion. You must come to understand there are things you cannot learn until your mind has travelled far enough to recognise the truth of what is being said."

"I'm going to get nowhere if you keep talking shit like that," moaned Llyat.

The youth looked up to the night sky and smiled as Mona broke through the cloud cover.

"So, if you won't speak of my history then tell me more about yourself. How long have you and Atropos been followers of Fatumai and why has your friend decided never to speak? Has he lost his tongue?"

Lachesis smiled and placed his hand on Llyat's shoulder.

"Let me first tell you of Atropos," he began. "I will whisper such that only you can hear. My fellow brother still has acute hearing and he is a little sensitive when others discuss his life."

"As am I" interrupted Llyat as he rolled his eyes.

"Quite so! Atropos was left in a basket upon the steps of the Temple when no more than a day old. He has known no other life. For some reason that he has never wanted to explain, he chose not to speak. This happened way back in his formative years and the messages he sends out on parchment never explain the true reasons behind his decision. This lack of verbal communication has allowed him to focus his learning and he has become a master in all things relating to the Ancients. He is well versed in their history, the cult of Fatumai, and her daughters. Yet there is another who knows even more than Atropos and you must meet him before your confrontation with the Moirai. He holds some of the truths you so long to hear."

Llyat closed his eyes and pondered. This had to be the hermit that Thias had mentioned.

"So, who is this other that I must seek and where will I find him," asked Llyat.

"His name is Clotho and he was one of our order until some forty years ago when he decided to isolate himself from the world and study the meaning of life from observations of both the earth and the heavens. He is the only one alive who can give you the knowledge you will need to begin your search for the door to the Underworld."

"I thought that was why I was going to see the Moirai."

"The Holy Three can be mischievous and fickle," mumbled the priest. "They may or may not decide to talk with you. I understand from the bard that they have communicated to you through your dreams. If this true, then I expect them to at least agree to a meeting. Legend says the Moirai will ask you a riddle which you must work out and answer before they will reveal the knowledge that you seek.

Clotho must prepare you for such a riddle for he alone knows how their minds think."

"This is getting more ridiculous by the day," snorted Llyat. "Why does it a l have to be so fucking complicated? Life was once so simple."

"This is the way it must be. Clotho will reveal all, especially if he hasn't got around to wearing clothes! The habit he wore on leaving Parandor fell from his back years ago, and the last time I met with him he was walking around naked. That was about ten years ago..."

"What was the purpose of your last visit?" probed Llyat.

"Atropos and I met with him to discuss the implications of your arrival in Parandor."

"What!" exclaimed Llyat?

"The Historian had turned up with you in tow, a boy of eight years. The Cuvar cult, led by Enguerrand Fullbane, were sniffing around you like dogs on heat and Clotho was most interested to hear that news. We have been watching you from a distance ever since but I will speak no more of Clotho at this time. Any questions you think of from now on, you must ask him. You will find him most accommodating if like us he believes you to be the Marked."

Llyat looked to the front of the small vessel. Theoplous and Atropos continued their skilful rowing as Lachesis held the rudder and pointed the vessel towards the fast-approaching shore. At the bow Llyat noted that Heliana had put her arm around Irabo as the pair looked beyond the water and out into their uncertain futures.

"Before we leave this boat, please tell me about yourself Father; how did you become a follower of the Fates," asked Llyat. "Were you born in Falahorr? I ask because that's where Irabo is from and he swears by the will of The Three."

"No lad, I am not from Falahorn. I have been in the order since I was ten years old. My father was a chandler and part of his work was to supply the Temple of Fatumai with the candles they required for the worship of our deity. He was not a follower of the faith but I used to visit the temple with him as he conducted his business. I always enjoyed going there and one day I spotted some cards that had been left on a small table to one side of the inner sanctum. I began to look through them and was fascinated by their images. Then, while my father was busy in the crypts below the temple, three old priests asked me if I wanted to see how the cards worked. I had no idea at that time that they were about to play Fortunes Fate with my soul but that is what they did. By the end of the game three cards had been revealed.

"And which three had been chosen?" asked Llyat.

"The Inquisitor, Selflessness, and the Priest."

"And what did they mean for you? Is that why you joined your Order?" said Llyat.

"I cannot tell and you shouldn't ask. Each man's destiny is his own.'

Llyat went on to describe the end of his time inside the Wizards Guild, how he too had found a pack of similar cards, and had dropped them to the floor. He told that only three had been revealed to him and that he had at once replaced them back with the rest.

"That's very interesting," replied Lachesis. "Tell me just as I have told you, which three cards did you turn up?"

"Truth, The Cutter, and The Lover," answered Llyat with a calmness that surprised the priest.

"Speak of this to no one other than Clotho, and not even him should he not ask."

"Why? Are these games for real? Should I believe in this message?"

"That is for you to decide lad," replied Lachesis "The choice must be yours alone."

The boat ran aground on a sandbank some thirty paces from the shore.

"Right, everyone out," shouted Irabo. "We will wade in from here and carry the boat between us. Then we will hide it in the bushes beyond the beach in anticipation of our return."

The lands south of the estuary contained the greatest oak woods in the Realm. The gnarled trees had first been planted by the Ancients, or so the bards had sung for a thousand years. As the centuries had passed other trees had found their way into parts of the great forest that swept up before the Howling Hills but most were still oak. The vast expanse of woodland covered the flat land and some of the north facing slopes of the long range of hillocks. It was said by the few who had tramped the through woods that it would take a full week to walk from east to west and yet but a couple of days on the ridge path above the tree line. In parts the oak woods were so dense that no one ever ventured inside them, all that is except the hermit Clotho.

Once they had secured their boat and concealed it under a covering of brushwood, Llyat and Lachesis lead the party of six on down the track that led towards the Howling Hills and beyond those mounds to the Badlands. The Marked had asked the priest how they would locate the hermit amongst the congested forest in the depth of a dark night. He had been told not to worry for there was a large boulder with a witching sign chiselled onto its surface half a day's journey along the trail. At the rock, they would all turn to the east and enter the thickest part of the woods. Clotho would be aware of their presence long before the group sensed his; he would be waiting for them.

The trek from the estuary was both slow and arduous. The track was narrow and although once straight it now deviated through and around clumps of trees that had taken root upon the seldom used road. After the first league Heliana moved forward to link Llyat by the arm for she said she was frightened by the whistling noises made by the trees and the snorts of the animals that hid within them. Llyat understood how she felt for as Mona cast her light upon the thick and twisted trunks it seemed as if faces were embedded in their woody bark. Heliana reckoned that there must be real people trapped inside the ancient trees but Llyat would have none of such fantasies. His new found confidence eased Heliana's fears.

The dark and treacherous walk continued through the night while the strange noises grew ever louder. Most of the woodland creatures seemed to be on the move, some no doubt were looking for a kill. Lachesis who had travelled this path before was able to recognise many of the sounds and put a name to the animals and birds that created them. Those he identified included badger, deer, boar, fox, owl, woodcock and goose. There were plenty that the priest did not recognise and their voice caused Heliana to tremble and grip Llyat's arm even tighter. There was one that Llyat recognised himself for he had heard it often enough in Maplehill. It was the distinctive cry of the skyfawn, somewhere away in the distance. At least he had not heard sign of the scuttling kulkulkath said to roam some of the more remote vales of the Howling Hills. Nor did he detect any of the grunts of the mighty mathulath who Denius Castor, amid one drunken stupor, had said turned aggressive during the night. Heliana revealed her childhood fear of wolves and bears but Lachesis reassured her that of recent such beasts confined themselves to the southern slopes of the hills. Llyat prayed that was still the case.

As the morning broke and the clouds moved away, Solaris cast light upon the forest trail which grew clearer as dawn flourished. The weary wanderers stumbled upon a great stone boulder to the left-hand side of the dirt track. It was coated in lichen and part covered by an accumulation of fern. There chiselled into the rock was a fire pointed star overlying three circles that resembled the brand mark of Kha.

"This is the stone I told you about last night," said Lachesis as he pointed the sign out to Llyat and then to the others.

"It's a pity Thias isn't here, he would have liked to see that," chipped in Irabo. "He is fascinated by all that ancient writing kind of shit."

"This is like the runes we saw in Barad Elestor," added Llyat.

"I see!" said the priest as he dismissed the comments. "Perhaps you will get to tell him of it one day. Look, see over there, Atropos has already entered the thickest of the forest. Come, let us follow at once for we must not get separated."

The six intrepid explorers had not walked more that fifteen minutes amongst the dense forest before they stumbled upon an area the size of small house that had been cleared of vegetation. In its centre lay a single old oak trunk that had been carved into the form of a seat. Upon the wood sat a very old man in the strangest clothes that Llyat had ever seen. But at least he wasn't naked.

Lachesis stepped forward and made his way towards the stranger. They whispered together for several minutes until at last Llyat was summoned to greet the one he assumed to be Clotho. As he approached he looked at the bizarre clothes that the hermit had chosen to wear. His wizen limbs and body were covered in a tight fitting single suit of green-brown wool. Llyat assumed it had been spun from the coat of sheep and dyed to give it is distinctive colour; one that matched that of the bark of a young oak tree. The wool had then been knitted to produce vertical ribbing that reminded Llyat of the grain he had seen on oak planks back on old Chirth Hardra's farm. It was when he noticed what the man wore on his head and feet that Llyat realised what hermit had tried to recreate. Atop of his head and made from similar wool he wore a tight-fitting bonnet with a stiff tail that pointed backwards. There was no doubt as to what it represented. It was an acorn cup and the man's face with its sallow complexion was the acorn itself. It was a remarkable living representation of the ancient oaks under which the hermit lived out his days and studied the natural world. Llyat's eyes wandered down to Clotho's shoes, made from green dyed leather with spare flaps of material sewn onto its uppers, all cut in the distinctive shape of oak leaves.

"Great clothes," said Llyat as he approached the hermit.

"I think so too," Clotho replied. "Lachesis tells me that you are the Marked, the one spoken of in the Enderdetag Prophecy. It appears he is taking you to Harico where you intend to meet with the Moirai. Is that true lad?"

"My name is Llyat and yes it is true. If you know the Prophecy you will also understand what I have to do. I carry with me the five Gems of Thamous, those created by the Wyvern that lives no more. The Moirai ought to be able to tell me how I may weld the five Gems I carry into the key that will once again seal the Underworld. There I must destroy Urthanock for all time."

"Those I must see; show me them now so that I can believe you to be the one sent by Raulyn."

Llyat pulled his travelling bag from off his shoulders and placed it on the earth before the man-tree. He delved inside and from out of its top pulled the smaller shoulder bag that Thias had brought with him from Avolire. One by one he pulled out the precious objects that few had ever seen. Each passed through Clotho's soil engrained hands and the first to do so was the sceptre of Urthanock. Before leaving Parandor Llyat had wrapped a small cloth around the diamond at its head and which he whipped off for less than a second before replacing it.

"It is too dangerous to stare at the stone," said Llyat. "I was told by one I trust that the Vessel that now carries Urthanock spent too much time looking into the stone's milky depths."

"I have heard legends that speak that same truth," replied Clotho without further challenge. "So this is the Seer's stone, an item of great torment from times long past."

Llyat dipped into the shoulder bag and pulled out the dagger of Kha. He passed it over to the hermit who examined its emeralds with even greater interest. Then it was the turn of the sapphire from Raulyn's axe, then the ruby necklace, and at last the amethyst.

"Thamous told me that the sapphire has the power to keep me hidden such that Urthanock cannot detect my presence," said Llyat as he collected the gems and replaced them into his bag.

"I sense there is another object you have yet to show me," said the hermit. "What is it that you hide from my old eyes?"

"A Dragon Whisper, cloaked inside a lead trinket box. It is part of our plan to deceive Urthanock. I am happy to share that plan if you then tell me all that I need to know to enable an audience with the Moirai."

"So be it, but first I need to get you to Harico undetected," said Clotho. "You must gather your party together for time is of the essence. Follow me in silence for even the forest has ears. We will walk for four hours after which we will stop to rest and eat. There must be no dawdling for we have a great distance to cover before we reach the glade of the most sacred oak, the one on which the mistletoe grows and which legend says was planted by Sir Raulyn himself in memory of the mother of his child. There as we rest I will tell you all that you need to know.

One last thing, the girl who is with child; do you intend taking her with you to meet the Holy Three?"

"I do!" replied Llyat.

"I guessed so!" replied Clotho as he shrugged his shoulders and cast a scowl.

A short time after Solaris had scaled the zenith of his transit Clotho led the group of six into the sacred grove of the oaks. The march through the forest had been most bizarre. Gaps between the mighty trees seemed to form and close in response to Clotho's will and not one of the group believed they would be able to find their way back to the witching stone. Llyat immediately realised the value of this route; it would be impossible for anyone to follow his trail. Thias had indeed been smart when devising this part of the journey. Once in the sacred grove Heliana, Irabo, and Theoplous sat together under the shade of one of the majestic oaks at the edge of the glade. Lachesis sat a few paces away with Atropos and as they ate they communicated with their hands in a language that only they could interpret.

Llyat had been called to sit with Clotho under the oldest tree he had ever seen and the one from which the mistletoe grew. It was across the glade from his friends for the hermit said that his words were only for the Marked. Heliana had protested and despite Llyat stating he was happy for her to hear all, Clotho had been most insistent that it was just Llyat that heard what he had to say. Once seated next to the Clotho, Llyat rummaged inside his bag and pulled out a selection of bread, cheese, and meats that he offered to share with his new teacher. Clotho declined the fine food for it was not what his stomach was used to eating. Instead he munched upon a handful of acorns and dried wild berries that he had carried with him under his unusual bonnet. Once both had eaten their fill, Clotho pulled out an old and frayed parchment which he proceeded to lay on the grass before Llyat's feet.

"Concentrate and remember all," began the old hermit. "Here s what you must know and understand if you are to succeed in your quest. Let me first ask you a question; do you have any knowledge of geometry?"

Llyat stared at the strange symbols on the parchment and was bewildered.

"Not a clue." he exclaimed. "I have never heard of 'jommy-tree' and my writing skills are shite. My father kept me away from all learning although my mother did from time to time try to teach me to read a little."

"Pity!" replied Clotho. "Never mind."

Something most unusual then began inside Llyat's head. Memories that had been passed down through generations began to pop up and impregnate the youth's thoughts. As the seconds passed they coalesced into a meaningful message.

"The mind block that my father placed on me was unlocked by Icotrix of the Wizards Guild," blurted out Llyat. "Because of that I now have some understanding of what this geometry is all about."

The youth stared down at the parchment and the symbols meaning became clear.

"Shit, I can read it," he giggled. "How in the name of Solaris did that that happen."

"Strange indeed. You are without doubt the most interesting person I have met in a very long time," replied Clotho who then wasted no time in explaining his drawing. "Do you see the three circles lad?"

"Yes I do."

"Have you seen anything like this before?"

"They are the like the Mark of Kha that my friend Thias often talks about," replied Llyat. "The one that was found on all the victims of that shapeshifter who disguised himself as the Fool."

"Indeed. Have you seen them anywhere else?"

"I am not so certain, but they are similar to the birth mark that my best friend Methladon Heyn carried on the back of his neck until the day he was killed by the Knights of Avolire."

"I see; that is also interesting," continued Clotho. "This information before you is but a snippet of the secret teachings of the Ancients and those that followed them. It has taken me a life time of studying the stars and reading the runes they left hidden in the ground to create this one page of vital information. All of this I did for the time when the Marked would reveal himself to the bards."

"It doesn't look much," replied Llyat although he guessed that was about to change.

"This is a projection of the Realm onto what is called a map Llyat. The Ancients surveyed these lands a long time ago when they first journeyed over the seas. They did not build willy-nilly and most of the settlements that you know of today grew from places that fitted in to their heaven sent design. They worshipped Solaris and the movements of their Lord reflected what they saw on the ground. Do you see how the lines from the centre points of each circle create a perfect triangle with three sides of equal length? Do you recognise anything else interesting about those three points?"

"Yes I do, I'm not that thick!" snapped back Llyat. "The Ancient's home, Barad Elestor, is at the apex point of what looks like and arrowhead. The other two points were of relevance to my quest; the Gathering where I met with the wyvern Thamous, and Harico where I intend to question the Moirai."

"Would you not agree it is an interesting alignment? Now look at the line that drops from Barad Elestor through the midpoint of the bottom line of the triangle. Do you see how it passes through places you know of, including your home of Maplehill? That line then travels out into the far distant ocean. I hope you can see that. Look, the line points to the Lotus Isles. This is a direction finder. Follow that line in a seagoing vessel for a month and you come to those islands. They are too far away to be shown on this small map. In fact, they are so far south that Solaris shines bright there every day. The people there have coloured skin like your sailor friend."

Llyat glanced up to where Theoplous sat and then refocused on the map.

"It's quite interesting that Barad Elestor, Avolire, Griginor, Maple Hill and Parandor all sit on that same line. I guess it's just one of those freaky things that happen from time to time. I guess it's just a coincidence."

"No Llyat, it is all deliberate, although the Cuvar would argue otherwise," said Clotho. "Search your forefathers' memory and tell me if you know what is meant by a solstice line."

Llyat paused and thought "It's something to do with Solaris at a certain time of the year."

"Yes, you are on the right track lad. I will try and explain," began Clotho. "Having worked on a farm you will have noticed how the seasons change. Solaris rises in a slightly different place each day as the seasons of the year progress. On the longest day of each year, in the middle of our summer, Solaris's progression stands still. After that day, the direction of Solaris's rising is reversed. The Ancients, being devotes of the great yellow disc, knew this and built Barad Elestor in a direct line from the rising of Solaris on that one day of the year to the Lotus Isles across the vast ocean. You see lad, that's where the Ancients came from. If you thought your ancestors a thousand years ago were white skinned, then be prepared to be shocked. Those Ancients did not come from the east as is told in the history of the Realm. They were a dark race and their home was the Lotus Isles."

"No fucking way!" exclaimed Llyat.

"It's a pity Rukave Emgar failed to give you a vocabulary to match your status!" snorted Clotho. "Have you understood what I am trying to tell you? The portal that you must close is somewhere on the Lotus Isles. It is not just how to weld the Gems that you need from the Holy Three; you need their help in finding where on those islands the portal has remained hidden from the knowledge of men."

"I think I understand all you are saying," said Llyat after a moment of reflection.

"There is more of this geometry that you must understand..."

Llyat glanced to his friends and then to the two priests who had delivered him to the great forest below the Howling Hills. As all were content he refocused on what Clotho had to say.

"Once you reach the Barrow of Harico you must descend into the bowels of the earth. I will deliver you to the outskirts of the old town but then Lachesis, Atropos, and I will leave you and return to our work. You and your three colleagues must then go on alone. Once underground you must pass beneath the cave that houses the remains of the ancient wood folk. Then you will need to locate the 'Corridors of Traps", a devious maze that guards the 'Chambers of the Risen'. Both those places you will need to negotiate before you can get to speak with the Moirai."

"Will the two be easy to locate and what will I meet down there?" asked Llyat as he tried to avoid dwelling on the perils that lay ahead.

"I cannot give you more detail for I know nothing more. There is however something else that may help you and your friends survive the journey."

"Then tell me that secret for that is why I am here," answered Llyat.

"Of course, and that is my purpose also," said Clotho as his bony index finger once again pointed to the old parchment. "Do you see where the three circles meet? They form a shape. It is like a triangle with lines that curve inwards. You see it now, don't you?"

"But what is its meaning?" asked Llyat.

"According to the ancient texts that were chiselled into stones that I unearthed as I searched these lands, this symbol is said to be the shape of the portal to the Underworld. This is the door you must locate and seal with the gems that you carry."

"I thought it was somewhere else, not down there with the Moirai," said Llyat as he rubbed his chin and tried to recall what he had been told just seconds earlier.

"As I have already said, the ancient runes talk of it being somewhere on the Lotus Isles and they mention two other phrases that you should try and remember. The first is as follows: *'One day the Marked shall come and seek out the Lords of Light.'* I do not know what that means but I understand your sailor friend is from the Lotus Isles. He should be able to take you there to continue your search. I also expect the Moirai will explain more if you can persuade them to talk."

"I understand that and will discuss this over with Theo once I have met with the three crones. Sorry, I meant no offence in calling them that."

"None taken. The second was as follows: *'First the Marked must face the fire, high above the clouds in secret Bryngaer Henuriaid'*. Again I know no more. Ask the Moirai if you dare."

"Then at least answer one question," continued Llyat. "How does the incurved triangle help me negotiate the Corridors of Traps and the Chambers of the Risen?"

The hermit Clotho paused for moment, inhaled and then spoke again, his voice softer yet more serious with each word uttered.

"There have been other brave souls who have made the same journey before you. Their intent was to leave signposts for you, the Marked, to follow. They were the bravest of the brave for none ever returned. There are runes that tell the names of the many who contributed to the task. It is written that they etched the incurved triangle upon the rock as direction finders at various points on the path to the Moirai. All you need do is locate the signs that they left for you."

"So, I just look for the strange triangles and follow them?"

"Exactly!"

"Who were these brave souls that sacrificed their lives to help me on my quest?"

"This is how it has been told for hundreds of years and it is most interesting," continued the smiling hermit. "Those who left the marks on the rocks in anticipation of your visit called themselves after the curved lines of the triangle. For a long time, they were known in secret circles as the 'Curved' or 'Guardians of the Arc', but over the years that changed and those who followed this particular faith became known as the 'Curvre'. As many more years passed they became what they are today, the Cuvar."

"Fuck!" exclaimed Llyat. "I cannot wait to tell Thias that. He will be astounded."

"Quite!" replied Clotho as his eyebrows lifted.

"But there is something that has been puzzling me ever since you showed me the three circles," said Llyat. "Why did the ancients choose the circle Mark of

Kha as the basis for their sacred geometry? It seems strange to pick a representation of evil when trying to be a force for good."

"I cannot answer that lad. It is something that has also worried me for many years. I did once think that each of the three circles represented one of the Moirai but that was just speculation on my part."

Llyat tried to process the information he had been given and to make sense of it all. While he struggled he noted that his companions were back on their feet.

"I see my friends are beginning to stir and are ready to move on," said Llvat as he looked across the glade. "Is there anything else you need to tell me before set off?"

"There are two further gifts I will give you. First off, you must remember this map and its geometry as best you can. It has always been whispered that the Moirai will test the Marked with a riddle. If you do not answer it as they intend then you will fail in your quest for they will not then let you back into this Middle Realm."

"And what is the riddle?" asked Llyat in hope of an easy answer.

"I do not know what the riddle is nor what the answer could be," said Clotho. "The runes talk of it being linked to the sacred geometry and that is why you must study this parchment. Without its hidden knowledge, you will go no further. You will also need to keep your wits about you for the riddle will not be easy to solve. I suggest you search through the unlocked memory of your blood line and listen to all that it tells you about circles and triangles."

"And what is the second gift you have for me?" asked Llyat at once.

"If and when the Moirai release you and your sailor delivers you to the Lotus Isles then be prepared for a further test. The runes suggest you will be asked for a code. What form that will take I do not know. I suspect it will have something to do with the Lords of Light and the place called Bryngaer Henuriaid. Perhaps it is a code from a Cuvar wheel, a circle, a triangle, or may be something very different."

"One last question if I may Clotho," said Llyat as he lifted his travel bag onto his shoulders. "I sense a great father-like reassurance when I am in your presence; did you ever have children yourself.

"One boy, a very long time ago. He went off to seek his fortune and never came back."

"Did he have a name? I mean of course a real name, not made up ones like you and the two priests use," asked Llyat.

"He was called Denius Castor and I miss him very much."

Clotho turned before he could witness Llyat's jaw drop.

"Come, we must away to Harico," shouted the hermit who dressed like a tree.

In the late evening of the second day, the group of six emerged from the great oak forest to the north of Harico. At intervals throughout the trek Llyat had shared much of what he had learned with Heliana. He kept certain key points to himself however and never once told her of the dangers they would face beneath the Barrow of Harico. He deemed it best that his lover stood before the Moirai in a state of ignorance rather than one of heightened terror. During periods when the group had stopped to rest Theoplous shared a little of basic geometric knowledge he had picked up as a seafarer. The sailor's skill in navigation helped Llyat to a greater understanding of the inherited memories that now filled most of his thoughts. As night fell they stared at the distant lights of the ancient town which twinkled in the dark of yet another lonely night. Clotho, Lachesis, and Atropos communicated their farewells in their own unique manner and in an instant the three were gone.

"I think we should stay under cover of the treeline until morning," suggested Irabo. "It will be much easier to do the right thing by the light of Solaris.

"I agree," replied Llyat and with that said the remaining four prepared to spend one last night amongst the root beds of the ancient oaks.

Llyat held Heliana in his arms and from time to time stroked her swollen belly. When his hand felt the tremble of his unborn child's movement, tears welled in his eyes. It took great resolve not to think of the dangers ahead and the evils he would force Heliana to endure. Sleep was slow in coming.

13

It should have been the blackest of nights for the snow leaden clouds sat low and the surrounding mountains seemed intent on strangling the ancient town. Yet from where he sat on his horse the distant buildings were visible and outlined. Fires that raged from its centre cast a blood-orange glow over the settlement, melting what snow had had already dropped on the low rooves. A distinct aroma drifted on the air and it caused the Lizardmen warriors to open up their snouts and drool. Urthanock watched and witnessed the ash plumes as they rose high into the night sky and he knew at once what was cooking. The smell was the distinctive mix of meat and bowel gas that that always lingers when a great number of people are incinerated at the same time. It was obvious to the Lord over Fear that the ogres dispatched by the Lady of the Silverwynn were busy.

Urthanock watched, sniffed, and savoured the destruction of a people he had never met, knew nothing of, nor had ever wronged him. Yet inside his warped and depraved mind, one that now teetered on the brink of total madness, none of that seemed to matter. Those that were being slaughtered were of the man race and that's all that was important. A string that held his mind together then snapped. Urthanock, the personification of the foulest of the foul, sat in his majesty on his frightened horse and laughed out into the night.

"My Lord, Bane of Dragons, what is it that causes you so much merriment?" asked Ssonsh.

The appointed Hochnar of the Eastern Marsh sat next to his Lord atop of his snorting steed.

"You have no idea Toad how much pleasure it gives me to witness the destruction of men. But what you see out there is nothing compared to what I will bring to the gates of Parandor. It will not be long before I rest on the marble throne and declare my rule over these lands of the Middle World. None who are of the man race must be allowed to live. I will rid the realm of their sort for they are the most base of all species, the very excrement of the gods."

"And yet you travel in your Vessel, one who was of their kind," replied Ssonsh. "Will that not be an issue if all others are destroyed?"

Urthanock turned, glared, and forced the toad to avert his eyes.

"Do not push your luck, Hochnar. Once I have destroyed Parandor and the Marked, opened the portal to connect the dimensions, and freed my remaining essence from the infinite dark, I will take on another form. I will become like Kha himself for during my enforced incarceration the Black Lord as good as promised me that honour. Once fully formed I will take on the pious rulers of the Heavens. It is my destiny to unite the three dimensions."

Urthanock turned to expose the flesh of his neck that had been covered under his half helm.

"Tell me toad, what do you understand of the Mark of Kha that is etched onto the neck of this Vessel?

"I am not sure that I follow you," replied Ssonsh. "Can you clarify what you want me to understand? I do not want to interpret your words in an inappropriate way, given that you may ask me to share such insights with your army."

"A bold statement toad," huffed Urthanock. "This information is for you alone Hochnar. Of all the scale covered shits that I lead, you are the one I trust the most; you and the Gator Lord. I need you to understand something important. The three circles of the brand represent the three dimensions of existence; the Heavens where most of the gods the pass their time in play, in drunken fuck fests, and all other manner of perverted debaucheries; the Middle World where the living creatures irk out their pathetic existences, fighting each day to survive while an elite few live off the fat of the land; and the Underworld where Kha rules over the spirits of the departed and the collective evil built over an infinite number of reincarnations. Then there are the three."

"What three?" croaked Ssonsh, his voice stumbling.

"The old crones, the daughters of the Fickle Fate, they who transcend the three dimensions. Look at my mark. See the strange curved triangle in the middle, it represents the Moirai who I intend to seek out and destroy. Then I will take possession of that sacred central space and all shall then be mine."

"I see," replied the frog creature as it moved in close to examine its Lord's neck. "I am pleased that you mean this information for my ears alone for tripe-talk of gods would unhinge our troops."

"It matters not what the reptiles of the gruesome gods think," guffawed Urthanock.

"Forgive me Lord, but time moves on. We cannot sit here all night looking to the flames of Griginor. What orders do you have for me?"

The Lord over Fear stared towards the burning town and smiled.

"Take a hundred or so reptiles and race ahead. Scout out what has transpired there and find the ogres. I want to reward them myself, but also ensure they move on and clear out the Old Pass. They may well be tempted to desert for many times past they fucked off before the fighting proper began. That is of course unless they are doing that already. Find out if anything useful remains that we can salvage before we move through this town."

"I obey Lord and with your permission will leave at once," replied Ssonsh as his limbs trembled.

"Good, so do it now. I will lead the army to the centre of Griginor and make camp."

Ssonsh turned his horse around and departed at speed. Urthanock looked towards the burning buildings in the distance as the familiar voice returned.

"I will destroy you, in the end."

An hour later Urthanock stood in the middle of the ancient town while surveying its burning structures. His army had fanned out, unordered but with their Lord's consent, to loot, to pillage, and to slaughter. From the screams of men, women and children, it was obvious that some citizens had escaped the initial assault of the ogres. Those who had stayed in the city would not live to witness the dawn. As time passed Urthanock grew impatient, frustrated that Ssonsh had not yet brought him news of the whereabouts of General Brozisrug and his ogres. He pulled five Lizardmen to one side and ordered them to seek out his Hochnar. A reward of promotion was offered to the first to find his pet toad but he also threatened them should they fail in their task. Urthanock's knot awaited the quintet should they return without the frog-priest by the time he had erected his tent. The Lizardmen trembled but set about their task, dividing the city in to sectors, and leaving the central square in agreed directions.

Urthanock tied his horse to a hook that had been attached for that same purpose to a statue in the centre of the main square. For several minutes he looked at the cast of the figure with more than a passing interest for he had little else to do but to prepare his camp. The depiction was that of a man, cast in bronze and placed above a marble plinth about half of Urthanock's height. He guessed that he had been once of historic importance for he wore a hat and a chain of the type popular amongst those of the man race who called themselves mayor. He would not have given the statue a second glance had his eyes not then focused on the sword that hung from its waist. He tapped his own with his hand for the one he had brought from Avolire was identical to that on the figure before him. His sword could also have been forged in Griginor but perhaps that would be too much of a coincidence. Then in a moment of deep reflection, Urthanock stepped forward to touch the statue. The first step his right foot made crunched on some small animal. When his eyes looked to his boot he saw the flattened residue of a gecko while a dozen others darted into nearby hiding holes. His lips snapped into a sick affected smile for this was just the beginning of the destruction he was about to unleash upon the world.

Urthanock was adept at erecting his tent for it was something he had practiced often during his first incarnation and battles with the Ancients. He had forgotten little during the aeons of his incarceration. His Vessel carried out the work with significant efficiency for it too had knowledge of such shelters from the time it had spent protecting the lands around the Tiaryer. The Vessel had passed many a night with its father and brothers amongst the open grasslands south of the river.

Soon the rough and ready canvass shelter, slung over two vertical staves and anchored to the floor with rocks, stood erect and proud beside the ancient statue. Urthanock fed his horse with a bucket of meal and another of water which he had drawn from a nearby hand pump. This beast needed care, at least until t had borne him before the walls of Parandor. He made a fire from some wood that he took from one of his army's supply carts, constructed his pot holder over it and began to prepare his evening meal. Into the pot of water that sat above the fire he placed a handful of twisted turnips, wild garlic, and some strips of human flesh that his sword had sliced from the leg of one of the ogres' recent kills. He adjusted the height of his pot once the water began to boil, raising it such that the mixture would then simmer. Finally he fixed its lid to contain the goodness of his soup. With everything done he soon became bored and so it was that Urthanock decided to take a walk, stretch his legs, and gaze upon the destruction left in the wake of the ogres sweep through the town. A tour of the devastation would help fuel his appetite.

The foul Lord's feet set off in a random direction. It was in fact south but he was unaware of that fact for he was lost in his thoughts. He began to think and plan on the destruction of Parandor and how his victory would be accomplished.

Wandering through close packed buildings he at last came upon another small square. So far he had yet to see any ogres but here was at least evidence of their work. The centre of the open space was a very antechamber to the underworld. There before him were the dead of the Griginor, those at least who had not yet been incinerated. It was a masterpiece of ogre artwork and a sight that brought a great smile to the uncovered half of his face. Twelve makeshift crucifixes had been erected and onto each a naked elder of the city had been nailed. All were dead but Urthanock guessed that Cutter had not come in haste. He decided in that moment to replicate the foul monument to murder once he had taken in Parandor, but on a grander scale. This was how the pompous highborn would end their days in fitting recognition of his power over their pathetic lives.

Around the tight knot of crucifixes, a circle of stakes had been rammed into the ground. The wooden staves were the height of the tallest of men and upon each a naked girl of virginal appearance had been impale through the quim. Urthanock looked on with reverence as he imagined how following his victory he could outdo such a depiction of ritual deflowering. He would so relish watching Parandor's bitches squeal their last as he himself rammed the wood deep inside their nethers. Around the circle of stakes lay the rest of the naked dead, men, women, children, and all of them defiled in one way or another. They were lain like spokes of a wheel with their heads pointing to the centre. There was makeshift outer circle which then captured Urthanock's focus. At first he could not make them out. While two eyes scanned a heaped-up pile of bones, furs, hides of many kinds, he at last realised what he was looking at. The mess comprised the domesticated animals of Griginor and as he looked closer he saw that all bore evidence of ogre teeth marks. The mountain swine had gorged on the innocent creatures before tossing them aside at the edge of their work of art as would highborn Lords tossing food scraps from the table.

Standing back in approved wonderment, Urthanock realised what it was that the ogres had tried to create. Their concentric circles represented the levels that had to be negotiated in order to access the door to the underworld. He counted nine. He sensed it had to be a morbid representation of one of the circle's that marked his Vessel's neck. Yes, it had to be that. Urthanock's concentration was then broken by a sudden shout from a Lizardman that approached from behind.

"Lord, please come, we have been looking for you everywhere. Follow me Bane of Dragons for Ssonsh has found the ogres and begs you come and see what they have been up to."

"Where is my pet toad?" demanded Urthanock as he glared at the unfortunate messenger.

"Just a ten-minute walk to the south Lord," hissed the creature. "He has found the ogres in the cellars beneath Griginor's winery."

"Then take me there at once if you value the skin that you walk in," snarled Urthanock.

The trembling reptile led his terrifying leader on through the narrow streets of the old town in an area devoid of light. It proved easy for the Lizardman for its eyes had evolved to see well in the gloom. Urthanock on the other hand struggled to keep up for the Vessel's eyes were not well designed to cope with the black. On numerous occasions he bumped against a passing wall or door that had been left part open. Once he tripped over a corpse that had fallen out of an alleyway and fell to the ground. This caused an upsurge in his anger and the ground shook with great violence as ripples of hate spread out through the earth.

"How much further before we reach our goal?" demanded Urthanock.

"We are almost there Lord; it's just around the next corner."

The creature was indeed correct for as Urthanock turned off the street to his right he entered a short-cobbled passageway that led up to an imposing stone building. Ahead stood two impressive wooden gates, left open to reveal an intervening courtyard. Through these gates the Lizardman strode, beckoning his Lord to follow. On they moved to the building at the far side of the yard and entered through its door, one constructed like those that guard prison cells. Even in the dark Urthanock saw that it had been forced open. Nostrils sniffed the foul smell of ogre in the air. He entered with unknown expectations for on his journey to the winery he had asked his guide what Ssonsh had found but the Lizardman had declared his ignorance. The scaly nonentity was just a messenger and not party to what had been discovered within the cellars of the winery.

"My Lord, I am ordered by Ssonsh to go no further," whimpered the reptile. "Take that burning stave that is fixed to the wall and follow the passage to the steps a short distance ahead of you. They will take you down into the cellars where you will find your Hochnar waiting."

"Then fuck off," ordered Urthanock with contempt. "Don't let me cast eyes on you again."

The reptile turned and ran while Urthanock reached out to the wall took a firm hold of the burning torch, lifted it from its bracket, and made his way deeper inside the constricting black. Once again the voice popped up to remind him of its continued presence.

"Ssonsh is taking the piss. He knows like me that you are mad. You had best be on your guard."

"Fuck off and get out of my head," shouted Urthanock but none but the walls heard his words.

A minute later Urthanock stood before the stone steps that led to the cellars. Light seeped from below and Urthanock saw shadows moving across the distant opening. Strange tremors reverberated through the stone and it took him a while to work out its origin. The ground trembled with deep growls which grew ever louder as he descended the long flight of steps. It was the heavy resonant snoring of many sleepers and given the intensity of the noise they had to be ogres. The moment that he stepped inside the vast cellars of Griginor he was greeted by the frog priest Ssonsh who strode forward with heavy purpose in order to engage with his Lord.

"Urthanock I am so pleased my messengers managed to find you. We found these oafs almost an hour ago but have been unable to wake them. It seems they decided to take advantage of Griginor's store of strong wine and attempt to drink themselves into oblivion. We have tried everything to wake them but they are as pissed as brewery mice."

The Lord over Fear scanned his new environment. The cellars were indeed vast and stretched as far as the eye could see in all directions. The number of casks containing wine was incalculable as they stretched from floor to ceiling, row upon row, into the far distant shadows. A heavy mixed scent of sweet intoxication and ogre excrement hung in the air and weaved it presence into his nose. He tried to estimate whether the atmosphere was potent enough to ignite in the presence of the Lizardmens' torches. His hand let hold of his light and he extinguished it with his foot for he did not want to be the one to cause yet another fire, at least not before he had emptied the cellar of its precious contents. There were numerous other reptiles present besides Ssonsh and all were engaged in seeking an alternative exit in order to remove the casks. It was unlikely that Griginor's vintners would have used the steep stone steps to extricate their produce nor indeed bring the casks down to mature. Urthanock then focused his attention upon the twenty or so ogres that lay about on the floor, all adjacent to several opened casks that they had drained down their gullets. The grotesque swine had stripped themselves of their armour and now in their stupor wore nothing but loin cloths.

"Which one of these worthless lumps is General Brosizrug?" demanded Urthanock.

"That one over there Lord," replied Ssonsh as he pointed forward with a webbed digit to the third prostrated heap to his right. "It would appear that having gorged on the towns pets, he led his troop down here and quaffed 'till they dropped."

"Have you tried to wake the stupid buggers?"

"Yes my Lord, we have tried everything. We have kicked and punched, prodded them with pointed sticks, and even tried burning them with our torches. You will see from the amount of damp that surrounds them that we have even drenched them with buckets of water. Their stupor is so deep that nothing we have done has brought a response."

"But you didn't try this toad," snarled Urthanock.

The crazed purveyor of evil strode forward until he towered over the legs of the unconscious General. He pointed his hand at the creature's groin and unleashed a bolt of ice blue fire. The intense flame shot from the Vessel's hand and fell upon the ogre's oversized scrote sack which happened to lie exposed beneath its displaced loincloth. Within a second the ogre's great muscle bound limbs began to convulse. It's already grotesque and fearful face then contorted as every one of its deep facial furrows pulled its surrounding skin into a projection of intense agony. Two seconds later the great beast sat erect, opened its vast cavernous mouth and screamed through the gaps in its yellow peg shaped teeth. It was a noise so loud and so foul that it threatened to wake the dead. Yet it had little effect on the rest of the ogres who slept through the insult to their drums.

"Who the fuck dares wake me?" bellowed Brosizrug as two hands the size of plates began to massage his frazzled bollocks.

"It was I and I need you to get up, you pathetic excuse for a mountain warlord," snapped back Urthanock as he stood with great menace.

"You better tell me who you are," snarled the General, "before I rip that half head off your fucking shoulders."

Urthanock reached out his arm, grabbed the General by the throat. Fingers squeezed with iron like strength. The General fought for breath as the scared faced towered overhead.

"I am Urthanock reborn. I am the Lord over Fear and you will bow to my will. Watch and take note dolt. You serve me now for I have disposed of the Lady of the Silverwynn and the knights of Avolire. My reptilian army slaughtered all amongst the ruins of that once putrid pile. You are not of the man race and for that reason I spare you and these other dim-witted piss brains that surround you. All you have to is obey and swear your allegiance to me."

Urthanock released his grip on the creature's throat. The General made as if to answer but another bolt of energy shot from Urthanock's hand. It hit the ogre in the mouth and the intensity of the pain caused its massive body to shake.

"All that our new lord has said is true," said Ssonsh, fearing the General would resist and be terminated. "He has indeed dispatched the Lady and destroyed her army. More than that, he has killed the great wyvern called Thamous, all with his own two hands. He has even consumed the beast essence. Where Avolire once stood there is now nothing and he has even destroyed the room that powered the Silverwynn; the fracture within our reality. The Lord that stands before you is omnipotent and cannot ever die. He is the Lord over Fear. Urthanock, Mighty Lord of the Lizards, has returned and soon we will march on Parandor to finish our work.

"Thank you Hochnar," said Urthanock, his eyes glowing red. "I do hope that General Burned Balls will heed your advice. Now ogre, do I have your undivided and complete loyalty. Will you obey my every command or should I extinguish your miserable existence with one more jolt to your groin?"

"Lord, spare him," pleaded Ssonsh as he stepped forward. "The beast of the mountains may be stupid but he has always been a loyal servant and carried out the orders of the Silverwynn without question. Of course, like all of his kind he can act like a cunt, but he and his kin's strength will be of great value once we begin to storm Parandor's defences."

Others may have believed that the ogre was dim of thought, but that was not the case and the brute had already calculated what it had to do to stay alive. It's time would come and the ogre buried its desire for revenge. It would wait until the right opportunity presented itself.

"I am yours to command and will serve you to the end," swore the General as he struggled beyond his knees to prostrated obedience.

"Excellent," replied Urthanock. "Then listen with care to the orders I now give you…"

Urthanock then proceeded to define all that he expected of his new General. While he spoke the ogre listened and concentrated as best it could. It held its oversize head in its hands in order to somehow mitigate the extent of its pounding headache. The others of its kind were to be woken by whatever way Brosizrug thought would work best. They were then to smash a hole through the cellar's ceiling and extricate as many wine casks as they could. These would be taken on the journey to Parandor. Urthanock then threatened the General that the ogres would pull the carts themselves had they eaten all the horses or oxen that once supported life in Griginor. Once the casks were loaded onto all available carts

Brozisrug was to lead his ogres up and through the Old Pass that cut through the Grey Mountains. They would toil hard in punishment for their debauchery, clear and repair the trail, and eliminate any wild beasts that would be a potential threat to the movement of Army of the Eastern Marsh. Brosizrug nodded in acceptance of his new orders and was about to wake his fellow beasts when another Lizardman shot down the stone steps and rushed forward to report a new development.

"My Lord Urthanock and once mighty Ssonsh, I bring you great news,"

"This had better be important for you disturb our battle planning," replied the Hochnar.

"It is, once great leader of the Marsh," jabbered this new messenger. "It concerns the reworking of the suits of orichalcum armour that we have dragged all the way from Avolire."

"Speak at once, what is this news that you wish to tell me?" shouted Urthanock.

"We have found a factory of metal workers, well-hidden in the south of the town and whose furnaces have not yet been extinguished. They have pleaded for their lives saying they know everything about the forging of the metal. We can force these blacksmiths to rework the orichalcum to meet our requirements and save much time."

"I see," grunted Urthanock with a smirk. "That news pleases me. Take me there at once. "

The foul Lord relished this additional boon of war. Not only did he now have vast quantities of wine with which to keep the army content but his warriors would be able to leave Griginor better protected than any that he had led in the past. He would make the smiths of Griginor submit to his will. Urthanock turned again to address the ogre.

"Do not let me down Brosizrug, I neither forgive nor forget and my vengeance is swift."

The foundry had been built at the southern edge of Griginor lest the fire from its furnaces escape and destroy the town as had once happened in times almost forgotten. There was another reason it had been placed there. It stood in the centre of a circle of enormous stones each the height of three grown men and separated from each other by a distance of two outstretched arms. These stones acted as a shield from the heat generated by the furnaces and allowed the town buildings to be built closer to the factory than would have been otherwise possible. The stone circle was so large that it took a man fifteen minutes to walk its circumference. The massive granite slabs were so heavy and thick that even the Ancients had been at a loss to explain how the structure had been created. Such rock was found in just one place in the Realm, at the base of the three peaked mountain known as the Gathering. No one ever knew how the circle had been built nor indeed why. The people of Griginor had long referred to it as the Eye of Solaris for on the longest day of the summer the god rose in a direct line between its nearest neighbour Avolire, and the old pass in the opposite direction. In its centre and almost filling its space a vast stone walled complex of workshops had been constructed. There were in addition three furnaces that had not been extinguished for a thousand years. The chambers that housed these fiery pits had the tallest of walls, built so high so as to allow their slated rooves to resist the heat that rose from the ground. All the surrounding workshops were however roofless and there men had laboured to produce all which they were tasked to forge.

Every bit of metal needed to support the town's wealth was created in this one spot, farm implements, weapons, pots, pipes of every dimension, and even works of art. Close to the base of the Grey Mountains were the only copper and tin seams ever discovered south of the Dirmark and with this monopoly Griginor had prospered. It did not however have a glut of iron nor any orichalcum. The wood used for the furnaces had to be brought from far distant and diminishing areas of woodland. What additional precious metals the smiths could extract from the earth they reserved for the creation of swords which they made to their own unique style. Not many were named but all were revered and some were said to have magical welded into their core; so told the local patter.

It was to this metalworkers' factory, set amongst the circle of ancient standing stones that Urthanock hurried. He noted the great pillars long before he passed through them for even he had never seen the likes of such before. Soon he was ushered into one of the larger workshops near to the three buildings that housed the furnaces, the heat from which caused his skin to leak. He was reminded of the flames of Thamous and sneered at the thought of the creature's demise. .

Forced to sit huddled on the floor were some fifty or so workmen, those brave or foolish enough to have refused the chance to abandon the fires that had been the life blood of Griginor. An equal number of Lizardmen surrounded the workmen with weapons pointed. Urthanock strode forward and shouted at the weary souls who as one sat with heads hung low and limbs that trembled. None sought to make eye contact with the fearsome invader.

"I will speak with your leader," bellowed Urthanock. "Which one of you can talk for all? I have an offer to make to you. Comply and I will spare your lives. Now who is your leader?"

No answer came and so Urthanock stepped forward and kicked the first prisoner in the ribs.

"You, tell me which of you buggers will work with me to save the rest?"

The man winced with pain. Not wishing to receive further blows he shouted back.

"That would be Gof. Talk to Gof for he is the one who owns and manages this enterprise."

"Stand up now Gof," ordered Urthanock. "Should I have to wait, I will begin killing those who work for you, one each second, until you are all no more."

None of the prisoners moved.

"Let me demonstrate my power," shouted Urthanock.

Raising his hand Urthanock clicked his fingers. The one he had kicked then rose into the air. Arms and legs were stretched and snapped at the hip and shoulder. Then a neck cracked. A bolt of blue light shot from the evil one's hand and the prisoner exploded in a shower of flesh and bone. Prisoners and Lizardmen alike shook in the presence of the demonic youth that now had power over the elements that formed the Realm.

"I am Gof," shouted one from the centre of the huddle. "Please stop your killing. Tell me what I must do to save us all?"

A single figure stood and Urthanock lowered his hand. With a sick grin he beckoned him over.

"Come, I wish to talk with you alone. I want to know if you are capable of meeting my needs."

The man called Gof was tall, but fat. At a guess, Urthanock reckoned he was at least in his sixtieth year. A once muscular frame was now well passed its best, no doubt having gorged for many years on the fire wines of Griginor. The owner of the forges stepped through the ring of Lizardmen. Urthanock led him on to one side of the vast room where both then sat together on stones that over time had been worn in to comfortable seats by a thousand arses.

"Is Gof your first name or that given by your father?" asked Urthanock.

"I have no other name than Gof. If I had a father no one ever told me his name. I have worked within the circle ever since I can remember and I became the best at my trade."

"Then I am talking with the right man. Can your people refashion orichalcum? I have a vast amount of armour stripped from the Army of Avolire that I have just destroyed. I need it reworked into the style worn by the Lizardmen of the Eastern Marsh, those who now hold you captive and who are ready to flay the skin from your back should I give the order."

"Yes we can my Lord," replied the trembling Gof. "We are skilled in working with all metals although orichalcum seldom comes our way. The exotic kinds we reserve for our speciality work, the manufacture of swords considered to be the envy of the gods themselves; just like the one you carry at your side."

Urthanock hesitated for he sensed the intervention of the Fates.

"Say more; was this sword made in Griginor?"

"Indeed it was but from the subtleties of its design it is very old. Where did you come by it Lord, if I may be permitted to enquire?"

"It was brought to me in Avolire by way of the creatures that now drink your cellars dry. It has already proved most useful," replied Urthanock as he recalled the death of the wyvern.

"A Griginor blade will always prevail," answered Gof.

"I have not time for small talk. I will deliver several cart loads of armour within the hour. The Lizardmen that guard you will show you how the metal is to be reformed to meet my needs. You have two nights and one whole day to complete the work. Succeed and you all shall live to continue your work. Fail me and your life will be forfeit. You have already seen the terrors that your men will face. You alone are their salvation and work will set you free. Do we have an agreement, bastard of the bellows?"

"My lord, I do have one concern," stuttered Gof. "You are expecting us to work nonstop until you return. I fear the labour and heat will finish off the weakest of my men. Can you perhaps give us more time?"

"No I cannot so do as I command!" shouted Urthanock with eyes that glowed furnace red. "War waits for no one. I will leave on time and you will deliver. Understand?"

Gof nodded as his limbs quaked.

"Before we part, I have a couple of other questions for which I demand answers." ordered Urthanock. "Passing through the great stones I noted there are runes caved upon their surface. I am curious to know the message that the stones convey?"

"My Lord," stammered the fearful Gof "There has been none in this town able to read them for a thousand years. There are however stories passed down through the children who have always played at the base of the mighty ancient monument. I fear that if you persist, I will speak what you consider to be nonsense and I do not wish to incur your wrath."

"I understand these limitations but indulge me and tell me what the children say."

"It is a strange rhyme that they sing," the blacksmith continued. "It goes something like this…"

Round and round the circle,
We dance with all our skill.
Yet never can we stop this rite,
Lest our bodies should get ill.

We dance with passion and delight,
To please the wondrous Lords of Light;
And so we skip and twist and leap
Lest death comes calling in our sleep.

But on the day the disc stands still
We stop our dance and eat our fill;
Then again, we prance and thrill,
The sparkling diamond on the hill."

"What the fuck is that supposed to mean?" demanded Urthanock.

"It is just a child's song for dancing around the circle but it is supposed to be very old," replied Gof. "Some of the more educated of Griginor claim there is a true story behind the simple verse but I do not know what that is."

"It just a bag of shite, but no matter," laughed Urthanock.

"Like I said my Lord, it's a children's song."

"Then answer my other question," added Urthanock. "What happened to the once great river called the Wistulla? Why does it no longer flow past this town and into the great gorge it carved through the Dragonas?"

"Once again indulge but do not punish me when I speak the legend we were told in our youth,"

"Just spit it out dolt," snapped back Urthanock as his patience waned.

"So be it Lord. It is told that long ago, soon after Sir Belquin had taken the dragon Xenvagen's head, a swarm of the flying beasts descended upon the mountains south of this town. They came seeking revenge against the dragon hunters that would in time form the order of the Knights of Avolire. The beasts pummelled the peaks with rock, sulphur, and fire until the earth could take no more and began to shake in a most horrible way. The violent tremors caused the ground to fracture and to shift. A whole mountain fell and it blocked the path of the Wistulla. Its headwaters were diverted and they joined with those of the Awyth which was until then but a puny stream in comparison. So the river left Griginor forever and raced to the east."

"That is at least more believable than your nursery rhyme and it would account for the flooding of the Eastern Marsh," replied Urthanock as he pondered this new information.

"But was not the Marsh was already there?"

"You are too smart for your own good metal man," snarled Urthanock

"Thank you Lord," grovelled Gof as he fell to his knees and kissed the beast's feet.

"When I return make sure your work is done or be prepared to meet your gods."

The beast who would rule all, jumped to his feet and shouted his last order.

"Make these bastards sweat and toil. I will not accept excuses."

Urthanock promptly left the circle and made his way back to his tent. As he did so, the voice that plagued his mind whispered in his ear.

"Call yourself the Lord over Fear? You are denser than a rustic dullard. You missed all the clues? Even that simpleton Gof could have worked it out."

"Fuck off and get out of my head!" the beast snapped back.

Urthanock woke late and crawled from under his shelter in the central square of Griginor. He tended to his horse, fed it, and checked the soundness of the shoes on its feet. Then he began to caress its neck but the horse seemed to sense the evil that flowed from his hand and it pulled its head away. The Dark Lord was too preoccupied to notice for his mind was on other things. The first was the messages from his stomach and the second his need to address his body functions. He checked on his pot and noted the residues of his previous night's supper. It had long gone cold as the fire had gone out but what remained would have to do for now. He strode across the square and emptied his bladder over several corpses. Having shaken himself dry he returned to wash with water drawn from the hand pump. Soon the pot was on his lap and with his ladle he scrapped its bottom clean and devoured what was left of the man-meat and turnips.

Sitting by the statue he began to reflect on the destruction of both Avolire and Griginor. For some unknown reason he found that a difficult task. It did not please him as much as it had before he went to sleep. For just one moment a fleeting semblance of guilt rippled through his soul and Urthanock knew it was not of his own doing. It was either the lingering essence of his Vessel or that of the wyvern, refusing to continence his behaviour. There had to be a way that he could be rid of that which messed with his mind. He sensed it had to be gone before he could prosecute his war with any certainty of success. However, before he could dwell further on those thoughts Ssonsh waddled over from across the square as fast as its toady bulk permitted. Urthanock slipped his ladle into his pot and awaited the arrival of his Hochnar.

"I am so pleased to see you awake Lord," began Ssonsh as soon as Urthanock was in earshot. "I have important news for you regarding the functioning of the Rift and the movement of the ogres; both of which I am sure you will find interesting."

"You don't look so good to today Hochnar. Are you well my pet toad? You seem to have aged and lost weight."

"All I can say is that it must be related to events back in Avolire," replied Ssonsh.

"Say more!" added Urthanock as his curiosity grew.

"Ever since the connection to the rift in Avolire was silenced, when the explosion sealed the crack between the dimensions, I have not felt quite the same. I feel like I have lost much of my usual energy. Have you noticed anything different about me Lord? "

"Should I have done?"

"Given that your Vessel was the room's favourite and upon which it showered its magic, I thought perhaps you may have noticed something too," replied Ssonsh shuffling from foot to foot in an agitated dance of nerve tingles.

Urthanock stood and thought a while as he tried to decide how and whether to indulge the frog priest's paranoia. Then a thought flicked through his head.

"Yesterday, when I fried Brosizrug's balls, I had expected a much greater impact. I have not thought about it until your question but I will watch and take note of how I feel over the coming days. I still feel the power flowing through my mark. Kha continues to favour me so put any thoughts of my decline well behind you."

"Yes of course my Lord."

"And do not speak of this conversation with anyone else lest I rip you limb from trunk."

"I understand and obey Lord," croaked Ssonsh.

"Good, what news do you have of the Rift?"

Ssonsh did not answer and it was clear he was hiding something.

"Spit out your words toad. Don't make me force them from you."

"Ssobekk tried to send three Lizardmen with messages over to me this morning as we wished to coordinate our rendezvous beyond the mountains. He has already passed the Grey Keep."

"And?"

"Only one of his messengers arrived intact," added Ssonsh as he coiled his fists

"What are you trying to say?"

"The Rift malfunctions; it is not safe to use."

"I will be the judge of that," ordered Urthanock. "Tell me what happened."

"One came through, intact in both mind and body. The second arrived a minute later inside the next building. I'm sad to say, not all of that one turned up!"

"Go on!" exclaimed Urthanock.

"If you were to imagine a line drawn from right shoulder to left hip, then it was the bottom half that materialised near where it should have done. The other half could be anywhere and we have so far failed to find it."

"And the third?"

"At first it seemed the creature was complete but it then stood still and aimless. It appears to have no mind or essence. It is but an empty shell. The issue we now have is that unless we can fix the Rift then we dare not use it as a means to access the Citadel of Parandor."

"I beg to disagree," sneered Urthanock as he fixed his sword to his belt. "If the Rift stays as it is then one in three reptiles would get through. I estimate we need a force of two hundred to sack the Citadel. We would lose four hundred if we continue with my plan."

"My Lord, these are our kin. That would be a hurtful sacrifice. There must be another way."

"No there is not Toad," bellowed Urthanock. "You will be leading the six hundred through yourself, so if I were you I would seek to fix the problem.

"You're the fucking problem, watch the toad doesn't fix you," laughed the voice.

"Hochnar, we will talk further on this matter when we approach Parandor. What news do you have of Brosizrug and his ogres?"

"They did not sleep all last night," began Ssonsh as a smile spread across his amphibian face. "Once you left, Brosizrug woke them all himself. It took him a while for he first used many of the techniques that we had tried earlier. We then reminded him how you had assaulted his balls and suggested he did something similar. We provided him with a hot brand and when applied to their scrote sacks it soon did the trick. All, including the General now walk with bowlegs and there was only one death as a consequence of their waking."

"And how did that happen?"

"There was one who was a friend of the brute called Ikeg, that funny looking bugger with a chain from nose to an ear," continued Ssonsh while savouring the moment. "It woke with a start and clutched at its balls for Brosizrug had left the brand against them for a second or two longer than the others. The creature was incensed and lunged at the General. Brosizrug then thrust the hot metal into this ogre's throat. The swelling stopped it from breathing and within five minutes it was dead. There appeared to be no love lost between the two and not one of the others ogres flickered even an eyelid as their comrade fell."

Despite the smile that sat upon his half exposed face, Urthanock was displeased.

"Have the ogres done as I ordered, that's all I need to know?"

"Yes they have Lord. They soon broke through a tunnel they found which slopped up to great doors that secured the contents of the winery. By dawn they had extricated every single one of the barrels they could fit onto dozen carts. The number was limited by the amount of animals we found but we have enough wine to celebrate with the Gator Lord when we meet with him beyond the mountains. Once that task was finished the ogres left to clear the way through the Old Pass, just as you instructed."

"I sense you hold back more information Hochnar. Don't make me regret your appointment."

"There is indeed one more thing Lord," said Ssonsh.

"Well, spit it out!"

"I think Brosizrug holds a grudge against you for using his privates as target practice. He has asked many questions about you and spits to the floor whenever your name is mentioned."

"Then he is a fool," laughed Urthanock. "Once Parandor has fallen I will kill the fat fuck and all his kin. Only the Lizard race will walk these lands. Now is there anything else you wish to add?"

"There is just one piece of news I still need to surface Lord.

"Speak it at once then for I am already bored with your drivel."

"There has still been no message from Ssleptaz in Parandor. This is of significant concern to me. He has to be dead for there can be no other explanation for his continued silence. Our ability to enter the Citadel in the right place at the right time has been lost."

"It is not an issue for me," snapped back Urthanock, "It may be for you as leader of that assault group. Sort it and don't mention it to me again. Now, enough of all this shite. Come, let us walk and discuss the strategies that will bring us victory in the war that is to come."

The Lord over Fear walked on with his Hochnar in tow. The voice that was the bane of his waking hours whispered away inside his head.

"It's all going wrong, isn't it? Your plans are falling apart and your powers are waning. You should never have destroyed the room that linked you to the Rift. That one stupid act will be your downfall for your life force no longer feeds off its power. You will have to enter the Underworld to regain what you have lost. That is the only way to reunite yourself and become whole again. Half-helm? More a half-wit!"

Urthanock knew it had been a mistake to seal the crack but it was done and there was no going back. The voice was right.

The next morning Urthanock woke early, packed away his field shelter, loaded his horse, and road off to the circle of stones. The squares and the streets were crammed with the Army of the East, all waiting for the order to begin the long march into the Old Pass. The ogre's art of contorted human form had been left where he had found it as a warning to any who had escaped Griginor and who wished to re-establish the town once his army had moved on. The stench from the rotting flesh hung hard and caused all who approached to wretch and many of the reptiles to expel their stomach contents. It was so foul that the beasts that now accompanied his battlegroup screeched with alarm whenever the wind blew in their direction. Urthanock passed the carts that were loaded with casks of wine and noted that many of those for which there was no transport had been opened and their contents drained. This accounted for the stagger of a great many of the Lizardmen warriors that he passed on route to the circle. He vowed to make the swamp swine march at speed, not that he begrudged them their revelry. Many would soon be dead so what did one more headache matter. He would amplify their suffering just because he could. He was all powerful. He was Urthanock. All would bend to his will.

"They will turn against you if you don't learn how to lead," whispered the voice.

Urthanock tethered his horse up against one of the mighty stone uprights. He noted five carts, four of which were filled with reworked armour but one which was empty. He wondered what excuse Gof would come up with but then was distracted as he tried to remember the rhyme that the blacksmith had told him the previous day. The first two lines were all he could recall.

Round and round the circle,
We dance with all our skill.

The rest had been lost from his memory. There would be no more children to dance around these stones. The song was dead, Brosizrug had seen to that. Urthanock strode at pace through the workshops of the factory until at last he found the metal workers pounding away amid the grime, still guarded by half a hundred reptiles. He wasted no time and summoned Gof over. The blacksmith looked exhausted, his body broken, his spirit shattered, and his skin stained with soot and ash.

"My lord we have toiled without rest and are buggered," wept the old man. "We have served you as ordered and even lost several to the Underworld for they could not keep up with the crack of the slave master's whip. We have filled four carts for you and the craftsmanship is first class."

"Yet you haven't finished it all as I instructed," snapped back Urthanock. "We struck a bargain you and I and you have defaulted. You leave me no option but to slaughter the lot of you."

"Mercy Lord, Please!" cried Gof, falling to his knees. "Those lizards who have watched over our work say that you have some portable furnaces. Take us with you as slaves. Better that than killing us and we will continue with our labours whenever your army stops to rest."

Urthanock thought about the merits of Gof's proposals and then called over the Lizardman in charge of the troop of guards.

"Captain, take this man and let him choose ten of his best blacksmiths who will then accompany us on our journey to finish their work. Chain the ten to one another. If one falls then so will they all. Have the rest load the armour that is yet to be reworked onto the empty cart outside the circle. Then slit their throats."

"No Lord. Please no, they are all good men."

"Stop winging Gof. For every minute you protest I will take away one I would otherwise save."

Gof gasped and tried to control his fear.

"Lord, I have a present for you. It is something of enormous value to the people of Griginor and it will help you in the battle ahead."

"I like presents, go fetch it then," shouted Urthanock for he was beginning to lose patience.

Gof walked off to an area that contained many baskets of metal weapons of every conceivable shape and size. Soon he returned with a very long sword.

"Take this as a gift from my people in the hope that you will spare more of us."

Urthanock looked at the strange weapon in his hand while tapping the sword at his waist.

"Why should I want another when I have this one by my side?"

"With respect Lord, the one you already have is not suited to combat with an enemy that boasts a forest of halbards, pikes, and claymores, not to mention a thousand long swords," began Gof, stumbling over his words as he pleaded his case. "This magnificent two handed battle sword was said to have belonged to none other than Pietos Qrakus, friend to Sir Belquin the dragon slayer. It was due a polish and repair of a small crack in its ivory hilt, but it is ready for war and may assist you in your slaughter."

"Why does it have so long a blade and why is it wavy and not straight like all other swords I have ever seen?"

"It was designed to be effective against pikes and halbards," answered Gof. "When struck against other steel, the waves of the blade induce unpleasant vibrations in an opponent's weapon, causing it fall from the hands that hold it. It is as if the blade sings."

"Does this sword have a name?"

"These rare and special swords are known as flame blades from their wave like appearance" said Gof as his confidence began to grow. "This is the most famous of them and it has always been called White Hilt, given the ivory used in its construction."

"What metal is its blade made from?"

"Iron, with a trace of orichalcum, a little copper, and more than a sprinkle of tin" replied Gof.

"Orichalcum?" questioned Urthanock.

"From a trade with Calistorn in the days of legend."

The Lord over Fear examined the blade once again and smiled.

"I thank you for this gift and I must test its swing at once."

Urthanock took two paces back and swung the sword in the opposite direction. It cut through the air with a great rush and it felt perfect in his hands. It was as if it had been forged for him alone. Then without warning Urthanock turned, took a pace forward and swung the blade clean through Gof's neck. The old blacksmith's body dropped like a sack of turnips while his severed head hung in the air for a second before following it down to the ground. There it rolled on until coming to rest two paces from its body. Urthanock turned to the Lizardman Captain.

"I like it; I like it a lot. That'll teach the fucker to try and get familiar with me. Now, take the ten who have shown the most skill and shackle then to the carts. Load them, slaughter the rest of the smiths, and then drink your fill of wine. However, be ready to move out within the hour. I must leave you now to find Ssonsh. Do not disappoint me or you will end your days as the next target for this singing blade."

Dragging his new toy across the dirt floor behind him, Urthanock left the foundry work shop and headed back to his horse.

"Beware a blacksmith's paltry presents, but you should know that already, moron of Maplehill!" sneered the voice.

The Army of the East moved through the Old Pass without significant problem. The ogres having gone on ahead, had done a most thorough job. Vegetation had been cleared, potholes filled, embankments reinforced, and log bridges repaired. The battlegroup travelled at a pace that none had deemed possible. It passed many fires where the ogres had disposed of the trees and bushes that would have otherwise hindered its passage. Urthanock led the column with Ssonsh ever present by his side. Every hour or so the Hochnar looked to the ivory topped blade, strapped to Urthanock's back, but never once did the frog-priest have the courage to ask where it came from for his Lord was in the foulest of moods, tormented by the voice inside his head. Urthanock smiled just once when passing the remains of several kulkulkath, no doubt destroyed by the ogres. The beast was troubled by reports that the hype of geckos still tracked his army, never creeping closer than a league and said to be increasing ts number by the hour. It took two days to traverse the pass between in the Grey Mountains and descend onto the lush grasslands. There Urthanock ordered his army to break camp and await Ssobekk's arrival. The ogres, having done their job, had deserted and vanished into the mountains.

14

"Who is it and what the fuck do you want at this time in the morning?" bellowed words from behind the wood.

"Hotch, let me in. There is something of the utmost importance that I need to ask you," replied the youthful voice from the street. "The future of the Realm depends upon that which I seek and it is possible that you may hold the key. Even a lard lump like you may be of use in the war that is coming."

"Go away whoever you are," replied the stern voice. "I had only just nodded off after a night's toil when you started hammering at my door. The first cock is yet to crow, so again I tell you fuck off."

"I will not, and I will continue to hammer at your door until you open it and listen to what I have to say. It is I, Thias Calavan, envoy from the Sovereign Council, and I must speak with you now," bellowed the bard.

"Phauless Gylewu is as dead as my dick," came the response. "Just fuck right off."

A small window opened on the upper floor of one of the houses across the street from The Murdered Wolf. It was followed by several others in different buildings and from which angry heads poked out into the street. Some spat, some swore, and one even threw the contents of his piss pot which missed the bard by mere inches. Yet all this did not deter Thias from continuing to hammer upon the wood.

"Let the bastard inside Hotch," shouted the loudest of the disturbed, a comment that was affirmed by a further dozen voices.

"Put the fucker out of his misery; slit his throat," shouted another.

Thias heard the bolts to the door of The Murdered Wolf sliding back. The wood soon part opened and a large hairy hand was thrust out through the gap. It grabbed the bard's jacket and dragged him inside the shadows of the temple of sin and debauchery. The door was then slammed shut and Thias pushed into the nearest chair which almost toppled due to the force inflicted on it. Isambard Hotch moved to his serving counter and retrieved a small lantern which he then lit with a flint and brought with him to the table at which Thias sat waiting. At least the bard had gained entry and would get to ask his question.

As Isambard Hotch towered over him, the first thing that Thias noted was that the barkeep smelled better than he had in a long while. Then as the lardy lump sat to face him across the table, the bard could not help but ask why.

"Hotch, have you had a bath?" he said while sniffing in air.

"Piss off bard and no I haven't," grunted Hotch as he thrust his nose into his right arm pit and then laughed. "If you must know, yesterday I went to the docks to see if there was any fish left from that brought ashore by the Master's Catch, what with war coming and all that. A group of Underscroft's brats pushed me into the Tiaryer saying my stench was driving the fish away and putting their livelihood at risk. The salt water did the rest and not even my whores can resist me now!"

"Quite so!" replied Thias.

"Now, tell me what you have to say so I can return to my bed. What is so fucking important that it couldn't wait till opening hours?"

Thias did not hesitate "I need to know this; in all your many years listening to drunken sea shanties and the like from across the far reaches of the Realm, have you ever heard a tune or a song titled 'The Ballad of Predestination'?"

The barkeep rose from his seat and roared with laughter.

"You're the fucking bard, not me. I thought you buggers were said to know all the songs," Hotch scratched an itch between his legs.

"I can in all truth say it is one I have never heard of. It is most important I find and examine its words, because as you already put it, with the war coming and all that," said Thais as he leaned across the table. "All our lives depend upon the message that is hidden in its verse. For fucks sake man, try harder and see if you can help me. If it was ever sung anywhere it would have been here."

"Well I have never heard of it. Why don't you go and search the Royal Library. If it is anywhere, then that's where you would find it. There is bound to be some form of record in that dust filled rats nest. Why such a ballad is important would be the other question I would ask myself."

"That is what I think too and where I am heading next but the building doesn't open until the birds cry," said Thias with disappointment.

"Then why the fuck did you knock me up then, you crooning arsehole?"

"I thought you could save me time Hotch for it is running short, what with war coming and all that. Now I will have to spend hours amongst piles of ancient writings and the tedious tomes of the highborn, time I could have spent on other tasks of equal importance."

Thais looked across the table to the ruffian opposite and waited for an answer.

"Well?" demanded Thias but Isambard remained silent and just glared. "Well sod you then."

At that, Thias raised himself from his chair and prepared to leave but Hotch's large right hand shot across the table and pulled the bard back down again.

"You think you know everything don't you bard. There are things you need to be aware of, things that concern you more than you would think."

Thias was puzzled for it appeared that Hotch was threatening him. If so he had missed the point that had triggered this sudden change in their conversation.

"What are you blathering on about?"

"I'll keep it simple such that the likes of a tune tart can understand. While I have you here there is something important you need to know about the Thieves' Guild. I have grown to like you bard, and your friends, even if they almost cost me my business. Listen to what I have to say for these matters are of great concern to you."

"My ears belong to you," replied Thias as his interest grew.

"I, as you realised after the incident regarding Nedes Karoly's head, have a tenuous link to those who pride themselves in the art of undetected theft. I have a message for you, from those who lead the Thieves Guild. It was passed down to me by a whisper here and a rustle there. It is not meant as a threat unless you do not heed it. No, in fact you could call it more of a gesture of friendship to a child of one of their number. So consider it well and contemplate its meaning."

"Hotch, this is most unlike you," replied Thias, taken aback by the clarity of the innkeeper's words which somehow implicated his father. "Say what you must convey, then I will make my own mind up as to whether the message is benign or of evil intent."

"Then do not interrupt me until I have finished," continued Hotch as he picked a kipper bone he had just located in his ever-growing beard. "Do not repeat this anywhere else for should you do so and folks come enquiring then I will deny all that I now tell you. I will make you out to be a slanderer and although you may find it hard to believe I have contacts in the highest of places; even in the Sovereign Court who tasked you as their envoy."

"Just get on with it Hotch. Your words will speak for themselves and I will not judge you until the last has been uttered."

"Then listen with care bard. Those who have been inducted into the Thieves Guild are aware of the Enderdetag Prophecy, what it means for us all, the coming of the Marked, and the resurrection of Urthanock. They wish you to know that some of them are also members of a secret society who work hard to ensure that the prophecy will be fulfilled. They call themselves Cuvar."

"What the fuck..." exclaimed Thias but Isambard Hotch ignored him and continued.

"They too have watched over the years and the Order's Head monitors your activities. They wish you well in your endeavours, as do we all given what is at stake, yet at the same time their own needs are paramount. Should anything you do compromise their business then they will not hesitate to eliminate you and any who follow your orders. I hope that is clear."

"I thought you said that you were not delivering a threat," answered Thias as his hand move to the hilt of the blade.

The bard assumed that Hotch was also now a threat like the mysterious thieves. It would be easy to eliminate the lard lump but Thias was interested to hear more and therefore continued to listen to what the barkeep had to say.

"Your father was of the Guild. You no doubt remember him as low life scum, one who would steal bread and end up hanged. He no doubt taught you some simple tricks on how to pick locks, steal purses, and the like but you didn't know him like the elders who run the Guild. It is not for me to tell all of it but your father was a subversive, secreted into the slums to listen and later pass information up to those who are the real power behind this city. You may be surprised to learn that your father was well connected with a highborn lady, more than you could ever suspect, but it is not within my power to say more without fear of death. You will never know the full story unless you discover the identity of the Guild's Grand Master and that is not going to happen."

"You are losing me with this tripe Hotch," replied Thias as his frustration grew. "What is the real message you are trying to give me?"

"The Thieves Guild intends to profit from the war that is about to descend upon us. There are always winners and losers at such times and those I speak for intend as always to be beneficiaries. Do not get in their way. Stick to fighting and prophecies and keep away from the profiteers. Then we will all work as one."

"Given I may have need to deal with your Grand Master, are there any clues you can give me as to his identity? I would not wish to fall foul of the Guild's justice and end my days with my head in a barrel of your firewater."

"My master has eyes and ears and influence. The Guild's will is present at the highest tables of the Citadel, although our Head has yet to infiltrate the Sovereign Council. That is all I will say."

"Fuck me!" exclaimed Thias.

The bard sat back in his chair. His mind raced and his heart beat at a gross a minute. In a matter of a few moments Isambard Hotch had changed everything he had come to believe about the Thieves Guild. When the war was over, and if he survived, the identity of the Guild's Grand Master would become his priority.

The position of Royal Librarian had not been filled following the death of Mathias Amberstone and nor would it be anytime soon. This action had first been put on hold to allow a respectful period of mourning. All who worked in the ancient repository believed that their leader had been innocent of the crimes for which he had been executed. The other ten shelf fillers and scribes were just about to hold an election, to choose one of their own, when both the Sovereign and Amberstone's daughter Tonousa had been murdered in quick succession. This meant once again that a wake and period of respect needed observance and then of course there was the issue of impending war. So it was decided that no official replacement would be appointed until the battle for Parandor was over and of course should the right side win.

Once Thias had described the importance and the relevance of his search, the ten guardians of the words of the Realm set about aiding the bard with all the energy they could muster. Each took a section of the library that was thought to contain records of any ballads, songs, poems or short stories in the hope of discovering the elusive tune that included the word 'predestination' and which held the key to the defeat of Urthanock. Thias and one other had chosen a specific section to search, a dark corner thought to hold the most ancient of scrolls. The bard believed that if the tune had ever existed then it had to have been very old to have slipped from the memory of man. So it was that he sat on a three-legged stool beside a pyramid of old parchment that stretched from the floor to the height of a full-grown man. His companion was the most junior of the ten who now ran the library, a mere snot of a lad called Amren, and who Thias reckoned to be no more than twelve years old. As the two set about their task they generated a haze of dust that rose from parchments that had not been disturbed for hundreds of years. The specks caught a ray of light from the one window that lit the pile and they sparkled like an army of insect souls released in the slaughter of some great forest battle. Many of the parchments were so old that they crumbled when touched. Others had edges nibbled away by the booklice and to such an extent that the first letter of each line had been taken. Many at the bottom of the pile had been cratered by the jaws of termites or revealed evidence of the bore holes of the powder post beetles. It was into this mountainous insect home that four hands delved and out pulled documents one by one.

"What are we looking for again," asked the young boy Amren.

"An old poem that is called the Ballad of Predestination," replied Thias.

"What does that word mean?" asked the lad.

"It's the belief that everything that will happen has already been decided by the fickle Fates and cannot be changed," answered Thias as he pulled out another scroll, scanned its contents, and then threw it onto an ever-growing pile of rejected material.

"Do you believe in that kind of stuff?" asked Amren as he mirrored Thias's actions.

"May be! May be not! I did at one time, but no longer."

Thias looked at the stack of parchment in front of him and sighed.

"This is going to be a boring unless we play some sort of game to keep our mind focused."

"So what do you suggest," the boy asked. "I like games."

"Whenever you find a ballad with a funny name then we show it to each other. When we work through to the end of this pile we will agree who found the funniest."

Thias smiled and thrust his hand back into the centre of the paper pyramid. If only the Great Library of the bard's still stood, but that now fed the fish. Parandor's would have to do.

Some five minutes later Amren thrust his right hand into the air and squealed with delight.

"What about this one," he cried out. 'The day after Ragman was stretched, his wife at last got to look him in the eye'."

"Right, put it to one side, I'm sure we can better that one.

An hour later the youth shrieked again.

"The Mermaid's tail and the fishmonger's rampant tongue!"

"Very infantile, but keep looking for we still have a mountain to get through," sneered Thias. "Oh wait! I've got one too. How about this one. 'The cobbler's party and the maiden's rarebit,"

"We should stop and read that one," smirked Amren." It sounds funnier than mine."

"Save it to one side. You can read it yourself later. We have far too many to get through before we can pause for rest. So far we have but scratched the surface."

So, it went on hour after hour, their intense concentration broken only by the occasional odd title. 'The Stinging Wick and the Fire Down Below', 'Coniferous Flaps and the Buzzard's Hand-me-downs', and 'The Courting of the Spider by the Fly', were a few of the better ones. By mid-afternoon the plie had been searched but there was no hint of anything called the Ballad of Predestination.

Having completed their task Thias gave the helpful lad five groats in recognition of both his hard labour and the cheerful manner in which he had contributed to the sense dulling work.

"So who wins the best title then?" asked the youth, a question that seemed of more immediate value than the five coins that he held in his hand.

"Which do think should win?"

"When Connor divorced his Father's Goat,"

"Somehow, I knew you were going to choose that one," laughed Thias. "Here is a silver penny as your prize. Now run along while I see if others have had better luck than we have."

Amren did not have to be told a second time and with the reward for his morning efforts clutched in his hand he scuttled off to deposit his coins in some remote and secret hideaway. Thias then toured the vast expanse of the library where he interviewed all the others who had joined him in the quest to find the words that would defeat Urthanock. With his heart at its nadir, and having no positive response he approached the two final librarians who had been searching the shelves that contained the oldest poetry, including one long forgotten collection by Anyle Belanore.

"We didn't find the ballad, Thias," began the elder of the two, "but in this anthology of Belanore's poetry there does appear to be reference made of it. It is in old manspeak but you can just about make out what it says."

"Let me see," replied Thias, unable to contain his excitement.

The bard took the open book from the librarian and stared at the words at the top of the page.

"If my translation is correct then it says something like 'For the Song of Predestination, seek the Inevitable Truths amid the Lore of the Dead'," replied Thias as a thought sprang into his head.

"Well done bard," added the aide. "That is just how I would read it. We have been looking in the wrong place."

"So it would seem," replied Thias as he rubbed his chin. "Have you found any other references? Anything at all?"

"No we have not Thias," said the librarian. "This clue is all we have discovered throughout our long hours of toil. If the Lore of the Dead were here then we could help you search it for these so called 'Inevitable Truths'; but it is not. I assume you are aware of its history and that it was last reported to be in the care of the wizards. They say it was taken there after it was stolen and returned by the one who murdered Amberstone and his daughter?"

"Yes I have heard that, and also that the wizards have studied the tome in great detail. I am surprised they haven't raised the issue of these Truths if they are as important as they seem to be."

"I suggest there is just one thing left for you to do bard; you must go and confront the arrogant Iqotrix and have him show you that accursed book."

"You're right. I will track down the Archmage and see what he has to say."

A smile spread across Thias's face. At last he sensed a breakthrough and it made him feel excited. It appeared the answer had been under his nose all of the time, even though not where he expected. Turning to the librarian his words continued to flow.

"I thank you and all your colleagues for all your assistance this morning, especially yourself and young Amren. Now I must take my leave and I hope the next time you see me I will have the answers which we sought here today."

The two shook hands and Thias left in a hurry. He knew at once where he had to go.

The bard raced through the corridors that connected the old library to the main complex of the Citadel. On reaching the doors to the throne room he almost collided with Llys Emeny who exited the hall in a hurry and continued on in the same direction that Thias travelled. She soon felt Thias's presence behind her and turned to her right as he drew up alongside.

"Excuse me Llys, but have you by any chance seen Iqotrix this morning?"

"Yes, I have," replied Lady Emeny as they walked on together. "About fifteen minutes ago and I know where you can find him. He was with Commander Townsforth when I saw him. The two said they were heading to a meeting in the Council Chamber with that buffoon Ystafell who still thinks he is in charge."

"Do you know what their meeting is about?" asked Thias as he struggled to keep up.

"Something about rations for the slum dwellers but if you will excuse me bard, I have some urgent work of my own that I must attend to. I have a meeting with those who arrived from Falahorn and Berserkers do not like to be kept waiting."

"Thank you for your help Llys," shouted Thias as he allowed the woman to race off.

Thias turned and scuttled away in the opposite direction. Up the stairs he then went until at last he reached the door to the Council Chamber. He rapped on the wood and waited for an answer.

"Who is and what do you want," demanded the unmistakable lisp of Gilebin Ystafell.

"It is me, Thias Calavan and I must speak with you all, and in particular the Archmage if he is still with you. It's about the verse, 'The Ballad of Predestination' that will destroy Urthanock and help us win this war."

Several seconds later the sound of a key the lock helped lower the anxiety that coursed through the bard's veins. The door then opened and Thias was welcomed inside.

"You look flustered young man," said Ystafell as he ushered Thias to the table. "As you can see, the Archmage is here and so is Townsforth of the Watch. Speak with freedom. I am pleased to have the opportunity pause our protracted pontifications as to whether a family should get one loaf a week or every six days! Tell us at once, what if anything have you discovered."

Thias glanced to the others present before he spoke again.

"I have spent most of the day with the librarians of Parandor, searching through every ballad known to have existed," began Thias.

"And?" interrupted the Archmage.

"There is no copy of Ballad of Predestination to be found anywhere," continued Thias, "However, in an old book of poems by Anyle Belanore we did find a reference to it and by some perverted whim of the gods it is said to found in the book that started this bloody mess. There the song is referred to as 'The Inevitable Truths'."

"What," exclaimed the Archmage

"The full quote was, 'For the Song of Predestination, seek the Inevitable Truths amid the Lore of the Dead'."

Thias saw that he had the Archmage's full attention "I need your assistance Iqotrix. We must go at once to the Wizards Guild and interrogate the Lore of the Dead."

"There is no need to leave this room bard," replied the odd man. "I have it here with me now. It's in my sack beneath the table."

"Why is it here with you and not locked away where it can do no harm? What purpose did you intend for that obnoxious thing?"

"After our discussion on rationing there were a couple of things I wanted to discuss with Ystafell. In particular, some spells that I found within its pages of flesh, yes flesh. It is said these spells arrest the decay of food and may be employed should we be caught in a protracted siege."

Thias looked at the wizard with great suspicion but recognised that he must hold his tongue. He needed the Archmage's help in deciphering the text of the Lore. Iqotrix wasted no time, delved into his bag, and then pulled out the ancient tome; a heavy book bound in brown leather and embossed with intricate brass designs. When opened Thias looked to its pages, each made of thin strips of mummified flesh.

"So, that's what the bugger looks ike," muttered Townsforth. "No wonder it's called the Lore of the Dead."

"Open the book and see if you can find these so called Inevitable Truths," ordered Thias.

"I have read this text so many times that I know its exact location. Take a breath bard, I will find it in a few seconds," replied the wizard who then thumbed through the pages of skin.

As Iqotrix searched the Thias scanned the runes and incantations written upon its pages, all stained dark red and written in the blood of some long forgotten soul. A noise from the Archmage then indicated that he had found what he sought.

"So you knew of this passage already! Why did you not tell me about it earlier?" demanded Thias. "It could have saved us valuable time; time that we don't have."

"You will understand when you hear it." replied the Archmage. "You may all be more than just a little disappointed."

"Just read it man," lisped Ystafell from across the table.

"This is the best translation I can give you, given the age and style it has been written in. Remember though, it is a very rough rendering and it goes as follows;"

They sang this song for a thousand years
And it was always short;
Don't analyse its meaning,
Or you will end up caught.
The five inescapable ones are clear,
To those who bring us hope or fear.

> *So listen well, remember all,*
> *Or else like them, you too shall fall.*
>
> *The first of these is that you're born,*
> *The second that all must die.*
> *The third you choose, the fourth is given,*
> *And the last, you know's a lie.*
>
> *So sing it well and sing it loud,*
> *Never cut it short.*
> *Play each note as if the last,*
> *And keep your life strings taught.*
> *The five inescapable ones are clear,*
> *To those who bring us hope or fear.*
> *So listen well, remember all,*
> *Or else like them, you too shall fall*

"Now do you see why I paid no attention to it?" added Iqotrix. "I did warn you not to expect much."

"Is that it? All if it?" asked Thias as his head dropped.

"I'm afraid so,"

"Then we must seek to make sense of it. Read it again," ordered Thias as he stood from the table and began to pace the room.

"I know what Sir Byddin would say if her were here now," moaned Ystafell.

"Dog's bollocks," replied the other three in unison.

Then discussion began in earnest. It went on for some fifteen minutes before the Archmage suggested a break and a recap. Ten minutes later when all returned from the privy, Iqotrix summarised his interpretation of the so called 'Inevitable Truths'.

"Well, the first thing we have agreed is that there is nothing in this text that helps us formulate a plan to defeat Urthanock in battle. We are without doubt no further forward. The second is that it is just the middle four lines that have any significance and that we think they refer to the debate on fate and self-determination.

"Run it past me again; how did we reach that conclusion Iqotrix?" asked Brynn Townsforth.

"Because," began the wizard in frustration. "The first line states we all are born and the second that at some point in time we all must die. These are indeed inevitable truths. Now 'the third you choose' must refer to us having a choice in what happens in our lives, whereas 'the fourth is given' means that the Fates have predetermined all that will happen to us. They cannot both be right and I think that is the clue given in the fourth line. I myself believe that the message in that last line 'and the last, you know's a lie' refers to the fourth truth and refutes it. That means that the Fates have no say over anything that we do in life. They likely do not exist and are nothing but dullards' claptrap."

"Well many would disagree with you there, Archmage," said Townsforth as he too looked disappointed at the outcome of their inquisition. "Our visitors from Falahorn would state otherwise."

"But if this conclusion is correct, and the more I think on it I hope it isn't," began Thias. "What does it all mean for The Marked? We have sent him off to Harico with the Gems of Thamous to seek out the Moirai, the Fates, or if you wish, the Daughters of Fatumai. What if the buggers don't even exist? What then? What if the gems are mere baubles and this prophecy we are so wedded to is no more than a bag of shite? What then? Fuck, I wish I had never found this sodding piece of worthless scribble."

Then as he snapped, Thias picked up the Lore of the Dead and tossed it against the nearest wall where it landed and closed itself with a thump.

"Steady on bard," squeaked Ystafell. "We can't lose our heads at a time like this. Let's us stick to facts and base our decisions on where we have come from. First off, a vast army approaches our gates. We must fight it as best we can, whether or not they are led by some pox ridden demigod. The lad Llyat must continue on his quest for we cannot abandon what has been started just because we have read some blood scrawled runes in a book that we all revile. You Thias, once you have set in motion your deception, and by the grace of the gods survived the battle, must hurry on after Llyat. If there are no Moirai then all may lost. Who knows what will happen if we are unable to seal the Lord of Fear behind the door to the Underworld."

"If any of it exists, including the so-called gods we follow like brainless cattle," sneered Thias.

"Come on bard, snap out of this self-inflicted torture," ordered Townsforth. "For once, I'm with Ystafell."

"And me," said the Archmage with a level of confidence that took others by surprise.

While the wizard moved from the table to retrieve the Lore of the Dead the Commander of the Watch made his way to the bard.

"Thias, I will arrange for you up to meet with Lolye Throissler in my room in the barracks at first light tomorrow. Then we will send him on his way. Ignore these so called Inevitable Truths that we have heard today. There is in fact just one. If the Archmage's interpretation is correct we are fucked."

"No I disagree. There is one truth that I am now convinced of," answered Thias. "Whether what happens is predetermined or not, we have the chance to change it. We must carry on with our plan. We must defend this city."

"Good for you Thias, let us work for a successful outcome to our endeavours," responded Ystafell as he moved forward and patted Thias on his back. "And if we have nothing left to debate, let us get back to planning the distribution of loaves. I wish you all good fortune amid the many terrors that we are about to endure."

An hour later Thias stood on the battlements of the highest tower of the Citadel of Parandor and stared towards the horizon. His mind was elsewhere, back pondering the content of the Inescapable Truths that he had linked to the Ballad of Predestination. Two lines of the verse would not leave his thoughts.

The five inescapable ones are clear,
To those who bring us hope or fear

He could not be sure of anything. The interpretation of the middle verse as voiced by the wizard had some merit but Thias could not bring himself to believe that after all his efforts there was nothing more tangible hidden in the gaps between the lines and words. The other two verses had been ignored but in his reflective state atop of the tower he began to see meaning in their construction. There were just two people who would be able the understand the truths, the one who brought hope, Llyat Emgar, and the one who brought fear, the essence of Urthanock that walked in the body of Methladon Heyn. Thias thought back to happier times, an evening in the Red Mare when three lives had intersected. He trembled as the realisation of the last line of the first and final verse struck home.

Or else like them, you too shall fall

They were both going to die! Whether he joined them in that end seemed undecided. The thought of losing Llyat caused a tear to form in the bard's right eye and he wiped it away with his sleeve.

Once again he fixed his gaze to the north east and a strange black shadow that lay across the land gripped his attention. At first he was not sure but the longer he looked the more convinced he was that it was moving, although at such a slow pace that at a glance it would easily be missed. He looked to the sky but saw no clouds. Soon he realised what it was he was watching. It was the Army of the Eastern Marsh and it was but a day away. Tomorrow would be the perfect time to despatch young Throissler but his immediate priority was to warn Sir Byddin of the imminence of war.

Thias ran down the tower's spiral steps and raced on through the Citadel. Then as if by some fated coincidence, he met the Head of the Army on the stairs beneath the great stained glass window.

"Sir Byddin, I am so pleased to have bumped into you, in fact I was searching you out. I have been watching from the tower and the enemy's army is visible on the horizon. They will soon make camp for the night but will be at our walls by the end of tomorrow."

"Let the bastards come, I just wish we had a few days longer to prepare," replied the knight. Thias noticed a sudden change in Sir Byddin's his demeanour.

"I sense something is wrong. What is it?"

"Oh, nothing that is of importance to you," replied Byddin before attempting to leave.

"But it is, and you know that you need and want to tell someone what troubles you," said Thias using the deep magic of his voice to overcome the knight's self-imposed mind block. "Tell me what it is you find difficult to speak of, it will go no further."

The voice trick worked and Byddin's words flowed like river melt in a spring thaw.

"We have been inspecting the integrity of the walls and have found a weakness in its construction. Should the enemy become aware of its existence then they may not need their Rift to get inside the Citadel."

Thias's brow furrowed with concern. "Tell me all," he said using controlling tones.

"When the first Citadel was built in Parandor it had its own gate, one which was quite large for its time and it faced to the west. It was blocked in when the Citadel was expanded and the western wall constructed. The old west face of the edifice now forms part of the Great West Wall, but the gate filling has not worn well and the stone is crumbling. I should have spotted it earlier but if what you have seen is true then we do not have time to fix it now."

"Believe me Sir, I have seen the enemy on the horizon," said Thias. "Now finish off what you need to say about the damaged wall."

"There is little more I can say. Should it be discovered it will take but three men with picks a mere ten minutes to clear the crumbling stone that was deposited there. The walls that surround the old gate are five cubits thick, but the door filling is less than half a forearm. I cannot believe we missed it. We have been most lackadaisical in our preparations."

"Can it not be reinforced from the inside without disclosing the weakness to the enemy?" asked Thias.

"There just isn't time lad and it would scare the shit out of the highborn. You must tell no one of this Thias. Now if you don't mind I have other things to do."

"My lips are sealed," answered the bard.

In that briefest of moments Thias considered that Byddin could be Head of the Thieves Guild.

"If only we could say that about the fucking west wall," moaned the knight as he left and climbed the stone steps.

Thias looked up to the stained glass image of Sir Raulyn.

"Now see what you've done." he shouted, but the window did not answer.

The bard made then his way to his room inside the Citadel as Solaris gave way to Mona and the corridors darkened. It had been another long and exhausting day but those that were to come would no doubt be much worse.

Thias woke the next morning and ate a hurried breakfast of berries and a small slice of bread over which so little honey had been spread that its taste was undetectable. Having attended to his toilet he completed his dress by attaching his blade to his side. He then ran some fine powder through his hair in an attempt to lighten the colour for Llyat Emgar was known to be fair of head. The first cock crowed and so the bard left the Citadel. It was still dark as he made his way over to the Barbican and up to the sentry who stood half asleep while guarding its gate.

"A good morning to you sir," began Thias as the young warrior held his blade forward as a warning. "And who do I have the pleasure of addressing this fine morning."

"Are you always so bloody cheerful at his time of day?" responded the youth mid yawn. "And for your information my name is Ambrose Bluehill. My friends call me barmy Bluehill but if you address me in that manner you will feel the point of my blade in your gizzard. Now state your business or move along."

"I have an appointment with your Lord Commander at sunrise, in his office, and along with Lolye Throissler of your order," began Thias. "Check you admittance sheet. You should find my name there. It is Llyat Emgar."

"Then just wait here a moment while I fetch it," replied the youth as he stepped into his sentry box. "Yes... all seems in order. However, I cannot let you pass until Solaris has shown his face. Please wait in silence or I will arrest you for disturbing the peace."

"You must be joking!" snapped back Thias.

"No I am not sir," chirped the efficient and proud youth. "I am in earnest. Do you not realise a war beckons and there are dangers everywhere?"

And so Thias waited until the morning sky turned red. Barmy Ambrose opened the gate at last and Thias rushed on to his meeting.

"I apologise for being a few minutes later than I intended this morning Commander but your sentry was at his most efficient best this morning," began Thias as he sat opposite Townsforth on the second of three chairs inside the small room.

"No problem Thias for as you see Throissler has not yet arrived. Young men were much more punctual when I was a lad."

"You must try your best not to mention my real name when we meet with Throissler. Remember Brynn, I am Llyat Emgar. Our whole plan depends on Throissler believing that I am the Marked."

"Quite so! I think it best I say as little as possible and leave all the talking to you, young Thias, I mean Llyat..."

A sudden knock at the door broke the flow of the conversation.

"It opens," shouted the Commander.

Lolye Throissler entered the room and closed the door behind him.

"Excellent, come over here lad and sit with us. This person in front of me is the one everyone has been talking about; the one Irabo Basquin fished out of the bay. The lad known as er... Llyat Emgar. You may have seen posters about the town, maybe even distributed some. Well, this is he, the one referred to in the Prophecy and on whom the continued existence of us all depends. Now don't stand there any longer with your gob wide open, sit down and say hello to the Marked."

Throissler did as commanded and with a voice weaker than a dormouse he said "Hello."

Thias thrust out his hand and the two men shook in the manner of the common greeting. Townsforth said no more and left it for Thias to do all the talking. It took less than fifteen minutes for Thias to convince the youth that he was the Marked and to deliver his background story. The Marked would stay behind the walls of Parandor for protection against the foul forces from the east. This message was to be passed with the utmost urgency to the town of Valameer with the Marked's personal request that the Lady Flurdiana attack the rear of the enemy at the earliest opportunity using the full complement of her Trident Guard. Throissler was then told that he had been selected for this most dangerous of missions due to the faith that Commander Townsforth had in his courage and abilities. He would not carry paper lest it fell into the hands of the enemy. Should he be captured it was important that he resisted torture as long as possible. If he could get away with spinning lies then so much the better.

The youth puffed out his chest and questioned nothing, so proud was he at being chosen. So it was that Thias departed but not before Throissler had prostrated himself before the bard and dedicated his life to his cause. Thias smiled, Llyat the great hero, worshipped by all; who would ever have believed the once dim dolt from Maplehill would turn out so revered.

The bard, having done all that he could to try and buy Llyat time, wandered through the tight compact streets of the southern quarter of the city. His life had been but a short one when compared to those who had lived into their dotage. As he contemplated the coming war and confrontation with Urthanock his resolve weakened for he had experienced a portent of his own demise. The image came from nowhere. In it he stared into the shadow-beast's eyes while a fiery sword pushed through his heart. He thought of Tonousa and for some reason her death caused him much greater distress than the many others who had succumbed during this most brutal of years. So it was that his mind drifted to the memory of his father's execution and as he looked to see where he was he knew he was not far from that very spot.

A couple of twists and turns, an odd change of direction here with a short cut there, and Thias found himself in the small square where in years past the swine called Danisun Dain had strung up his father. It did not seem right that a man's life could be taken for just stealing a loaf of bread. But then he remembered what Isambard Hotch had told him yesterday; that his father was not just a simple opportunist, but a member of the Thieves' Guild and in league with someone of significance. How he wished the Guild had exacted their revenge for the death of his father upon Danisun Dain and the others who the warrior had killed over the years. For some unknown reason they had not and the bard could not understand why. So it was that on the eve of the greatest battle for a thousand years, Thias swore an oath to himself. As no other, would take the life of the Man-at-Arms of the Watch, then he would do it himself. He would talk to the Guild directly and offer them his services, but first he needed to discover the identity of their Grand Master.

From out of a dingy tavern on the far side of the square, one known as the 'Beggars Bowl", an enormous man staggered forth. Thias recognised him in an instant for his size and shape was unique. Sir R chemanus of the Nightfall wobbled on melting legs before falling head first into the dirt. The bard rushed over to the drunken executioner, rolled him over, and then sat him back against the wall of the tavern. A passing whore shouted to Thias in order to give him advice.

"Don't be bothering with old dickdroop there, he's like this every afternoon now, pissed, and broke. Leave him be sir and go on your way."

"I know this man and must help him to his rooms, war is coming you know," answered Thias, his mind twirling with confused thoughts.

"I know that sir and I am free at this time should you require business. How's about it? One last shag before you die mister?"

"Later... maybe, but now leave me to care for my friend," ordered Thias as he dismissed the wench who then disappeared down a ginnel in search of a more willing customer.

Beside the slumped executioner stood an ancient stone horse trough with a wooden pail floating on its water. Thias filled the bucket with the cold liquid that still showed residues of horse spittle on its surface. He then threw the water with great force into the face of the once fearsome knight. It took three buckets before the monster stirred and swore.

"Will you stop fucking doing that, I haven't yet learned to swim. What are up to?"

"I was just trying to work out if my father, who was once hanged in this very square, was a good man or a bad one. Then you came along and collapsed into my life," replied Thias as he threw another pail full into Sir Richemanus's face.

"If you stop throwing piss at me I can help your there," slurred the inebriate amid the befuddling influence of vast quantities of beer.

"If you can sober up a little then please share your insights, oh great philosopher of the wooden block."

"I am an expert on such matters. I would have you know sir... Is that you bard? Fuck it is isn't it. See I am not as far gone as you thought I was Thias... I still recognised you."

The bard saw no point in trying to respond and so just listened to the sot's sad prattle.

"Now where was I? Yes... good and evil. I'll keep this short for I don't feel too good and may soon puke. Form all my years observing those I had to kill, I learned one fact that has as much certainty about it as that one day we both shall die. Are you ready for it bard? Here it is..."

Richemanus threw up but then composed himself and continued.

"All of us are born as equal blank pages. All have the potential to be just as good as they can be swine. Any babe could turn out virtuous or a thieving murderous piece of shite. It's all about life events; what that child experiences as it goes through its life, and most of that it has little say in. But all can flip. If big things happen, even the pious may turn evil, even a shit may become a priest, just look at Teulu if you don't believe me. I've seen it all, I know it for a fact. You father was both good and evil at the same time, as are you, and as am I."

Richemanus then threw up again.

"You are a far better philosopher when pissed than when sober sir. Now let me help you to your bed," laughed Thias as he allowed the executioner's wisdom to sink in.

Thias helped the knight to his feet and supported the large man around his shoulders as they both staggered off away from the trough. It would prove to be a slow and arduous trek back to Richemanus's rooms.

15

The four shrouded figures, each dressed in their habits with cowls pulled low, walked with their heads bowed as they left the sheltered tree line of the great oak forest that caressed the base of the rolling Hills of Harico. Llyat led the group forward while he oozed the confidence brought on by a crisp morning and the warmth of the watchful eye of Solaris. He headed for the town that shared its name with the hills. The sky god had begun a new day watch over the lands south of the Tiaryer and in the cool of the breaking day a light mist clung to the ground, reluctant to leave the caress of the sweet earth. Llyat's imagination toyed with his senses for he did not see the mist as low cloud but rather the breath of the Moirai as they exhaled through soil pores; holes created by an infinite number of the dirt worms that tended the ancient ground. He imagined the three old crones sat in the belly of some great beast as they smoked dried weeds on three enormous clay pipes while casting enchantments over the land. The mist rose to the level of Llyat's waist. Anyone watching from afar would have seen four ghostly torsos floating across a sea of white. The Marked tramped on towards the old ruins, a cluster of stone derelicts similar in style to those he had encountered in Barad Elestor and which lay to the east of the inhabited hamlet of Harico. The closer he got to the ruins the more certain he was that they were identical to those he had dreamt of just a few days earlier.

Heliana followed next in line as the curious procession of priors crossed the grassy slopes. Her lips were close enough to Llyat such that she could speak and be heard. Behind the young woman trudged Irabo and Theoplous brought up the rear; both with hands on their weapons should danger present itself. All had eaten before breaking from the tree cover and were in good humour. Llyat sensed Heliana begin to fidget and so he turned his head and whispered;

"What's up my pretty swamp duck?" he asked with a cheeky air.

"Stop using such names Llyat," she moaned. "You know I don't like you calling me them. I much prefer Heliana if you don't mind but if you persist I will think of something just as insulting."

"Like what?"

"How's about something your simple head could understand like... pizzle pate!"

"Children, please stop this nonsense," ordered Irabo whose loud, stern voice echoed from behind. "We have an important task ahead and we must try and remain focused."

"Go cool your blood Irabo," replied Heliana. "Llyat and I were just indulging in a bit of fun chat. I recommend once all this is over that you find yourself a bit of quim and settle down. You need the wit of girl to lighten you up."

"I'll bare that in mind Heliana, if and when we succeed in our quest; but until then please try and be a little more sensible. This is hallowed ground that we approach."

"Hallowed ground? You're sounding more pious by the day," chipped in Theoplous who had followed the banter. "You've spent too long in the company of Lachesis and Atropos."

"In answer to your question Llyat," added Heliana. "I have an itch on my arse from these course clothes and would so love to scratch it, but I am not in the mood for giving Fatumai-fearing Irabo a flash of my charms. The last thing I want to do is to corrupt his prissy senses."

Llyat laughed and then all fell quiet as the group began to skirt around the main town of Harico. Lights were beginning to appear in windows and doors to open. The hamlet was stirring and as the four recognised that fact they tramped on in silent haste. The priestly procession snaked its way through the ruins of Old Harico and thereafter began its ascent of the largest of the hills that stood guard over the town and the oak forest at its feet. They passed no one and once half way up the steep climb Llyat called for a break for he could sense the laboured nature of Heliana's breathing.

Just as in his dream Llyat turned to gaze upon the valley below. There the light of Solaris caught the top of the thatched rooves of Harico and caused them to glisten. Here laid out for admiration was the legendary hamlet said to have been forged from golden light. Now in the real world he watched inhabitants of the mystical community move like dots amid the buildings that surrounded the town. His gaze fell to the narrow river that ran through the centre of the town and the small stone bridge over which he had walked in his dreams. He smiled as if in recognition of an old friend and knew at once he was in the right place.

After their brief rest the four companions continued their climb and fifteen minutes later as Llyat mounted a small overhang below the rock-strewn summit, he saw the crest of the hill and the unique structure that sat upon its peak. Ahead just as in his dream lay the sausage like construction, older than time and built from mighty boulders by a long-forgotten people. He stopped, took Heliana by the hand, and pointed out its rock walls and roof over which turf had grown for more than a thousand years. Then as Irabo and Theoplous joined them Llyat pointed to the end of the great mound where several large boulders created a gateway into the structure. The entrance was an impenetrable black. It beckoned and yet threatened to swallow. With sagging jaws the four stared at the long famed Barrow of Harico with both awe and reverence.

"It is just as in my dream," said Llyat.

"It is just as the legend described," confirmed Theoplous.

"Let us hope the Oracle is at home," added Llyat as Irabo's hand rested on his shoulder.

"Is this the site of the Oracles Crypt as mentioned in the Prophecy?" whispered the warrior of the Watch into Llyat's ear.

"I do believe so," the youth replied. "When I sat on that chair inside the Wizards Guild, despite my mind being bombarded, I was told that the so called 'Crypt' was deep below this earthen hill. The Moirai will be waiting."

"I do hope you are right," replied Irabo. "It is too pleasant a day to die."

Some minutes later the group stood before the boulders that formed the barrow's opening. Six sequential upright stones of diminishing height, set in the ground to the left and right of the entrance, supported six roof slabs that had somehow remained in place despite the storms and winds that had battered the sacred sight for as long as man could remember. Beyond the last pair the entrance disappeared beneath the mound of earth. Llyat entered through the black door and found that the granite walls and ceiling stones continued well inside the barrow. Once the four had entered the space Llyat used his fire incantation and ignited his hands. He then searched each inch of the ancient stones. The light reflected off the uneven surfaces of what appeared to be roughhewn rock and created moving images of people and animals. It soon became obvious that the carvings and been created by a most precise and intricate method. The three men stared in wonderment at the moving images but Heliana was not impressed.

"By the will of the gods!" she lamented. "Can you all please stop gawping at this pathetic picture show and find the way to the Moirai lair. You are like babes catching sight of their first rattles. Come on, move your scrawny limbs; concentrate on finding a way forward."

Llyat proceeded to focus his light on the floor. Within minutes he spotted a small opening with narrow stone steps that descended deep into the earth.

"I have located the way down," he squealed. "But there is a problem; how are we going to light the way for none but I know the Promethelumous spell?"

"Then it is a good job others have been more diligent," shouted Irabo from the rear.

"What?" demanded Llyat while turning in the narrow space and almost setting Heliana alight.

"Watch it dick-dolt," she cried as she pushed back against the wall.

Llyat turned to face the young warrior who then removed his back pack from off his shoulders. Once deposited on the ground Irabo took out four oil lamps. He lifted the first to Llyat's flaming hand and then repeated the action with the other three. Now they had enough light to continue without the youth's cumbersome flame.

Llyat checked all were ready to descend. To his surprise and concern he noted sweat pumping out from Theo's forehead. The sailor had turned a most unusual duck grey.

"Are you feeling well, Theo?" he asked. "You look pretty spooked. Is there something you haven't told us about this place? Given your knowledge of the Cuvar, do you want to tell us anything before we go on?"

"I'm fine Llyat, let's just get moving," replied the sailor in a manner that hinted at untruths.

"If you are ill I would rather you remain up here than put our mission in peril," ordered Llyat. "We do not know what terrors we will be meet below ground. Having come so far I cannot allow anything to hinder our progress."

"I am fine, lead on and stop wasting time. It must be something I ate."

"You know your body best," answered Llyat as he began to move in to the depths of the hill.

There were three hundred and sixty-five steps down and Llyat counted them all for something in the back of his mind told him to do so. The descent had been broken by twelve extended stone walkways that connected each of the sets of steps. Llyat did not share his thoughts on the numbers. There was a further quarter step right at the bottom and on its surface, had been chiselled an incurved triangle.

Here Llyat stopped and pointed out the symbol to his colleagues. Irabo bent down low and waved his lamp before this smallest of the steps.

"We are in the right place for sure, given what you were told by Clotho," the warrior began. "We need to look for more of the same for many have sacrificed their lives to point the way."

"Then let us begin our search without wasting anymore time," replied Llyat as he took in the immense proportions of the cavern they had entered.

"This is going to take some time," said Irabo as marvelled at the many stalagmites.

As the group were about to press on, Theoplous dropped to his knees, vomited, and shook.

"What's wrong with you man?" asked Heliana while jumping to the sailor's aid.

"Nothing, I am fine," replied Theoplous as his puke flowed. "Just as said before, it must have been something I ate for breakfast, either that or I have been off the sea too long."

"Are you sure Theo?" whispered Irabo.

"I know fear when I sense it," said Llyat. "I have felt it many times in my life."

"Let's find more of these triangles," shouted Theoplous as he clambered back to his feet. "Just focus on what we came here to do and stop worrying about me. I am expendable. Your meeting the Moirai must take priority."

"If you are sure then so be it," answered Llyat. "But if you're going to puke again then make sure you miss my feet next time."

A quarter hour later, opposite a side tunnel and carved into the rock face, Irabo spotted another incurved triangle about the size of a fist. Llyat and Heliana had walked passed the sign and it was only the young warriors vigilance and keen eyesight that had stopped them from missing this most important of clues. Much to their collective relief they regrouped and headed off along this new passageway that sloped down beneath the hill. On and on they trudged, always following the triangles that had been chiselled out every ten paces. The passage way opened up into yet another cavern. This was smaller than the first and around its walls there were quarried niches each of which contained the offerings to some deity or another. The walls surrounding the niches and the whole expanse of the ceiling had been smoothed by the timeless pounding of rocks and this expansive canvass had been covered in paintings. The vaulted ceiling was blanketed by hand prints, an equal mixture of red and black. It was as if a thousand souls had raised their hands to the heavens or else the dead were trying to claw their way out of the ground. Llyat could not decide which as he stared but soon his interest waned and he switched his gaze to the walls. Their most outstanding feature was the vast number of triangles depicted on their surface and as Llyat examined them he noted other images.

"Come and look at this one Llyat," shouted Irabo from the opposite side to that which Llyat was exploring. "It's the same design as the one on Raulyn's tomb back in Barad Elestor, remember that which we assumed depicted you, the five gems and the Kundalish Aura. This one is however much clearer and easier to make out."

"Let me see that," shouted Heliana as she raced over to Irabo's side and stared at the wall. "Bugger me, it is you Llyat; but how did the person who painted this know what you look like?"

"I guess there are somethings in this mystery we may never get to understand," replied Llyat as he joined the others to look at the painting. "If I were to guess then I think this must be a sacred space of the Cuvar. The ones who have led us here must have been responsible for all this painting. If you look around there are other interesting depictions, all of which seem related in some way to the Enderdetag Prophecy. What do you say Theoplous, you've long been Cuvar. Does any of this mean something to you?"

Theo did not answer for he too was fixated on the crude art upon the walls. His pallor persisted and it took a violent shake by Heliana to halt his trembling.

"Oi!" she hollered. "Deaf lugs; Llyat is talking to you."

Theo snapped from out of his trance.

"No, it doesn't," he replied. "These paintings are much older than we think. My guess is that they are many hundreds of years old. Their meaning has no doubt been lost from the minds of man. Perhaps some of the Lotus Isle Sages would be able to give insight should we ever make it out of this dreadful place."

"Are you alright?" asked Llyat again. "Are you certain there nothing you need to tell us?"

"No, no, no," replied the sailor while shaking his head. "Why don't we search the niches? If the Cuvar were responsible for their creation and yet never returned to the surface, then where are all their bones?"

All then began to search, shining their lamps to the far edges of the cavern.

"You make a good point," said Irabo as he rubbed his chin. "Let's see what else we can find."

Llyat and Heliana chose to explore the tomb's alcoves together and soon found many objects that pointed to the past presence of the Cuvar and their pilgrimage to the Fated Crypt. Most contained small bowls of crystals and stones, all in the colours of the five Gems of Thamous. There were pot beakers containing dried grass seed and bunches of desiccated herbs, all of which puzzled Llyat. Heliana was intrigued by a multitude of coloured ribbons, tied into small bows that had lost their meaning through the passage of time. Some niches contained small collections of animal bones which Llyat reckoned were either mice, shrews, or the like. Many contained three Fortunes Fate cards, all faded. Llyat assumed that those who had left them had followed the diktats of the game. The lovers continued their exploration of the weird hall of the dead and in one section Heliana found strange symbols and runes. When pointed them out to him the youth understood what they meant for he was able to tap into inherited memories passed down through a thousand seeding cycles.

Llyat ran his fingers over of a set of the carved out lines and smiled.

"You can read them can't you?" whispered Heliana.

"Yes, and some are easier than others. It is a gift from Sir Raulyn."

"Have you found anything that will help," she asked. "That last lot made you smile."

"Yes I think whoever wrote it may not have been as serious as some of the others."

"What do you mean?" said Heliana while pushing for an answer.

"It's just a rude comment about the Marked, and the size of his manhood."

"You're not telling me they even knew the secret that I thought was mine alone," she giggled. "What of those scribblings on that wall over there? Their pattern reminds me of what you see in verse."

Heliana led Llyat over to the closest wall where he sought to make sense of the runes.

"These ones are difficult to interpret but my best guess would be as follows:

> The first of these is that you're born,
> The second that all must die.
> The third you choose, the fourth is given,
> And the last, you know's a lie.

That's about it. Have you got any idea what that could mean?" he asked.

"It's just another pile of shite to me," said Heliana after which they both laughed.

"Hey, over here!" bellowed Irabo from the distant reaches of the cavern. "Come and look at this. I found a most interesting door."

The four friends regrouped before a vast metal portal. It stood the height of Irabo and was wide enough to allow the passage of three men abreast. It was a brown, coppery colour with a smattering of green and it looked like it had stood without being opened from the day it had first been fitted. The stone on the floor before it had been eroded by the presence of many who had stood there over the years and it's one handle seemed more polished than the rest of the metal; no doubt in Irabo's opinion from the hands who had once tried to open it. The rock surround into which the metal door was fixed was covered with incurved triangles.

"This must be the way to go but that door doesn't look like it will move," said Llyat as a wave of disappointment coursed through his heart.

"What do those runes on the door say Llyat?" asked Heliana.

"Only those who have been marked may enter."

"Well I guess that just means you then Llyat," said Theoplous.

"Perhaps, perhaps not," said Irabo. "Heliana is carrying your child Llyat which is also marked with Raulyn's seed. Come Theo, help me get it open."

Without hesitation Irabo and Theoplous threw their full weight against the metal portal but the door would not budge. Heliana and Llyat then joined in the push but even four working together could not shift the barrier. As they began to tire and to contemplate what they should do next, Llyat began to search the surface for any hidden clues, instructions, mechanisms, or the like. Theoplous and Irabo slumped to the floor from exhaustion. Youthful eyes scanned the metal surface from top to bottom but there was nothing to indicate how the door could be opened. Llyat turned his back on the portal and leaned against it. The door then moved an inch and so Llyat turned and began to push by himself.

"It's opening," shouted Irabo, jumping up from the floor. "How did you do that?"

"I didn't do anything in particular," replied Llyat. "I just touched it and it opened. It seems that it recognises me."

"Fascinating, I wonder how it did that?" said Theoplous as he too rose to his feet.

The door had moved enough for one person to squeeze between its open edge and the stone surround. No light came from behind and a musty whiff of decay seeped out into the nostrils of those who stood and waited.

"Have a peep in side, wave your lamp in there," suggested Heliana. "I'm not going through until I know what's behind the door. I know we are on a quest but I don't like this one bit."

"We have come too far to back out now," replied Llyat as he squeezed his lover's hand. "I'm happy to be the first to look inside but don't stand too close behind lest I lose control of my arse with fear.

"Just do it Llyat," moaned Heliana, "I may faint from boredom if we wait any longer."

Llyat pushed his head through the door and then his right hand. He moved it around inside in an attempt to illuminate the passage beyond the door.

"What can you see?" demanded Heliana.

"It's a bit black in there. There's a narrow tunnel about shoulder high as best as I can make out. We will all have to stoop as we move through it so as to keep our heads on our shoulders. Heliana take hold of my hand and follow me inside. We will explore together. Theo, Irabo, just wait until we are in and then follow."

"I'm right behind you." answered Irabo.

Theoplous, who had remained seated on the floor screamed without warning. It was a guttural howl that echoed through the cavern and it caused Llyat to jump and spin around as he sought to identify the cause of Theo's distress.

"What is it?" shouted Llyat as he rushed to comfort his friend. "What the fuck's the matter?"

"The dark... the darkness beyond," cried the sailor in panic as the others tried to console him. "The darkness beyond.... the ninth level.... the sight of the door. The sight of the door."

"Theo!" cried Llyat. "What is it?"

"What's wrong with him?" screamed Heliana.

"How the fuck do I know," snapped back Llyat.

The sailor had turned flour white. His limbs shook with great violence and he continued to cry out as if warning of some passing evil. Llyat held Theo and attempted to stem the shaking and all the while his ears were bombarded with the same words.

"The ninth level... The ninth level... The ninth level..."

Llyat looked to Irabo.

"We can't take him in there with us," said Llyat. "Not like this."

"We can't leave him here alone either," added Irabo.

"We have gone through too much to abandon the quest," added Llyat.

"But we cannot leave him," added Heliana as she too trembled.

"I'll stay with him," ordered Irabo, while pushing Llyat towards the door. "Go and fulfil your destiny and let fortune guide your way."

Irabo then threw his arm around the sailor. Llyat did not argue and pulled Heliana with him into the darkness beyond the door.

"Good luck Llyat..." began Irabo but the door closed and cut off his words.

"I guess Irabo was right; we are the only ones permitted to enter," moaned Heliana. "I'm having second thoughts about this fucking quest of yours Llyat Emgar. What have you led me to now?"

Llyat did not answer. Then, with some considerable difficulty, he squeezed past his lover and tried to make the door open again. He could still hear the occasional cry from Theoplous and he feared for his wellbeing. Whatever has happening to the sailor Llyat would have to confront it later. He tried the door to see if it would open again but he soon gave up for the portal would have none of it. There was but one option left, to keep going forward. He squeezed back past Heliana a second time and then began to pull her along the tunnel. All the while he stooped so as not to crack his skull on the uneven rock that formed the roof.

On and on the young couple trudged, minute after long minute, while their necks began to ache. Llyat's concern grew for the oil reservoir in his lamp was already below halfway and he would need to factor in a return journey. He came to the conclusion that they needed to extinguish Heliana's lamp in order to save fuel and thus for another fifteen or so minutes they persevered with the guidance of a single point of light. There was always the Promethelumous spell to call on but he did not want to waste energy in case he needed it later. Then, just when things looked desperate, Llyat became aware of another source of light. It came from out of the tunnel ahead and as they approached it grew in intensity and lifted Llyat's spirits.

A few minutes later the pair stood before an opening formed of two vertical stones with a lintel of equal thickness. Upon this cross stone's surface further strange runes had been chiselled. The two vertical stones each displayed an incurved triangle, the grooves of which had been painted red while the fill of triangles had been coloured black. They were different from the ones left by the Cuvar on the outer side of the metal door. These had been made with a precis on that left Llyat dumbfounded for he knew of nothing that could cut into stone and leave such clean edges. The opening between the two uprights was as narrow as the tunnel they had just navigated but beyond the portal the room expanded into a much larger space. There was something about its walls that looked most strange and Llyat struggled to make out the nature of the material that had been used in their construction.

"What do those ancient scribbles on the lintel say?" shouted Heliana from behind Llyat's shoulder.

"Stop – Here is the Realm of the Dead" he read.

"I don't like the look of this," squealed Heliana. "May we go back now?"

"Whatever is in there, we will face it together," replied Llyat as he pulled her through the gap between the stones. "We two must succeed where so many before have failed."

Tentatively the pair of lovers moved into the dark. Using the light from the lantern, Llyat noted that the walls and ceiling of this new passage were covered in grey rounded bumps whose precise form and origin was not immediately apparent. A minute later the pair arrived at the source of the light and all was revealed. A shudder passed up Llyat's right arm as Heliana trembled at its distal end.

"For the love of mercy!" cried out the young woman, "Did you ever see anything like that before? The three old crones we have come to chat with are about as head sick as you can get."

"They must have collected all the Cuvar ever to have visited this cave and bought them here for amusement," replied Llyat as he regained control of his jaws. "Let's have a look around but keep your wits about you for I sense we are close to the lair of the hideous hags."

Llyat stared ahead into the circular temple of death. Two large cauldrons of burning oil stood to Llyat's left and right and it was from these that the room was lit. The walls and roof which had so confused him now revealed their secret. The rounded bumps were the ends of long bones. Llyat was not an expert on the bony bits of man but from what he remembered from the odd rotted corpse he had seen during his time in Maplehill and the diagrams in Abrahamus Marus's books, they looked like the knee ends of thigh bones. Vast numbers were piled up one on top of another, thousands upon thousands of them. There were more that formed the roof and given that they were packed to close together it was impossible to tell if those high ones were complete bones or just the severed ends. The pattern they formed was quiet appealing in its own macabre way although the thought of so many Cuvar having contributed beggared belief.

"What is this place?" Llyat gasped.

In the flickering light of the cauldrons Llyat saw a mound of human bones twice his height with a base was just as wide. This structure sat in centre of the bizarre temple. On closer inspection this one had been formed into a perfect barrel shape. Its base was a circle of skulls over which some eight layers of thigh bones had been placed such that once again only their ends were displayed. Then there was another circle of skulls, then more layers of long bones, and this pattern continued to the top of the barrel. Still grasping Heliana's hand he led her around the right-hand aspect of the structure. At the point opposite the entrance portal they came across a narrow plinth, waist high, and upon which had been fixed a red and black streaked marble bowl. This had been filled with water. The object seemed to tremble as ripples of water spread across its surface from no apparent cause. Heliana pointed to the wall behind this font of sacred liquid. Deliberately placed amongst the ends of the thigh bones, and made from skulls that stared back, was the pattern of the incurved triangle.

"I guess this is where the Moirai make their sacrifices," whispered Llyat as he stared and pointed. "Brave as we are, sense tells me that we should not linger here."

"I couldn't agree more. I like this place even less than the last," moaned Heliana. "Look over there. Shit, there are several skeletons so small that they must have been ripped from their mother's womb before their allotted time."

"I think you're right," gasped Llyat as he examined the foetal remains. "We shouldn't stay here; I am becoming more fearful by the minute. Fuck knows what we have got ourselves into!"

"What should we do then? I for one want to go home."

"Just stand still and don't move. I'll circle around this monstrous barrel and come back to you. There must be some other way out of here, either that or we missed a turn off the dark tunnel."

"Okay, but be quick about it, this place is the creepiest I've ever been in," she replied. "It beats anything I saw in the service of the Grand Physician."

Llyat began his circumnavigation of the barrel in the centre of the ossuary. He scanned the wall and floor for evidence of another portal. Without finding anything it took him less than a minute to return to the font where he had left his lover. There he stopped in utter confusion for Heliana had disappeared without trace. He had left her with her lamp and that too had vanished. He looked to the wall below the incurved triangle of skulls and there saw a small black hole, one just large enough to permit the passage of a man if crawling on his belly. He bent low and shouted through the opening and into the black beyond.

"Heliana, are you in there?"

No answer came back and Llyat sat on the floor in silence not knowing what to do next. He knew he couldn't sit there forever and at the point of reverting to his old inadequacies something deep and ancient kicked his mind in to focus. He jumped up, ran around the bony barrel, and shouted down the tunnel that had led him to this ossuary temple of the dead.

"Heliana, stop messing about, where are you," he bellowed but other than the echo of his words there was no reply.

Fear sought to manifest itself in an outpouring of sweat beneath his priest's habit and despite the cool and constant temperature of this subterranean world he began to overheat. In that brief moment, he was thankful to be naked under his habit, the way that the Lachesis had directed. Or was he? Did he not put the habit on over his own clothes? Llyat was confused. He could not think straight but he knew that he needed to do something. He ran back beyond the font of water, drooped to the floor, and decided to crawl through the narrow opening that led into the black. First, he removed his bag from his back which along with his extinguished lamp, both of which he then pushed on ahead. He called up the flame in his fists and lit the oil wick such that he could see where he was going.

On he crawled through the passage until after a distance of some fifty paces he sensed the tunnel open up into a much larger space. There he found himself able to stand and as he looked around he saw he was in a brick lined tunnel, similar in appearance to those he had encountered beneath Avolire.

Llyat looked into his bag and checked that the satchel containing the gems of Thamous was still there. If he was to lose them in the dark there would be no chance of finding them ever again. Fixing his travel bag back over his shoulders he then took a few tentative steps forward. It was still dark and so difficult to know where to go next. He put his hand to his mouth and shouted.

"Heliana, are you in here? Stop fucking about and answer me."

In an instant he was surrounded by light although its origin was not evident. Now he could see all. There ahead of him the tunnel led to a door in the distance. It was so far away as to look small but yet large enough that he could see it was part open. The brick lined tunnel seemed innocuous enough at first until a forest of clawed hands passed through its wall and threatened to tear him apart should he attempt to move to the distant door.

"Llyat, help me," screamed a voice from behind the distant portal. "Save me! Come at once, they have me!"

"Who?" he shouted back with all the force he could muster.

"The monsters in cloaks," Heliana screamed back. "I need you now!"

"I'm coming. I will save you," he bellowed Llyat as he ran forward.

"They are coming to tear me apart. They want to feed on my flesh."

Heliana then let out the most soul wrenching scream while Llyat's beating heart threatened to burst out through his ribs. Then all was silent save for his own breath. The rotting arms that pushed through the walls sought to grab Llyat as he raced forward. They scratched, gripped, and tore at his clothes until the only fabric left against his skin was a small patch beneath his travel bag that somehow managed to stay fixed to his back. Despite his nakedness, Llyat rushed on and when about one third of the way to the distant door the floor ahead begin to shimmer and the ceiling moved. As the hands clawed away at his skin the path ahead became a sea of slithering black snakes of many shapes and sizes. The roof was awash with an army of hideous red spiders that all sought to bite with gigantic razor shape fangs. Amid his growing terror Llyat turned. A wall of fire advanced, cracking, spitting, and billowing acrid smoke that smelt of burning flesh. Turning to run he headed towards the oncoming snakes and spiders for he had decided it would be preferable to die a quick death from poison that the agony of being burned alive. Still the hands clawed as ran towards the door. His legs functioned by their own will and amid the collective torments he called out to himself;

"These are all my worst fucking fears. All I need now is for the light to go out."

The light inside the tunnel disappeared and to make matters worse Llyat dropped his oil lamp. It shattered on impact with the ground and the only illumination left was an orange glow from the fire that chased him. The wall of heat cast a feeble light, one insufficient to cut the impenetrable darkness that lay ahead. He tried to light the fire from his fists but the spell didn't work. On he ran as the claws snatched and a thousand snakes snapped and bit at his bare feet. Spiders rained down from the roof and sank their fangs deep into the skin of his neck and shoulders. Then without warning the roof began to drop and the walls inched inwards. In this corridor of traps and terrors the darkness seemed all encompassing. Had he a blade with him Llyat would have driven it through his own heart to end the torture that engulfed his mind. His body was ravaged and evil threatened to suck the essence out of his soul. Perhaps he was amidst a Moirai ordeal but there was no way to determine the truth of the matter.

Pushing forward Llyat somehow managed to reach the metal door without succumbing to the poison of the many bites that the beasts inflicted upon his naked body. He forced the solid portal open and allowed his body to squeeze between the door edge and its stone surround. Despite his intense fear and focus on escape he still recognised that the door was identical in all respects to the one that Theo and Irabo had been left behind. As soon as he had pushed through the gap he turned and slammed the door shut for the fire had caught up. Flames forced their way around the door edge before he managed to seal it in back in place. The fire raged and the metal began to turn red. Llyat stopped pushing against it and turned to see if he could locate Heliana inside yet another strange space.

His senses took a turn for the better. Here there was light, albeit dim, and it emanated from the far end of the large rocky cavern that he had now entered. A wave of relief swept over him as he noted the absence of the eight-legged swarm and the slithering carpet of hissing scales. Llyat then looked to his legs and then his shoulders. Bite marks covered his skin and yet he felt no ill effects. He felt no poison coursing through his veins. Much to his relief his quest would continue and his innate confidence returned. Far away in the distance he heard Heliana's voice cry out.

"Llyat I need you. The beasts are after our baby."

"Who are they?" he shouted back.

"Foul creatures, the most hideous of swine."

"What are they?"

"The undead. The place is crawling with the undead. Rescue me before all is lost. I am over here at the far end of the cavern."

"Where exactly?" asked Llyat, straining his eyes through the dark. "I cannot see much for the light is poor and I have lost my lamp."

"For fucks sake Llyat, fire up your hands. Use your promethy-lethy spell or whatever the fuck it's called. For once in your miserable life do something helpful. If you don't save me soon there will be nothing left of me."

"I have just tried to create the flame but nothing happened. Magic doesn't work down here. Some greater power supresses my energy."

"Try again Llyat, they are close now and there is nowhere for me to run."

"How many of them are there?" shouted Llyat as his heart began to thump inside his chest.

"Thirty, maybe forty; they smell my fear. Wait... They are turning. They are coming for you!"

"Promethelumous," screamed Llyat while shaking his fists but once again nothing happened.

"Don't worry I am coming," he shouted.

"Go back, save yourself, I am lost. I am not worthy and you must live to complete your quest. Find another to love and fill her with your seed. Flee before they catch you... Do not fall victim to the undead."

"As frightened as I am I will not desert you now! We will live or die as one. '

Llyat strode forward into the gloom of the cavern. He moved as fast as he could but the uneven floor caused him to stumble often and the black stalagmites, many as broad as tree trunks, impeded his momentum. He bumped into several, cracking his forehead against two, and cried out with intense pain. The second time his forehead connected with the rock he heard a noise from behind which caused the hairs on his neck to erect. He span around and stared into the dark. That was when he saw the first of them.

It approached in a menacing manner and yet with a slow and deliberate gait. The dark spectral form inched closer while Llyat stood rooted to the spot and gazed in trepidation at this most unholy of sights. Covered in a black hooded cowl it approached and oozed the stench of evil. The skin over what little of its face he could see was also black, mummified from aeons of time limbo. So fragile was it that fragments of bone protruded through its surface. The monster's grim red eyes added the only colour to its presence and the crimson orbs stalked Llyat while it continued its advance.

Then the hideous beast opened its mouth to reveal two rows of razor sharp teeth between which dripped globules of congealed blood. The foul monster's stomach issued a belch of fetid air so horrendous that once it hit Llyat's nose it made him wretch from as far down as the bowels in his pelvis. Then came the sound, a deep, guttural, inhuman, screech that reminded him of a pig being squeezed in a vice. In between screeches the hideous beast sucked in air. Llyat had no option but to flee.

Through the cave, he staggered until more heavy breaths and screeches caused him to look back once again. Now there were five of the blood thirsty beasts and they had shortened the distance between themselves and their prey. Llyat passed a gap in the forest of upright rocks and saw another twelve moving towards him in the darkness from the right. Llyat involuntarily screamed but did not stop moving. He had to keep going. He had to survive for the sake of Heliana and his unborn child. Soon he found himself in a more open space within the cavern complex and then the light returned. Undead beasts in their tattered shrouds now came at him from all directions. All were identical in appearance, rotten and decaying, just like the first he had seen close up. The horde of the dead marched forward and their circle began to close in around him. Now there could be no escape from these Children of Gebez, those that Archmage Iqotrix had feared would make their presence known. Llyat now understood why the wizard had been so concerned.

"Heliana," he screamed. "I'm surrounded by the buggers... I can see no way out... I'm so sorry...I love you."

No answer came and Llyat dropped to his knees. His mind began to cloud and yet just before it shut down, he remembered something significant that Thamous had once whispered. It was as if Sir Raulyn had prodded Llyat's thoughts and ordered him to recall the wyvern's words. He tried to remember the detail of the message for his life now hung on the short distance that separated his frail body from the army of the undead. One of the Gems in his backpack, so the wyvern had said, gave its handler the ability to control the dead, but which one was it? He raked through his thoughts in an attempt to remember as the breathing of the beasts grew louder. Throwing his bag to the ground he snatched at the satchel and pulled it free. He rummaged inside until he pulled out the amethyst he had stolen from the shrine to Urthanock. Lifting it high into the air he bellowed:

"Look what I hold you fucking bastards. Come any closer and I'll unleash the power of Thamous. I am your master and you are now my puppets. "

Still the creatures advanced until the unknown light source focused upon the facets on the jewels surface. The stone began to glow with an intensity not previously revealed. A second later thin rays of purple shot from its centre and connected with the eyes of the Children of Gebez. Each and all then stopped and stood like statues while Llyat took his first breath in over a minute.

"There we go!" he hollered with a canyon-wide smile stretched across his face. "Now let's see what tricks this stone will let me do. How does it work I wonder?"

Llyat then proceeded to wave the amethyst to the right and all the while the purple strings connected the creatures to the stone. In unison, the staggering unholy horde moved to the right. He pointed it next to the left and they obeyed as one, turning and marching in that direction. A couple of minutes later he had worked out how to bend the horde to his will. Wasting no further time, he sent them all off in the direction of the door from which he had entered this last and most dreadful of caverns.

"Llyat where are you?" shouted Heliana's voice from amid the rocks. "Are you still alive?"

"I'm coming, hold on," he shouted back. "Where are you?"

"Follow my voice towards the next door, I am just beyond it."

Llyat replaced the amethyst back into the satchel which he then placed inside his travel bag. The waving beams of purple were then snapped and the Children of Gebez once again began to advance towards him.

"I'm coming," he shouted. "Keep hollering and I will find you."

"Please hurry for the three are sharpening their knives."

"Leave her alone," he screamed. "She is not yours to take."

On Llyat scuttled, bouncing off rock after rock, and despite his nakedness he did not stop to care for the injuries that their ragged surfaces inflicted. He could hear the monstrous horde gaining on him again, their screeches and screams echoing throughout the cavern. Then ahead he spotted another part open metal door. It was identical in all respects to the previous two but he did not stop to reflect on that interesting fact.

Pushing through the portal with the beasts close at heel he turned and slammed it shut. Looking to its inner side he saw an enormous bolt which he then moved across to secure the door. Almost at once the hoard began to hammer at the door and it began to buckle under their combined weight. Once again he realised there could be no going back. A second later he remembered Heliana and so turred to search for his lover. There was no sign of the woman who carried his precious child just three sets of fire red eyes that stared back at him

"We have been waiting a long time for you Llyat Emgar," said a strarge and yet familiar voice.

16

Ssobekk having been schooled in the art of war had erected his command tent on a position that overlooked the intended battlefield. There under the ever-constant scrutiny and supervision of Urthanock he would assist his Lord in plotting the destruction of the race of men who dared to claim the Realm for their own. The tent was a majestic canvass construction, decorated with blue and white stripes that radiated from its raised central pole. The canvass covered three sides, kept out the elements, and provided a focused view out through its open fourth aspect. This vantage point faced the flat ground before the northern wall of the fortress of Parandor. There was but one significant hillock between the Capital and the verdant grasslands of the plains and it was atop of this raised pimple that Ssobekk had decided to direct the scale skinned force that he had marched all the way from the Eastern Marsh. The Gator Lord had been most surprised to find this lonely hillock unguarded for he would have never left it to the enemy had he been the one in charge of the city's defence.

The open side of the tent gave an excellent opportunity for the Commander of Urthanock's Army to witness the war and decide on tactics that would no doubt evolve as the battle progressed. A large awning, supported by six stalwart poles, gave shade to the eyes of those who plotted the destruction of all they had come to despise. Ssobekk scanned the moving mass of reptiles before him as they took up their battle formations some five hundred paces before the stake palisade. The General was most impressed at this construction, built by those who sought to defend themselves against his mighty force. The enemy had been astute in assuming there would be no mercy shown for Ssobekk's troops had already been given strict instructions to spare no one who was not of lizard kind. This order had included ogres and any other creature brought to battle once their usefulness had been served. Knowledge of the decision had however been restricted to the Lizardmen elite. The beasts and ogres would enter the fray on the side of the Marsh without knowing that they had already been betrayed. The crossbred evil that walked inside its human vessel was intent on killing all.

Ssobekk was not alone under his canvass for Urthanock had commandeered the tent for himself. The "beast who heard voices", as he was now known to the common reptile warrior, had chosen to dictate how the battle would be fought. He stood to Ssobekk's right and licked his lips in anticipation of the upcoming slaughter. To Urthanock's right stood the Hochnar, the frog- priest of the Marsh, and through whom messages would be dispatched to ensure the success of the battle.

"That's quite a spawn swarm we have down there Lord," croaked Ssonsh. "There is not a single blade of grass upon which a Lizardman's foot does not rest. I have never seen the like before and we should complement Ssobekk for his remarkable efforts in raising, training, and getting such a horde of death so close to the walls of Parandor. See how the black shadow ripples as his Captains force their formations into position. I would like to recommend that you reward our General with a new title. I suggest something like Marshal of the Field. If that doesn't please you Lord, then perhaps…"

"Cease you croaking," ordered Urthanock after which he spat to the ground. "Old timber toes, our most perverted peg legged plotter, may stamp his stump around this pimple of a hill as much as he likes. Let him strut and pose and order his swine into war, but both remember it is I alone who will dictate how the battle unfolds. It will be my orders that you both will prosecute or else be the first to feel my wrath. I hope you both understand that; unless of course you wish to experience my knot."

"Of course, we understand," replied the Gator Lord without hesitation or hint of wavering loyalty. "Your Hochnar speaks out of turn for he is fat and foolish. I want no titles, nor do I seek any reward. To serve you in the defeat of the smooth skinned shits that have dominated these lands is all that I wish for before I depart this world. I want nothing more than to see you triumph Lord."

"Good, then no more talk like children," replied Urthanock as he turned to face the dawn and bask in the god's fiery morning light. "You do not need personal power now that you have me. So, tell me Ssonsh, how many ogres did your troops manage to bring back into the fold? Did they catch that bastard Brosizrug?"

"We were able to round up fifteen of the monstrous swine including Brosizrug," replied the Hochnar, unsure as to how Urthanock would take the news. "They didn't desert our cause after all. Once they had cleared the Old Pass it seems they had gone on an orgy of indulgence. With no one to order them otherwise they ran amok amongst the farmsteads and the part abandoned Keeps that lay closest to the Grey Mountains."

"So they just went off to get pissed again!" asserted Urthanock.

"That they did Lord, but other things too,"

"Like what?" the Lord demanded.

"They say they ravaged quim and ripped off any tit that came before their eyes," continued Ssonsh. "Those Lizardmen who found the ogres say it was not a pretty sight, even for reptilian eyes. Not one who was penetrated by the foul beasts survived for it is impossible for even the slackest to take an ogre and live. As for the men that our scouts found, it seems some of the ogres have perverted tastes for some were found with arses ripped asunder. Most however just had their heads torn from their shoulders."

"Excellent news Honchar," said Urthanock with a smirk, the vision of suffering brightening his thoughts. "And are these magnificent fifteen ogres prepared to support our cause?"

"It seems they are Lord," replied Ssonsh.

"My advice Urthanock, would be to keep the ogres in reserve," said Ssobekk, trying to second guess what his Lord was planning.

"And so what would you advise instead if we are to win this day?"

"If the decisions were mine alone Lord, given that we have far greater numbers of warriors, I would suggest attacking on many fronts to dilute the enemies' defences. We may not have siege engines but we do have wild beasts to unleash at the same time. We can stretch the defenders thinly around the circumference of their city."

Through his half helm Urthanock smiled and pondered on the thought.

"Say more oak leg."

"Split the beasts up, the grey nose and kulkulkath, and form them into three battle groups, each supported by two thousands of our best warriors. Then attack as one before the north, west, and east of the city. Have the rest of the army split into equals and ready to follow on behind the initial assault once our troops they have breached the stake palisade that the smooth skins have erected. Then we can flood the middle ground before the walls and slaughter the golden knights before they can retreat inside their mighty fortress."

"An interesting plan" sneered Urthanock, indicating he was not impressed. "What do you say Hochnar? Do you support the Gator Lord or do have ideas of your own?"

"General Ssobekk's plan is a good one and I think it could work," croaked the stuttering frog with legs a quiver. "Our original plan had been a two-pronged assault, from both without and within. However there has still been no word from the Dragon Whisper and we have tried the using the Rift again but it remains unpredictable."

"And?" spat out Urthanock, for it was clear the frog was stalling for time.

"We dare not risk the loss of a substantial force by invoking the Rift's unpredictable energy. I say we go with Ssobekk's ideas."

"I have told you before Hochnar," growled Urthanock as he displayed his ire. "Fix the Rift or you will forever regret that you didn't. We will use it when I am ready, but given the risks, you will lead your team through it when I have worked out where best to strike behind their walls. Had we a good supply of black powder, we could have taken Parandor with ease, just as the few reptiles did at the Bards' Guild."

The Hochnar and the Gator Lord kept silent and that fuelled Urthanock's temper.

"I ask you once again," he shouted. "How much black powder do we have? Do we have enough to breach their wall?"

"We have none Lord," croaked Ssonsh. "If you remember, you ordered it all used when we destroyed the room that sat over the crack between the realities…"

"Had you been a braver toad, you would have warned me against such an act," screamed Urthanock. "Your pathetic inability to speak up for yourself has put our whole endeavour at risk."

"But my lord…" stammered the Hochnar.

"Did we not find any black powder in Griginor?" bellowed Urthanock.

"No my Lord," answered Ssonsh. "The alchemical secret never made to that isolated place."

"Your actions displease me Hochnar, as do yours Gator Lord. Your plan reeks like your father's arse. Do I have to think of fucking everything? Now listen well. The beasts will lead off as we attack the palisade before the North Gate. We will have a single point of attack and by concentrating our force at that one place we will degrade their defences in no time at all. We will be inside the killing ground in less than fifteen minutes."

"Yes, my Lord," answered Ssobekk while Ssonsh shrugged shoulders.

"Order the warriors to their places and have the battle ready to start on the hour. Now, leave me alone while my head makes sense of your inadequacies."

Ssobekk and Ssonsh bowed in submission and left to deliver their orders.

"Well that went well!" sneered the voice. "Consensus decision making at its best. I'm so pleased the Army of the Eastern Marsh has at last formed a plan!"

Some thirty minutes later both Ssobekk and Ssonsh returned to the command tent and confirmed Urthanock's orders had been passed down the line. All was set, the battle would soon commence and the full impact of the reptilian force would be directed against the north sector of the palisade. However, when Ssonsh had walked in behind the limping Ssobekk, Urthanock saw that the Hochnar dragged along beaten young man who wore the distinctive leather armour of the City Watch of Parandor. The frog-priest threw the wretched warrior before the feet of his Lord and then stepped back as the prisoner sought to free himself from the ropes that bound both hands and feet.

"Why have you brought this piece of scum before me Hochnar?" demanded Urthanock as he sharpened his blade on a leather strap. "What do you intend?"

"Some of our spawn were scouting the far western edge of the palisade, adjacent to where its drops into the Tiaryer. They spotted this sly bugger break out from Parandor and head off on the old coast road that maps say leads to Valameer. We believe he is a messenger sent with instructions to the Lady Flurdiana, battle plans perhaps."

Ssonsh thrust a webbed foot forward and kicked the young man in the middle of his back.

Urthanock stared without emotion at the terrified wretch. His piercing eyes probed the warrior as his ears followed the Hochnar's report.

"Given your decision to take full command of this war," continued Ssonsh. "Both the Gator Lord and I thought it best you interrogate the bastard yourself. The human filth will not speak nor answer our questions and he carried no written instructions that we have yet been able to find. Our next resort would be torture but we are fearful we could kill him before he divulges anything of use."

Ssonsh looked to Urthanock but the Lord of over Fear did not speak. Red eyes began to glare.

"You have greater power and skills way beyond our capabilities Lord. Perhaps your magic would work better and that is why I have dragged him up this hillock."

"I see," replied Urthanock. "Given we have a little time I will amuse myself as you suggest."

Urthanock moved his arms forward and then pointed them at the prisoner. Then he lifted them up to the horizontal after which the bruised and beaten youth then rose from his knees until suspended upright in the air with his feet a few inches off the ground. Urthanock moved his hands to the sides and the prisoner's arms stretched out wide. The Lord's red eyes then stared at the man's feet and forced them to cross at the ankles. This was the pose that Urthanock had decided best for his interrogation, the appearance of one nailed to a cross for the purpose of crucifixion.

The man's eyelids opened and he stared back at the beast that stood before him. Then amid the spittle and blood from his broken teeth he began to utter words.

"Kill me now, whoever you are, for I will tell you nought."

"Oh yes you will lad," laughed Urthanock. "See toad, the prisoner speaks to me and I have yet to cause him pain. What do you say Gator Lord, are my powers not so amazing that I can get people to talk at will?"

"Of course Lord."

Ssobekk raised an eyebrow and exchanged a knowing glance with the Hochnar. Urthanock moved closer towards the young herald, his foul breath forcing its way up the prisoner's nostrils.

"Do you have any idea who I am," demanded Urthanock.

"Some pox ridden, trumped up shite from a whore house. A cunt who likes to play at soldiers."

As the words flew out so did blood and spittle from the warrior's busted mouth.

"Wrong answer I afraid."

Urthanock stretched open his arms as if to beckon the young man to him.

"You have the honour of being brought before the Great Urthanock. That is who I am and I here to take my revenge on the race of men for the cursed deeds of Sir Raulyn more than a thousand years ago. You must understand that I am omnipotent and you are lower than a worm."

"Fuck you," sneered the prisoner.

More clotted crimson left with the words and a large globule hit Urthanock about the mouth only to be licked clean without concern.

"I can and will indeed kill you with a click of my fingers but first you will tell me all that I need to hear," gloated the beast. "I want to understand what secret message you were ordered to deliver to Valameer. What does Parandor want with the Flurdiana?"

"Go fuck yourself," snapped back the youth and Urthanock laughed again.

"Make no mistake in understanding my intentions. You will tell me all. If you want to experience great pain then so be it, but your death will be the easier if you answer my questions."

Urthanock moved in towards the suspended youth, their faces almost touching.

"Now here is the first; who am I and who are you?"

"As I have said already, you are no doubt the bastard child of a pustulent whore who no doubt liked nothing better than to have her quim filled with grain and have the pond geese peck away at it until crying out in rapture. I on the other hand am a Nobel servant of the House of Gylewu and you are not fit to lick my boots."

Urthanock laughed, Ssobekk laughed, and Ssonsh quaked at what was to come.

"You've got balls, I give you that," sneered Urthanock, "But for not much longer."

The foul Lord lowered his right arm, pointed his first finger at the prisoner's groin, and unleashed an unseen power that ripped the youth's testicles from his body. Urthanock flicked his hand forward and the scrote sack and its contents flew out though the opening of the tent and fell upon the ground before the edge of the hillock's summit. The still suspended youth screamed in agony.

"Now let the fucking geese peck on those," bellowed the fearsome Lord.

Ssobekk no longer laughed and Ssonsh trembled even more. As the sounds of agony died away Urthanock saw that his captive had fainted from shock. An evil smile formed on the Vessel's face for Urthanock had no intention of leaving the wretched lad be. A bolt of blue light shot from his hand and the prisoner snapped back into a tortured reality. Eyes opened and drool dribbled from his mouth.

"I know what works best in situations such as these," said the evil one as he smirked. "It is pain, intense pain, pain like you could never imagine. Isn't that so Honchar?"

"Yes Lord, pain always works best."

"Now lad, listen to me with the greatest of care. I am going to cause your bones to expand from the insides, one by one, and starting with your right shin. The pain induced will be so great that you will tell me everything I want to know. Now we needn't do this if you speak with freedom, so just answer my questions and you will have a quick death. Do you understand me?"

"I do," snivelled the prisoner.

"And one last thing. Always refer to me as Lord in each response. Now tell me your name."

"I am called Lolye Throissler and I am an officer in the City Watch of Parandor. I follow the diktats of Commander Townsforth and it is his orders that have brought me before you...Lord"

"Good, very good." chuckled Urthanock. "You are a quick learner young Throissler. What orders were you given and why were you heading off on the old coast road?"

"I was sent with a message, handed to me by Phauless Gylewu. I memorised the content for I was told it could on no account fall into the hands of the enemy. I will tell you all if you let me leave and disappear from this dreadful war. I was to tell the Lady of Valameer to march north through the Grey Mountains and attack Avolire in your absence."

In the next instant Throissler's right lower leg exploded in pain so unimaginable that no one would ever want to feel it's like again. He tried his best to lose consciousness but Urthanock would not permit the messenger to miss one second of the agony he had brought to bear. The fearsome Lord took a step forward and his eyes burned hate red.

"We know for a fact that Phauless Gylewu is dead. One of my marsh underlings took the pompous prick's life. Therefore, I must assume that everything else you have told me so far is a lie. I will ask you once again, what message were you instructed to take to Valameer.

"An order for the Lady Flurdiana and her Trident Guard to attack your rear without delay."

Urthanock turned away and laughed.

"Ssobekk, pull back a thousand warriors and have them march north to cover our backs," ordered Urthanock without stopping to think. "I will not have the bitch interfering with my plans."

"But my lord, that is too many and we may yet need all the warriors we have in order to break through Parandor's defences," replied the frustrated Ssobekk. "We were led to believe after the attack on the Guild at Valameer that she only has about one hundred under her command."

"Are you questioning my orders Gator Lord," snarled Urthanock.

"No my Lord, I will do as you command if you are sure that's what you want."

"Then go and give the fucking order and be quick about it," shouted Urthanock.

Ssobekk limped out of the tent while Ssonsh continued to tremble and keep his head low.

"Toad, leave me to have some sport with young Throissler. Go and prepare the horn to sound the start of our battle charge. But do not begin without my order for I desire to see all of it. I will be finished with the lad soon enough."

Ssonsh bowed low and then waddled out of the tent. Once the frog had gone, Urthanock turned his attention back to his new toy.

"You have felt the pain of the bone bubble now lad. Don't let me have to use it again. There is one more thing more that I need to know. Where is the Marked?"

"I have no idea who you mean."

Throissler's left shin exploded and amid his agony he screamed out his answer.

"The Marked is in Parandor. He has taken refuge in the Citadel."

"I thank you for your honesty."

"Kill me and end this pain lord; I beg of you with all my heart," wept the terrified prisoner.

"As you so wish!"

Urthanock thrust his right hand forward and took hold of Throissler by the throat. A surge of blue light shot through his arm and his prisoner exploded in a burst of flesh and crimson that resemble the crushing of a ripe plum. The whole of the inside of the command tent was splattered as was the front of Urthanock's face and body. The beast of destruction smiled and licked his half human face with a tongue that extended further than should have been possible. Urthanock then marched from his tent to where Ssonsh stood shouting orders.

"Sound the war trumpet," bellowed Urthanock. "It's time to go to war."

"Do you in all honesty believe the Marked would allow himself to be caught like a rat in barrel? The lad was lying and you fell for it!" said the voice from within.

"Oh no he wasn't," snarled Urthanock. "No one ever lies when in such pain."

Ssonsh kept his amphibian head down as the trumpet rang out and ordered the start to the long awaited battle. Three blasts from the great horn of the Eastern Marsh resulted of a tumult of noise that rose from the land that stretched right from the summit of the hillock down to defences of Parandor. Thousands of voices cheered and a thousand more screamed in excitement. The wall of noise sought to quash the response of the enemy whose whistles and jeers of derision where soon overwhelmed. Then the noise was then overtaken by another, the sound of over nine thousand warriors stomping their way towards the stakewall that separated them from their foe. Urthanock wiped his half covered face free of the remnants of Lolye Throissler for the larger of the lumps had begun to irritate his scale covered skin. He wiped, smiled, and stood in anticipation of great sport.

"Unleash the beasts and drive them forward," ordered Urthanock after which four blasts on the trumpet were heard by all below.

From his vantage point the Foul Lord licked his lips as on the plain he witnessed a wave of fearsome creatures charge towards the palisade. Ten juvenile kulkulkath and a dozen mathulath raced forward at the head of the charge. They were followed by six leathery longnose who, despite being less fleet of foot, covered the ground at a frightening pace. Each longnose carried a box on its back hump, strapped around its girth, and in which a handful of archers had been primed to fire their bows. The Lizardmen had few archers and all had been committed to this first wave of attack, much to Ssobekk's consternation. The foot warriors now began to run in order to keep up with the creatures while a pack of some twenty skyfawn took to the air and flew over the front of the beasts as they headed towards the palisade. The air resounded to their screeching as they swooped from left to right. How Urthanock had waited for this time, the moment he would crush his enemy and leave not a single one alive. Yet a moment later his confidence was jolted for his enemies Battle Captain had also been planning for this very moment as the weeks had passed since news of the fall of the Grey Keep and the Bards Guild of Valameer had reached his ears.

The Lord over Fear snarled and cursed as the enemy's pults unleashed a devastating salvo of rock and scrap metal that landed amongst the beasts and the reptiles that charged on towards Parandor. The Lizardmen took the full force of the bombardment for most of the beasts managed to overrun the drop zone. It took a full two minutes to reload a pult and this gave ample time for more reptiles to charge forward and trample their way over their fallen comrades. The defenders rushed their pike men forward to bolster their stakewall at the point of imminent threat.

Far more devastating than the pult salvo was the defenders next tactic and Urthanock snarled as he watched it unfold before his eyes. The one weapon that Parandor had in abundance was the longbow. There was an untold number of high quality arrows which were soon deployed to murderous effect. A forest of steel tipped wood rained down for at least five minutes until the Battle Captain of Parandor ordered his forces to halt its storm of death. The effect had been stunning and Urthanock cursed while as his anger grew; all was not going as he had hoped.

The lethal arrow storm had decimated the swarm of skyfawn who fell as one within a single minute, each hit by at least fifty projectiles. The mathulath had also been slaughtered but not before some had turned tail and ran back into the advancing reptiles. The reverse charge caused much death and mayhem. An unintended battle struck up between those that were covered in scales and those that smelled of pig. Death came in large numbers and not one of the mathulath survived. The kulkulkath and longnose meanwhile accelerated their run, incensed by the myriad of pinpricks that stunned their hides. The Lizardmen archers in their boxes on high were instantly taken out as they were each transformed into something that resembled a pincushion.

The worst was yet to come. Many of the arrows unleashed had been lit before being fired and when they fell deliberately short they ignited a river of oil and wood that spread to engulf the entire northern aspect of Parandor just a short distance before the stakewall. Amid the arrow storm, the intensity of the screams of the wounded, and the acrid smoke that in an instant coved the battlefield, the kulkulkath and longnose raced on. Urthanock stamped in his rage and the hillock shook with an intensity that was less than the Dark Lord had expected.

"Your power is significantly weakening," teased the voice

"Fuck off!" bellowed Urthanock.

The beast's voice rolled down the hill, so loud that it was noticed by those who stood before the walls of the Capital.

The young kulkulkath and the longnose raced on until they fell into the burning pits of brush and oil. The scorpion beasts were unable to fight their way free and soon just added fuel to the fire. Their screams drowned all other noise and those who heard that sound would never forget the impact in had on both their drums and their souls. Two of the six longnose manged to climb out of the far side of the fire pit and hurled themselves at the stakewall but they got no further. Both had their underbellies ripped asunder and their entrails popped upon the pikes of the defenders. Urthanock was one of the few to witness their demise as a break in the smoke caused by a stiffening of the breeze gave him a clear line of vision if only for a few seconds. Those lizard warriors who still swarmed forward saw nothing but smoke. Some however soon witnessed something far more terrifying for the three longnose that had clawed their way out from the rear of the pit began a new charge back amongst the reptilian swarm.

Urthanock focused on the three behemoths of annihilation as they cut through the Army of the East. Minutes later they left the field of battle and disappeared in the direction of the Grey Mountains. The stakewall had remained intact, a thousand of Urthanock's warriors had perished under the storm of arrows, and the defenders had lost not a single knight.

"My Lord it is madness to continue like this," snorted Ssobekk who had returned to claim his rightful position on the top of the hillock. "The smooth skins will annihilate us if we persist."

"I am not fucking blind," snarled Urthanock. "Sound the retreat while I think through how to extricate our forces from this debacle."

Two short Blasts on the war trumpet, repeated three times, sent the signal to fall back. The black shadow on the ground began to roll back from the area before the stakewall. The Army of the East retreated in complete disarray and cries of exultation rose from the ranks of the defenders.

"Their arrow storm was devastating and most unexpected," croaked Ssonsh as he joined Urthanock upon his vantage point. "The fashioning of orichalcum in the style of our ancestors left too many exposed gaps. You will recall how keen the Knights of Avolire had been to eliminate such penetration points. We should perhaps have followed their example."

"Maybe we should camp here until we can rework the armour back into the style of the knights of old," added Ssobekk as he winced at the chaos unfolding below.

"They both know you are a fool and yet because of your powers they dare not answer you back," teased the voice. "If I were you I would listen to Ssobekk. Too many years have passed since you last took commanded in the field and the way that men fight has long since changed. No more do they just rely on the strength of their sword arms. They have learnt to defend themselves."

"Piss off and leave me alone," snarled Urthanock as both Ssonsh and Ssobekk made to leave. "No, not you two cretinous cruds. Stay where you are."

"Of course Lord," croaked Ssonsh who then bowed and returned to his place.

"As you so wish," added Ssobekk.

Bewilderment spread over the Gator Lord's face and it stoked Urthanock's discontent.

"You think I'm fucking befuddled, don't you General? Well I'm not... I just like thinking aloud. You need to know Ssobekk that I hold you responsible for the events that we have just witnessed. You are in part to blame Hochnar but not so much as this leather hide lump ..."

"How so me?" croaked Ssonsh.

"Shut up and do not speak again until I have finished; either of you. Do you understand?"

Both nodded their obedience and neither dared utter a word.

"Hochnar, it was your idea to refashion the orichalcum collected from the Knights of Avolire. Had we left it as it was many more of your kind would have made it to the stakewall and now we would be rejoicing in victory! But no, you wanted them to fight in the style they have always preferred and now see the slaughter you have brought about. I never should have listened to you, you bloated nabob..."

The Hochnar's eyes bulged but still he dared not speak despite the falsehoods his Commander threw at his webbed feet.

"As for you Gator Lord, had you agreed to go with my first plan and execute it well, then we would not be in such a mire. Call yourself a military man, why I remember a dimshit back in Maplehill who would have fared better than you. His name was Denius Castor and..."

"Oh, how strange you should think of that place at this time," sniggered the voice.

Urthanock ignored his tormentor and continued with his rant.

"I still do not know why you thought a single head on assault would have been a better plan than attacking on three fronts." bellowed Urthanock as he attempted to drown out the voice that teased his mind. "Even an egg laying snoutskull that eats his own clutch should have anticipated the outcome of such a foolish plan. Now I have to salvage this mess before it is too late. Do you both understand what I am saying?"

Once again the General and the Hochnar nodded their understanding amid their confusion.

"Fail me again and you will both be flayed. You Ssobekk will be made into a collection of boots that I will wear while I trample on any others who so disappoint me. Your skin Hochnar will be dried and stretched to create a dozen drums that will play at my victory feast. Now I will ask you both the same question and you may answer, but say either yes or no. Will you prosecute my new plan to the best of your abilities?"

"Yes," they answered in unison.

"Then give your ears full attention onto what I have to say. Given that we still have a far greater numbers of warriors, by at least a margin of eight to one, we will attack on several fronts to dilute the enemy defences and stretch them in a thin line around the circumference of their city. Ssobekk, send riders out and recall the thousand you sent to engage with the Flurdiana bitch. My new plan will give us victory and we will be finished here before she gets wind of what has happened. Remember, her messenger's jewel case lies on the dirt before this tent while his essence is at this very moment seeking access to the Underworld. Ssonsh split our assault force into three and have them regroup. You have two hours to prepare before we try again. We will attack together before the north, west, and eastern gates. Have the remnants of the army ready to follow on behind the assault troops once they have breached the stake palisade. You need to work out how you can protect them from the rain of wood for we will not stop to refashion their armour. A three pronged attack will allow us to flood the middle ground before the walls and slaughter the golden knights before they can retreat inside their mighty fortress, just as I had always wanted. Now go about your preparations and report back to me in two hours when I will give the order to recommence this war."

"What of the Ogres and Brosizrug?" the Hochnar dared to ask. "You have not yet factored them into your plans. They could be most useful. Some of my observers believe they have spotted a group of Berserkers moving around in front of the stone walls; giants from far away Falahorn."

"Come on, wake up dolt," sneered the voice but Urthanock closed it down at once.

"I have not forgotten them," he growled. "I'm contemplating where best to deploy them."

"May I be permitted to offer a suggestion Lord?" quaked Ssonsh.

"No, you may not," snapped back the Lord over Fear. "Your ideas and decisions are what led us into this mess. I alone will decide what we will do next. Split the ogres into three groups. From what you said earlier then that would mean five at the head of each assault group. If anything can break through that stakewall it will be the ogres. Have the bastard Brosizrug lead four others from the north. The ugly one with the chain from nose to ear can lead four in from the west. Then pick another of the swine and have him lead the left overs before the Eastern Gate."

"As you desire Lord," bowed the Hochnar without question.

"Tell me, how immune are the ugly buggers to arrows, do either of you know?"

"Permit me to answer that question Lord," replied Ssobekk as his nostrils twitched.

"Go on then, spit it out,"

"I am led to believe that their hide is thick and that arrows may not penetrate to a sufficient depth to kill for the points have to go through their armour first. However their eyes are vulnerable and it I were coordinating Parandor's defence I would have my archers aim for their faces. That is where they are most vulnerable."

"Well you're not!" barked Urthanock as he shifted his gaze back to his retreating army. "The ogres are expendable and we just need to keep them alive long enough to penetrate the stakewall. Equip them with hooks and chains and have them secure an attachment to the staves. Then all we need to do is to pull on the chains and rip their pointed sticks out from the ground."

"That may work," croaked Ssonsh.

"Of course it will fucking work. Once the stakes are down our victory will be assured. Now leave me and return when your plans are complete and the next phase of the assault is ready to go."

Neither the Gator Lord nor the Hochnar moved; it was clear they had more to say.

"Well!" snarled Urthanock, his ire ignited. "What the fuck are you waiting for?"

"Do you intend to join the battle yourself Lord?" asked Ssonsh in his weakest of voices."

"A good question Hochnar. You are indeed a brave toad today. I shouldn't need to intervene if you do your job well but if I have to then I will. Once I know where the Marked is I will go there for we have unfinished business."

"Are you sure you're not on Parandor's side" teased the voice.

"Fuck off!" bellowed Urthanock, causing the General and Hochnar to scuttle out of the tent.

Two hours later the tested twosome had returned and with them Urthanock surveyed the latest deployment of his troops from the top of the hillock. As he did so his right foot ground Throissler's scrote sack into the dirt. The eyes of the foul Lord looked to his army, now split into three sections and awaiting the signal to start.

"Are we ready to go?" demanded Urthanock. "I am growing impatient and want this battle over and done with by the end of the day,"

"Yes my Lord we are as prepared as we could ever be," replied Ssonsh. "However, those who oppose us have been mirroring our tactics and have redeployed their archers and knights in response to our manoeuvres."

"Then sound the trumpet and let's make sure we do the job right this time," ordered Urthanock. "We cannot afford another failure."

Three blasts from the great trumpet resounded across the land and seconds later the battle recommenced. Urthanock noted the five ogres at the head of each charge. The thick skulls raced on faster than the Lizardmen foot warriors and he felt pleased with his decision to use them as his vanguard. While he stood and watched the madness unfold, he switched his gaze from one assault group to the next and tried to assimilate the effectiveness of his new plan.

The battle group that attacked the northern palisade had shifted to the right to skirt around the reptiles and the beasts that had fallen during the first assault. The pults of Parandor unleashed a devastating salvo that took out many and when in range the rain of wood dropped many more. The thousands of arrows unleashed from behind the stakewall and from the top of the battlements swished into the reptile horde. It was however a lighter rain for there were one third less archers focusing their bolts of death at those who ran toward the north palisade. The reptiles continued their advance with weapons in one hand and make shift wooden shields in the other, held above their heads to withstand impact of the feathered missiles. This wood had been stripped from supply wagons and any other source available although some Lizardmen possessed metal shields of their own which were smaller and of limited effectiveness. The death toll grew as the Lizardmen ran up to the burned out trenches. Here they threw their wood down in order to create a solid bridge across the small but significant gap. The bottle neck this created increased the cull rate but soon the assault force began to stream over their bridge. Led by the ogres that now resembled the giant porcupines of the Lotus Isles, and despite their losses, the battle group began to mass before the stakewall where the rain of wood ceased to fall. Here the ogres and the lizards faced the sharp tipped oak stakes that angled forward but also a line of densely packed pikes and long swords; all readied to push through any flesh that came within reach of their steel.

Urthanock smiled when the assault troops made it to the stakewall. Once it was breached the rest of the battle group would be ordered to move forward. However, the ogres seem to be having significant difficulty in attaching their hooks and chains for the defenders of the city lobbed jars of flaming oil at the beasts who then, being set alight, retreated and rolled in the dirt to extinguish their burning leather armour. In this respect, General Brosizrug seemed no more capable of reaching the stakewall than his subordinates and soon the ogres were swamped by the reptiles who raced passed them and began to engage with the pike and the long swords of Parandor's defenders. It was then the Lizardmen revealed their surprise tactic.

"Watch what happens now my Lord," sneered Ssobekk. "You will be surprised at how much we have learned since you last walked upon this Realm."

"For both your sakes I hope that you are right," grizzled Urthanock as he stared ahead.

As Parandor's long pikes stopped the Lizardmen from using their short swords and axes to good effect, the assault troops each pulled from their back a small crossbow. They carried half a dozen bolts in a quiver at their waist and these they then began to fire at will, aiming for the gaps between the stakes that made up the palisade. The horizontal wave of destruction was well deployed but was not as devastating as either Ssobekk or Ssonsh had anticipated.

Urthanock looked to compare the progress of those at the norther assault with that made by those that attacked from the both the east and the west. The situation was unfolding in identical fashion although delayed by some minutes. On these other two fronts the defenders had ignited their fire traps but the Lizardmen knew that would happen and had a plan of their own. They had rolled forwards all of their water butts which they concentrated at a single point doused the fire before backfilling the pit with their makeshift wooden shields. Soon they had created bridgeheads over which they raced to their targeted portions of the stakewall. Here the ogres fared no better than those led by Brosizrug and in a similar manner the reptiles unleashed their crossbow bolts.

Across the three fronts many bolts never made it through the oak wall for in their haste and exhaustion the creatures' aim was not as accurate as when they had practiced. Yet over one third of those discharged did make it through. Most deflected off the bronze coloured armour but some found points of weakness and at last the defenders started to take casualties. As the knights of Parandor fell at a steady rate, most from bolts that had passed through their eyes as they looked to steer their weapons at the enemy, the battle of three parts ground to a stalemate before the wall of wood.

"At last we are beginning to inflict casualties Lord," croaked Ssonsh.

"But this is going to take for fucking ever," snarled Urthanock. "See... look...They have turned this into a slogfest. The ogres have not been able to get close to the stakes and most seem disheartened and at a loss to know what to do next."

"I thought they were smarter than this," offered Ssonsh. "They could move up and down in front of the wall until they either find an unmanned section or the knights run out of fiery oil jars."

"I am sorry to say this Lord, but I think I should go and lead from the front," said Ssobekk, no longer caring if he incurred his master's wrath. "If I were to take charge of one of the battlegroups on the ground I would be able to coordinate a decisive attack."

"I agree," smirked Urthanock. "Get yourself down there and set about winning this battle for me. You have been no help up here, just an irritation in my ear. Go and make things happen."

"From here on this hill it appears the west side is the least defended," croaked Ssonsh. "I would advise you take charge of that group. It also seems that the ogres there, the team led by the weird one Ikeg, is putting up more of a fight than the others."

"I agree," said Ssobekk as he prepared to leave the top of the hillock.

"Take this with you and use it to good effect," ordered Urthanock.

Lifting the sword he had been given by the blacksmith Gof from off his back, he thrust it into the hands of the Gator Lord.

"Legend says this sword with its wavy blade will cause those who hold either pike or longsword to drop their weapons should they clash on the field of war. Use it well and punch a hole in the stakewall for me."

"Does the blade have a name Lord?" asked Ssobekk, taken aback being given such a gift.

"White Hilt! Now be gone."

Ssobekk bowed and left to descend the hill. He had not needed to be told twice. Once the general was out of sight, Urthanock turned to Ssonsh.

"Hochnar, you are also of no use to me here. Take the thousand Lizardmen you can see over there, those returning from defending our rear. Kit them out with the gold bracelets of our kin and lead them through the rift. Now is the perfect time to open a second front."

"But my Lord, the rift malfunctions," trembled Ssonsh.

"Do it now!"

"At once Lord", whimpered the frog priest as he waddled off to meet his fate.

17

The bard, the acting Regent of Parandor, and the Archmage of the Wizards Guild, stood together at the summit of the highest tower of the Citadel and watched the battle as it progressed from its inception and following a series of blasts from the marsh army's horn. They had observed the first attack on the northern stakewall and had been most heartened when Sir Byddin's trap had been sprung. The enemy's battle beasts were either slaughtered or dismissed from the field. A deluge of wood rain had also taken out a vast number of reptiles. After that first attack, and following the cheers raised by Sir Byddin's buoyant troops and the armies of the Fifteen Keeps, the three had exchanged glances of satisfaction for the battle had so far gone better than any of them had expected. None however believed for one second that it would continue to be so one sided. Because of that reason alone they held back from any meaningful conversation, save for the odd comment about Sir Byddin's obvious skill in defending the capital.

During the realignment of the Army of the East, mirrored in its movement by Sir Byddin's force, Thias noted that the Archmage held a strange object to his right eye. He kept it there through the beginning of the second attack, unleashed on the palisade from three simultaneous directions. As Thias looked closer he noted the object had been constructed from two glass balls bound in leather to make a single tube-like object. There were however far more pressing issues at hand than the strange object held by Iqotrix. As all fronts headed to a slow and steady stalemate Thias's concerns began to mount. Although a vast number of Lizardmen had already fallen and the effectiveness of the stakewall demonstrated, the sheer size of the enemy's black shadow meant they would be able to continue to suffer a high casualty rate for many hours and by which time the defenders of Parandor would be exhausted and unable to further resist.

Having deduced this critical point in the battle the bard felt the need to seek the views of the Regent and the wizard. He sensed they too saw how all now hung in the balance.

"I have never seen conflict on such scale before," Thias began. "How do you two think it is going? How long do you think it will be before they break through our defences?"

"I don't believe anyone alive today has seen the likes of this before," replied Gilebin Ystafell. "I am not a military man but all seems locked in an impasse. I fear the enemy may just grind us down. The wearier Sir Byddin's troops become the more the swamp scum will grow in confidence; their reserves are endless."

"I wouldn't say endless," chipped in Iqotrix as he continued his stare through his strange toy. "But I understand the point you are making. I believe we all now realise that if this stalemate continues much longer we are finished as a race and that is without any new tactic they may deploy."

"What do you mean?" asked Thias as he tried to interpret the wizard's meaning. "Have you spotted something we two have so far missed and what is that strange object you have been looking through all this time?"

"I have been observing the body movements and expressions of those who command the reptile swarm from on top of yonder hillock."

"How are you able to make out such detail?" asked Ystafell as he ran his fingers through the forest of hair that covered his cheeks."

"Put this to your eye Lord Chamberlain and then let the bard have a turn. It is a seeing glass and it makes distant images appear much larger."

Ystafell raised the leather tube to his eye and looked through it. His jaw dropped as his gaze roamed over the battlefield and then up to the tent that was the enemy's command post.

"How does this thing work, it is amazing?" demanded Ystafell.

"Curved glass bends the image before the eye and enlarges it. I have been working on this for some years now and this is the first time I ever found a practical use for it."

"Well, it's amazing and I must have one when this war is over," lisped Ystafell. "Bard, you have to have a go with it."

"I would love to Gilebin if you could part company with it."

"I'm glad to see you keep your sense of humour in this darkest of times," sneered Ystafell.

As he handed the seeing glass over to the bard the wizard uttered a half stifled laugh and continued to scan the battlefield without his aid. Thias raised the tube to his eye and was shocked at how close the distant images now looked. He moved the focus of his enhanced vision from one area to the next and then at last made to pass the seeing glass back to the wizard.

"No, you keep it for a while if you wish," said Iqotrix. "I have seen enough of their command to understand they fight each other as well as our forces."

"Really!" exclaimed Thias, "How interesting; now let me locate their tent... Ah, there it is. It appears there is just one of them there at present and through this implement, as far as can I make out, it is Urthanock himself. The two other dots that were there earlier have departed, perhaps dismissed. What do you reckon Archmage?"

"I think perhaps they have been sent forth with new orders with which to break the current stalemate. What do you say Lord Chamberlain?"

"That would be most logical," replied Ystafell while fingering his whiskers. "What orders do you think could have been issued?"

"Let me scan the ground beyond the palisade and see if I can spot anything that would give us a clue to Urthanock's intentions," replied the bard.

"Yes, you just do that, and then share your wisdom with us," sneered Ystafell.

Thias ignored the sniping comment and put it down to the anxiety. Then in a most methodical manner he searched the ground as if covering a grid and began to search for the unusual. Unable to resist looking to the blue and white tent, he began to watch Urthanock pace before it and trample something red amongst the dirt smeared grass. The foul Lord looked agitated and stamped with violence on the ground beneath his feet. Thias found it hard to believe that he now looked upon the youth that had been seeded from the loins of Vostag Heyn and whom he had once called brother.

The story of the angry child and the hammering of nails into fence posts broke through into his conscious thoughts. For the first time he felt relieved that

Vostag was dead for the old blacksmith would have wept to see what his son had become. No father should be forced to witness such shame. The whole Realm did not contain enough iron to make the vast number of nails needed to allow Urthanock to manage his anger. Thias reflected on the relationship between the Vessel and the beast that could not be turned. It was beyond evil and it had to be destroyed; as would the Vessel that was once Methladon Heyn.

"You've had that seeing glass too long, let me have a go for a while," muttered the frustrated Lord Chamberlin.

"In a minute Gilebin, I'm still looking for something useful," snapped back.

"Well, focus on the fight to the west of the stakewall," said Ystafell. "That is where most of the action is happening."

Thias looked as directed and saw something most curious taking place within the enemy's ranks. The Lizardmen and the small group of ogres disengaged from the skirmish at the stakes and parted as if expecting something or someone to come between them. With the enhancement offered by the seeing glass Thias at once recognised the unforgettable face of the ogre leading the fight.

"I know the swine who leads the enemy at the west wall," began Thias. "He is called Ikeg and I hope before this battle is over I get to stick my blade through his heart, even should another beat me to it and kill him first. We have an old score to settle."

"Fuck the Ogres!" exclaimed the Archmage. "What's happening down there?"

"Listen bard," moaned Ystafell. "If you are going to keep hold of that object then you must tell us what you see so that we too may evaluate what's going on and make decisions of our own."

"Yes I can do that," replied Thias as he tried to work out all that was happening.

"I also have a suggestion," said Iqotrix. "I will watch the fight at the east wall and Ystafell can watch what's going on at the north. We will let you know if there is any change in our sectors but you must talk loud and tell us what you observe through the seeing glass. Do we agree?"

"Sure," replied Thias.

"Sounds good," added Ystafell, "and I will keep scanning their command tent."

"A great plan," sneered Ystafell in his usual pompous manner.

"Oh, I forgot to tell you both something when we first climbed this tower," added the Chamberlain.

"What now," exclaimed Thias?

"Inside my pocket I have some charcoal sticks, strips of linen, some stones, and a small slingshot. I have a prior understanding with Sir Byddin that should we spot anything of importance then I will write a message and fire it down to him or one of his Field Captains."

"That's good idea but let us not waste your tools on trivia," added Thias, "though it is good that you remembered to tell us."

"There's no need to be sarcastic lad!" lisped Ystafell as he drew attention back to the battle outside the city walls. "Anyway, what's happening over yonder?"

"There is a group of reptiles approaching the palisade," answered Thias. "They are carrying a large piece of wood over their heads, protecting someone or something that moves below it. The reptiles are moving in a very slow yet deliberate manner... Now they are taking a heavy shower of wood although so far the storm of arrows has failed to have any effect."

"That will be their legendary turtle manoeuvre," suggested the Archmage as he continued to look to his own area of reconnaissance. "Can you see any clues as to what the swamp swine may be covering and seeking to get to the palisade?"

"Not as yet... Oh, but wait," said Thias with mounting excitement. "Several of the support lizards have been downed, just after the group traversed the defence pit. That's interesting, I can see what looks like a wooden leg moving under the wood."

"What kind of weapon is a one legged beast?" sneered Ystafell. "Is this their campion, a stump walker sent in to take on what five ogres and a swarm of swamp scum couldn't better?"

Thias paused as memories of his conversation with Llyat returned to influence his thoughts.

"I think I may know who's under the wood and will soon be able to confirm my suspicions for the arrows are beginning to abate in fear of killing their own. The group approaches the stakewall... They are discarding their wood protection and have pushed it before the palisade.

"What do you see now Thias," asked the Archmage. "What is wooden leg doing down there?"

"That must be the one!" exclaimed Thias. "It has to be the same bastard that Llyat said killed my friend Einar. You must remember, the Berserker that I told you went into the swamps with the Marked to find the amethyst."

"What about it," asked Ystafell? "What has it...?"

"It is about to take charge of the assault," added Thias.

"How do you know it's the same one?" questioned the Archmage.

"It fits Llyat's description very well, a large scale hardened beast with a snout and thick tail that gives it the appearance of a Badland gator," answered Thias. "This without doubt is the General known as the Gator Lord; the one who leads the army of the swamps and had a pet kulkulkath that took his leg."

"But what could it bring to the battle that the others have not," asked a bemused Ystafell.

"Perhaps he will instil greater energy to those he leads although the buggers at the west wall already seem far more dangerous than the others," continued Thias as he once again stared through the seeing glass. "Wait, there is something else..."

"What," demanded Ystafell?

"The Gator Lord is carrying an enormous sword and seems to be showing it to his troops in an attempt to rally them to his cause. I wish I knew what he was saying."

"And what are our defenders doing while all this is going on?" demanded Ystafell. "Have they stopped for breakfast?"

"No, Byddin has taken the opportunity to rotate some of his troops. Our front line now consists of pike men alternating with Eerickk Jarl's Berserkers, about twenty of the giant men, and all with two axes. They are being led by Jarl himself who I know from my time in Falahorn. He is smaller than most of them and more like us, yet he is reputed to be as fierce as those that he leads."

"So what's happening now?" asked Iqotrix. "What does the Gator Lord's sword look like? That fact may be of some significance. It may give us an insight into their strategy and Urthanock's ultimate plan."

"It is a great two handed beast of a weapon with a white hilt and a strange wavy blade, the likes of which I have never seen before."

"That has to be a flame sword," answered the wizard. "I have heard legends that talk of them. They were forged in this manner so that when they strike they set up vibrations that make it difficult for those who face them to keep a grip on their long swords and pikes. What is the Gator Lord doing now?"

"It looks like it's about to lead a charge... here we go..."

Thias fell silent as he watched, much to the distain of the Lord Chamberlin.

"Well man." exclaimed Ystafell. "What the fuck is happening?"

"The peg-legged swine is at the palisade with ogres to his left and right. The thick skulls still cannot penetrate the spikes and attach their hooks but now the croc is hitting the ends of our gallant defender's pikes, and they are dropping. It seems what you have heard of this flame sword is true Archmage."

"Yes, yes," squeaked the Lord Chamberlin. "For goodness sake man. What is he doing now?"

"The long snout is pulling back and the ogres are sweeping in with their hocks before more pike can be pushed through the stakes."

"This does not sound good," lisped Ystafell.

"Well, you asked," added Thias.

"Enough of your lip bard," spat back Ystafell. "Has the stakewall been breached? Is there any evidence our forces are preparing to retreat back inside the city walls. I feel a siege coming on."

"It is too soon to make such a prediction although this is a worrying turn of events," groaned Thias before crying out in surprise; "By the first of Fatumai the man is crazy!"

"What is it, what can you see now?" demanded Ystafell.

"Eerickk Jarl and ten Berserkers have clambered up the stakes and are preparing to jump forward onto the enemy... there they go... now they are in hand to hand combat with the ogres and the Gator Lord. Shit, that took them by surprise."

"How are they faring?" asked the Archmage.

"Eerickk is swinging his axes like a windmill in a storm... He has severed a hand from one of the Gator Lord's arm. Now he has picked up the flame sword and is... He has thrown it back over the palisade into the midst of Byddin's troops..."

Thias gasped and fell silent.

"What is it man?" demanded Ystafell. "What has happened now?"

"Oh fuck, he's down," groaned Thias.

"Who," demanded Ystafell? "For mercy's sake tell us. Oh, how I wish we had three seeing implements and did not have to rely on your eyes."

"Jarl is down and it looks like he's dead!" cried Thias.

"Did he manage to get the blade to our side of the wall?" bellowed Ystafell.

"Yes, he did and the Gator is retreating. "They have taken back possession of their makeshift roof and a team of Lizardmen are covering his retreat as yet another shower of wood descends ... The stakewall still stands and the fallen pikes have been replaced. I think it was the brute Ikeg who delivered the fatal blow on Eerickk; crushed his head with a great stone club."

"And what of the rest of the Berserkers, it is impossible to believe they could climb back over the stakewall while still engaged in a fight to the death," said the wizard.

"You are right," replied Thias "They are making no attempt to flee. They are sacrificing their lives for our cause. There are but four of them left standing but they have taken out three of the ogres. The bastard Ikeg is still going strong... Now were down to two... But there are only two ogres now and more of the reptiles are moving in... Shit!"

"What?" exclaimed Ystafell, as he attempted to snatch hold the seeing glass. "What do you see now?"

"Those brave Berserkers are no more. Yet we must be grateful for what they have delivered at this critical hour. It's back to stalemate but at least we have control of that flame sword."

"That was a close one," stammered Ystafell. "No doubt the enemy will have a few more surprises for us but right now I am concerned about a ground shadow coming down from the north. It's my turn for the seeing glass, at least for a minute, and I will tell you if I can make out what it is. My guess is it's another Lizardman battalion."

Thias wasted no time and passed the awesome instrument over. Ystafell focused his gaze into the land beyond the command tent.

"The shadow is the group of Lizardmen we saw leave earlier in the day," he said at last. "It appears that wherever they went their mission has been completed for they are returning at great speed. Wait, there is something very odd happening out there."

"Describe it to us as best you can Gilebin," said Thias as he focused his eyes beyond the tent.

"There is a fat frog like creature leading a team of Lizardmen and an open cart towards the returning horde. I assume he is one of their leaders."

"It is possible," added Thias while deep in thought. "What is the frog doing?"

"Well as far as I can tell, the cart is full of golden objects, but even with this seeing glass I cannot be sure what they are. Wait, I do believe they are bracelets or something similar. This is most peculiar."

Thias let out a deep sigh for he knew what was about to happen

"Fuck!"

"What is it Thias," enquired the Archmage. "What knowledge do you have of these things?"

"They are about to open their second front," snarled Thias. "Things are about to get much worse."

"What do you mean," asked Ystafell.

"As I earlier told the Council, the Lizardmen use the Rift to move great distances and to overcome obstacles. I had considered they would perhaps try and send a strike force of maybe some thirty or so inside Parandor's walls, just as they did to the Bards Guild of Valameer. I never once though them capable of sending in a whole battalion."

"What are you jabbering on about boy," demanded Ystafell.

"Listen and take all this in," began Thias. "That cart that the frog is taking toward the black swarm must mean they are going to attempt a mass attack using the Rift. We will be caught between the hammer and the nail."

"May the gods have mercy on our wretched souls," trembled Ystafell as he paced around the tower top like a decapitated cockerel. "How has it come to this?"

"Calm yourself dolt," sneered the wizard. "We need to keep clear heads and make some important decisions. Thias, while this heap of hairy lard shakes like ferret in a bear trap, tell me the extent of the number of defenders left inside our walls. How many do we have who can wield a weapon?"

"There are about thirty of the Royal Guard left," began Thias. "Twenty or so have been deployed to the battlements to help support the warriors of the City Watch."

"So, there are just ten allocated to guard the highborn and the citadel." lisped Ystafell. "We will be at the mercy of the slit-eyed bastards."

"As far as I am aware, the City Watch can count on some two hundred swords," continued the bard. "If you remember what Townsforth told us, a hundred of them are pretty raw and have been rushed through their training. That being so, the best are deployed to the battlements and are supervising the peasant archers which number about one hundred and fifty."

Thias moved the Lord Chamberlin to one side and directed the seeing glass to where he pointed.

"Look to the battlements. They are split into groups guarding the four main gates and a few to the narrow one. The less experienced guard the main buildings outside the Citadel, and if you also remember they are listening and watching for Lizardmen who may seek to gain a subterranean entrance. I doubt all this will be enough against a battle group. Let us hope the peasants of Parandor put up some resistance or they may find they will likely be slaughtered without mercy."

"I now understand the extent of your concerns bard," replied the Archmage. "Yet we cannot just stand here and weep for what is to come. There is something we must do at once. I need your help Thias to complete a most import task."

"What could be so important at a time like this?" squealed Ystafell.

"It is vital that the Lore of the Dead does not fall into Urthanock's hands," said the wizard with steel to his voice. "If the Eastern Marsh breaches the Wizards Guild they will find the book of knowledge. There are spells and incantations within its pages that the evil one could use to destroy everything we have ever cherished. The tome lies in the centre of my Guild and it is chained by magic to the Ovumchair. Only I have the key to release it. Urthanock has greater powers and may be able to access the work. It must be destroyed at once."

"What is the best way to ensure its total destruction?" asked Thias.

"That at least is simple to answer," replied the wizard. "Fire! We will unlock the tome and burn it using whatever means necessary. I had grown attached to it and hoped that through victory the book could be preserved. It has a magic of its own that gnaws away at my thoughts..."

Thias was lost inside his head and did not hear the end of Iqotrix's sentence. Instead his thoughts focused on the book of skin and blood and the possibility that the Eastern Marsh were now ready to use the rift. There was no time to delay.

"Then we must leave at once and destroy it before the Lizardmen arrive," said Thias.

"Do you need me to come with you for added protection?" lisped Ystafell.

Thias couldn't help but laugh, much to Ystafell's disdain.

"No, I don't think so," smirked the Archmage. "I am grateful but your offer however your lack of prowess with a blade is legendary throughout Parandor. I think you would be a hindrance that we cannot afford."

"You are most rude young man," screeched Ystafell but Thias interrupted the exchange.

"There is something else I implore you to do instead Lord Chamberlain," he began. "The highborn will no doubt be scattered throughout the Citadel. Given the impending attack on its interior, I need you to round them all up as best you can. Have them make for the throne room and bolt the doors from the inside. No one should then be allowed to enter without the use of Townsforth's secret knock."

"Herding that lot could take forever," moaned Ystafell. "Seeing that you will not accept the protective presence of my small and humble sword, I will set about this new task with great vigour. I will not however forget this insult should any of us survive this war. No one tosses aside a Gilebin."

"I'm so scared," sneered the wizard.

"Please gentleman, our lives are in peril and yet you both act like dimwits," roared the bard. "Not another word please. Come Archmage, let us hurry to your Guild. I suspect we do not have a great deal of time before the slime of the Underworld descends upon us."

Thias grabbed the Archmage by the sleeve and dragged him to the head of the tower's steep steps. The wizard offered only token resistance and down the spiral stairway the pair raced.

"Move as quick as you can Gilebin," shouted Thias over his shoulder as his face drew level with the floor of the tower. "The highborn are laggards at the best of times and you need to get them moving."

Thias descended the steps as Ystafell's reply echoed in his ears. "You can rely on me, which is more than I could say about that red head. Good luck in your quest Thias Calavan and I hope we may live to meet again."

The distinctive lisp disappeared as the bard and the Archmage rushed to take possession of the Lore of the Dead. Once they reached the bottom of the spiral stair case they ran on, shouting to any highborn they passed to make for the throne room for an attack was imminent. Most, true to form, just stared back in total disbelief although a few did make to move.

On the two raced, past the stained-glass window depicting Sir Raulyn's defeat of Urthanock and through the maze of rooms and corridors that led to the main door of the Citadel. Those of the Royal Guard they passed were ordered to be vigilant. Through the courtyard they sprinted until at last they came before two warriors of the City Watch that were guarding the way through the Barbican. It took some time to persuade the pair to let them pass but then at last they were through. They cut through the streets of Parandor with ease as all were deserted except for several beggars asleep in the gutter. An occasional fearful face poked from out of a window and Thias tried to sense if the populous was up for a fight. The destruction of the foul book overrode all concerns for the denizens of Parandor. Some ten minutes later Thias stood panting before the door the Wizards Guild. Wasting no time the weird Archmage whispered a spell and the portal of the ancient tower opened. He led Thias on through the strange maze of sliding white wall panels until at last they arrived inside the wizard's laboratory with the Ovumchair sat in its centre. Iqotrix ran to the chair and uttered another incantation under his breath. The Lore of the Dead then twitched and jumped an inch into the air before falling back after which the wizard snatched it up with his right hand.

"Burn it," screamed Thias.

"I cannot. It is too valuable an artefact and my hands say no!"

"Fuck that!" bellowed Thias. "Promethelumous."

The bard's hands ignited in a flash of energy which Thias directed towards the evil tome. The book burst into flame with a ferocity that suggested it begged for such an end. As the heat from the book grew, Iqotrix dropped it to the floor where it burned until there was nothing left but ash.

"Thank the god's it is gone at last," exclaimed the Archmage.

"Tell me, would you have been able to destroy it on your own?"

"We'll never know."

"No we won't, so let's now try and make it back to the Citadel. I do however have one other question for you. Where are all the other wizards that I saw when I came here with Llyat?"

"It's very interesting that you pick up on that…" began the Archmage, but he never got around to finishing his answer.

Amid a stream of crackles and flashes of blue light multiple parts of reptiles began to materialise within the room. Thias and Iqotrix stood mesmerised as an intertwined mass of fetid intestines appeared before their stunned eyes and then fell to the ground where they lay and reeked. A stack of spine bones dropped into one corner and the belly skin of another reptile covered the Ovumchair. A leg then made its appearance and several half heads slew down the parchment walls creating crimson streaks like wine dribbles on an old man's shirt.

"By the balls of Belanore, what is happening?" stuttered Thias as his bottom jaw dropped.

"It seems something has gone amiss with Urthanock's plan," replied the wizard as he surveyed the body part piles. "We may yet be saved. Let us hope this is happening everywhere the creatures are attempting to enter."

No sooner had the last word sneaked over the wizard's tongue than a complete and intact Lizardman, in full armour and with sword and shield, appeared before the two astounded comrades. In the split of a second, Thias drew his blade from his belt as the creature advanced but before it had the chance to launch an attack a bolt of blue light flashed past Thias's right shoulder hitting the reptile in the chest. The creature dropped to the floor with a thud.

Thias turned and saw the Archmage holding a small cube of polished silver.

"What is that?"

"Just a toy I have been working on," mused the wizard. "That was the first time I have used it and I am most impressed. However, just like magic is has a limited time of use before it needs to recharge."

"Tell me about it later for we must get to the Citadel while we can."

Off they ran again, the Archmage leading them through the sliding maze to the great door that would lead them out of the Guild. As they traversed the many blanched rooms they came across more reptilian viscera, bone heaps, and severed limbs. Through some rooms they fought with great ferocity for more foul creatures appeared by the minute. Thias swung and thrust his blade to great effect while the wizard fired bolts of blue from his silvern block; that was until it faded and ceased to work.

"Promethelumous," shouted Iqotrix as he tossed the cube to one side while his right fist ignited in a wondrous golden flame.

On they moved and never once did Thias see another wizard. At some less critical time that fact would have bothered the bard but so preoccupied was he with survival that the observation failed to register on his bucket list. Several minutes later they arrived before the ancient portal that had stood guard to the Guild for millennia. The wizard mumbled words that Thias's ears couldn't catch and the doors opened. Two Lizardmen crashed through the walls behind them. Thias turned and decapitated the first with a single swipe of his blade and caused the other to retreat. Then flame shot past his right shoulder. This time it was of the yellow kind and it was directed at the first of the parchment walls. The material ignited in an instant and soon the fire began to spread at speed. A hand then gripped the bard by his collar and dragged him out of the Guild.

"Close!" shouted the Archmage and the portal obeyed.

"But you have set your Guild alight," shouted Thias with memories of the Bards Guild flashing before his eyes.

"I designed it that way!" replied the wizard as a sly smile crept across his face. "The inner walls will burn hot but for a short time. All inside will be destroyed but the flames will be insufficient to damage the outer stone or the great door. Any more of the reptile scum who seek to enter my Guild will be fried or locked inside without air once the fire has gone."

The sounds of screeching Lizardmen filled Thias's ears, so intense that they resonated through the solid wood of the ancient portal; they were the death cries those being cooked alive. It was a small victory, but a victory none the less.

"But what of your fellow wizards," bellowed Thias, "They too will perish?"

"Do not trouble yourself with wizards; there are none in there just now and I will explain all when we have more time," snapped back Iqotrix as he ran the fingers of his left hand through his cherry red hair.

A sudden clatter from behind brought an immediate end to further questioning. Thias turned as more Lizardmen entrails appeared amid further crackles and blue Rift flashes. Two attacked at the same time and as Thias began to defend himself the wizard used the last of his flame on another that sought to take him out. Thias defeated his two in less than a minute and sustained no significant injury although he was tiring fast.

"Let's make a run for it," shouted Iqotrix above the distinctive crackle of further arrivals.

The pair moved off into the network of narrow streets that led to the Barbican. No help came from the citizens of Parandor who no doubt cowered behind their doors. Slipping in a pot deposit, Thias clawed his way upright once again and looked back for a brief moment towards the Guild.

"Oh fuck! It's come itself!" he gasped.

"What," replied the wizard whose eyes followed the bard's finger?

"The one we saw with the cart of gold," replied Thias. "I am sure it is the one, perhaps thinner and older looking, but there cannot be two of the buggers."

The frog like creature had not come alone. Lizardmen warriors of all shapes and sizes began to appear in ever greater numbers. All were armed and looking for a kill. They gathered around their leader as Thias and Iqotrix took the opportunity to run back into the shadows. When the streets opened up before the Barbican's gate they came upon a group of some ten reptiles who were trying to work out the best way to breech the portal.

"Shit, the gates are closed and there are more of the buggers than two can handle." whispered Thias so as not to attract the attention of the enemy.

"We cannot go back for there are even more behind us," replied the wizard.

"What are we going to do? Should we make our last stand here?"

"I guess there's nothing else we can do," spat back Iqotrix.

Thias's ears picked up the distinctive sounds of the portcullis being raised. The reptiles heard it too and turned to face the iron grille. The metal teeth lifted to knee height off the ground and from under it rolled out half a dozen members of the City Watch who then proceed to engage with the enemy.

"Over here bard" bellowed the familiar voice of Commander Townsforth. "Get under the gate before we close it again. Move you scrawny arses; your life hangs on the fleetness of your feet."

Thias and Iqotrix ran towards the skirmish. The wizard skirted around its fringes and when he reached the portcullis he dropped to the ground. Iqotrix wasted no time and disappeared in the direction of the Citadel. Thias however remained to fight alongside Commander Townsforth and his gallant warriors of the Watch. The exchange was fierce but the attackers soon paused to regroup. This brief hiatus allowed Thias, Townsforth, and the two remaining members of the Watch to roll under the teeth of the portal. Townsforth immediately gave the order to drop the metal gate and it fell with a great thud. Seconds later a wall of Lizardmen began to gather on its far side.

"Come we must get you to the Citadel," shouted Townsforth while pointing to where Iqotrix had disappeared. "It seems our brave wizard is well on his way there already."

"You are wounded," cried Thias.

The bard winced as he saw the Commander's left arm hanging limp.

"The sinews are sliced through at the shoulder, but I will live," replied the Commander. "Let's keeping moving bard and talk of my injuries later. We need to regroup inside the Citadel. These scaly shits are popping up all over the place and there are far too many of them for us to cope with in the open. The citizens of Parandor have not rallied to our cause as I had hoped and we have left our heart exposed. We should have retained more of the Royal Guard behind the walls."

"Perhaps," said Thais as be moved towards the inner portcullis, already raised to allow passage of the Archmage. "Let me get you inside the Citadel and tend to your wounds."

Townsforth turned to the two surviving warriors of the Watch.

"Atheas, Bruge, you must both stay here and defend the Barbican with your lives. None must pass. Do you understand?"

"Yes Sir," replied two trembling mouths.

"Once the bard and I are in the courtyard keep the iron door shut. Hide if you must for you will likely be attacked from both sides. You must keep the way to the barracks closed until I return. If somehow the Barbican is breeched then destroy the workings such that the gates cannot be lifted. I pray we live to meet again."

Thias assisted the Watch Commander under the portcullis and on into the courtyard. No sooner were they through when the grille thudded into its ground slots.

"Look, Iqotrix has almost made it to the door," shouted Thias as he stared ahead. "It has always surprised me how fast the fearful flee."

The courtyard then filled with an intense blue light and the thunderous crackles of the Rift. Several hundred intact Lizardmen began to fill its space in addition to an outpouring of body parts from those that had not may it through in on one piece. Townsforth pushed Thias into the shadows to the right side of the Barbican tower. There within the darkness of the black cloak cast by the Citadel's outer wall, Thias watched as the ageless wizard became surrounded by the reptiles. The Archmage used his lightning bolts to take down several of the Lizardmen but one warrior was too quick for the wizard. Sneaking in from a blind spot the beast swung its jagged blade and decapitated the sorcerer.

"No!" bellowed Thias in an attempt at warning the wizard.

It was too late for the Archmage. No sooner had the blade passed through the wizard's neck than a pulse of invisible sorcery, a shock wave of released unworldliness, flew across the ground, and caused the surrounding walls of the Citadel to tremble. Thias quaked. Those Lizardman nearest to the wizard dropped to the ground, never to move again. As the dust thrown up by the explosion abated, the two separate parts of the once venerable Archmage glowed with the most intense display of Kundalish Aura that had ever been witnessed anywhere in the history of the Realm. That too at last passed. Thias's jaw dropped as he stared at the remains of the wizard.

"Look at that Brynn!" he exclaimed as he pointed ahead. "What is that on the front of the Citadel and what the fuck does it mean?"

"I'm buggered if I know," replied the astonished Commander

Burnt into the stone across the expanse of the Citadel's south wall was the three circle mark of Kha.

"What do we do now?" demanded the befuddled bard.

Despite their losses there were still too many intact Lizardmen inside the open space that separated the two defenders from the potential sanctuary of the Citadel's Keep. The creatures had been taken back by what they had just witnessed and appeared to be struggling to decide what they should to do next. The Commander, even though wounded and shocked, somehow managed to keep his mind working.

"This is what we will do bard," he ordered. "We will skirt around the Citadel and seek to enter by the backway into the Underkeep. As luck would have it I have a key to the door for that is how we take our prisoners to the cells. Follow me and move without making a sound. Do you understand?"

"Err... yes... of course," replied Thias as his mind struggled with all he had seen.

"Come on, then," ordered Townsforth. "My arm is still bleeding and I am feeling a little light headed. We must go at once before it is too late. "

Thias followed Townsforth through the shadows as the pair moved in silence. Their footfall was so light as to be absorbed by the dirt beneath their feet. All the while Thias glanced over to the swarm of confused reptiles who began to gather before the main door of the Keep. The bard and warrior continued to move towards the back of the mighty edifice. Three quarters of the way to their goal, the shadow thinned as they approached the full glare of Solaris. They still had some two hundred paces to cover until they reached their goal and both realised they would have to take a risk and run for the door.

"I don't know that I can make it," whispered Townsforth. , "I am having a bit of a dizzy turn. My vision is blurred and all seems so far away."

"We haven't got time for this shit," snapped back Thias. "Drop your sword and throw your good arm over my shoulder. We will do this together for I will not leave you here to have your carcass desecrated. But first find me the key to the door. We will not have time to search it out once we get over there."

Townsforth delved into a hidden pocket of his leather armour and pulled out an iron ring onto which half a dozen keys had been attached. He thrust it into the bard's hand.

"It's the one that's just a bit longer than the others," he said without hesitation.

"Are you sure?"

"Yes, I am Thias." affirmed the Commander. "As sure as I could ever be."

The bard wasted no time and soon separated the one key he needed from the rest. He then placed what he hoped was the right one between his teeth and with his left arm supported the injured Commander.

"Now, let's go," he ordered.

The bard and the warrior struggled on as if two young children in a three legged race. The further they went the heavier the burden on Thias' shoulder became. Yet still they pushed on, their goal only seconds away. Thirty paces from the door a loud screech from Thias's left caused him to stop and look to the direction of the noise. Several Lizardmen on moving around the corner of the Keep had spotted them and soon began to approach at speed, weapons drawn, and tongues flicking out in anticipation of a new kill.

"Oh, fuck!" exclaimed the bard.

Thias dragged Townsforth across the remaining part of the courtyard until he reached the small flight of steps that led down to the base of the Citadel wall. There lay a solid iron door with a small barred window in its middle.

"Brynn, you need to focus and do something for me as the enemy approaches. I need to distract them while we gain access to the Underkeep."

The bard thrust the key into the commander's still functioning hand. "Somehow you need to make it down those steps and unlock the door."

"I'll try," groaned Townsforth.

The three Lizardmen pounced and Thias readied himself for the attack. "Promethelumous," he shouted, thrusting out his blade which then ignited.

So preoccupied was he in his defence that Thias did not hear the Commander fall at the base of the door. Swords clashed, lizards hissed, the bard screamed, and scales were melted. The fight was intense and yet still more lizards came to join in fray. Thias found himself being pushed down the steps by the frenzied onslaught of his opponents' blows. Despite his approaching exhaustion he would not drop. At last his heels touched Townsforth's body.

"Brynn, open the door now or it will be too late."

"I've lost the key," groaned the Commander.

18

As Thias fought for his life he did not hear the door behind him open, nor the scraping of leather across the ground as Commander Townsforth was dragged inside the Underkeep. Only when it seemed he would at last succumb to the ever growing number of assailants did he become aware of the deep voice that thundered from behind.

"Move through the door at once or you are dead flesh for the carrion,"

Thias wasted no time and did not look back. He took one giant stride in reverse while slashing his fiery blade in every conceivable direction. With one last crash of steel on steel he stepped back into the shadows of the Underkeep. The door slammed shut and as Thias's eyes tried to adapt to the gloom he saw a mountain of a man close the bolts that would hold the door fast, at least for a time.

"I suggest you help your friend up and out of my cesspit," grunted his saviour.

Thias began to help the Commander back onto his limp legs as the large man shouted above the hammering at the door.

"What's happening out there?"

Tharik Mastisan, the mass of muscles, yet dim of wit custodian of the Underkeep, helped sling Townsforth over the bard's left shoulder as Thias answered the question.

"The Army of the Eastern Marsh has penetrated the outer wall of the Citacel and are massing in the courtyard. Soon they will seek to force entry through the Underkeep, now that they have located this door. This woodstop will be far easier to breech than the main one."

"And yet string plucker you were stupid enough to show them the way." sneered Mastisan with menace. "Get thee gone with Townsforth and I will seek to delay the bastards as long as I can."

Thias glanced into the gloom of the Underkeep while seeking clues that would lead him to a safer place of refuge.

"Which way is it?" he demanded. "How do I find my way through this maze of tunnels?"

"Head straight up the passage until you come to the steps, go up five, and then turn left." barked the gaoler pointing off into the dark. "Then keep turning left at each meeting of the tunnels. After some minutes you will find the main stairs that ascend to the Keep. Make sure you secure the door as you leave."

"But what of you," shouted back Thias as he began to ease Townsforth down the dark tunnel? "And what of the other prisoners? We can't leave them to be slaughtered by the Lizardmen."

"In all my long life I have never once left this place," snorted back the monstrous man. "I was born in this stinking womb of the defiled and I will die happy in it, if that is to be my fate this day. My world has been limited, but here I have been master of all. Keep moving bard for it will not be long before the swamp swine find a way to break the door."

"But the prisoners," shouted Thias as the sound of screams grew ever louder.

"They are my business, now fuck off while you still can."

"And how will you alone hold back all the reptiles that will soon enter your world," shouted Thias as he reached the first flight of steps that the gaoler had described.

"I have a store of oil for the lamps by this door. Tonight I will gorge on roasted reptile."

Thias struggled on and left the gaoler to get on with his task of denying the Lizardmen entry. The banging and hammering of the reptiles on the door began to fade the further the bard journeyed into the belly of Parandor's infamous Underkeep. With only the light of his flaming sword to show the way forward he negotiated the tunnels and expended what was left of his precious energy. While Thias laboured hard, Townsforth, still weak but alert, tried to express his feeling of gratitude to the bard who's arms held sway over his destiny.

"Thias, I will never be able to thank you enough for what you are doing, but if you find you can no longer support me then just leave me here. Should the Lizardmen break in then at least my death will be a quick one. They won't give me a second thought and I will not suffer long."

"Keep your mouth shut old man," snapped back Thias as his words rattled out at pace. "Save you strength for the more you have then the easier for me. I do not do this just for you alone but in the memory of another. Should Tonousa Amberstone be watching from some other world existence, I know exactly what she would expect of me? How could I ever face her when the time comes for my essence to depart my body if I did not strive to keep you alive? She looked to you as a daughter does to a father and I will be buggered if I do not do all I can to save your illustrious soul."

"Then let us move in silence," replied Townsforth as Thias caught sight of a tear trickling down the hard man's cheek.

Further through the Underkeep they trudged amid the maze of tunnels that seemed to branch off in every direction. Soon the way forward was lit by flaming baskets identical to those that illuminated the windowless corridors of the upper floors of the Keep. The flames flickered and cast dancing shadows on the walls and ceiling of the arched conduits that were filled with screams of men and the noise of scuttling rats. Thias knew that Mastisan would never release those locked inside their cells for he did not have a Court Order to do so. His simpleton's wits were known to be incapable of independent action and yet when it had mattered most he had proved all wrong; he had opened his door and saved two lives. The bard wanted to stop and free the incarcerated but he had neither the time nor the energy. It took all his strength just to follow the gaoler's instructions.

"Left... left... left... always left," Thias mumbled under his breath, knowing that just one aberrant move, one brief delay in their progress, would mean the end of all he had strived for. "Hear me Children of Fatumai, do not impede what destiny requires of me. Give me the strength to fulfil all that I need to do this day."

Just as Thias reached the final short flight of steps that led up into the main body of the Keep, the sounds of a great commotion suddenly rattled his eardrums. He paused and tried to make sense of it all. An intensification of the screams of the incarcerated followed the explosion of hissing shrieks from a multitude of reptiles. Then there was another sound, a clap like thunder as if something had exploded. A couple of seconds later, just as he pushed open the door that gave access to the Keep, a wall of hot air first enveloped and then shot past him. Mastisan, it seemed, had triggered his trap and his pursuers had walked straight into it. With renewed effort and with what little energy his body could still generate, Thias then dragged Townsforth clear of the door and dropped him in a heap in the centre of the corridor. He then returned to the portal and slipped the three great iron bolts that shielded the Keep from whatever was happening below. Feeling safe at last he sank to his knees in exhaustion and called across to his companion.

"When this is all over Brynn, you owe me a bloody stiff drink."

Minutes passed and Thias began to hear the footfall of two men that approached from the passageway to the right. Two armoured knights appeared and the bard recognised them both despite their faces being part obscured by their helms.

"Berthelemy, Cragtalon, one of you help me get Townsforth to the throne room," Thias bellowed. "He is wounded in the left shoulder and that arm is now useless. He has lost much blood and its flow needs stemming. Help me Digory, come-on we have no time to waste."

"What's happing down in the Underkeep?" demanded Sir Cragtalon as he moved over and put his ear to the wood. "We heard an explosion."

"A significant force of Lizardmen have broken in and will soon be at this door," answered Thias. "You need to barricade it; stuff anything in front in order to delay their progress. We must then get to the throne room, find respite, and then re-evaluate our options."

"It smells like there's a fire burning down there, what about the prisoners?" shouted Sir Cragtalon.

"Forget them!" replied Sir Berthelemy as he lifted Townsforth onto his shoulder. "They would wouldn't be down there if they were worth saving. Come on bard, get under the Lord Commander's other arm and help me move him."

Thias struggled back to his feet and did as instructed while Sir Cragtalon pushed a large court cupboard several paces along the corridor wall until it covered the door to the Underkeep.

"Did Ystafell issue orders for the highborn to gather in the throne room?" asked Thais.

"Yes, he did, but you know how slow most of those buggers are, especially the lardy one," replied Sir Berthelemy. "But they must all be there by now I reckon."

"I'll join you as soon as I've finished constructing this barricade," shouted Sir Cragtalon. "Then I'll go and check on the main door. No lizard scum will penetrate these walls."

The journey to the throne room was uneventful in comparison to all that had gone before. Thias was most thankful for the assistance provided by Digory Berthelemy for the knight took most of Townsforth's weight and all of the strain. The corridors of the Citadel were unerringly quiet, so much so that Thias's senses were seriously stressed. Only two servants raced ahead of them to join their masters in the safety of the regal retreat. The respite from carrying Townsforth alone allowed Thias to recover some of his spent reserves. He was part lost in his thoughts when jolted back by the hammering of Berthelemy's fist upon the vast metal doors that gave entrance to the place chosen to protect the highborn. It was the Lord Commander's secret code and without which no entry could be granted. When the knock-knocking had ceased a voice called out from within, heavily muffled by the bronze plates of the doors and barely perceptible to the bard's battered senses.

"Who's there?"

"Digory!" screamed back the knight.

"Digory who?" came the voice from behind the bronze.

"Stop playing that fucking infantile game and open the door at once," bellowed Sir Berthelemy.

"Then identify yourself. Are you alone and if not who is there with you?"

"It is I, Sir Digory Berthelemy and I have with me the bard, Thias Calavan, and Commander Townsforth of the City Watch who has been wounded and is in need of urgent care.

"Have the others speak up and identify themselves."

"I am Thias, Royal Bard and once Phauless's secret investigator," screamed Thias. "Townsforth is too weak to be heard. You must take it on trust that we three are who we say we are."

"Wait a minute while I check with Ystafell," mumbled the voice behind the door.

As the three waited for what seemed like forever their frustrations mounted. They were joined at last by Sir Tobye Cragtalon who came racing up the corridor.

"Why are you all stood as if in a queue for the petty," shouted the bemused knight as he clocked sight of the others. "We need to get inside at once. The Army of the Eastern Marsh is at the door to the keep and although my make shift barricade will hold them back a while, it will not keep them out for ever."

Sir Cragtalon then strode to the bronze and began to hammer out the secret knock.

"Who's there?" came the muffled reply.

"Tobye!" hollered the furious knight.

"Tobye who?"

"If you don't open this fucking door at once I will dice your dick and feed the bits to the guardroom cat."

No reply followed and just before Thias was about to try reason rather than insults the door began to open. The head servant, Wil Geddings, peeped from behind the door.

"Ystafell says you can come in but you must hurry. The door will not be opened again until we know the Lizardmen have been routed."

The door had been part opened such that one person at a time could pass through. The bard went first and Berthelemy then pushed Townsforth through and into Thias's waiting arms. The Commander rallied and managed to smile as he felt the security of Thias's embrace.

"Put me somewhere in a corner Thias and go and find out what's happening," said the Commander. "Find Ystafell and secure the room. It's up to you now lad to save the day."

Sir Berthelemy entered next followed by Sir Cragtalon who then assisted young Geddings in the closing of the door and the sliding of bolts. On completion of this most important of tasks the burley knight stood still before the young servant. Without warning he whipped the back of his hand onto the servant's nose. The youth recoiled in agony as the knight's steel gauntlet smashed into his face and induced a crimson fountain.

"My nose!" exclaimed Geddings. "You've broke my fucking nose."

"That'll teach you to piss me off," sneered Cragtalon as he marched off into the throng.

Berthelemy took charge of Commander Townsforth and led him to one who had knowledge of the healing arts. Thias scanned the hall and sought to take in all that fell before his eyes. The first demand upon his gaze was the great carrying chair upon which sat the oversized Lady Thinata Fullbane. The solid ornate box was bolted onto two steel poles, the best that Parandor's smiths had ever forged. It took a dozen of Fullbane's little boys as she liked to call them to lift the contraption once she had sat in its midst. These muscular men, the prime meat of the Badlands, surrounded the chair and part obscured Thias's view of its owner. Intrigued as he was by the rasping of air from her throat he paced forward until he stood within a couple of paces of the object of highborn derision. Thias did not feel that same revulsion for he saw the beauty of her character and refused to listen to stories of her reported perversions.

Lady Fullbane's chest rose and fell like storm waves over the Bridge of Athuna. Her signs of exhaustion were mirrored by the twelve who had, just fifteen minutes previous, somehow managed to carry her to the throne room. Thias smiled at the distress of her breathing for he could not believe she had even so much as walked a single step.

"My Lady, are you well, you seem so laboured of breath?"

"I am exhausted young Thias," she replied. "You've no idea how it tires me so being lifted and carried. My little boys were in a great hurry this morning. They have bumped and battered my chair here, there, and every sodding where. Tell me honestly, are our lives really at risk given that the City Watch and Royal Guard are at full strength? I do hope this rushing and congregating was necessary."

"It is Lady; the Lizardmen have breached the Keep and will soon be at the doors behind you."

"Well I hope it's all over by dinner for I am famished."

"It may be a considerable time before you eat again Thinata," replied Thias as he attempted to divert the Lady's thoughts away from food. "Tell me, have you seen Ystafell since you arrived?"

"Yes, he is over on the west wall, half way up a stack of chairs, and hanging out one of the windows. I will never forgive the swine for having dragged us to this desolate hole that is devoid of food. We could have easily have all been sent to kitchens and barricaded ourselves in there. At least we would have had much to sustain our vigour while waiting for the swamp scum to leave us be."

"I'm sorry to admit that it was my idea to have you all muster here," apologised Thias. "The reptiles are not going anywhere lest we kick them out somehow. I am sorry to affirm that you may be considerably lighter if and when you ever get to gorge again."

"Never trust a crooner my Enguerrand always used to say," growled the fat lady. "I will never forgive you for this young Thias."

"I am sorry my Lady but should we both survive this ordeal then I will seek to make amends for any inconvenience this may have caused you."

"Is that so," she giggled as she winked her eye and stared at Thias's groin. "In that case I know exactly what I will hold you too!"

"Please excuse me," stuttered the embarrassed bard. "I must speak with Ystafell on matters of great importance to our survival."

Thias moved away as fast as he could. At the far end of the marble hall he saw a most precarious construction, a pyramid of well-balanced chairs and tables at the apex of which the Lord Chamberlain perched in order to thrust his head through an open window. The bard set off at a pace, noting as he passed that Commander Townsforth was being cared for by Heward Teulu, Calandriel Lorst, and Antivane Rirert. Part way across the hall his path through the highborn was interrupted. Lady Emeny moved in front of him with her escort and made to block his way.

"Where are you off to in such a rush Thias," she began once in voice shot. "Is it true the Archmage is dead and the Lizardman army has breached the Citadel? These are the words that have rippled through the throng ever since you arrived with Cragtalon and Berthelemy."

"I am grieved to announce both are true," Thias answered as he attempted to break away from Dustfury's sudden restraint. "If you will excuse me, I must talk with Ystafell to understand how the battle progresses. I assume that's what the slaphead is up to, hanging out the window over on the west wall. Somehow we must think of a way to drive the reptiles out from inside of the Citadel."

"Quite so and I will not delay you further," replied Emeny while signalling the bard's release. "Should you need any assistance seek me out and I will be glad to help in whatever way that I can."

Thias smiled and ran on. Soon he stood at the base of the creaking stack of furniture and at once began to attract the Lord Chamberlain's attention.

"Ystafell," he shouted. "What is happening? What can you see?"

The Lord Chamberlain could not hear Thias's voice as the clamour of battle beyond the walls hammered against his ear drums. Thias looked around for something to throw and he soon spotted a discarded shoe on the floor. Who it belonged to or why it lay alone on the marble was a mystery but in that moment such truths seemed of little importance. Thias wasted no time, bent forward, and lifted the piece of malodourous footwear. He took a careful aim and threw it with all his strength at the ample arse of the Lord Chamberlin. The bard's aim was perfect and soon a head retracted back inside the room like a startled tortoise. The oaf nearly toppled from his makeshift scaffolding, his face flushed, and his ginger mutton chop whiskers turned a deeper shade of russet.

"Who the fuck did that?" he bellowed. "Who threw that shoe? By witness to my mother's paps, I will flay the bastard should I find out who it was."

"It was I Ystafell," shouted Thias, his neck straining to keep his focus on the lisping lump at the window. "We need to make urgent plans, but first tell me how the battle progresses. What have you witnessed through the seeing glass?"

"How dare you throw something at me; I can have you hung for that bard!" yelled Ystafell. "I am acting Ruler in case you have forgotten. It is within my power..."

"Stop acting like a wazzock and just tell me what you witness. What has happened since we last spoke?"

The Regent hesitated and forced his anger to disperse.

"From this window, I can only see what is happening to the west of the city. It's still very much a stalemate. The Lizardmen assault team still cannot get close enough to attach their chains and hooks despite the efforts their two remaining ogres. The enemy's infantry will not deploy for fear of being decimated by our bowmen or pults. We continue to take small numbers of casualties but they are mounting and as time passes they cannot be replaced. Our peg-legged friend has retreated from the field and is most likely seeking attention for the injury to his arm; either that or he has returned to the command tent to report his failure to Urthanock. Rather him than me I say! There is however one new development which I think could be critical to the outcome of this battle."

"And what is that?" shouted Thias.

"There is a fleet of some twenty fishing vessels sailing up the estuary from the ocean. Through the seeing glass they are flying a flag that could be that of Valameer. I do hope so although until they get closer I will not be able to say for certain."

"Where are they making for?" yelled the bard.

"Straight for Parandor's harbour."

"If they are not from Valameer but rather part of the reptile's plan then they will have landed a force behind the stakewall and will have Sir Byddin's troops in a claw grip," answered Thias as his anxiety mounted. "We must warn Sir Byddin at once. Use your agreed method of communication and slingshot him a message."

"I have tried already and used up all my notes," replied Ystafell as he flushed again. "The arrogant bastard reads them, then just tosses them aside and continues on regardless."

"Then we must think of another plan, let me ponder a while."

No sooner had the words left Thias's mouth than the pounding on the throne room doors began. The Lizardmen had penetrated the Citadels walls.

"They're using some form of ram," shouted Berthelemy from the opposite end of the room. "The doors will give unless we do something."

"Ystafell!" bellowed Thias having weighed the options that cascaded through his thoughts. "We need to do two things. First build a significant barricade in front of the great doors. Then I must find an alternate way out of this room and confront Sir Byddin in person. I must make him see sense. Any plan needs to provide a means of escape for the highborn for they are trapped in here like maidens in a tyrant's whorehouse."

"Then quick about it young bard. Go talk to Enemy, she's usually good at coming up with ideas when others are clouded by the fog. I can see that the ships coming up the estuary carry the flag of Valameer although it may of course be one of Urthanock's devious deceptions."

"I will seek out Lady Emeny then," bellowed Thias.

The bard turned and moved away only to be enveloped by the throng. It took him many minutes to locate the Sovereign Adviser and all the while the strikes against the outside of the doors rose in intensity and fuelled the highborns' terror. Suddenly the throng parted and as he pushed forward he once again came upon Lady Emeny and her escort.

"By my mother's corns am I pleased to see you Llys," shouted Thias. "I need your advice on two urgent issues; please spare me a moment of your time."

"I would but Dustfury, Lightmain, and myself, are in a hurry to bolster the doors. We must barricade them with whatever we can find sufficient to seal the entrance. We do have a few ideas…"

"I see," said Thias. "Creating a barrier was the first issue I wanted to talk about, but it seems you already have the answer."

"Then follow us bard; come we have no time to lose," added Sir Dustfury. "We think we have come up the perfect solution."

Two minutes later the group stood before Fullbane's carrying chair. Sir Lightmain called out to the Lady's boys who lolled about waiting further orders.

"Which one of you is the captain of the whale's litter?"

"I beg your fucking pardon…" sniffed Lady Fullbane.

"It is I sir," replied a particularly muscular dimwit.

"Then by our command, take your positions on the poles and move the Lady and her chair against the doors," Sir Lightmain continued. "They must be secured this way as they only open inwards. We must protect the highborn until such time that this siege is lifted."

"Don't you fucking dare!" screamed Fullbane. "You're not using me in that way. I will not forget this Llys, you swine of the first water. If my Enguerrand was still alive he would tie your tits to a skyfawn and have them ripped from your chest. Why if I was only more mobile…"

Lady Thinata Fullbane never got the chance to finish her sentence for Sir Dustfury rammed an old rag he had been carrying deep inside her mouth. At the same time Lightmain threw a thick rope around her monumental chest, pulled tight to restrain her arms, and then secured her bulk to the chair. The lifters had gathered in close and without further discussion the team of muscle bound simpletons lifted the chair and then placed it in front of the great doors.

"Now pretty boys, fuck off," shouted Lady Emeny as she pulled the filthy rag out of her victim's mouth and threw back to Dustfury."

"I'll kill you for this, you ungrateful bitch," bellowed Fullbane.

"Of course you will dear!" sneered Emeny as she dragged Thias away from the irate mountain. "That's your first problem solved, now tell me about the other issue you have identified."

As Thias was pulled back into the throng he was distracted by Fullbane's rant.

"I get you back for this Llys, you scrawny witch."

"I need to find a way out of this throne room," began Thias. "There is only one other door out of this place, to the back of the throne room itself, the one that leads to the Sovereign Ruler's apartments. Do you know if there is a way out through those rooms for I have never been granted access to that most private of inner sanctums?"

"I been in there a few times but I have never seen one," replied Lady Emeny as her brow furrowed. "Someone once told me there could be a secret back exit but I would have no idea where to start looking for it. It could take days to find. Dustfury, Lightmain, have either of you heard of an alternative way out?"

"Blackfayer once said the Royal back passage had been blocked years ago, and I'm not referring to Phauless's renowned constipation," replied Sir Lightmain.

"Stop being such a dolt," growled Lady Emeny. "What say you Dustfury?"

"I know of no such alternative way to salvation," replied the knight.

"Then I must revert to my first plan," replied Thias as he stopped walking.

The bard pulled on Lady Emeny's arm and pointed up to the great candelabra that sat high above the throne; one that was talked of throughout the Realm for its intricate metal work.

"That I believe holds the key to our deliverance but I will need help to make it work."

"I'm sorry but I am at a complete loss as to what you intend Thias," answered Emeny. "I hope this is not another of your fanciful ideas. Please explain your intentions for we have no plan other than reliance on Fullbane's bulk. Do not have us light fifty candles and pray or I will spit on your feet. I have listened to far too much nonsense from Teulu over recent months."

"Fear not Llys, it is far more practical than that," sniggered Thias. "It's time to take our fate into our own hands. Fuck Fatumai and all her zealots. Come, Wesmin, Watcyn, gather around and listen for I would much value your opinions on my idea... The candelabra is, as you will note, suspended from a pulley attached to the roof rafters. The strong chain passes through it and then onto the winding mechanism fixed to the west wall, quite near to where Ystafell still protrudes through the window."

"Yes, I see that," said Lady Emeny, "but what of it?"

"If we lower the candelabra to the floor as if putting in new candles, we can detach the metal circle, then rewind the chain all the way through the pulley, shift Ystafell from his perch, and drop the end of the chain through the window. Its anchor points on the wall should be secure enough to take the weight of one person at a time and using the chain we can drop down between the wall and the stake palisade. Then at least we will be out of this death trap. What do you think?"

Thias sensed Lady Emeny assimilating the information.

"I like it bard and for once you have come up with something useful. What say you boys?"

"I'm all for it," replied Wesmin Lightmain.

"Me too!" added Watcyn Dustfury, "but let's waste no time in enacting this plan. The Lizardmen are beginning to inch open the great doors despite Lady Fullbane's bulk."

"Then let's do it," said Thias. "I must insist that I am first out. It's imperative that I get to talk with Sir Byddin. Just before the fighting commenced I met him in one of the lower corridors and he told me of a weakness in the Citadel's wall. I need to have him loan me a significant number of men such that I can lead them back inside and retake the city. I also need to warn him of the fleet of boats that Ystafell has spotted heading into Parandor's harbour. They may not be as friendly as their flags indicate."

"I can agree to that, but I will be out second," said Lady Emeny. "Dustfury and Lightmain can then oversee an ordered evacuation,"

"What about Lady Fullbane," asked Sir Lightmain?

"She must be left by the door for she would never fit through the window; nor would the whole of Parandor's army be able to lift her to the portal. It serves her right in my opinion, old guzzle guts has had this coming. What say you Thias?"

"I see no alternative." replied the bard, "Come we have work to do!"

Ten minutes later, having mobilised a significant cohort of the pampered to help him complete his preparations, Thias began his decent from the throne room window on the outer wall of the Citadel. The speedy climb down took less than twenty seconds during which time several steel tipped bolts clattered against the stone to both his left and right. Once away from the chain and on solid ground Thias looked up to the window in order to signal for the next to descend. Soon Lady Emeny's legs appeared through the window and as she pushed outwards her dress caught on the window frame causing it to ride up and expose her scrawny rear. This unexpected target proved an immediate focus for the enemy and a volley of bolts sped towards the most novel of bullseyes. Most missed by some way but one hit the inner circle, plum in the centre of Lady Emeny's right buttock. Even the clamour from the surrounding battle failed to prevent the Sovereign Adviser's screams from penetrating Thias's ears. Emeny was immediately pulled back inside the throne room and no one else tried to leave. If the highborn were to be saved, Thias would have to do it by himself. Without further delay he set off to find Sir Byddin.

Thias looked about the battlefield in search of the Head of the Royal Army. Amid the screams, the shouts, and the clashes of steel on steel, he tried to temper his heartbeat and avoid dissolving into mental mush. He kept close to the walls of Parandor as it seemed much safer there than the melee around the stakewall before the West Gate. A wounded knight staggered to his right. Thias winced at the cherry red liquor that dripped down the man's face from under a half crushed helm.

"Is that you Redglade?" Thias shouted.

"Yes," replied the knight. "I cannot stop for I need to find a healer and have him stitch up my head unless it is beyond saving."

"I need to speak with Sir Byddin at once," shouted Thias over the clamour of battle. "Do you know where I may find him?"

"Over there, behind the slaughter at the palisade. By the gods balls I swear we are giving our all. The lizard spawn are still trying to break us and show no signs of giving up. Go quickly if you want to talk to Byddin for we are beginning to wilt under the pressure of their onslaught. I'm not sure how much longer we can keep them out of the city."

"Thank you, good luck with your head," bellowed back Thias.

Redglade took two steps forward and then collapsed into thick treacle ground that had once been verdant pasture. Thias had not had time to tell the fallen knight of the Lizardmen presence inside the city walls. On he ran to the fallen knight and with care removed the fractured helm from off the stricken man's head. Then he wished he had left it where it was. The wound he revealed was the size of a small platter and resembled a dish of mashed beetroot and turnip, stirred and beaten as a child would do when forced to eat such a taste threatening combination. Thias knew then that Sir Jasper Redglade was dead. Looking up to the ongoing battle ahead the bard then set off once again to find Sir Byddin. Soon he approached the thick of the fighting and at the rear of the pressed defenders he saw his target shouting out orders. Just as he closed in to engage with the warrior he tripped over an object that had remained part hidden in the mud and below his line of focus. Picking himself up he looked back to see that which had caused him to stumble. His gaze fell upon an enormous white hilt of what was obviously two handed battle sword. He checked his side and saw that his own blade was missing, left in the throne room as he had hurriedly exited its window. Thias snatched at the hilt with both hands and pulled the beast of a sword from the ground. As he marvelled at its unique curved blade he realised he had found the one that the Gator Lord had wielded earlier in the battle. It was the weird weapon that Eerickk Jarl had sacrificed his life to neutralise.

"This is indeed a fortuitous find," he mumbled to himself. "I claim it as my own."

A minute later he called out to Sir Byddin.

"Rayner, it is I, Thias Calavan"

The great man in blood splattered armour turned, his weapon raised and ready.

"Fuck off Thias, I am busy and do not need you to sing to me. Dog's bollocks, is there no peace this day. Save your eternal prattle for another."

"I have two vital messages to give to you. You must hear me out!" bellowed the bard. "Ystafell tried too..."

"Then tell me what you have to say but be quick about it," growled the knight.

"There is a fleet of small boats heading for the harbour. They may be flying the flag of Valameer but we cannot be too sure from the Throne Room window."

"How have you got out of the Citadel?" demanded Sir Byddin as he turned to look to the walls. "Did you come down that chain?"

"Yes I did, but what of the fleet?"

"I was informed of its presence a few minutes ago; it is Lady Flurdiana and her Trident guard. The sullen sow finally answered our call for aid. God bless Danisun Dain and that other fellow that went with him. The Trident Guard may well bolster our defences; we are beginning to tire."

"Yes, I did use the chain and nearly took a few bolts in the process," replied Thias as he pointed to the window. The Lady Emeny followed me but got shot in the arse before being pulled back in."

"Why are you lot trying to get out? It's fucking dangerous down here! I ordered them all to stay put!"

"It's even more dangerous inside," bellowed back Thias. "A reptile battle group has entered the Citadel, no doubt through the Rift. All our highborn and their servants are holed up in the Throne Room. We need a force to enter by the wall weakness you earlier told me you had located. You need to loan me some men so that I can break in and lead a counterattack. How many can you spare?"

"I cannot afford a one," spat back Sir Byddin as he dodged an enemy arrow which grazed his ear. "We are hard pressed as it is, just to keep the bastards pulling down the palisade. I was just contemplating a strategic retreat back behind the city walls but that would leave us at the mercy of any tunnel diggers or those burrowing Kulkulkath they seem to have tamed. If they have black powder the walls could soon topple."

The great warrior Byddin paused his rant as the seriousness of the situation screwed his facial muscles. He then sighed and spoke again.

"Given that the enemy are inside in significant numbers, I need to rethink my strategy."

"Do your archers have many arrows left?" asked Thias amongst the continued screams of war.

"That's one thing we are not short of," replied Byddin while pointing a corpse that resembled a pin cushion. "Why do you ask?"

"I would suggest you coordinate a rapid disengagement from the stakewall and then unleash a volley of the wood rain upon the enemy assault force. That should even the numbers up a bit!"

"Don't you fucking dare tell me how to run a battle bard," growled the grizzled old war dog. "Now if you want some men to lead, go and beg the use of Flurdiana's pickle pronged guard. See, they approach between the palisade and the stone walls. It didn't take the buggers long to disembark."

"Yes, it is they and I am sure that is Danisun Dane running at their head. I'd know that bastard anywhere," bellowed Thias above the continued screams of slaughter. "I will seek to rally them to my cause but first show me the weak patch in the Citadel's wall. "

"Two hundred paces to your right, almost below the window from which you made your escape. You cannot miss it." snarled Sir Byddin. "Now piss of and leave me to fight... but wait, where did you get that sword you are dragging behind you?"

"I found it over there in the mud," replied Thias.

"It has a power of its own," gestured Sir Byddin. "I suggest you use it against the wall infill and see what happens."

"I will and now I leave you to your work. Danisun approaches and I need to action my plan."

The bard turned to his left and thrust himself before the man who had killed his father. With his hate for warrior dismissed from his heart he arrested the progress of the Man-at-Arms.

"I'm so pleased to see you're still alive Thias," shouted Danisun Dain. "I saw you talking to Byddin. How may we best serve Parandor and help turn the course of this battle."

Thias talked like a gale at full tilt. He told of the battle group that that invaded the inner city and how the fate of the highborn hung in the balance. He then spoke of his plan to re-enter the city and that Byddin was too preoccupied to give thought as how to best use the men from Valameer; that he had been given permission for the use of Flurdiana's reinforcements in an attempt to drive the reptiles from inside the walls of Parandor. Danisun Dain immediately saw the value of this plan and wasted no time in discussing it further. Lady Flurdiana, dressed in her fine armour, had arrived in time to hear most of Thias's words and had not once interrupted their flow. No sooner had Thias finished than the Lady spoke.

"Are you sure this is how you wish to use my Trident Guard?"

"Yes, how many have you?"

"Two hundred thereabouts," she replied. "They should keep the lizard scum at bay for a while at least."

"It is imperative they are deployed and time is critical," replied the bard.

Under her helm Thias saw a face determined to extract vengeance.

"Lead on young man!" she shouted in her excitement. "For Raorick and House Gylewu!"

"Follow me," bellowed Thias as he turned to move.

A short time later they stood before the weakened wall by the infill of the long forgotten portal.

"Are you sure this is as weak as Byddin suggests?" demanded the Lady.

"It looks pretty solid to me," added Danisun

"And to me," added a second man in the uniform of the City Watch.

Thias looked with suspicion at one he did not know. "And you are who?" he asked.

"Darchus Arillius of Valameer..."

"Yes indeed," interrupted Lady Flurdiana. "Skip the pleasantries and share your thoughts as to how we break through the stone."

"Sir Byddin told me that in just fifteen minutes a few men with picks could clear the weakened stone and poor mortar," continued Thias. "But even such a short time may be too long."

"What do you suggest then?" asked Danisun Dain.

The voice of the man responsible for his father's death grated on the bard's soul. Should they both survive this day Thias vowed he would challenge the Man-at-Arms about his connection to the Thieves' Guild and the reason his father had to die. Turning his thoughts back to battle he held aloft his new sword.

"The power of this blade will clear a way for us. Stand back while I unleash it."

"How can this be?" demanded the one called Darchus.

"My cordwainer asks a valid question," said the Lady.

"I witnessed its power earlier in the battle," answered Thias. "It had a devastating effect on our brave defenders. It has magic sufficient for our needs."

"Then we must trust you bard," answered the Lady.

Thias pushed the waved blade forward with all the strength he could generate. The ivory hilted sword hit the wall hard and in the midst of a mighty impact it sang. The noise produced from its curves set up intense vibrations, so severe that all except Thias held their hands to their ears. It was as if a thousand mountain gongs had been hit as one. The impact of the sound deafened Thias and his right ear began to bleed yet still he gripped the blade as shock waves caused the weak wall to crumble as eggshell under a boot. Without warning the blade then shattered into a myriad of slivers which vaporised in the heat generated by the vibrations it had itself generated.

"I wouldn't have believed that had I not witnessed it myself," screamed Danisun.

Thias stared at the hole in the wall, one as tall as a man and equally as wide. Smoke billowed from out of its centre while he gathered his senses. He dropped the white hilt that once held a majestic blade and then shouted out further instructions.

"Follow me inside and have your tridents ready. Who knows where this portal leads for it has not been used in over a thousand years. We must find a way into the main body of the Citadel."

"Yes, go now," ordered Lady Flurdiana. "We have an opportunity to save the lives of my highborn brothers and sisters. I could not live with myself should we fail to deliver them from the evil that pounds on their door."

The legendary Trident Guard of Valameer poured through the darkness beyond the hole. Thias, Danisun, and Darchus moved in amongst them and soon located a flight of stone steps up which the warriors raced. The top was blocked by light wooden panel which too was in an advance state of decay. It was felled in no time and as it dropped it took with it a large tapestry that had hung on its far side. Light and fresh air flooded this new entrance and as the wave of warriors rolled on they entered and passed through a number of opulent rooms.

"Phauless Gylewu's private chambers, I have been here many times," yelled Flurdiana.

Cheers resounded in the throne room as the wave of pickle-forked warriors entered.

19

Llyat's naked form stood amid a wondrous space the likes of which he had never once imagined. The cavern was circular in form and its curved interior wall was both solid and dark. Its colour reminded Llyat of rotting meat although composed of highly polished stone. Life sized statues chiselled from white stone stood every few paces. He assumed that they depicted the fabled gods and their various children. The midpoint of the circular temple, for that was what he assumed it to be, was some ten long strides from the door in which he had entered. He walked to that centre with stealth and as a cool breeze cooled his exposed skin Llyat searched the gloom for the origin of the voice.

"We have been waiting a long time young Emgar!" the haggard voice repeated, this time coming from his right.

Llyat turned and stared into a recess in the wall behind a stone table with the same hue of putrefaction. There sat three pulchritudinous women, all dressed in identical flowing robes of gossamer. Their clothes enhanced their beauty tenfold and Llyat was awestruck for never had he imagined anyone could look so beautiful. The thin material did not hide much and as his eyes roamed from breast to breast his cock began to twitch.

"Oh shit," he mumbled to himself.

Remembering his nakedness Llyat dropped his hands and sought to cover his manhood.

"Who are you?" he exclaimed. "I seek the Moirai; are you their handmaidens?"

The tallest laughed before answering; "we are they, the ones you have come to meet."

"Oh no you're not," replied the youth. "I have talked with many about you, including the mighty Thamous and this is not how you were ever described. I also have distant memories given to me by Sir Raulyn, locked deep inside my head and only recently freed by an Archmage. You are not the Moirai. They are old wrinkled crones and I even saw them once, watching my progress in a tavern called the Three Sisters."

"The boy is smart," chuckled the middle one.

"We must drop our pretence and introduce ourselves," laughed the tallest.

In the blink of eye, the three beauties transformed into ancient hags, their skin leathery and furrowed like freshly ploughed meadows. Their demeanour changed, their eyes reddened and Llyat felt the presence of a most potent of power. No longer, it seemed was this to be a benevolent meeting.

"If I am to address the Moirai, I would like to know your names," demanded Llyat.

"Our true names are not for you to hear," cackled the middle of the three. "Though in the tongue of mortals I am known as Allotter. To my right, the tallest of us three, is the one spoken of as Spinner. Say hello to Llyat Emgar, the one it seems is marked by Raulyn's seed."

"Hello Llyat," groaned Spinner after which she spat on the floor.

"To my left our sister goes by the name of Cutter, but she is mute," continued Allotter with eyes that radiated sinister intent. "Flash him your blade simple one. Take note Llyat Emgar, this is the last thing you will see when my sister calls to cut your strings."

Cutter lifted a scythe from under the table and winked at Llyat. He could not be sure but he sensed more empathy in her soul. It was then that Llyat realised that the white statues had disappeared and the circular wall had changed its appearance. It seemed the Moirai had begun to play tricks. Carved deeply into the wall's surface every few paces was the familiar image of three circles, one sat upon the other two and all touching. The circle outlines cut into the rock had been highlighted in gold paint as had their centre which clearly displayed the incurved triangle of the Cuvar.

"I don't get it," exclaimed Llyat as he looked upon the new wall. "What's with all this three-circle shit? The pattern is like the birthmark that my dead friend Methladon carried on his neck. It is also the mark that appeared on the victims of the Death Tubaria murders. I was told it was called the Mark of Kha so what purpose do you have in showing it to me now. Is this another of your foul deceptions?"

The three hags flickered their eye globes as Spinner smiled.

"The boy has got this far, explain it to him," she cackled.

"I don't mind doing that if you think the farm boy can make sense of it all!" replied Allotter.

"Just try me," snapped back Llyat, frustrated at the wasting of his time.

"The three circles represent the Moirai, always have and always will," began Allotter. "It has never had anything to do with Kha. That bastard enjoys his underworld too much to be bothered with what happens in the middle dimension. We three created this special symbol and bound within it is a most powerful spell that underpins the greater meaning of the Lore of the Dead. When that book's spells were first incanted in the presence of the Dagger of Kha, it awoke in the emerald a recognition of its long-forgotten role inside a deeper realm of magic. We wanted the mark as part of our game and sought a way to bring it back into being. Thus were set in motion the murders you know as Death Tubaria."

"A silly name if you ask me sister," snorted Spinner.

"And the Cuvar mark?" interrupted Llyat.

"The golden centre represents where our mother Fatumai sits. She watches over our games but very rarely interferes. It was something the ancients who built Barad Elestor recognised when they first swore to protect the Marked."

"But I don't understand the link to the Death Tubaria murders," began Llyat. "Why would your symbol appear with each murder? Were you three responsible for all those foul crimes rather than the Lizardman from the Eastern Marsh? I understood it to be that creature's magic that caused the mark to appear?"

"It is all part of our current game."

"Game?" questioned Llyat, but Allotter was quick to stifle his words.

"The first series of Death Tubaria murders, led by Jonas Tullage, were carried out in the presence of the dagger's emerald. The brand marks were created by its deep magic. We have watched your life history and know that your friend Methladon was branded by the dagger in a way that did not fit with our game plan.

He was rescued by certain members of Parandor's Watch for we needed him to live to fulfil the destiny our Fortune cards had chosen for him. When the dagger went missing we arranged for the changeling known as Ssleptaz to begin the pretence of the cult's resurgence. Through our influence he was ordered to divert attention from the rise of the Eastern Marsh and the Knights of Avolire. The slime used his own well developed skills to brand his victims in an imitation of the power of the emerald. He was the most cunning of his race that we three have ever known."

Llyat tried to take all in as Allotter continued.

"Remember this young man; those with a powerful ability to generate their own Kundalish Aura also display our mark somewhere close to where they die. This is what will happen to you Llyat for you are full of it."

"Full of what?" spat back Llyat, uncertain of where the conversation was going.

"We have been busy of late and we must keep this meeting short," interrupted Spinner. "There are many dying right now and many strings for Cutter to sever."

"You are sick fuckers," moaned Llyat amid his confusion

"No, we are not young man, this is just how life is," answered Spinner.

Llyat paused and attempted to refocus.

"So if I understand what you are saying, the dagger of Kha was responsible for my friend Methladon's mark. You stopped it killing him but later finished him off?"

"As it would seem," said Allotter as she raised an eyebrow.

"But why?"

"Simply because of his role in our game," she continued.

"And what role did you design for him," demanded Llyat, gesturing with his hands despite his nakedness. "Why did you have to end him in his prime? He was one of the greatest people I have ever known; he was my best friend."

"His role in our game is not for your ears young Emgar," said Spinner. "Concentrate on your own destiny for we sense you now have a much greater insight into what is expected of you."

"I still don't get the link to Death Tubaria. Why did the reptile copy the brand?"

"We cannot reveal all," said Spinner. "Some answers are best eft unknown. Let us give you some insight for then you may understand the game a little better."

"Our games always involve the Lore of the Dead," began Allotter. "This one more so and as already said, one of the tome's incantations activated the evil contained within the emerald."

"I have heard much of the foul book," said Llyat as his mind raced. "It was first brought to Parandor by that sick quack Tullage? That was when the cult first surfaced and claimed many innocents."

"Very good," sniggered Spinner. "So let us tell you how that all came to pass. We needed a good start to this phase of the Game of Fates. One day my sister went up to walk in the lands above, to clear the soot from out of her pipes. You tell the lad what happened next."

"Very well, but listen carefully for time is short," cackled Allotter. "I was out walking the Harico Hills when I decided to drop down into the village for inspiration as how best to slip the Law of the Dead into our latest iteration. It was there that I met the easily deceived Tullage. He had begun to take an interest in the unnatural and had developed an unhealthy desire to learn more about our resting place. The moron sought to bargain with us for the return of his dead wife. The rest was soon done for he was easily duped. I sat with him by the side of the stream that runs out through the village and there I pretended to need his help. Disguised as an old washerwoman I convinced Tullage that I wanted to visit the Barrow and pay my respects to the memory of the Moirai."

"Allotter has always been the slyest of us three," added Spinner.

"He was hooked at once and wanted to hear all I knew about of the power over life and death, resurrection and such stuff. Anyway, he was fooled by my teasing and eventually we reached the mouth of the Barrow. There I told him certain things and sent him on his way. As reward for joining the game I gave him a copy of the Lore of Dead. I told him that within its fleshy pages he would find the answers to all his questions pertaining to the resurrection of the deceased."

"Did you tell him of its power?" asked Llyat. "Why is this book so important to your plans?"

"It's just a tool, a trick, something that a flibbertigibbet would use to tease you mortal fools," laughed Allotter. "It has become the first move in all the games we play. 'Give the book to mortal man, and he'll destroy all that he can.'"

Llyat's concern began to fester. "Is my life real?" he demanded to know.

"That is something you must decide yourself," answered Spinner. For some unknown reason Llyat looked to the Cutter who nodded her affirmation and winked large so as make her message clear. The gesture did not go unnoticed.

"Stop it sister, the lad must be allowed to make his own mind up," snarled Allotter.

"Exactly so," added Spinner.

"I would like to know more of the sick game that you three play."

"Quick then sister tell him, but we must soon move on," grumbled Spinner.

"I will try and make this as simple as possible although in reality it is far more complicated," began Allotter, her face contorted by ancient memories. "We play in cycles with stories that are usually related and intertwined. Each game focuses on different characters for that keeps our interest fresh. All cycles are kicked off by the introduction of the Lore. The book is like a catalyst for the intense reactions we induce in mortals. The fates of each are dictated by the role of dice and the turning of cards. And so it is with you young man. You have done very well to have got this far for when we first drew your image from the pack our hopes for a good game were not high. I have to tell you that we are pleased with your progress so far."

Llyat's rage echoed through the cavern.

"So all that has ever happened to me is due to three fucked up wizen crones sat playing with cards and dice?" snarled Llyat.

"Yes, if I understand the eloquence of your words," sneered Allotter.

The mute Cutter shook her head from side to side and once again winked at Llyat.

"Sister, what are you doing?" growled Spinner.

"Yes, why are you acting in such a strange way with this child," demanded Allotter. "This is not something you have done before."

Cutter looked to her sisters and then back to Llyat. Once again she turned but this time she could not hide the wide grin that had formed on her face. Her two siblings could sense something significant but were at a loss as to what was behind the mute's odd behaviour. Then as if a golden nugget sparkled in the mire, Llyat observed Spinner's moment of realisation.

"It's been you all along hasn't it?" she screamed out. "You are the one who has been interfering with the game. Go on, deny it you rancid prune."

The smile on the Cutters face beamed ever wider as she tried to stifle her laughter. The smothered guffaw was picked up by all. Spinner and Allotter sat is if struck dumb and amid a silent hiatus Llyat focused his thinking.

"If the dumb one can laugh why can't she speak?" he asked.

"We'll sort her out later, lad" began the incensed Allotter. "We'll get to the bottom of it when you've gone. She knows the rules well enough."

"Rules? Games?" exclaimed Llyat. "I came here seeking questions anc…"

"We will tell you no more lad until we are convinced you are ready for the next stage of the game," snapped out Spinner.

"And I will do nothing, nor say anything further unless you tell me where Heliana is and whether you have done anything to harm her."

Llyat's concern for Heliana mounted as the three crones laughed.

"The girl and her baby are fine and will stay so as long as we conclude our business in a satisfactory manner," replied Allotter with equal strength of voice.

"When will I get to see her and make sure you have not harmed her?"

"Let's just get on with it," shouted Spinner. "First we need to understand what is in the bag slung over your back. If it contains that which we think it does then we will be most pleased to see them again, for it is said they are reunited. After that you must pass a mind test which will confirm you have sufficient insight and knowledge to carry on with your quest. We have tested your courage on route to our temple but we must also ensure your intellect is also up to the task. Now show us the jewels that you carry in your sack."

Llyat was immediately reminded of his nakedness and that his hand still rested in front of his own precious baubles. With great haste he lifted both hands up and removed the bag from his shoulders. He pulled it around his body such that it rested between his legs and hid his cock from the hags prying eyes.

"Reveal the contents of your sack for we grow impatient," ordered Allotter.

Llyat watched as a stream of spittle leaked from the cracked corner of the hag's mouth and dribbled onto the wispy beard hairs of her chin. His hand dropped inside the satchel and one by one he lifted the objects out. Each was held high for inspection and then replaced. First came the amethyst, then the heart shaped ruby. Next the sapphire taken from Raulyn's mighty battle-axe.

"Do you know of the powers that these stones can give to the Marked?" asked Spinner.

"Yes, Thamous told me."

"Good, don't ever forget. You may yet need them before your quest is done."

Llyat pulled out the Sceptre of Urthanock and finally the Dagger of Kha for the six myopic eyes to savour. The Moirai smiled, licked their lips, and drooled in anticipation. As soon as dagger was back in his satchel he noted Spinner's expression change.

"You are hiding something else in there?" she grumbled while her eyes sought to penetrate Llyat's soul. "Be honest with us for we have the ability to tell if you lie,"

Llyat thought for a while and realised he had no option other than to tell the truth.

"It is a box constructed from lead," he began in haste. "It hides a stone, a Dragon Whisper, given to me by one of the Berserkers of Falahorn. Urthanock knows I have it and he seeks to use it to track and destroy me. My plan is to reveal the stone once I leave this place. That will distract him from his war with Parandor and perhaps alter the outcome of the battle. But it will also bring him here while I journey elsewhere. It is a plan worked out by a bard, my friend Thias. I ask you not to interfere."

"Ah yes, the lousy crooner from the Three Sisters! We could not stay and listen for it was too painful to our ears," sneered Spinner as the others laughed.

"So, it was you!"

Llyat's comment elicited no response. Allotter and Spinner retreated into a whispered huddle out of which they then broke free.

"We support this plan," said the Allotter. "We do so hope Urthanock decides to visit this place for we would like to converse with the creature that has named himself Lord over Fear. However, once you open that box on the surface you must flee with great haste. If he uses the Rift he could arrive within seconds and you must be well away by then. I suggest you let one who you brought here, and who remains behind the locked door, open the box for you. But only when you have put several hours march between your feet and the Barrow. It must not be the sailor given his mental state and you will need him to navigate to where you are to go next. The other is more expendable."

Llyat thought of his two companions and Theoplous's behaviour.

"Irabo, the warrior of the Watch with whom I have shared many adventures will be the one to open the box. Yet you three seem to have forgotten that the sapphire I carry will hide me from Urthanock's sight."

"But perhaps not your friends," answered Spinner. "The warrior is fated to carry out this most important of tasks so let us not waste further time on it. Now, you must answer our riddle."

Llyat closed his eyes and took a deep breath. It was time.

"Ask away and let's get this over with."

"The three of us each have a twelve-sided die in our right hand," began Allotter as she opened her hand to reveal her bone carved object. "I will roll first and

Spinner will go next. Having seen the results of the first two throws you must predict the number that the mute will throw next. You will try and guess the answer, but should you get it wrong your quest ends here and you will never return to the surface."

"Will you give me any clue as to how I can do this?"

"If as you say, you have access to Raulyn's secret memories, then search there for the answer. I'm sure that Clotho of the Oakes would have told you the same thing."

Llyat was stunned. "How do know that I met with him?"

The Moirai did not answer and instead Allotter threw her dice towards Llyat's feet.

"What number does it show?" she demanded.

Llyat glanced to where the dice had stopped. "Five" he shouted.

Spinner took aim and second later another bone landed by his feet.

"What number shows on mine?" she shouted.

"Three" called back Llyat.

In the sinister silence that enveloped him, Llyat stared back at the three sisters.

"Well." he began. "Now what?"

"You have one minute to tell us what the number Cutter will throw," answered Spinner.

Llyat searched his memory from times when he had played such games in the Red Mare but he could not remember this particular riddle. Given that both the Moirai and Clotho had both hinted he should explore Sir Raulyn's secret store; that is what he then did. Yet, as crazy as it seemed he at last came across one memory that could be of significance. It had been filed deep and secure under the title 'Shape Secrets of the Ancients' and titled 'Raulyn's Triangular Law'. He rapidly scanned the memory's contents for he was aware that time was running out.

"Four!" he bellowed.

"Just in time" screeched Allotter as Cutter unleashed her odd shaped bone.

As if by some magic of its own, the final die landed, bounced, and then dropped. It came back down on to one of its many points and began to spin n a most haphazard way. It danced, it swayed, it teetered, and it swaggered. Then after what seemed like forever it revealed its face to Llyat.

"What is the number shown?" shouted Allotter.

Llyat was dumbfounded.

"Four" he replied.

"Well done, but now you must explain why four was the correct answer such that we know you were not guessing," said Spinner.

"I didn't have time to study the memory properly," said Llyat.

"Well you had better have a stab at an answer, and remember you only get one chance,"

"Is a method of calculating the unknown length of one side of a triangle that has one angle that looks like a capital L," he continued. "The side opposite the L angle is related to the other two sides in a complex way."

"And what is that way?" asked Allotter

"The length of side one multiplied by itself and added to the length of side two multiplied by itself then equals the side of the one opposite the L angle multiplied by itself," mumbled Llyat.

"Not the best explanation we have ever heard but it will do for a farm yacker" sneered Spinner. "So tell us how you came to the answer four,"

"The first dice was five. Five times five is twenty five. The second was three. Three times three is nine. Twenty five minus nine is sixteen. The only number on a dye that when multiplied by itself will give sixteen is the number four. Therefore the answer had to be four."

"Not bad for an uneducated half-wit, eh sister?" chuckled Allotter.

"More luck than sense me thinks," laughed Spinner.

"So, what does this prove?" demanded Llyat.

"He is the Marked though, without any doubt." continued Spinner

Cutter then decided to clap in a most excited manner. She winked over and over again as the broadest of smiles wedged itself deep within her face. Her two sisters scowled and their wrinkled brows furrowed.

"What's got into the mad bitch today?" asked Allotter of her sister.

"It must be that time of month!" replied Spinner.

While the two crones sat and debated their sisters' behaviour Llyat's thoughts drifted back to the end of his visit to the Wizards Guild. His memory of the three cards had not faded and images of them lying on the floor were as clear now as they had been at his feet. Truth, The Cutter, The Lover, all called attention to the fact that something important that was about to take place and he wondered what link they had to his current predicament. He would remain vigilant despite the Moirai being less threatening than he had initially expected.

"It is time for us to tell you a story Llyat Emgar and you need to pay attention," began Allotter. "You now know, having had your mind unlocked, that you are descended from the seed of Sir Raulyn. What you haven't guessed is that you are also descended from a child conceived in our mute sister's womb."

"What!" groaned Llyat, but his call went unheard.

"Raulyn, to gain the knowledge he needed, was required to give up a child. So behold the mother of your line, the egg layer from which your furthest descendant was hatched."

Llyat's memory returned to the temple of Barad Elestor, the runes he had seen there, and the story Thias had related; one that told of Raulyn giving the Moirai a child. It had not been a sacrifice at all. It was something more natural. Once again stories had been distorted by the passage of time.

"How can I be related?" he asked.

"Don't fight the thought," sniggered Spinner as Cutter smiled and winked. "We find it hard to believe some days but it was part of one of our earliest games."

"It has been a very long time since Raulyn came to this Barrow and reclaimed his child after it had been weaned from our dear sister's tit," continued Allotter. "The shock was so great to her that it destroyed her ability to speak. We suspect she regretted ever volunteering to be the one to carry the babe but it had to be her for we two have always been barren, cursed by the bastard Kha, may he be one day sewn inside the hide of a flayed camel and left to suffocate in the deserts of Badlands."

Spinner spat to the floor as then did Allotter while Cutter smiled like a rat at the milk.

"Why are you telling me all this shit?" demanded Llyat as he grew ever more uncomfortable.

"Because you need to understand the goal of our game, how the dice will roll and therefore what we seek to bring to pass," answered Spinner.

"And what exactly do you intended to do with your magic dice?"

"It may have taken many years but at last we are almost at the point where a descendent of the Moirai, spawned from the loins of Raulyn the Grand, will sit on the throne of this Realm," said Allotter as she too at last smiled.

"That is you Emgar," added Spinner. "Your line, beginning with the unborn in the wench Heliana's belly, will create a Moiraic dynasty that will rule the middle dimension until such time as we tire of the game."

Finally, all made sense to the youth from Maplehill.

"So Sir Raulyn never sacrificed a child and you are not expecting me to give up mine. What then do I have to give to gain the information that I need. With your help I will fuse the gems and control the doors to the Underworld... Please tell me where I should look."

Two sisters sniggered.

"We will tell you what we need of you quite soon," said Allotter. "If you play the game well your future will be one of greatness, not just for you but for all who will spring from your loins."

"Then you need to understand this," snarled Llyat. "I have neither the intention nor desire to sit on some lofty perch while surrounded by sycophantic arse lickers or devious profiteers filling my ears with shite from one minute to the next. No, that is not what my life is about. It works on a much simpler level and I will have none of your interference once I have sealed the door to the Underworld and saved my fellow men from Kha's intended annihilation."

The candles flickered as the three crones grew within the shadows.

"You will do as your told lad," ordered Allotter, her voice thundering and spittle full. "We, with our cards and dice, dictate all that will happen. You have no choice in the matter."

"Oh yes he does!"

A new voice flooded the temple with a shockwave as great as if the world itself had exploded.

Llyat was stunned while Allotter and Spinner looked to their sister in disbelief.

"I am so pleased to see you Llyat," said Cutter crisply. "I have waited so long for this moment while playing stupid games with my moronic soul sisters. At last, that which once passed through my legs has returned and stands before me."

"But you were not my mother," snapped back Llyat.

"Not directly, but you are still a product of one of my womb."

"What did you mean when you said 'Oh yes, he does'?" demanded Llyat

"Why have you never spoken before?" asked Allotter, her mouth barely working.

"I didn't want too. Now let me answer his question."

"First explain yourself…" began Spinner but her once mute sister ploughed on.

"My sisters have implied that you have no say in what will happen to you. Well that is not true. I am telling you now Llyat that should you wish, you can make your own choices. That means you will have to take full responsibility for those that may turn out to be foolish as well as those that bring you benefit. I will continue to watch over you but you must take care in all that you decide to do. All choices are precious, even the most trivial, so make sure you think things through."

"No he can't" shouted Allotter. "You cannot make up rules like this toward the end of our game. It's not fair… you're not allowed."

"I changed the rules at the game's inception," sneered Cutter. "He has always been making his own choices, as have many other pieces of the game we have been playing."

"Just wait while mother gets wind of this," bellowed Spinner. "She will be furious."

Cutter laughed as her sisters sat aghast.

"I cleared it with mother at the outset," she continued. "As soon as I realised the farm boy we had chosen for the game was descended from my own sweet child."

"You devious cowpat,"

Spinner bellowed her contempt after which she attacked her sister with claws that scratched and a spittle shower that flew through toothless gums.

"Stop this nonsense at once," screamed Llyat. "I am in a hurry to leave this place and you still need to answer my questions. You three are also short of time and the longer you prolong this needless nonsense those dying amid the war will suffer terribly until you get to sever their strings."

Llyat's words cleared Allotter's mind and she set about restraining her incensed sister. From out of nowhere, Cutter produced a rolled up piece of paper and threw it to Llyat. He caught it, opened it, and scanned its scrawled message before raising his eyebrows to express his bewilderment. There were just four lines that he could understand. The remainder was in a language the Realm had long forgotten.

The first of these is that you're born,
The second that all must die.
The third you choose, the fourth is given,
And the last, you know's a lie.

"Think about it when you have time," smiled Cutter.

"What devious trick are you up to now?" demanded Spinner. "No more of this cheating."

"Nothing, just some encouragement for the lad as he seeks to complete his quest."

"Enough of this," boomed Allotter. "We must move on and address our grievances later. Llyat, we know what you want us to divulge. But just like Raulyn you must first donate a prize, something we will need for a future iteration of this game. We the Moirai require some of your seed with which to impregnate our sister a second time, although given her sudden outburst I feel we may live to regret it. Yet the seed we must have if we are to twist another tale from the legend that was Sir Raulyn."

"And how would you have me produce this for you, leave a sample in a cup?" sneered Llyat.

The three hags laughed as only the demented can.

"Don't be stupid, you will fuck her of course," replied Allotter "Now drop your satchel and stand proud before us in your nakedness."

"Piss off," snorted Llyat.

The bag and satchel were both pulled away by some unseen force and dropped at the base of the sisters' table. Llyat had lost control of events.

"As you so wish, perverted monsters of the mire."

"Insults have no effect here so stop wasting time with them," continued Allotter harshly. "Now stand sister and let young Llyat feast his eyes on your wondrous charms.

Cutter stood and moved from behind the table, wobbling forward on ancient spindly legs. Llyat watched her every move until she stood alone half way between him and her sisters. She then dropped her sack cloth and revealed all. Llyat's emotions sank as his eyes scanned the cachectic skin covered bone rack. There was not a morsel of lard on her hips and when she turned to show her arse there was none there either. Where had once been breasts were two empty leather saddlebags that hung vertically to below the waist, allowing two blacked nipples to rest against the skin of her ancient belly. There was more hair on her chin than on the parts that attract young men. Llyat felt his cock shrink as if trying to hide from the world and escape the torment that was about to be forced upon it.

"I cannot fuck that; how could anyone get hard looking at a corpse?"

"You should not have challenged our original appearance, things could have been so much easier for you," sniggered Spinner. "You must do what needs to be done or we three will have to take your child instead and we will not wait for it to be born. We will rip it in a most untimely manner from out of its mother's womb."

"But I cannot cope with the sight, the thought, the smell," pleaded Llyat. "It's too revolting and the idea is making me gip."

"Being made from immortal flesh I will ease your discomfort," began Cutter. "I will transform myself and become the body of one from your memory. My sisters will watch your manhood rise and fall. Whichever provokes the greatest response will be the one you will impregnate."

"No I won't," snapped back Llyat.

"Get on with it sister," ordered Allotter.

Without further ado Cutter transformed into the lean naked form of Tonousa Amberstone. As Llyat's eyes wandered from her small boy-like breasts across her rippling abdominal muscles he struggled to get aroused and thought perhaps the deed could be done if she turned around and bent forward. Cutter anticipated this thought and as she turned Llyat's gaze fell upon the deep scars that covered the back of her torso. Any hopes of a stiff one vanished. The next transformation was into that of Heliana with bulging belly and engorged tits. Llyat's cock stood to attention but he closed his eyes, bit his lip, and slapped his manhood down.

"No fucking way you evil hags," he shouted from behind the darkness of his eye lids. "I will not shag the living dead on the belief that it is the woman I love."

"Then how about this one," suggested Cutter.

Llyat open his eyes and immediately wished he had not done so. The sight he beheld was so shocking that he could not help but keep staring. There in her wobbly wondrousness was a naked Catriana Darcha. His eyes wandered over her pudding rumps, down the deep cleft that separated her low hanging breasts and on to a thick bush that resembled Thengar Forest. Llyat's cock made a run for it and hid somewhere behind his balls.

"Try another," yelled Spinner.

Llyat blinked and when he opened his eyes the contrast of image was as wide as the vast ocean to the west. There stood Arnkatla Jarl, a naked vision of female perfection. Llyat's cock pumped to full capacity. The beauty opened her legs and her scent wafted up the tortured youth's nose. Somehow his manhood increased another third and drool dripped from his open tongue. He tried to push his manhood down but it would have none of it for it was already moist at the end.

"Matta dagomota baline enata," squealed Allotter and Spinner roared with laughter.

"Moni gnatha gabi; budduton imon. Geneta marcosior," replied Llyat with no understand of what this strange language meant or what he had just said.

"Right, let's get the job done!" shouted Allotter.

Llyat immediately turned his back on the three sisters and focused on remaining in control of his actions. Once again the three cards entered his mind. He just had to work out the meaning of the combination, Truth, the Cutter, the Lover. Suddenly he understood what they had been trying to tell him all along. Truth mattered most. He could not live the life he wanted if he could not be true to himself, Heliana, and their unborn child. He had a choice to make, to remain true to Heliana or give himself up to Cutter. Despite his persistent engorgement he continued to resist the drive to fuck. He turned once again to face the three women but Arnkatla was still there.

"I will not do it and nor will I let you harm Heliana," he shouted through his whirling emotions.

"Then help me back to my table while I discuss with my sisters what we should do next," croaked Cutter as she transformed back into her ancient self.

Llyat stepped forward and offer his hand. The crone winked, smiled, and took his hand. For a moment she seemed transfixed by its stickiness. Then as she sat, Llyat returned to his place before the three.

A great argument then broke out between the sisters. On it continued for several minutes and was ended only when Cutter declared that she had already cleared this particular outcome with their mother.

"If this is how you want to play the game then so be it," bellowed the incensed Allotter. "The talons are sharp sister."

"Yes, and don't expect us to support you when it all goes arse up," shouted Spinner.

"As you wish," said Cutter before fixing her attention back on to Llyat. "Ask all that you wish to know Llyat and I will answer for the Moirai."

"At last we can broach that which I have come to discuss," snarled Llyat as he began to rant. "I have been through many trials to meet with you all. A good number of people have died supporting my cause and I feel a great weight of responsibility dragging me down. Yet still the three of you sit and smirk as you dabble in what you think is nothing more than a game. I am not frightened of you. Your pathetic meddling has led you to the point where the Middle Realm may be destroyed and on that day you three will have no purpose left to exist. Did you ever considered that? I will open the portal to the Underworld, I will destroy Urthanock, and I will allow you to have meaning; but you must stop fucking with me and give me the information that I need."

"So where do you wish to begin?" asked Cutter.

"With my long-lost ancestor," began Llyat. "Clotho the oak man recited some ancient words he had once found; *'One day the Marked shall come and seek out the Lords of Light.'* Tell me what you know of these Lords. Who are they and how will they help with all that I have to do?"

"They are the last link to the Ancients and they dwell upon one of two mountains at the western end of the Lotus Isles," answered Cutter while the other two glared amid their fermenting hate for their sister. "They are the guardians of many of the old secrets and they have the 'diamond in the sky', that which you must use to weld the five Gems of Thamous into the one key that will control access to the Underworld. It alone has sufficient power to generate enough heat to match the belch that Thamous used in the last iteration of The Great Game."

"Stop calling this a game," ordered Llyat. "Tell me more about the diamond."

"When Raulyn the Grand had defeated Urthanock and sealed him in the underworld he knew that a day would come when the Moirai would once again seek to play a similar ga..., plot a new eventuality," continued Cutter. "He tried to hide the five jewels from us sisters and the eyes of men. If the gems ever needed to be forced together again then he knew he could not rely on Thamous. The wyvern could have passed away, indeed just as it has done. He was clever you know and..."

"And the diamond?" interrupted Llyat.

"Oh yes, forgive me if I ramble. I have not spoken for so long that my tongue is racing."

"Get on with it sister," snarled Allotter. "Then find a way to keep silent again for I much preferred it that way."

"I agree," growled Spinner. "The mumblecrust was much better muted."

"As I was saying, Sir Raulyn travelled to see the priests who had first sent men across the ocean to this Realm. He met with them high in their hillfort at the edge of the Lotus isles. With him went a vast uncut diamond, the size of a large boulder and the likes of which has never been found before or since. He had discovered it when trading with the diminutive miners of the Dirmark, but that is another story and I must remain focused."

"He doesn't need to know this shit," mumbled Spinner.

"Silence!" shouted Llyat and the two spurned crones fell dumb.

"Raulyn asked the priests to begin the process of cutting and polishing the diamond to create a lens powerful enough that when it focused the light of Solaris to a single point its heat would match that of the breath of Thamous. Do you know what a lens is lad?"

"Yes, Sir Raulyn's memories tell all; curved glass that can bend light. He was a clever sod."

"You need to take the Gems to the Lords of Light," continued Cutter. "Once you have convinced them who you are and told them of our meeting this day, they will then create the one key for you. In fact they have been waiting a very long time to do so."

"Clotho of the oaks also spoke of another ancient clue; *'First the Marked must face the fire, high above the clouds in secret Bryngaer Henuriaid.'* Is this yet another trial I must overcome and what is Bryngaer Henuriaid?" asked Llyat, sure that he had remembered the precise quotation.

"There is little to concern you there" reassured Cutter. "The words just confirm the power of the fire that the diamond will produce, and that you must both deliver the Gems to this fire and be present during the weld. It has to be the Marked who places the Gems together for no one else will fit the rules of the ga…, I mean it will not otherwise work. Bryngaer Henuriaid is just the name of their ancient hillfort, the enclosure in which their Temple of Light is located. As I have already said, it is on the top of one of the twin peaks at the west of the Lotus Isles. Be most careful to climb the right one for you have limited time."

"What do you mean by that?" asked Llyat.

"There is only one day each year that the rays of Solaris are strong enough to fuse the crystals of the jewels. It is the longest day, the one on which Solaris pauses the progression of his morning rise and then begins his slow retreat. The final day of the Enderdetag Alignment is but one month off and you must be in position on that day below the diamond, ready to begin the transmutation of the Gems. Do not miss it for you will have to wait another year for Solaris to be in the right place but a thousand life times before the sacred alignment of the stars returns. This is your one chance to tap the full power of Solaris and I don't believe you could escape Urthanock's evil grip for so a long time. Remember this verse Llyat, it will help you to recall that fact. It is from a child song passed down from ancient times and left as a pointer for you by Raulyn himself."

"But on the day the disc stands still
We stop our dance and eat our fill;
Then again we prance and thrill,
The sparkling diamond on the hill."

"I have seen this before on a wall before the first of the metal doors," replied Llyat. "I will think on it later but will you not tell me which of the twin mountains to climb?"

"No she cannot," sneered Spinner. "The dice and cards do not permit t."

"The sailor, Theoplous, who is a native of those Isles may well be able to guide you in this matter, or at least take you to someone who knows something that may help you make your choice," said Cutter as she cast a knowing wink at Llyat.

"Will you free him from the torment you have imposed on him so that he may help?"

"What torment?" snapped back Allotter.

"He's..." began Llyat as the eyes of the three hags flared red. "It doesn't matter."

"Well," continued Cutter. "Do you understand what you must do?"

"I do, but where is the location of the door to the Underworld?"

"Time is running out so listen very carefully," Cutter continued. "The Lotus Isles are comprised of three islands, one large and two small. The largest contains their towns, harbours, and farmsteads which are still as they were before the Ancients first visited this Realm. The beaches of the island are covered with the whitest and purest of sands, while the sea is clear and resembles turquoise paint. Its rolling hills are covered in the most verdant of grass, a unique variety that gives off a hint of cinnamon. A sweetness will fill your nostrils that you will find nowhere else in this world. The main island, close to the Twin Mountains is where door to the Underworld is concealed. However it has been long buried under the cumulative detritus of aeons and may not be easy to locate. The Lords of Light will however be able to show you the way."

Llyat listened intently as Cutter changed her demeanour.

"Now remember this for it is the only way that the portal works." she began. "Whosoever places the key on the lockstone of the great door will cease to exist. That includes you so think of a solution before we sisters next roll our dice."

"But how..." mumbled Llyat as Cutter continued?

"Only inside the Underworld can you defeat Urthanock. If you get that far then to seal the portal there is a similar lockstone inside. Think of another way for if you dear child place the key down upon it, then again you will die. If somehow you do manage to seal the door with Urthanock inside then the cracks that appeared between the dimensions will be healed. What has seeped out will we believe cease to exist. I hope you understand that this no small task that you must undertake!"

"Then I must leave you at once and go to fulfil my destiny," replied Llyat.

"Thank fuck for that," moaned Allotter. "Men and Lizard kind are dying in in bucket loads before the gates of Parandor and we have a forest of strings to sever."

"I intend to leave now. Do I have to pass back through all the terrors that I faced to get here?"

"No, you do not, they were all in your mind," snarled the impatient Spinner.

Llyat stepped forward to reclaim his bag and satchel of Gems. The weight of what he had to accomplish pressed heavy on his youthful shoulders. Without waiting for permission he stepped back towards the centre of the temple. He looked to his nakedness and found it hard to believe that all he had suffered had been but fabrications of his mind. They had all seemed so real and he longed to be reunited with the woman that carried his child.

"What about Heliana, you promised to return her to me?"

"Step through the door and she will be there," said Allotter with granite like authority.

Llyat hesitated. Could the three be believed after all that had been said?

"You may trust us Llyat but take care and remember all I have told you child," said Cutter as a tear rolled out of her right eye.

Llyat took a deep breath, made his way to the copper streaked door, and pulled on its handle. He stopped as if to say something but the thought alluded him. Once the door had moved a sufficient distance to allow his passage he was expelled from the temple in a flash of brilliant light. The door slammed shut with a mighty thud and as an unseen force pushed him forward into the embrace of his friends' arms.

"What's behind the door Llyat, did you get to see anything at all in the few seconds you were inside," squealed Heliana as she held the love of her life. "Is that the way we need to go?"

"Seconds?" he questioned.

Llyat's face betrayed his amazement. His bewilderment was compounded when he realised that he was fully clothed.

"Yes, no sooner did you step inside than you jumped back out again," said Irabo, wondering why Llyat looked so confused.

"In and out faster than Highroar in bathtub," confirmed Theoplous, seemingly recovered.

"Our work here is done," ordered Llyat. "All is not what it seems. We must away at speed and I will reveal all when we reach the surface and set the trap for Urthanock. The plan is altered a little but I will explain later. Come we must leave at once."

The climb back up the calendar steps was a struggle for Heliana given the extra load that sloshed inside her womb, the puffiness of her ankles, and the bones of her pelvis that didn't somehow feel as tight as they should. She would have kept all this information quiet had Llyat not kept enquiring of her condition every ten steps or so. With a great stoic resolve she never slackened her pace, despite her heavy breathing and the offer from Irabo and Theoplous to carry her the final third of the journey. In the end she swore at them all and so they desisted in their displays of concern. No comment was passed regarding the sailor's health.

Once they had broken the surface and exited the Barrow the weary group rested on its grassy slope adjacent to the portal. With nothing better to do they all looked down towards Harico in the distance. Ten minutes passed before Heliana had recovered from her climb and Llyat took the opportunity to summarise what had happened from the moment he had first passed through the Moirai door. He did not include his naked ordeal or the cock reaction test. He squashed all thought of Arnkatla's naked form and did not speak of his blood relationship to the

Moirai. These he felt ashamed of despite them being no fault of his own doing. There were however certain facts that Llyat was willing to share. He told his comrades about the Lords of Light, the diamond, its location, and the approximate whereabouts of the door to the underworld. Theoplous agreed that he was the best person to take Llyat to the Lotus Isles. Irabo immediately saw the logic in the plan to gain Llyat two hours of travel time before the Dragon Whisper was triggered. Their last act together would be to find a suitable crevice for Irabo to hide once he had taken the stone out of the lead casket. A cluster of boulders some thirty paces towards the far end of the Barrow was chosen as Irabo's hide.

"I will wait until the Lord of Fear has entered the Barrow before racing to catch you all up," said Irabo when all was finalised. "I suggest you avoid the village. Head west along the line of the Harico Hills until you reach the road to the south. There you can drop down through the oaks. You will never get to Parandor if you try the route we came on."

"I agree and that is what we will do," replied Llyat

"Keep your wits about you for the bastard may not use the rift but come on foot," added Irabo. "If I have not caught you up by the time you get to the north-south road then he has not yet made the Barrow and you should then take even greater care. You all understand that don't you?"

"Aye lad, we do," said Theoplous gruffly.

Llyat passed the lead box over to Irabo and the group bade their farewells.

"Do you think we will ever see him again?" whispered Heliana as they moved away.

20

The gathered throng of Parandor's highborn moved to the sides of the throne room in one collective parting. It was as if the master puppeteer had pulled both hands in opposite directions. From behind the marble throne where once sat the bony posterior of Phauless Gylewu, the Trident Guard of Valameer swept out to secure the room. The troops marched forward in prefect formation. With precision timing all turned inward to face the crowd on either side of the passage that their entrance had created. Each wore the distinctive dress of distant Valameer, white tunics with green cloth cloaks around their shoulders and buckled under the neck with shimmering bronze broaches. Attached to their belts the warriors carried a short sword. In their left hand they gripped a wooden shield while in their right a gleaming silver trident that pushed forward towards the crowd. They left nothing to chance as Lady Fluridana entered into the space between the two ranks of her famed fighters and began to take stock of the situation that fell before her gaze. Stood by her side as she scanned for danger were her Captains with whom she then began to discuss how best to bring relief to the Citadel. It was not without difficulty that she made herself heard over the whoops of joy from those to which she had brought salvation.

"Valameer... Valameer.... Valameer," servants began to chant, low at first and then growing in intensity as more joined in.

"Thias, Danisun, what should we do next; you know the Citadel better than most."

"Look to the far end by the great metal doors," began Thias. "They pulse and you can hear the thuds of Lizardmens' ram as they try to push the portal inwards. Say some words to the crowd and then let us immediately take battle to the reptiles."

Thias looked to the doors. They still held fast as Lady Fullbane and her litter continued to deny entrance to the reptile hoard. The man the bard now knew to be Darchus then sought to make his voice heard.

"I agree with the bard's assessment. We have time to plan our offensive for as much as they batter away it seems that they cannot shift that most marvellous of barricades."

"At last the gods have found a use for Thinata Fullbane," laughed Lady Flurdiana. "This is one sight that will stick with me until the end of my days. Should we survive this day remind me to award her some sort of medal, although it may take time to think of the most appropriate one."

"I will go at once to the doors and plan her removal if that is how we intend to exit this chamber," added Danisun Dain. "Then I will and ready the Trident Guard into their triple wall and begin the coordination of the two."

"Excellent," replied the Lady as she turned to address the crowd.

Facing the idle elite she raised her hands high and so silence fell.

"Highborn of Parandor. Sing of this day for as long as breath passes over your lips. Soon all will be as it should and the reptilian swine will be no more. By the end of this day we will have enough scale hide to give work for all. We will churn out shoes and bags in such numbers that all may wear them and have several to spare.

Remember forever who it was who came to your aid in your darkest hour. I, Flurdiana of Valameer, the saviour of the Realm."

"Valameer... Valameer... Valameer," rose the chant.

Thias's attention was drawn to the waving hands of the Lord Chamberlain who along with others rushed forward in relieved excitement. Lady Flurdiana lowered her arms and ordered he guard to stand at ease and then muster by the great doors. Mobbed in an instant by those who would touch the self-imposed new Ruler of the Realm, the lady could not help but smile. Thias took several paces forward in order to intercept Ystafell and as he did so his eyes fell upon Lady Erreny who was being comforted by several Ladies of the Court. The Sovereign Adviser lay still and moaned, her eyes half closed and her face screwed in the throes of agony. The iron pult bolt still protruded from a bare exposed cheek and had been padded with several lace and silk scarves donated by those who attempted to ease her suffering.

"Pull the bolt out," shouted Thias to the woman. "Unless you do so the wound will not heal. It will fester and the black creeping flesh will appear. All then will be lost."

Ystafell stopped at the bard's side and whispered in his ear.

"We have tried, but the tip of the bolt is firmly embedded in some deep bone or other. The one chance she has is if we can get her to the healing priests in the Temple of Fatumai and have their holy men extract it under the influence of poppite."

"Then do the best you can for her while we seek to clear the city of Lizardmen," answered Thias. "That may take some time but we will work as fast as the Fates permit."

"Good fortune," replied Ystafell as without warning as he threw his arms around the Bard and squeezed out his admiration.

"The Fates too hold me in their embrace this day Ystafell," replied Thias as he broke away. "I must leave now for I have much to accomplish if we are going to defend this city."

Thias ran to catch up with Lady Flurdiana and Darchus who were now half way across the throne room on route to the iron doors.

Some five minutes later preparations were well underway to remove the barricade that had frustrated the enemy's advance. Lady Fullbane's lifting team made ready to move their load at Danisun's command. Fullbane blasphemed in a muffled manner as she screamed into the old rag that be reinserted inside her mouth. Spotting her discomfort, Thias immediately moved forward and removed to obstruction. He expected to be target of the whale's ire but as the rag fell from her voluminous lips, she began to thank Thias for his prompt intervention.

"I am for ever in your debt young bard," she began as her voice revelled in its freedom. "I will not forget this kindness you have shown me in the moment of my triumph. I expect you to write the most marvellous of ballads about the day that Thinata Fullbane saved the highborn from annihilation. Now let me think of a really good title to help you get started. I know of old that songs are best made once the first words have been penned. Now let me think... How about you call it 'The doors could not be shifted?' No I think we can come up with something much better than that... Perhaps 'Thinata the hero of the holy hour?' No far too priestly; there must be better ... 'An ode to the overweight saviour of the ungrateful.' Yes, that sounds more like it. What about you Thias, do you have an idea of what such a master piece could be called?"

"When her mouth stood full, the Realm rejoiced!" replied Thias without thinking.

"You cheeky young bugger," she squealed back in her excitement. "Do you think you could untie this rope for it its crushing my tits?"

"Of course Thinata, as soon as you have been lifted clear of the doors."

"Then while we wait Thias, please answer me one question. While I was acting as the barricade to the Court buffoons I overheard some interesting conversations although most were difficult to follow due to the repeated banging on the door."

"What is you would like to know?" replied Thias.

"This marked boy they are talking about," she began. "They say that this war is all because of him and that the beast out there called Urthanock is determined to stop him fulfilling some shit ancient prophecy."

"That is all true," said Thias as he checked on the completion of the trident triple wall.

"Some have whispered that this marked one has left the Capital and others that he was my sister Lyrusa's lad who disappeared many years ago. What say you to that Thias?"

"Both are true Thinata and I will seek to join with Llyat Emgar as soon as this battle has run its course. I know the boy well and have pledged to support his quest. I am now Cuvar just as your husband was, may the gods watch over his ever endearing essence."

"Then I am his step aunt and no doubt his only living relative," said Lady Fullbane as a tear formed in her eye. "You will watch out for him won't you Thias? He is all I have apart from my servants."

Thias's answer was lost in the midst of a sudden commotion. On Danisun Dain's orders the team of muscular dimwits lifted the whale's chair and with surprising speed moved it a dozen paces clear of the portal. The vast metal doors were immediately pushed open as the Lizardman swarm attempted to rush the room.

"Advance!" bellowed Danisun

The Trident wall sprung forward with deadly effect into the midst of the onrushing reptiles. Thias expected such success for while in music training in Valameer he had heard of tell of their most deadly honed technique. The triple wall of Valameer was a formation that had been developed over centuries and in both attack and defence it was a war tool second to none. He looked on as the front line of warriors interlocked their shields as they bent or stood at three different heights. Those who stooped lowest formed a shield wall at leg level while between them partially bent warriors created the next at torso height. The third rank stood behind the alternating first and second and locked the wall before their heads. At the top of each of the three shield segments the Trident Guard pushed their three pronged forks forward and created a killing zone before the wall. Behind the front ranks followed the rest of the guards and with ever increasing pressure they forced the wall forward against any opposition that dared to stand against it. And so, it was that the Lizardmen of the Eastern Marsh found themselves rushing an organised formation that decimated their attack.

Soon the front of the triple wall resembled a plate of skewered gherkins and still the wall trudged forward. Those that fell from the pickle prongs were simply marched over and as the new blood-green carpet swept underneath a forest of short blades descended from the fists of the Trident Guard and ended the lives of any that the points of the tridents had failed to extinguish. On into the corridor the men from Valameer pushed without sustaining a single casualty of their own. After something less than five minutes the remaining Lizardmen, one third of their initial strength, turned and fled as one. Out through the main doors to the Citadel they ran while the Trident Guard kept their discipline and did not once seek to charge and leave their flanks exposed. Thias followed as the last warrior left the Great Hall. Once the relentless tide of death reached the main doors to the Keep they stopped under Danisun's command and waited for their leader to catch them up. Thias stood by his side, ready for the next phase to begin. The battle for the Citadel was as good as over but the war to regain the city was about to begin. Lady Flurdiana fought her way through to the front of her troops.

"Excellent Danisun. What's happening outside and what do you advise next?"

"There are about fifty or so of the reptiles that fled across the courtyard and who now seek to find a way through the Barbican. The will be easy pickings if we attack at once."

"Then take the majority of the Guard and wipe the bastards out," she ordered. "But leave fifty for the cordwainer Darchus Arillius. I want him to sweep through the rooms in the Keep and the rest of the Citadel. None must be left alive who could later attack from our rear. These shits will rue the day they murdered my betrothed."

Thias mused. The attack on Valameer seemed so long ago and as he inwardly smiled the Lady Flurdiana moved to his side.

"Thias is there anything else you think I should do?" asked the fearsome woman.

"My Lady there is potential threat that we need still to nullify. Give me twenty of your guard and I will secure the Underkeep for you. This is how the bastards gained entry to the Keep and there could still be some down there."

"Excellent Thias. You shall have fifteen of my finest. Join us in the courtyard when done."

Lady Flurdiana signalled to her troops, some of whom soon broke away and followed Thias down into the dank domain of the Parandor's Underkeep. The bard was greatly relieved to find the dark tunnels and passages devoid of the enemy. The air stank with the heavy sweetness of fresh spilt blood, mixed with the acrid after bite of burnt wood and lamp oil. Feelings of hatred towards the Lizardmen continue to swell Thias's chest as cell by cell, torture chambers, laboratories, and store rooms were searched in the most systematic and efficient manner. The evil reptiles had slaughtered every prisoner behind their locked doors, all shot through the window by however many crossbow bolts it took to complete the task. Soon Thias arrived at the door that led up into the rear courtyard and there he saw what the foul creatures had done to Tharik Mastisan.

The poor brute of a gaoler who had known nothing of the world beyond his place of employment, had been fixed to the wall by the door he had earlier tried to defend. A brazier had been ripped from its bracket. Its metal had been bent into the shape of a hook and onto it Tharik's ribcage had been fixed. His eyes had been ripped out, as had his tongue. His private parts lay on top of his intestines. The stink tubes spewed from out of his belly through the gash of his evisceration. Tharik smelled worse dead that he had ever done alive and that was remarkable in itself.

Thias threw up and then sought to hide his intense nausea from the Trident Guard. When recovered he then sought to force his way out of the Underkeep and up into the courtyard. He screamed insults to the heavens although doubting any of the gods gave a shit about him or his words.

"No one may have cared about you Mastisan, but I fucking did. I will avenge this foul deed, so help me I will."

The bard was not given time to stand amid the rays of Solaris, nor to contemplate the extent of his intended revenge. Trident Warriors began to gather around him and as they confirmed the Underkeep cleansed of swamp swine. He led them through the courtyard, around outside of the Keep, and on towards the Barbican gates. There before the portcullis he witnessed the final slaughter as Danisun Dain and the main force of the Guard disposed of the remaining contingent of Lizardmen who had dared to enter the Citadel. The fight had been one sided and of short duration. Reptilian corpses were dragged away from the portcullis along with the few Trident guard who had fallen in battle. A noise from the right of the Keep's doors gripped his attention and as his head turned he saw Darchus approach, his blade blooded but with a smile that indicated his sweep of the Citadel had been successful.

From amongst the mass of white uniforms, now splattered as if sprayed by over ripe tomatoes, stepped the ornately armoured Lady Flurdiana. She immediately hailed the return of Thias, Darchus and their warriors.

"Good to have you back with us," she began. "I hope all went well; you seem to be both intact and have taken few if any casualties."

"I can report that the Underkeep is secure and sound," replied Thias. "They are the most evil of creatures for they even stopped to slaughter every last one of the prisoners. We must show them no mercy."

"Quite so," Flurdiana replied in a calm and dismissive manner. "What about you Darchus, I see from your smile you have been equally successful."

"I have indeed my Lady. We found a few of the slime scale lurking in the shadows but left none alive.

"Good, Danisun is in communication with the few from the City Watch who barricaded themselves in the engine room of the Barbican," continued the Lady. "The gates will begin to rise on Danisun's orders. I have instructed him to split his force, one third to end the battle that rages inside the barracks and relieve the beleaguered Watch. The rest will attack in triple wall formation the Lizardmen who are gathered in the square beyond. I want you Thias and Darchus with your groups to protect the wall's flanks and at my signal push forward and encircle the swine. Is that clear? Do you understand what you have to do?"

"Yes my Lady," both replied.

Thias marvelled at the authority that Flurdiana carried amid of the chaos of war.

"Thias, pick up a trident and shield from one of my fallen heroes as you pass through the Barbican. You will be even more useful if you can blend in with our tactics. Danisun, when you are ready get your men to form the wall and lift the gates."

Lady Flurdiana then turned to speak to Thias. She pointed to the bizarre remains of reptiles.

"What's with all these bits of Lizardmen lying scattered about," she began. "This is not the work of my Trident Guard nor the effects of battle for most were there before we engaged in the fight?"

"They used the Rift, the connection to the Underworld's magic appears to be malfunctioning," replied Thias as the portcullis began to lift in front of the triple wall. "From what I can tell, only a half or so of the reptiles seem to have arrived intact."

Thias sensed the Lady to be in no mood for superfluous dialogue. As his voice tailed off she cried out to her Trident Guard and Parandor's Man-at-Arms.

"Danisun, begin the advance."

Onwards the triple wall stomped and the reptiles beyond the Barbican quaked as they realised death was coming. Half way across the circular inner vault of the mighty edifice, the fearsome fighters split with a small continent diverting into the barracks. Thias, as ordered, picked up a trident and shield from the nearest of the fallen and marched behind the advancing behemoth. From time to time he exchanged a knowing glance with Darchus. Now inside the city Thias knew the tide of the war was changing. Amid his heightened excitement he could only hope that Sir Byddin continued to hold on behind the stakewall. The battlements were still held by the City Watch who continued to rain down arrows upon the horde beyond the walls. The sudden appearance of the Trident Guard at the entrance to the Barbican had not gone unnoticed. Those Lizardmen who had been fighting to gain the battlements now abandoned their attempts and sought to re-join their fellow spawn. The scale force fell back and created a formation ready to meet the expanding triple wall as it pushed into more open space. A volley of crossbow bolts clattered against the circular shields of the men from Valameer. It was an ineffectual attempt and yet seemed to at least to give the reptiles something rally around. A collective screech echoed off the walls of the surrounding buildings and rattled Thias's ear drums. The few heroic defenders on the battlements rained down volley upon volley of arrows from their long bows and the Lizardman realising they would be cut down if they remained in the open began to retreat into the crowded, slop slithering streets of the Capital.

"What is happening ahead Danisun?" shouted the Flurdiana as the triple wall halted its advance.

"My Lady, there is a large fat frog like creature ahead, organising his forces in order to retreat."

"A frog you say?" she replied, hinting of prior knowledge of the creature.

"That is correct my Lady."

"That will be Ssonsh; the High Priest of the Marsh."

"Do you know…" stuttered Thias, but his part question went unheard as Danisun continued.

"From the direction that their backs faced and knowing Parandor as well as I do, I believe that this Ssonsh is intending to retreat through two of the gates. He will seek to regroup before the South Gate by the harbour where you landed your fleet, and the Narrow Gate that leads out by south west corner of the walls. The Narrow Gate will be the lighter defended and that is where the bulk seem intent on heading. Our frog fiend and a smaller group seem to have aligned more to the South Gate. Perhaps he has charge of the best of reptilian warriors. Who knows how their minds work?"

"Go back at once and advance at pace Danisun," replied Flurdiana. "When the scum brake and begin their race for the gates then you and your wall must chase after them, but keep to an orderly formation lest it is a trap. Do not allow yourself to be ambushed. Thias and Darchus, take your groups of warriors and pursue Ssonsh and his force."

"If we can take the toad out the others may well loose heart," said Thias as the Lady paused for a breath.

"Good, but at all costs we must ma ntain control of the gates to the City. Go now and let us finish this. I will follow behind Danisun's group and if you both succeed, then join us before the Narrow Gate, if that is indeed the focus of their next attack. Let us pray all still goes well outside the walls."

Danisun made his way back to his command position immediately behind the triple wall. Thias watched as the Man-at-Arms peered through a small gap in the shields and gave his order to advance. The Trident Guard moved forward at walking pace towards what Thias presumed was the retreating enemy. A dozen paces from the line of buildings Danisun's force broke from its wall formation and began to form a column, four abreast as it raced into the street that led in a diagonal line to the Narrow Gate. As the white wave veered off Thias could see the fleeing group led by Ssonsh as it headed straight into the city an on towards the Southern Gate.

"For Parandor!" shouted Thias as he set his troops off in support.

"For Valameer!" screamed Darchus as he mirrored Thias's order

"For the Realm!" hollered the carpet of white as it raced to confront the enemy.

As ordered Thias and Darchus led their pursuit of the frog priest Ssonsh and his minions but the Lizardmen did not just run. Every several hundred paces, they stopped and half a dozen or so would put up a fierce resistance in order to buy the main group more time with which to reach the Southern gate. After the first such skirmish Thias realised that if he held back a few paces the bulk of the fighting at each encounter would be borne by the warriors of the Trident Guard who demonstrated far greater skill in the handling of both shield and trident than Thias could ever hope to match. Despite the killing of many Lizardmen as they progressed south Thias soon realised that instead of their numbers being gradually degraded, they were in fact increasing as more reptiles rallied inside the old town and in response to the shouts of their toady Commander.

"I'm not sure I like this," shouted Thias to Darchus in the midst of yet another scrap. "If their numbers keep growing we may soon find ourselves in considerable difficulty."

"But we have no choice bard," shouted back Darchus. "Come bard, stick your prongs in, the more we slaughter the greater the chance we have to even the numbers."

On the fighting raged until at last the buildings fell away at the base of the infamous Stukeley Knoll; its summit still set up for further executions upon the stage of the Folly. Covering the slopes of the grassy Knoll lay at least two hundred corpses, peasants and lowlife of the Capital. At the mounds base the gathering the army of the swamp stood defiant as Ssonsh screamed out his orders. Thias scanned the seventy or so warriors from Valameer and realised they were outnumbered almost two to one. He then turned to his new comrade in arms.

"They have the high ground and the numbers, do you think we have a chance."

"Form the wall," shouted Darchus and the warriors of Valameer responded without question.

"Good Fortune Darchus," said Thias.

"And may the Fates also be with you," answered the cordwainer.

The triple wall began its methodical trudge forward. Thias looked through gaps in the shield wall and his eyes became fixed on Ssonsh's antics. The frog priest was seeking to maximise the advantage of the high ground. From this vantage point he sought to organise those reptiles with crossbows for their high position would provide a devastating angle of fire over the shields of Valameer. So it was that as the triple wall continued to roll on the Lizardmen backed up the hill, passing between the bodies of the slum dwellers as they did so. Soon the front rank of crossbows were readied and Ssonsh prepared to unleash the first salvo. Then something most unexpected happened. A monstrous figure appeared at the top of the Folly. Thias watched as Sir Richemanus, mighty axe in one hand and bottle of firewater in the other, stood legs apart and screamed like a mathulath in full rut.

"Come on ye scale covered Silverwynn shaggers, let's see what you're made of!"

"What is he doing?" said Thias.

"Getting himself killed, the drunken oaf," answered Darchus.

Ssonsh then waved his webbed hands again and croaked out orders that were too far away on the wind for Thias to make out. Some twenty or so Lizardmen, those nearest to the Folly, moved up the hill at a run in order to take out the Royal Executioner. Still the triple wall edged forwards but Thias could not take his eyes off Richemanus whose axe swept in great circles and slaughtered all who approached. Then a volley of bolts took their toll on the inebriate monster who had for some reason forsaken his armour. Two hit him in the chest and one in the belly. Richemanus dropped on his own wooden stage. He raised himself up for one brief second as expecting a curtain call, bowed forward, and then crashed with a dull thud. The Lizardmen turned and reloaded. Ssonsh raised his hand again, ready to give the order to fire when in an instant the battle turned on its head.

The lowlife of Parandor that Thias had presumed dead, raised as one between the formations of Lizardmen. How the attack was coordinated the bard could not tell but the magnitude of its surprise and the speed of its execution left it impossible for the reptiles to respond. Daggers flashed, daggers slashed, daggers thrust and cut deep. So many throats were cut that the spray produced turned the grass of the knoll into something resembling a glade of trampled cherries. Guts were opened, eyes poked through, and golden bracelets stolen. It all happened so quickly that Thias was forced to wipe his eyes in disbelief. Ssonsh was immediately surrounded by several of his captains and fled from the Knoll in the direction of the Narrow Gate. Any other Lizardman who avoided the blades of the unsavoury and who descended the grassy slopes fell foul of the triple wall which took no prisoners. The battle for Stuckeley Knoll was over and as the wall of Valameer was stood down Thias moved through it with two purposes in mind. The first to thank the ordinary people of Parandor and the second to give aid to the Knight of the Nightfall.

However, before Thias could engage with those who had changed the course of history, the peasants of Parandor raced away over the back of the knoll and lost themselves in the buildings that abutted this most ancient of spaces. That is all except one. From the top of the Folly a man stopped for a brief moment, turned and shouted down to Thias.

"I am the Dead Collector and I will be back later to collect the fallen. The Thieves Guild hope you accept this intervention in the spirit it was given. Having done our bit, leave us be."

Then the man was gone. Thias and Darchus redoubled their efforts to offer aid to the fallen executioner. Some few minutes later Thias cradled Richemanus's head in his arms and whispered words of comfort. The once most feared Knight of Parandor struggled to stop his eyes from flickering as his life force began to ebb. Yet he had one final message for Thias.

"That's you, isn't it bard? I would recognised your silky sentences even after a thousand years in the afterlife. I can see the strings and there are three dark shadows hovering behind you, waiting to take me away on my last journey."

Thias turned his head but there was nothing to be seen.

"Let's keep this short," continued the weakened executioner. "Your father was a good man deep in his core, as was Danisun Dain who took his life for reasons more complex that you will ever be able to understand. Forgive Danisun and move on, otherwise you will torture yourself and perhaps like myself begin to drown your distress in drink. So with this parting gift I ask you to now fuck off; the Cutter's scythe is about to sever my…"

The last breath of Sir Richemanus of the Nightfall left in a gurgling rush.

"By the will of the gods, what was all that about?" asked Darchus who had listened at the end.

"Nothing," replied Thias as he jumped to his feet. "Come, Ssonsh is making his escape. We must chase him down."

Thias and Darchus collected the warriors under their command and soon set off in the relentless pursuit of the frog priest and his personal guard. They re-entered the warren of intersecting alleyways, overhanging houses, and ginnels of gloom which provided the most perfect places for ambush. However apart from the occasional body part there was no evidence of the presence of Lizardmen. It soon became obvious that the slitherers from the swamps had given up on the hope of taking the city and were now desperate to escape before their total annihilation. Then as Thias approached The Murdered Wolf, and with Ssonsh's noisy flight still audible in the distance, a different sound reached his ears. It was the unmistakable voice of Isambard Hotch venting his full range of earthy expletives. The profanities rolled out of the door of his establishment like some foul fog over the great river of death. There was no doubt about it, Hotch was in a fight for his life and that could only mean one thing, reptiles. On reaching the door, Darchus called a pause to the chase and barked out an order to the Trident Guard.

"Fan out and scour this area for the toad," he ordered. "Thias and I will see what's going in inside this tavern. If you spot our prey then give three blasts on your whistle. Now, go."

As the warriors departed, Thias was the first to enter The Murdered Wolf where Hotch continued to curse and bellow. The bard's eyes soon adjusted to the unlit interior and at the far corner of the bar he spotted the lardy barkeep. Hotch swung a large spade in an attempt to keep four lizard men at a distance. From the blood that oozed from his right sleeve it was obvious he had already taken at least one blow to his good arm. Thias took aim with his trident and threw it as a spear across the room. By more luck that skill the three prongs flashed through the back of one of the reptiles' necks carried it forward two paces, and impaled the creature on the wall to Hotch's right. Thias then drew his blade and readied his shield. The three remaining Lizardmen turned to face the attack from their rear and as they did so Hotch brought his great spade down upon the helmetless head of the nearest beast and divided it from crown to neck. The remaining two then sought a means of escape. One in blind panic ran onto the prongs of Darchus's trident. The remaining swamp warrior dropped his sword and raised his hands as in surrender but Hotch was having none of that. His spade swung around in a horizontal plane and it removed the head which flew across the room and bounced into the hearth.

"I thank you for your timely intervention," grunted Hotch as he recognised his saviours.

Moving forward to shake Thias's hand he added, "I will not forget this day bard. I am forever in your debt. If you ever need a favour of me then feel free to call it out."

"Who is the Grand Master of the Thieves Guild?" asked Thias, a question that brought a look of surprise to Darchus's face and one of fear to that of the barkeep.

"Better you would have left me to die than force me to answer that question," replied Hotch as he perspired at an even greater rate of leakage. "If I were to answer that I would be a dead man walking and your hours with the living would be few."

"If I survive this day I will need to thank them…" began Thias but the barkeep would not give up his secret.

"That is knowledge I will take to my grave."

Before Thias could press for an answer, three short blasts on a whistle penetrated the interior of The Murdered Wolf.

"Come Thias, it seems we have tracked down the toad," shouted Darchus.

"Hotch, join us," said Thias. "There is much more killing to be done this day and we can use you spade in our endeavours. You wield it like an executioner would an axe."

And so it was that as Thias stowed away his blade and extracted the reptile from his trident. He and Isambard Hotch, the most unlikely new recruit to the Trident Guard, followed Darchus back into the narrow streets of Parandor.

"It appears the toad is doubling back on himself. He and his body guard have been spotted approaching the Temple of Fatumai," shouted Darchus as soon as Thias had cleared the door to the tavern."

"There are innocents in there," exclaimed Hotch. "We cannot leave them to their fate."

The barkeep was right. The slum dwellers were using the temple as refuge.

"I guess the Toad is not intent on praying to Fatumai," added Darchus.

"He must have some devious plan, "replied Thias. "Whatever it is we must thwart it."

Some five minutes later the regrouped Trident Guard, Thias, Darchus, and Isambard Hotch approached the square in front of the ancient temple. The space was still filled with the squalid camp of refugees that had earlier poured in from outside of the city. On the steps before the closed doors of the edifice, Ssonsh could be seen waving his arms like a sheet on a line amidst a storm. From his movements Thias knew the swine was directing what was left of his force to slaughter the innocents amid their hovels. Thias pulled Darchus to one side and they at once began to plan how they would best react to this emergency. A snap decision was stuck as the pitiful peasants of Parandor fought against swords and crossbows with sticks, and for a lucky few, stones. Darchus led the charge of the Trident Guard deep into the mass of ramshackle dwellings. Triple prongs set about destroying the reptiles before their slaughter of the innocents could be completed. Hotch held back with his spade swinging, lest any Lizardmen sought to escape. Filled with the energy of battle Thias set off alone. He raced around the perimeter of the great square until at last he approached the toad from its left flank.

So preoccupied was Ssonsh in pointing out where it wanted his force to exact its revenge that the priest failed to notice Thias's approach until the last second. The bloated croaker raised its hands as if to unleash some diabolic spell of destruction but Thias beat the toad to the draw. Thrusting his right fist forward he bellowed 'Promethelumous' and a fraction of a second later a fireball shot from his fiery palm and hit the frog priest in both eyes. A second later Thias's trident swept in a low arc and connected with the back of Ssonsh's ankles. The blow dropped the slime covered ball to the floor. Standing tall above the creature Thias drove his trident down into the foul beast's right shoulder and pinned it to the wood that lay before the temple doors. In the blink of an eye Thias whipped his sword out from his side and sliced open the toad's belly from chest to whatever it had between its legs. The hideous screech that broke from its mouth would be long remembered by all whose ears endured it. But Ssonsh was not yet dead. Thias looked to the priest as it watched its own entrails slither like a great coiled snake. Leaning forward he whispered a final message.

"On behalf of the Cuvar, the Marked, Thamous, Einar, and Tonousa, I sentence you to pain eternal. With the Fortune bestowed on me by the Fates themselves I condemn you to everlasting suffering."

Ssonsh then made as to reply but Thias was not in the mood to hear the creature's babble. His blade flashed down, then up, and entered the toad's head below the chin. It exited through the soft bone of the creature's skull after which Ssonsh twitched for several seconds and then went limp. Energised and gasping for breath Thias revelled in the moment. He felt so good that the feeling began to cause him concern. Before he could dwell further on the sensation he heard Darchus call from the foot of the temple steps.

"The swamp swine here have been eliminated. Let's race on to the Narrow Gate and finish these cunts off once and for all."

When Thias passed into one of the three cramped streets that fed down to the Narrow Gate the sounds of battle were so intense that it was almost impossible to think. Never before, despite his experiences at the Bards Guild, the sounds of the war above the prison in Avolire, his observations of the first phase of the battle from the Citadel Tower, and his rampage with the Trident Guard through the old town, had his ears had to bear witness to such dreadful sounds of mayhem. He had entered the middle and main thoroughfare to the Narrow Gate and there ahead he looked on as the white forces of Valameer pressed its triple wall in its most efficient and relentless manner against the warriors of the Eastern Marsh. At the rear of the advancing juggernaut, standing out of cross bow range and surveying the scene before her, stood the Lady Flurdiana. Highly animated she sent runners with instructions into the fray and to where Danisun Dain still dictated the flow of battle.

Thias ordered his warriors to join those of Darchus and the man more accustomed to making shoes led a secondary charge to add weight behind the pressing wall. Thias raced on a pace behind but once he got level with Lady Flurdiana he stopped to engage her and to give her an update on all that had occurred. He covered the pursuit of the frog priest Ssonsh, the events on Stuckeley Knoll, and the toad's evisceration before the gates of the Temple of Fatumai. He kept his sentences short for he did not want to inhibit the Lady's remarkable control of the battleground. Once he had finished Flurdiana nodded to indicate her understanding but then wasted no further time before appraising Thias of what lay ahead.

"The Lizardmen are making their last stand," she began. "They obviously planned to take this gate, either to escape, or to bring in reinforcements. I reckon it's the former for the battle outside has not been progressing as Urthanock had no doubt intended. When we first chased them here they began their rear-guard defence while several stormed the room that controls the raising of the portcullis. They got it to shift but a few inches when it got stuck and no matter what they do they cannot get it to lift again."

"The new cogs that Sir Byddin had welded have probably slipped again," replied Thias. "It will not work again unless they know what they are doing."

"This is good to hear Thias for we have them trapped and soon there will be none left inside the city for us to worry about; that is of course unless they send in another battlegroup using the Rift."

"Most unlikely, replied Thias, "Not given its obvious malfunctioning."

"Good, I have lost enough of my warriors to the enemy's bolts," growled the Lady, dodging one that flew inches passed her head. "Praise the gods Thias that I arrived with reinforcements."

"Indeed so," my Lady.

Thias smirked as he recalled the sniping between Byddin and Townsforth in the war room.

The battle for the Narrow Gate raged on but soon the noise of the wounded began to fall. Sometime later all fell silent save for the suck and slurps of the blades of the Trident Guard as they ensured no fallen reptile remained with breath about its scales or blood in its heart. As the triple wall was stood down and parted Thias gazed upon the pile of swamp dead piled high against the portcullis, the aftermath of their frantic attempts to somehow pass through the solid metal grid. The stench of body fluids pervaded all for the smell of lizard blood is like no other, sweet, sticky and yet with an after sting of sulphurous eggs.

"Danisun, take control of the gate's mechanism," bellowed Flurdiana, "Let me know if you can fix it. If not I will send up the bard for he seems to have some insight into the problem.

"At once my Lady," came the reply.

Thias watched as several of the Trident Guard followed Danisun on a climb up the wall and onto the battlements. Through the door they raced that led to the lifting mechanism. All went well until Danisun pushed open the portal expecting little resistance. Just when it was wide enough, five Lizardmen stormed out. One of the creatures thrust his sword through the Man-at-Arm's stomach and pushing him over the edge. Like a sack of sods it fell before the metal gate. The lives of these reptiles was equally short lived as tridents thrust, swung, stabbed, and cut deep. The gate was secure but Thias was aghast.

"Danisun," he screamed.

The bard ran forward to where man who had killed his father's lay mortally wounded. He cradled Danisun in his arms and offered comfort. The warrior groaned from the intense agony that the gut wound had induced.

"Is that you Thias?" he asked through eyes that glazed by the second. "Say it is you."

"Yes Danisun," stammered the bard. "You're going to be fine, I will get you to the Temple of Fatumai and into the hands of the priests that work miracles."

"No you will not bard; I have an appointment with the Fates and you cannot keep me from it. Come close and listen well for my voice is fading."

The warrior writhed in the throes of agony but Thias still leaned forward and put his ear to the dying man's mouth.

"I am sorry for killing your father all those years ago. Take your revenge and finish me now. This pain is too intense and my time of usefulness has passed."

"I forgive you Danisun," sobbed Thias.

The bard felt a burning need to ask the one question that had haunted him over the years.

"Tell me the name of the Grand Master and I will then release you from your suffering."

The man who had done so much to save Parandor moved his lips as if to answer.

"Who is it? Give me one name for you must have some idea," pushed Thias.

"No I cannot... I..."

It was over. The warrior had left the Realm of the living.

A hand rested on Thias's shoulder. It was the gentle touch of Lady Flurdiana.

"Both Parandor and Valameer will remember the heroic deeds of our servant Danisun, may the gods take care of his essence," she said with softness. "But now bard, move your arse for we still have much work to do. Get yourself up to the mechanism and see if you can fix it. We may yet be able to use it to our advantage."

No sooner had Thias regained his feet when the voice of one of the Trident Guard echoed down from on high.

"My Lady! If we can lift the grate there is a chance we can finish this war.

"I'm coming to see for myself," she hollered. "Come bard, what are you waiting for? The rest of you clear a way through the swamp scum and get ready to move should we get the gate to rise."

Thias dried his eyes on his sleeve. Taking a deep breath to hold back further flow he followed the Lady up the wall on a rope dropped by the Trident Guard. As soon as Thias gained the summit he crossed the battlement and together with Lady Flurdiana looked down to the battle beyond the walls.

"I need you to lift the portcullis now," she ordered before the bard could speak.

Thias ran off to see what he could do. Once inside the stone chamber he set about his task of inspecting the old workings that controlled the raising of the metal gate. He had seen the like before in his youth so the sight was not altogether confusing. Thias knew what to look for. The problem had to be due to the new pieces that Sir Byddin had ordered and so he focused on the shiniest of metal amongst the rusting tooth cogs, wheels, and pulleys. Then at last he found them, two cogs, one of which had been displaced but a few inches and yet sufficient enough to induce a malalignment that stopped their teeth from connecting. Against the stone work of the adjacent wall rested a large metal hammer and as Thias noted its presence he realised it had been left there to remedy the same recurring problem. Three heavy blows and the cogs were reset. Satisfied with his efforts Thias raced over to the wheel that needed to be turned. Much to his relief the portcullis began to rise and an excited chant rose from the courtyard below.

"Valameer…Valameer…Valameer."

21

Urthanock stood before his command tent and watched the battle for Parandor unfold. From what he had observed and from the many incoming reports over the past hour, all was not going as he had neither wished nor expected. He had witnessed Ssobekk the gator lord fail in the task he had given him. To say he was angry would not do justice to the intense venom that coursed through his Vessel's veins. He was way beyond mad; in fact he was distraught with fury. Urthanock could not begin to think what pathetic excuses old timber leg would give for his failure to dismantle the stakewall and destroy the enemy before the West Gate. The beast sneered. No one else but he knew of the Gator Lord's most intimate of secrets. The kulkulkath had taken more than the Gator Lord's leg! It served the bugger right.

Closing his eyes, the Lord over Fear replayed the visions of Ssobekk's retreat from the stakewall, his loss of the flame sword, given to Urthanock by the blacksmith Gof. He sneered with distain at the lack of progress made by his army as they had attacked on three fronts. A new plan was needed for despite sending Ssonsh to use the rift to gain entry behind the city walls, the Army of the East had failed to make inroads into the degradation of Parandor's inner defences. The voice inside his head continued to berate his ears and accused him of great inadequacies, framed in the most demeaning of language. Profanities flew, ones never before heard by the ears of either reptile or man.

The Lord over Fear clenched his fists and the command tent trembled So furious had Urthanock become that he wished for nothing more than his foes to be impaled throughout the length of the stakewall. He would march before their screaming ranks, rip off their privates and ground them into the dirt with his boots; just as he had done with the messenger called Throissler. Such was the sickness that clouded the beast's mind. The Vessel's eyes opened and once again Urthanock looked to the battle below. To his surprise he saw Ssobekk marching up the hill towards him. The General clutched his injured forearm to his chest as if carrying a babe to a place of demonic sacrifice. It was obvious from his purposeful stride that the Gator Lord had something to report. Whether it was important or not Urthanock decided to wait and hear rather than prejudge and execute the bloated beast on sight.

"My Lord," began Ssobekk as soon as he was within ten paces of his master. "We need new tactics. The Army of Parandor is too well prepared. We lost the beasts without them having any impact and I fear the ogres are not yet fully committed. Only one of the thick skulls fights with determination. It's an ugly swine, even by their own standards, and goes by the name of Ikeg. The rest just prance like peacocks before the pointed staves. We should have built siege engines and giant ballisters. Their pults are keeping most of our forces back and out of battle range. Unless we come up with something soon then I believe the battle will be lost."

"You are the most pessimistic of creatures," snarled back Urthanock as he refused to countenance talk of defeat. "I watched as you lose the flame sword that I entrusted to your care. You failed to use it to any great effect, despite the fact it contains great powers for use against the enemy's weapons. What excuse do you have for letting it fall into their hands?"

"I didn't know it had," began Ssobekk, raking through his memories. "I remember the attack of the Falahorn dragon fuckers. Had the Knights of Avolire been with me, as the Lady's originally intended, they would have pushed Parandor's Army back with ease. Forgive my insolence Lord, but remind me again why we had to destroy the black knights."

"Because they challenged my authority. Do not go there should you wish to see this day end."

"When the sword vibrated I thought we had a chance," hesitated Ssobekk, "but then I lost my right hand. By the will of the swamp wisps, I swear to you the pain in my stump is excruciating."

"Did you not see what happened next to the blade? The Berserkers, those Falahorn Fuckers you refer to, threw it back over the stakewall and any advantage it may have given us is now forever lost."

"My Lord, one curved blade alone would not the turn back the defeat that lies before us."

"I will have none of this defeatist talk," snapped back Urthanock.

The voice then awoke with a vengeance.

"Has the Lord over Fear forgotten how to fight?"

"Fuck off!" bellowed Urthanock. "...No not you Ssobekk."

"What advice do you have for me General?" he demanded before the gator could move.

"Retreat to the Marsh and come back next year when we have better refined out tactics. We need to build machines to breach the sake wall. If we scorch the lands between the estuary and the Grey Mountains we will starve these bastards to the point of collapse," spat back the flustered gator.

The Lord over Fear clenched his fists, the tent trembled, yet Ssobekk stood his ground.

"No! Absolutely not. You will win me this battle, this day, this hour, this minute, or by the evil I channel from Kha, I will rip your body apart."

Ssobekk clutched his bloody stump and staggered two steps forward before dropping down to his knees. Urthanock saw that his General's pain was great. Part of his fractured mind wanted to prolong the suffering of the one creature who could perhaps yet turn the tide of batte. The Lizardmen had still to fully commit all of their warriors and so there remained a fair prospect for victory. He knew that he needed the General's continued support, if only to communicate effectively the next phase of plan.

"Hold your stump forward and I will heal it with the power of Kha. I will relieve your suffering and then we will decide what needs to be done to turn this battle in our favour."

Ssobekk trembled as he thrust the bleeding end of his forearm forward. Lumps of clot fell from its end. White bone and crimson marrow poked though the flesh beneath the ragged sheds of hide that had once connected to a distal claw. Urthanock's right hand extended towards the pulp and when but a few inches away it began to emit a green glow that turned to wisp like vapour. The ethereal fog surrounded both limbs. It cracked and popped as it worked its magic, all the while hiding the transformation taking place within its cocoon of weird healing.

"What is happening in there?" stuttered Ssobekk, fearful of his Lord's intentions. "The pain has gone but what will you leave me with?"

"I cannot restore that which lies in the mud of the battle," began Urthanock as the green fog extended upwards to envelope the gator's elbow. "Is there anything you would have me fix to the end of the limb, something practical, a hook perhaps?"

"No, not a hook my Lord; a pirate I will never be."

"Do you jest Gator Lord?" growled Urthanock. "This is not the time for jokes."

"I mean my Lord…" stammered Ssobekk amid his bubbling fear. "I would prefer something long and straight. Something with a pointed end for this was my sword arm."

"Do you mean a blade?"

"Yes, that is exactly what I need. One like that small dainty sword you always carry."

Urthanock looked to the weapon that hung from his side, the one that had killed the wyvern. He laughed in memory of the ease of Thamous's dispatch.

"You're not having that one," replied the beast. "There are others inside the tent."

Urthanock pointed his left hand backwards towards the tent's interior and in an instant a long dagger, the length of a man's forearm, floated out on a stream of magic until it came to the green fog.

"This one seems to have chosen you itself," sneered Urthanock. "What do you think?"

"Yes, that one will do!" answered as the General amid a squint of suspicion.

The mysterious miasma, charged with the mixed stench of metal fume and roasted meat, crackled and then exploded in a flash of light that shocked both Urthanock and Ssobekk. The two staggered back from each other. Three paces later the mysterious fog blew away on the wind. As the Lord over Fear looked to review the outcome of his operation he saw the delight on Ssobekk's face as his right arm swished one way then another while trying out its new appendage.

"Thank you, my Lord," hissed the Gator Lord. "I am without pain and this blade will indeed serve me well. Now I will return to the battle and thrust this gift into the hearts of any men who should dare to oppose us."

"First we must test the power I have imbued into the weld," said Urthanock as his face contorted into one of maniacal malevolence,"

"What do you mean Lord?"

"This!"

The foul Lord twisted his right wrist. Ssobekk immediately experienced an intense burning pain that radiated out from his new arm. It soon enveloped his whole being and dropped him to the ground. Then, just as it had appeared it was gone.

"What in the name of all that is unholy!" exclaimed Ssobekk?

"I have embedded a pain trigger into the weld," sneered Urthanock. "Should you fail to carry out any of my future orders you will not have to wait until back in my presence to receive punishment? You have felt but a little of what I will inflict should you disappoint me a second time."

"I will not Lord."

"Seriously?" sneered the voice. "A pain trigger? You think you have this General under your control but you are mistaken. Do not turn your back on him for one moment or that blade will find its way into your heart; if you have one left."

Urthanock chose not to reply.

"Come Ssobekk, we have wasted too much time in play. Let us take stock and work out how we will destroy Parandor."

Urthanock led his General by the arm in order to gaze upon the battle below. The pair stepped to the edge of the hill and once again began to monitor the stalemate at the three points of their attack. After several minutes of contemplation Ssobekk drew his attention to a small fleet of fishing boats, loaded as best he could make out with warriors dressed in white. Soon with the tide in their favour the flotilla passed the south west corner of Parandor's walls and disappeared from view.

"They are making for the harbour and will no doubt disembark there," said Ssobekk with a calmness that hid his inner concern.

"Who are they?" asked Urthanock. "Who comes to the aid of Parandor?"

"My guess would be that they are from Valameer. The messenger you tortured was either a good liar or more likely had been given false information. It seems that Lady Flurdiana never intended to attack our rear. I wonder what other lies that little shit spat from his tongue."

"Indeed," replied Urthanock as he watched the first of the white reinforcements round the corner of the wall and head towards the skirmish before the West Gate. "As we noted earlier, the palisade ends in the estuary at both ends of their south facing wall. Why did we not plan to attack from the south?"

"I will remind you of the reason if you permit me Lord," began Ssobekk as he looked to his new blade and prayed that Urthanock would not torture him for his response.

"Yes, do that!"

"First of all we have no boats. Also, where their palisade hits the estuary to the east of the city the cliffs over the water are too steep to allow an assault around its edges. On the west side we believe the water to be above head height, even at low tide. The golden knights knew exactly what they were doing when they planned the lay out of their stakewall. I do not wish to incur your ire, but we could come back next year having built our own fleet of river boats"

Urthanock grunted as he recalled Ssobekk's earlier assessment and yet he held his tongue. His urge to inflict pain on the moaning Gator passed as his eyes were taken by the sweep of the white warriors who progressed north between the city walls and the palisade. There he watched them pause for a short time before then setting off at pace to where the base of the Citadel formed part of the Parandor's outer wall.

"One is wielding the flame sword," said Urthanock, trying to make sense of his observations.

A sudden flash of blue at the base of the Citadel wall was followed by the appearance of a hole in the stone work and through which the white robed warriors then began to pour.

"Did the flame sword do that?" asked Ssobekk as he rubbed his eyes with his good hand.

"I believe it did. It seems fortuitous that you lost it and with it they have defiled their own defences. If we could get to that hole behind the stakewall we could enter the Citadel directly. We could destroy all as we join up with the Hochnar's battlegroup which must be inside the city walls by now. It would be a perfect pincer movement. What do you say General?"

"I would like to concur Lord but we are no further on in deciding how to breech their palisade."

"Use your reptilian hoard and create a bridge and skirt around the end of the stake wall; kill some and lie them on the riverbed," suggested the voice. "There are enough of the shits and it doesn't matter should you waste a few,"

"This is what we will do General. Listen with great care and implement my orders without delay," snapped out Urthanock. "Fail me and you will suffer unimaginable pain."

"Of course, my Lord," answered Ssobekk as his wooden leg began to quivertap.

"Pull the assault groups back from their three points of attack. Have them join the main bulk of the army and keep them out of range of the pults. Then sweep the whole force around to the south west and have them mass at the edge of the estuary. We will storm around the end of the palisade and attack between it and the city wall.

"But Lord, our forces will drown, most are poor swimmers despite a lifetime in the swamps, and with armour and weapons they will just sink to the bottom."

Urthanock sneered and tweaked Ssobekk's weld sufficient to shock the gator into compliance.

"I have thought of that. Press your warriors forward to fill the river. Yes, many will drown and sink but their number will displace the water and eventually form a bridge over which the vast bulk of our force will then pass. Those that die will honour my cause and for that they should consider themselves martyrs. The number who die will be minimal compared to those who will then march through to secure our victory. We will sweep all away before us so make sure that when you round the stakewall you have any remaining ogres at the vanguard of your charge."

Urthanock waited upon Ssobekk's obedience. He would tolerate only compliance.

"I will carry out your orders My Lord, but what will we do next?"

"Isn't that obvious General?"

"That's it treat him like a hatchling," laughed the voice. "Have the bloated buffoon see how stupid he is."

"Once you have destroyed the defenders, for they will have nowhere to run, head for the breech in the Citadel's wall. The idiots have opened the way for us without us having to storm the gates, climb the walls, or tunnel beneath them. This is the perfect time to strike and you must not delay another minute."

"My Lord, may I be permitted to point out one other small detail?" replied the General.

"Just as long as it's not an excuse!"

"The moronic fool mouths off again," whispered the voice.

"Once we near the stakewall we will come in range of their pults and bowmen," trembled Ssobekk. "We will take heavy casualties."

Urthanock clenched his fists, his knuckles blanched, and the tent shook once again.

"Just get on with it swamp Lord, I grow weary of your excuses."

"I have said all that is important," moaned Ssobekk. "I will carry out your orders but please Lord no more punishment."

Urthanock sneered and Ssobekk knew not to answer back.

"I will need a clear head to lead this most perilous of attacks," rambled the General as he swished his new blade back and forth to show he was up for the task. "I do have one final question Lord. Will you be with us for this final assault or will you still stay here? Your presence amid the battle would give the Lizardmen heart and strengthen their resolve. With you beside them they will do all that you command. Your presence would inspire our warriors to victory."

"This battle is yours to win for me and you will deliver Parandor before my feet. This is how it was in the past and this is how it will be today."

"But legend says you fought hand to hand with Raulyn the Grand, so you must have once joined the fray," said Ssobekk.

"I always waited until I saw Raulyn take to the field," began Urthanock. "He was the only one I was interested in fighting. Sometimes I would set myself on a high mound so he could see me, sometimes I saw his movements and rushed to take him on in single combat."

"Raulyn is long dead so why do you still hold back?"

"Some time ago in Avolire and when these eyes were forced to look into the Seer's Stone I had a recurring vision. I fought with a knight in golden armour, one who carried the sigil of Parandor on his pauldron. The stone played tricks with my mind for when at last I defeated the bastard amid cascading rivers of blood it was my own face that I unmasked beneath the knight's visor. Yet I knew in that vison I had fought the Marked, the last of Raulyn's line. I must wait until he reveals himself on the battlefield. Only then will I join in."

"Idiot!" screamed the voice. "He won't be there! He won't turn up."

"Then I must hope he reveals himself soon," answered Ssonsh as he saluted his Lord, turned, and prepared to move away. "Until then watch and see how I will crush the enemy for you."

The peg legged General sloped off the hill and as he limped away he swished his new blade from side to side. Urthanock watched each peg stomped step just to be reassured that Ssobekk would do as intended. Minutes passed before he saw the General engage with his Captains amid the reserves held back from the pults that guarded the Parandor's West Gate. He noted runners making off towards the north and east and sometime later four blasts on the war horn ordered the

Army to disengage. The three stakewall skirmishes ceased at once. Lizardmen and their ogre muscle machine began to retreat and to join in with the main scale force, held back while waiting for the palisade to be breached. A forest of arrows was unleashed by Parandor's defenders and as the pults let fly they took their toll on those who fell back on the order of the horn. Few reptiles from the assault groups made it to safety and the voice continued to criticise the prosecution of the war.

Urthanock then noticed the hunger pains that squeezed the convoluted coils constrained inside his belly. He had not eaten for some time, not in fact since supper the night before. Given there would now be a lull in the fighting as his forces regrouped, he took the opportunity to prepare something to sustain him through the coming hours. He marched back inside his tent and over to the small fire that burned in its centre. He looked to his cooking pot, saw that it was empty, and so began to search around the scattered detritus that part filled the canvass shelter. He sought anything he could throw together to create something palatable and he searched for many long minutes until at last he found an open box, its lid having been lost who knows where, and which was of the type that the Lizardmen used to hold their provisions. Looking inside he knew he was part way to inventing a dish to tickle the buds of his tongue. There inside he found a small slab of mathulath lard, a sprig of dried nettlegrass, a turnip that resembled his Hochnar, and a large frying pan that had been through happier times. With a smile forming on his face he balanced the pan on the rocks that that form the ring within which the charcoal burned. Into its centre he dropped a slice of lard, cut with the sword that he now carried everywhere. He peeled and diced the turnip, all the while imagining he was skinning his Hochnar. Then he stood back and listened with relish to the sizzles that rose from the pan.

If only he had some meat to give it a kick he would dine in style. So it was that his mind turned to Throissler's jewels, those that he had ripped from the young messenger and trampled into the grass before the tent. Urthanock rushed outside and retrieved the squashed and bloodied remains and without stopping to wash off the soil and grass stems he threw the bollock patty into the pan with the diced turnip. Once seared on both sides he added the nettlegrass, tossed the contents in the pan, and then carried the concoction outside as he sought to check on the progress below. While staring at the moving swarms of reptiles he used the tip of his blade to lift the contents of his battle breakfast to his mouth.

"You foul creature. How can you eat your own," said the voice.

"I am Urthanock, not man. I find the taste of their flesh most suited to my palate."

"Not even dragons eat their own," snarled the voice.

"Piss off and bother me no longer."

Once his stomach had been quietened Urthanock threw the pan to the floor, sheathed his blade, and focused on the troop movements before the walls of Parandor. The back shadow that was his army swept slowly from the east, rounded the north wall and then descended towards the south west. It grew larger, longer, wider, and denser as it marched forward at pace, driven on by the Captains that controlled the flow of both scale and metal. As the Lizardmen moved over the land, the pults of Parandor unleashed a steady barrage of anything and everything that could flatten and maim. They kept the reptiles at a distance. Urthanock then looked beyond the stakewall and noted that the golden knights of Parandor mirrored the flow to the south west.

"Whoever is leading and marshalling his resources knows what he is doing, unlike you, you half faced dimwit." sneered the voice.

Ignoring the constant undermining of his ever-present tormentor Urthanock continued to monitor the defenders who stopped once they got level with the West Gate. It was obvious, even from such a distance, that they had anticipated what was being planned and had already decided how to counter this new threat. The Army of Parandor spread out in formation across the land between the city's walls and the palisade. They locked shields, pushed through a forest of pikes and filled in behind with the rest of their armoured knights. Some twenty paces behind them bowmen massed, all prepared to unleash another storm of wood. Before the shield wall and the first to face any attack stood a line of giant men in wolf pelts. Urthanock guessed they had to be more of the Berserkers that he had first encountered at the Gathering. Although he could not be certain given the distance, he felt sure that each carried a large bottle in their left hand. If this was the same drink used in the Dragonas, he had underestimated his enemy.

"It's too late now arsehole," sneered the voice. "They chose their friends wisely."

"Fuck off and leave me alone; what do you want?"

"You took my essence and you took my life," replied the voice. "It was not yours to take. You should not have done that for now I am part of you and I intend to destroy you from within."

"I am omnipotent. Try all you might but you will fail."

"We shall see about that! Look and learn before you are defeated in battle. Your tactics are as solid as a wyvern's fart. They are all noise, they stink, and are blown away on the slightest of winds."

"Fuck off," screamed Urthanock. "Victory will be mine and I will force you to acknowledge it. You died in battle; your powers were mine for the taking."

"You know nothing; you are nothing; you will die nothing" continued the voice as it sought to drive the Lord over Fear insane.

Urthanock threw his hands to his ears and screamed aloud,

"No...No... No..."

Rushing back inside his command tent Urthanock sought out the bottle he had spotted when searching for food some minutes earlier. Within seconds he found what he was looking for, one of the last remaining bottles of the fortified wine that had been looted from the cellars of Griginor. Once in his hands he trudged back out to watch the battle progress. There he ripped the cork from the bottle with his teeth and proceeded to down the first half of its contents in one prolonged series of gulps. Two seconds later having taken a deep breath he finished the rest in a similar manner.

"If you won't go of your own free will, then I shall fucking drown you out."

Two minutes later Urthanock felt very queasy but at least his mind had stilled.

"Bye for now," slurred the voice as Urthanock's legs wobbled and the hill began to move as if attached to some monstrous wheel.

With his senses fighting the onslaught of the Griginor grog, the self-proclaimed Lord over Fear dropped to his hands and knees, forced his lungs to pump in air as if through a smithy's bellows. Without warning projectile puke of such ferocity shot from his belly. A red fountain sprayed for a good ten paces. More air was pumped through his heaving chest before at last he felt able to raise his head. The voice remained still and Urthanock in that short hiatus of peace realised at last how he could rid himself of his torment.

Forcing his eyes open, burred images swirled from left to right. He vomited again, more drool this time than wine, and as the minutes passed the rotation slowed and images became ever clearer. Forcing himself focus on the most critical phase of the battle, Urthanock looked to the south east where his dark forces had gathered on the edge of the estuary, still kept at distance by the repeated firing of three pults that guarded this section of the palisade. Raising himself back onto unsteady legs he heard the blasts on Ssobekk's war trumpet that signalled the charge to the edge of the stakewall.

Squinting to take all in, Urthanock watched the dark shadow surge forward. The three pults took a significant toll and Lizardmen flew through the air as each projectile smashed amongst the racing riot of reptiles. Given that it took five minutes or longer to reload each of the pults the vast majority of the army arrived at the stakewall inside the range of the mighty war engines. The formation of the scale bridge began at once. Lizardmen swarmed into the water. Those at the front made a valiant attempt to swim. The press from behind came so fast and furious that bodies were pushed down. They began build up upon the river bottom with bubbles rising as water in a boiling pan. Just as Urthanock had expected the ever growing underwater accumulation soon created a causeway over which the bulk of the Army of the Eastern Marsh then tramped at speed. The volley of arrows that flew from the battlements added to the build-up of the scale bridge but still the reptiles swept on. They swarmed until most had gathered by the base of Parandor's walls and there waited in anticipation of Ssobekk's arrival.

Urthanock somehow managed a smile. This day would be long remembered; the moment his army walked on water and he vowed to write a song about it once the battle had been won. He would ensure that the bards sang about him rather than their usual inane prattle. They would be forced to obey for he was the Lord over Fear. Bleary eyes then spotted Ssobekk in the distance as he crossed the scale bridge. The General was surrounded by his captains who shielded the Gator from the constant volleys of arrows by interlocking their shields above their General's head. After a few minutes Ssobekk stood once again on dry land and the Lizardmen began to separate his forces into two groups. Urthanock figured out what was happening. The General intended to split his force. He would order half through the harbour to the south, have them circumnavigate the walls and hit Parandor's army from behind. The other half of his force would commit to a frontal assault before the West Gate. Urthanock was pleased although unsure as to why he had not thought of this tactic himself. The two battle groups were quickly formed and the distant figure of Ssobekk once again ordered the horn to be blown. The first group to be unleashed were the wall circlers. The others would wait and coordinate their attack in a simultaneous pincer strike. That was how it was supposed to be but that is not what Urthanock witnessed.

Parandor's archers at the south west corner and all those along the south wall second guessed enemy's intentions. In a coordinated counterstrike they unleashed a volley of incendiary arrows which rained down onto the slums and buildings that surrounded the harbour. Within minutes the route ahead of the swarming Lizardmen turned into an inferno. The vanguard of the southern battlegroup was at once engulfed in flames while the rest retreated at great speed to the point where Ssobekk stood cursing. Urthanock too swore under his breath, still transfixed as the battle took yet another downward twist. Ssobekk began organising his remaining swarm for the last option available. At the front of his group he placed the six remaining ogres. Even from his distant viewpoint Urthanock recognised General Brosizrug and the one called Ikeg who had excelled at the stakewall skirmish. Now there was no barrier between the ogres and the forces of Parandor.

Urthanock rubbed his hands in anticipation of the fight. In the battle between ogres and Berserkers he expected that the mountain beasts would prevail. Behind the ugly giants Ssobekk formed his troops into three ranks of warriors. Once the ogres had punched a hole in the defender's shield wall it seemed he would send his reptiles forward in waves, each one bringing new energy and impetus to the end game. The Lizardmen, despite their losses, still greatly outnumbered those who sought to defend their ancient city.

An involuntary hic shot out from Urthanock's mouth while the horizon blurred. The inebriated personification of evil then switched his focus to the ranks of the golden knights, their shield wall, and the Berserkers that stood before it. He reckoned that given the imbalance in numbers the battle would be over within the hour. Somehow staggering to his feet, he tried to make himself as tall as possible so as not to miss any of the action. The battle horn sounded and the Ssobekk's charge began. The ogres ran forward, followed by the three waves of marsh troops. Through his troubled vision he could just about make out the row of Berserkers who raised bottles to their mouths and gulped, just as he himself had done with the Griginor grog. The Berserkers crouched low and howled so loud that even Urthanock could hear the bestial bellow. The giant men of Falahorn then formed into a round, swinging battle-axes as they did so. A circle of the crazed beast men began to move forward at walking pace to meet the onrushing ogres. The final stage in battle for Parandor had begun.

A rain of wood from the rear of the golden knights flew beyond the heads of the Berserkers and began to degrade the reptile charge. A crossfire of more arrows was unleashed from the battlements and despite their reworked orichalcum armour there were too many gaps between the plates to prevent the losses that mounted. The short line of ogres reached the circle of wild and insane Berserkers who then broke rank suddenly and sucked the Ogres into their midst before encircling them. The giants from Falahorn had a numerical advantage of at least six to one. Urthanock was exhilarated by the ring of fighting but not so the terrified swarm of reptiles who raced around it on their mission to crush the shield wall. The ogres had not made it to that target, the wall had not been breached, and in that moment Urthanock feared for the outcome of his war.

The Dark Lord felt his anger grow. The mark on the back of his neck burned like never before. Ignoring the severe pain he focused on the two armies, locked together before the shield wall. A dust storm created by the powerful interaction of ogres and Berserkers hid the outcome of that conflict.

"Admit it, you've lost," slurred the voice as it returned.

"Piss off!" snarled Urthanock.

"You thought that by getting me drunk you would get rid of me. I'm happy to inform you I am back. Yes, I went for a while for I couldn't think straight after you poisoned me... Do you know you look like an iguana? I knew one once... sexy little bugger with a flicky, sticky tongue. Always posturing and whipping its tail, the dirty little whore... Let's share another bottle and I swear I will look it up and fix us a tryst."

"I said piss off."

Urthanock growled as he clutched his head in the forlorn hope of driving the voice away.

"Come on, let's be friends. You know you need some... I never had many but I always had more than you," continued the almost incoherent mumblings of the confused essence. "You didn't bring any with you to the battlefield you know and if you did they won't be friends anymore, or play with you, or..."

"Leave me be!"

"Okay, I'm going for a sleep now," slurred the voice. "I'll come back when I feel better."

"Fuck off!"

With a deep sigh the foul Lord turned his attention back to the battle. Much was still as it was as the two armies fought to the death. He knew the enemy would demand unconditional surrender but was still convinced of his own ultimate triumph. He began to imagine the slaughter of all those who did not die in battle. None would be permitted to survive. Any girls found alive would feel the power of his vessels manhood, for despite being Urthanock reincarnated, strange bestial urges flowed through his balls and urged him to conduct a rampage of vicious deflowering. This feeling had been welling for some time and the slaughter before his eyes only served to inflame his lust. Just as his mind drifted into more detailed imagery, the course of the battle changed.

He looked beyond the Lizardmen and saw the Narrow Gate open after which the white warriors he had seen enter by the breech in the Citadel's wall now streamed out behind the rear of his army. He was at a loss to understand why Ssorsh's battle group had not destroyed these warriors of Valameer. The bloated toad would answer later for this crime but for now he had far greater concerns. The white troops formed into a strange wall like formation that stretched from the city's stone work across to the oak of the stakewall. It began to move forward towards the ongoing fight between the Berserkers and ogres. The main reptile force also continued to move forwards and remained oblivious to this new threat. Urthanock saw it all.

The dust storm abated and blew away on the stiffening breeze, kicked into existence as the tide turned in the estuary. The Berserkers, noticing the approaching white wall, began waving their battle axes in frenzied motions of recognition. At their feet lay what had been Ssobekk's shock troops, all now wasted, diced, and sliced. Several Berserkers had also lost their lives but so great had been their numerical superiority and the coordinated assault of their juice fuelled axe strikes that the ogres never stood a chance. The fight at the shield wall continued with great ferocity and would have been yet another stalemate had the Lizardmen not found themselves attacked from both sides. There was something about the ends of the pikes of the golden knights that seemed most strange to Urthanock. Their steel tips glowed blue and their collective presence seemed to form a blanket force that repelled the reptiles' weapons. Urthanock reckoned it could only be result of the magic manipulation of metal using some technique he had never heard of. He would consult the Lore of the Dead about it once it fell into his hands.

Amid the howls the Berserkers reformed their circle and sprinted into the rear of the reptiles. There they pushed through into the middle and began a great slaughter. The wall of white, with three rows of shields and a killing zone of tridents before it then slammed into the rear of the Army of the Eastern Marsh. Screams of terror filled the air. So loud did the cries become that Urthanock was sure they would have been heard as far away as the Grey Mountains. The battle for Parandor was as good as over. The reptiles had nowhere to run and minute after minute Urthanock watched their death toll mount. In the middle of the melee the Berserkers exterminated everything with scales while the two shield walls, one golden and one white, squeezed the reptiles between an ever tightening vice.

"You buggered that one up didn't you," said a voice less pissed. "You've lost the lot. Not one single swamp swine will survive. How could you have let that happen oh wondrous ruler of the lands that stink of fart."

"Leave me be, I must think what to do next!" bellowed Urthanock as his anger stung his mark.

"My advice would be to stick that sword you like so much up under your ribs and skewer a few bits to cook later," giggled the voice. "Start with the spleen, maybe pick up a bit of kidney, liver, and then a bit of heart. Wriggle the blade about and you may even secure a bit of tasty sweetbreads."

"Just fuck off," screamed Urthanock as he held his head in his hands.

"Stick them in your frying pan and eat them, Lord of the Lost Lizard Loons."

Urthanock shook his head until the pain so induced caused him to stop. He stared in disbelief at the devastation of his army. Growling from deep within he looked to the victorious defenders, all cheering as one as they then began to break formation and revel in their victory. Never before had an army of the Marsh been so overwhelmed in such a short time. It seemed that even Ssobekk must have perished for nothing moved that was not of Parandor. At least that would save him the trouble of killing the General himself. Now he had to decide what to do next. It was imperative that he found the Marked, the Gems of Thamous, and stopped the upstart from sealing the door to the Underworld. The Marked had not appeared on the battlefield as had happened during his Seer Stone visions. Something was not right. Soon he witnessed two figures walk out from the Narrow Gate, one female and the other with the swaggering gait of the bard he had left back in Avolire. Thinking perhaps he should attack Parandor himself, a new vision began to form inside his head. He knew what was happening for he had experienced it once before.

Despite the grog that sought to befuddle both his thinking and his vision, a moving picture settled behind his eyes. It was the area around the entrance to an old and ancient barrow and the beast knew at once where it was. The Dragon Whisper, the link to the thoughts and power of the wyvern, had revealed itself to him at last. It lay wedged in a rock crevice before the entrance to the Barrow of Harico. He scanned the picture for signs of life and for a brief instance he thought he saw the shadow of a young man although given his mind altered state he could not be certain. The battle had been lost but as if by some strange coincidence at the very moment of his defeat Urthanock saw his way forward. The Marked had not appeared on the battlefield as predicted for he wasn't in Parandor but instead at Harico. The Dragon Whisper must have fallen out from whatever device had concealed it and revealed the location of the one he needed to destroy. It mattered not that the battle was lost for he now had had the Marked in his sights.

"It's a trap," said the voice as it too saw the image. "Now you know where he is but how are you going to get to Harico? Perhaps if there were still wyverns in this world you could have asked for a ride but there are none. It's a long way to go on foot and first you would have to cross the estuary."

Urthanock ignored the voice for he saw no purpose in engaging with its attempts to push him beyond the edge of reason. Instead he sought to think about his options while his eyes continued to watch the scenes of jubilation before the walls of Parandor.

"Use the Mighty Rift," sneered the voice. "I know it isn't working as it should, but that was your fault for destroying the fracture. Give it a whirl. It could get you to Harico in seconds or of course not at all. It would be just like tossing a groat. Crown side you arrive; cross side you die. Come one let's play."

Urthanock continued to ignore his tormentor and promptly marched back into his now redundant command post to seek out anything that could aid him in his journey to Harico. After some minutes looking for nothing in particular he realised he was wasting time. He had his trusty sword, his half helm, and the gold Rift band around his right wrist. Around his torso rested the reworked armour, fashioned by the smith called Gof way back in Griginor. Yet there was one other find he was determined to take with him, a bottle of fortified wine.

"So, when do you intend drinking that?" asked the voice. "Give me good warning so that I have time to hide."

"Fuck off!" snapped back Urthanock as he rotated the gold band and focused on the image of the Barrow that still played out behind his eyes.

The air snapped, crackled, and popped. A blue ring of light formed around Urthanock and then he was gone. The journey through the Rift was unlike any other that he had experienced before. He was stretched, twisted, and deformed as he moved between the dimensions. Bits of him separated and rotated from his body as a cyclone of air threatened to spit him into a myriad of minute particles. Then the wind reversed and the separated flesh began to reunite. The blue lit tunnel reformed and Urthanock was spat out onto the ground before the Barrow's entrance. The air crackled and the surrounding rocks trembled. As the great stones moved, the Dragon Whisper fell from its hiding place and rolled before Urthanock's feet. The Lord over Fear reached down to pic‹ it up with his left hand but then pulled it back with horror. Half his hand was missing. Urthanock had arrived, he was alive, but he was not quite whole.

22

Thais the bard had changed. The slaughter and bestial viciousness he had been forced to witness during the battle for Parandor had hardened his soul and taken the sheen off his essence. Death and mutilation now held no terrors and a tacky revenge held his thoughts like honey refusing to leave the knife. That sickly glue encapsulated one issue and cocooned it in the centre of his fractured mind. That thought was Methladon Heyn, the beast that now called itself Urthanock. Flesh and blood that had once been the dearest of touchpoints in his early life had become the object of his jet black hatred. He had no wife, no family, and no children. The Heyn's, the Bards of Valameer, and the wyvern Thamous were no more. There was just Llyat and the beast, both innocents of loathsome circumstance.

There were a dozen dead bodies that lined the street before him; both reptilians and men of the Realm. The bard raised his eyes over the slaughter and looked to the heavens above the high crenulated walls of Parandor. There in his anger his mind dared to challenge Fatumai and her monstrous malevolent Moirai.

"Fuck Fate. Fuck Fortune. I am the master of my own destiny and I swear to you all that I will not rest until I have destroyed what remains of Methladon Heyn."

"A groat if you'll share your thoughts," said the Lady Flurdiana.

Both stood some twenty paces behind the heaped gore that was her field of victory. Thias cast a glance to the carnage and then shifted his focus to the Lady.

"I must search for Urthanock," rambled Thias as his grip on the hilt of his sword caused his knuckles to blanch. "I have to find his corpse so that I may then defile it. The swine must be somewhere here amongst the dead. With your permission Lady, that is what I will now do."

"In a minute perhaps Thias," she answered while raising her hand. "First there are orders you must hear, as must the rest of my captains. Go forward and return with Darchus, he being the most trusted of men from Valameer. I will then pass my instructions on to the Trident Guard."

Thias did as instructed and several minutes later he had returned with the bloodied cordwainer. The honourable man who had spent a lifetime in shoe leather and dye now dripped with the crimson spoils of war, splattered from helm to boot in gory chunks and slices of reptilian decimation.

"My Lady, I believe you have further orders for the brave men of Valameer," began Darchus as soon as in range of ear. "Say all that you wish and I will have it done."

"Then listen well, most trusted of Valameer. I intend to rule this Realm as offered to me by acting Reagent Ystafell in his bird-sent request for my assistance. I cannot rule a disease infested plague hole so the priority must be the cleansing of the dead. Enlist my Trident Guard, the Berserkers, Sir Byddin's Golden Knights, and what's left of those from the Fifteen Keeps. Arrange for the destruction of all bodies, ours and the scale swine that dared to threaten our very existence."

"Do you have any preference as to how we dispose of them?" asked Darchus.

"First have the Trident Guard collect the fallen good and create the greatest funeral pyre in the history of this Realm. Have them rip up the oak palisade and use it for fuel. The Berserkers will be best used in that task. The stakewall saved the city but it is now redundant. Be ready to ignite the fire by the first morning light and we will give our heroic dead the send-off they deserve."

"And the Lizardmen, what will you have us do with them?" asked Darchus.

"Once the Berserkers have removed the stakewall before this West Gate have the Army of Parandor strip the reptiles of their armour and drop their remains in the fire pit that Sir Byddin built in front of the palisade. Enlist the peasants of Parandor for it is also in their interests to get this job done as soon as possible. Also approach all the Guilds; if they want to be part of this city's future, then they must share in this work. We must avoid the killing stench at all costs. This will be day for the dead collectors to toil and sweat."

"I will carry out your orders immediately my Lady," replied Darchus while bowing low, "With your leave Lady, once I have set all in motion, I beg to be released for an hour in order to find those most dear to me."

Thias noted the Lady raise an eyebrow.

"And who would that be?" she asked without pause.

"My wife, son, and a friend, the warrior of the Watch called Tonousa Amberstone."

"So be it," answered Flurdiana.

Thias coughed and spoke with a heavy voice; "Tonousa is dead. The shapeshifter killed her."

"Dead!" exclaimed Darchus. "But how?"

Thias did not answer and turned to the highborn woman from Valameer.

"Excuse me my Lady but I too must leave and search out Urthanock."

Without waiting for release Thias turned and marched off towards the vast heaps of slaughter while Darchus stood dazed and rooted to the spot. The bard was lost in his own need for retribution and oblivious to Lady Flurdiana's anger that rushed from her mouth as without permission he had left her side.

With his thoughts a jumbled morass, and without conscious intent, it took Thias just a dozen paces to reach the area of ground where the Berserkers had terminated the lives of the remaining ogres. The impact of the amber crazed giants lay before him. The scene resembled the abattoir of the gods. Frenzied axe blows had left none of the mountain beasts intact and had Thias not been desensitised to such sights he would have added to the ogre's degradation with the contents of his stomach. His gaze fell upon the head of the ogres' General, the beast known as Brosizrug. It had been part severed from the neck and as his eyes sort to piece together its body parts from the many that lay around. He sneered when he noted the beast was without legs. A sudden gasp of air revealed one of the ogres to be still alive. A limb twitched beside the General's corpse.

Ikeg the ogre was the easiest of the beasts to identify being devoid of hair and with its distinctive chain from nose to ear. The ogre's eyes were part closed but opened fully when Thias's shadow fell across its monstrous face. Despite the deep wounds to its chest and one great slice taken from its right shoulder the beast tried to communicate. In a faint whisper words bubbled out amid the pink froth that seeped from between its darkening prune like lips.

"Water, I need water," groaned the fetid savage.

"Do you recognise me swine face, or should sing for you again?" demanded Thias as he knelt down and thrust his words into the creature's ear.

"Stop fucking me about and wet my lips. Help ease my dying moments," begged the ogre.

"Only once you recognise who stands before you and ready to ease your suffering."

"I've no fucking idea who you are, nor do I care. Just give me water."

Words gurgled out of the throaty froth while Thias began to sing.

> There was a cat,
> That often sat,
> Beneath an old oak tree.
> And there it meditated all its days,
> And came to understand the ways,
> Of how it could be free.

Thias did not begin his next verse for he noted Ikeg's recognition.

"For fuck's sake bard, I know it's you. Just give me water."

"No, I will not give you water," snarled Thias, "But I will give you this."

As he had previously promised himself, Thias gripped his sword and rammed it with all his might into the ogre's mouth. It found an exit between the bony joints of the ogre's neck. The frothing ceased and the bard spat on the face of the beast that he had grown to loath. For one brief second he felt the slightest feeling of regret but the sensation departed on the wind, kicked out of his head by the intense desire for revenge. Sweeping his blade between his index finger and thumb he cleansed his sword of its vermillion stains and moved on.

A brief commotion to his left caused Thias to turn. The Berserkers had torn down a section of the stakewall as instructed by Lady Flurdiana and were in the process of retrieving the bodies of the gallant defenders who had fallen beyond the palisade. First to be brought back was the body of Eerickk Jarl, still adorned in his wolf pelt as it passed. Thias asked the Berserkers to stop for a brief moment. The man who had offered him hospitality in Falahorn now lay lifeless before his eyes. He stroked the once great man's head and mumbled a prayer, not that he believed, but just because it seemed the right thing to do. The body then moved on, carried on its final journey by those who had fought by his side. Thias grimaced and set off to locate Urthanock's remains.

Soon the bard was in the thick of the heaps of rancid bone and scale. It was impossible to move through the slaughter without immersion in rivers of swamp blood. Thias's trousers soon turned the deep colour of squashed cherries and to his utter dismay all those on which he trampled looked the same. Lizardmen were difficult to distinguish from one another at the best of times but once part of a quagmire of severed destruction it was the most impossible of tasks. The Golden Knights of Parandor began dragging the reptile remains out to the trench beyond the palisade and Thias decided to join them. He instructed them to let him know should anyone find a reptile with half human face. Only one corpse looked different from the rest and was one of the first to be dragged into the pit. The beast was larger than the rest. Thias recognised the creature having seen him through the wizard's seeing glass at the commencement of the battle. It was crocodilian in form save for one wooden hind leg and a front limb somehow welded onto the hilt of a sword.

Two hours later most of the Lizardmen had been dumped into the pit. Thias had an uneasy feeling in his stomach as he realised that Urthanock had not taken to the battlefield. He looked up to the enemy's command tent on the crest of the small hill where with the aid of the Iqotirx's seeing glass he had earlier watched the enemy supervise the battle. Thinking Urthanock was perhaps still up there he set off explore the hill. It didn't take Thias long to realise that the beast was not there either. He searched the tent to see if there was anything that could point to where the foul Lord could have gone but there was not a single clue to be found. Even the shredded remains of Lolye Throissler offered no hint as to The Lord of Fear's location.

Thias concluded that the next part of his plan must have been enacted just as he had hoped. Llyat must have been successful in getting to meet with the Moirai. Even more important, he had survived the ordeal and released the Dragon Whisper from its box. That had to be the answer; Urthanock had gone to Harico to search for The Marked. Whether or not he knew of his army's complete obliteration did not matter. Thias's plan had been set in motion. At the earliest opportunity he would cross the estuary and seek out the Marked. Then, armed with information given by the Moirai he would take Llyat to the door to the Underworld, wherever it in the world it happened to be. But first he had loose ends to tie up in Parandor.

The bard stood on the edge of the hill and gazed down on the same vista that would have greeted Urthanock's eyes earlier that morning. He was just about to return to Parandor when he noticed a dark ground-shadow approaching from the north. It had not been formed by any cloud cover and it moved across the land as if alive. Those who continued to clear the dead from before the city walls saw it too and began to retreat at great speed towards the still open Narrow Gate. As Thias watched the shadow sweep past his vantage point he began to make out what it was. Every gecko that inhabited the Realm had gathered together and they moved as if an unstoppable tidal wave towards the trench into which most of the Lizardmen had been deposited. The gecko's swarmed relentlessly on and soon covered all ground where Lizardmen corpses lay. It was a final reckoning for those responsible of the death of Thamous. The wyvern's horde did not however approach the funeral pyre of the fallen defenders of Parandor.

A noise then drifted out on the wind. From where Thias stood it sounded like the rustling of barley grains falling from a barrel. A quarter of an hour later it ceased and the ground-cloud began to retreat. Some fifteen minutes or so after that, once Thias was convinced the shadow had gone, he raced down the hill in order to see what had transpired. On reaching the defensive ditch he peered over the edge. The Lizardmen had been stripped clean of all flesh and all that reminded were bones and any clothes that went in there with them. He had heard stories from the Badlands and other faraway lands where it was said that vast swarms of insects could devour crops, but never before had he heard of geckos devouring the dead of battle. In the midst of a shocking mental disquiet he reflected on all that was happening. The conversation that he had been party to in the Great Observatory of Anyle Belanore jumped back into memory. The Enderdetag alignment had arrived. The Lord of Fear had returned and he stalked the Marked. Many other fucked up things were happening too and perhaps this really was the 'End of Days' that the Prophecy spoke of.

Snapping out of his sudden melancholy Thias scuttled over to the Narrow Gate. As he approached the portal it began to open again having been closed by those who fled the gecko horde. On passing through he saw at once that the three narrow roads that funnelled into the gate had yet to be cleared of most Lizardmen who had perished there. The clearing operation had been interrupted by the arrival of the geckos but at least there was some reptilian meat to be buried with the worms as an insult to Kha. Then amongst one particular pile of corpses Thias spotted Isambard Hotch who, without shame or cause for concern, severed the right wrists of the dead to remove the gold bracelets that each of them wore.

"Be care as you do that Hotch, lest you fall ill of the magic they each carry," warned Thias.

"These are fair pickings bard, leave me be. I will smelt this lot down before the morn and don't even think about interfering."

"Do as you please," laughed Thias. "I have no intention of denying you the spoils of war. Just don't slip one on your own wrist and twist it for that is how the marsh scum travel the Rift. You will only kill yourself. Much better you melt the metal as you intend. But one last thing; have you seen anything of Lady Flurdiana."

"She has gone to Stuckeley Knoll and taken a large crowd of slum dwellers with her?"

"And why would she have done that?" demanded Thias.

"Her Trident Guard found six unharmed Lizardmen hiding in the disused apothecary down on Shaylotte Street. She means to execute them on the Folly such that all will fear her presence. Rumours say she will soon be crowned and it appears she is laying down markers as to the nature of her rule."

"Then this I must see," replied Thias as he walked away. "You had best warn your thieving friends there is a new law coming and they may fall victim to its power."

"That I will bard," laughed the innkeeper. "That I will."

A short time later, breathing heavily from his race through the slippery ginnels of the southern quarter, Thias surfaced once again into the open space around the Knoll. A vast crowd of lowlife had gathered, part in celebration of the salvation of their city and part to witness the first executions of their new ruler. Rumour and half-truths had flash-spread and all now knew that Phauless Gylewu was dead and that Lady Flurdiana's reign had started. Even Thias was intrigued to understand how she would stamp her mark on the collective mind-set of her new subjects. He began to wonder if she would show mercy as perhaps great rulers had in the past. His own fire for revenge against the reptiles, one that had burned like a furnace but a few hours earlier, had eased after the gecko's feast; but he could not predict what the Lady Flurdiana would do next. The Eastern Marsh had killed her betrothed, Raorick Gylewu, and for that crime he sensed forgiveness was the furthest thought from her mind. Looking to the Richemanus Folly, Thias was reminded of the last conversation he had had with the monstrous executioner and the insight he had gained on the nature of learned evil. Suddenly the bard felt an overwhelming need to forgive as he remembered the depth of his hate for Danisun Dain, now slain and lost to the world.

Thias was snapped from his musings as the crowd began to cheer for the sport they had come to witness. The Folly was then filled with a dozen white robed Trident Guards who proceeded the fix oak staves taken from the palisade into 'X' shaped crosses. These were then tied with secure ropes to the upright gibbets that were a permanent feature of Richemanus's stage. From the back of the Folly six naked Lizardmen were then dragged forward and nailed through the wrists and ankles to the crosses. They were fixed facing the wood with their rears exposed to the crowd. With each nail driven home the crowd cheered and drowned out the cries of the reptiles. A party-like atmosphere began to permeate the lowlife. Thias frowned for somehow despite seeming wrong it was also satisfying.

Once the carpentry had been completed most of the Trident Guard retreated down amongst the crowd to join in the anticipation of a great show. Besides each Lizardman remained a single member of Flurdiana's Guard. All brandished a butcher's knife which they held aloft for the eyes of the baying audience to see. Still in her armour Lady Flurdiana mounted the Folly and bid the scum to be silent by raising her right arm. All the gathered then fell silent and mirrored her action, raising their own right arms in spontaneous salute. Thias did not join in.

"Great and good people of Parandor," began the Lady. "Today we have won the most marvellous of victories. The gods I serve have favoured me and allowed me to take control of this city and all who dwell within its walls. I will immediately rebuild the little that the enemy managed to destroy and my reign will bring you all peace and great prosperity. My lineage will be founded on strength and never again will those with weak livers dictate the course of your lives."

A loud cheer rose from mouths filled with carious teeth and gumboils. The malnourished puppet-pulled crowd was captivated by the Lady's charisma.

"What you are about to witness here today, I invented in my childhood for such an occasion as this. The demonstration you will witness is called the 'Red Eagle'. I want you to enjoy it and remember it until the day you breathe your last. So cheer loudly and let all in this Realm know that no one ever fucks with Flurdiana."

Then to more cheers the Lady mounted the highborn viewing platform, raised her hands high, while the show began to the accompaniment of whistles and much clapping.

Each of the six bladed guards stepped forward towards their scream-hissing victims and in synchronised slashing slit the skin of their allotted reptile in a vertical line from neck to waist. Then they cut from neck to shoulder and from waist to hip on both sides of the spine. On each Lizardman, two flaps of skin were then pulled back exposing the ribs. Dark red juices began to drip. Through the upper apex of each sheet of scale a hook was passed and its end secured with string around the oak stake to which its adjacent arm was nailed. The crowd cheered, the reptiles screamed, and Thais wondered what would happen next. His stomach turned in spasms.

Each member of the Trident Guard, with a skill well practiced, slit through the joints that linked ribs to spine and when the Lady then clapped her hands again those ribs were pulled outward to create the appearance of blooded wings. Again, the crowd cheered, the reptiles screamed, but this time Thias retched. Squelching rose from coloured lungs soon pulled from out of their cavities while the reptiles suffocated, their limbs thrashing wildly against the stake posts. It was all soon over and the crowd went wild with excitement. Some minutes later, surrounded by her Trident Guard, Lady Flurdiana descended from the Knoll. As she made her way to the edge of the crowd that cheered her ever step she spotted Thias and beckoned him over to her side.

"Tell me bard," she began. "Did you manage to find Urthanock's remains? Can you confirm he has been slain?"

"Well, I..." began Thias as Lady carried on regardless.

"But first apologise for leaving my presence earlier without being formally dismissed."

"I apologise in full recognition of your authority," grovelled Thias. "It will not happen again my Lady. It's been a trying day and I was preoccupied with finding the Lord of Fear. Unfortunately, he is nowhere to be found and must have used the Rift to escape from Parandor."

"Come walk with me then; where were you heading?"

"To the Citadel," replied Thias.

Striding alongside the woman who now held sway over the Parandor's future, its fortune, and its fate, Thias felt obliged to add:

"I need to see a few people and tie up some loose ends before this day ends."

"Then do that at once young Thias for I have a task for you."

"What is it you would have me do?"

Thias, prayed that she would not divert him from his planned reunion with Llyat.

"I know from my spies, and some of my own digging, that you were Phauless's private investigator and trusted informant. The Ruler thought you more trustworthy and capable than the Sovereign Council although they would not see it that way. I need you to hunt down Urthanock and kill the swine. It was his army that was responsible for the massacre of the Grey Keep and the slaughter of my betrothed. I want the vile creature's head on a spike. Will you do that for me?"

Thias stepped to one side to avoid a pot fall.

"I will begin by the end of this already long day. Before I do so may I be permitted please ask one question which I hope will not cause annoyance?"

"What is it Thias? I hope it is important for I have much to think about. My head needs to be clear for I am to reign tomorrow."

"Quite so," said Thias, stifling a smile. "Was it really necessary to conduct your Red Eagle demonstration? Such savagery drags us down to the level of the swamp scum."

Lady Flurdiana stopped walking while her Guards surrounded both herself and Thias. Nostrils blanched with anger and Thias knew at once that he had over stepped his mark.

"Bard, this is your last warning. Never question my actions again or you shall feel three prongs penetrate that scrawny arse of yours. I need to start off with the respect and fear of those that I now rule and what you just witnessed was the first step on maintaining peace in this city. For too long there been has been intrigue, theft, murder, and mayhem; but no more. I demand obedience from all on pain of death and that includes you Thias Calavan, son of a common thief. Now you know where we both stand. Serve me loyally and you will live. Challenge my authority again and I will have your fucking tongue ripped out and fed to the crows. I will then fix a stone inside your mouth such that your ballads will be reduced to muffle-grunts, lost in the burbling spittle that will spew from your mouth until you depart this world. Do you understand?"

"I do my Lady," replied Thias, biting his lip to contain his frustrations. "I will leave as soon as possible to locate and destroy Urthanock."

"Have you any idea where he may have gone?" she asked as they started walking again.

"I have already set a trap for him. At this very moment I believe him to be seeking an audience with the Moirai beneath the Barrow of Harico."

"Oh really! Tell me more Thias," she ordered as the group continued their journey on towards the Citadel.

Sometime later that day as Solaris passed his watch over to Mona, the bard wandered the still congested throne room deep inside the Citadel. Servants had been dispatched by Ystafell to every room and corridor to ensure that no Lizardmen had been missed during the Darchus led sweep of the building. None had been found alive but there were some whose corpses had made a bloody mess and therefore Ystafell had ordered a deep clean of the building. A number of the Royal Guard had been dispatched by Sir Byddin to clear out the Underkeep of all things unpleasant and the trumpet had yet to sound to give the all clear for the haughty highborn to return to their private rooms. In the eyes of many, Ystafell had redeemed his cornucopia of inadequacies by ensuring the kitchens had been cleansed first and that whatever food possible had been brought up into the impressive marble hall. The highborn were as content as the lowlife were around the Folly. Their impromptu feast was accompanied by the remaining contents of Phauless's once great wine collection and which Ystafell deemed his mission to drain.

So it was that when Thias at last got to talk to the Lord Chamberlain and still acting Regent, he found the whiskered sot to be pickled with port. He had located the lisping inebriate trying to engage in a serious conversation with Sir Byddin, Heward Teulu and Darchus regarding the good and not so good bits of Lady Flurdiana's personality. The debate hovered as to whether or not her reign would bring positive change for all in Parandor. Thias joined in as best he could but struggled to make sense of Ystafell's slurred words. Following a hiatus in the conversation the bard was able to describe the debut of the Red Eagles at the Stukeley Knoll. Ystafell's colour turned pea green and he soon sloped off to the privies and did not return. Even Darchus was surprised by the description of such a gruesome execution but Sir Byddin was adamant that it showed the woman had bal s and that he was in full support of her actions. The old knight also made it clear that her intervention on the battlefield, even though her force was small, was the key to what in the end proved an easy victory. It was then that Heward Teulu asked the one question that stunned those who heard it.

"Tell me Thias, what will happen to us should the Marked destroy Urthanock and seal the doors to the Underworld as predicted by the Enderdetag Prophecy? I would assume he would return to Parandor and claim dominion over this Realm; given that he would have saved it from annihilation. We may yet then face another war and further slaughter. So, tell me bard, whose side would you take, the Marked or the Flurdiana?"

"I would rather not say for I have already angered the Lady to the point where she threatened to remove my tongue."

Thias's fingers begin to tremble as he teetered on the edge of the priest's verbal trap.

"Do not worry bard, you need not answer for I already know what you would say," replied Teulu with the expression of a sentencing judge. "Your secret is quite safe! What about you Darchus."

"I will not play your nonsense game," replied the honourable cordwainer.

"Again, I know the answer seeing that you hail from Valameer. So, what about you Rayner?"

"I would support the Lady over some snot of a lad any day. I have seen her in action."

"I knew it, there's going to be another fucking war!" laughed the priest.

"So, who would the holy one back?"

Byddin sneered and let his one eye roam across the twisted priest's face

"I would have to consult the cards,"

"And I'd like to shove them up your arse," shouted Thias to the astonishment of the others. "Now where is Lady Emeny? There is something important that I need to ask her."

"She has been carted off to my temple," replied Teulu "The bolt that pierced her buttocks needs removing and I fear for the bitch's life. If you want to talk with her I would advise you do not delay."

"I thank you at least for that," answered Thias after which he moved off towards the doors.

Just before he reached the great metal portal Thias made a gross error of judgement. He allowed his eyes to connect with those of Lady Fullbane. Her chair still stood where it had been left following the dismantling of the barricade that had saved the highborn from extermination. Thinata smiled and her eyes sparkled like an excited schoolgirl as she waved Thias over to her side. Feeling unable to ignore the monstrous mathulath, Thias took the few necessary steps to yet another diversion.

An arm the size of his torso thrust forwards as he approached. At its end was an empty silver salver that had minutes before held pies but now only residual traces of gravy, crumbs of pastry, and a collection of pigeon bones sucked clean of their meat.

"Pass the plate to one of my boys will you Thias, there's a good bard."

As the perfect eating machine wiped globules of grease from her chin with the sleeve of her gown, Thias complied with the ladies request.

"There my Lady," he began. "It was a pleasure to be of service once again this day. Please excuse me; I must away for I have important tasks awaiting my attention."

"Not so fast Thias. I must thank you for your timely intervention earlier this day," she began as she thrutched her great arse upon her chair. "Together, you with your quick wit and I with my bulk, have ensured that the highborn of Parandor live on. You must write a ballad about it when you have a minute to yourself."

"If only I had one my Lady, I most certainly would do so."

"Before you go rushing off to probable certain doom, I need you to tell me something about my sister's boy; the lad that came to Parandor with the Historian; the one who you believe to be the Marked. What is Llyat like now that he has become a man?"

"He is fair of hair and spotty like most of his age," began Thias "From what I am told, the maidens say he has what it takes to satisfy, but he is dim of intellect and weak in courage."

"A typical Fullbane then," giggled the Lady.

"He is not of your blood…" began Thias, but Lady Fullbane continued.

"Tell me though bard, does he have what it takes to defeat Urthanock and can you protect him for me? I will reward you handsomely should you bring him back to Parandor in sound body and mind. I am not the wealthiest of the highborn but I have ample flesh and it can be all yours. I consent to being your bride should you succeed in your mission."

"Then how could I possibly fail," laughed Thias. "Yet if I am to help him, you must allow me to leave Thinata. There are still many trials ahead for young Llyat, many mysteries to solve, and unknowns to discover. First I need to find him and work out what to do next."

"Do not fret Thias," she replied before releasing a belch so powerful that Thias felt its shock wave hit the cheeks of his face. "A path will form for you bard as it has and will again for Llyat."

"I do not understand what you mean Thinata," replied Thias as his fingers twitched.

"There is much you have yet to know bard, despite all your learning and travels. Should you survive then seek to understand a little of the true reality that underlies our everyday existence. I once had a gift and it helped me see into troubled minds. My husband was also Cuvar and he shared much of their insights. I know how the other world works although you would never understand me should I share my knowledge. Watch for the path opening, that's all you need remember."

"I thank you again for your wisdom," replied Thias as he dismissed the ramblings of the woman that none considered sane. "I must leave you at once for there is something I need to ask Lady Emeny."

"Ask her to tell you about your father," shouted Lady Fullbane as Thias strode towards the metal doors. "Ask her about his dealings with the dark shadow that he sought to unmask."

The Lady's last sentence failed to register in Thias's consciousness. He heard it but his thoughts were elsewhere.

Racing on through the now dark streets of Parandor Thias sought to make sense of all that had happened on this most unique of days. His mind ached from the fatigue of intense concentration, his limbs pained from their continued use while his essence felt crushed by the slaughter it had been forced to witness. Yet the battle had gone better than he could have hoped and he began to realise that was part due to good fortune but also the inept tactics employed by Urthanock. Dodging drunken revellers in most of the narrow passageways, all bent on celebrating the victory over the swamp life, a strange possibility began to form in his mind. Urthanock walked inside its Vessel, that which was once Methladon Heyn. Was it possible, he thought, that somehow part of Methladon was the cause of the beast's ineptitude and failure to prosecute an effective war? He eventually dismissed the thought for it seemed most improbable that the foul Lord could be influenced by anything other than Kha. He then began to dwell on Lady Fullbane's words about paths opening up before him. Allowing his imagination full reign he thought of hidden routes to the Underworld. Perhaps the lard mountain was not as stupid as she appeared. That line of thought was then dismissed as began to focus on the purpose of his intended meeting with Lady Emeny.

Thias knew that he could not return to Parandor should his mission to support the Marked fail. Indeed, the challenge ahead was so great that he feared there was little chance of a positive outcome despite the defeat of Urthanock's army. In a moment of clear thinking he realised he had just one last hour to find the answer to the question that had begun to gnaw away at his innards; who was the master of the Thieves Guild? He tried to work out why this was so important to him and kept coming back to the memories of his father's death. It was then that a brief and long suppressed whisper from the past resurfaced and teased his thinking.

While he had been sobbing amongst the crowd as his father danced and dangled, a voice from amongst the onlookers had cried out; 'Such was the order of the Guild Master." All then became clear, just as if a path had indeed opened up before him. Yes, it had been Danisun Dain who had kicked away the milking stool but he always knew deep inside that the Master of Thieves had set his father up. That was why he had to find out who the swine was. Then, before he could think further, he arrived before the doors to the Temple of Fatumai. Wasting no time, he immediately entered and began his search for the Lady he needed question before it was too late.

"Is that you Thias?" said a soft sweet voice from amid the rows of groaning wounded that clogged every available space under the temple's mighty dome.

"Arnkatla," said Thias as he turned and smiled at the healer. "You have your hands full I see. I wonder if you can help me."

"Sure, but I cannot stop and chat for as you see I will be busy for many days to come."

The young woman flicked a lump of human flesh from off the surface of her apron.

"I am looking for Lady Emeny; have you seen her?"

"She is in that small room over there but she is weak and toxic. You may not get much sense from her."

"How come she is so ill from a single bolt to the buttocks," asked Thias?

"It was hard to remove it from the bone of her pelvis. Whoever ever fired that bolt had dipped its tip in excrement before letting it fly. The poisons that cause the putrid stench have travelled through her body and she drifts in and out of delirium. We have given her up and are concentrating on those we can save. I must go now Thias, please excuse me."

"Have Atropos and Lachesis returned?" shouted Thias as the nurse rushed away.

"No, not as yet," came the answer and then the girl was gone.

Thias made his way to the small room and entered through its open door. There he found Lady Emeny lying alone on a makeshift bed constructed from boxes, planks and an old canvass sail. Her eyes were open and although weak she did not appear to be in significant pain.

"Llys, it's me, Thias Calavan, how are you doing?"

"Hello Thias, I think I'm done for," she replied with mouse-like weakness. "They say we won the battle. That is good."

Lady Emeny coughed and blood flowed from her mouth.

"I feel like shit;" she whispered. "Come hold my hand."

Thias did as requested and knowing time was short began to ask his questions.

"Llys, in all your dealings as Court Judge and as a junior in law before then, did you ever unearth any clue as to who runs the Thieves Guild. I wish to discover who ordered the death of my father and why they would do so. I have had a premonition that my time in this Realm may be limited and I would like to discover this greatest of secrets before my life comes to an end."

"What was that you said," she mumbled as she squeezed Thias's hand.

"Who is the Master of the Thieves Guild?"

"Why does that bother you so Thias?"

"Because whoever the bugger is, he ordered the execution of my father."

"He was not who you thought he was," groaned the Lady, her eyes now closed.

Thias shook the dying woman with as much force as he dared. Her eyes flickered.

"Who? What do you mean? Tell me all that you know."

"Your father was employed by my predecessor to try and discover that very same fact. The Guild Master realised the double game that your father was playing and had him hung because of it. It was the thieves who tipped off the Watch that he was stealing bread for his family."

"But after all these years you must have some idea who the evil mastermind is. Those who know are too terrified to speak his name. Are you sure you don't know something that could help me?"

Lady Emeny drifted once again towards death's portal and without regard for her suffering, Thias shook life back into her.

"I will not let you die until you reveal your suspicions."

"Keep the fucking noise down," bellowed a gruff voice from just outside the room.

"Asking such questions will be the death of you," croaked Emeny as Thias lifted her head, rammed a pillow under her neck, and forced the near-corpse to concentrate.

"Could it be one of the Council or someone who got close to them ike that shit Lolly?"

"I can in all honesty swear on my last breath that have no idea who it is," she croaked in the faintest of whispers. "It could be anyone. What the thieves do with all that they steal the gods alone know. Once valuables are taken in Parancor, most are never seen again. Let it be Thias. I like you too much to think of you ending your days on the back of Underscroft's cart."

"We all, those of us not highborn, will all end up there one day. It's just a matter of when. Do you have any advice for me at all?"

"When the war is over and the slums reoccupied, talk to the children. Should anyone know it will be them," she added before her eyes closed.

"What do you mean by that?"

"They make up rhymes you know. I bet you've never heard this one...

Master Danisun, show us the way, to pick a pocket by night and day.

Thias smiled. "I don't believe Dain was the Guild Master and he's dead anyway."

"Of course, it wasn't him you simple pap. It is just the type of rhyme that get gets men hanged, if you see what I am alluding to. Seek out what other songs they sing and they may turn out more illuminating than the tripe you have entertained us with over the years. Now enough of this thieving nonsense, it is time for you to tell me something."

"Then we had best be quick," answered Thias as he squeezed the Lady's hand.

"I have always held a desire to visit Avolire and I have a collected many artefacts from that ancient city. It appears that pleasure has been denied me forever by a turd smeared pult bolt shot by bastards from the swamps. I know you have visited the place, so as I close my eyes I want you to describe to me all that you saw there."

Thias complied with the dying Lady's wishes and began to describe the few ruins of Avolire that he had seen during his theft of the Gems of Thamous from the Silverwynn's enchanted chamber. Throughout his tale he sensed there was someone stood beside him listening to his story. He felt a breeze like disturbance of the air but when he looked there was no one there. At the end of his second stream of sentences Llys Emeny's light was forever extinguished.

Having spent some minutes in reflection at the loss of one of the best that Parandor had raised to high office, Thias wiped the tears from his eyes and with a heavy heart he trundled out of the temple. He had failed in his attempt to gain a name but vowed as he entered the refugees' encampment that once his quest was over he would return and renew his investigation. On he trudged towards the South Gate in the hope that despite the harbour being destroyed he would find some means to ferry him across the estuary. He was a good swimmer but the water was cold, the night was dark, and his energy had been drained.

The alleys and ginnels of the southern quarter closed about the bard and cut out all light save for the occasional flicker from a candle that burned in a rare window. Heavy clouds had settled over the Capital and hid any light from Mona or her sister stars. All was temple quiet. Most of the townsfolk were in the taverns, the brothels, or celebrating in their homes. A muffled sound bounced off the cobbles ahead and Thias guessed that only the rats had turned out to bid him farewell. Three dark shapes appeared out of the gloom as Thias passed through the narrowest of Parandor's passageways. It had not been rats after all. The shadows held club like objects in their hands and in that moment Thias knew they posed an immediate threat to his life. As always happened at such times his mind raced as he sought to think of the best way out of his predicament. In a fraction of a single second he decided to turn and run but then realised that way was blocked by more of the sinister shapes. He figured it best to surrender all his possessions in the hope that having gained spoils those who blocked his way would then let him pass unharmed. If reason would not work then he would try his voice trick and seek to gain control of their actions. In the end he decided to use flame.

"Prometh..." began a word never to be completed. The bard's world turned black.

Thias woke with a headache so severe that would have crushed an ogre. Where the back of his skull joined with his neck, a pain throbbed with such ferocity that he had to fight the waves of nausea that threatened to empty his intestines. He sought to see and realised all was black. Then he remembered what the bards had once taught him back in Valameer, that a severe blow to the back of the head could cause a person to go blind. This it seemed was his fate. Soon he remembered the shadows that had appeared before him in the narrow alley and that there had been others behind him. One of those must have felled him with a club. He tried to move his arms in order to feel the extent of the damage to his skull but they seemed tied to something, yes it was a chair. The rough wood was noticeable as his arms and arse struggled against its grain. With his head clearing he realised two other important facts. His feet were tied to the chair legs and an impenetrable hood had been placed over his head. The coarseness of the sackcloth rubbed against the skin of his cheeks and tried to resist he outflow of air from his mouth. There could be a chance he was not blind as he first thought.

Wriggling in his chair he heard the footsteps of another within his place of confinement. The point of a dagger pushed firmly against the hood that covered his head and neck. It pressed on his windpipe, hard enough to cause fear and discomfort yet not so much as to pierce both cloth and skin. The sounds of a chair being moved in front of him gripped his senses and still the dagger pressed into his throat. Thias then knew there were at least two others present. A voice spoke to him, muffled as if uttered through a pillow. It delivered its message without change in tone or pitch. So unusual was it that Thias was unable to decide if it belonged to man, woman, child or indeed beast. The presence of the hood further impaired his hearing and added to his frustrations.

"Thias Calavan, I know very well who you are," the voice began. "This meeting has been arranged such that I can give you a message, one that you will ignore at your peril. Should you wish to hear all I have to say and leave here alive you must on no account speak. Your questions will remain unanswered and your throat slit. I ask you to confirm your understanding of what I have just said by nodding your head. Now let us test this rule. Do you understand me so far?"

Thias did as instructed and affirmed his agreement. The movement brought more pain.

"You have been asking too many questions about me of recent," the mysterious voice continued. "I will not permitted this to continue. Should I ever find you trying again then your life will be terminated. You only live now because of all you have done to help save the Realm and I know that you must journey on to meet with the Marked. In that quest, I wish you all success..."

The bard's heart pumped at twenty to the dozen as he realised the probability that the one who spoke was none other than the Grand Master of the Thieves Guild. His life hung by a thread and all he could do was to sit and listen for clues that would point to the identity of the one he would one day kill.

"... Should you manage to succeed in closing the doors to the Underworld do not ever think of returning to Parandor. When you leave this city tonight you must never comeback. This is the price you must pay for your snooping. Nod if you agree."

Thias did not hesitate and with his head he accepted the price of his freedom.

"Good, very good," continued the voice of the Guild. "As you will be aware the harbour was destroyed by our own troops' fiery arrows. You will not perhaps be surprised to learn that I have been able to obtain a small rowing boat which my servants took from two priests returning from the south this evening. You will find it tied to what remains of the jetty. This boat will save your life bard. Should you choose not to use it then you will not live to hear the first cock crow. Nod if you agree."

Thias indicated his acceptance.

"Excellent. Never let me cast my eyes on you again Thias Calavan. I am leaving now. In five minutes my shadow-brothers will cut the ropes that bind you. You will not move until you hear them leave and close the door. Only then can you stand. Try to be clever and they will show no mercy. Do you understand?"

Thias nodded.

"Before me is a small table. On it you will find a token of recognition for the agreement we have just sealed. Take it as a reminder of our pact. Should you ever renege or be seen north of the Tiaryer again then something else will appear on this table... your tongue. I bid thee farewell bard, and once again I wish you well on your quest."

Thias fought to contain the pounding of his heart which he was convinced all others in the room could hear. The second chair moved and a soft footfall retreated until at last it disappeared from his hearing. Some minutes later he felt the dagger lift from his throat and cut the ropes that secured his legs and those that held his arms. Still he dared not move. The sound of numerous other feet retreated behind him and a short time later a door slammed shut. Thias heaved the deepest of sighs and with great care stood to his feet.

The sack that covered his head had been tied with thick twine and secured with a devious knot. It took Thias many more minutes to unravel it and had he wanted to follow his captors it would have been impossible. All were long gone. Once the hood was removed he looked a few paces ahead where he saw a small table with a single candle burning on its surface. Stepping forward he picked up a thin golden ring that he had not seen since his childhood. It had belonged to his father and around its edge had been engraved letters that spelled out the word 'Calavan'. Tears welled in Thias's eyes as he slipped the ring onto his left little finger.

Then in the gloom, sat on a chair some ten paces away, Thias spotted a figure dressed in black robes. Despite great fear he edged towards it, not knowing if the person was dead or alive. He prayed it wasn't yet another evil trick sent by those who had threatened him. Waving the candle ahead he stopped with a start as he looked into the glazed eyes of middle aged corpse. The man's mouth was open, the jaws forced apart by what Thias assumed to be a swollen tongue. But then he realised what he was looking at. The tongue had been removed and a large stone sat in its place.

"Oh fuck," he mumbled as he left in haste.

23

As Solaris played hide and seek amid the clouds of early evening, Urthanock lifted his disfigured left hand toward his eyes. He felt no pain from it despite its bizarre appearance. The only digits that remained were the thumb and first finger. The other three had disappeared as had the half of the hand that would have rooted them to his wrist. There was no blood at the raw end just hard reddened pulp which when he played with it seemed as tough as leather. He could still pinch with what he had left but any attempt to use the hand to carry either sword or shield would be impossible.

The journey through the Rift had been both disconcerting and dangerous. His Hochnar, Ssonsh, had not told lies when he had talked of problems traversing it. Urthanock realised he could not dare to use it again. The golden bracelet, glinting as rays of light hit its polished surface, was still wrapped around his right wrist. Using the thumb and finger of his half-hand Urthanock pulled it off and threw it to the ground. It landed close to the pale pebble-like Dragon Whisper. He then kicked the golden band into the morass of small boulders that surrounded the dark entrance to the Barrow of Harico.

The beast stared again at his half-hand and a smile formed as he considered it a good partner for his half-human face. Then he checked to see if he had any other bits of his body missing or altered in some way that would cause him concern. Thrusting his good hand down his trousers and much to his relief he found all to be intact. Seven remaining digits roamed across his body with care but found nothing else of concern. Believing himself to be fortunate to have lost so little, he smiled; pleased that since the Vessel's childhood both hands had been equally dextrous. Urthanock's eyes were drawn once again to the Dragon Whisper that lay upon the rocky ground. He reached forward and picked it up for closer examination. It did not glow as it had in the past nor did it seem in anyway interested in his presence. The foul Lord's frustrations continued to mount as he scanned the surrounding hilltop and the valley below. The Vessel's eyes saw no danger although as the seconds passed Urthanock became ever more concerned. He sensed a trap had been set and that he was walking straight into its jaws. Yet here he was and there seemed no alternative but to enter the Barrow. Spitting to the ground he cursed aloud. If the Marked had gone in before him then it was he who was trapped for there was no other obvious way out. With one last look to the Dragon Whisper he pulled his right arm back and then threw the stone. Like a startled bird it flew a great distance and on hitting the bottom of the hill disappeared out of sight, deep amid the trunks of the ancient oak forest.

"Fuck your precious bauble Thamous," he muttered under his breath
Urthanock stepped into the Barrow's entrance.
"Pompous prick!" sneered the voice.

Drawing his sword the beast began his search of the short dark tunnel, walled by giant stones. He floundered without success until hidden behind a large boulder he found a small opening with stone steps that descended deep into the earth. Given he had no candle or other means of illumination he hesitated before then drawing on the powers that had been bestowed on him by the Underworld. He looked to the blade that he carried and he willed it to glow, to lead him on his predestined fate. Soon the tempered steel fired with a strong white light. It was as if Mona's full face had become an extension of his essence. Given he now had ample luminosity he began his descent in search of the Moirai Crypt. This was where legend indicated it would be found. It was here somewhere as was he.

Down the calendar steps he raced, all the while looking for evidence that would indicate the presence of the Moirai or the Marked. There was no sign of the living; only a sense of the dead. As he reached the last of the cut stone steps his eyes were drawn to its surface. On it had been chiselled an incurved triangle.

"Excellent," he mumbled to himself.

"Arsehole!" replied the voice. "What good is that to the likes of you?"

Waving his bade to cast the light forward he saw that he stood at one end of an immense cavern in which columns of stalagmites rose like the cobbled trunks of a petrified forest. His nostrils began to twitch as they picked up the scent of something on the floor, an odour that begged his attention. Pushing his sword down he spotted and pool of vomit which he was sure was human rather than that of some other beast. To confirm his suspicions Urthanock pushed a finger into the deposit and felt its lingering warmth. He estimated it had been there no longer than a couple of hours and just to check it was from man he sucked the tip of his finger. Whether it had come from the guts of the Marked or some other he could not say, yet its warmth on his tongue confirmed it had not lain there long.

Some minutes later Urthanock spotted another incurved triangle by a side passageway that dropped in a most precipitous slope down beneath the hill. In some strange way it had glowed as he had approached and as he journeyed on others appeared in a similar manner. He began to suspect that the wall marks were somehow aware of his presence. A part of him knew the stones were inanimate and yet he sensed some lived and were taunting him. The voice sneered at the absurdity of such a thought.

More minutes passed before Urtharock entered a second smaller cavern amid whose walls a multitude of niches had be cut. All contained offerings left by those who had gone before. The Vessel's eyes then scanned the cavern's ceiling with its red and black images. Amongst the palm prints inverted triangles seemed to fill every other space. The beast of the swamps then checked some of the niche offerings and sneered at the pathetic collections of bones and herbs.

"What kind of morons would create such shite?" he mumbled to himself.

"Those who carried great secrets from the past," replied the voice.

Sometime later, amid the far distant reaches of the cavern, Urthanock stood before a great metal door; one high enough to just allow him to walk through without having to lower his head. Its copper green colour was like no other he had seen and it looked about as old as a door could be. He noted the stone surround, covered with incurved triangles of all shapes and sizes. His focus then switched to scratchings on the door itself and he guessed they were what the Ancients had referred to as runes.

"I bet you wish you could read them," mocked the voice. "Then again, I'm not surprised you can't for reptiles are renowned across the Realm for the smallness of their brains."

"If you know what they say then tell me, or are you also ignorant of their meaning,"

"Even if I knew I wouldn't tell you for I detest the foulness of your essence."

Urthanock sought to ignore the bane of his new existence but the voice would not desist.

"May be it is a warning for a thick-skull like you. Perhaps it says something like 'only the Marked may pass, and reptiles should piss off back where they slithered from.' Yes, that's the sort of thing they would say. If I could read them of course."

Ignoring the noise Urthanock leaned against the door and pushed. Nothing happened.

"Why don't you try the handle," teased the prattler.

Urthanock looked to the door's single handle, the one part of the door that was highly polished, and tried to move it. Nothing happened and this just fuelled his anger further. He kicked the metal, spat at it, and then when he could think of no alternative way forward, he raised his arms and threw bolts of pure energy in its direction. The door began to glow red and to emit fumes that his Vessel recognised from its time at the blacksmiths forge. Yet still the door did not move. Retreating back into the cavern Urthanock began a detailed search of the niches in the hope of finding some clue as to how he could open the mighty metal portal.

"You'll not find anything amongst that holy heap of sacred shite," said the voice.

"Leave me be," bellowed back Urthanock. "I must find a way to get behind the door."

"Go back and push with a gentle touch; that always works for me."

Without arguing Urthanock retraced the path to the portal and pushed with the fingertips of his right hand. The door opened of its own accord and Urthanock stepped inside. There in the darkness he pointed his sword forward but the portal slammed shut and his sword ceased to glow. Slowly his eyes began to accommodate to the all-pervading blackness. Focusing his strength upon the magic centres of his body, he tried once again to power up his blade. Nothing happened. His senses still functioned yet he no longer felt imbued with the power of the Underworld and it seemed that Kha had abandoned him. For the first time in a dozen or more centuries he felt both vulnerable and mortal. It was a sensation that shocked the beast until anger kicked back and forced his evil to the surface.

Ahead, a circle of burning candles, each as thick as a Lizardman's arm and as tall as a Dirmark dwarf, materialised out of the ether. They formed a fiery circle some ten paces beyond the door and from its centre the voice of a woman called out with the strength of youth.

"Stranger, you have entered the Oracle of Frasteria, the abode of the Daughters of Fatumai. Your uninvited presence defiles the sanctity of the Temple of the Moirai. Step into the circle and state your business. You will need to think well before you ask any questions for the Oracle will not grant you many answers. In return for our words there will be a price you must pay. The Oracle will in due course decide what that will be. These are the terms of Frasteria. Step into the circle should you wish to continue; if not return through the door but never dare to come back. No one has ever entered twice and lived."

Urthanock curled his lip, snorted, and strode into the circle of light. Once in its centre he stopped and turned to all directions.

"I intend to continue," he shouted out to the black beyond the candles. "Show yourself such that I can see who dares to treat me with such contempt. I demand to speak with the Moirai themselves and not a cackling spirit of the cave."

"So be it, foul Lord," replied the woman's voice, this time from away to the right and outside the circle. "I sense much anger and hate for others in an essence that is both tormented and confused. Watch how you speak in here for we will not tolerate disrespect."

Urthanock turned towards the voice while a grey light diffused out from the walls of the weird and strangest space that Urthanock had ever encountered. The Temple's interior had curved walls of great solidity. Amid the grey light their colour resembled rotten meat and yet they seemed made from well-polished stone. Urthanock sniffed and his nose was stung by a smell of death that complemented the colour of the walls. Every few paces around the temples circumference stood statues of the gods that had been carved from a crystal white material. Then in the shadows between the sculptures he noted a circle of other worldly figures, each with a hooded cowl that part hid hideous faces, mummified over aeons of time. Then as one, the creatures pulled back their hoods to reveal grim red eyes and open mouths of razored teeth. When they all then began to hiss, Urthanock smiled at the Oracle's theatrical show.

A brighter light, like that from Solaris, broke forth from the ceiling and illuminated an area just beyond the circle of candles. Its beam fell upon three beautiful women, dressed in the finest of gossamer robes while sat behind a white marble table. They oozed a sensuous presence but that had little effect on Urthanock whose preference was now for something with more scales.

"I seek the Oracle of Frasteria!"

"Step forward and make yourself known," spoke the beauty on the left.

"Are you three the Moirai, for if not, fuck off and don't waste my time," he shouted.

Urthanock checked that those with gnashing fangs had not moved closer.

"I am Allotter, and to my right is my sister, Spinner," schmoozed the middle of the three beauties "And who might you be?"

The siren ran her finger through her long black hair while her eyes sought to tempt.

"I am Urthanock, Lord over Fear, Disciple of Kha, and Ruler of the Eastern Marsh. I have come to demand the knowledge that will help destroy the Enderdetag Prophecy," he stated, unable to constrain his contempt for the three that held his gaze.

"Did you hear that my sisters?" smirked Allotter. "He has come to demand things of us; so little does the jumped-up half lizard understand. Sister say hello to Urthanock before I make the upstart grovel."

"Hello, You-rank-cock. Is that how I should pronounce your name?" sneered Spinner.

The second brushed her auburn hair away from her face and drank from a pewter goblet that had stood on the table just inches from her hand.

"To my left, the blond one is Cutter, but she is dumb," said Allotter. "Produce your blade, simple one. Take note Lord Rank-cock, this is the last thing you will see when my sister calls to cut through your life strings. You would do well to be careful how you address us."

The Cutter lifted a scythe from under the table and snarled.

"My name is Urthanock," bellowed the foul Lord of the Swamps as the Moirai's threat left no impact. "You will address me with respect for I shall soon hold dominion over your souls. You have deemed yourself more important than you ever were meant to be. I have had the ear of Kha, the Great One. He talks of you as if nothing more than lugworms casting their coiled heaps upon the sludge of the primeval Realm. You Moirai will bend to my will or else be destroyed."

"Hark at this one," responded Allotter as she too took a drink from a goblet. "It seems this iteration of our game has finally produced the means we have been seeking. What say you sister?"

"I do believe that Lord Rank-cock is worthy of his place within our plan," laughed Allotter. "Although not quite in the form we had first intended. This puny prick bite of human prepuce will serve our purpose well."

"You should have kept your mouth shut," shouted Urthanock, unable to control the wave of anger that swept through his presence.

With his sword waving like a whirling banshee in a storm, Urthanock sprang from out of the candle circle, rushed forward, and then thrust sword arm towards Allotter. The blade swished through her neck without sensing any resistance and in an instant the three beauties disappeared. The foul Lord stood rooted to the spot while the laughter of aged voices echoed around the temple's walls. He twisted, turned, and then looked to all directions. All was still until the reeking, emaciated creatures with eyes of beacon red, began to move as one and close in around him. Their hands extended from beneath their black habits to reveal long and pointed talons. Their lips retracted and needle like teeth snapped and bit. The blood-soaked spittle of previous victims sprayed before them as they marched towards their prey.

Urthanock retreated back into the centre of the candle circle while the creatures advanced to its edge and then stopped. The sword he so cherished was then ripped from his hand by an unseen force that was a deeper and more powerful than his own. It clattered to the floor by his feet. In the next instant, all light but from the candles disappeared. It was gone for a less that a second but when it returned it revealed a different set of images.

Where once sat three beautiful women now perched three ancient hags, their leathery skin furrowed like freshly ploughed meadows. Their eyes had reddened and their breath turned fetid. An aura of evil seeped from out of their gaping pores. Urthanock sensed the strength of their presence but refused to be intimidated. The white statues had disappeared and the circular wall had changed its appearance. Carved deeply into it, and where the statues had stood, was the image of three circles, each one sat upon the other and all touching. The cut marks had been highlighted in gold paint as had their centre which clearly displayed an incurved triangle.

"Our time for play is over Lord Urthanock of the Eastern Marsh. We must settle our business and have you understand why we have brought you here," said the hag that replaced Allotter.

"I came to this bug hut of my own volition," snapped back Urthanock.

"No, you didn't," growled the one in the place of Spinner.

"Silence" commanded Allotter.

The old crone raised her hand and Urthanock obeyed the witch's order.

"Do you have any idea what the three circles and the triangle represent?" asked Spinner.

"It is a depiction of the Moirai?"

"That's not a satisfactory answer. Not good enough by half. Try again for we cannot make progress until you grasp its meaning. Understanding the mark is the first step to winning the..."

"Stop playing games you malevolent moron," jeered Urthanock.

"This is your last warning before we throw you out and begin anew," replied Allotter. "What do the symbols mean to you?"

The beast hesitated while a memory stirred.

"During my long incarceration in the Underworld, for one brief moment I got to interact with the essence of Kha himself," began Urthanock as he recalled his thousand year torture. "He told me that that I had been fated to unite the three dimensions. He forced me to remember the three-circle mark, the very same one etched onto the neck of this Vessel. The mark would be my destiny. The Vessel I reside..."

"Okay, carry on; we will return to discuss the Vessel a little later," interrupted Allotter.

"As I was about to say before your wart encrusted tongue struck up, the three circles depicted in my Vessel's brand, and displayed upon your temple walls represent the three dimensions of existence; the Heavens where most of the gods play their foolish games; the Middle World where simple creatures irk out pathetic existences and strive to reach heights that the gods deny them; and the Underworld dominion of Kha where the spirits of the departed linger within a collective evil created over infinite reincarnations."

"Kha was indeed informative," smirked Allotter.

Urthanock took a step forward, his story not yet finished.

"Kha then told me of the other three, the old crones that transcend the three dimensions. He explained that the strange curved triangle in the middle of the circles represents you Moirai, the Oracle of Frasteria, and that which I need to destroy if I am to claim the Middle World in his name. That was the mission he gave to me on the promise of an eternal life amongst the gods. It was Kha who let half of my essence leech out between the cracks and into the Middle World. The rest he retains as hostage. I am here to take possession of that sacred central space that you have coveted for so long."

"Poor deluded reptile," sneered Spinner.

"But at least he does understand the symbol," added Allotter."

"Explain the problem with the Vessel," said Spinner as she turned and spat at Cutter.

"What problem?" asked Urthanock, but Allotter's words were already flowing.

"The Vessel whose body you inhabit should not be here. We planned that the boy should have died many years ago but something powerful began to change the rules of our game, didn't they mumblecrust?"

Cutter smiled back with the look of the inane yet still continued to sit in silence.

"It all related to the time of Lord Jonas Tullage, he who propagated the cult of Death Tubaria. It was his fate for we three rolled his dice and turned his cards," continued Allotter. "Amid the chaos he had caused, manipulated always by the one called Ssleptaz, the youth known as Methladon Heyn had been selected for early termination. He was to have been ripped apart by four fearsome stallions and we dispatched Cutter to slice through his strings. Yet the sly fox next to me deceived us and went against the rule of the game, she says with our own mother's permission…"

"Just a second, are you saying Ssleptaz was in Parandor even back then?" asked Urthanock.

"There has always been one Ssleptaz in Parandor, but I'll come to that later if I remember."

Allotter shifted her aching bones upon the marble plinth and continued.

"Only now do we realise the rules were changed by our dumb sister who we find after all these years can speak if she so wishes. Tell Lord Rankcock why you choose to behave in such an underhanded way. Never before has a game been so spoiled."

Cutter's features remained those of the befuddled as she sat amid the silence of the dead.

"Perhaps she is dumber than she looks," snorted Urthanock, glancing to the circle of creatures who waited with menace beyond the ring of candles.

"Are these cunts intent on causing me harm?" he asked, trying to stare out at the red eyes.

"They are there to keep you in your place until such time as we dismiss you from our presence," replied Spinner as she picked out a piece of maggoty cheese from between the few pegs that still grew from her lower jaw. "The Children of Gebez will not harm you unless we order them to do so."

"Let me continue," ordered Allotter as she tapped out her impatience on the table. "This is not the only game in which we have toyed with your essence, Lord of the Marsh. In the first game of the ages, you lost to Sir Raulyn and this time around it was our intention to leave the outcome in the balance. Two of us support your success but it appears that our third sister and mother are pushing for a different outcome."

Urthanock was confused and the more the creatures spoke, the more it deepened.

"Explain!"

"We wanted you, the reptile, to win but we are not yet able to throw the last roll. Our closed lipped sister has hidden the dice. She will only give them back when the final play must be made."

Urthanock looked to Cutter who appeared to laugh in silence.

"So now you understand our predicament," finished Allotter

"Not really," sneered Urthanock. "I have no time for games for I inhabit the real world. What is all this shit about the Vessel? What is it you are not telling me?"

"We had another lined up for you to inhabit, but sister here buggered that up too," growled Spinner. "The line of the Silverwynn was supposed to take the powers of the Underworld and with it your essence, yet the boy Methladon Heyn came into existence and with our sister's interference disrupted the balance of the game."

"And this body that holds me, what is it about him?"

"We suspect the Vessel you now possess is being manipulated by Cutter, although we cannot prove it or determine how. She may look stupid but underneath her leathery skin there sits a devious old intellect."

"But what of this one they call the Marked," demanded Urthanock as he contemplated reaching for his blade. "How does he fit into all of this? Is the Prophecy of Enderdetag real or just part of your game? My Vessel knows the lad of old; a whelping coward by all accounts. Does the pathetic snot pose a threat to me?"

"Very much so, in fact we would goes as far as to say it's all down to the roll of a dice between which of you will succeed," answered Allotter.

The crone flicked her wrist and caused the Children of Gebez to hiss. The undead opened their mouths and flashed two rows of razor sharp teeth. Their breath emitted air so fetid that it even turned Urthanock's nose. A deep, guttural, whipped-pig screech burst forth from between their pointed fangs and cut the air.

"You say you wish to help me, to have me win this game of yours. If that is true then tell me all you know about him such I will triumph in my final confrontation with Raulyn's seed. What happened while I was incarcerated in the underworld? How was it possible to bring this Marked into being?"

"Raulyn fucked our mute sister and left a child in her belly," began Spinner after sipping again from her goblet. "Do not interrupt Marsh Lord, and I will tell you all you need know. Once the dumb one had played long enough with her child and weened it from her tit, we introduced it to this game, although not against her will. Now do you see how long we have been playing? Raulyn was clever. He enchanted his seed with a gamespell of his own, a deeper magic he had no doubt learned from that interfering snake called Thamous. He made it such that this fated game could never end until the stars we know as the 'Fortunes' slipped into the Enderdetag alignment. We, Allotter and I, have been trying to break that spell for over a thousand years but still it defies our magic. Raulyn was the most untypical of his race, those dark ancients from across the sea. We still seek to outsmart his fiendish race even after all these years. Down through the seed of his descendants the deeper magic passed, and as the years rolled on, protectors and believers in the Prophecy gathered to try and thwart us. They became the Cuvar and the impudent swine even stole our symbol. They began to use the incurved triangle for their own ends. Somehow they even managed to hide many of Raulyn's blood line from our eyes."

Silence filled the cavern as Urthanock sought to assimilate this information.

"Are you following all I am saying?" said Spinner.

"Stop stalling and tell me that which I wish to know. The lad Llyat, what are his weaknesses? How can I defeat him?"

"He is the one descended from the union of Raulyn and Cutter. It is he who has come into being during the Enderdetag alignment and in doing so has triggered the gamespell. The youth you knew as Llyat Emgar has undergone significant growth since the Silverwynn took away the influence of his protector, a Historian from beyond the Dirmark called Rukave. While you and your vessel have been idle, the Marked and the Cuvar have been putting in place all that they need to bring about your destruction. He has reunited the Gems of Thamous and now seeks to seal the door to the Underworld once again. Now perhaps you will understand why our dear sister has been protecting her own and seeking to undermine our intentions. We are still on your side and to compete with Emgar you must gain further insight."

Urthanock reflected and a question formed. "You said you would say more about Ssleptaz's involvement; what more can you tell me?"

"Ah yes, so I did," chuckled Allotter. "We three not only turn the cards and roll the dice for men, we also do it for the Lizard kind and indeed all other creatures that move through the Middle World. We needed one who could flush out the Marked and so we created the Silverwynn. Then we had her influence the creatures from the swamps and those from the old order, the Knights of Avolire. We helped them to set her up with the opportunity to feed off the power of the Rift and we implanted the idea of sending in a shape changer to find the Marked. He nearly did so. After the manipulation of Jonas Tullage and his Death Tubaria cult, the changeling Ssleptaz got a sniff of where the Marked was hiding. The Historian sensed our interference, and being trained in the art of Cuvar, he disappeared along with the child. With the help of his fellow conspirators the Marked was once lost again from our sight. They hid him along the banks of one of the great rivers. Sometime later without our influence or insight your Vessel came to know the child well. Should you choose to communicate with the Vessel's essence it may give you useful insight into how the lad thinks. Remember however, he is not as he was. The power of the wizards saw to that."

"I dispatched the Vessel's essence to the underworld. Ssleptaz has also failed you. The changeling disappeared and my Hochnar has lost contact with his pet chameleon."

"Yes indeed," added Spinner. "The creature is long dead, killed it seems by another of our dear sister's interventions; a protector sent to watch over the Marked; another direct descendent of the infernal Cuvar."

"Do I know this other? Have I met this person?" demanded Urthanock

"No!" jumped in a new voice. "And neither shall you."

Cutter had spoken for the first time.

"So what can you tell me about the string plucker, the bard who has been interfering in my attempts to destroy the Marked and gain control of the Gems. He seems just as great a threat as the fucked up Marked and the Cuvar."

"Indeed, he does, replied Allotter as she twisted a strand of wispy crone-hair around her little finger. "He is the second of the guardians that our sly and devious sister introduced to this game, again with the intent of protecting Llyat Emgar. We suspect she rolls his dice and turns his cards in secret for we have tried on numerous occasion to destroy him but always he has somehow survived. Why, we even threw boulders at him from the steep cliffs besides of the Valmuhsh and…"

"Enough of Thias Calavan dear sister," interrupted Spinner between sips of wine. "I am still working on a way to limit his impact on the outcome we wish to promote."

"Shut you foul mouths; all of you!" bellowed Urthanock as he held his head in his hands. "I want no more of your mystical claptrap. Tell me only that which I need to secure my victory over the Marked or I swear by the power of Kha that I will rip your rotting flesh from your bones."

"You are no threat to us, no matter what you think Kha promised you," shouted back Allotter, her spittle crackling as it hit candles flames. "We three alone unite the dimensions; we are the Fates. One last time, minion of the Dark Lord, do you wish to continue this game?"

At this the crones, including the dumb one, cackled in a display of maniacal madness.

"You misunderstand my intentions," answered Urthanock, baring his teeth as if to strike. "I will unlock the portal and unite the dimensions; then I alone will occupy your space and time. I may however spare you should you be complicit in my goals. But first tell me this, what is it that you three want? What is the ultimate outcome that you seek? Why do you two seek to help me?"

"Do you listen to nothing," spat back Allotter. "To us this is just a game. It is how we pass our time and amuse ourselves. It is all in the dice and the cards. We play such trivia all the time but this one game is special because of its links to Raulyn and the fate of the Enderdetag Prophecy; words that should strike terror into your heart."

"They are just words and mean nothing."

"Mean nothing!" laughed Spinner. "They were penned by Belanore, one of the first of the Cuvar after Raulyn and Thamous. They are far more powerful than your puny mind could ever imagine. When your essence was incarcerated, Belanore envisaged your eventual return. He saw it manifested in the movement of the Fortunes having constructed the Great Orrery of the Bards. Now here we all are as predicted."

"I must and will open the portal." bellowed Urthanock. "Only half of my essence leeched out through the cracks in Avolire; Kha made sure of that. I need to feel whole again and once I am complete, all will stand in awe of my presence. Even Kha will quake before me. Then you will all understand was is meant by 'the End of Days!'"

"Fucking megalomaniac!" growled the mute crone to the surprise of her sisters.

"Spinner and I will help you on the condition that you give us that which is not yours," said Allotter with steel in her voice. "Otherwise there is no deal and you must leave at once."

"Tell me what it is that you require of me?"

"A great power, something you stole."

"Yet more riddles," snapped back Urthanock. "What is it you want?"

"We demand that you give up Thamous's essence, that which you purloined in Avolire," snarled Allotter. "It sits in limbo and cannot pass to its afterlife. Give it up and you may yet succeed."

"Take the fucking thing if you know how. The wyvern sits inside my head and its voice threatens my sanity each and every hour. Take it; take it now. I wish to be free from that eternal plague."

"Then stand still and do not move," ordered Spinner.

Urthanock inhaled, fixed his stare upon the Moirai, and did not twitch a muscle. A purple mist began to ooze from his pores and it coalesced one arm's length before his eyes. It swayed as if floating like fog on the still river in the first hours of morning. Its colour then changed as the ghost-mist began to float ever higher. On it rose, forming every few seconds into smoke shapes that resembled a wyvern in flight. A memory stirred and it forced Urthanock to focus. Despite a vastness in scale it resembled the smoke figures puffed into the still air of the Red Mare as one called Denius Castor suckled on his old pot pipe. Purple changed to blue, to green, to turquoise, and finally the hue of devilled kidney. The swirl of ethereal mist rose to the roof of the Moirai Temple and passed through the rock as if it were no barrier. A shudder knocked through the marrow cavities of Urthanock's skeleton. It rattled against hard bones while conducting a symphony of release. The Lord from the swamps then trembled with its aftershock until a stillness pervaded his Vessel's inner being. He checked his body to ensure he had not lost anything of importance

"Has the serpent gone? Will I at last have peace of mind?"

"Thamous has gone and we will never sense his presence again," replied Spinner with satisfaction. "The great beast that once knew Raulyn can now rest in peace."

"Now fulfil your part of the bargain," insisted Urthanock.

"For this gift, which you gave freely, my sister will now give you the knowledge needed to enable a successful outcome of your endeavours."

Children of Gebez screeched and Allotter paused until they fell silent. As seconds ticked by she bided her time picking flakes of dead skin from her hairy chin and flicking them forward.

"Listen with care for I will not repeat myself. The first thing to understand is that the Underworld's portal is located far away from this land. It lies amongst the Lotus Isles, way to the south west across the Great Ocean. There the ancients tapped its power and profited from what its presence bestowed upon them. You must understand this; there had been a previous leach from that place of darkness.

Raulyn sealed it with help of Thamous's key and he locked you inside its black space."

Urthanock looked at the three wizens and scoffed. "I do not remember ever having been there, what is it like? How should I travel?"

"Use the Rift," replied Spinner. "Although I see you have no bracelet."

"I will not use it again; just look at what it did to my left hand," he declared as he revealed his deformity.

"Then you must travel by boat," said Allotter without a pause. "Yet you must hurry for the Marked has a head start on you. In one month from now, Solaris will be at its midsummer zenith, directly over the Isles and the portal. The golden god's power will be used to weld the Gems in to one. If that time is missed then you will have failed. You would have to wait another millennia for the alignment of the Fortune Stars and another summer solstice. Without the two together the key cannot be formed by mortals. Thamous is no longer around to help thanks to you."

"Where will the Marked create the Key?"

"You do not need to know," replied Spinner. "First we must show you something. Hold your hands out to your sides and watch closely. This is will be a great privilege as mortals only ever see this once."

Urthanock did as ordered and looked first to the left and then to the right. His eyes widened as they gazed upon the strangest of all phenomena. Around his entire body wisps of unreality began to form. Soon he was surrounded by a massed tangle of tiny strings. They reminded him of the cords of puppets that had been twisted during the play of pampered brats. As they became ever more distinct he saw they were formed from vibrant shafts of coloured light. Attached to his body they rose up and disappeared through the stone roof high above his head.

"These are the strings of your Vessel's life force," said Allotter in the most serious tone. "Those that were linked to your reptile's body were severed by Cutter when Raulyn locked you in the Underworld. I have never seen such a mess of tubules before and I must assume it is due to the twistedness of your foul essence as it interacts with your Vessel's flesh. However, the point of this demonstration is to make you aware that we three, my dumb sister especially, can terminate your existence should you not do as we bid."

"What would you have me do then," screamed Urthanock. "Would you have me fuck you three? Is that what you want?"

"Not I," growled Cutter.

"Then tell me, where on the Lotus Isles will I find the door to the Underworld? You must at least tell be able to tell me that."

"We will give you a clue for that is no more than we did for he who came before you," answered Spinner. "Look for the shadow of the Lords of Light. Seek a place beyond the settlements, across the expanse of the cinnamon grass and the lush verdant forests. When you see the Twin Peaks of Enlightenment you will then be close. We cannot say more for the game must have a semblance of balance."

"You stinking corpses," screamed Urthanock amid his whirlpool anger. "I have waited a thousand years and all I hear is drivel. Tell me something useful. I have surrendered Thamous's essence for fuck all. Come on, give me value in return."

Both Allotter and Spinner laughed.

"Think of what we have already said, swine of the swamp," screamed Allotter. "We have told you the day that the Marked will seek to use the key to close the portal. We have told you where in the world to find him, within the range of your eyes. We have also told you that you must procure a sea going vessel and journey to the Lotus Isles in great haste; get there before the Marked and set your trap. Then all will be yours unless you fuck things up like you did with the battle at Parandor, where you turned the most glorious of reptilian victories into dunghill of defeat."

Urthanock's ire boiled and the Vessel's mark began to burn.

"What do you know of that battle, were you there with me?" he demanded.

"You will never understand how our dimension works so I will not bother to explain," snapped back Allotter.

"Then at least tell me this; if your intention is to see me win this game of yours, what sort of a trap should I set?"

"Do we have to spell everything out for you?" moaned Spinner while rolling her clouded eyes. "Dig a spike pit; roll a giant boulder ball at him; fire an arrow up his arse from a racing humpy. Come on scale brain, use what little sense you have. This is not difficult."

Urthanock thought for a moment while Spinner continued as if bored.

"We are tired after the cutting of so many strings from the battle. We wish to rest."

"You mean the battle for Parandor is over?" asked Urthanock but no answer came.

"It is time you buggered off back to where you came from or to where you need to go next." added Allotter.

"I thought you wanted me to win this time?" snapped back the Dark Lord.

Cutter spat to the floor, snarled, then banged her fist down on the table.

"Well I for one do not," she screamed from the pit of her putrid stomach. "But you do at least deserve some honest advice. Here, catch this."

A crumpled piece of parchment flew from out of Cutter's hand and landed before Urthanock's feet. It came to rest by the tip of his sword that still lay where it had fallen. Without hesitating he picked it up and having opened it, gazed down on a strange language that he couldn't read.

"What the fuck is this?"

"It is a clue, written in the secret babbling tongue of the Cuvar of the Lotus Isles. When you arrive at your destination look out for the man with a dark cratered face. Ask him to translate it for you. If you are kind in your approach and offer reward for his services you may be given further insight. But be careful, for as with every force for good there is an equal and opposite evil. Handle him well or you may die to regret it."

"And what the fuck is that supposed to mean?" spat back Urthanock.

"I will say no more for it is time to seal my lips for another thousand years."

That said, Cutter slumped in her chair, pulled the cowl of her mouse-munched shawl over her head, and hid from the conversation.

"What do you know of Raulyn's Ratio?" asked Spinner.

"I have no idea what the fuck you are talking about," sneered Urthanock.

"That's a pity," she replied.

In that moment of ignorance, the Lord over Fear realised that the voice that had so plagued him over recent months had at last disappeared. That was at least one positive he could take from his meeting with the three old crones. He sensed he would get little more from the decaying dames and so decided to eliminate them forever. Raising both his hands he thrust them forward. His intention was to summon up the powers bestowed on him by Kha. He would start by entwining the three in Urthanock's Knot before ripping them asunder. Yet nothing happen and amid his anger and frustration he began to stamp his feet upon the ground.

"We have told you already Marsh Lord," cackled Allotter. "You are powerless inside this temple. Kha cannot touch us here."

"Fuck off home," spat out Spinner. "Return to your swamp."

The Children of Gebez screeched and hissed and began to move through the circle of candles with claws extended and jaws that snapped.

"Take your sword and run to the door or they will claim you as one of their own," laughed Allotter.

Urthanock hesitated but then realised that without his powers he had no hope of surviving the wrath of the hideous guardians of the Moirai. He snatched up his sword and raced to the portal which opened before him. All the while the stinking breath of the Children of Gebez pulsed against the nape of his neck. He jumped through the orifice, turned at once, and pushed against the great metal door while his eyes stared into the soulless sockets of his pursuers' skulls. Then all was quiet. Alone amid the offerings that filled the Cuvar cavern Urthanock felt the power of Kha flood back into his being. To test his might he launched a ball of fame through the subterranean space. As it passed it scoured the walls and roof, stripping off the art work of a thousand years and fully illuminating the dark.

"Now you hideous hags, prepare to cut your own fucking strings."

Urthanock pulled on the handle of the door and it slowly began to open. He readied himself to leap amid the Children of Gebez but once again his intentions were thwarted. Behind the door was nought but rock, as solid as the hardest of mountains. The hags had said that no one ever entered twice and so it was for the beast. He kicked the wall in frustration as the door began to close. Soon it looked as if it had never been opened and when he again tried to pull, the portal would not budge.

Realising he had no option but to head for the surface he decided to race back to Parandor in order to procure a ship to take him to the Lotus Isles. So incensed was his mind, that his upward journey passed as in a blur. Once he hit the air of a new morning he paused to take stock. For a while he contemplated using the Rift but in the end decided the odds were against him surviving intact. No, he would have to go by sea despite such vast swathes of water having long held terrors of all of lizard kind. He scanned the surrounding landscape, knowing that Parandor lay to the north and the west of his current position. Checking where Solaris rose he realised that a bird's line of flight would take it over the vast oak woods that lay beyond the hamlet of Harico. He pointed his face to his distant target and set off towards the trees.

"Well that visit went well; I think not," sneered a voice.

Urthanock stopped and closed his eyes.

"No it cannot be. You were exorcised and taken from me by the crones. You cannot still be here vile worm."

"I am not the voice of Thamous, nor have I ever been," replied the voice.

"Then who the fuck are you?" demanded Urthanock as he held his head in his hands.

"It is I, Methladon Heyn, and I intend to destroy you."

24

The trek across the high ridgeway that traversed the Harico Hills passed without significant incident. It took two full nights and a day for the weary travellers to complete the journey for despite the cloudless sky and Mona's guiding light the three had walked with more care than speed. The trail had not been maintained since first being created by the Ancients and for centuries had been left for the wild goats to wander back and forth upon its surface. Erosion had also taken its toll and made parts treacherous with both land slips and potholes. There was no doubt however that this choice of route had been the better of the two options. Navigating the vast oak woods at night would have been nigh impossible. By the first hint of daybreak on the second morning Heliana began to struggle, both from staying awake and from the back pain induced by her belly load. In addition, the joints of her pelvis felt more unstable as each hour passed. So it was that Llyat ordered camp to be made at the base of the ridge, hidden in the tree line of the oak wood, and within sight of the road from Parandor to the Badlands.

Theoplous was despatched to find kindling and fallen branches. The promethelumous spell was enacted and Llyat soon had a fire going on which to cook what little food they had left. The sailor was then sent away a second time, to find game with which to feed three hungry mouths. As Llyat warmed his hands before the flames he began to take note of the surrounding land and in particular the road to the south. He would remain ever vigilant as the thought of Urthanock stumbling upon them filled him with dread.

All through the long and arduous nights the sounds of the woodland animals had filled the forested valley below, some benign, and some that hinted at the presence of more malevolent beasts. Around the camp fire and without any footfall to distract his hearing, Llyat began to pick up even more distant sounds. Some reminded him of the snapping of jaws, others the cries of animals caught by an unknown prey. He thought at one point that he had heard the distinctive flapping of skyfawn wings but it turned out to be bats returning to roost for the upcoming day. At one point an owl with a great white face and saucer sized eyes swooped through the make shift camp and caused Llyat and Heliana to recoil in fright. Llyat's imagination was in danger of exploding as he envisioned a hoard of kulkulkath marching up the old road to reinforce Urthanock's army before the walls of Parandor. He bit into his cheek and forced himself back into reality.

"I wonder why they call the lands to the south the Badlands?" he whispered to Heliana who sat beside him on the soft grass with her head resting on his right shoulder.

"I know the answer to that," she replied. "Old Marus once told me it when I was attending to his bedtime rituals."

"What exactly did he tell you?" demanded Llyat as his thoughts of the old man's possible perversions took him to places best left buried.

"The Grand Physician told me that he had been there once on his travels," she began. "Apparently beyond the Harico Hills the grass fades away and after some twenty or so leagues it disappears altogether. It never rains there for some reason. There is just sand and rock and nothing grows save for some strange trees around a number of remote waterholes. These islands of liquid sustain the few weird folk who wander its sandy surface on strange back lumped animals they call humpies and which legend says have feet that resembled a woman's quim."

"Bollocks!" sneered Llyat.

"No, quim," giggled Heliana.

"But why call them Badlands?" asked Llyat as he struggled to imagine such a possibility.

"Because nothing grows there, dolt," winced the young woman as her unborn kicked hard against the inside her belly. "They say that there are mountains there as tall as the Grey ones that we can see from Parandor. There are monstrous hils of sand that move on the will of the dust storms that blow with great vengeance on an almost daily basis. Old Marus said he was never as glad as when he returned from his exploration of the sandy dung heap. He vowed would never set foot in the awful place again."

"It's just as well we will be taking the road to Parandor," said Llyat as he placed his right arm around his lover. "It sounds a really shit place to visit."

Some thirty minutes later Theoplous returned with a brace of plump ground birds he had trapped at the edge of the forest. He said proudly that they had been roosting in the low branches at the forest's edge and that he had used sa lor's stealth to capture them. As if boarding an enemy ship he had rung their necks without them even waking. Theo sat in a shell of contentment and plucked away at the feathers until all were gone. Then in no time and with deft flicks of his knife he gutted and cut the two nude birds into halves. Holding one over the fire with his blade he began to cook it in the hot smoke that rose up to the still star filled sky. Soon the outer layers began to brown and a most pleasant aroma drifted out on the wind.

"I'll do one at time," he suggested as he smiled at his handiwork. "The first will be for the girl, the second for you Llyat, and the third for myself."

"And the fourth?" asked Heliana, "Do we fight over that one?"

"No, that's for young Irabo," reasoned the sailor. "As I returned with the birds I caught sight of his silhouette. It was just a small speck on crest of a distant hill but he will be with us soon."

"That's really good news," replied Heliana while looking up to the mounds they had earlier descended. "I wasn't sure if we would see him again and I was growing to like him, what with all he'd been through, nearly dying and all that!"

"Can you be sure that it wasn't Urthanock you saw?" cautioned Llyat.

"No, I am not, but for all our sakes let us pray that it wasn't," replied the sailor as he turned his blade to cook the other side of the bird.

The next ten minutes passed amid triple infused tension as the three ate their birds and waited for the arrival of the one who followed them. Although Llyat was hopeful that it was Irabo he readied himself against other possibilities. His right hand fell to the hilt of his blade while his left arm held his shoulder bag in close in order to protect the Gems of Thamous. The sudden sound of approaching feet caused three hearts to pump faster but then, much to the relief of all, Irabo at last strode into their camp and slumped exhausted to the ground. He rolled onto his back and stared into the heavens. While his breath returned he pointed to the stars that had formed a straight line and which were still visible in the virgin morning light.

"Sorry I was so long in catching you up," he began, "But half way through the first night I sat down to rest awhile and then fell asleep. I was woken by the sound of a distant nighthowler and after that raced on as fast as I dared to catch you all. We had better not linger too long here."

"Eat your share of the bird, it will sustain you on your journey later today," responded Llyat. "We cannot stop for sleep until we clear the other side of the oak forest and find shelter. We are not far enough away from Harico and must avoid any encounter with Urthanock."

As Irabo's teeth sank into the moist flesh of the bird Llyat began to question him about events at the Barrow and how their plan had played out.

"Did you reveal the Dragon Whisper and did Urthanock show as we had hoped?"

"Indeed, he did. Just some ten minutes after I had hidden the strange stone amongst the boulders, and having just made it to my hide, a crackling blue flash announced the beast's arrival. For a brief second, I thought Urthanock had seen me but he obviously hadn't. He soon found and examined the stone, looked around but saw nothing amiss. Then he entered the Barrow no doubt to seek out the Moirai. I waited for about a half an hour. Believing it to be then safe I set off to catch you all. There is nothing more I can add. It seems Thias's plan worked just as intended."

"Yes, so far so good," replied Llyat as he rose from the grass and pulled Heliana to his side. "Come on girl, you will seize up if we don't get moving again. Plenty of time to rest on the ocean, if we can find a ship willing to take us to the Lotus Isles."

"Let me run on ahead," suggested Theoplous as the group broke camp. "The girl is the slowest and you should go at her pace. I will seek out Ligart Highroar and the Banshees Wail and inform the letch what is expected of him. Knowing Highroar, he would have deserted Parandor at the first sight of trouble and anchored somewhere further down the estuary."

"Are you sure you are well enough?" questioned Llyat as soon as they had begun to move.

"What are you implying," answered Theoplous. "I am fitter than all of you and can travel at five times the pace as we are now. Don't underestimate me Llyat."

The sailor kicked out the fire and set off on the road that led south. Llyat sensed something bothered Theoplous despite the sailor's unwillingness to admit it.

"I refer to your collapse in the barrow," shouted Llyat, loud enough so all could hear.

"What about it, I fainted that was all," muttered the sailor as he walked a little quicker and thus caused Llyat to step up his own pace. "I've not been sleeping..."

"Theo, it was much more significant than that," countered Llyat. "Both Irabo and Heliana were witness to what transpired and will correct me should I speak false words. You were sat on the floor and you bellowed like a nighthowler. Then you started rambling and I can remember the words that came from your mouth... 'The darkness beyond.... the ninth level.... the sight of the door.' We tried to snap you out of your trance but then you turned white and shook with great vio ence. We all reckoned you were possessed by some evil essence or perhaps the dark magic of the Moirai. Your fits continued for many minutes and still you ranted. Over and over again you shouted the same words; 'The ninth level... The ninth level... The ninth level...'"

"Is what Llyat says true Irabo? Did I really mention the ninth?"

"Yes, Llyat has told it exactly as it happened," replied the young warrior.

"What does it all mean Theo," demanded Llyat as Heliana fell behind. "You owe us an explanation."

"I am not permitted to speak of such things," snapped back Theoplous. "Not at least until you have set your feet upon the land of the Lotus Isles."

For the first time in days Llyat felt angry for he knew that the sailor hid a great secret.

"I'm sorry but that's not an acceptable answer," he shouted. "At least give me a morsel of insight or I swear by the gods you will go no further with me on this quest, Cuvar or not!"

"This is all I dare say at the moment," growled the sailor. "Long before I took up with Highroar and the crew of the Banshees Wail, I once worked on part of a dig. It was an excavation by those who hold sway over the Lotus Isles. It has been going on for a very long time and it is close to the mountain on which the hill fort of the Lords of Light was built. I cannot tell you more at this time but the workings are reputed to contain nine levels; nine steps of terror that lead into the unknown. Ever since my time there I have been tormented by hideous nightmares. Something evil was woken during that dig. I do not sleep well because of my time there and sometimes when exhausted I pass out in a manner you just described. No more questions please; I will explain all in due course so please trust me. I'm sorry but I must leave you now and secure the services of the Banshees Wail."

On finishing his words Theoplous sprinted off down the road. Irabo set off after him in order restrain the sailor but Llyat screamed out for the warrior to stop. Soon there were just three as Theoplous disappeared over the next rise in the land. The trees then seemed to close in on Llyat and he saw in their black shadows omens of the darkness to come. He tried to work out what this sudden change in the sailor's behaviour meant, for Theo's flight had induced a cascade of confusion. The dark skinned First Mate, he who had declared himself to be Cuvar, was supposed to be one of his guardians. Yet now he had deserted and put their mission at risk. Something was not right but Llyat could not work out what it was.

"I think he may be a threat to us," panted Irabo on his return.

"Quite possibly," answered Llyat while Heliana waddled amongst them.

"Well I don't think so," she began. "I suspect he may have vital clues that must never reach the ears of our enemies. I trust Theo although I now fear for him more than I have ever done. I just hope he never comes face to face with the Urthanock."

"Do you know something about these nine levels?" quizzed Llyat as the group moved on.

"Yes a little," she replied before dipping into the trees to relieve herself.

A few minutes later she returned, readjusted her habit and set off down the road at a gallop. Llyat and Irabo chased after her, surprised at the new found energy that sprang from her lithe legs.

"What do you know?" he demanded.

"Do you remember me telling you about Ailith on our voyage to Valameer," she began.

"Yes I do. I dream of it often but what relevance is she to this?"

"She used to tell me things after, you know, afterwards. Ailith told me she had once met a strange man down by the docks, fresh arrived from the Lotus Isles. He was apparently on the run and in hiding for having betrayed a great secret."

"Was that secret related to the ninth level?" asked Irabo, sensing something important.

"Yes, it was," she continued. "Apparently there was a creepy group of holy fanatics on the Lotus Islands that had been looking for some weird door buried deep within the rock for a very long time. They kill anyone who breaks their secrets. The stranger told Ailith that they had been digging in the base of an old iron quarry and discovered ancient ruins that went down at least seven levels. Writings on some of the walls suggested that there were nine in total. Strange objects had been found at each step of the way down but all who ever worked there were in fear of ever speaking of what they knew. Ailith was both excited and terrified having had this secret shared with her."

"Did she ever say what happened to this stranger from the islands," asked Llyat as he rubbed his chin and tried to work out if this was in any way significant.

"Apparently, he was found floating in the Parandor's harbour the very next day," replied Heliana with a nervous giggle.

Llyat hesitated as he realised that Heliana had known about the Underworld portal for longer than he cared to believe possible.

"Why didn't you tell me about this before?" he demanded.

"Because you never asked."

"But..."

"Come on Llyat, get real," she snapped back. "First the stranger is found dead in the water, then Ailith disappears, surrounded by some bullshit story that she was executed in secret and her corpse fed to the Royal Hounds. There was no way I was going to talk of such things but now I sense that Theo is in danger from the same holy nutters I felt it best to speak of that which may carry the curse of death. I hope I haven't put either of you in danger for it is a fearful secret and I have carried it alone for too long."

"Shit," exclaimed Irabo as his sword hand dropped to the hilt of his blade.

An eerie silence strangled the three until Llyat found the means to speak.

"We must find Theo as soon as possible for I now suspect he knows far more than he has let on. Try your best and waddle fast. The sooner we get to the Estuary of New Beginnings the better."

By the early evening of the following day the three travellers dropped out of the root margin of the ancient oak forest. All were pleased to be out of the shadows that throughout the long and difficult march had prevented the warmth of

Solaris from refuelling their cores. There at last, bathed in the radiant red and orange of the waning sky god, their eyes feasted upon the beauty of the estuary and to mighty edifice of Parandor in the distance. Llyat extended his right arm and pointed out several plumes of smoke that drifted high into the air. It was a day without breeze and the smoke mixed with the few clouds that dared to mar the splendour of the evening's sky.

"Funeral pyres!" exclaimed Irabo, the second of the three to spot them. "They are outside the walls of Parandor and the battle is over."

"How can you tell that?" replied Heliana as she gawped at the most unusual vista.

"There is no noise and Parandor itself does not burn," replied Irabo as a broad smile stretched to the extremities of his cheeks. "Can you not sense the scent, cooked meat mixed with bowel gas?"

"Look down there to where the road meets the estuary," bellowed Llyat as he tried to drag the eyes of his companions away from the mountainous plumes of cremated ash. "I'm sure that's Thias down there waving his arms like a windmill in full sail."

The three companions focused on the embankment and the figure that approached.

"I do believe you're right," answered Irabo. "Let's rush on and hear what news he has to tell. I'm sure he will have much to sing about."

Some ten minutes Thias embraced each of his three friends as they were at last reunited. The bard stood beside the very same rowing boat that had ferried Llyat and his party across the Tiaryer under the guidance of the priests. Heliana dropped to the ground, rested her back against the side of the boat, and within seconds had fallen asleep. Llyat looked deep into Thias's eyes and saw a troubled mind. This was not the same bard he had left a week earlier. A great fear sat within his pupils and pulled on the wrinkles on his face.

"Leave her to her dreams," said Llyat as he pointed to Heliana. "We haven't slept for a couple of days and her lump adds to her exhaustion."

"I understand," replied the bard as his eyes roamed across the woman's belly. "But please, no more than an hour. Then we must move off if we are to catch the tide."

"How long have you been here and have you seen anything of Theo," whispered Irabo?

"The sailor passed here in the early hours of the day, just as I had dragged my boat out of the water," began Thias. "He stopped briefly for an update on the battle and then realising it was all over raced on to find Highroar and The Banshees Wail. If you look down the edge of the estuary you will just be able to see the tops of its masts over that distant hillock. He told me you would be coming this way sometime soon and that I should wait and then lead you on to his master's boat. He did in fact return but half an hour ago and was a little disappointed you had not yet arrived. Then he was off again to make more arrangements. The tide will soon turn and as I said earlier, we need to be away as soon as possible. I suspect

Urthanock may not be far behind and if he uses the Rift then he could arrive at any moment."

"Yet we still have to let Heliana rest and take a chance the Moirai will detain him a while longer," cautioned Llyat as he too rested against the boat. "I propose we exchange summaries of our adventures while we wait, but be alert and ready just in case the bastard appears."

The three began an earnest conversation, competing as they did so with Heliana's hogsnores.

"I came over during the night," explained Thias. "There is much I need to tell you about the battle and other things. The Lizardmen have all been slaughtered and Urthanock fled from the battle."

"That's at least one good outcome." added Llyat.

"Did he turn up at the Barrow as hoped?" asked Thias.

"Yes he did," interrupted Irabo. "Your plan worked as you intended it to and..."

For the next half an hour, the three men talked and outlined all that had happened since Llyat had left Parandor to seek information from the Moirai. Llyat promised to give greater detail once he had slept and got his head around the key messages the three old crones had passed on to him. Irabo pushed Thias for more information once the bard got into detail about the battle. In particular he sought after the welfare of Commander Townsforth whose shoulder had been wounded. The young warrior wanted to know more of Thias's dark encounter with the Thieves Guild but the bard clammed up and would say no more except that he could never return to Parandor. That was the price he had to pay for his freedom.

Heliana stirred. Having rolled to one side and with drool seeping from the side of her mouth, her eyes flickered open. She grimaced as she then tried to rise to her feet.

"Bugger me but these pebbles are uncomfortable to the arse," she moaned. "I bet they've left scars on my best asset."

"I'll have a look and confirm that if you like," replied Llyat.

"Fuck off you perverted toad," she snorted.

As Llyat laughed Heliana struggled to move her feet and then cast a glance to the bard.

"Hello Thias, I forgot you were here."

"You have been out for half an hour or so but now you are awake we should get moving," replied the bard. "We will leave the boat out in the open. Perhaps if Urthanock comes this way it may confuse him and induce him to cross the Tiaryer."

"Then let's move," ordered Llyat.

An hour later the four sleep deprived wanderers came before yet another rowing vessel. There to greet them stood Theoplous and Ligart Highroar, both smiling and yet with an urgency to their movements that indicated much underlying tension. Beyond the shingle beach Llyat saw the Banshees Wail still at anchor but with its crew waiting to unfurl the vessel's sails for a hasty departure. Bobbing in the changing waters of the estuary it provided a most welcome sight.

Theoplous still looked sheepish and the Captain as lecherous as ever. Once Highroar had shaken the hands of the men, he looked to Heliana's belly and leered, no doubt imagining the act that propagated the belly-mound. Heliana turned her head away in disgust.

"We must board the Banshees Wail without delay," ordered the Captain while pointing to his ferry craft. "My ship is ready to sail and we have the good fortune to be able to take the tide before it turns. Otherwise we will be stuck on the sandbanks for hours while the shit storm that chases you has chance to catch up. I for one want to be well out of here before that happens."

"Whose is that other ship over there," asked Llyat as he pointed to a smaller vessel a league further down the estuary."

"That is the Masters Catch, old Amos Whitebeard's fishing ketch," replied Highroar as he scratched his groin. "I told the dim fish sniffer to clear off, that trouble is coming, but he would not listen; said he had not got to sixty-four by being afeard of swamp scum."

"Then let us hope that once we leave he will come to his senses," added Theoplous as he helped Heliana into the small boat that would take them to the Banshees Wail.

Llyat then clambered on-board while Thias scanned the bay.

"Did any other vessels survive the war?" asked Thias.

"Not a one," replied Highroar.

"I must thank you for taking us to the Lotus Isles, Captain," said Llyat. "You do realised I hope that you are helping save the Realm from destruction."

"Given all that Theo has promised me, I would be mad to refuse?" sniggered the Captain.

"What is it you have promised Theo?" asked Llyat.

"I'll tell you later," replied the first mate.

Theo pushed the craft away from the beach and at last jumped on board. Wasting no further time the First Mate began to pull on the oars and the small boat cut through the rising swell.

For the next day and night Llyat and Heliana lay together in the small cabin that Abrahamus Marus had occupied during Llyat's first sea adventure. They had slept for most of the time save for using the slop bucket and drinking from a pitcher of water that Theoplous had provided. Some stale bread and pungent ewe cheese had been left on a platter beside the water which both had nibbled at but hadn't the appetite to finish. When at last they both felt the need to venture from their cabin they arose to a bright clear morning. Solaris shone bright and couds raced past the yellow god, pushed by a wind that came from behind. The lovers held hands and watched the distant horizon change as the Banshees Wail pitched and rolled amid the ocean swell.

"I'm glad to see you are back with us," shouted Thias from high up on the deck that covered the Captain's quarters. "I'll be down with you in a second. Breakfast has been prepared and is waiting in the Highroar's cabin. We have much to plan and we may as well start now, even though our journey will be long. You should be pleased to hear that the wind favours us at present and Highroar says we are making good time. Pray that it doesn't drop. We must not fail to reach our destination before the solstice day."

Llyat watched as Thias leapt down the stairs that led to the main deck. Linking arms with both Llyat and Heliana he began to pull them to the door that led into Highroar's inner sanctum. The lovers complied without comment for they were much fatigued and their minds still slow to function. Once inside they were ushered to the Captain's table and encouraged to sit on two of three vacant chairs. With nods of their heads they acknowledged the presence of the others who had gathered there. Thias took the third chair as Highroar, Theoplous and Irabo pecked away at food on the plates before them.

"I do not expect you to immediately take a liking to this sea food but you will get used to it as your bellies empty and hunger starts to shout in your ears," declared Highroar. "It's important that the lass carrying the babe eats regularly and gets much sunshine and sea air. That will be necessary to keep both mother and child well while at sea."

Llyat looked to the extensive platter that covered much of the table. He then switched his gaze to Heliana whose face showed her apprehension at all that lay be for her. A great pewter plate was covered in fish of various types that had been recently caught and then grilled on the deck mounted charcoal griddle that Llyat remembered from his first trip on the Wail. Soon his mind drifted back to the sword lesion with Tonousa and Irabo. The image of Tonousa's face was crystal clear and induced a tidal wave of sadness that battered his emotions.

"Not bad," muttered Heliana as she took her first bite. "I would prefer chicken but fish is okay. Come on Llyat stop dreaming; wake up and get with the meal."

Highroar leaned across the table, snatched a lemon from the bowel beside Heliana and sliced it in half with his knife. He then squeezed the juice over the young woman's fish.

"It's hard to catch a chicken at sea," said Highroar as he smiled and revealed the few rotten pegs that passed for his teeth. "Make sure you squeeze lemon on all you eat young lady for that is how we sailors keep away the gum rot."

Llyat tried the food and found it to be good. Despite his background ocean nausea the more he ate the more he began to satiate his hunger.

"It is time to put our thoughts and plans in motion," insisted Thias as he shuffled in his chair. "Llyat, if you able, and if they permit, it may be best if you summarise the messages given to you by the Moirai. If we understand their full implications we can then help you plan what needs to be done once we reach the Lotus Isles."

"So be it," the youth replied. "Perhaps you can help me make sense of it all."

Llyat then explained to his captive audience the details of everything that had occurred once he had entered the door that led to the Oracles' Crypt. He avoided mentioning Theo's collapse for he somehow sensed it better to hold that information back, not least for the sake of the sailor's embarrassment.

"So, in summary," he added at the end of his long saga. "First off, being the Marked of the Prophecy, I have to search out some people called the Lords of the Light. They dwell on one of two mountains at the far end of the main island where two big ones stick out from the sea. They are the guardians of ancient secrets and they possess what was known from the beginning as the 'Diamond in the Sky'. This massive polished stone is the only object that can weld the five Gems of Thamous into the one key that will give access to the Underworld. The power to do this work is only possible at the summer midpoint of an Enderdetag so we must be with the Lords of Light by then. These strange Lords live in a place called Bryngaer Henuriaid. Theo, I believe you can will tell us which of the mountains to climb."

"I can, when needed," replied the First Mate.

"Then there is the issue regarding the precise location of the door to the underworld. The Moirai would not tell me where it was for two are against me and only one of them appears to be working for my victory."

"Is that true Llyat or are you just making that up?" demanded Thias.

"Sadly, it is true."

"Fuck!" exclaimed Theoplous as he jumped to his feet. "We must get you to these Lords of Light as soon as possible. We cannot allow the Fates to move against us. I can take you directly to the Lords for I have met and worked for them in my youth. Ligart, aim your ship directly for the tallest of the two island mountains, we want the one whose summit sits permanently above the ring of cloud that surrounds it. Only the Lords can direct Llyat to the Underworld's portal."

"Consider it done." replied Highroar, nodding his head.

"Yet Theo, you and I both know where it is," countered Llyat. "It's at the bottom of an old iron quarry on the main island and close to the Twin Mountains."

"How the fuck did you know that," demanded Theo?

"It doesn't matter," answered Llyat "but I see from you face that it is true."

All eyes turned and stared with intent.

"I will take you to the Lords but ask me no more for I am not yet reacy to die," uttered the First Mate as sweat beads formed on his lips and forehead. "I will not speak more of that most evil of places."

"Let me fill in some gaps," said Llyat. "We must locate the quarry and seek the ninth level."

Theoplous gasped and slumped back down into his chair.

"The final message from the Moirai was that whosoever places the key on the lock stone and opens the portal will die. That includes me, even being the Marked. Whoever then closes it from the inside will also die, and so it seems I'll be fucked twice over.

"Then I will open the door for you," announced Thias with great bravado.

"And I will enter the underworld with you and when you have defeated Urthanock I will close the portal as you leave," added Irabo proudly.

"You guys need to think about this a bit more," sneered Highroar.

"I think we do need to consider all our options and not decide anything unti we have talked with the Lords of Light," answered Llyat, "There may other ways we have not yet explored but I do thank you for your support. Let us leave this for now and do much more thinking. I would like a little fresh air, and then Captain if you would be willing, I would like a lesson in navigation and the calculations that you use to know where you are at sea. I am to be tested by the Lords of Light and I must learn all that I can about numbers, shapes, and such things.

"Sure, let's take a brake then and meet up again after lunch," replied the Captain.

Highroar ripped the head off the largest fish on the platter and sucked out its eyes. Heliana threw up onto her plate.

"Come in and join us," said Captain Highroar as Llyat, accompanied by the ever dutiful Heliana, arrived for his lesson. "Theo has brought his astrolabe, cross staff, and sunstone along with books on numbers that will hopefully explain all we know of such things. I will leave Theo to impart his vast knowledge, for I have some other issues I need to address with the crew, like where are we going, and the payment they are demanding for such an extended voyage."

"I thank you once again Captain," replied Llyat as Highroar left the room. The youth looked to the table where Theoplous sat amid a number of leather bound books and objects, the likes of which he had never seen before.

"Heliana, my dear marsh muckle, sit at the opposite side of the table and amuse yourself in silence while Theo and I talk."

"Of course, master," sneered Heliana. "You're such a prick."

"I'm sorry, I didn't mean to demean you."

Llyat attempted to kiss his lover on the cheek. Heliana pulled away.

For the best part of the afternoon Theo talked and drew on paper. He covered all the number work he had ever been taught and a little of what he had discovered for himself. He drew triangles, circles, images of the sun in relation to the horizon and showed how to calculate what he called angles. Llyat sat and absorbed it all, only stopping to ask occasional question when memories embedded from Sir Raulyn's seed stirred some new thought process in the swirling soup that filled the cauldron of his expanding mind. Heliana did as instructed and sat in silence. After some time had passed she began to examine the many wooden objects that the sailor had said he used to make his calculations. Then in a state of boredom, she reached across for a spare piece of parchment, one discarded by Theo on completing an early section of his lesson. She also picked up a straight rule and a hinged two-pronged device that had a metal point embedded in one of its slender arms and a pencil attached to its other. There in her personal seclusion she stated to doodle and create designs. Llyat looked at her from time to time but thought nothing of her work until Theo at last stared across the table and called out with surprise.

"Let me see that paper girl," he shouted as he reached forward and snatched her art work away. "Who taught you to draw a prefect pentagram using just a compass and a straight stick? This is sacred knowledge of the Ancients and the likes of you should not carry such learning."

"It just a sodding five pointed star," screamed back Heliana. "You have no right to challenge me like this."

"Tell me now, who gave you that skill," demanded Theo as he rose shaking from the table.

"Steady on Theo," cautioned Llyat as he looked over the sailor's shoulder at the star picture.

"This is very important Llyat, I must know who taught Heliana how to do this."

"If you must know arsehole, it was taught to me by a past girlfriend."

Heliana stood up and moved to the window at the back of the cabin. There she stared out to the distant horizon without registering its presence.

"Was it Ailith?" asked Llyat.

"Yes! She was taught this trick by the man she befriended down by the docks, the one who knew of the iron quarry."

"He knew off the dig!" said Theo as his face whitened.

"Apparently, he did," answered Heliana while stroking her bump.

"What are these doodles at the point of each star," asked Theoplous as he looked again at the parchment in his hands. "Did this friend of yours also draw these?"

"Yes."

"Do you know what they mean?

"No."

"For fuck's sake Theo, what's this all about," demanded Llyat with growing concern.

"The symbols at each point are secret representations of the five Gems of Thamous that you carry in the shoulder bag that never leaves your side. This figure with the symbols attached is the secret emblem of the Lords of Light, something know only to a very select few. I believe Heliana to be more than she has so far admitted. Own up girl, who are you and what is your connection to the Lotus Isle Cuvar? What do you know of the Golden Ratio?"

"I know fuck all! Apart from realising you too are not who you seem," spat back Heliana. "You are no simple seafarer."

"That is all I am lady!" shouted Theoplous.

"And I'm just a servant, a gazunder girl to the great."

"In that case I will leave," continued Theo while collecting his instruments and books. "I cannot divulge more and now you must wait until you meet the Lords of Light. I have said far too much already but I will be watching your every move from now on girl."

Theoplous stormed out from the cabin almost flattening Thias who had just opened the door and popped his head inside.

"Out of my way bard!" yelled the First Mate as he raced on.

"What's the matter with him?" asked Thias. "How did do make him so mad. What have you said or done to make him act so?"

"Nothing, he is having a man gush," snorted Heliana.

"He's lost the fucking plot," grumbled Llyat. "There is something about the dig site that troubles him; all is not right."

"Okay, I understand" said Thias without compounding the issue. "We have a more immediate problem than Theo's strange behaviour. I have come to warn you. There is a storm blowing in from the west. Highroar reckons that soor the decks will be unsafe for us landies. Its best you both return to your cabin and sit tight until it has blown over. I will come and get you once the danger has passed."

There was little room for much else apart from the bed and a large wooden trunk in the cabin that Llyat and Heliana now called home. The bed was large enough to accommodate one person with some comfort, but for two it was at best a crush. For two and a bump it was decidedly overcrowded. Heliana had lain down as soon as the squall had hit the Banshees Wail while Llyat had sat on the chest. However, once the storm hit its maximum Llyat had squeezed in besides his loyal lover. Now as the ship tossed and turned, all the while groaning from its every joint, Heliana spooned into Llyat's back as they both lay on their sides. His unborn child did not take kindly to the sea god's torment and repeatedly kicked Llyat in the back.

"It's a feisty little bugger," he exclaimed after several violent thuds over his right kidney. "It's bound to be a boy."

"Don't be so cocksure, we girls can kick like the best of you dick danglers," giggled Heliana as she tried to allay her fears of the boat capsizing. "Will you still love it as much if it is a girl? I would hate for you not to."

"Of course, I will my little duck dumpling," sniggered Llyat. "Just as long as she is as beautiful as her mother."

"Fuck off Llyat, I am being serious. And give over with bird name calling or I shall invent worse shite with which to get my own back. Now, tell me from your heart; what hopes and aspirations do you have for our little one? Please be kind for I am beginning to feel the sea sickness coming back and you could help take my mind off it."

"Now let me think for a minute," responded Llyat while moving to sit on the edge of the bed.

"I would like it to have more opportunity and a happier childhood than we both endured. The thought of it being a servant or swineherd does not fill me with great joy. Obviously I wish it to be healthy and that it's got all the bits it needs in the right places. After that I pray it has some talent of one form or another which it can use it to fulfil its dreams and aspirations."

"So you don't buy into Irabo's shit that everything is predetermined," said Heliana as she too tried to sit up. "Please pass the slop bucket. I may yet puke."

"To be honest, he talks pure bollocks when he delves into religious claptrap."

Llyat passed the pot, grateful he had emptied its contents before the tempest hit.

"Don't you believe in any gods at all? You've met the Moirai so you have proof that at least they exist. I do feel sick Llyat... You were such a tart on your first trip so how come the sickness doesn't bother you now?"

"Ok so I believe in three, but only because I have seen them; no others though," he responded, taking her hand in between his own. "Yet in answer to your other question, just before we sailed I had Irabo do his wrist squeezing trick and it has stopped the illness from coming. Would you like to see if I can get it to work on you? I have had Irabo do it three times now. I know where he puts his thumbs and squeezes."

"I would very much like you to try," she replied after which she emptied the contents of her stomach contents into the pot between her legs.

"Okay, but I'll wait until you've finished throwing up... I have been thinking of what Theoplous said my love. Is there anything you have failed to tell me about your past, from your tryst with Ailith?"

"No Llyat, I have told you everything. You must believe in me and trust in my words; otherwise our future together will be dark."

"Okay, pass me your wrists bog booby, let's sort you out good and proper."

Heliana thrust her arms forward, took a deep breath, and tried to smile.

"Do your worst snake groin!" she snapped back.

Llyat took the pot and placed it on the planks. He glanced at the matted mush of undigested fish and then set about trying to relieve his lover's discomfort.

Three weeks later Llyat stood on the aft deck of the Banshees Wail and stared towards the island that the vessel fast approached. With him stood Heliana, Thias, and Irabo. Two paces to their right Highroar shouted out orders to the rest of the crew and to Theoplous in particular who steered by means of the great wheel. All had gathered as the first sight of land in weeks warmed their hearts and gave hope of an imminent journey's end. A group of dolphins played ahead of the vessel as it cut through the water and they brought much joy to Llyat and Heliana who had never before known such creatures even existed. The weeks had passed quickly and had given time for both reflexion and recuperation. Heliana's bump had continued to grow such that now she had a belly to match that of Highroar.

Like her companions, Heliana showed a darkening of her skin where it had been exposed to both the wind and the rays from Solaris since the storm had abated. Theoplous had kept himself to himself and barely grunted in Heliana's presence. Whenever the sailor's eyes fell on the girl they oozed malignant suspicion and mistrust. Thias had tried to revert to his old self but it was clear to Llyat that something sinister still held sway over the bard's emotions. He had tried several times to get Thias to talk about whatever it was that worried him but the bard would not open up. As for Llyat, he continued to grow inside. He had spent much time seeking the knowledge of geometry, implanted at his conception by the seed of Sir Raulyn. He even had Heliana teach him how to draw a perfect pentagram despite her continued denial that she knew anything more than she had revealed to date.

"I am aiming for those two mountains to the right of the main island," shouted Theoplous above the noise of the waves. "The peaks are actually islands separated from the main Lotus Isle by a short channel of turquoise water."

It was the first time the sailor had spoken since he had stormed out of the geometry lesson and the words caught Llyat off guard.

"It's bloody hot out here, even with a sea breeze," remarked Llyat.

"It's nice though," added Heliana, elbowing Llyat in the ribs.

"Do you see the clouds around the biggest?" added Theoplous. "They have always been there and always will be. That is where we will find the Lords of Light. I will anchor the Banshees Wail as close in as I can to its base and then arrange for us to be rowed ashore from there."

As the islands came ever closer Llyat began to make out a large town at the opposite end from the mountains and he asked what it was called.

"That is Ula'ree" answered Theoplous. "That name is known only to the Cuvar. To all others it is the town without a name for it has never needed one. It is the place of my birth, of my boyhood, and in where I did many other interesting things before I set off on the sea. Once Highroar has dropped us off by the twin peaks, known locally as the 'Enlightened Ones', he will head for the town and tie up in its harbour. There he will wait until we seek him out, give him payment, and plan our return journey."

The conversation then dwindled as a gathering of eyes scanned the coast alongside the vessel's approach to the distant mountains. Llyat marvelled at pristine white beaches, the turquoise sea, and the swathes of grass lands from which a hint of cinnamon drifted over the waves on an offshore wind. There were the areas of dense green forests, full of trees the likes of which did not grow in the Realm. Closer to the peaks, high craggy hills rose above the tree line and it was there that Llyat sensed he would find the iron quarry. The farm boy from Maplehill had come a long way but now his journey was coming to an end. He squeezed Heliana's hand and could only wonder what final challenges lay ahead for him. Without realising what he was doing, he tapped on the shoulder bag that always hung from his side.

Thias and Irabo pulled on the oars that propelled the small boat through the crystal-clear waves that rolled on to the silver beach that surrounded of the island mountain whose summit never revealed itself to the world. Theoplous sat in the rear with his hands on the rudder and eyes fixed on the outcrops of rock that broke through the shimmering sea. Llyat sat at in the bow alongside Heliana who looked into the water for minutes on end, mesmerised by the multitude of coloured fish that she spied there. She tugged on her lovers arm whenever something new and interesting came into view. It happened so often that Llyat started to get a little frustrated but finally the boat reached its destination. The smell of cinnamon grew stronger, carried from the main island on a breeze wind only to then swirl around the Peak of Enlightenment that was to be Llyat's new challenge. The youth jumped from the boat and let his feet land in the soft sand. Then he turned to face the sea one last time. There he saw the Banshees Wail making sail and heading off to Ula'ree. In that most fleeting of moments Llyat pictured Highroar quaffing and whoring in the island's town, hoping that those he had left behind would not rush to end their quest. Theo and Irabo pulled the boat out of the water and heaved it across sand so fine that it made walking difficult. At last they dragged it inside one of many caves that lay at the mountain's base.

"We will camp here for the night," insisted Theoplous once the group had recovered their land legs. "The change between night and day happens almost at once this deep into the ocean. It will also rain once Solaris passes for it does so every night. That is why there is so much vegetation on the mountain slopes. We must light a fire to keep away marauding crabs and other beasts who may wish to sample your flesh. All of us will all take turns to stand guard, except the woman, and in the morning, we will make the climb. It will take most of the day even though the path is good and well maintained."

"So, you've been here before," reasoned Llyat. "Why and for what purpose?"

"All will be revealed by the Lords of Light," replied the sailor as he then left to collect firewood and fruit. The others began to gut the fish they had brought with them for supper.

Day changed to night in the blink of an eye and Llyat agreed to take the first three-hour watch. The fish and strange fruits had gone down well and Theoplous had brought enough wood to keep the fire going all night. After their collective meal, all except Llyat lay in the soft sand, wishing the early arrival of sleep. The pressure on Heliana's bladder however required her to leave the cave. No sooner had she departed than the chorus of night creatures struck up outside and Heliana wasted no time in returning to Llyat's protective embrace.

"It's a bit more frightening in dark," she whispered so as not to disturb the others. "I was so scared that a crab would nip my arse that I dribbled down my legs. You know, I thought this place was a paradise when we first arrived but now I am not so sure."

"Everything will be fine," answered Llyat as his arms held her close. "It's just different."

"Llyat, I want you to answer a question but I only want the truth,"

"What is it that troubles you? What exactly do you want to know?"

"Did the Moirai demand a sacrifice? Do they want to take our child?"

Llyat began his tale. He told how the three old crones had desired a child of their own and that they expected he would provide it from the seed from his loins. He talked of their temptations, how they had posed as others to entice him, but how through the strength of his will he had refused to play their game and yet still gained the information needed to help him on his quest. Then he explained that this was why he no longer believed that the three fates controlled his life decisions. He had stood up to them, said no, and lived to tell of it. Heliana listened and although she could detect no evidence of lies, she found the story hard to believe.

"You fucked them, didn't you? Oh you disgusting bugger... Don't come near me with your poxy cock," she raged after which she raced to a corner of the cave and began to sob.

Llyat was about to go to her when a sudden clamour revealed Theoplous having another of his fits. The violent shaking, mixed with his guttural grunts and groans, disturbed all and prevented further sleep. Within seconds the sailor's tormented body was surrounded by his companions who together held his head and limbs. Trying to prevent him from inflicting harm on himself or others, they pushed him into the soft sand. Then Theoplous began to utter strange words. Most were undecipherable but some could just about be understood.

"The darkness beyond.... the ninth level.... the sight of the door."

The rambling continued for several minutes and once the shaking ceased Theoplous lay still upon the sand.

"I have witnessed several people who have suffered the demonic shakes, but none of them could talk in the midst of their fits," said Thias. "This was the strangest example I have ever seen."

"It's exactly what he did before the Moirai's door," added Llyat as he rolled the sailor onto his side in order to stop him choking. "What do you make of all that shit about darkness, the ninth level, and the door? My guess is he was making reference to the dig at the iron quarry and that the door he mentioned is the portal to the Underworld."

"I agree, that seems a most logical answer," added Thias. "What say you Irabo?"

"Spot on," replied the warrior. "But there is something not right about all this and I wish I knew what it was."

25

Solaris rose and cast a cosy warmth upon the weary travellers who lay within the sheltered cave beneath the Mountain of Enlightenment. Thias, being the last to take the watch, moved from his position at the cavern entrance and looked out upon the sea. Gentle waves lapped across the crystal waters while several sea turtles swam in silence through the ebb and flow on route for the second of the mountain islands. Dawn passed in an instant and as the temperature of the air jumped in leaps so did the monkeys that woke from within the foliage that hung over the entrance of Thias's temporary home. Theoplous was the first of the slumbering comrades to stir. He nodded to Thias in stuporous recognition of all being well, then rose to his feet before leaving to find a more secluded place to void his bladder.

"Are you okay?" asked the bard as the sailor passed.

"Couldn't be better, why do you ask?" came a half asleep reply.

"You had an attack of the shakes last night," said Thias calmly.

"Did I say anything that I need to be aware of?"

"Just the usual shit. The darkness beyond…. the ninth level…. the sight of the door. That stuff."

"I see," added Theo as his moved away and shouted back. "Raise the others. We will set off in half an hour. Your journey will soon be at an end bard. I will explain more during our climb."

Thias took a moment to reflect on the sailor's words as he sought to work out if they were as benign as their intent suggested. Then, as instructed, he began the process of waking the others. First he shook Llyat by the right boot and then Irabo by the shoulders while kneeling in the sand. He then moved to the back of the cave where he found Heliana lying on her side, her belly resting on the soft sand and appearing far larger that it had the previous evening. With a gentle hand that once caressed the lute he gently moved his fingertips over her exposed left hand. Heliana woke without haste and her eyes soon flicked open. Thias smiled.

"It is time to rise," he whispered softly as the young woman pushed herself up onto her rump. "Theo says we must leave here soon so you'd best move and do whatever you need outside."

Heliana stretched through her morning stiffness, yawned, and then scratched at the habit over her belly hump

"How is Theo this morning? What do you think's wrong with him?"

Thias just shrugged his shoulders and moved away in order to brake camp.

For two hours Theoplous led the climb up the steep mountain trail as it cut through the jungle of lush palm and fruit trees that provided a walking breakfast for the hungry trekkers. Thias marvelled at the sailor's knowledge and the quality of the strange fruits that he provided for them to eat. Most memorable were the yellow skinned crescent fruits that once peeled offered tasty cream-white flesh. There were strange green pods that when opened revealed hairy hard rocks. When these were cracked a sweet milky drink and a hard white inner crust were revealed which Theo showed how to eat with skillful insertions of his blade. All the while vast numbers of monkeys and beautiful yet odd looking birds monitored the group's progress as the heat of the day caused the jungle to steam.

At one of the frequent stops, made to allow Heliana to regain her breath, Theoplous spoke of his time spent in the excavations of the old iron quarry and how the nearer he had dug to the bottom, the more it had begun to affect his health. He also warned Thias to prepare himself for what he would feel and see there, should the Lords of Light agree to aid Llyat in his quest.

The jungle eventually gave way to rock and shale and by late afternoon the group entered the cloud that permanently shrouded the mountain's summit. There the temperature dropped several levels and the watery mist soon soaked all to their skin. It was a most welcome relief from the heat of the day but the visibility was poor and the path narrow and dangerous. Thias was reminded of their journey through the Ivory Pass and the events long past that had led them to Falahorn.

It took a further hour to navigate the high fog but eventually, having walked slower than even the small salamanders that crawled amongst the rocks, the mist cleared and the summit revealed itself to the ten eyes that gazed upon it. The trail plateaued a couple of hundred paces below the hillfort that was now visible atop of the mountain. On this flattened area of ground stood an enormous curved horn, an instrument the likes of which Thias had never heard of, let alone seen. At one end its mouth piece could be accessed via a raised platform and a series of ladders. Away at its distant end the opening of the instrument was so large and black that it reminded Thias of the cave's entrance he had left only hours earlier. It was secured to the mountain by means of massive timbers, taken from the hard wood trees of the mountain's slopes and which glistened apple red under the rays from Solaris. Thias looked on as Theoplous mounted the platform and gave three blasts on the trumpet. The noise was deep, thumping, and it caused the floor of the mountain to tremble. Jaws dropped and legs shook, so awesome was the impact of the blasts on the visitors' senses.

"Now they know we are here and will open their gates to greet us," shouted Theoplous from besides the horn's mouthpiece.

"And who are they?" shouted Thias despite knowing the answer.

"The Lords of Light, my masters. Prepare yourselves for a most interesting encounter!"

Theoplous climbed down from the platform and led the group on towards the summit. Ahead were earthworks the size of a small village. From where he stood on the path of slippery shale Thias assessed its manner of construction. Five concentric ditches and rolling banks of gathered scree surrounded the outer defences of the Lords of Lights' hillfort. At the top of each of these loose mounds was a wooden wall, also constructed from the red trees that grew on the slopes of the mountain. Strong gates were built into each wall and it was to first of these that Theoplous strode with much renewed energy while others plodded on in his wake. What lay beyond the highest of the five gates remained a mystery for it was impossible for Thias to judge due to the angle of his approach.

A great creaking of wood announced the opening of the first of the doors. It pushed forward and outwards and hid from view whoever or whatever lay behind them. The group continued on and some twenty paces from the out-turned gate, three figures stepped from behind the wood. Thias was taken aback by the sight that then met his eyes. Never once had he imagined the Lords to look like this and was surprised that Theoplous had not forewarned him of the nature of those who could weld gems. There before him stood three giants, at least third taller than himself. All were dark skinned, a shade deeper that Theoplous, and wore black leather tunics, trousers, boots, and thick aprons. Their arms like their faces were bare and rippled with muscles, no doubt honed by the great physical work that the three carried out each day upon the mountain's summit. Their skin was oiled with the sweat of their labours and their hands calloused and grime stained from the use of the hammers that they carried in their hands. Heads had been shaven save for a strip grown in a line from the centre of their foreheads to the napes of their necks.

Theoplous stopped before the giants and waited for the straggling others to catch up.

"Behold the Lords of Light," he declared with authority as he pointed to each of the giants in turn. "Here stand before you Maponos, Iovantucarus, and Lugus, Guardians of the Mountains of Enlightenment, and they whose help you have come so far to seek."

"And who are these people from the north lands that you have brought to our gates?" asked the one called Maponos with a voice deeper than any Thias had ever encountered. "Speak now for we are busy. There is much work we need to complete on this most special of days."

Theo bowed in deference to his masters.

"As you had instructed and as the alignment foretold, I have returned with the Marked," he began. "With him are companions who have remained loyal to the Enderdetag quest. The one we have sought has possession of the Gems and begs your aid in creating the key that will manipulate the door to the Underworld."

The three strange smiths stood motionless while their six eyes scanned their visitors.

"Step forward Marked and identify yourself," boomed Iovantucarus. "We have long wanted to meet you. The Moirai have played this same game many times and always the Marked was an imposter. Come and present yourself."

Llyat stepped forward before the three and without fear spoke out.

"I have proved myself before the Bard's of Valameer, the mighty wyvern Thamous, and the Moirai themselves. My likeness is to be found on the side of Sir Raulyn's tomb in the temple of Barad Elestor and within the Cave of Offerings before the portal of the Moirai Crypt. The wizards of Parandor unlocked my mind and released the ancient memory of those descended from Sir Raulyn the Grand. I have collected the Gems and brought them across the ocean in my shoulder bag. The Cuvar with me have facilitated my journey and I ask you to work with me to seal the Underworld for all time."

"That is all good but have you yet defeated Urthanock?" demanded the third Lord. "This must happen to satisfy the Enderdetag."

"Not as yet Lord Lugus," replied Theoplous, "The foul beast from across the water no doubt makes its way here as we speak its name."

"And who are these others with the Marked; the ones he identifies as Cuvar. Do they have names?" asked Iovantucarus.

"I am Thias Calavan, Royal Bard, friend, and trusted advisor to the late Phauless Gylewu," began Thias. "This young warrior is Irabo Basequin, a proud member of the City Watch of Parandor and believer in the Fates. The woman is the lover of the Marked. Her name is Heliana Pulchra and as you can see she carries his child. Her time to open up is but a few months away."

"The Marked has a child! This is most unexpected," said Maponos as he rubbed his chin. "This was not prophesised and we need to think through its implications."

The Three huddled and whispered. A moment later Maponos beckoned the visitors forward.

"Hurry inside for there is much to discuss. There are but two days until Solaris stands still and then begins the retreat into winter. As dictated by the rules of the three crones' game, we three must interrogate the one who calls himself the Marked. Let us hope for his sake that in this version of Fortunes Fate he passes the test."

Thias looked to Llyat who held Heliana as she teetered from the effects of a belly spasm.

"Is she alright?" Thias asked as he moved towards the couple.

"I sense the baby is as tired as I am," replied Heliana before addressing the three dark giants. "Do you have somewhere so I could lie down and rest for a while? It has been a most weary climb."

"Of course" replied Iovantucarus. "Follow us now as we enter our sacred domain. We will do all we can to make you comfortable."

The giant stepped forward, cradled Heliana in his muscular arms, and lifted her from the ground. Through the first gate they all went while Thias's eyes scanned for danger. Bridges led from gate to gate, all supported by arches that spanned the ditches between the ramparts of loose stone and the stake walls. Once through the final gate Thias took in all that lay before his eyes. In the centre of the space stood a dome, built long ago from a heavy white stone. Its surface had been smoothed but at regular intervals, at the height of the heads of the Lords of Light, pentagrams had been carved into the hard rock. Around this papular pinnacle three giant timbered smithies belched out white steam which then rolled over the ramparts and formed the clouds that surrounded the mountain. Though Thias tried his best to identify the nature of the Lords' labours he saw no evidence of metal which caused him much consternation. In between the smithies were four houses and together the seven completed an outer ring of buildings.

"They each have their own private space," whispered Theoplous into Thias ear as he watched the bard trying to make sense of it all. "The fourth building is the guest house, the hostel where we will rest during our stay. You will find it basic but not unpleasant."

"Theoplous," boomed out Maponos as the group approached the door to the hostel. "Make your friends comfortable, especially the woman and her precious cargo. Have the men meet with us by the diamond when Solaris sinks behind the ocean's edge; but not the one called Irabo. He will guard and watch over the girl."

"Of course Lord," answered the sailor. "Is there any food and drink available for them?"

"You will find a little if it has not rotted away," replied Lugus. "Go down amid trees first thing tomorrow Theoplous and return with whatever food you deem appropriate."

Iovantucarus gently placed Heliana on her feet before the hostel's door after which the three giants left and moved towards the central dome

"Do they not eat?" asked Thias.

"No, they do not," replied Theoplous as he opened the door to the hostel. "They feed off the energy that they forge in their smithies, that which nourishes the dragons and is the basis behind all magic in this Middle Realm."

One hour later the meeting began. Solaris had set and the night was calm and cloudless. Theoplous had directed those permitted inside the dome of stone while Irabo, as instructed, had stayed with Heliana. The woman had been left lying on a white sheet upon a straw mattress positioned on the ground floor. Once rested her pains had begun to subside. So it was that Llyat felt less guilt in abandoning her to meet with the three strange giants. Entrance into the dome was achieved through its one door, the thickest Thias had ever seen, and which once sealed was almost as dense as the stone walls themselves. The room was dark and foreboding, lit only by a slit of Mona's light that pierced the apex of the dome. Soon the great door opened a second time and the three Lords entered. Maponos pulled on a serpentine rope, coiled around a large hook at the side of the door. The thin slit in the roof opened into an oval aperture which let in sufficient of Mona's light to allow the occupants to gaze upon six chairs, three large and three more normal in size. All had been arranged in a tight circle beneath the oculus. A sudden gesture from Lugus's arm was all that was needed for Thias and his friends to take their places upon their chairs. Llyat took the middle of the smaller three with Thias to his right and Theoplous to his left. Iovantucarus took the chair opposite Llyat with Maponos to his left. Lugus placed his massive frame upon the last. Thias inhaled and tried to breathe away his tension; his nerve endings tingled as he prayed they had not walked into a trap.

"Theoplous has told you of the Cuvar, those who swear to protect the Marked," began Iovantucarus.

The giant stared at Llyat with whirlpool eyes that sucked in all they saw.

"However, he will only have told that which he is permitted to disclose. We will now seek to fill in the gaps. Maponos will now explain the truth behind the creation of the Cuvar and the conspiracy we have kept secret for so many years. Brother, please continue."

"Before I begin," said Maponos. "You need to understand who we are. Once in eons past, long before the birth of the Ancients there was a group of giants who lived in a vast land far to the west of these islands. Some, three so legend says, were caught on the edges of the greatest of all sea storms and their flimsy craft was sent across the vast ocean until one day it smashed upon the rocks of this mountain.

They had been blacksmiths in their land of origin and one day on climbing this very mountain they noted something most interesting. When they built their first forge they found it interacted with a dark energy that permeates the space between the stars. As they hammered away they created something new, a dark light, invisible to the eyes of men, and which had the most remarkable properties. Once produced in sufficient quantities it spread across all the lands and seas in which the primitive beasts of the Middle Realm thrived. The Ancients later learned to harness its powers by using their energy centres and this became the basis of all magic that you know of today. Then Chalis, having heard of the work of these great smiths, dropped her tears onto ground where dragons and wyverns could feed off this hammered out energy. Overtime the smiths were themselves effected by the dark light that as they forged and they ceased to age, or suffer sickness. They no longer had need for food and struck a pact with the dark force."

"You are those three, are you not," suggested Llyat as he sought the truth from out of the giants eyes.

"Yes we are," answered Lugus as he picked up the tale. "We will remain forever immortal as long as the door to the Underworld remains closed. That was the nature of our pact. Only once did we almost succumb to the fate of mortals. That was the time that Raulyn locked Urthanock behind the portal. The door can be opened but must be closed immediately. We sense that Urthanock seeks to capture the rest of his essence. In his deluded thinking he intends to leave the portal open for all time and usurp the power of the Moirai. This is how it was prophesised but as yet never come to pass. If you truly are marked by the Fortune Stars then all our fate is in your hands. So understand this; the conspiracy was always about keeping the portal closed. The Cuvar watched and in the end thwarted any attempt to open it in the many games the hags have played. The conspiracy was formed to ensure the maintenance of the dark light, the magic, and of course the dragons."

"Do you intend to thwart Llyat, the Marked that sits before you now?" demanded Thias.

"This game is different bard," added Maponos. "Look up through the oculus and see the perfect alignment. This is Enderdetag and it may indeed be the End of Days. We have blocked all others but if the lad convinces us he is of Raulyn's seed then we may yet help him."

"Continue then," ordered Llyat, devoid of fear and keen to hear how he would be tested.

"We were here when Raulyn came for our help," added Iovantucarus. "That knight was a great sage as well as a warrior and man of science. He had worked with the Great Thamous but unlike the wyvern was mortal. He saw in the Fortune Stars Urthanock's second coming and debated many long nights with us as to how he could ensure the beasts failure. We suggested that he stayed with us in the hope that we would bestow immortality upon his flesh but he decided to pursue a different end. He would encode his seed and seek out the Moirai. Once he had fucked one of the eternal hags the descendants of that fateful fornication would ensure a line of those who would forever seek to keep the portal closed for all time."

"You are the first Cuvar, aren't you?" proclaimed Llyat.

Thias noted the power of the youth, no longer the Maplehill nonentity.

"In deed we are," replied Iovantucarus. "There were five of us at the beginning; we three, Raulyn, and Thamous, although Cuvar was not the name we first used. Then Belanore came to see us when Raulyn went home to die. He was a great mystic, reader of the heavens and purveyor of prophecies. He took Raulyn's place and became the progenitor of the Cuvar cult."

"And how does Theoplous fit into all of this?" asked Thias.

The bard sensed that Llyat needed to hear the truth while the sailor sat with eyes part closed.

"Theoplous has been our chief emissary for the past twenty years," continued Iovantucarus. "We cannot move beyond the cloud and we have always had a go-between ourselves and the Cuvar. Theoplous is the current holder of that role and he fulfils it well. He has great respect for his masters."

"Where is the portal located?" demanded Llyat.

"Raulyn buried it with our help, using vast quantities of iron ore that we forged from out of the dark energy," added Maponos. "For many winters as Raulyn grew older we rained down ore from our forges in the sky and for a thousand years thereafter the slaves of the Ancients have mined it, not to find the Portal but enhance their wealth and science. As the ore became less dense the first cracks in the portal began to appear and those that worked the quarry began to suffer. Each hundred years that passed another plague befell them until the iron had all gone. Now only Theoplous knows which plie of remnants hides the door amid the belly of the nine level dig."

"Have any of you ever heard of the Ballad of Predestination?" asked Thias without warning.

"No, how does it go?" answered all three giants together.

"When will you test me?" demanded Llyat as he stood from his chair, "I am ready for anything you may ask."

"I understand your impatience lad but we need the light of Solaris in order to do that," replied Lugus for the three. "Return here tomorrow when the Lord of the Heavens climbs his peak. You should all rest now after your long journey but I advise the Marked to search through all that Raulyn encoded into his seed. We need poof you are the One."

"Would you like to see the Gems of Thamous?" asked Llyat as he slipped the strap of his shoulder bag from off his right shoulder.

"No, not until they are placed before the diamond," answered Iovantucarus. "Sleep well mortals, but please excuse us for we three brothers have still much to forge."

Morning eventually came and as Thias woke he heard a familiar sound from his youth, the pounding of hammers on anvils. The Lords of Light it seemed, continued with their eternal labour. Llyat lay beside Heliana whose belly cramps had dissipated. Irabo was already awake and sat in deep thought, no doubt thinking through all that Thias had told him of the conversation inside the dome. Soon Thias realised that Theoplous was absent and Irabo confirmed that the sailor had set off in the middle of the night to collect food, for that which the giants had kept had long been destroyed by the invisible rot that lingered in all air. Thias then spent the morning reflecting on all that had transpired since Phauless Gylewu had despatched him to the Grey Keep as a consequence of the Death Tubaria murders. He thought of those who had already sacrificed their lives to the Cuvar cause and the maintenance of magic in the world.

Amid that precious morning, a seed of enlightenment crept from out of the mountain peak and entered the bard's soul. Perhaps the Realm would be a better place without the mystical interference of those who both created and tapped into the dark light of magic. However, before he could develop his thoughts further Theoplous returned with a feast of jungle produce and clear cool water. Breakfast was not rushed and lasted until late morning. At last Theoplous declared Solaris to be approaching the Zenith and so led Thias and Llyat from out of the hostel and on to the Lords' dome.

Soon all were sat in the same seats as they had occupied the night before. Thias looked about the strange space and saw that Llyat was equally attentive. The walls were covered in geometric images; circles, triangles, curved lines, and straight ones. There were dots with ellipses around them, some larger than others and as their centres grew in size, so did the circles that surrounded them. Pentagrams were present in abundance as were incurved triangles. Thias hoped that Llyat had studied his memory well for the Lords of Light seemed well versed in the intricacies of shapes and numbers. The bard then looked to the stone flagged floor and beneath the circle of chairs there was yet another pentagram. This one however revealed a hollowed-out pit in the shape of the pentagon at the centre of its star. At the five points, there were further shaped pits of different sizes and this puzzled Thias until a second seed crept from out of the mountain. They matched the shapes of the five Gems of Thamous. Channels of black something, a strange substance that reflected no light connected the shapes at the tips of the five points with that of the pentagon which sat a foot lower in the floor. Thias then looked up to the oculus and noted an array of strange metal beams, rods, cogs, chains, and wheels. These it appeared would allow an object the size of a large boulder to be swung in front of the oculus. His eyes then drifted to one side and there he saw it, the pig-sized diamond whose rim was encased in a frame of the strange black substance.

"Tell me Theoplous, what leads you to believe that this youth is the true 'Marked' for whom we should weld the Gems?" asked Iovantucarus as he leaned forward.

"I sensed a powerful destiny when I first met the lad on the Banshees Wail and was soon convinced when he glowed in the presence of Masslewort before of the Bards of Valameer."

Theoplous spoke for many minutes and told of all that had happened to Llyat while in his presence. He related the disaster at the Bards Guild, how he had been entrusted with looking after the Gems when the Marked had returned to Parandor via the Rift. Finally, he mentioned the youth's encounter with the hermit Clotho and the visit to the Moirai Crypt at Harico.

Thias had then been asked to give his evidence in support of Llyat and he spoke for even longer. He retold events at the Bards Guild, the visit to the Gathering and what Llyat had shared of his conversation with Thamous. He talked in length about the runes and glyphs around Sir Raulyn's tomb and how Llyat had reacted when holding the sapphire; how he knew where to find the Amethyst. Then Thias told of the strange happenings inside the Wizards Guild, the unlocking of youth's mind and all that he had been witness to on the strange paper like walls. He spoke of his encounter with Urthanock in Avolire but did not declare the true identity of the Vessel lest the knowledge deflect Llyat from his mission. The Lords of Light listened, remained impassive, and did not respond.

"Tell us of your visit to the Eastern Marsh?" requested Lugus.

Llyat responded and talked in detail of all that had happened within the foul swamp. He related the details of Einar's death and as he did so tears flowed. The three giants showed even greater interest when Llyat spoke of his rescue by Thamous and how the wyvern had flown him to Avolire. When Llyat told of the special properties that each of the five Gems held, the Lords of Light leaned even closer and listened with such intent that Thias felt unnerved.

Maponos turned to his left to address his two brothers.

"Only Thamous and Raulyn, knew of the gift each carries."

"Look to the floor Llyat Emgar," ordered Iovantucarus. "Tell us what it is that you see. Be careful for this is the beginning of the test you must pass."

Thias looked on with trepidation as Llyat gazed upon the five-pointed star. After only a few seconds he began to describe the nature of the pentagram, the pentagon in its centre, and the shapes at its points; all much to the satisfaction of the three dark Lords.

"Clotho the hermit told me you would challenge me, but your question was not as difficult as I had imagined it would be," stated Llyat, knowing he had been correct so far.

"What precisely did the old man say?" asked Lugus.

"*If and when the Moirai release you, and your sailor friend delivers you to the Lotus Isles, then be prepared for a further test. The runes suggest you will be asked for a code. What form that will take I do not know. I suspect it will have something to do with the Lords of Light and the place called Brygaer Henuriaid. Perhaps it is a code from a Cuvar code wheel or may be something very different.*"

"Now however did he know that?" asked Iovantucarus as he rubbed his great jaw with his fingers. "Yet he was correct. Now for the key piece of knowledge that the Great Knight expected his heir to know. What is the value of Raulyn's Ratio?"

"What!" screeched Thias? "What kind of a question is that to ask a farm boy?"

"One point six two eight" answered Llyat without hesitation.

"Finally the Marked has revealed himself; he knows the golden ratio," grunted Maponos as the three giants smiled as one. "Welcome to our abode, although I must say you have left it to the last minute. We will weld the five into one tomorrow, at the high point of the equinox, amid the rare alignment of the Fortune Stars."

"I don't understand what just happened," shouted Thias as he twitched on his seat.

"You do not need to," answered Llyat as the Lords broke into spontaneous laughter. "I have one further question to ask so please indulge me."

"Only one?" replied Maponos. "We wait to hear it."

"I was given a message by the Moirai, some of which is in a language I cannot read even with the help of Raulyn's memory," said Llyat as he passed the paper over for the Lords of Light perusal.

"Some of this is written in our language; that of our original home in the west," stated Iovantucarus. "I translate the repeated elements thus; *'To manipulate the black, search for commonality inside the Vessel. Seek the Vermillion Mount.'* Then it changes to the language of the Ancients and next four lines are in verse: *'the first of these is that you're born, the second that all must die. The third you choose, the fourth is given, and the last, you know's a lie.'* It then continues to repeat the message about the Vermillion Mount"

"Do you know what that means?" asked Llyat as he scratched his head.

"No we do not," answered all three.

"What about you Thias, Theo, can you add insight to these words?"

The sailor shrugged his shoulders and looked nonplussed. Thias did not answer for it no longer seemed useful to contemplate the existence of the Ballad of Predestination.

"Be here an hour before noon tomorrow and bring the Gems of Thamous with you," ordered Iovantucarus after which the three Lords stood and promptly left the dome.

At the appointed hour on the most unique of celestial days, Thias sat beside Llyat on two chairs that had been positioned against the back wall of the dome, directly opposite the door of the welding room. Theoplous did not join them for he had left the mountain on the order of the Lords of Light. He had been despatched with a large spade and sent to the old iron quarry to clear the ground of the ninth level that covered the portal to the Underworld. The sailor had been unhappy to have missed out on being witness to the creation of the one key, but being a loyal servant of the 'Three', he obeyed without question. Theoplous's mission was to clear the way for Llyat to fulfil his destiny.

Heliana had continued to experience intermittent belly cramps yet insisted all was well before Llyat and Thias had left. Irabo had reassured Llyat that having a first baby was always a long and arduous experience and that he would care for Heliana during the upcoming meeting with the Lords of Light. Llyat was relieved to be able to leave for watching Heliana in pain caused him great distress.

"Are you ready for this?" asked Thias as his limbs twitched with anticipation of the long-awaited fusion. "I find it hard to believe that the day has come at last. I hope you have the Gems with you!"

"Of course, I have," replied Llyat with a smile on his stubble face. "Take deep breaths and calm yourself. We will soon have that which we need."

"Do you trust these buggers?" Thias asked as he clenched his fists. "Do you believe them to be a force for good or for evil?"

"That matters not," replied Llyat as he dismissed his friend's concerns. "We have a job to do. Whether in the fullness of time the outcome produces a better reality depends upon those that follow us. We do what we do in good faith and believe in our hearts it is the right way. Fuck all that fate, and destiny shit; today we have the chance to make our mark on this world. Now, be quiet, I hear footsteps approaching."

The door pushed open and the three dark giants strode into the structure they had long past built for this most special of days. They moved to the centre of the floor and checked the pentagram in detail. Maponos returned to the door, slid the bolts and then uncoiled the serpentine rope that hung on the hook beside the portal. For several minutes he pulled the rope one way and then another causing the diamond to at last swing into place beneath the oculus. Lugus then beckoned Llyat to join them and had him empty his shoulder bag. Iovantucarus reached into the folds of his black leather tunic and removed a strong steel pointed implement. The giant then proceeded to extract the largest emerald from off the hilt of the dagger of Kha and place it in the small pit that matched its shape at one of the pentagrams points. Then he did the same for the diamond, freeing it with great deftness and without apparent concern over its powers. The ruby was detached from its chain and laid to rest on the floor after which the sapphire and amethyst were dropped with care into their slots. Lugus gave Thias and Llyat a strange black hood for each to wear. They reflected no light and were like no others found in the Realm.

"We are almost ready now," began Lugus after he had demonstrated how and when the hoods were to be donned. "The Fortune Stars, as we three have always called them, now sit in perfect alignment as Solaris approaches his maximum. The Enderdetag is with us."

"Can you explain more about the alignment," asked Thias as memories of events in the Orrery of Belanore returned. "What causes them to straighten in such away after the passage of so many years?"

"The stars you see in the night sky are all part of a spiral cluster, one so big we cannot envision it with our eyes, only with our thoughts," answered Lugus. "The Fortune Stars are in the spinning tail of the cluster and as all rotate through long and ancient cycles so from time to time the line appears. The stars are of seven types and when aligned created a force that acts upon the three Realms of which we occupy the middle one. The stars seek to unify the three yet we must ensure they remain separated or the world as we know it ceases and the end of days will be upon us. You understand this Llyat don't you, even if it is too much for the bard?"

"Yes I do," answered Llyat without emotion.

"May I ask about the diamond?" said Thias as he looked to the stone below the oculus. "How does it work? How does it weld the Gems? What exactly will happen today?"

"We still have some time before Solaris is directly overhead so let me answer your questions," replied Maponos. "Sir Raulyn left us a great uncut diamond he had found on his travels to some far distant shore. We had previously debated with him how best to fashion a gemstone onto what we call the Lentiloid, that which shaped like a lentil it can bend and focus the power of Solaris onto a single point. We calculated we needed a vast diamond to do such a job and he said at once that he knew where to find one. However, to generate the power needed, the surface of the jewel had to be cut and curved precisely and then highly polished. You will no doubt know already that diamond is the hardest of all substances and will therefore understand why it has taken a thousand years to get it ready for its moment of destiny."

"But I still don't understand how it the weld will work," added Thias as he looked from ceiling to floor and then back again.

"We created dark matter from the dark light, and it is a substance most strange, neither metal nor anything else," interrupted Iovantucarus as he pointed to the black channels and the pentagonal pit on the floor. "We will focus the light of Solaris, using the diamond and alignment of the Fortune Stars, onto the pentagon pit. The intense heat generated will travel up the black up channels and melt the gems which will then flow down and meet together to form one whole. Solaris will then move past the oculus, the one will cool, and the key to the underworld will have been created. Thamous used his fire, but Raulyn sensed the wyvern would be dead by this day. So as you will see, we have but one chance to get this right."

"Have you ever tried this experiment on any other stones and did it work?" asked Thias.

The bard was concerned he and Llyat were stepping into an unknown world of fantasy.

"No we haven't," responded Iovantucarus as he shrugged his shoulders. "But it is too late now to change the course of your fate. Look how the light increases. Solaris will be at zenith in less than a minute. Put on your black hoods or else be blind for the rest of your lives

Thias, like Llyat, wasted no time and pulled the strange black material over his head. He was just about to ask what would happen next when the whole dome shook. The ground seemed to tremble as if threatening to turn into quicksand. The bard's feet felt the heat from the stone floor as sounds like the cracking of burning wood and the bubbling of porridge in the pot banged against his eardrums. An odd smell filled the air and although similar to burning iron, it was uniquely malodourous and acrid. Soon all fell quiet and a moment later a voice boomed out.

"You may remove your hoods and gaze upon what we have achieved," shouted Iovantucarus.

As he did so Thias opened his eyes and looked to the floor. The Gems had gone and left empty black pits. The central pentagon remained and in that moment Thias believed he had been cheated.

"There is nothing there," he screamed. "What do we do now?"

"Look back to the floor," replied Llyat. "Lugus is lifting something with the edge of his knife."

A moment later a pentagon of intense black was thrust into Llyat's hand.

"The five are now one," shouted Maponos as a wide smile spread across his face.

Llyat held the strange object in his grip. His jaw dropped in a trance of wonderment and awe. It was then passed to Thias who examined it in minute detail, looking for a surface yet just seeing black. A minute later Thias passed it back to Llyat and then moved forward to examine the floor. It was as if nothing had ever been there and as he looked to the Lords of Light it became clear that they were equally surprised at the ease with which the key had been formed. Maponos strode towards the serpentine rope and began the process of retracting the diamond from in front of the oculus. Soon all was as it had been before the welding process had begun. Thias returned to Llyat and they began to contemplate what the door the portal to the Underworld could be made from to require the use of such a bizarre key. A thunderous knocking on the door ended their conversation.

"Who dares disturb us?" boomed out Maponos as he moved towards the portal.

"It is I, Irabo, and I have important news for Llyat."

"Open the door Lugus and see what agitates the warrior so," ordered Iovantucarus. "We have finished most of what we came here to do."

In an instant the door was pulled open and Irabo shouted from its edge.

"Heliana is in severe discomfort and there are signs of blood."

"The red mark shows at the time of the welding," mused Lugus. "How very interesting."

Llyat jumped up and made for the door. Irabo took a pace forward and beckoned to his friend. The black pentagon still rested in Llyat's hand, an object so light as to be barely noticeable and soon forgotten in the madness of the moment. One very muscular arm extended out across the door, followed by Maponos's massive frame. Thias rose to his feet and followed in Llyat's footsteps, expecting there to be trouble.

"No so fast, Marked of the Maples," thundered the giant. "We still have instructions to give before you care for the woman who carries the seed of your loins. These words are of vital importance so you must listen carefully to what we have to say."

"Can they not wait, at least until we are sure that the child is well," pleaded Thias.

"Only if you return within the hour, ready to proceed to the portal,"

"I agree to your terms," shouted Llyat before forcing Maponos to one side.

"Do not be late," ordered the giant while Llyat raced off to hostel.

Thias entered behind Llyat and was relieved to see Heliana smiling.

"She looks much better than she did five minutes ago," whispered Irabo into Thias's ear.

"What has happened love?" demanded Llyat as Heliana sought to rise and remove the blood stained sheet upon which she had lain.

"I popped an arse grape that's all," she responded. "I will need something new to wear. It had been growing since the time of my last gush. I know them to be commonplace when a child is in the belly. It was the main cause of my discomfort as we climbed to this place but I feel much relived now it has burst."

"It seems I worried over nothing," whispered Irabo as he took the bloody sheet from Heliana's hands. "I will dispose of this and see if the Lords of Light have any more; perhaps something to replace your priest's garb."

"Let's do that together while Heliana cleans her nether regions," suggested Llyat. "That is of course if you are sure all is well my love."

"Yes please do that and let me wash in private. Llyat go on ahead with Irabo but I just need a few words in private with Thias. Do not worry, I just want to ask him to look after you and I have a message for him should he not return."

Thias watched as Llyat shrugged his shoulders yet did not stay to question his lover. The Marked looked down to the black key clutched in his right hand, slipped it into his shoulder bag, and left the room in haste.

"I want you to listen carefully Thias for I know you and Llyat must soon leave and I may never see either of you again," she began. "I have some things to say to you but first you must promise to keep all of my words secret and never speak them to anyone else. Will you agree to hold my confidence?"

"Yes I will, answered Thias," unsure as to whether this was the appropriate answer.

"I think there is a chance that I may be losing the baby. I want you to know that just in case you and Llyat succeed in your quest. You could then forewarn him on your return, to the possibility of bad news. But if he is to die he must do so in the firm belief his child will carry on in his place. Do you understand?"

"Yes I do and I will honour the trust you have paced in me."

"There is something else that you need to be aware of Thias," she continued. "When I was in the Moirai Crypt and their door was opened for the briefest of moments in time, an idea came to me."

"What are you saying, I'm not sure I understand?"

"Could it be that you and I have been but counters in a game that the old hags began many years ago. Perhaps we too have been manipulated by the Moirai. Even if that is the truth we must support Llyat despite any costs to ourselves. Do you understand what I am saying?"

"I hear you but I am not sure I agree," responded Thias while his thoughts whirled like a twister in the Dragonas. "I for one am sure I control that which I chose to do."

"I fear that Llyat and our baby are to be taken by the wrinkled witches," continued Heliana as she took hold of Thias's hand and squeezed. "My future appears black and my mind is being tortured. I have no idea how Llyat can defeat Urthanock, especially given we still have no knowledge of the ballad that can kill the fucking beast. Thias, you must do all you can to help Llyat, even if it means sacrificing yourself to his cause. This is what I ask of you now. It is your fate; it is your destiny. Will you do that for me? Will you do that for Llyat?"

"I promise on all that has ever been dear to me and yet I do not plan to die," replied Thias with as much bravado as he could muster. "Should Llyat fall, he will do so only once I am dead. As long as breath moves through my throat, I swear I will protect the Marked. But what of Irabo, do you sense he too could be being manipulated?"

"No chance, he is just nobody; although a most honourable and loyal nonentity. He just happened to be in the wrong place at the wrong time; caught up in this unholy mess by no fault of his own. He will however be by my side while you and Llyat seek out Urthanock. I know he will care for me as best he can."

The door to the hostel burst open. Llyat and Irabo returned with a pile of sheets they had obtained from the Lords of Light which were soon placed on the bed before Heliana's feet. The Lords had suggested that dresses could be fashioned from the sheets with a little thought and care. Llyat then proceed to kiss and hug Heliana until she at last pushed him away.

"Llyat you must go now," she said with tears welling. "Go and make the world safe for us. We will be here waiting in expectation of a victorious return."

"No," replied Llyat, "I will come back for one last hug once my business with the Lords of Light is concluded."

A little later Thias and Llyat made their way over to the dome for their final meeting with the giants. The encounter lasted for half an hour during which the Lords of Light did most of the talking. The first thing they had Llyat do was to demonstrate that he still had the black pentagon and were content when it was lifted briefly out of the shoulder bag and passed before their eyes. They went on to describe the route the two travellers would need to take to locate the old iron quarry. First they must use the boat which Theoplous should have left in the cave where they had spent their first night under the mountain. The sailor had several others hidden on the landward side of the island, one of which he should have used for his own passage onwards. Once they had crossed the shallow waters to the main island they were to head to the south and west and on towards the range of brown hills that would soon meet their gaze. The walk was a significant one and would perhaps take half a day. If longer they would likely have gone astray. The quarry sat amid the hills and would be easy to see from any of the taller summits.

Thias asked what they would find there and why there were nine levels. The answer that came was unexpected. Every one hundred years or so as the ore was extracted, great disasters fell upon those who sort to profit from the Lord of Light's deposits. Amongst the ruined building at each level they would find skeletal remains that would explain what had befallen the unfortunates present when those disasters came to call. Thias asked why or who or what had caused such evil slaughters only to be told it had not been the doing of the Lords of Light. Llyat asked if the recurring deaths were a consequence of being close to the portal of the Underworld, a question that was answered by an affirmative nod of the head. Thias then asked about the portal's appearance and it was Maponos who chose to answer this final question.

"Theoplous should have cleared away the soil over the umbilicus of the ninth level. There you will see, flat against the bedrock a large incurved triangle as wide as the base of this dome. In its centre is a depression that matches the pentagon you carry in your bag. Once the key is pushed into place the portal will open but for the world to continue as we know it you must close it immediately and lock it forever. Just lift the pentagon from its resting place and the door wil close. You will have very little time to place Urthanock inside. Do you understand what I say?"

"Yes, I do," said Llyat. "But what if Urthanock doesn't show?"

"He will, of that we are certain," replied the Maponos.

Throughout the conversation Thias thought of all the dangers that lay ahead. Heliana's words and the promises he had made to her rested at the forefront of his mind. He pondered on the concept of self-sacrifice and whether he would be brave enough for such a heroic act. His thoughts swirled and he tried to imagine a life of meaning should Llyat, Heliana, and their baby fail to survive the coming hours. At risk of mental paralysis he then stopped thinking about the immense challenge that lay ahead. He recalled Heliana's message that perhaps he too had been conceived and manipulated as if a counter in a devious game of Fate. If this was all just play, then nothing really mattered at all.

26

On his release from the darkness of the barrow, Urthanock skirted around the edge of Harico and thereafter entered the dense oak forest that surrounded the quaint village. The beast was determined to keep walking in a straight line. The Vessel he had occupied, had aligned itself to the north and west using Solaris as its guide. It expected little problem in maintaining that direction. However, as night fell and the trees closed in, the Lord over Fear became disorientated and no longer felt so confident. After an hour of darkness Urthanock realised he had made a mistake in trusting the skill sets of his Vessel. It would most certainly have been better to have walked west upon the ridge of the Harico Hills and then north once they had intersected with the road that led from Parandor to the Badlands. As he stumbled through the dark, strange animal noises seeped out of the black, teased his senses and brought back memories of primordial times. Between the massive ancient oaks shadows crept and although he was without fear they heighted his awareness of being lost. Upon the trunks of the gnarled old trees, where shafts of Mona's light had penetrated small patches in the tree canopy, faces of captured spirits formed. They tormented the Vessel's eyes as its feet pressed on regardless. The Vessel then crashed through an area of dense foliage where the trees were thinner but where thick growths of flowering bushes had sprouted.

"Once again you made the wrong choice," said the voice of Methladon Heyn. "It must be true what they say about reptiles; their brains are no bigger than those of marsh bugs."

"Fuck off," snapped back Urthanock's essence.

"I will go when I am ready and not before. You destroyed what I once was, but now I have a chance to thwart your plans. Try as you might you will never rid yourself of my presence. As the years turn to thousands you will wish you had never heard the name of Heyn."

"Fuck off!" screamed Urthanock; so loud as to cause the beasts of the forest to fall silent.

"These are my woods and I will make as much noise as I like," laughed a different voice from high in an adjacent oak.

The Vessel swung around and stared in the direction of this new an unexpected sound. Then as its eyes grew accustomed to the darkness between the oak's branches a wizen face appeared, lit by Mona in the one place she had managed to penetrate the dark.

"Who the fuck are you and what do you want?" snarled Urthanock. "Piss off before I fry you and your fucking tree."

"My name is Clotho. These are my woods and I thought you may want some help given you have been walking in circles for some time now."

Urthanock felt his anger soar.

"What are you doing in this forest so long into the night?" demanded the beast. "Who exactly are you?"

"I am but an old hermit of these woods and I know things others do not. The trees are my home and those that dwell beneath its canopy my friends. I see you wear the armour of those who fight the cause of the Lizardmen yet you only have a half-scaled face and limbs of the man race. From those facts alone I know who you are."

"Then say who," snapped back Urthanock as he pulled his sword from its sheath. "You cannot possibly know who I am old man."

"You are the blacksmith's boy from Maplehill, infected with the spirit of a long deceased swine of the swamp," continued Clotho as his face moved higher into the trees. "I also know where you have been and where you are heading. You however no nothing of me."

"How do you know such things," demanded Urthanock while lifting his blade high. "Who has spoken about me? Have you also met with the Moirai?"

"No I have not." sniggered the old man. "A youth by the name of Llyat told me all about you."

"So the bastard that calls himself the Marked has passed this way. How long ago was it that you met with him?"

"Who can say?" laughed Clotho as the beast fumed.

"Tell me old man, before I run you through."

"A day, a couple of days, a week perhaps, no a month; it makes no difference," laughed Clotho. "By now he should be at sea and well beyond the reach of your foul claws."

"Lead me out of these woods and I will make it worth your while?" ordered Urthanock as Clotho's face disappeared and disorientated the beast further.

"I could do so if I so desired," answered the hermit as his voice grew more distant.

"Then do it,"

"I said I can, I didn't say I would," came a reply as quiet as a whisper.

"Come back you old cunt," bellowed Urthanock into the black. "I will skin your wrinkled hide and fashion boots out of your entrails should I ever get my hands on you. Have you no advice for me?"

"Beware the Vermillion Mount," echoed a faint whisper through the ancient oaks.

"Whoever that was, you handled him well," sneered the voice of Methladon. "You need a new title for no longer is Lord over Fear fit for purpose. I propose 'Urthanock the Unstable, Usurper of the Ugly, and Underling of the Useless.'"

"Give me some fucking peace!" screamed the foul Lord and with that the voice went away.

Four days later, a dehydrated Vessel cashed out from the oak forest and staggered down to the Estuary of New Beginnings only to throw itself into the water and drink until it could take no more. Then it threw up and started to guzzle again. It had been the most difficult of treks given that the trees in the forest had seemed to constantly move and form barriers in whichever direction had Urthanock had attempted to travel. It was as if nature itself had turned against him. Only once did he eat, having found a fawn that had a fractured leg, no doubt also lost and seeking safe passage out of the dense sylvanian prison. He had ripped off its fur in temper, leaving only scrag ends of meat attached to the skeleton which he had flash cooked with fire from his hands. He had found no water in the woods and so it was with great relief he fell into the Tiaryer. Throughout all of the Vessel's meanderings Methladon Heyn's voice had hammered away inside its head, always tormenting Urthanock to the point where he had begun to inflict wounds on the smooth skinned side of the Vessel's split face. Some cuts went deep and had bled profusely but most were now scabbed over.

Once the Vessel's thirst had been satiated Urthanock looked around for signs of activity but saw nothing that would pose a threat to his presence. To the west and on the opposite bank, a thousand paces from his current position, stood mighty Parandor, all intact as if no battle had ever been waged there. Before its walls a vast swathe of people were busy reconstructing the harbour. There was not a Lizardman, ogre, or other beast to be seen and as he stood and stared Urthanock could not comprehend how his army had been obliterated with such apparent ease. Some minutes later he began a forced march along the shoreline in order to seek out a means, other than swimming, of crossing the water amid a fast out-going tide. Soon he came upon a small rowing boat pulled up onto the beach above the high-water mark. The tethering rope at its bow had been anchored to the ground by a moveable but significant rock. He decided his best course of action would be to cross the river and under the cover of darkness make enquires as to the whereabouts of any seafaring ships that he could later purloin. Without wasting further time, and despite a constant barrage of insults from Methladon's perpetual chatter, Urthanock freed the boat from the rock and dragged it down to the water's edge. Jumping in without great skill or thought, the current caught hold of the flimsy craft and began to whisk it away towards the ocean.

Night approached quickly and with the low cloud it was soon dank and dark. By the time Urthanock had forced the oars into the rowlocks and gained some semblance of control the boat had drifted a significant distance downstream. As he turned to strike back for Parandor, Urthanock spied an impressive vessel. The Masters Catch lay at anchor where it had been since before the start of the Battle of Parandor. For the first time in several days the swamp beast felt a surge of positive energy and despite the insults that bombarded his ears, Urthanock knew what to do next. He turned the rowing boat again and with the tide doing most of the work he used just one oar to steer towards the rear of the ketch. On the darkest of all evenings he approached the fishing boat in silence. Soon he had tied up to its rudder and prepared to board the vessel. First off he listened for noise of the crew which was not easy given Methladon's background prattle. Just as he was about to climb aboard he heard the sounds of many men talking and so decided to wait until all fell silent.

"You take the first watch Farrell while the rest of us turn in," ordered a voice of authority that carried with ease over the graveyard quiet of the estuary. "Rotate as follows, Dudley next, then Norwell, Manton, and finally Terrel. We will sail for the fishing grounds as soon as Terrel's watch is passed. Rest well for I will crack the whip o' the morn."

"Five plus the Captain," screeched Methladon into the Vessel's ears. "Five, five, you'll never take five; they'll cut you, and skewer you, and burn you alive."

Urthanock shook the Vessel's head in a forlorn attempt to block out his persecutor. He then sat back down in the dinghy to give the fishermen ample time to fall asleep. It was perhaps an hour later when he made his move on Farrell. The fishing ketch had resounded to a concert of snoring for some considerable time and as the Vessel sneaked onto the deck, even the sentry slept.

"Wake him gently," whispered Methladon. "He probably has a large family to feed and a doting wench who panders to his vices, unlike you who are loathed by every creature that walks, crawls, or slithers over these lands."

"Shut it," snapped Urthanock and the voice fell quiet.

Urthanock crept behind the unfortunate soul who sat in peaceful oblivion against an empty fish barrel that stood upright between the two masts. His blade flicked forward and then up. It entered Farrell under the jaw and pushed with a crunch into the fisherman's brain. It was a clean kill and left no mess. Nor did it make significant noise. The Vessel caught Farrell before his body clattered to the deck and it then laid the limp weight down while retracting the blade that had brought death in the night.

"You are one cruel beast, do you know that?" mind bellowed the voice of Methladon.

Urthanock ignored his tormentor and proceeded to strip off his armour and the rags he wore beneath the plate. He made sure that he recovered the crumpled paper given to him by the Moirai and which he still needed to decipher. Having stripped Farrell he dressed the Vessel in clothes that reeked of stale sweat and rancid fish.

"So, what are you going to do with his body?" sneered the voice. "You are hungry so eat it."

"I'm going to hang him from the fucking mast," snarled Urthanock, "and when I get you into the Underworld you are going to regret every fucking word you've said this day."

"Suck on my soul, slime scale of the swamp!"

Captain Amos Whitebeard had never in all his years expected to be woken by a face half lizard. He jumped bolt upright with a heart ponding so fierce that it echoed off the walls of his small cabin. He made to scream but a greased rag was thrust into his mouth after which a fist slammed against his bulbous nose. The flesh of the Captain's nostrils ruptured in several places and crimson shot to both left and right. As Whitebeard's whiskers turned red, the old seadog was dragged with contempt from out of his cabin and thrown upon the deck of the Masters Catch. There the confused and bewildered Captain writhed in pain, his groans shaking the bulwarks while his tears dripped upon the salt caked deck. The rest of the crew stirred, scuttled, and seconds later emerged through the door that led to the crew's quarters. All four rushed forward brandishing knives but stopped as their eyes looked upon a half-scaled face atop of a man that wore their shipmate's clothes. A sword pointed down to the throat of their whimpering Captain.

"You're next in command Dudley," shouted one of the fishermen. "What do we do next?"

"Who are you and what the fuck are you doing," shouted Dudley as his eyes glared, his face flushed, and his top lip retracted to expose a row of blackened teeth. "What have you done with Farrell?"

"If that is the name of your sentry then gaze upon the top of your main mast," replied Urthanock as he pointed up with the index finger of his deformed left hand.

The four deckhands looked up as directed. So also did the Captain despite water filled eyes turned on by the insult to his nose. There hanging from the tall pole, a third of the way to its high point, was the sentry who had failed his watch. A thick rope had been fixed to the mast by a great and complicated knot. Hooks attached to each of its free ends passed through the chest skin and under the collarbones of the naked Farrell before re-emerging in his neck. As the wind blew strongly down the estuary the corpse swayed before the eyes of his comrades like some diabolical flag of war.

"You bastard," screamed one of the other crew and as all took a menacing step forward.

Yet that was as far as they got. Urthanock pointed his blade forward and from its tip he projected a bolt of blue fire that engulfed the four fishermen and forced them into the air. There he held them, arms and legs stretched wide as their weapons clattered upon the deck. As all experienced the pain of the floating stretch, Urthanock kicked Whitebeard in the ribs and snarled through a spray of venomous spittle.

"Crawl over there and throw their weapons over the side," he ordered with more than a hint of reptilian lisp. "Do not attempt anything foolish old man for I am not in the mood to waste time on scum such as you."

"You wouldn't speak like that if the odds were more even," whispered the voice. "I wager they will have killed you by the time you reach the Lotus Isles.

"Fuck off Heyn!" bellowed Urthanock and the shock wave from his voice rippled out across the flowing waters of the Tiaryer.

"What does that mean," asked the terrified Captain. "Do I continue as ordered?"

"Yes, you fucking do; just get on with it."

Once the confused Amos Whitebeard had completed his task he was lifted in the air by the same force that held and stretched the others. As the five hung in agony Urthanock began to spell out the means by which the fishermen could save their lives.

"There is a task that I require of you. You will sail to the Lotus Isles and should you deliver me there before the summer solstice then you will be free to return to your homes. Fail and you will all die the most horrible of deaths. I have great power and you now feel but a morsel of its ferocity. Do as I demand and you shall live. Now answer one by one for we have not the time to waste on written contracts."

All answered aye, except for one.

"Dudley, say aye," ordered Whitebeard as he looked to the man.

"The fuck I will," snarled the fisherman. "He will need to stick the islands up his arse before I will bend to his will."

Urthanock laughed and Dudley exploded. Flesh, bone, and entrails splattered on all including Urthanock, but the demonstration had its desired effect.

"We will take you there as soon as you release us from your spell great Lord," said Whitebeard having lost control of his bladder. "We can still make the ocean before the tide turns."

"So be it," snapped back Urthanock as he dropped the four to the deck.

The weeks at sea passed in relative calm. The Captain and his remaining crew worked hard to ensure the Masters Catch sped across the ocean as fast as it sails could carry it. They all prayed each long day and restless night that they would soon reach the Lotus isles and see the beast depart without further recourse to murder. The Catch had left the estuary with few provisions, not more than one week's worth, even on rations. Given their short supply of potable water the Captain had proposed that all pots, buckets, and empty fish tubs would all be left open on deck in order to collect any rain that fell during the voyage. Whitebeard had confirmed that the further they progressed upon the seas the hotter the air would become. They need to collect and conserve water from the outset. Urthanock had agreed to this strategy and much to the relief of the fishermen the mid ocean squalls and storms provided ample water to fill every available container.

Food was more of a problem. Despite dangling lines from the rear of the Catch, few fish were caught, mostly due to the absence of any quality bait with which to lure them to the hooks. By the end of the second week hunger was rife and starvation only kept at bay when a large shoal of flying fish dropped a significant quantity of their relatives upon on the deck of the ketch. These were all quickly gutted and salted with the small amount of the white crystals found in the ship's galley. The diet of salty fish at least kept the hunger pains away for another week but the thirst induced depleted the water stores at a faster rate than either the Captain or Urthanock had deemed safe. All throughout the long days and restless nights the voice of Methladon's essence hammered away inside the vessels skull, forever criticising, constantly sniping, undermining, and always seeking to push Urthanock further from the safe constraints of sanity.

By the end of the third week all were hungry again. The heat was becoming intense and the putrefying corpse of Farrell became so offensive that the Captain begged Urthanock to cut it down. He stated it would be best to throw it to the large fish with the grey back triangles that now followed the boat and circled it like the scavenging bald necked birds of the Dragonas. Urthanock did not see what all the fuss was about but after two days of constant demands and the growing lethargy of the crew he at last relented. And so it was that the beast of the swamps shinned up the mast late one afternoon and severed the rope that held the corpse aloft. It fell with a thud and as it hit the deck its gross purple and swollen belly burst open and scattered entrails so putrid and foul smelling that all except Urthanock immediate voided anything that was left in their stomachs. So, debilitating was this stench to the fishermen that Urthanock himself had to swab the decks clean with buckets of salt water hauled from the sea; much to Methladon's delight.

The crew looked on as the job neared completion and to a man they tried to second guess why Urthanock had cut off Farrell's head and kept it after feeding the fish with the rest of the body. Soon it became obvious for Urthanock was determined to terrorise his captives further. Taking hold of the head in both hands the beast smashed it against a metal ring that circled a section of the mizzen mast. The bony container cracked open after which Urthanock extracted the brain with several flicks of the point of his blade. He then placed the rotting gloop inside an empty bowl filled with rain water and fired the pot with blue flame from his hands. The water boiled fiercely and soon a ghost-grey soup had formed in the pot. He stirred it and allowed it to cool while eight eyes watched in horror. The remains of the head was in the meantime thrown to the fish.

"Soup anyone? You're most welcome to try some. I am not a selfish Lord."

Urthanock scooped some liquid from out of the pot with a cup that had also been collecting rainwater. None of the fishermen accepted the invitation and the one who went by the name of Manton began to vomit all over again.

"That's it, the shows over," shouted Urthanock as he finished the contents of the bowl and ended his feast with a thunderous belch. "Now get back to work."

"You really are one sick fucker," shouted the voice.

Four days later the Lotus Isles appeared on the distant horizon as Urthanock and Amos Whitebeard stood at the bow of The Masters Catch while it rose and fell amid the ocean swell. A dozen large and strange fish with holes in the back of their heads escorted the Catch as it cut through the foam that its bow created. The Lord over Fear looked to the distant island with twin peaks at one end and then turned to the old sea dog beside him.

"Have you ever been to these islands before?"

"Only once, many years ago when I was chartered to carry some cargo there," replied the Captain. "We make our living from what we catch in waters much closer to Parandor. Anything caught this far out would rot down to a stinking pulp by the time we returned."

"I don't need to hear your fucking life story old man. What do you know of this place? Are those two mountains the only ones in the lotus Isles? I seek the 'Twin Peaks of Enlightenment'. Is that they that stand out to the right?"

"Yes Lord. That is what they were referred to on an old chart I once had in my youth. There are no other mountains, just a few low lying hills, much verdant jungle, and a mass of cinnamon grass. At the far end of the island, furthest from the twin peaks you will find the town of the dark people, one which has no name for the natives have never had need for one."

"You talk too much old man," snarled Urthanock. "I advise you to keep your answers short and to the point."

"Are we to drop you off in the harbour of that town?" asked Whitebeard as he shuffled a pace to his right.

"No, head for the mountains. I wish to make landfall on the main island as close to the peaks as possible for the place that I seek is said to lay in their shadows."

"Where exactly are you seeking?" the Captain dared to ask. "Perhaps I have also heard of that place and may be able to point you in the right direction once you are ashore.

"I seek the door to the Underworld."

Urthanock stared with eyes of fire red, so hot they threatened the Captain's soul.

"I cannot help you there my Lord," answered Whitebeard as he moved another pace away.

"I thought not, now fuck off and steer this boat into a safe cove or sheltered beach. Then I will leave you be."

"As you command Lord," replied Whitebeard as he dropped his head and scuttled away to give out further orders.

Urthanock gazed out from the front of the boat as it forced its way through the through gentle waves and as the mountains loomed ever closer. The crew whispered to each other as they carried out their tasks and Urthanock was certain they were plotting his demise.

"They'll never let you off this ship," said the voice of Methladon. "If you keep your back turned for much longer you will miss the push from behind. Then you will spend the rest of eternity swimming for your life."

"Fuck off Heyn, I will listen to you no more," screamed the Dark Lord

Turning away from the salt spray Urthanock began his trudge back through the boat. He forced his Vessel to the back of the ketch and once there stood beside the Captain who had taken back the role of helmsman from the fisherman called Norwell. After another hour had passed and the twin peaks loomed large to the right, a bay with a beach of platinum sand approached at speed.

"I'll take the wheel from here," ordered Urthanock, "just on the oft chance you decide to double-cross me. I have heard you all whispering, no doubt intent on thwarting my plans."

"We would do no such thing Lord," replied the Captain as his limbs began to tremble. "We just desire to return to Parandor."

"Move now arsehole or I swear by your mother's soul I will rip you limb from limb."

Amos Whitebeard fled for his life, gathered his crew and together, then stood in terror on the deck between the main and the mizzen masts. Pointing the Masters Catch towards the beach and with no attempt to slow it down, Urthanock lifted his good hand from off the wheel and pointed it directly at the fishermen. A blue bolt of light shot from his finger tips and lifted the four into the air. Then limbs were stretched, trunks extended, and necks snapped as Urthanock created another of his knots. When he was at last content with its configuration he snapped his fingers and the ball of crushed humanity shot out to sea. The ocean splashed, the boat careered on, and the sounds of maniacal laughter scattered the monkeys in the trees that lined the fast approaching beach. The Masters Catch ran aground upon a reef some two hundred paces from the shore proper. The sudden deceleration and shock to the old boats timbers caused Urthanock to fly forward over the ship's wheel where the Vessel's head then connected with the main mast. Urthanock was stunned, a mere mortal would have died, but Methladon's voice was unimpaired.

"Now what dullard? What plans does your cracked skull have for us?"

Urthanock staggered to the back of the ketch and with some difficulty climbed down into the rowing boat which was still tied where he had left it despite its long crossing of the ocean. He untied his complicated knot and as the small boat drifted away from the ketch he slipped its oars into the rowlocks and pulled against the water. Then in a moment of tormented temper he fired a blast of fire at the Masters Catch. The intensity of the strike set the craft alight in an instant and it burned with a ferocity that threatened to singe Urthanock's clothes. Shocked into action, he redoubled his efforts with the oars until finally the heat began to subside.

"A sailor's life for me, upon the boiling sea; I'll burn the boat and singe my scrote, a sailor's life for me," sang Methladon into the Vessel's ears.

"Fuck off and leave me be," bellowed Urthanock so loud that the beach ahead rippled and the palm trees shook.

Many arduous minutes later Urthanock pulled his rowing boat ashore and dragged it up beyond the high water line. There he stood in silence and watched as the Masters Catch skeleton burned its last and surrender to the sea. Vast emissions of steam accompanied it's its passing. The beast then stood for a few moments and looked around the strange land on which he had just planted his feet. He stared at the turquoise sea where white horses galloped in the far distance. His gaze then fell upon the two offshore mountains, one whose summit was hidden by a halo of white cloud. For a moment he wondered why that should be. Looking down to the platinum sand his gaze fell upon numerous large pig-pink crabs that foraged for food amongst the outcrops of rocks that broke through the land at the meeting of beach and sea. Then he turned inland and sought to see through the curtain of moss green trees and bushes, the likes of which he had never imagined existed. He felt the hot humid air as Solaris held sway amid an azure sky devoid of cloud save for that around the mountain. The sea salt that had made its home in his nostrils gave way to the pungent aroma of cinnamon, an odour force strong enough to repel the prevailing offshore breeze. Never could the beast have imagined such a foul and inhospitable place. The south of the Realm near Parandor was bad enough, but his place was a lizard's worst nightmare.

"I like this island," teased Methladon's voice. "It is like the paradise of my dreams."

"Give me swamps, the smell of the marsh gas, the mist that hides the wisps; then I will be contented," snarled Urthanock. "This place is not for the lizard kind... Seeing as you're such a smart arsed fucker Heyn, which way should we go?"

"What did the Moirai tell you?"

"*Look for the shadow of the Lords of Light. Seek a place beyond the settlements, across the expanse of cinnamon grass, and even the lush verdant forests. There look for the twin peaks of enlightenment and then you will be close,*" mumbled Urthanock.

"Then look to those mountains over there... see where their shadow falls," began the voice. "Follow that pointer as you would a sundial... I don't know why I'm telling you this and I'm pretty pissed off at what you did to those fishermen that I liked so much. You're on your own now scale face and I won't be back until I feel the need to push you over the edge."

"Piss off then and never return," screamed the Lord of the Swamps.

So dense were they in parts that Urthanock pushed through the fringe of trees only with considerable difficulty. He could not help but compare them to the oak forest he had been trapped in one month earlier. These at least contained fruit that he could pick although the thorns of some of the plants had enough of a sting to make the journey less than uncomfortable. After perhaps an hour the jungle gave way to an expanse of level land that was filled with grass. The smell of cinnamon was of such a magnitude that it stung Urthanock's senses. Beyond the edge of this savanna to his right began a series of hills which lay in the shadow of the Mountains of Enlightenment. He set off towards them at a rapid pace and when he had travelled half the distance the Vessel's ears began to pick up new sounds. They came from voices, talking and laughing as if one had told a memorable joke. Soon he saw before him a group of seven workers busy cutting down the tallest of the cinnamon grass and stacking it into heaps as high as a pitchfork could throw. On his approach, the men downed their scythes and forks and began to greet this stranger in the manner of seeking friendship and communion. That was until their eyes fell upon a face half covered in scale and a body blood splattered. At that point their enthusiasm dampened.

"Hail traveller," shouted one. "We do not see many strangers in these lands. Are you in need of water or sustenance? As is our custom, we the people of the grasslands, share what we have. I'm sad to say that today that just happens to be bread, water, and cheese."

"No, thank you," replied Urthanock as he moved ever closer. "I do however need directions to the place that I seek. I hope you will be able to help me with that request."

"Where is that you hope to find?" asked the spokesman for the group, a middle-aged man with dark skin but with the belly of someone older.

"Tell me the way to the door to the Underworld," ordered Urthanock.

The seven men laughed.

"I'm not sure where you mean," answered the man with much suspicion in his voice. "There is not much around here save for the grass and the old iron quarry away yonder in the midst of those hills."

"The quarry is bound to be what he seeks Trim," shouted another; one near enough to hear the words of the conversation. "There's enough strange shit there to fit such a description.

"Point the way out to me," demanded Urthanock. "Then I will leave you in peace."

"What does he want Trim," shouted another from much further away.

"Just head for the highest hill and look down; you cannot then miss it," the spokesman replied as a smirk spread across his rustic face. "We bid you good fortune and hope you are successful in your quest."

Urthanock thought to move on but something disturbed him. He was not sure if the vessel was playing tricks but there was a strangeness about the farmer who was generously offering his help and support without realising who he was talking too. Then he realised what was bothering him; the name.

"What name do you really have?" asked Urthanock as his eyes narrowed. "Trim is one I have never come across before."

"My name in truth is Trim. In full, Trim Tealeaf-Tosscobble."

"He's taking the piss," laughed Methladon. "Just like me, he sees you for the idiot that you are. You're no Lord over Fear. You're just like that fool Ssleptaz. A lizard in jester garb."

Urthanock snapped. Just like every other soul that walked the ground he could not remain in control of his actions when anger came to call. The mark on his reck burned with ferocious intensity. He thrust out his deformed left hand and forced the farmer who had dared to tease him high into the air. Without registering any of the peasant's pleas for mercy he exploded the wretch into a myriad of sticky globules that rained down upon the rest of the grass cutters. The others turned at once and ran off in different directions. They screamed in terror as their legs circled in rapid motion, far faster than ever designed to move. There was however no escape and all were pulled back towards the beast's feet by invisible chains that not even Urthanock's Vessel could see. All six were forced to kneel before the Dark Lord, unable to move yet still capable of feeling pain and vocalising their terror.

Holding the farmers still as if frozen in time Urthanock drew his blade and one by one destroyed the dozen eyes that were forced to look upon his foul and evil presence. The peasants' screams rose to such an intensity that that Urthanock grew weary and so six tongues were sucked forward. As they protruded out between uncared for teeth the noise of their terror was muted. The same blade; the wyvern's bane that the foul Lord had carried with him all the way from Avolire, sliced along the line of tongues. The crimson flowed and throats coughed out blood. Urthanock then smiled in recognition of a job well done. He then released the tortured souls from his spell. Off he strode without further ado, on towards hills in the distance and his appointment with fate.

"Did you have to kill the first of them; you sick bastard," demanded his tormentor?

"He shouldn't have taken me for a fool."

"But perhaps in the end it was his real name," suggested the voice.

"Fuck off and leave me alone. I've had enough of your persistent twaddle."

"And the others, did you have to blind them and leave them mute? Who will care for their families now?" asked the voice.

"You promised to leave me alone!"

Urthanock picked up his pace and sought to block out the impact of his persecutor. He then sought to refocus on the words of the Moirai, for if he could remember them well the better his chances of success.

"You must journey to the Lotus Isles in great haste. Get there before the Marked and set your trap. Then all will be yours."

He had then asked them what sort of trap and they had dismissed him as if he were a dumb child before a frustrated teacher. Their voices were clear.

"Do we have to spell everything out for you? Dig a spike pit; roll a giant boulder ball at him; fire an arrow up his arse from a racing humpy. Come on scale brain. Use what little sense you have. This is not difficult."

He would remember this insult to the last moment of his existence. Once he had mastery over the three dimensions he would torture the old crones into obedience; decedents of the gods or not, they would pay for their insolence. Then he would torture them even more, just for the pleasure. Walking further he then remembered the paper that the last of the Fates had given him. He reached into the recesses of his sailor clothes and pulled it out. Stopping for a moment as Solaris began a rapid dive behind the distant hills he sought to use the last of the light to gaze upon its writing. Once again he remembered what the Moirai had told him.

"It is a clue, written in the secret babbling tongue of the Cuvar of the Lotus Isles. When you arrive at your destination look out for the man with a dark cratered face. Ask him to translate it for you. If you are kind in your approach and offer reward for his services you may be given further insights. Handle him well or you may regret it."

The peasants that had worked the fields had dark faces and Urthanock then realised he may have already made the gravest of errors amid the anger that had consumed him. Words that he had thought belonged to Thamous also came back to haunt him.

"It's all going wrong, isn't it? Your plans are falling apart and your powers are waning. You should never have destroyed the room that linked you to the Rift. That one stupid act will be your downfall for your life force no longer feeds off its power. You will have to stand before the gates to the Underworld to regain what you have lost. That is the one way to reunite yourself and become whole again. Half-helm? You're more a half-wit!"

Urthanock began to laugh. It was maniacal evil sound, the likes of which had never before rolled across the yellow cinnamon grass of the Lotus Isles. Night had fallen but the insane laughter continued until at last the Vessels throat demanded rest. Then once again the lands fell silent. In the hiatus of stillness that followed the voice of Methladon chose make its presence known.

"You're right on the edge now, one push and your gone."

It was night-dark when Urthanock scaled the summit of the highest of the hills that had been the focus of his forced march. The night had started clear and a full face of Mona shone with harvest intensity. The stars in the heavens appeared to have multiplied tenfold and together with Mona they lit up the bowl created by the circle of dark hillocks. There below, just a league away, had to be the location of the door to the Underworld. Here on a faraway island stood a wonder of the world, an enormous hole dug into the ground. It was as if one hillock had been inverted and then hollowed out. Even in the light of night Urthanock could make out the nine levels of the terraced sides of the great scar on the land; one that had been inflicted by the hands of men as the centuries had rolled ever on. His eyes scanned the nine and as they did so they picked out what appeared to be stone ruins, each more sophisticated in construction the deeper the levels progressed. At the very bottom Urthanock was sure that a lantern burned. Its light glinted off the surface of something metal and convinced him that someone or something was active in the base of the quarry below.

Sat pondering his next course of action, the beast experienced a moment of insight which did not go unnoticed by the Vessel. In the south of the realm his powers had been fading, ever since the destruction of the Silverwynn's chamber within the ruins of Avolire. Yet as the Masters Catch had closed in on the Lotus Isles he had felt a resurgence in the forces that gave him his unique powers. He thought back to the knot he had produced from the fishermen, the firing of the ketch, and the destruction of the farmers. Now on the summit of the hill he sensed an even greater return of his abilities. It had to be due to his proximity to the portal he had come so far to open for all time. The beast had no doubt that this was the place where the fortunes of all would transfer to his to control.

"What now then?" asked the voice. "You have no key and you will not progress without one. The Marked may never come so what will you do then? I will have driven you to destroy yourself before the Moirai could send another to play their insane game."

Urthanock did not respond for he knew it would take very little to now turn his malevolent powers in on himself. So it was that he started to move down from the summit of the hill and on towards the gaping gash in the ground. Soon the foul Lord stood at the edge of the first terrace. The hole looked immense, far wider and deeper than it had from his vantage point upon the hill. The levels were connected by a multitude of steps cut into the rock and which for a thousand years feet had worn smooth. Urthanock kept to the shaded side of the vast crater as he descended through the levels, never stopping to examine in detail the ruins that the miners had left behind nor the varied skeletal remains to be found within them. His focus never wavered from the lantern and the glinting metal. By the time he was down to the seventh level he began to make out a solitary figure digging and searching the ground of the ninth.

Down the steps Urthanock crept as all the while the man by the lantern continued to dig. Soon he was but ten paces away, hidden behind a large boulder, one that it seems had not been of the right type or quality to have been hauled to the surface. Several similar yet smaller ones lay on the ground between him and the one that he sought to ambush. The man turned into the light cast by his burning candle. His face became illuminated such that Urthanock could see its surface with great clarity. It was a dark-skinned face that was covered with the scars of the pox.

"Look out for the man with a dark cratered face"

Urthanock knew at once that this had to be the one spoken of by the Moirai. He would seek to remain calm but he would get the answers he needed by whatever means were necessary.

"Hello," shouted Urthanock as he stepped from behind his hide. "I'm sorry to have startled you but I wonder if you could help me. I am lost in these parts and have instructions on paper that are not in my own language. Seeing you down here I thought I would ask if you would translate it for me."

Having at first jumped from the shock of hearing another voice the man readied his shovel as a weapon. He reached down and lifted his lantern from the ground. Waving it aloft he sought to obtain a better view of the one who approached this seldom visited place.

"Let me see it and I will do my best to help you," answer the man as he thrust his left hand forward.

Urthanock passed the paper over without further comment and the man studied it before raising and eyebrow in surprise.

"The message is written in the secret language of the Lotus Isle Cuvar," replied the man as his vocal cords quivered. "Wherever did you come by this I wonder?"

"It was given to me by an old hag who said it would help me on my quest," replied Urthanock with as much restraint he could muster. "But can you read it?"

"Yes I can for it is only a short message that is repeated twice."

"Then what does it say?"

"The first of these is that you're born; the second that all must die. The third you choose, the fourth is given, and the last, you know's a lie."

"What does it mean," growled Urthanock as his eyes began to redden.

"I have no idea," replied the man as his grip tightened on the shaft of his shovel.

"Then answer me this, where will I find the door to the Underworld? Tell me now or suffer the consequences,"

The crater faced man began to laugh.

"What's so fucking funny?"

"I know who you are for I am acquainted with someone who has met you and described your appearance," replied the man as he took a step back and tightened his muscles. "You will learn nothing more from me, spawn of the Underworld. Even if you do take the appearance Methladon Heyn!"

The Lord over Fear was immediately incensed and his mark fired.

"I am Urthanock, not some turd from the arse end of the Realm," screamed the beast in his fury. "You will tell me where the fucking door is or you will fucking die this fucking instant."

"I am digging to try and find it but its exact location seems somewhat elusive. You can have a go and help me it you like for I am weary and have been at it for hours,"

The man sneered and lowered his lantern to the ground. He raised his shovel to attack only to find it ripped by unseen forces from his hands and thrown some distance away.

"Get there before the Marked and set your trap. Then all will be yours," echoed around Urthanock's head.

"I have a great dislike for shits who think they are so smart they feel they can disrespect me," screamed Urthanock. "You will regret the moment you tried to get one over on the Great Urthanock, Lord over Fear, and one soon to hold dominion over the three dimensions. You are nothing but a discoloured turd face of the bastard isles."

"Thias said you were a cunt! And you prove him right."

The man's fear had gone, no doubt in acceptance of his fate.

"How do you know of the bard? Is that fucker also here?" bellowed the beast of the swamps.

"Rant all you like but you'll get no further information from me. You are finished for the time of the Enderdetag is..."

The native of the Lotus Isle did not have chance to finish his sentence before Urthanock's temper exploded in a maelstrom of rage. He raised his hands to wield his powers and threw the dark skinned man across the ground where he landed amongst numerous other rocky prominences. The beast then walked over to his unconscious victim who lay on his back with arms and legs splayed wide. He levitated a large boulder and dropped it on to the man's left forearm, crushing the bones and fixing what remained to the ground. The beast then repeated the same action until all the man's limbs were pinned to the ground. Next he placed a rag in in victim's mouth lest he begin to scream. After a short search Urthanock found the spade he had only minutes before ripped from the man's hands. He planted it by the pit that the man had been digging before extinguishing the candle in the lantern. When all was done he retreated back behind the large boulder that had been his original hiding place and began to contemplate the likely effectiveness of the trap he had just set.

An hour later he heard two voices that spoke in a whisper. They came from the top of the quarry.

27

Having concluded their business with the Lords of Light, Llyat and Thias returned to the makeshift hostel to say their final farewells; both equally anxious about the trials ahead. Pushing through the door Llyat moved to his lover. Heliana had washed and fashioned a dress from one of the white sheets that Llyat and Irabo had earlier procured. The bed cover had also been changed and upon its cream white smoothness Heliana lay with her hands folded across her lower belly. Llyat sat down beside her and with a tear forming in his eye he hugged her close. His salt and sun cracked lips kissed her cheek. For one last time he forced his eyes to roam from her head to her toes and then back again. Where her dress lay part-opened at the join of her legs Llyat noted a further spot of crimson which begged notice against the contrasting white material.

"I see the grape still oozes," he said smiling, not knowing how else to comment. "I must leave now and with Thias go to save the Realm."

"The bleeding is nothing my love," replied Heliana as she peered over her belly hump. "Go now for if you stay longer I will not let you leave. I have already come to terms with the fact that I may never see you again, so please do not make this harder. Do what you need to do and focus all your strength upon your task. Thias will watch your rear and you must not think of me or the baby until you have finished and are free to return. Do not come back if you fail Llyat for I do not wish to end my days with one who wallows in a life time of regret. Go now before I collapse into a wailing mess."

Llyat did not reply. He stood and walked back to the door in order to join his friends.

"Come Irabo," he said as he moved through the door without looking back. "I need a few words; they are important."

"Of course."

Irabo followed Llyat out into the crisp air surrounding the mountain top.

"Thias and I may not return," began Llyat once far enough away such that Heliana could not hear his words. "Should events not go as I hope, I want you to try and take Heliana back to Parandor. I cannot imagine what foul forces of evil will descend upon this world if I do not close the portal. Nor do I know if the swine Urthanock will show. Even if he does it is not given that I will destroy him. The Moirai are fickle and if you believe their shite, then they are still to decide on the outcome of their game. I charge you with the care of sweet Heliana and my unborn child. Are you up for the task?"

"Of course," replied Irabo as he took Llyat's right hand squeezed. "I will protect her until my dying breath. Despite the Fates trying to finish me off I am still here and will be to the end of days. I will keep her amused and comfortable until your return; of which I have every confidence. I sense the Fates are with you and will guide you to success, despite what you told me about your meeting with them. Go and do what you have to in the knowledge that I am here to care for her."

"There is one more thing I ask of you Irabo. Can you play Fidchell?"

"Yes I can but why did you think of that, at this moment, in this faraway place?" answered the bemused warrior while Thias looked equally nonplussed.

"I don't know why it seems so important right now but it I would be grateful if you could teach Heliana how to play it while I am gone. I spotted a dusty game board and counters in the hostel, in the small area where we stored the food that Theoplous had brought us. I would like to play it with her if and when I return."

"Are there not more important things to think about?" asked Thias.

"No, not at this precise moment," replied Llyat as he turned to Irabo. "Promise me you will do that for me my friend."

"As it means so much to you, I will occupy her with the game," answered the warrior.

"You must also seek permission from the Lords of Light to descend the mountain for fresh food and water. Will you do that also?"

"I had worked that one out myself Llyat. Thias, take him away before he speaks more drivel."

"Of course," added the bard while nodding his head. "This is goodbye."

With that Thias and Irabo embraced. After all they had been through they squeezed each other until both could hardly breathe.

"Goodbye dear friend," replied Irabo with a tear in his eye. "The Fates will protect you."

And so, it was that Llyat and Thias left the confines of the hillfort and began their trek into an uncertain of future. They passed the successive gates, crossed the wooden bridges between the ramparts, and then the great horn that Theoplous had used to announce their arrival just two days earlier. The halo of cloud loomed large before them and as they entered is cool and spectral domain Llyat kept his eyes fixed to the shale floor lest he fall off the edge of the mountain. All the while he kept as close to Thias as he dared, his concentration cutting through the mist as would a spade through a midden. He remembered only too well the near disaster on the high reaches of the Ivory Pass when he had contracted the sweating sickness and Irabo had fallen during the Skyfawn attack.

Once out of the cloud and back into the light, Llyat gawped at the stunning vista that greeted his eyes, the vast and beautiful pea-green ocean that changed through ever deepening hues before kissing the sky on the far distant horizon. He turned to look at the main island, its brown hillocks which where the target of his trek, the vast grasslands with the hint of a town in the distance. Finally, his eyes drifted to the pristine coast with beaches like nowhere in the Realm. With his thigh aches needing a break from the steep descent the youth stopped and pulled on Thias's shoulder. As the bard turned with a quizzical eye Llyat raised his right arm and pointed to a fire amidst the waters of a sandy bay upon the main island.

"Look there," he ordered as he sought to make out the structure beneath the smoke. "I reckon that's a ship on fire."

The bard raised his hand to focus and diminish the glare from Solaris.

"Yes, I agree. Look, as the smoke clears a little, you can make out the shape of the burning timbers. It looks like a ketch to me. "

"What's a ketch?"

"A fishing boat of the type built in the boatyard of Parandor," answered Thias.

Llyat could sense there was something wrong with Thias's tone.

"What is it?" he asked.

"I have a sense of great foreboding," continued the bard. "The best of such vessels that served Parandor was called the Master's Catch. If that is her on fire then it can only mean one thing; the bastard Urthanock is here already. We must assume this is his work and that he has beaten us to the main island. Keep your wits about you Llyat for I sense we will have company sooner than perhaps we would have liked."

"Look to the beach, could that black speck that moves upon its surface be him"

"Perhaps, and we must assume it is so," answered Thias as he began to walk forward. "Come we have a job to do and a long trek ahead of us. Snatch food from the trees as we pass for we do not have time to keep stopping and admiring the view. The time of the prophecy is at hand."

The descent of the mountain proved much quicker that its climb. The small dinghy was still where they had left it in the back of the cave. It was immediately launched into the turquoise swell as Thias took to the oars and began the journey around the island peak and across the channel to the fated isle that reeked of cinnamon. Once ashore Llyat and Thias carried the small boat over the sinking sands and hid it amongst the trees. Llyat was insistent it still be there when he returned to collect Heliana and Irabo. Thias smiled at his companion's outward confidence but Llyat knew his friend did not share his conviction that all would turn out well.

Sometime later they pushed through the last of the jungle that skirted the island shore and entered the vast swathes of grass. Marching toward the distant hills Thias began to ask a number of questions to help pass their toil.

"You've met the Moirai so you know them to be real, right?"

"You know I have," answered Llyat as he ran both hands through the tips of the long grass. "What do you think happened at Harico?"

"Do you believe we have any say in what happens in our lives or is all predetermined?" asked Thias. "I for one am confused. Irabo has always been certain that the Fates dictate everything, yet I sense that in most of what has come before me, the choices I made were mine and not the whims of others."

"There is much I do not understand Thias but I tell you this if nothing else. Right now, in this place and time of great peril, I couldn't give a damn about such ideas. We have to do what we need to do. It would be better that we believe we can determine what happens in each moment. If pushed, I suspect the three crones were but figments of my imagination."

"How can you say that Llyat when you have seen them with your own eyes?" demanded Thias.

"I was only behind the Oracle door for seconds according to Heliana. The Moirai told me that the terrors I faced before I met with them were but the result of my furtive mind. So why not they also? There is only one thing that makes me consider they could be real, the paper note that one of them gave me; that which contains the rhyme."

"I agree; that paper is proof of their existence," answered Thias. "I have heard the lines upon the parchment before. They come from the Lore of the Dead and I believe that they are of great importance. I just wish I could work out their significance."

"You'd best hurry up and do so. It will soon be dark and we have many leagues to go."

The two friends marched on and pushed through the grass over which no discernible tracks could be seen. They talked about their fears and anxieties, not only for what lay ahead of them, but what the world would be like should they fail in their mission. Soon Llyat switched the focus of their musings into a more positive space and pushed Thias to speak of his hopes and aspirations for the future. All the bard wished for was to live a long and fruitful life. His main desire was to find a home where he felt safe, preferably back in the Court of Parandor, and settle down to entertain and compose heroic ballads. Should he be lucky enough to find a partner and raise a family then that would be a bonus, but having survived alone for so many years he had little expectation of such an idyllic ending. Llyat on the other hand refused to speak of what could be. He had all he wanted already, Heliana and a child growing in her belly. Anything else would be froth on the ale.

Night fell quickly and while stopping to release the growing pressure in his bladder Thias asked yet another question which took Llyat by surprise.

"What do you think is the purpose behind our existence?"

"Fuck me Thias, I have no fucking idea. I will have to think about it..."

"Well don't take too long," laughed Thias. "We may not get another chance to work it out."

Some minutes later Llyat came up with his answer.

"There is no purpose to life other than to create children to follow in our footsteps."

"Really! Is that all you reckon there is to it?" replied the bard. "What about..."

The discussion ceased abruptly when a poor wretch staggered from out of the long grass and bumped into Llyat. The youth threw the man to the ground with the deftness of a well-trained warrior after which the stranger lay floundering with pungent froth burbling from a mouth devoid of tongue. Neither did the unfortunate have eyes and where they had been Llyat saw only sockets filled with a macerated mush. In a reflex action he took a giant leap back, and with Thias copying his actions, drew his sword and scanned the dark lands to both sides. There was nothing to see apart from the tragic rustic who pleaded with his hand for mercy and release.

"Urthanock's work I think. Theo would never have done this," said Llyat. "It is too painful to watch, see how he begs for an end to his suffering."

Thias stepped forward while his blade made ready to enter the man's chest.

"I cannot do it," cried the bard with tears running down his cheeks. "I have seen too much suffering to last a dozen lifetimes. My days of killing are over."

Llyat acted at once. He stepped forward and thrust his sword into the man's heart. The end came quickly and the peasants last moment ended with a smile of contentment.

"For fucks sake get a grip," ordered Llyat. "This is not how you must react if we come across Urthanock. Now let's move on and see if we can find other evidence of his passing."

The hills ahead proved to be a helpful sign post. The pair walked in silence lest they gave warning of their passing. Once amidst the tallest of the mounds Llyat pointed to the distance. There a flame flickered in the centre of a deep depression in the earth. He reckoned it to be a manmade fire but what concerned him was who may have lit it. He hoped it had been Theoplous.

It was the middle of the night when Llyat and Thias arrived at the rim of the iron quarry. All appeared quiet and the burning light they had seen from atop of the hills had since disappeared. Llyat stood on the edge of the first tier and sought to work out the best way to descend into the belly of the great pit

"It looks like Theo has turned in for the night."

"I hope that is the case," replied Thias. "Let's move with stealth. Keep your eyes alert and your blade at the ready. I will go first. If by chance Urthanock has beaten us to the bottom it will be my sword that will make first contact."

Llyat followed Thias down the cut-out steps as they dropped from one terrace to another. He had not objected to Thias's order despite his concerns over the bard's wavering emotions. By following in Thias's footsteps he was able to better observe the ruins he moved amongst and the strange skeletal remains offered up at each level. It gave him time to second guess the nature of each of the disasters that had decimated those who had mined the quarry. The oldest of the ruins fringed the rim of the first level and they became more sophisticated in construction the deeper Llyat dropped. He would of have taken more notice of these buildings if it were not for the skeletons present. They spoke much of what had terminated the work as a series of slaughters had followed one upon another. Despite Llyat's musings the truth remained as elusive as the origin of the people who had once toiled to extract the iron deposited by the Lords of Light.

Amidst the ruins of the first level all exposed skeletons were missing both hands. Llyat imagined the reason that none had been buried or burned was to provide a warning to the generations that followed. A myriad of arms all been severed at the wrist in a deliberate and unique manner, evidenced by the slash marks of blades on the ends of the forearm bones. The skeletons of those of the second level were interspersed with those of giant land lizards, not the upright forms of the Eastern Marsh, but rather those that like the geckos of the Realm, moved on all fours. It was as if a battle of species had raged but as to who the victor had been it was impossible to tell.

Down into the dark they dropped and amid the ruins of the third level Llyat winced at the means of death of those who had faced this particular plague. Jaws had been nailed shut and all had a scorpion the size of a foot placed inside their mouths. On the fourth level, the dead had been impaled on iron stakes that had been thrust up through the rear and positioned to overlook the mine although some had since toppled over. Llyat imagined the time when the miners had first been impaled. The sight, the smell, and the clouds of flies would have turned the sky black. Down amongst the ruins of the fifth level there were signs of great trauma, holes ripped through rib cages and skulls cracked open. Soon Llyat came up with an explanation, for what his eyes saw next was the bony remnants of the biggest of beasts, a mighty auroxorn. It appeared the great animal had been deliberately set against the sad souls that worked the mine. The envisioned screams of those subjected to the rampant beast hammered away inside Llyat's ears. Amidst the sixth level the dead exhibited evidence of a severe infection of the long bones, great abscesses that would have led to the most painful of deaths. Those of the seventh level had been subjected to fire while the skeletons of the eighth revealed ghoulish signs of starvation. Sir Raulyn's memory served up an ancient clue. There were clear signs of knife scrapes. The starving had stripped the bones of their meat. They had resorted to eating each other.

So, it was that the pair dropped in amongst the ruins of the ninth and there Llyat realised the foul depths to which miners had sank. Here the evidence was clear; they had gone beyond eating each other and for generations had eaten children and babies. Where these unfortunate young ones had come from or who had brought them such a dreadful end inside the belly of the earth, Llyat could only speculate. Yet he sensed a connection behind all that he had witnessed. The closer to the portal the miners had dug, the greater were the depravities inflicted on or by them. The presence of the evil that lay below the surface had manifested itself in those that dug out the iron. It had been a dreadful price to pay for providing a wealthy elite with the resources on which to grow fat and idle. Llyat realised the importance of his mission for he had now seen the likely consequences of his failure.

Llyat and Thias wandered around the vast open space of the bottom of the great pit and searched for signs of both Theoplous and Urthanock. They talked rarely and then only in the quietest of whispers for they were determined as best they could to keep their presence secret. At any moment Llyat expected a surprise attack from out of the mist that had now begun to settle in the open bowl. The temperature had dropped several degrees and he began to shiver. He could not decide if his reaction was due to the cold for fear had begun to tease his senses. The two moved in a systematic manner so as to cover all the ground without missing anything significant. Backwards and forwards they went until after some thirty minutes an upright spade against a rock appeared out of the mist ahead.

"That's the very one that Theoplous took from the mountain," whispered Llyat as he walked over to the tool and lifted it from the ground.

"How can you be so sure?" answered Thias?

"Look at the handle, see here the incurved triangles," continued Llyat. "This must be where Theo was digging before he decided to leave for the night. Help me down into this hole."

Theoplous had indeed been busy. His excavation was as deep as the height of a man and it covered an area the size of a large bed. Thias held Llyat by both wrists and then lowered his friend down into the foggy depths of the pit Once Llyat had reached the bottom he began to rub his hands over the soil's surface until he came across an area where metal had been revealed by Theoplous's spade work. Feeling across its surface he found a deep groove which he then began to follow. It moved inwards as an arc and Llyat soon realised what he had found. It was a section of an incurved triangle.

"Pass me the spade Thias, and I will continue the dig. We are in the right place but all is not yet uncovered. You keep guard and let me know if I make too much noise," whispered Llyat as passed his shoulder bag up into the bard's hands. "Here, you look after the key while I dig."

"Do you want to take it in turns?" came the reply from above.

"No, this should not take long and I don't understand why Theo didn't finish the job. There doesn't appear to be much more to uncover. Besides, physical effort always helps me take my mind off problems and focus what I need to do."

Llyat set about clearing the earth with great energy. A short while later he had uncovered a large and rusted iron key from amongst the dirt. He recognised it as the kind that opened the Underkeep's doors to Abraham Marus's chamber. It was of no relevance but in the moment of its discovery Llyat took the decision to place it in the pocket of the habit he still wore. His intention was to give the key to Heliana, as a keepsake of his visit to the Lotus Isles. No sooner had he secreted it away than he felt the urgent need to take a piss. Not certain if that was all he wanted and not wishing to foul the portal, he asked Thias's help extricate him from the hole. The bard reached down and pulled Llyat out. Through the fog to his right Llyat noted a collection of large boulders and so leaving Thias to stand guard over the dig he strode towards the stones.

Just as he finished emptying his bladder he heard a muffled sound that crawled out from amongst the rocks. Going at once to investigate he came across Theoplous, pinned to the ground by large boulders. Shocked at the sight of his friend lying there motionless, Llyat retreated several paces until he could see Thias's shadow through the mist.

"Thias, come over here at once," he said as loud as he dared while stressing the urgency of his message. "I have found Theo and he is in a bad way. Something must have happened. I think Urthanock has been here and for all we know he may still be lurking nearby."

The shadow immediately approached and as Thias's image came into focus Llyat was relieved that it was his friend and not the beast of the swamps.

"Where is he?" whispered Thias as soon as he reached Llyat's side.

"Over there. Quick, let's see what we can do for him."

A minute later both knelt beside the unfortunate sailor who groaned through a cloth that filled his mouth. Llyat put his right index finger to his lips and then slowly began to drag the obstruction from out between Theoplous's lips.

"Don't make a noise Theo; can you understand me?" said Llyat in his most reassuring voice.

The sailor nodded to show that he had indeed understood the instruction.

"What happened Theo?" asked Thias as the last of the material was pulled clear.

"That bastard ambushed me and when I wouldn't provide him with the information he wanted he threw me over here and pinned me with these boulders."

"Theo who did this?" asked Llyat, realising it had taken magic to shift the boulders.

"The swine that calls itself as Urthanock." spluttered Theo as blood poured from his mouth.

"Let Thias and I see if we can find some way to free you."

"Do not waste time with such nonsense lad," answered the sailor. "My limbs are crushed and my back was broken when I was thrown over here. Something bleeds inside me and I can see the strings beginning to form. The Three will soon be here. Before I go you need to listen with great care to what I have to say."

Thias placed Llyat's shoulder bag under the back of Theoplous's head in an attempt to offer some comfort as the sailor spoke through his pain.

"I was clearing the portal when he turned up," groaned Theoplous. "He just came from behind and started asking questions. The swine showed me a piece of paper and ordered me to translate it for it was written in Lotus Isle Cuvar, a language few know or can speak."

"What was written on the paper," asked Llyat.

"The first is you're born; the second that you die. The third you choose, the fourth is given, and the last, is a fucking a lie… or something like that"

"That's most interesting," said Thias as he turned and readied his sword.

"Thias, let me finish," continued Theoplous. "He has set a trap for you and I am the bait. The swine ordered me to finish digging out the portal but when I refused he did this to me."

"What happened after he pinned and gagged you?" asked Thias as he moved closer to compensate for Theoplous's fading voice.

"He staggered off clutching his head, ranting, raging, and talking to himself like the madmen they lock up inside Parandor's Underkeep. Thias, these next words are for your ears only," said the sailor, so soft that Llyat could barely make them out. "It was him, just as you had described him. I did right not to tell Llyat, didn't I?"

"Who," shouted Llyat? "Who was it?"

No further words passed the sailors mouth, for Theoplous Danmar had breathed his last. As life departed so Llyat looked up before mumbling into the mist.

"If you three witches have come for this great man's essence then listen to me now. As Thias is my witness, I will fucking thwart your plans whatever they are, even if I have to unleash the horrors of the Underworld to do my bidding."

Thias stood up straight, returned to Llyat's side and led the youth away from Theo's corpse.

"So, what should we do now?" he asked, wiping the tears from his eyes.

"We have no choice but to continue to dig," answered Llyat who then turned and began his journey back to the hole. "This is what we have come for and we will just have to be ready for Urthanock when he shows; which he no doubt will before this night is over."

Llyat worked as fast as his spade would fly. He shovelled and scraped and threw the earth he had loosened up and over the rim of the pit. Thias continued to scan the surrounding mist for signs of Urthanock but the Lord of the swamps did not make an appearance. The only sounds were those from the spade as it scrapped across the metal portal and the thuds from the thrown earth as it landed beside Thias's feet. Llyat dug and dug but after some time he realised he could no longer sense Thias's presence. The longer his absence continued the more concerned Llyat became until at last he decided to climb from his pit and seek out the bard. No sooner had he done so than Thias re-emerged from out of the mist in the direction where Theoplous still lay pinned by the boulders. Angered that his friend had disappeared without warning, as soon as the Thias was back within whisper range, Llyat vented his ire.

"Where the fuck did you go? I thought for a moment Urthanock had taken you. You left me unguarded and I fail to understand why you would have done that?"

"I also needed a piss," replied the Thias as he moved to the edge of the hole and peered into its depths. "I see that you have finished the task."

"Yes, I have," answered Llyat. "The portal is ready for the Lord of Fear to make his appearance. I intend to fulfil the Prophecy once and for all time."

"I cannot make it out clearly from up here," said Thias as he peered down. "There is a swirl of mist that obscures the detail. Can you describe it to me?"

"Sure," began Llyat. "The door is made of thick metal. It appears stronger than iron and does not scratch when the spade moves across it. Nor does it show any signs of rust or similar ageing. It is the weirdest of portals for there are no hinges and there could be a door within the door."

"What do you mean?"

"There is a large incurved triangle that sits in the middle of the metal plate. Its etched edges go deep and I have a suspicion it may be what moves for in its centre is another of the blackest of pentagons. It is identical in shape to the one we forged on the mountain. It is so black I thought it to be a hole but when I thrust by hand forward it was as solid as the metal that surrounded it. Fuck! My shoulder bag; where is it?"

"Under Theo's head," answered Thias whose lack of anxiety caused Llyat concern. "Look, before we go and retrieve it there is something I must tell you about Urthanock, a secret I have been keeping from you for some time."

"What are you talking about? What devious game are you playing bard?"

Thias sensed that Llyat was thinking about everything that had led them to this point and the conspiracy that surrounded the actions of the Cuvar. It was time that Llyat knew the truth.

"You're talking about Theo's last words aren't you Thias."

"Llyat, you need to trust me," began the bard. "Please listen to what I have to say."

"No more riddles. Who was Theo was referring to? What have you been keeping from me?"

"Remember when we talked of the essence of Urthanock taking over a Vessel, one whose body the foul Lord purloined?" said Thias as he took hold of Llyat by both shoulders and stared into his still youthful eyes. "The difficult truth you must face is that the beast walks within the body of your once great friend and my brother, Methladon Heyn. You must prepare yourself to be reunited with one you thought long dead."

"Fuck off," snapped back Llyat in disbelief. "There is no time for stupid bollock talk; the swine may be here at any moment. Stop winding me up and let's go back for the shoulder bag."

"I tell you the truth…" began Thais.

"You forget I was there in Maplehill and that I saw Methladon fall."

"You may have seen him drop but think back, did you actually witness him die?"

"I'm sure I did," answered Llyat. "But if this is true, why did no one tell me before?"

"Because we would never have got you this far.

"How can you be so certain it is him?"

"Because I met him again in Avolire when I stole the Gems."

Llyat became quiet. Thias could see the youth was dumbfounded.

"I will not believe it." the youth exclaimed.

"The bard speaks the truth," growled a new and ominous voice.

Llyat looked beyond Thias's shoulder and recoiled in shock. A figure appeared from out of the mist.

"Hello Llyat, Thias. It's been a while!"

Llyat immediately recognised the voice for those dear are never lost from memory.

"Shut the fuck up," snarled a deeper version of the same voice. "I will deal with this. Get back from whence you came and bother me no more."

"The beast, the man, whatever he or it is, has descended into madness," whispered Thias.

"It can't be…" began Llyat.

"It is and you need to focus," added Thias as he sought to break Llyat's fixed gaze.

An unseen force shot from Urthanock's hands and threw both Llyat and Thias down into the pit and onto the solid metal portal. Both winced as they landed on the hard surface and as soon as Llyat had recovered he looked up to rim of the hole. There sat the beast on the edge of the pit with fire red eyes that stared with a crazed insanity.

"I am pleased to find you here, Marked of the Maples," snarled the beast. "There will be no escape for either of you. Your deaths will come easier should you comply with my demands. I have slaughtered a great many to get to this place and two more will make no difference. I give not a toss if you once meant something special to this Vessel that I occupy. Now, which one of you has the key?"

"I do," responded Llyat as he held up the rusted iron key that he had found earlier.

"Throw it to me so that I may examine it," ordered Urthanock as an evil shadow oozed from his scale exposed face.

Thias snatched the key from out of Llyat's hand and pushing Llyat back behind him shouted to the creature that had once been his brother.

"Methladon, if you are still somewhere inside that depraved being, listen to me for the sake of all who have ever loved you. Fight the beast that has attacked your mind and come back to us."

Urthanock laughed so loud that both Thais and Llyat were forced to cover their ears.

"He is nothing but a torment to my drums," growled Urthanock as the Vessel's right hand thrust forward. "Give me the key and show me where the lock resides for I cannot see the hole from here."

"There isn't one Methladon," screamed Thias, determined not the acknowledge Urthanock by name. "What would Vostag, our father, say if he could see the depths to which you have sunk? Find pride, seek courage, and turn away from the dark one's influence."

Urthanock laughed again before sternly commanding the pit.

"I will ask you one more time bard, where is the keyhole?"

"You do not have to be like this Methladon; you have a choice in all this," continued Thias. "Search for the essence that is you. A philosopher told me something special just one month past. He said 'All of us are born as equal blank pages. All have the potential to be just as good as they can be swine. It's all about life events and all can flip. The pious may turn evil but even the greatest of shits may turn out good in the end.' I know you of old and you are a good man Methladon. Let go of the beast that controls you."

"You test my patience bard," answered Urthanock with just a hint of hesitation.

Two fingers clicked and the key flew from the bard and into the claws of the Lord over Fear.

"That is not the real key," laughed Thias without fear of what the foul Lord would do. "Another guards it, a sailor from the Banshee's Wail and who is now untouchable. If I knew where it was I would have returned to that sailor, taken the key, and have it with me now."

Thias then turned towards Llyat and winked. He tapped his left hand over his trousers in a way that only Llyat could see and understand.

"I and the Marked both need that door opened so stop fucking with me bard."

Urthanock jumped down into the hole and faced the two that dared to tease him."

"Llyat means to close it again once the key has healed the fractures that threaten to destroy the Realm," screamed back Thias.

"You speak too much," snarled Urthanock.

Without warning the beast drew the sword from his side and thrust it into Thias's belly.

"You bastard," screamed the Vessel's lighter voice.

"You fucking bastard," screamed Llyat, as he moved to offer aid to his fallen friend.

"Forget about me Llyat," coughed Thias. "Finish what we have started."

Llyat turned on the Lord over Fear. He looked to the sword and as Thias knelt dying a look of realisation spread across the Marked's face.

"That sword is mine you thieving swine," he cried.

Llyat prepared to attack Urthanock but with one hand on his belly and with his other on Llyat's leg, Thias somehow manged to hold his friend back.

"Do you remember its name Llyat?" moaned Thias as he sought to make mind connections."

"Destiny's Song," answered Llyat. "It was old Abrahamus Marus's blade but what has..."

"Cut out the babbling shite," ordered Urthanock as he wiped the b oodied blade across his fish caked trousers. "Give me the fucking key!"

"What would Ruta say if she were alive to see what you have become?" whimpered Thias as he crawled toward the centre of the portal. "She would have flayed your arse 'til it was raw. You are a disgrace to your mother's memory. You were my brother Methladon!"

Urthanock's mind snapped. The beast's right hand rose into the air and an orange ball of flame shot from the fingertips of his good hand. It hit Thias in the face and boiled the front of his eyes, blinding him in an instant. Thias screamed but did not retreat from his position over the blackest of all shapes. Llyat then lunged forward, desperate to kill the beast. The Marked's anger flared and in that brief moment any thoughts of saving the Realm vanished into the mist. Revenge was all that mattered. The beast turned his hand and in that same moment pointed it towards Llyat. An invisible shield blocked Llyat's advance and as Urthanock flicked a finger, the youth was thrown back against the wall of the pit.

Llyat's head began to swirl as the impact of the hard earth stunned his senses. Yet in that very moment of mental confusion, connections formed out of the fog of coincidence. Words hammered away inside his thoughts as he tried to work out the answer to the riddle that Thias had tried to communicate. Then as his head began to clear, more messages implanted by Sir Raulyn's seed began to germinate and grow in the forefront of his mind. The first to come through described the nature of the Underworld, its emptiness, the black, and the swirling essences of an infinite number of those who had gone before. Minds swept like dark storm clouds and where they met they formed the interfaces of shared experiences.

"Seek the commonality" whispered Sir Raulyn. "Seek commonality with the Vessel."

"Look to your friend, Marked of the Maples," laughed Urthanock amidst an explosion of mania. "See how he squirms and how much pleasure it gives me to watch him die. The blade has pierced his stomach and as his juices leak into to his belly. The pain intensifies and it will take a long time for this arrogant string plucker to die. Much suffering will have to be endured before his release. I would have preferred he watched his own strings severed; but in my haste and anger I took away his eyes."

Llyat focused on more images that formed within his inherited memory. A knight in silver armour stood before a white horse a waved to a frenzied sea of admirers. Two squires moved forward and placed a brilliant scarlet cloak around Sir Raulyn's shoulders.

"Vermillion... Vermillion... Vermillion," screamed the gathered multitude.

The image changed and the knight climbed upon his mare and let his cloak fall around its body.

"He has turned his mount to vermillion." shouted a lone voice from the crowd, one that sounded just like Llyat's voice.

Llyat felt a hand grip his throat. His head cleared and his eyes opened. He looked into the red orbs of the beast and shuddered at the evil that rushed out through the blackest of pupils.

"Now it's just you and me," bellowed Urthanock. "You and I are going to finish off what we came here to do, once we open this fucking portal?"

"Do it now Thias," shouted Llyat to his dying friend. "I know exactly what to do. Open it now?"

Llyat sneaked a quick look as Thias placed the pentagon into the matching space at the centre of the portal. The ground then convulsed with great violence. The bard's head and body swelled in a fraction of a second to twice its normal size before exploding into a boiling mist of pink droplets which then disappeared out of existence. Llyat's jaw dropped, his right hand rose to cover his shocked mouth while tears welled in his eyes. The ground of the vast quarry then began to tremble and Llyat and Urthanock began to sink down as the incurved triangle descended below the surface of the middle dimension. The beast let go of Llyat's throat and a visage of insanity ripped through the Vessel's face.

"And so the last battle begins," screamed Urthanock amid an aura of demonic rapture.

As he was sucked into the black, Llyat reached out and with his right hand grabbed the pentagon from its position on the surface of metal door. He thrust it deep inside the pocket of his habit in anticipation of a return journey. Then all went very black.

The Marked found himself floating in a void. There was no sound, no smell, not a hint of wind upon his face. The Underworld was nothing more than an all-encompassing black. It was as if all his senses had been switched off and yet his thoughts seemed clearer than they had ever been. No longer could he feel Urthanock's presence and he wondered where the body of Methladon had gone. Soon his thoughts switched back to Thias and a feeling of intense sadness washed through his soul. The prophecy had been enacted and the one who triggered the portal had died as foretold. Thias had made the greatest of all sacrifices and surrendered to the Moirai such that he, Llyat Emgar, could enter the one place from where no mortal had ever returned.

Llyat thought back to the Bards Guild of Valameer and in the passing of that second, he retraced all his time with the man he had grown to love and admire. The pain of Thias's death took seed in his heart as he realised that should he manage to destroy Urthanock and seal the portal, his life would for always be half empty. Forcing himself out of his self-inflicted torture, Llyat felt for the pentagon tucked away in the pocket of his habit. He began to think about closing the portal. It seemed an impossible task give the black that surrounded him. He reached down to locate the matching hole but the metal floor was no longer there. In fact, there was no floor at all. Suspended amid an empty nothingness and not knowing what else to do he shouted out the words given to him by the Moirai.

"To manipulate the black, search for commonality in the Vessel. Seek the Vermillion Mount."

"What the fuck is the Vermillion Mount," screamed Urthanock from somewhere distant.

28

"It's the fucking Red Mare you arsehole," screamed the Marked.

Amid the dark nothingness of the Uncerworld void, Llyat had heard the quietest of whispers tickle against the taught eardrum in the recess of his right ear.

"Vermillion, vermillion, reddest of the reds; women call it scarlet when they add it to their threads. Vermillion, vermillion, reddest of his mounts; the name of the tavern that you must now recount."

Whose voice it was he could not tell but he thought it was most likely female. It was not one he recognised but it carried a quiet authority that would not be dismissed. Whether the voice had made the connection through coincidence or deliberate intervention mattered not for it had given Llyat insight into the riddle that had previously stumped his reasoning. And so, it was that Llyat realised what he needed to do to be able to confront and destroy Urthanock within the Underworld. There amongst the black he had to fuse the commonality of thought and image with the beast. Together their memories would reconstruct a place that they both knew. It would be the one best known and shared. It would be where they could meet and reach final settlement.

"If we both focus on a place we know best, we can make it form around us," shouted Llyat into the black. "Only then can we end this."

"Then let us reform the battlefield on which I last fought with Sir Raulyn," replied the beast from afar. "No doubt he implanted that memory somewhere inside your ignorant boy's head; a field of blood and carnage is fit for this purpose."

"He did but the image is weak and unclear," bellowed Llyat, desperate he would not lose his nemesis amid the swirling void. "Methladon knows the Red Mare in Maplehill well. Have him focus on a vision of its interior. That is how we may fuse something useful amid this infinite madness."

"No it must be Urthanock and Raulyn who decide the place of reckoning, not a pair of fucking rustics from the arsehole of the Realm."

Llyat sighed for he had no way of knowing amid the black what the beast's intentions were.

"Methladon, if can you hear me and I hope that you can, force your will upon the beast and come talk with me, friend to friend."

A small sparkling ball the size of a thumbnail popped out of nothingness before Llyat's eyes. He looked at it closely as it hovered without moving and in its centre he thought he saw the fleeting image of a building.

"That's it, keep going Methladon. Keep focusing on the Red Mare. I am here with you and together we will make its presence known."

"If this wizard's folly lets me find you than I will not interfere," growled the deeper voice. "The Vessel has control."

"Focus Meth, focus," screamed Llyat and the brown ball expanded with a pop until it was the size of a man's head. "I can see the familiar door inside this sphere of reality. The sign of the Red Mare is swinging in the wind. Focus on the inside and we will make it happen. Remember when we were last drinking there; you taught me how to play Fidchell for you had fashioned a new board for yourself and wanted to try it out. I was the one that you came to and it holds fond memories."

The ball popped again and expanded to the size of a barrel. Llyat looked to its centre and saw the long table, the fire in the heath, the gaming board, and two tankards whose froth cascaded onto the black aged oak. In the dark, the beast growled again but yet Llyat was sure he heard Methladon's softer voice urging him to continue the process of union.

"Remember the banter you had with Catriana. Focus on that and we will soon be back in the Red Mare," continued Llyat.

"Which words do you refer to," said the distinctive voice of the blacksmith's son.

"You told her that you loved it when she talked of perverted play. You told her that if she played her cards well that you would fuck her that night. She had sneered and told you to 'fuck off and tug on your twig!' We laughed long into the night."

Without further warning the sparkling brown filled Llyat's senses and he found himself sitting across the table from the beast Urthanock whose half-scaled face snapped and snarled while green lips dripped fetid swamp drool. In the sepia toned light of the Tavern, Llyat was reminded of the features of Cvyler Olin of the Dragonas and the facial changes that had followed living long in the proximity of dragons. Through the ghostly flickering flame light Llyat saw similar changes. Methladon had lost most of his defining features.

Urthanock tightened his grip on the familiar sword that he clutched tight in his right hand as it lay across the Fidchell board.

"Well done Vessel," the deep voice growled. "He is now ours to destroy."

Llyat realised in an instant the seriousness of his predicament. He had believed that Methladon's essence still held onto the goodness that had once rested within his heart. Now it seemed that the Vessel and the beast had colluded to trap him on their terms. He needed to devise a means of escape and yet somehow destroy the evil that sat before him. Time was not on his side for he also knew that the continued existence of the world he had left behind depended on him closing the portal as soon as possible. He felt to his pocket and touched the pentagon. He would need to find the keystone but realised he had no idea where to start looking. If he failed to locate it then all would be surely be lost.

Llyat looked into the beast's eyes and recoiled at the demon within. For a brief second, his gaze switched to the sword on the table. He thought perhaps Urthanock had noticed and guessed his intent yet no other option seemed viable. Llyat's past association with the blade flashed through his memory with the speed of a discharged arrow. He first remembered seeing it in his master's trunk as he and Heliana had prepared for the journey to Valameer. It had been given to the Grand Physician and its name had been passed down through generations. It had been there when his master had been slain and he had used it for his first kill during the fall of the Bards Guild. He recalled picking it up and taking it with him through the watery tunnel, then holding it inside the Ivory pass when threatened by the kulkulkath. It had then been taken into keeping by the Berserkers of Falahorn when he had fallen ill with the sweating sickness. Later when given back to him it was by his side when he had met Thamous beneath the Gathering. It hung from his hip as he had inspected Sir Raulyn's tomb in Barad Elestor. The last time he had seen it was when he had thrown it to Thias during the ogre attack. How strange it seemed to see Urthanock turn up with it in the depths of the iron quarry and that it should now lay on the table before him in the altered reality of the Underworld.

The Marked sought his inner strength and acted without concern for any dangers he may face. Seeking to distract Urthanock he flicked his eyes to the right. The Vessel's eyes followed and in that fraction of an instant he snatched at the handle of one mug and threw the ale into Urthanock's face. His plan had been to get the beast to drop the blade but instead Urthanock's grip tightened while madness burst from flaming eyes like fiery embers.

Screaming with intent to startle, Llyat then jumped up from his chair and kicked the table forward. The second mug was propelled across its surface and hit Urthanock in the chest. The Fidchell board and counters flew into the air as the table rocked and creaked. The board dropped from the table and revealed a distinctive shape embedded within the oaken planks, one which should not have been there but nevertheless was. It was the blackest of black pentagons from which no light escaped; the keystone that he needed to terminate his quest.

In an instant Urthanock was on his feet, his stolen weapon swishing through the air as it swung from left to right. Llyat fell back without any possibility of placing the pentagon in its home. He had no other option left but to run. Having scrambled to his feet he made for the door.

"There will be no escape, Marked of the fucking Maples," hollered the beast as it jumped first onto the table and then down onto the floor beyond.

Llyat reached the oak door several seconds ahead of his pursuer and raced out into the open. He had intended to head for Vostag Heyn's smithy for there he was sure he would find a weapon with which he could at least put up some semblance of a fight. Yet when he ran forward in the direction he knew it to be, he entered a strange world that was full of spectral shadows and dark shapes. Undeterred he raced forward and as Urthanock crashed through the door behind him the ghost like realm began to change. There before his untrusting eyes the village of Maplehill formed out of the shadows, its definition and clarity increasing with every step across the dirt track between the tavern and the blacksmith's workshop. Despite Llyat's many years in his village and the fact that he had passed the smithy at least twice each day, he had never taken much notice of anything that went on inside, nor of its layout. Most of the times he had passed it was usually filled with steam, the great body of a horse being shod, or the imposing figure of the smith who did not welcome the likes of Llyat loitering outside his establishment. In this surreal version of his home, other than Urthanock there was not another soul to be seen.

When Llyat entered the workshop he at once began to assimilate his surroundings into his thoughts. He saw that the building's ceiling was supported by two large wooden struts and that its planked roof was pierced by a central chimney that rose up from the glowing stone furnace below. Why, he wondered, had the fire been lit given there was no one to work the metal. He noted the anvil lay that in its centre and then beside the furnace the mightiest of bellows he had ever seen. The sound of Urthanock approaching at speed forced him to find what he was looking for. There before him stood a rack of weapons. He prayed that their points were as real as the beer had been.

Llyat picked up the nearest of the tools of war, a long wooden shaft that had been converted into a spear by the insertion of a blade at one end. The weapon was a tall as a man and Llyat wasted no time in putting it to good effect. He turned and threw it with all his force as Urthanock closed in for the kill. The shaft flew from Llyat's hand and rippled through the shimmering world into which it had been launched. The throw had been a good one, no doubt guided by Raulyn's essence. It struck its target as intended but the aim had been less than perfect. The spear entered Urthanock's left thigh, pierced the skin with butter-like ease, crunched as it glanced the beast's thigh bone, before one third exited between the hamstrings.

Urthanock dropped to the floor and Llyat armed himself with a sword that happened to be the next weapon in the line of those that had been created for his attention. The youth moved towards his nemesis, intent on decapitation, but the beast rose quickly from the floor and bellowed like a fire drake. The noise stopped Llyat's momentum just as if he had hit a wall. The Marked then began to move back as Urthanock reached down and snapped the section of the spear's shaft that protruded from the front of the Vessel's thigh. Llyat hesitated for he was not skilled in the art of war unlike his illustrious ancestor. In that brief gap in time and space, Urthanock reached behind and pulled out the rest of the spear. The beast howled and Llyat gasped. Gipping his new sword with all the strength he could muster Llyat decided that fleeing was still the best option. Given that the beast was now far less mobile, he would run it into the ground. He was about to take flight when Urthanock clutched his head and screamed out as if in agony. Words followed the screams while Llyat stood bemused and bewildered.

"Get out of my head you fucking piece of shit," yelled Urthanock. "The Underworld is my domain to control, never has it nor ever will it be yours."

A significant pause was followed by more words.

"I don't give a fuck if this was your father's anvil," spat out Urthanock as he stared beyond Llyat as if not seeing him. "Stop this fucking nonsense for I have a more important swine to slaughter."

Amidst a second pause Llyat realised that Urthanock was arguing with the conscious thoughts of his lost friend Methladon; an essence that had survived and which refused to leave the creature.

"I know what you're playing at boy," continued Urthanock. "You are trying to aid your puny friend, but I control your body now. Soon I will reconnect with the other half of my essence that I was forced to leave behind when I entered your mind through the cracks in Avolire. Then I will rid myself of your infernal presence. Mark my words lad, you will come rue the time you sought to interfere with the plans of Urthanock."

Llyat decided to inflame the beast's mind further as Urthanock attempted to place weight on the Vessel's damaged limb.

"It seems unfortunate that I should be the one chosen to kill one who is mad. Those suffering such mental torture should be treated as sick and should not have to forfeit their lives just because of their insanity," mocked Llyat as he took several paces backwards. "A mad reptile with one good leg makes for an unequal contest. Maybe you should return to the marsh from whence you came."

"Laugh as much as you like," snarled Urthanock despite the crimson rivulet trickling from out of his leg. "This wound is of no consequence to your eventual fate."

Llyat backed around the furnace and past the great bellows. He then stood behind the anvil as Urthanock trudged forward. Here he decided to test the sword skills of the maddened swine. It was time to see if Methladon's Vessel would inhibit the creature that had taken his it as its own. Urthanock's blade lunged forward and Llyat countered with a move taught to him by Tonousa Amberstone on the deck of the Banshees Wail. Then as the beast rocked back onto its one good leg, Llyat swung his sword down in an arc from behind his right shoulder. He expected it to cleave Urthanock's skull but the beast's skill with the sword had not been diminished by the passage of time. A counter up thrust caused Llyat's blade to fly from out of his palm, made slippery from the sweat of battle. He may have been imbued with Sir Raulyn's courage but for a moment the old Llyat had returned. A wave of distress shot through his core as his sword clanged against the furnace stones. Manic screams, half human, half lizard, shot from the Vessel's mouth while eyes fired even redder than before.

"Prepare to die, spawn of an ancient fuck,"

"Catch me if you can you scale faced bastard," screamed back Llyat as he turned and prepared to make his escape. "Methladon, meet me at the old watermill down by the Tiaryer. Let us see if we can wear this bugger down. There is only so much he can take."

"We'll see about that lad," hissed the reptile. "We'll see."

Llyat ran as fast as his legs would move. The shadows of the Underworld began to fuse into a new reality the more he concentrated on his memories. Even so there were parts of the landscape that did not form completely, for despite less than one year's absence he could not recollect it all with certainty. Amongst those minutes of intense trepidation he somehow still managed to find the space to chastise himself for not having been more observant in the past. Soon many of the gaps then filled in and he knew that Methladon's memory had begun to contribute to what was being created.

Once he reached the house that belonged to Denius and Mal Castor he stopped and turned. Sure enough Urthanock followed, dragging his dead-leg in a frustrated attempt to catch his prey. Off Llyat sprinted again and while he increased the distance from his pursuer he realised he had never once been inside the old mill that he was making for, even though he had played around it too many times to remember. It had always been bolted but he had been able to see through cracks in the walls and view its contents. Just once he heard his father describe its interior when talking with his mother and Llyat tried as best he could to recall that conversation. Once again, he realised how unobservant and disconnected with his world he had been as he had wandered through his feckless adolescence. The mill soon formed into view and a minute later he stood before its door. He had worked out a plan but first he needed to gain entry. A heavy padlock secured the door although the surrounding timbers showed signs of age and decay. Hearing the steady drag of Urthanock's leg across the dirt, Llyat thrust his shoulder against the ancient portal. The lock attachments ripped clear and the door bust inwards amid a fog of disturbed dust and the accumulated detritus of this never time.

The plan that he had formulated on his run was intended to further degrade the beast's mobility. The kernel of it was that he would climb to the top floor of the disused mill and begin to pelt the beast with whatever objects he found there. Once Urthanock had struggled to make the climb he would jump from the upper window that he knew from old was always open and across onto the maple trees that encroached within a few feet of the building. That would cause further weakening of the beast's ability to continue the chase. At least that was what he hoped.

Entering through the broken door it was immediately obvious that the watermill had not been used for a considerable time given the layers of mouldy muck that covered the wheels and cogs of the ancient machinery. It was a damp interior and fungus had taken hold in patches across the lower portions of the wooden support beams that held the building up. Llyat fixed his gaze upon the ladders that led to the floor above and a second later he began his climb. No sooner had he reached his goal than Urthanock forced his way over the collapsed door and entered the confines of the old mill. The detail of its interior then became much clearer as Methladon continued to aid in the formation the alternative reality.

Stood on high, Llyat watched as Urthanock paced and searched the ground level, thrusted his blade between whatever debris he considered his prey could be hiding. As the beast finished its search, Llyat began to look for objects he could use as projectiles. He collected numerous short planks of old oak, several plaster covered stones that had fallen from the walls, and one large rusted cog the size of a bucket's rim that had fallen from the off the grinding mechanism. This last object Llyat considered the most lethal for it had jagged points and was of significant weight. He lifted it with some difficulty and made his way to the top of the ladder where he waited for Urthanock to begin his climb.

He did not have to wait long. A few minutes later the beast limped its way toward the base of the rungs. Llyat was determined to aim for Urthanock's head but the creature wavered at the last second and Llyat released his missile a fraction too early. The rusting piece of iron fell from his arms, clipped the bottom of the ladder and hit the dirt an inch from Urthanock's good leg. The beast cursed, then screamed in the manner of an incensed lizard. Llyat gulped in air and raced back to collect his other missiles. By the time he had returned to the top of the ladder Urthanock had struggled half of the way up. Down went the first brick which hit Urthanock on the left shoulder and only caused the beast to speed its climb. A second followed and this time it glanced off Urthanock's right temple. Neither blow had been enough to slow the creature's advance.

As it the fiend reached the top of the ladder Llyat turned and ran for the upper floor window. Running at full speed he launched himself out through the hole in the wall and across the void to the nearest of the maple trees. He brushed through the outer foliage without difficulty until coming up against a major branch with a bone crunching thud. Hanging on for his life Llyat finally opened his eyes and sought to work out the best route down through the branches. This was to be no easy matter for his ribs and arms throbbed from his impact with the iron hard tree. A half minute later he stood at the base of the sweet-smelling maple and looked up at the face that watched him from the high window.

"There will be no escape for Raulyn's drip of mucous," screeched Urthanock. "Run all you like but there will be no respite for you. You cannot leave this place and my chase will last for eternity if needs be. Sooner or later I will cut the strings that hold your life."

"Well you'd better move your arse for I am out of here," yelled back Llyat, unable to resist the tormenting the beast and as he held the pentagon aloft for the Vessel's eyes to see. "I am off to close the portal. There is nothing you can do now that will stop me."

Urthanock roared. So intense was the beast's anger that its sound caused Maplehill to shudder. Llyat almost lost his balance but as the tremors subsided he remembered Methladon's presence and contribution.

"Meth, I thank you for helping me navigate this foul world and I will never forget you," he shouted to the face at the window. "You were dead to me until this day and so will be again. I will try to forget I left you here with Urthanock but please understand that I have no other choice."

"Run as fast as you like," laughed Urthanock as a further wave of mania roared from his throat. "There is no escape Marked of the Maples."

Llyat did indeed run fast. The beast's words began to fade as he headed back towards the Red Mare. Passing Castor's house for a second time he glanced back to see if he was being followed. To his great surprise Urthanock was still in pursuit and seemed to be coping better with the injury to his thigh. The rock strikes to the shoulder and head seemed to have had no significant effect but Llyat was almost at the door to the tavern and the strange portal that he had been destined to close. He could only hope he wasn't already too late to save his world. Then just before he reached out to push the door, the building burst into flame. So did the Castor's house, the Heyn workshop, and all adjacent buildings. Llyat jumped back and looked first towards Hadra's farm. That too was ablaze. He sought out his own house on the hill and saw it was as yet untouched.

"Fuck," he exclaimed as he looked to Urthanock and retreated from the flames.

As the limping Vessel passed Castor's house Llyat realised he had no time to think of another plan. The only sanctuary that came to mind was his family home, the one place he had been secure until the night that the knights in black armour had arrived and murdered his family. In this alternative dimension, there was nothing beyond the confines of Maplehill; there was only the village itself. Without seeking to rationalise his decision, Llyat set off up the path, past the village stocks, and up the incline that would take him home.

"My Vessel has burned the buildings," bellowed Urthanock, still some distance back. "It's the last thing he remembered. No, wait… It was night when the destruction came!"

Then darkness fell in the blink of an eye as Llyat too remembered the time of great slaughter; the night he had been cast into the Tiaryer.

"Fuck," he exclaimed as he redoubled his efforts to escape.

It took but a few minutes for Llyat to reach the top of the hill on which Rukave Emgar, the Historian from beyond the Dirmark, had settled and built his secret hideaway. It was a place intended to protect his adopted son, the seed of Sir Raulyn, from the very creature that now pursued him. Memories of happier times flashed thought Llyat's mind as he strove to reach the rustic door. He remembered standing beside his father, looking to the sunset and listening to his words of wisdom. Then there were the frequent chastisements, for being idle, for not applying himself to his work, and for seemingly having little ambition. With great fondness he recalled his mother Lyrusa, stood with her arms folded and her foot tapping by the door on those nights he had stayed out drinking with the Heyn boys, only to stagger back up the hill on rubbery legs. How he wished she was there now to give Urthanock a lashing of her tempestuous tongue. Images of sitting by the hearth while his favourite chicken cooked on the spit caused tears to well in his eyes. The liquid jewels tumbled over his reddened lids when he recalled the dream that came to him on Mount Feorhread; the one which showed how those who had loved him had sought to protect him from the beast which had vowed to hunt him down.

Pushing through the door Llyat entered to the place he knew best. All was recreated as it had been and without any semblance of a gap, error, or anything missing. Turning back to look for the beast he stood and stared. Urthanock continued in his chase and was already half way up the hill. At a loss Llyat tried to think what to do next. The insights of Sir Raulyn had deserted him and once again he was alone in the vastness of the strange yet familiar world. He thought of Heliana and his unborn child but the pain of never seeing them again squeezed the reflection out of his consciousness. Then another memory stirred, one where his father had given him advice on how to survive the threats of skyfawn and similar fearsome creatures. Desperate to do something positive he tried to imagine exactly what Rukave would have done had he found himself in such a predicament. The knowledge of the hidden space beneath the floor came flooding back and Llyat focused his concentration upon creating it within the replicated rustic cottage. Now he knew exactly what to do; he would hide below and take Urthanock by surprise.

The Marked approached the hiding hole near the hearth and seconds later he lifted a section of floor boards to reveal a gap large enough the permit the entry of a single man. Just as he was about to climb in he had second thoughts. Once inside there was no way out. He would be trapped in a prison of his own making. Amid his growing fear Llyat recalled a story once told to him by Denius Castor. To catch a mathulath out in the wild Denius had once romanced the tale of digging baited pits and covering them with a mat of a woven reeds. The pig-skinned beasts would fall inside and be finished off with a spear. In a flash, Llyat's hands reached down and hid the loose boards behind the family dresser. The rag mat that his mother had made and which lay in the centre of the sparsely furnished room was dragged over to cover the hole he had made. Stepping back, he began to examine his endeavours as the sound of the Urthanock's limping gait grew ever louder. Looking back to the mat he noted that it sagged inch in the middle but the colours and the knots of cloth sought to camouflage the indentation. Strange things happen to a mind in extremis. Llyat felt happy he had at least set his trap and although he had no weapon he was sure he could find something to destroy Urthanock if only he could induce the swine to fall.

"I'm almost with you," snarled the foul Lord from the black beyond the door. "Fear not, 'Marked of the Maples', your death will be a quick one, though you will spend an eternity of torment amidst Kha's taloned hands."

Llyat did not answer and slipped behind the door. There he waited, his heart pounding and his breath both rapid and shallow. He thought back to the night of his parents' murder and visions returned of his father's blood dripping through the cracks of the floorboards. As those images intensified, rivulets of blood began to appear on the walls, the floor, and the ceiling. The moving crimson sludge seemed to have a life of its own and as Urthanock burst amongst the confines of the small room a plum red shower descended from above and splattered both the scales and smooth skin of the beast's split face and the hairless mound of its head. Urthanock wiped the red from his eyes as the Vessel's feet slid through the bloody gloop. The beast bellowed.

"What is happening? Does this foul fluid belong to the Marked or has some other cunt been slaughtered here?"

The beast seemed to pause as if listening for a reply. Whatever words came back fuelled Urthanock's anger. The beast began to hiss as if a thousand snakes had nested in the Vessel's throat. Then spinning and without obvious aim it began to lash out with its blade.

"Fuck off and find another to torture, you piece of smooth skinned shite," bellowed the creature. "Once I have finished with the Marked it will be your turn to suffer. I'll find you within the underworld and..."

From out of the shadows Llyat pounced, narrowly avoiding the flurry of blade strikes aimed at the air created from nothingness. His intention was clear, to push the beast to the centre of the rag mat and have it drop into his trap. It was a move that if successful would rely on the benevolence of the Moirai for Urthanock's blade continued to swing in most unpredictable directions. Dice rolled somewhere and a card was turned. When the blow came the beast was taken by surprise and it staggered after Llyat's youthful frame had slammed into both chest and abdomen. The Vessel's wounded thigh buckled and forced the beast to retreat upon the mat. Lyrusa's colour-faded creation gave way and Urthanock dropped down into the hole. The beast somehow managed to hold himself part way out using the Vessel's good right hand and its left elbow. That was until Llyat took a step forward and unleashed his right boot into the burnt reptilian split face that was once his friend. More crimson sprayed and added to the art work inside the house of slaughter. Urthanock dropped to the bottom of the hole.

Llyat paused for breath and sought to contain the pounding of his heart. He felt a sticky flow move across the right side of his chin after which it dipped down onto his habit that was already sodden. He lifted his left hand to the right side of his face where his finger sank into a deep cleft that stretched from the centre of his right cheek up into his temple. Urthanock's final swipe had found its target and had missed his eye by less than an inch. Llyat's first thought concerned what Heliana would make of it. He doubted even one as kind as she could look upon his face now and continue to love him. This caused Llyat's anger to erupt and his lust to kill took over any residues of rational thought.

At the edge of the hole in the floor, Llyat stared into the evil that seeped from out of Urthanock's eyes. It was he who had trapped his foe and now all he needed to do was to finish the task. He looked to the corner of the room where the beast's sword had dropped following the impact of his charge. The blade glinted amongst several pans of various shapes and sizes, a pail, and a brush. Lying amid this pauper's pile lay the hilt of Destiny's Song. He moved across the room, gripped it, and returned to once again stare at his captive foe.

"You don't look as pretty now boy," snarled Urthanock as almost unnoticed two hands gripped onto the edges of the floorboards. "Your bitch will never force her eyes to look upon your face again. I would doubt even a hog sow could ever bring its globes to bear on one with such a canyon where a smooth cheek once lay."

"Goad me all you like," snarled Llyat while waving the blade. "I don't know if you have noticed but the roof is on fire, no doubt caused by the one who torments your mind. I did not start it so it had to him."

In the silent second that followed smoke began to fill the small building. The heat from the burning thatch pressed down upon Llyat's uncovered head and neck. He knew he would soon have to leave but the delay in any response from the beast meant that it was listening to Methladon's voice. A hideous howl of intense hate then erupted from the beast's mouth.

"I will suffer this fucking torture no longer," screamed an ancient voice as the complex creature pulled itself out of the hole.

Llyat staggered back from the shock of witnessing such demonic athleticism. His legs wobbled as his back reached the wall adjacent to the door that led to the outside unknown. Now he understood the full potential of the beast's powers and he sought to ready himself for its next attack. It was not long in coming for Urthanock then sprang forward, arms raised and ready to slaughter. Llyat dropped to the floor and rolled to his left. Urthanock crashed into the wall and caused it timbers to crack and groan. Llyat twisted, raised his sword arm, and swept the blade in an arc behind the Vessel's knees. The tendons that worked the lower legs were severed and as Urthanock turned to continue the fight his Vessel dropped face first and with a great thud. Llyat stepped back as burning debris from the roof fell and acrid smoke caused him to cough. He then thrust his blade forward into the Vessel's chest, striking just below the left shoulder bade. The crackling of the flames grew louder and as Llyat was about to strike again something strange happened and it froze his intentions.

Out of the Vessel's body, from the wound he had just inflicted, erupted a violet fountain. It was one not made from water, nor solid, nor gas, but something more indeterminate. Its colour forced its way through the wood smoke and it formed into the shape of a reptile's head. Then as Llyat watched transfixed, it hovered in front his eyes before rising on an up draft into the burning roof.

"The madness has left me!" cried the voice of Methladon from the crumpled heap upon the floor. "Finally, I am free."

For one brief second Llyat decided to leave his childhood friend to be incinerated but then his conscience pushed him toward a different stream of action. He grabbed the collar of the Vessel, Methladon, or whatever the form now was, and began to make for the door. Those final few laborious paces seemed the longest and most difficult of his short life. Llyat fought his through the stinging smoke that needled his eyes and the heat from the fire that seemed determined to cook his lungs from the inside. Once outside the door he redoubled his efforts and dragged Methladon's body to a safe distance from the raging conflagration. With no energy left to propel him forward Llyat dropped to the floor in utter exhaustion and wept.

"I think you've killed me Llyat; in fact I'm fucking sure you have!" exclaimed the body on the ground.

The few words smashed against Llyat's eardrums but his response was immediate. The Marked sat upright and then moved the Vessel's head to one side such that he could see all of it.

"Is that you Meth? Is it over? Has he truly left you?"

Llyat gazed into pale blue eyes, globes now devoid of the evil that had once sat behind them. For a distinct moment, he saw no spark of his former friend, then a glimmer of hope prevailed.

"Yes it is," replied Methladon, his voice a little weaker that Llyat remembered it. "I guess the bastard knew you were about to finish me off and fled for fear of an irreversible end. It will be out there somewhere and as we sit here talking will no doubt be seeking to reunite with that which it had been forced to leave in the Underworld when it took over my Vessel."

"Stop using that fucking stupid word," shouted Llyat as he rose to his feet and slipped his sword into the belt of his habit. "You are Methladon Heyn. Urthanock, Lord over Fear has gone and I do not accept that the wounds I have inflicted must end in your death.

"Well I cannot walk and you have popped my lung. You may well be correct, the wounds may or may yet prove fatal, but you have still not finished what you came here to do. You must hurry to the portal in the Red Mare. The building will be burned out by now and although still hot you should be able to deploy your strange key. Where ever did you get that from? … No, do not tell me, it is of no importance now. We must leave at once and you must carry me there. The door to the Underworld may already have been open for too long. We must leave now before it is too late."

"Why we? This is my task to complete," said Llyat as he sought to collect his thoughts.

"Because the one who triggers the door will be destroyed. Remember what happen to Thias when he opened it up for us. We have to try and get you back to the real world."

"The real world! What the fuck is that?" said Llyat as he slumped back onto his haunches. "I think I'd rather stay here and rebuild this village that the beast had you burn down."

"He didn't make me do it," replied Methladon as he sought to press his hand over his chest wound. "I just started to remember the last time that I saw you and how we fought together for what we felt was right, for what we felt was important. Then this place started to burn. Fuck, I wish we could go back to when we were innocent and free."

"We can stay here and rebuild what we need," answered Llyat.

Tears streamed from the Marked's eyes as he recalled all who he had grown up with. Those who had died for no reason other than being in the wrong place at inopportune times amid a senseless game and a fucking stupid ancient prophecy.

"Stop being the pathetic twat you were in Maplehill," ordered Methladon, gathering enough strength to bark out his words. "If you don't become a man now you never will. What is it that fucks up your mind and stops you from being strong? Despite all we have been through we still act the fucking same. If I asked you to protect the village with me you would only come up with some shit excuse about that not being you, or blaming fucking Rukave for everything bad that's happened in your shit filled life. Llyat just fulfil one thing for me before I cease to exist, become what you should be; a fucking man!"

Llyat rocked and retreated back into his thoughts. Methladon's words hurt so hard for they were true and he could not argue against them. Ever since his time in the Wizards Guild he had been imbued with the strength of Sir Raulyn, at least until he had entered the Underworld. After passing through the portal he had been reliant on his own resources. In this different dimension, even Urthanock had lost most of his power. Without the presence of the dark matter it was every essence for itself. Llyat was who he was. He knew he had to do whatever was expected of him, wimp, hero, nonentity, or someone worthy. It was in that moment of troubled thinking that he fully appreciated the true importance of friendship And so he bit his lip. Fuck the Moirai, he would decide what would happen next. He would be master of his fate.

"Move your arse Llyat," said Methladon as he tried to stand but then collapsed. "You are my one true friend and I love you for all your imperfections. In respect for Rukave and Vostag, shoulder me and get me to the Red Mare. We must finish this together. Give me the key."

"No way! I will take you with me to the portal but placing the key is my responsibility."

"Why does it have to be so?"

"Because it is I, not you, who is the Marked," snapped back Llyat. " will get us to the portal but before I do I will end your life. It is too painful to imagine you suffering until the end of time."

"We must leave at once," said Methladon as a soft smile spread between his cheeks.

Llyat lifted Methladon from the ground and threw his friend's arm around his neck. He then began his trek down the hill despite its further drain on his already depleted reserves. On he struggled, determined to save the life of the person who had most influenced his life. It was his responsibility to close the portal but his plan was to push Methladon back into the Middle Realm once he had activated the keystone.

Following what seemed like years rather than minutes, Llyat dragged Methaldon into the smoking remains of what was once the focal point of Maplehill.

The limp body of the blacksmith's apprentice was dumped on one chair beside the ancient oak table. Despite every other slither of wood being turned to cinders, the oak table, chairs, and Fidchell board had somehow remained untouched and had been replaced in their original positions.

"Do you remember when you taught me to play this game?" asked Llyat as he moved the board to one side to reveal the blackest of black pentagons. "I have thought of it often, each day since I first saw you felled by the blows of that bastard in black."

"Yes, I do Llyat but we cannot talk of games now. We have to close the portal at once."

"I know that my friend," responded Llyat, "When I place the key down my life will end but before that comes to pass I need to know what happened to you after Maplehill was destroyed."

"We haven't time for this shit Llyat, place the fucking key in the hole."

"Not until you tell me what happened to you," demanded Llyat as he reached into the recesses of his habit and pulled out the pentagon. "I will not die in ignorance of your story so you had better speak fast."

"For fucks sake Llyat, put the key in the fucking hole."

"No, not until I hear of how you became what you were."

"Then so be it, but I will keep it short and you must not interrupt. The Black knights took me to Avolire. A bitch called the Lady of the Silverwynn bewitched me in her room of power. She gave me access to the diamond in the Sceptre of Urthanock and inside that stone I saw visions of the future. That was when Urthanock's essence began to take control of my mind. The Silverbitch sent me to the Gathering and there I met with Thamous just after you had left. That bastard fired me with a belch so fierce that I barely survived. The room in Avolire, the Rift, healed me but the price I had to pay was immense. I became a prisoner in my own body and sent to the dungeons of my mind. The beast took complete control and although I tried to turn it insane, it always continued on its mission to destroy the Marked of the Maples. The cunt killed many, including the Silverbitch, a dwarf that had cared for me, and Thamous. It killed the wyvern with the blade you now hold in your hand. I was forced to watch as Urthanock waged war on Avolire and when that battle was over I was there when the swamp swine came before the Moirai. Two of the crones seemed willing to help the foul Lord and are no doubt still playing their game of cards and dice. I had to watch and endure the pain as Urthanock stole a ship called the Masters Catch and sailed it to these islands. The rest you know. Now, place the fucking key in the fucking hole and let us be done with this prattle before it is too late."

Llyat pushed his hand that held the pentagon forward but when it was inches away from its intended destination the burned-out ruins of the tavern began to tremble. Swirling mists of a violet swept around the two youths while Urthanock's voice boomed loud.

"You're too late, the door has been opened for too long. It cannot now be shut."

"Fuck you!" screamed out Llyat as he pushed the pentagon forward once again.

Without warning a second hand locked onto the black key and pulled.

"It is far better that I do this Llyat," shouted Methladon as he snatched at the object.

"No, it is mine to use. I am destined to close it. This is my destiny and you cannot interfere."

"My legs are gone, my chest has been pierced, and my mind has been crushed between millstones. Let go Llyat for unlike yourself I have no reason to live."

"Never," bellowed Llyat as the arm wrestle continued.

"No!" screamed Methladon as a wisp of violet entered his right ear.

"Let go Methladon,"

"Never."

The key fell into place and the violet swirls vanished amid a great hiss. One youth exploded into a boiling mist of pink droplets which immediately disappeared out of existence. The other was expelled through the portal where it lay limp and lifeless amid the depths of the old iron quarry.

29

It was several hours later when the man finally awoke from the coma induced by his reverse transportation through the portal; the door that had stood guard over the underworld since the beginning of legend time. His mind woke first and then his ears. The whistle of a light breeze that eddied within the confines of the pit tickled his senses. In the far distance, he heard the cry of one of the coloured squawkers that had no doubt sought to cross from one patch of verdant forest to another. Then his nose woke and the smell of blood crawled up both nostrils and forced him to remember all that had just transpired. His eyes soon began to notice light behind his lids and slowly he allowed them to open. Lying on his back he looked to the cloudless sky of morning and sensed with much relief that he was still alive. His right cheek began to sting with a viciousness that would not be ignored and so he lifted his hand to it and there felt the great gash that had been inflicted by the sword wielding swine he had finally vanquished.

Several minutes later he felt recovered enough to sit up and begin to examine his immediate surroundings. Destiny's Song lay on the ground beside him and he realised he must somehow have still been hold of it when Methladon had placed the pentagon within the keystone. He looked for evidence of the key's presence but it was nowhere to be seen, nor was it hidden in the folds of the priestly habit that now irritated his skin to such a degree that he felt an intense need to remove it. He ripped the dirt grimed material from his body and threw to a corner of the pit. It landed and yet still seemed to continue to move. Across its surface scuttled a myriad of fleas, companions that had multiplied during his presence in the Underworld. Stood naked apart from his boots and with sword still in hand Llyat looked down to the rash of bites that covered his skin. His thoughts jumped to memories of Methladon and then to Thias, once great friends who had given up their lives such that he would live. The pain dropped him to his knees and there he wept. Amid his uncontrollable sobbing, tears cascaded from his eyes like storm waves over the once mighty Bridge of Athuna. It was over; finally at an end.

When at last his tear reserves were depleted he began to inspect the portal through which he had travelled. Where the blackest of black pentagons had once existed, now there was only smooth metal. The incurved triangle was fading and was now much less distinct than before. Llyat then realised that somehow, he had achieved the impossible. The door had been sealed, the power of the Gems of Thamous destroyed forever, and the Lord of Fear left where its foul essence belonged.

Llyat smiled. His spirits were raised by these revelations and in his heightened euphoria he clambered out of the pit. The early morning warmth of Solaris caressed his skin and helped him forget the pricking itch, induced by the beasts that had sought to feed off his flesh. And so it was that Llyat then looked up towards the mountain, the place he had left the fair Heliana and his unborn child in the care of Irabo and the Lords of Light. He then rubbed his eyes as the shock of what he saw caused him to question the validity of his vision. The halo of clouds that should have surrounded the mountain peak had disappeared and the summit was clearly visible. Llyat struggled to understand the implications of this phenomenon until Urthanock's words came back to haunt his thoughts:

'You're too late, the door has been opened for too long.'

Lying on the ground, close to the edge of the pit, was the spade he had used to finish the work that Theoplous had started.

"Fuck!" he exclaimed.

It was in the midst of this frustrated utterance that he remembered the sailor, trapped and pinned beneath boulders just a score of paces away from where he now stood.

Picking up the spade he raced over to where the First Mate of the Banshees Wail lay bloating under the growing heat from Solaris and surrounded by a dense cloud of black flies. Extending his right hand Llyat then tried to summon up some magic in order to shift the boulders. Nothing happened and so he tried the promethelumous spell in an attempt to cremate the servant of the Lords of Light. Without success and he once again looked up to the cloudless mountain summit.

"Oh fuck!" he exclaimed as he tried to work out what to do next.

Llyat looked to his hands; in one Destiny's Song and in the other the spade. In an instant, he knew what he had to do, although the decision pierced the essence of his soul. He would need to cut and chop. It took all of Llyat's mental strength and heart felt courage to free Theoplous from his rocky constraints. First, he used his blade to cut the skin of the sailor's limbs as close to each boulder as possible. Once down to the bone he swapped the blade for the shovel and using it as an axe he hacked away. The bones of the old sea dog where toughened through many years of hard labour and it required considerable effort for Llyat to complete his gruesome task. When at last the body was freed Llyat dragged the corpse back and dropped it into the pit. There he joined it and positioned it as neatly as he could over the portal having first removed all the sailor's clothes. The incurved triangle had now disappeared completely and other than the metal slab there was no clue as to the previous importance of the object.

Yet again Llyat climbed out from the pit, his naked skin now caked in grime, blood splatter, and the fetid stench of death. Using the spade, he spent the next hour filling in the pit in order to create a fitting resting place for Theoplous Danmar. At the end of his toil he drove the spade into the finished grave mound and onto its handle he tied Theoplous's shirt for he had no other way of signalling who rested there. Having first removed his boots he pulled on the sailor's trousers, fastened its belt, and then reapplied his footwear. Llyat then recovered Destiny's Song from the scene of his butchery and set off towards the Mountain of Enlightenment. A switch flicked inside his mind as he realised that the knowledge passed on through Sir Raulyn's seed had deserted him. All that was left was Llyat Emgar.

By the time that Solaris reached its zenith, Llyat stood on a sandy beach and marvelled in being alive. A fresh onshore breeze cooled his face and was of great relief following his struggle through the jungle that joined the cinnamon grass to the ocean. He staggered past numerous large crabs and as fast as his worn-cut legs would carry him he threw himself in to the surf. Never before had water felt so good, despite the stinging of the salt upon his many wounds. The crevasse across the right side of his face stung like a slaver's lash. Having left the water his gaze fell upon some burnt timbers that pushed through the gentle waves of the lime green sea. Unsure that he had the strength to swim across to the Mountain of Enlightenment he set off to investigate further the remains of the ship that he knew had brought Methladon to the shores of the Lotus Isles. Walking briskly along the water's edge and when level with the wreck, he noticed a trail of drag marks that led from the sea, up over the beach and beyond the high-water line. Following it at once he soon came across an upturned rowing boat complete with oars. Wasting no time, he flipped it and then dragged it back down the beach where he launched it into the surf. Llyat had never rowed a boat before but he remembered how Theoplous and Thias had manipulated the oars in their rowlocks. It took some ten minutes for Llyat to master the technique but once achieved he set off in the direction of the mountain and the cave where he had spent his first night on this strange land.

Night fell just minutes after Llyat arrived at the cave beside the path to Brygaer Henuriaid. His next task had been to stow the rowing boat in the cave. He knew for certain that he was in the right place for he recognised the shapes and shadows that were cast by Mona's soft light. Sleep came quickly for exhaustion now ruled his domain. When the next day arrived, he had missed much of the morning. Every fold of skin and knotted sinew ached from the pounding it had endured. His muscles craved further rest yet Llyat knew he had to climb the mountain. With a throat as dry as thatch in high summer he sought the solace of the jungle and water to quench his thirst. The climb was arduous in the extreme until at last he found a small trickle of a stream, the remnants of the moisture that had fallen from the Lord's ring of cloud. Later he came across several of the trees on which grew the curved yellow fruits. He lifted three from off the nearest plant and sat down to rest while he ate. Then without thinking he placed the unpeeled fruit into a familiar pattern, an incurved triangle.

"Llyat what in the name of the gods have you done to your face," shouted Irabo's familiar voice from the trail ahead. "At least you are alive. What about Thias? Is he with you? Is he alive? Where is Theoplous? What went wrong? What do we do now?"

Llyat sat confused for he did not know how to even begin to answer the flood of questions. As he thought about what to say he pealed back the skin off one of the yellow fruits and finished it in two gulps.

"Tell me what's gone on!" shouted Irabo as he reached forward, threw his arms around Llyat, and squeezed out all his pent-up anxiety.

For the next two hours, the two companions exchanged stories as they climbed up the high peak. Irabo had earlier dropped down its sides in order to collect provisions with which to feed both himself and Heliana in the absence of others. He had already completed his harvesting of the jungle fruits and carried them in a wicker pouch that was fixed to his back. He also had two full water bottles made from the hide of some animal or other and the combined weight of his load inhibited a rapid climb, not that Llyat's weary limbs could have gone much faster.

Llyat spoke at length in order to answer Irabo's deluge of questions. He told all he could remember from the time he and Thias had left the mountain to seek out the portal to the Underworld. Starting with finding of the blind and dumb man he then spoke of the iron quarry and all he had seen in its various levels; the ever-growing presence of evil. Tears welled in his eyes when he spoke of Theoplous's death, pinned under boulders as bait within Urthanock's trap. Llyat cried openly when he related how Thias had then died, how he had sacrificed his life to open the portal such that he, the Marked, could fulfil the Prophecy. The description of the Underworld and Urthanock's chase caused Llyat to shiver and the longer the story progressed, the more Irabo screwed his brow. The youth spoke of how he had set his trap for the beast and having disabled the Vessel with his blade the madness had lifted. He forced a smile as he told of how Methladon had been freed of the evil that had possessed him. Then at last he got to the end of his story and told of his hand wrestle for the key; how Methladon had been the stronger of the two, and had closed the portal in another show of selfless sacrifice.

"And what of Urthanock's essence," asked Irabo as soon as Llyat had finished his story. "Did you manage to close the door in time to seal him in that Realm of Nothingness?"

"Sure," began Llyat. "Although I heard words in the black that now cause me to think again."

"And what words were they?"

"You're too late, the door has been opened for too long."

"I see; that is most interesting," murmured Irabo. "That may perhaps explain a little of what has happened at the top of the mountain.

"I think you had better tell me your story now," replied Llyat as the pair continued their slog.

Irabo first ordered a stop for a water brake and when both had drunk their fill he began.

"Two nights ago, the time that you no doubt entered into the underworld, a great storm began to gather across the Lotus Isles. Its centre was in the direction of the iron quarry but the greatest arm of the thunderous clouds crept across the water and enveloped the top of this mountain peak. Such a storm you have never witnessed Llyat, neither do you ever want to. It made the one we experienced at the Bards Guild of Valameer appear nothing in comparison. Lightning bolts the likes of which I would never have imagined possible rained down upon us and destroyed most of the buildings. I managed to create a shelter for Heliana and myself as the buildings fell about us."

"And Heliana?" asked Llyat as he sought to understand the words' implications?

"She is fine."

"So what happened on the mountain summit?"

"The Lords of Light flew into a panic," continued Irabo as he wiped rivulets of perspiration from his brow. "While Heliana covered her ears, and hid her face beneath her blanket, I looked out through the haven I had made from the fallen timbers and I saw the mountain top turn the colour of vivid violet blossom. It was as if the lightening had all collected together in one single entity. The air snapped, crackled, and popped. All the metal began to glow white hot and then the three giants disappeared into nothingness. One second they were there, the next they were gone."

"Interesting indeed, so what happened next?"

"The violet glow then swept down the mountain and within minutes the storm had passed. I returned to comfort Heliana who soon stopped shaking once the tempest had abated. Once the morning light of Solaris bathed the mountain again I ventured out to see what was left of the ancient hill fort. Most of it had been flattened but what concerned me most was the ring of clouds had gone."

"I have noticed that," replied Llyat. "What of the diamond? Is it still intact?"

"No Llyat it is not," said Irabo as he picked up a handful of pebbles from the path and held them before Llyat's gaze. "The full force of the storm, the god's lightening, struck fiercest over the oculus and the great diamond has been shattered into a myriad of pieces the size of these stones."

"What does all this mean Irabo?" asked Llyat as he looked up to the summit.

"I have no idea," replied the warrior "I guess we will have to wait and see.

Some hours later Llyat and Irabo approached the hillfort in the sky. Llyat realised at once how his friend had spoken the truth when he had told of the devastation that the storm had brought. The greeting horn had been split from its blow hole to its open end. It had been wrenched from its wooden supports and it lay in permanent silence as it teetered close to the edge of the mountain. The wooden palisades had been laid flat as if stamped on by some mighty kraken. The bridges that joined each rampart had also been much damaged but Irabo had used remnants of what had been left behind to create a way across the ditches. Once inside the fort's inner circle Llyat scanned the devastation that fell before his gaze. Wasting no further time he raced over to where the hostel once stood and where Heliana waited for him with open arms.

"Oh shit, what have you done to your face?" she exclaimed.

"I'm so sorry my love," he answered as he took her in his arms. "The fucker sliced me with Destiny's Song, but see, I have it now and I used it to finish him off."

"My poor sweet child," sobbed the young woman as she turned to Irabo and sought the warrior's advice. "Can you repair this with cotton and a needle if we can find one? You know somethings of the healing arts from your time in Falahorn; surely there must be something we can do."

"The wound has been open too long to sew back together right now," replied Irabo. "It is also full of dirt and much else that is putrid. If I were to stitch it now it would fester; there being no release for the pus that would form, Llyat would become toxic, the infection would spread, and he would then succumb to the fever that would follow as sure as we all breathe. The best I can do is clean it hourly and rub in salt. If there is none to be found here then we need to get him to the sea as soon as you feel able to leave."

"But that will leave a most horrendous scar," moaned Llyat as he pulled back and looked into the sadness that welled in Heliana's eyes. "How could you live with such a hideous monster?"

"Then Irabo, you'd better start cleaning straight away," she answered with a firmness that would not be denied.

As Irabo cleaned and Llyat winced, Heliana disclosed the secret she had kept from her lover when he had left her to complete his quest. She explained how the bleeding had been from her womb not her arse, and that how she had thought she would lose the baby. She explained that the blood flow had stopped about the same time as the great storm had appeared over the mountain and that she now felt it likely that her pregnancy would turn out well.

"Irabo has been good to me and saw to my every need."

Llyat expressed his gratitude as best he could, given the pain he was enduring; but he was far from happy that Heliana had kept this great secret from him.

"Why didn't you tell me," he demanded.

"Because you would never have left me."

"How long do you think it will be before you dare try and descend the mountain?" asked Irabo as he finished cleaning the wound. "After all that has happened here I do not want to stay any longer than necessary."

"We can leave now if you like," answered Heliana as she stood and made to collect her few belongings.

"The morning would be better," added Llyat. "I am absolutely, totally, fucked. I need more sleep. At first light we will collect what remains of the great diamond. The stones will be of great value to those who know how to cut and polish them and we need to pay Highroar for his services; unless he has buggered off already."

"No, the old sea serpent will still be there waiting for us," sneered Irabo. "He will not be going anywhere until he has news of our fate. I agree that some of the diamond will satisfy his need for payment and a little of the rest we can trade for clothes, food, and soft pillows on which to lay our heads. I support the idea that we set off tomorrow and am sure we can survive one more night on this strangest of mountains."

"Then I will make the decision for us all," reasoned Heliana as she held her belly following a strong kick from her unborn. "Tomorrow it is. We will set off as soon as Solaris has shown his face. Until then we will rest, but first I need to eat. Come Irabo, show me what you have in your basket."

Llyat rose early the next morning for he had suffered the most disturbing of nights. Heliana had tossed and turned for hours as he had shared her bed. Given his concern not to put any pressure on her belly, he had woken every time the lump made contact. Up before Solaris and he slipped back into some trousers. He noted Irabo still snoring, yet another reason why his own sleep had been so poor. Making a cloth bundle from out of a discarded pillow case he fixed it with a secure knot to the end of a shaft off wood that was lying close at hand. Then he set off towards the shattered dome within which he had welded the Gems of Thamous only two days earlier. Once through its portal he saw how its curved roof had exploded outwards at its apex and created a much larger and jagged oculus. The floor was covered in glass like pebbles, remnants of the once great diamond. His eyes then scanned the wooden mechanism that had held Raulyn's gemstone and which now lay in splinters amongst the objects he had come to collect. By the time he had filled his bundle Solaris had risen, and so without further delay Llyat made his way back to the shelter and kicked Irabo on the bottom of his feet. The warrior stirred and began to set his mind in motion. Llyat then woke Heliana in a much more gentle fashion, rubbing her left earlobe with his fingers until she too began to stir.

"How are you this morning, my princess?" he whispered as Heliana opened her eyes.

"Good, I think. I'll tell you more when I've come to my senses."

Heliana raised her hand and touched his wounded cheek with a caress of loving sympathy.

"Do you still think we can risk taking you down the mountain today?" he asked.

Heliana slipped her other hand under her makeshift dress and felt about her quim.

"Yes I think so; there has been no further bleeding and I have no pain. But we're not going anywhere until Irabo has cleaned your wound."

The three weary adventurers left the hill fort as soon as Irabo had finished attending to Llyat's face and after all had filled their bellies on fruit from Irabo's basket. The journey down to the beach took most of the day for the two men kept to Heliana's pace, not wishing to induce further complications to her every growing maternal mound. Irabo had stocked his basket with ripening fruits as they passed through the jungle, most of which already looked parched due to lack of moisture from the missing cloud. Llyat never once put his bundle down for he realised the value of what he carried. Without means of payment they could never leave the Lotus Isles. The rowing boat was where Llyat had left it but by the time the three arrived at the cave it was too late to contemplate putting out to sea. So, it was that Llyat and his two friends spent their last night on the Island of Enlightenment. They built a fire from drift wood but then found they could not light it. The promethelumous spell would still not work for Llyat and despite Irabo spending an hour rubbing two sticks together he failed to generate a flame. The night was long and cold but warmed by sharing memories of Thias and the others who had contributed to their quest.

The boat was launched at day break and the two men took it in turns to man the oars. Hugging the coast and always pointing south, it took them three days to reach their intended destination. They pulled the boat ashore each night and slept on the beach, shivering in the cool of the cloudless nights while gazing up to more stars than could fit into the heavens. The days were hot and thirsty and yet they still found time and water enough to tend to Llyat's scab filled canyon. In the mid-afternoon of their third day at sea Irabo rowed their small boat into the harbour of the town with no name. The Banshees Wail was soon spotted amongst the many other ships present, given its distinctive shape and layout. Llyat directed Irabo's stokes until at last they pulled alongside the vessel that they all hoped would take them back to Parandor.

Tying the boat to the jetty that serviced the caravel, the three disembarked and then set out to find Captain Highroar. It did not take them ong. The crusty old seaman was asleep in his cabin. The guard who greeted them confirmed this to be Highroar's routine ever since he had discovered the whorehouses and ale houses that surrounded the harbour. A week of heavy drinking and the repeated dipping of his dick had emptied both the Captain's sack and purse. Llyat looked to his bundle. Now he knew he would be able to control Highroar, for the diamonds it contained would bewitch the fat fornicator; and so it turned out to be.

They stayed a week in the harbour while the Captain lusted over the handful of diamonds he had been given as payment for the use of his ship. Highroar had been delighted with the price he had obtained for the gems in the open market, for those who dealt with such objects said they had never before seen such quality. It was soon rumoured that they had magical properties for the exposure of the diamond to the violet storm had given them a sparkle that when cut and polished, outshone anything the jewel merchants had believed possible. With such sudden wealth at his disposal Highroar no longer had to chase whores. By day the Captain busied himself and his crew, assembling provisions and all else that would be required for a return across the vast ocean. Highroar had procured good quality clothes for his three guests which they soon donned with great satisfaction. Irabo continued to address Llyat's wound while Heliana spent most of her time resting. The evening before they were due to sail for home, Highroar took Llyat and Irabo to his favourite tavern in order to celebrate the end of their time on the island that smelled of cinnamon.

It had been some time since Llyat had savoured a good pint of ale. In fact, he searched his memory to think when that actually was. He thought of his last encounter with Methladon inside the Red Mare when he had drunk far more than intended due to his fascination with the game called Fidchell. He remembered his time as a servant in Parandor and how he had drained the dregs from highborn idle's flagons once the pampered elite had retired to their beds. Then his mind jumped to the Three Sisters in Fallguard where he had quaffed with Thias and Irabo. That was the first time he had seen the Moirai but it was the memory of the beer served up by Kaylee which brought a smile to his face. If he had drank beer after that night he couldn't remember doing so and the anticipation of the Lotus Isle brew drew him in like a spell. Llyat was not to be disappointed. Highroar had said the beer was good but in fact it was exceptional. Made from fermented cinnamon grass with yeast that had been once been imported from some far away land, its taste was exceptional and a blend somewhere between Blessed Beast and bog-standard mead.

Five tankards took its toll on Llyat's actions and as he relaxed he became less inhibited. He soon began to join in the songs sung by the local sailors who filed the tavern that was known to all as the Loose Limpet in recognition of its whores and the barkeep's knack of sucking in money. It mattered not to Llyat that he didn't know the words, nor the language the songs were sung in. By the time each got to its fifth verse, he had sussed out the melody and made up nonsense words to the amusement of those sober enough to listen. When finally he got too loud, Highroar and Irabo each took one of Llyat's arms on their shoulders and they dragged the youth back to the Banshees Wail.

The evening had been a resounding success and only spoiled when one whore looking for business had made reference to the price needed to fuck the one with the scar. Highroar, who knew the harlot well from previous visits, soon sent her away and by then Llyat had been too pissed to care. He was dropped by the door to the small cabin he shared with Heliana at the rear of the Banshees Wail. When he woke the next morning with a head that thumped, Llyat had a vague recollection of being chastised. The beratement began again once his lover noted he had woken from his drunken stupor. Then a growing sickness inside his stomach caused him to realise that the ship was tossing upon the ocean. He had overslept and missed the Banshees departure. Staggering onto the deck he sought out his friend as fast as he dared without falling.

"Irabo, please squeeze my wrists," he shouted as he caught sight of his saviour.

The journey back across the ocean turned out to be both benign and pleasurable. The weather was good with not a single storm during the three and a half weeks it took the caravel to cross the blue desert. The crew were happy in the extreme for the payment they had been promised by Highroar filled them with expectations of new lives in a standard they had never before dreamed of. The Captain was the happiest of all for he intended to buy another two like the Banshees Wail and run the greatest trading fleet that the realm had ever witnessed. Llyat kept his cabin locked at all times for although the sailors were content, he did not want them helping themselves to the diamond pebbles in his oversized bundle, nor Destiny's Song which now held special meaning in his life. A south-easterly breeze kept the ship on a steady course for home and never once did it succumb to the doldrums. Llyat spent much time gazing out to sea, marvelling at the creatures that surfaced from time to time. Between such sightings he reflected on all that had happened during his brief visit to the Lotus Isles. Heliana continued to rest, to take in the rays of Solaris, and as her belly grew large she turned more the colour of the people from the islands. Each night Llyat, Heliana, and Irabo joined the Captain for dinner in his cabin. Highroar had spent wisely and the food served up was varied and of good quality. On one particular evening of their third week out at sea, Highroar finally persuaded Llyat to talk of his experiences in the Underworld for the youth had vehemently refused until that night to speak of what had transpired there.

All listened with great interest to his story including Irabo who had heard it all before on the climb up the Mountain of Enlightenment. Llyat began with the events at the bottom of the iron quarry and although the Captain was aware that Theoplous had been killed, he wept at the description of the torture that his first mate had endured. Heliana wept when Llyat spoke of how Thias has been stabbed by the Lord over Fear and then sacrificed himself such that Llyat could continue his quest. Then at last Llyat told of the chase. How Urthanock had cornered h m in his childhood home, a replica created by his own imagination. All ears pricked when he described how Destiny's Song had entered the Vessel's chest, driven out Urthanock's essence, and freed Llyat's once friend Methladon from the madness that had consumed him.

Suddenly Heliana began to chuckle.

"What's so funny?" asked Llyat as he stoked the healing cleft on his face.

"I cannot stop thinking of all those hours in which Thias tortured h mself trying to work out the message that talked of how Urthanock could be defeated," she began.

"What are you getting at?" asked Llyat.

"You know, the so-called Ballad of Predestination that the bard thought tc be some tune or song to which Urthanock had no defence," continued Heliana with the smile of the smug etched onto her face.

"The ballad of fucking what?" sneered Highroar as he downed his third tankard of ale.

"Explain yourself Heliana," added Irabo as a look of intrigue formed on his face.

"Predestination; Destiny. Ballad; Song, They are one and the same thing," laughed Heliana. "It was never a tune or rhyme. It was always that sword you have locked away in our cabin Llyat, the one that once belong to our old master Marus."

"Of course, that's it," added Irabo, face palming his head.

"Fuck me!" exclaimed Llyat as the coin dropped. "How I wish I had known that when I entered the Underworld. I could have used that knowledge and perhaps killed Urthanock sooner."

"But the Moirai had already decided your outcome," replied Irabo as Highroar poured another drink and scratched away at his crotch. "Just be grateful they rolled their final dice in your favour."

"The buggers do not exist," snapped back Llyat and the conversation moved on.

The friends talked late into the night and each took their turn. They each spoke in detail of the sacrifices others had made as their quest had progressed. It was Irabo's turn to weep when he recalled all that Tonousa Amberstone had done fo~ them, lost in her mistaken belief it was all simply the resurgence of the cult of Death Tubaria. Once back in control of his emotions he thanked Heliana for killing the Fool and exacting revenge for Tonousa's murder.

"Llyat, how do you cope knowing so many have died, your parents, your childhood friends, your master, Thias, Thamous, Einar, and all those others who helped you become the man you are today?" uttered Irabo as he wiped a fina tear from his eye.

Llyat though for several minutes as Highroar snored. Then he answered.

"It's because I had already witnessed them die in my imagination. I worried so much as I grew up about being left alone in the world. To ease my pain, I always imagined those whom I met and liked dying long before they ever did. Time and time again I felt the hurt from those imagined departures as if they were real.

So, to me, all were dead before they died and when their strings were finally cut, despite a transient experience of grief, I at once accepted the loss."

"Have you imagined my death and that of our unborn?" asked Heliana.

"Indeed I have and my heart has been crushed many times."

"Fuck me Llyat Emgar, you are a bugger of the strangest kind," she added as she wiped a tear from her own eye. "I love you much more than when I first met you, despite the scar that adds a bit of man to your laddish looks. Yet events have made you colder. You need to reconnect into the joy of the simple things of life and drop this emotional shite. That is how I like you."

"She is right," added Irabo.

"I know," answered Llyat. "Deep down, I have always known."

As the beer and emotions mixed, the three moved on to discuss their aspirations for the future. Irabo wanted nothing more than to return to the City Watch of Parandor. He declined a share of the diamond pebbles and told Llyat to keep them for himself and his future family. He did however ask that a donation be made through the Temple of Fatumai, to benefit the poor who no doubt still struggled in the aftermath of the battle. Heliana on the other hand wished to return to the life that she knew best. Somehow, she wanted to stay and serve the highborn but understood how difficult that would be with a child hanging on to her dress hem day and night. Llyat had no idea what he wanted to do. He spoke of his desire to be a good father and partner but other than that his future seemed as dense as the winter fog that rolls down the Tiaryer. Mouths and words exhausted, the three friends retired to their beds and left Highroar slumped over his table; the sounds of the waves drowned out by his drunken snores.

As soon as Llyat fell into a deep sleep, three visitors arrived to disturb his peace. Smoke like mists, not of the water kind, swirled around the storm grey creatures.

"Wake up lad, we have come to speak with you," whispered the first of three hooded figures.

"We have come to tell you all that will come to pass," added the second as her fetid breath slipped inside Llyat's nostrils and kick started his thoughts.

The third made a hissing sound, almost snakelike, but yet less threatening.

"Say what you must then leave me alone," Llyat heard himself reply.

"Our sister played the game better than we had expected," said the first as she too moved closer to Llyat's face. "You succeeded against the odds but there is a price to pay young Emgar, descendant of Raulyn's fortuitous fuck. We have come to tell of the role you must play should you wish your days to be free of the terrors that others faced on your behalf."

"Listen well to my sister," added the second as her gnarl-boned figure thrust its talon towards his eyes. "Should you not comply with the roll of the dice then we will not be held responsible for all that will befall your vessel."

The third hissed again and yet remained at a distance behind the other two.

"Tell me what you must, then fuck off," answered Llyat as he tossed, turned, and perspired.

"You are to sit on the throne of Parandor as Ruler of the Middle Realm," continued the first as her wrinkled hand ran its rough skin over Llyat's deep facial scar. "You will give the woman who sleeps beside you five children and we will come for the first girl that is born. Only then can you survive what you have unleashed."

"The girl babe will then be ours for we need the child to play a new game of mother's design."

"No… No… No…!" screamed Llyat as he shot upward from his sweat drenched pillow and into Heliana's arms.

"Wake up Llyat, you're having another nightmare," she whispered as she wiped the sweat from his brow while behind Llyat's eyes the three crones disappeared into the mist.

"Oh fuck!" moaned Llyat. "That was a bad one."

"What was it about this time?" demanded Heliana.

"You don't want to know."

Two days later the Banshees Wail tied up to the reconstructed harbour before the southern wall of Parandor. Llyat had noticed how the Members of the City Watch had monitored the ship's progress from the battlements that looked out over the Estuary of New Beginnings. As he and his friends prepared to disembark, a group of armoured knights approached the gang plank. It was obvious to all aboard that the City's troops remained in a heightened state of readiness following its recent victory over the forces of the Eastern Marsh. Llyat said farewell to Captain Highroar and wished him well in his future endeavours. The rotund fornicator reciprocated and once again thanked Llyat for making him the richest of all the pox infused sea swine. With his bundle over his left shoulder and Destiny's Song tucked into his belt, Llyat lead Irabo and his waddling lover off the ship and onto the jetty.

A knight moved forward to meet the new arrivals and once within touching distance the leader of the escort lifted his visor and exposed his face.

"Hello Irabo, Heliana, and I guess this must be Llyat. I'm so relieved to see you all alive," began the knight in golden armour. "What happened to your face lad?"

"Heliana told me that you had come to Parandor," answered Irabo has he stepped forward and shook the knight's gauntlet. "But for fucks sake Darchus what are you doing trussed up in all that metal?"

"Take no notice of my face," added Llyat as he too then shook the knight's gauntlet. "Heliana thinks it makes me look manly and the appearance is starting to grow on me, especially since my beard has started to grow back."

"The Lady Flurdiana promoted me Irabo!" answered Darchus as he beckoned the trio to follow him to the gates of Parandor. "She guessed it would be the 'Marked' returning and she sent me here to greet you. However she had also hoped that Thias the bard was with you for she wished to reward him for his part in defeating Urthanock's forces. Where is the man who led Parandor to victory?"

Darchus did not wait for an answer for Llyat's facial expressions said it all.

"That news distresses me," sighed the knight as he led the way into the Capital. "I will call on you later to hear all you have to say but right now you must meet with our new Ruler. She waits for you just inside the gate and has important matters to discuss with Llyat. Be prepared to answer her honestly lad and without hesitation. Be concise with your patter for she is not one who tolerates many words and will be direct when she speaks to you."

Glancing sideways, Llyat noticed Darchus look at Heliana with increased interest.

"Heliana looks like she is not far from parting with her load," continued Darchus. "Once you are settled in the Citadel I will send my wife Ailora to look to her needs; she was midwife back in Valameer."

"I thank you for that," answered Llyat as he marched on in deep thought.

"What does Flurdiana want to talk to Llyat about that cannot wait?" demanded Irabo.

"He will find out soon enough once we reach the gates. You and Heliana must not cross through the portal until the Lady gives her permission. She will only do that once she has spoken with Llyat."

"Be on your guard Llyat," warned Irabo. "I sense all is not right."

Llyat was escorted through the gate and into a ring of Trident Guard, all fully armed and alert. Then the ring parted and Lady Flurdiana appeared, stepped forward, and embraced Llyat.

"Did you seal the portal to the Underworld as dictated by the Prophecy?" she asked.

"Yes my lady."

"And did you slay Urthanock?"

"Yes my Lady."

"Is Thias Calavan dead?"

"Yes my Lady.

"Then I must offer the throne to you as Saviour of the Realm," she said with a firmness that concerned Llyat. "We will crown you tomorrow."

"No my Lady," answered Llyat in a manner that mirrored the Lady's tone.

"What do mean?" replied Lady Flurdiana, somewhat shocked.

"I do not want this honour and responsibility. You are highborn and will make a much better job of it. I require a more simple life and I wish to focus on raising a family. Do not try and persuade me otherwise for the only thing I want to rule is my own happiness."

Llyat gazed upon the formidable woman before him and wondered what would now happen.

"Are you sure lad?" she asked as her face softened.

"Yes I am."

"Good; in that case take your woman to the Citadel," she ordered with a wave of her hand. "Thinata Fullbane claims to be a distant relative of yours and has prepared a room for you both within her private apartment should you return. She always held on to the belief that you would, unlike most of us. But now you are here and we have settled our futures, enter as my friend and be reassured of my protection."

The Lady turned and departed with her guards. Llyat moved back to the gate and held Heliana's hand. He hugged Irabo with all the heart felt passion he could muster and said his farewell to the warrior would had pulled him half dead from the Tiaryer all those months ago.

"Come my little duck, Lady Fullbane is going to look after us!"

Llyat felt the blow on his shoulder as Heliana slapped him hard.

"Stop calling me stupid names Llyat or I swear I will finish what Urthanock failed to do."

Two hands gripped and remained entwined as the lovers swayed on towards the Citadel.

Four the next four weeks Llyat led the life of a devoted partner. Sequestered inside Lady Fullbane's private rooms while the great Lady was away at a nunnery on an imposed starvation, Llyat pampered Heliana and responded to her every need. There was another reason he failed to venture out into the city. His mood had dipped low and his confidence had been shaken. His melancholy, Heliana had told him, was a rebound reaction to all that he had been through and a coming to terms with all those he had lost. He saw the logic in her words but also knew that he had not yet resolved his feelings towards the deep scar across his face. The man Darchus, who Irabo finally introduced to Llyat as the one he had once worked for and from whom they had borrowed the horse Glorius from so many months ago, called in from time to time and his wife Ailora came every morning to check on Heliana's progress.

At last the day finally came when infant demanded to be born and began to knock on the door of Heliana's quim. Llyat was dispatched to fetch Ailora from the rooms she now shared with her husband in the Citadel. Once the midwife had departed, Llyat lingered to talk with Darchus for the cry of his lover's pains were too much for his ears to bear. Darchus entertained Llyat for several hours and they indulged in games of Fidchell, Fox and Geese, and the like. The olive skinned Ourri then appeared with a message that spoke of great progress was being made and that Llyat should return to the birthing room. Darchus took Llyat by the arm and led the trembling youth back to Lady Fullbane's quarters. There they waited outside the door to the bedchamber while Llyat squirmed every time Heliana wailed. The sound of a healthy infant's cry soon changed Llyat's mood and he began to pace in circles and clap his hands in great joy. Ailora's face then appeared at the door with a smile that stretched from ear to ear.

"It's a boy and all is well!"

Llyat jumped in excitement and made for the door. Once Heliana had been sat upright with her babe in her arms, Llyat rushed to her bed. He embraced his new child and the woman who had sparked this most magical of moments.

"Look how happy they both are," whispered Ailora, loud enough for all to hear.

"Was it an easy birth, it seemed to come in no time at all?" asked Darchus as Heliana smiled back and with great pride and satisfaction over Llyat's shoulder.

"It was as if it were her tenth," replied Ailora as she lifted her bloodied hands to confirm her role in the birthing process. "I believe it has come a little early but it is a good size and is well formed."

"And what of the afterbirth, did you deliver that also or do we still have cause for concern?"

"Do not worry, it's in that bucket in the corner," answered Ailora as she pointed to the pail.

"You'd best not show it Llyat, I don't want him going queasy on me," ordered Darchus.

Llyat took the infant way from its attempts to latch onto Heliana's tit, an act that caused it to scream out in displeasure, and he carried it to his new friends in order to let them gaze upon his prize possession.

"What do you think Darchus? Have you ever seen such a looker?"

"He's his father's son, of that there is no doubt," answered Darchus as he smiled down upon the babe. "Just as ugly and ginger as well!"

"But with a cock to match his father's by all accounts," answered Llyat as the friends continued their inane banter.

Heliana shouted from her bed as the child began to scream louder.

"Bring him to my tit or I swear by the gods I will rise from this bed and kick you Emgar."

Llyat obeyed for he knew this was not the time for further teasing.

"What shall we call him Llyat?" Heliana asked as a tiny mouth latched on as a limpet to a rock.

"He has a great voice, just like a bard," answered Llyat. "Let's call him Ffortiwin."

"I like that and so would have Thias," she replied.

Heliana smiled from ear to ear, one so full it spoke more than tome of words.

30

Lady Thinata Fullbane returned one week later. While the light from Solaris bathed her pale face as she sat on her chaise longue, she smiled at the infant that she held in her arms. The once large mass had lost a quarter of her weight but of greater importance was that she could now walk unaided; well, just. Her forced exile to a remote nunnery, run by those who followed the Faith of Fatumai and halfway along the coastal road between Parandor and Valameer, had induced a most remarkable change. Sent there by the newly crowned Lady Flurdiana as a reward for her saving the highborn in the Citadel, Thinata Fullbane had now seen the way forward. New rituals had been established in order to counter her addictive habits. Her life was no longer driven by the need to eat, drink, and satiate perversions. She was reborn and delighted to be reunited with the child that her husband and his fellow conspirators had sought to hide. The time of the Enderdetag alignment and the return of the Lord of Fear had passed, just as the Cuvar had predicted.

Llyat smiled as his adopted relative sat cuddling the infant he had named Ffortiwin. The babe was thriving from the hours spent chomping on Heliana's tits and it grew heavier by the day. The cleft across Llyat's face no longer cause him pain and his beard, fair in colour with a hint of ginger, hid the worst of its impact. He marvelled at how Heliana had taken to motherhood and how her energy and positivity kept him going through the dark thoughts that constantly reminded him of his failure. He had taken to spending several hours each day atop of the highest tower of the Citadel, staring out across the Realm, but always ending in the direction of Maplehill. Finding it difficult to venture into the city he imagined all would blame him for the death of Thias Calavan and all those others who had died protecting him. Both Heliana and Lady Fullbane tried to convince him that these were deluded thoughts but Llyat's melancholy ran deep and he was not minded to think otherwise.

So, it was with the babe cooing in her arms that Lady Fullbane had suggested throwing a grand banquet and party to cheer Llyat up. His response was far from positive but Heliana liked the idea and agreed to seek out the few friends Llyat had, and to ask them to come and celebrate the birth of their first child. Before a date could be set however a member of the Trident Guard arrived with a message for Lady Fullbane. The new Ruler had heard of her return and had summoned Thinata for an important audience with her Council. The child was handed to Heliana and despite the great struggle to stand and move, the onetime whale followed the messenger out of her solar.

Heliana fed Ffortiwin and once settled, laid him in his crib. Leaving her most precious possession in Llyat's care she set off in search of the few friends she thought he would be willing to entertain. Llyat was fine with that arrangement until the babe began to want another feed. By the time Heliana had returned he was beyond despair for he had tried everything he knew to try and settle its hunger. Heliana walked in and laughed as she looked to Llyat, a little finger thrust into Ffortiwin's mouth in the hope of convincing the infant it was a nipple; all the while pulling ridiculous faces in order to startle the babe out of its distress. Heliana wasted no time in taking charge of her son and fixing it to her breast. All fell silent and so Llyat sat down on the floor before Heliana's feet and enquired as to the success of her mission.

"Did you find anyone willing to come?" he moaned while half hoping the answer was no.

"Irabo was out with the Watch on something important so I left a message for him to contact me," began Heliana as she smiled gently and stroked Llyat's head with her free hand. "I found Darchus and Ailora in the courtyard and they both said they could come. Then I remembered the girl who had cared for you in Falahorn."

"You mean Arnkatla?" asked Llyat, unsure as to where this was leading.

"Yes, the one you said had a face like a plank and the arse of a mathulath! That's the one."

"You have invited her?"

"Yes, I have, I thought it would cheer you up because you are so fucking miserable these days," answered Heliana. "That's why I have been so long. I had to trek all the way to the Temple of Fatumai to find her. It was worth it though for she had much insight into what has been happening in Parandor, both while we were away and ever since we have been confined to Lady Fullbane's rooms. Would you like me to share what I have learned?"

"I suppose so... I mean yes... thank you," replied Llyat with the enthusiasm of a snail.

"I have to tell you first that she has suffered much these past two months since her father was killed in the battle for Parandor," began Heliana while she swopped the baby from one breast to the other. "Arnkatla described with great pride how he had died a hero along with several other Berserkers defending the stakewall before the West Gate."

Heliana fell quiet, and Llyat noticed the look of concern upon her face.

"What is it?" he asked. "What has happened?"

"There is something else you must understand Llyat although I am a little reluctant to tell you given your black mood."

"Whatever it is you must speak it, no matter what its impact, just as long as it is the truth."

"A messenger bird came from Falahorn some three weeks past. The dragons have fled, apparently in search of sustenance. The message from the Berserkers is that the dark magic they fed off has disappeared. They have all retreated to beyond the Dirmark and their leader, the one with the strange name, has died along with the magic."

"Do you mean Cvyler Olin," demanded Llyat as a heavy pain sat within his heart.

"Yes, that was the name she spoke. Arnkatla is devastated and sees no point in returning to Falahorn. In fact, she is going to become one of Fatumai's nuns and seek out the most isolated place in this Realm, possibly the Abbey on the coast road, where she can reflect with fellow Sisters of the Fates."

"When does she intend to leave?" answered Llyat.

"As soon as she has seen you one last time my love. She was interested to know what you intended to do with your life now that your quest was over. I told her you still had not made your mind up. She then asked if you intended to go back to Maplehill. I said that was unlikely given there was nothing left there."

"Perhaps she should build a nunnery there," added Llyat amid a rambling confusion.

"Oh really!" answered Heliana as she detected the slightest hint of sparkle in Llyat's eyes. "You may be interested to know what else she told me. Lady Flurdiana rules with strict enforcement of her diktats and everything is monitored by her Trident Guard. Apparently, this past week, the Lady has taken a lover and by all accounts she is wearing him out. It is said she was looking for a benign hero who would provide her with a child to continue her line."

"And does the poor bastard have a name for I would like to offer my sympathies."

"Prepare yourself for a shock Llyat. You will find what I am about to say hard to believe."

"Who is it? Spit it out," he shouted, startling the baby for an instant."

"It is none other than the Captain of her Trident Guard."

"Fuck me! The poor bugger," sighed Llyat as he raised himself to his feet and sought to climb out of the depths of melancholy."

"The Lady is rebuilding the Realm and starting first with Parandor," continued Heliana. "The wizards have apparently all disappeared and their home burned after their Guild Master and Thias destroyed the Lore of the Dead inside its centre. The great walls of their tower have however remained intact and Flurdiana is refashioning its interior to be her own private palace. Some say Irabo has had some input given all he has witnessed during his travels across the Realm..."

"Speak no more of such nonsense," moaned Llyat as he began to pace the room.

"There is just one other thing you need to be aware of my love. The truth is out and talked of across the Capital. All believe you have the right to rule the Realm and that you declined the Lady's offer of the crown. Many reasons are speculated and offered up for debate, but none know the truth. As a matter of fact, neither do I. Perhaps one day when you are better, you will explain it all to me "

"Perhaps," answered Llyat.

As dusk fell Lady Fullbane returned and summoned Llyat and Heliana to hear her news.

"You'll never believe it, I don't think I even do myself," she began. "I have to keep biting my lip to convince me I am not dreaming.

"Then tell us what you know and lower the tension," ordered Llyat.

"Flurdiana, no doubt amid the peak of one of her gush cycles, has appointed me Lady Chamberlain and given me a detachment of Trident Guard to pamper to my needs. Oh what joy! It is all in recognition of my heroic actions during the battle."

"You mean when you sat on your arse and insulted everyone in earshot?" replied Llyat as he conjured up a fake smile. "That's what Thias told me!"

"Quite so, and there is no need to be so rude young Emgar, even if you are my nephew," she babbled on as she made her way back to her chaise-longue and there collapsed from the effort. "There is just one snag, I am to continue to control my eating and lose more lard. The pickle prong guards are instructed to watch over my mouth and so I will need to rely on you two to sneak in provision when my body weakens. But oh my word, I will be responsible for organising all the parties and stuff that that idiot Ystafell used to fuss about and always cock up."

"That's wonderful news my Lady," chipped in Heliana, "but what of old ginger chops. What has happened to him?"

"That my innocents, is another of the mad bitch's new appointments," rambled Lady Fullbane amid her excitement. "Ystafell is appointed Sovereign Adviser as well as Court Judge to replace Lady Emeny who died most heroically from a bolt to her arse. I doubt myself that anyone misses the sour faced scrawn of skin and bone. Had she had a rump as big as mine the steel tip would never have reached her bones; what say you Heliana?"

"No one could argue with you on that score my Lady," giggled Heliana.

"I will tell you something else though my dears," the whale continued, "Legal judgements and council will now be far more entertaining, especially after lunch as the old fool drinks himself out of each day."

"Has Lady Flurdiana made any other new appointments?" asked Llyat.

The youth sat on the floor beside Heliana and tried to remain present.

"Has she? I'll say she has, the insane cow. In her womb induced madness, no doubt brought on by her constant demands on her stud who they say loses more weight as each day passes; she has appointed Heward Teulu to the position of Grand Physician as well as Royal High Priest. He is under instruction never to bad mouth Lady Flurdiana again for rumours reached her ear of whispers at the War Council before the battle commenced. You could say he is on a kind of probation and is expected to learn the healing arts as quick as his acorn sized brain will permit. Most of his healing work he intendeds to delegate to the two strange buggers under him who go by the names Atropos and Lachesis. Or so the rumours go."

"We know them, don't we love," added Llyat and Heliana nodded her head in agreement. "And what of poor Irabo, has he been given any title or role after all he had been through?"

"Your friend has this very day been appointed the new Commander of the City Watch. He certainly will be stretched to his limits."

"So, what of Commander Townsforth" asked Llyat as he ran his hand through his facial hair? "I had heard a rumour he had survived the battle although had been wounded."

"Sir Townsforth the Limp Arm, was knighted this morning and now heads the Royal Guard," continued Fullbane. "It is expected he will knock discipline and pride into those who had addled their minds with the Lillywort supplied by that bastard Lolly."

"And has our esteemed Ruler employed another Fool to replace the one I stuck down?" asked Heliana as she spat to the floor.

"No, for she now has a Court full of them," laughed Lady Fullbane.

"What of Sir Byddin then," asked Llyat as he sought to make sense of the chain of new appointments?

"He is to leave tomorrow and has been ordered to keep a garrison in Valameer now that Flurdiana sits in Parandor. He has been told to keep his good eye on the wellbeing of the town and his missing one on the rebuilding of the Bards Guild and Bridge of Athuna. The merry music men that survived the slaughter have begun their labours already. At least that what the birds say although such a task will not be completed in our lifetime."

"Are those all the changes we need to be aware of?" asked Llyat as he rose to his feet. "I could go and get us all a snack if you would like."

"There are just a few more to complete your necessary education. We have a new executioner, Isambard Hotch. By all accounts he can wield his spade like Richemanus could his axe. The order of the Knightfall are proud to have him in their numbers."

"No fucking way!" exclaimed Llyat.

"There is more that may amuse you," she continued. "Captain Highroar has been appointed Captain of the Royal Barge; I jest not."

"He'll turn the ship into a floating whorehouse," sneered Heiana, stroking her baby's head.

"I told you we are to be run by a Fool's circus," laughed the Lady. "Now what else, oh yes, that's it. Lady Lorst appointed Royal Librarian and Watcyn Dustfury will leave tomorrow to re-establish the garrison at the Grey Keep. He will defend the North and overtime create another great citadel where once the dismal tower once stood alone. Wesmin Lightmain will travel with him but then continue with a force of one hundred men with the task of destroying anything left in the Eastern Marsh. Not one of the lizard kind will be spared, if indeed there are any of the swamp swine left. The armies of the Fifteen Keeps, those that have not already left to attend to their farms, will be gone by the end of the week. The Berserkers left weeks ago apparently. Well, that's it, you're as up to date as I am. Now Llyat sneak off and bring us all cake and wine but don't let those pickle prong buggers see you. If they stop you then it's all for you and Heliana, do you understand?"

"On course I do Aunt Thinata," answered Llyat as he rushed off to find some comfort food.

Six months later Llyat and Heliana had finished their preparations to leave Parandor once and for all time. It had all begun at the banquet to celebrate the birth of Ffortiwin and when Llyat's deep melancholy had begun to lift following a conversation he had had with Irabo. The new Commander of the Watch had talked to Llyat about his future and what Llyat would do with the diamond pebbles that made him the wealthiest of all men in Parandor, should he choose to sell them. Llyat met with the warrior weekly and one afternoon while gazing out across the Realm from the highest tower he decided he would rebuild the three villages destroyed by the Knights of Avolire. He would go home.

As the months had rolled on, Llyat sold a few diamonds here and there and bought all that would be necessary to rebuild Maplehill, Ashview, and Oakwood. When ready to depart, the cart line was some twenty long. He had recruited others to join him in this new quest, Darchus, his wife Ailora, and their son Finian were the first. The once cordwainer of Valameer was not content to spend his days in metal plate and wished for a new challenge and a return to simpler freedoms. Lady Flurdiana was happy to release Darchus from her service on the condition that he continued to monitor the welfare of the 'Marked who had saved the world' and report back to her should Llyat ever express the need to try and claim the throne. After speaking to Llyat about what they would find in Maplehill, Darchus intended to rebuild the Red Mare, turn it into the most social of meeting points, but would also create a workshop in order to manufacture the best quality shoes that he would trade with the Capital. The leather would come from the large herd of cattle purchased by the sale of a single diamond and which Llyat would care for with his family as he recreated Chirth Hadra's farm.

One night, Arnkatla Jarl decided to join in Llyat's exodus. In a spontaneous instant, having heard much of Llyat's time in Maplehill, she decided to rebuild the old watermill in order to make bread for the three village communities. From the profits generated she intended to create a small convent adjacent to the banks of the Tiaryer and spend her spare time in refining her healing arts and understanding the teaching of those who followed Fatumai. She claimed there was nothing left for her in Falahorn, now that her father was dead and the dragons long since departed.

The thirty souls who prepared to set off for the verdant grasslands included several servants of the court that Llyat knew well. Among them was Arfon Caddick, Will Geddings, Tecwyn Hennion and the lad Mervrig who had no second name. They brought with them their lovers and despite this depletion of those that serviced the Court, Lady Flurdiana was happy to let them leave for it was said she intended to replace them with ones who would spy on those they were allocated to serve. Such was the culture of her 'New Beginning'.

Two days before the time of the great exodus, Irabo came to talk with Llyat. Lady Flurdiana was pregnant and he had been called before her and given new orders. He was to take a small contingent of the Watch and base himself in Maplehill. There he was also instructed to monitor the Marked and like Darchus, report back should Llyat show a desire to usurp her throne. Irabo fully understood this would never happen and was comfortable in revealing the Lady's plans to his friend. This amused Llyat greatly and the two embraced the opportunity to rekindle their friendship. Irabo was also instructed to establish a major weapons workshop in Maplehill, based on the site of the Heyn smithy, as the Lady wished to arm her forces to a level never before imagined in the history of the Realm.

"But what of your position as Commander of the Watch" asked Llyat?

"Sir Townsforth the Limp Arm will lead all three, the Trident Guard, The Golden Royal Guard, and the City Watch. They are to be combined into a single body of men, reporting directly through Townsforth to the Lady herself."

And so, it was that on the day of departure Irabo turned up with several younger members of the Watch who he introduced as Ambrose, Bruge, Fillias, Atheas, and Lothar. The rest of the travellers were made up from friends that Darchus's family and Arnkatla had made during their time in Parandor. Lady Fullbane had waddled down to the North Gate to witness the departure and to say farewell with eyes that overflowed with sadness. As she hugged Heliana close, the elder woman's nose twitched while the hairs of her nostrils detected a new scent that seeped out from Heliana's pores.

"Your pregnant again aren't you?" she whispered as she pulled back and smiled.

"Yes I am," replied Heliana, "but say nothing to Llyat. I want it to be a surprise for him when we reach Maplehill."

"I want to know as soon as it is born; promise me you will keep in touch."

"Of course we will, and thank you so much for all you have done for us."

The progress of the line of carts along the banks of the Tiaryer was slow in the extreme. In the first of the waggons sat Llyat and Heliana and it was the Saviour of the Realm who dictated the pace of the expedition. The melancholy hero was well aware of Heliana's discomfort at having left the Capital that had been her home for the majority of her short yet eventful life. Although his lover never moaned, Llyat reckoned that deep inside her soul she would rather have stayed in Parandor. Ffortiwin was a good child and Heliana rarely let the infant stray from her side, particularly as the child become a proficient crawler. So, it was that on the second morning of the journey Llyat decided his paranoia was getting the better of him and he began a conversation with the intention of exploring his lover's true feelings.

"I know we have been travelling the speed of a slug but by the time Solaris passes over his watch tomorrow, we should be in Maplehill," he began. "I know that there will be little left of the buildings and that the bones of the slaughtered may still cover the ground. Yet I do hope you will like the maples for their scent will astound your nose."

"I hope so too Llyat," replied Heliana while trying to raise a smile. "Most of all I want a safe place for Ffortiwin and our second that will come soon enough. Given there is nothing there of significance then we must educate our children in the ways of the world as best we can. However you occupy yourself during the day, you must make time for love, play, and teaching. I will not let you squash the child like your father did you. How do feel now about him having tried to closet you away rather than teaching you the ways of the world?"

"I understand what he was trying to do," replied Llyat as he ran his fingers through his beard. "He knew that evil would come looking for me and he did his best to hide me until that time came."

"We all know that story Llyat, but in my opinion he would have been better preparing you for the dangers you would face. I think you were very lucky that Irabo was there to fish you out of the river when he did. If Rukave had been my father I would have bollocked him daily on his failings..."

Llyat did not reply leaving Heliana to ask her next question.

"Do you miss him?" she asked.

"Of course I fucking miss him, he was the only father I ever had and as such he will always have a special place in my heart," snapped back Llyat as his eyes strayed back to the road.

"Do you ever wonder who your real father was? I mean, Rukave was just the Historian who took you away for protection. It was another who shot your seed. Then there is your real mother. Do you never wonder what she would have been like?"

"The past has passed just like the water through the old mill," answered Llyat. "There is no point dwelling on it for there is no one alive who would still have the knowledge. I questioned my Aunt Fullbane about it some weeks ago and she confirmed that Rukave never once gave up the secrets of his former life. Until the day my strings are cut I will always think of Rukave and Lyrusa Emgar as my true parents, for that is the only honour I can give those who did their best to protect me from the Lord of Fear; but enough of this tripe. Tell me what you really think of the prospect of living your life with me in Maplehill."

"From all you have told me about the place, I have to admit that its attraction to me is not the same as yours. I just hope that I can get to like it over time."

"You'll love it; I'm sure of it," answered Llyat as he forced a smile and squeezed Heliana's hand.

"Look Llyat, a turd is a turd. You cannot polish one and in fact the best you can do with yours is to cover it maple sap. Whatever you do don't get rid of the trees."

Llyat began to laugh and he continued for several minutes much to Heliana's surprise. It had been a most insignificant joke and yet it had acted as the key in unlocking Llyat's emotions. Months of mental darkness began to lift and by the time he had stopped laughing the Realm appeared a much brighter place in which to end his days. Whatever had happened inside his head had worked like magic and for a moment Llyat was convinced it had to have been another of Rukave's clever mind locks. Knowing he would never know the answer and so wasting no further time in thinking on it, he turned to Heliana with his eyes sparkling like the great diamond in the sky. His lips moistened with the anticipation of lingering once again on his lover's flesh. Heliana returned Llyat's stare and wondered what was going on inside her lover's head.

"Are you okay Llyat? I've not seen you look so happy for months. I only said 'don't get rid of the trees.' What's so fucking funny about that?"

"Covering a turd in maple sap," giggled Llyat and a further bout of laughter followed.

"I'm beginning to worry about you Emgar," laughed Heliana as Llyat's the mood infected her senses. "What's so fucking funny about that?"

"Those few words describe Maplehill in the simplest yet most perfect of ways," he replied as he pulled on his horse's reins and brought the cart to a stop. "I can smell it now. It's what I've really missed about the place, the scent of my home, my youth, my family, and my friends. We stank of shit and maple and so soon shall you my love."

Llyat leaned across and kissed his lover with more passion that he could remember. He tried to reach under Heliana's dress but she pressed Ffortiwin down into her lap. Her face flushed with embarrassment after which she whispered back.

"Llyat, not here, not now! Not with all those others behind and wondering why we have stopped"

"So be it, but when all are asleep tonight I intend to make you howl like a Berserker."

"I cannot wait," replied Heliana as she winked. "My cave will be ready whenever the dragon wishes to return."

"Wyvern!" giggled Llyat.

By mid-afternoon the clouds had begun to gather. It was one of those days in the Realm where all turned sultry and the river had begun to steam Llyat knew there was a storm brewing and so did Heliana as she looked to their infant with growing concern. The line of carts moved ever on and Llyat noted the sweat that formed on his horses back. A sense, a feeling, a hint of unease, began to subsume his mind. A great storm was coming and he feared for the safety of the two loves of his life. Irabo and Darchus also recognised the impending threat from the weather and leaving their carts in the hands of others they had raced forward to warn Llyat of the deluge, wind, and lightening that would in their opinion hit them before the day had ended. The conversation had been a short one but all in the end were in agreement. They would make camp as soon as the wind stiffened, which as Irabo had pointed out, always heralded a storm.

A short distance from Maplehill the line of carts stopped for the night. The storm clouds had continued to build throughout the afternoon yet still the wind had not picked up. The line of carts was forced to make a circle as the light from Solaris at last disappeared. Around this camp fire late into the night following a disturbance in a thicket close by, an old naked man was dragged before Llyat and Irabo. He had been spotted approaching the camp by the young boy Fillias who was on watch and facing south towards the nearby thicket. Llyat recognised the old man at once for it was Clotho, the hermit from the oak forest.

"It's okay Fillias, I know this man and have met him once before, leave him here and return to your post," ordered Llyat as he beckon the emaciated hermit forward and sat him by the fire. "Come share some stew with us and tell us what brings you to these parts. Cover yourself with this blanket before you scare the horses."

Clotho willingly accepted both the invitation to eat and the blanket. Then as he swallowed his first mouthful he answered Llyat's question.

"There was no need for me to stay near Harico, for having met with you and passed on my knowledge, my purpose in life was complete. The Prophecy of Enderdetag was fulfilled and with nothing else to do in my life, I set out to find my son, just in case he still walks this Realm alone."

"And what happened to your clothes?" asked Heliana with compassion.

"I was set upon by a group of have-noughts, not long after I had skirted around the capital," began Clotho. "They had lost everything as the Army of the Eastern Marsh passed through their hamlet on route to wage war on Parandor. They were but feckless and impoverished yobs, not yet adult but no longer children. One liked the wool I had fashioned into clothes and relieved me of it for having seen nothing of its kind before he reckoned he would wear it himself."

Llyat sought to offer some comfort.

"Tell me a little of your son," he said as the storm gathered and the air grew heavy and oppressive. "When we met in the oak woods I recall you said his name was Denius Castor. Should that be the case then it is possible that I knew him once. When did you last see him?"

"Although I cannot be certain, I think I have lived through at least thirty summers since I last cast eyes on him," began Clotho. "I will keep my story short for I do not want to bore you with it; and to be honest, it pains me to speak of such things... But for what it is worth I lived with his mother in the village called Ashview until some wandering peddler passed through. She left me and Denius to follow that swine to wherever he laid his head. My son was only ten years old at that time and he was devastated by his mother's desertion. No offence Heliana, but I told him this is how many women lead their lives, jumping from one cock to another."

"None taken," mumbled Heliana as she put young Ffortiwin to her tit. "Just don't judge us all to be the same."

"Quite," continued the hermit. "One day, some two summers later, I had a most strange dream. I was visited by the Moirai and in it we made a pact. Denius had caught the sweating sickness and was not expected to live the night. I made a treaty with the three in order to save his life. I would have to dig in the dirt and find ancient clues. Then I would stay in the oak forest until the day the Marked came to ask for advice. That is exactly what I did and I waited a very long time until you finally showed your face."

"Bollocks!" muttered Llyat.

"But what of your son" asked Heliana, before Llyat could insult the hermit further?

"He stayed with me in the forest for just one year," continued Clotho. "Then he too was visited in a dream by the three crones. They told him to wander and search the Realm for great stories and then to find the Marked. There he was to watch and wait, but for what I do not know. If you knew him once then he at least succeeded in his mission."

"It was he who told me all the mysteries of the Realm, for my father would not speak of them," replied Llyat. "It was he who first told me the stories of Urthanock."

Llyat rose before the camp fire while memories of Denius Castor's stories in the Red Mare flooded back into memory.

"Where was it that you met him and do you know where he is now?" asked the hermit.

"He lived close to me in Maplehill all the time I was growing up," answered Llyat. "I am sad to say that one day the Knights of Avolire came and destroyed our village. I barely escaped alive but your son was not so lucky. I saw him lying dead in the dirt and I took his sword, although I later lost it."

"I guess he was trying to protect the Marked as was expected of him. I think I will make for Maplehill and see if there is anything left of him to bury."

"That is where we are headed so journey on with us," offered Llyat. "I will take you to his bones, unless the skyfawn have carried them off. What will you do then?"

"Find somewhere to lay my head and wait for the Moirai to call."

"Stop talking such tripe," grumbled Llyat. "I will house you in what was my old home upon the hill that overlooks the maples, once I have rebuilt it. We intend to live at the farm and make our living there. I want you to listen to me old man. You have wasted your precious life dreaming of crones and sinking into fantasy. There are no Moirai. They are false ideas formed in the mind of the weak. The Fates and all that Fatumai stuff is just total bollocks. I know, for I have been before the door beneath the Barrow of Harico."

"He is right," added Heliana as she shuffled he arse upon the ground. "Come and join our small group and live out the rest of your days in the comfort of friends, before a warm fire, and with a tankard of Blessed Beast in your hand."

"I will take you up on your offer dear friends," replied the hermit. "If as you say I have wasted my days alone then I had better make up for lost time. I cannot remember the last time I had ale."

Midway through the night the storm blew in across the grasslands. All the weary travellers sheltered beneath their carts as a thick mist rolled in from the Tiaryer. It was one of those tempests where the lightening was almost continuous and yet there was little in the way of thunder. The constant flashes turned the swirling mist the colour of violet and so unusual was the display that Llyat couldn't take his eyes off it. The air crackled, the horses snorted out their discomfort, and Ffortiwin began to cry. Heliana put the child to her breast and closed her eyes in order to block out the terrors that had come once again to test her resolve. The blue lightening grew and the violet mist continued to thicken. The air began to hiss and to glow. Then something most strange happened. Everything that was made of metal began at once to glow. Depending on whether brass, copper, iron, or steel, the metals glowed green, blue, orange or violet. The horses began to tense and Llyat reckoned they soon would bolt should the storm not abate. A feeling of great dread seeped through his pores for this was a most unnatural and bizarre disturbance.

Without warning the old hermit, who had been hiding with Llyat and Heliana, threw down his blanket to once again reveal his leathery nakedness. Before Llvat could move, Clotho snatched Destiny's Song from its resting place on the ground besides its master. Gripping it firmly he ran into the circle of carts and stood before the glowing embers of the camp fire. Llyat made to follow, but Heliana held him back.

"No Llyat, let him do whatever he intends," she shouted through the violet mist. "You must stay with me and the babe. We must be protected from whatever is coming."

"It's just a freak storm," replied Llyat as he put his arm around his lover. "I'm sure it will pass."

"Fuck, what's he doing now," shouted Heliana.

The shrivelled and ancient oak dweller raised Destiny's Song aloft and pointed its tip to the heavens. The mist rushed in around his prune like skin and the crackling of the air intensified. Lightening seemed to coalesce above his head before focusing on the blade amid a single flash of light that lit the land as if it were day. Clotho exploded into a ball of white flame. A second later his fired remains dropped to the ground and the smell of cooked flesh drifted through its stilling aftermath. The lightening stopped. The crackling sounds disappeared and the violet mist began to disperse on the wind. One terrifying but prolonged rumble of thunder rolled out across the surrounding lands. Amid this cacophony of sound, a curl of violet vapour crept inside Llyat's left ear and tickled his drum. Then as the wind whistled it seem to Llyat that it formed into words.

"Somehow, someday, this vessel will be mine."

Llyat shock his head and then stepped out from under the cart.

"Are you okay Llyat?" shouted Heliana as the thunder finally ceased. "Where are you going?"

"The storm is over my love and so it appears is Clotho. That was the weirdest thing I have ever witnessed. Stay where you are until I have made sure all is well and I have recovered Destiny's Song."

Llyat strode over to the spot where the hermit had stood. There he looked to the ground and saw nothing but the charred shadow of what was left of the hermit. Of the sword there was no trace, no hint of molten metal, nor any shattered shards. Llyat began to scratch his head amid his confusion until a voice spoke from his side.

"I've never seen anything like that before," said Irabo as he too looked to the charred ground. "Do you think the old fool knew what he was doing?"

"I suspect he did," answered Llyat as he continued his search of his sword. "He took Destiny's Song and now it is gone."

"And that strange mist; I have never seen that before either," added Irabo.

"I have, in the Underworld as Methladon triggered the closing of the portal," stammered Llyat as a great unease began to test his thinking. "I don't like this one bit."

"I think your imagination is making more of that tempest than it warrants," uttered Irabo as he put his arm around his friend. "Now that it has passed, I suggest we try and get some sleep for tomorrow, with luck, we will reach our destination."

Three months later the villages of Maplehill, Ashview and Oakwood had been reborn. Llyat and his followers had rebuilt them just as they had been before, save for two exceptions. The watermill's extension in which Arnkatla and her nuns baked and prayed, added to the charm of the riverbank. Their singing drifted through the maples on still evenings when Llyat trudged from his labours on the farm to the Red Mare for ale, conversation, and Fidchell. The second addition was the large extension to the blacksmith's forge where Irabo and others smelted, wrought, and sharpened through every daylight hour. Heat and hard work provided many thirsty mouths and so it was that the Red Mare thrived as never before in its history. Darchus left the running of the tavern to his wife while he began to create the finest footwear ever seen outside of the Capital

One late evening as ale flowed and voices grew ever louder, Llyat, Irabo, and Darchus sat at one end of the long table and talked at length of all they had been through. The three had all achieved both happiness and success and through the heightened perceptions brought on by the Blessed Beast they could not have been more content. Before the glow of the fire the door to the tavern burst open and in strode a travelling bard with a lyre that look like it longed to be played.

"Is this Maplehill?" began the youth with slender fingers. "Is this the village where legend has it the Marked grew up?"

"It is indeed," answered Ailora from behind her serving counter. "His house was at the top of the hill if you want to visit it, but you would need permission from Arfon Caddick over there by the fire, for he now occupies its walls.

"I'll sing you the greatest of all ballads, if you will reward me with supper and give me shelter for the night," the bard replied in his excitement. "We are spreading a message across the Realm for all to hear and remember until the end of time. I cannot believe I have been chosen to cover this stretch of the Tiaryer where legend says it all began."

"Then food, ale, and a stone slab for the night shall be yours, young bard" replied Ailora. "But first we will hear your song and assess if you are worthy to carry such a message."

The young bard, dressed in the finest clothes of the Capital, moved to the centre of the Red Mare and began to pluck away on his lyre. Then the most beautiful of voices took control of the space and silenced the gathered crowd."

"He's got a better voice than Thias ever had," said Irabo as he smiled and reflected.

"Sssh, I want to listen," replied Llyat as he raised a finger to lips.

> On either bank of the river wide,
> Grew arbours of maple and oak,
> Forming visions to please the eye;
> And through that land the river ran
> On to the walls of Parandor;
> The ale and wine filled glasses
> The highborn pampered asses
> The bards who sang to lasses
> Form the essence of this Lore...

The bard sang long and the verses followed one upon the other while all those present looked on with a knowing smile; and so it was that back amongst the maples, Llyat Emgar first heard the Ballard of the Marked.

The End Game

"Well my dearest sisters, are we happy with how that game played out?" asked the first of the crones as she sucked on her pipe and filled the cavern with a grey impenetrable haze.

"It was an outcome we didn't ever once foresee," answered the second as she too contributed to the hanging cloud of sweet smelling backy.

What say you our silent sib?" demanded the first. "At least you got something out of it!"

The third hissed out her reply and scowled. She wafted the smoke away from the infant that sat on her lap while its bony gums sucked away on her gnarled little finger.

"She is besotted, the befuddled old bugger," added the second and as her ancient wrinkles forged a look of utter contempt.

"Use your pad and write," demanded the first while pinching the infant with her talons. "Tell us where you got the child from. How did you come by it?"

The third rolled her smooth surfaced tongue between her lips and blew out air.

"What plans do you have for the girl?" growled the second as she too sought to scratch it. "When do you propose to introduce her to the game?" asked the first.

The third picked up two dice and threw a twelve and an eight. Then she cut three cards from the pack before her and flipped them for her sisters to see.

"Laughter; the Thief; the Keeper of Secrets. That is a most interesting combination," cackled the first as she tugged away at the hairs on her grizzled chin.

"To restart the game we need the Lore of the Dead but the wizard destroyed it in Parandor," sneered the second.

A haze of blackfly hovered around the large ulcer that had formed on her scalp.

"That was but a copy, see I have the original here," chuckled the first as she reached within her dark cloak and pulled out a hefty tome. "We can start as soon as you are ready."

"What say you our silent one, are you also prepared for the off?"

An airy puff cut through the haze. The silent one giggled and pointed to the infant's arse.

"I'll take that as a yes," laughed the first.

"Roll the dice then," shouted the second

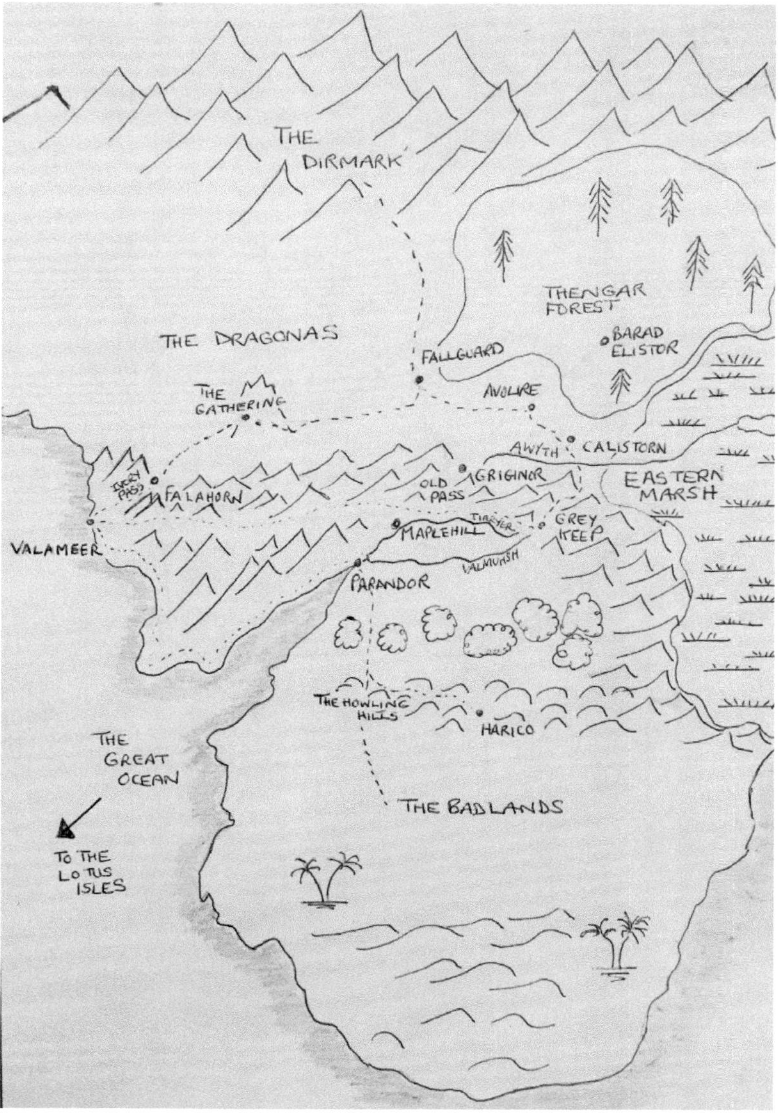
THE DIRMARK
THENGAR FOREST
BARAD ELISTOR
THE DRAGONAS
FALLGUARD
AVOLIRE
THE GATHERING
AWYTH
CALISTORN
GRIGINOR
OLD PASS
EASTERN MARSH
FALAHORN
VALAMEER
MAPLEHILL
GREY KEEP
PARANDOR
THE HOWLING HILLS
HARICO
THE GREAT OCEAN
TO THE LOTUS ISLES
THE BADLANDS

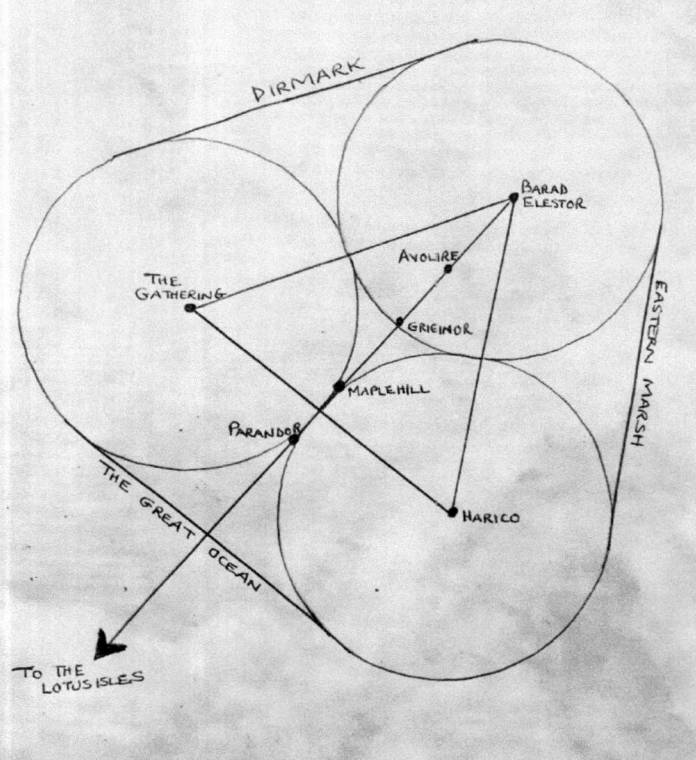